WHEN TOMORROW CALLS

OMNIBUS: BOOKS 1 - 3

JT LAWRENCE

ALSO BY JT LAWRENCE

FICTION

SCI-FI THRILLER

WHEN TOMORROW CALLS

• *SERIES* •

The Stepford Florist: A Novelette

The Sigma Surrogate (prequel)

1. Why You Were Taken
2. How We Found You
3. What Have We Done

When Tomorrow Calls Box Set: Books 1 - 3

URBAN FANTASY

BLOOD MAGIC SERIES

1. The HighFire Crown
2. The Dream Drinker
3. The Witch Hunter
4. The Ember Isles
5. The Chaos Jar
6. The New Dawn Throne

STANDALONE NOVELS

The Memory of Water

Grey Magic

EverDark

~

SHORT STORY COLLECTIONS

Sticky Fingers

Sticky Fingers 2

Sticky Fingers 3

Sticky Fingers 4

Sticky Fingers: 36 Deliciously Twisted Short Stories: The Complete Box Set Collection (Books 1 - 3)

~

NON-FICTION

The Underachieving Ovary

DEDICATION

This book is dedicated to the loyal readers and patrons of this series who first encouraged me to write a sequel to 'Why You Were Taken'.

It's been a ride! Thank you.

WHY YOU WERE TAKEN

BOOK 1

WHEN TOMORROW CALLS BOOK ONE

WHY YOU WERE TAKEN

JT LAWRENCE

CHAPTER 1

BRIDE IN THE BATH

JOHANNESBURG, 2021

A well-built man in grimy blue overalls waits outside the front door of a Mr Edward Blanco, number 28, Rosebank Heights. He's on a short stepladder, and is pretending to fix the corridor ceiling light, the bulb of which he unscrewed the day before, causing the old lady at the end of the passage to call general maintenance, the number which he has temporarily diverted to himself.

He would smirk, but he takes himself too seriously. People in his occupation are often thought of having little brain-to-brawn ratio, but in his case it isn't true. You have to be clever to survive in this game, to stay out of the Crim Colonies.

Clever, and vigilant, he thinks, as he hears someone climbing the stairs behind him and holds an impotent screwdriver up to an already tightened screw. The unseen person doesn't stop at his landing but keeps ascending.

The man in overalls lowers his screwdriver and listens. He's waiting for Mr Blanco to run his evening bath. If he doesn't start it during the next few minutes he'll have to leave and find another reason to visit the building; he has already been here for twenty minutes, and even the pocket granny would know that you don't need more than half an hour to fix a broken light.

At five minutes left, he checks the lightbulb again and fastens the fitting around it, dusts it with an exhalation, folds up his ladder. As he closes his dinged metal toolbox, he hears the movement of water flowing through the pipes in the ceiling. He uses a wireless device in his pocket to momentarily scramble the access card entrance mechanism on the door. It's as simple as the red light changing to green, a muted click, and he silently opens the door at 28, enters, and closes it behind him. In the entrance hall of Blanco's flat he eases off his workman boots, strips off his overalls to reveal his sleeker outfit of a tight black shirt and belted black pants.

The burn scar on his right arm is now visible. The skin is mottled, shiny. He no longer notices it; it's as much part of him as his eyes, or his nose. Perhaps subconsciously it is his constant reminder as to why his does what he does. Perhaps not.

He stands in his black stockinged feet, biding his time until he hears the taps being turned off. Mr Blanco is half whistling, half humming. A small man; effeminate.

What is that song? So familiar. Something from the 1990s? No, a bit later than that. Melancholy. A perfect choice, really, for how his evening will turn out.

He hears the not-quite-splashing of the man lowering himself into the bath. Tentative. Is the water too hot or too cold? Or perhaps it's the colour of the water putting him off. Recycled water has a murkiness to it, a suspiciousness. Who knows where that water has been, what it has seen? The public service announcements, now planted everywhere, urge you to shower instead of bath, to save water. It does seem like the cleaner option. If you do insist on bathing, they preach, you don't need more than five fingers. And then, only every second day. His nose wrinkles slightly at that. He takes his cleanliness very seriously.

Mr Blanco settles in and starts humming again. The man with the burnt arm glides over the parquet flooring and enters the bathroom. Even though his eyes are shut, the man in the bath senses his presence and starts, his face stamped with confusion. The scarred man sweeps Blanco up by his ankles in a graceful one-armed movement, causing water to rush up his nose and into his mouth. As he chokes and writhes upside-down, the man gently holds his head under the water with his free hand.

It's a technique he learnt from watching a rerun on the crime channel. In the early 1900s a grey-eyed George Joseph Smith, dressed in colourful bow ties and hands flashing with gold rings, married and killed at least three women for their life insurance. He would prowl promenades in the evenings looking for lonely spinsters and pounce at any sign of vulnerability. His charisma, likened to a magnetic field, ensured the women would do as he told them, one of his wives even buying the bath in which she was to be murdered. His technique in killing them was cold-blooded, clean: he'd grip their ankles to pull their bodies under—submerge them so swiftly that they would lose consciousness immediately—and they would never show a bruise. But where such care had been taken in the actual murders, Smith was careless with originality, and was caught and hanged before he could kill another bride in the bath.

A moment is all it takes, and soon Mr Blanco is reclining in the bath again, slack-jawed, and just a little paler than before. The man in black turns on the taps and fills the tub. Turns out five fingers is enough in which to drown, but it would be better if it looks like an accident, or suicide.

Mr Blanco's face is a porcelain mask, an ivory island in the milky grey water. Perhaps the person who finds him will think he fell asleep in the bath. Which he has, in a way. He washes his hands in the basin, wipes down the room. He throws on the white-collared shirt he brought with him and within five minutes he is out of the building and walking to the bus station, dumping the dummy toolbox and overalls on the way. He manages to hop on a bus just as it's pulling out onto the road. He's in a good mood, but he doesn't show it. This was one of his easier jobs. He wonders if the other six names on the list will be as effortless.

He slides his hand into his pocket and pulls out the curiosity he lifted from Blanco's mantelpiece: a worn piece of ivory—a finger-polished piano key. Engraved on the underside: 'Love you always, my Plinky Plonky.' It's smooth in his palm and retains the warmth of his skin. A melody enters his head. Coldplay: that's what Blanco was humming. The man finds this very satisfying.

CHAPTER 2

RAINBOW VOM

JOHANNESBURG, 2021

Kirsten, late for the appointment she's been dreading for weeks, taps her sneakers on the scuffed concrete of the communal taxi stop on Oxford Road. The taxis are supposed to collect passengers every fifteen minutes but the drivers don't pay much attention to the official timetable. Most of them are passive aggressive which, Kirsten thinks, is better than just plain aggressive, which they were in the old days. Taxi bosses, South Africa's own mafia, used to gun down their rivals —blood in the streets—as if our history doesn't have enough of that already.

They stay with her, the pictures. She doesn't know if it's part of her synaesthesia or if she just has a more visual memory than most. It comes in handy with her job as a photographer.

The exception, of course, is her early childhood, of which she can remember very little. It was before you could download and back up your memories. Her parents used to tell her what she was like when she was a child, describe her first word, her first steps, the outings they had been on, but Kirsten's early memory remains an odourless, flavourless blank.

One year, for their anniversary, Marmalade James gave her the first book she had ever read cover to cover. A hardbound, beautifully illustrated, vintage edition of a Grimms' fairy tale: 'Hansel and Gretel'. The pages are foxed, the cover bumped. When she holds it she can feel that the book contains more than one story. She was so touched by the gesture: as if he's trying to give her a small part of those early years back. She treasures the book. Reads it carefully, is appalled by it, falls in love with it, can't bear to read it again. Still dreams of toaster waffle tiles.

Kirsten's watch beeps with a reminder just as a minibus rolls up. She's supposed to be at the clinic already. She double-clicks the message and it dials through to the reception machine, letting them know she's running late. People are more flexible now that personal cars are practically extinct and almost everyone relies on public transport. At least that's what Kirsten hopes, seeing as she's terminally late. The irony of her period being precisely on time every month is never lost on her.

She lets a few passengers push in front of her in the queue so that she's last to board and gets a seat in the front row. She hates sitting at the back. All the smells: the perfume and aftershave and shampoo and worn pleather shoes and smudge and *atchar* and chewing gum. All the sounds: the tinny *kwaito,* jazz and retro-*marabi* on the radio; the different languages and dialects; the shades of skin; the mad hooting.

The close fabric of different textures and colours makes her giddy, sometimes ill. Overwhelming: like having to see, smell, touch and taste all the colours of the rainbow, in 3D, at the same time. At its worst, it mixes together to become a thick, soupy, smelly, bubbling, multi-coloured mess.

Normally she closes her eyes, pictures herself in a clean white room, and tries to cut herself off from her senses, but fellow passengers never like that. They either take offence or move a little away from her, afraid, perhaps rightly so, that she will hurl on them. Rainbow Vom, she thinks, and smiles, although the idea doesn't make the trip any easier.

With her LocketCam she takes a quick snap of the miniature disco-ball hanging off the taxi's rear-view mirror, which swings as they stop to pick up passengers. The driver makes a dangerous stop at a dogleg to offer a woman a ride. Probably because she's pretty, Kirsten thinks, till the door opens and she sees the woman's bulging stomach.

Christ. As if this morning isn't difficult enough.

The other passengers all snap to and make the appropriate noises. Not gasps, not quite, but something similar. They shift up in their seats, making space for her, dusting invisible crumbs off the cheap cracked upholstery seat.

The pregnant woman smiles shyly, thanks them in vernacular. The people on either side of her beam as she sits, and steal shy glances at her bump. The woman smiles, puts her hand on her belly. A special kind of smug, the way only pregnant women can be. Kirsten stares out of the hair oil smeared window.

The Infertility Crisis has hit the lower socio-economic groups the hardest, with nine out of ten couples battling to conceive. As the salaries climb, though, the infertility—bizarrely—decreases, with top earners having the reversed fortune.

Declining fertility rates are a problem the world over but nowhere is it as dire as in South Africa. No one knows the definitive reasons behind the crisis. Billions have been spent testing the various hypotheses: cell tower radiation, Tile and/or Patch use, hormones used in farming and agriculture, high stress levels, bad diets, GMO, people waiting too long to start their families. While there is some correlation, they still can't figure out why South Africa is so badly affected compared to other countries. The population is declining rapidly, and those fortunate few who do manage to conceive are treated like queens.

When they draw near to where she's going, Kirsten lets the driver know by shoving a hundred rand at him. They're supposed to use government tokens to pay for community taxis but drivers always appreciate cash. Old school style. She doesn't do this for the sake of the driver, but more as a small act of rebellion against the incumbent ruling party, the New ANC—known, regrettably, as the Nancies—because the idea of a nanny state makes the hair on the back of her neck stand up.

She jumps off onto the pavement, glad to put distance between herself and the bun in the oven. Digital street posters call her name and tell her to wait, they have a message for her.

'Kirsten,' a recorded voice says in an American accent, 'have you done something for yourself today?'

Bilchen knows her favourite ice cream flavour—rose petal—and showers her with 4D rose petals and a blast of cool air. A travel agency tells her that it's been 206 days since her last holiday—doesn't she need another one? Bolivia? Mozambique? The Cape Republic? The soundtrack is vaguely island style and she can smell rum and coconut. Has she considered a travelbattical? Workcation?

Tuk-tuks zoom past her, hooting as they go. The sky darkens. Kirsten shields her eyes and looks up to see a drone-swarm fly overhead. She doesn't like them, doesn't like the shadow they cast. Hates that they have cameras, as if she's living in someone else's bleak futuristic imaginings. Already she feels as if she's being watched, always has. She shakes her brain, tries to focus on the task ahead. The time has come.

Carpe diem, and all of that.

For as long as she can remember, she's always hated doctors. And hospitals, but doesn't everyone? She abhors it when someone says they hate hospitals. That's like saying you hate stepping in dog shit, or wetting your pants in public. Obvious. Or in local slang, *obvi-ass:* the stating of which usually just shows how little you know.

Yuck, I'm just grouchy. Nervous.

Her underarms are damp so she slows her pace, and thinks about the ice cream, the Piña Colada.

Besides, how can she say she hates doctors when she's practically married to one? Just one example of how conflicted (read: crap) her personality is. Anyway, Marmalade is different. He's a paediatric cardiologist and goes around fixing kids' hearts, like some kind of golden-haired scalpel-bearing angel. And it's not like he has ever been *her* doctor. Never going to happen (No, not even then).

inVitro looms before her. It's bigger than she expected. The pictures on the website made it look less intimidating. The architecture is beautiful, inspired by Petri: the disc-shaped building is built out of attenuated glass (Crystal Whisper), strangely transparent and reflective at the same time: as if the architect meant for it to look invisible.

Kirsten wipes her clammy hands on her jeans, wonders if she really wants to go ahead with this. All the electronic poster-projectors near her apartment have been advertising this place; it seems to be the best of the hundreds of fertility clinics around. The spambots hack your online social status, and as soon as they see you are in a relationship they bombard you with wedding messages. As if anyone gets married anymore. After a while they give up on you getting married and start with the fertility and baby *spiel.* A bit like parents.

Or—Kirsten sniffs—how parents used to be. Her pain is still jagged.

Two heavily armed guards stand at the entrance. They look more like American militants than security: top-of-the-range automatic rifles, Kevlarskin, tortoise-shell-shaped helmets that make them sweat. They don't take their eyes off the pedestrians walking past. Seeing-eye cameras swivel in Kirsten's direction and blink at her. A bit further in, a lesser-armed female guard scans Kirsten for anything suspicious, then points where to go.

The reception area of inVitro is plush but anaemic: decorated in the kind of soulless way a five-star hotel is. The walls are covered in vanilla wallpaper that feels flat, dry, and tastes sweet, like a wafer. Kirsten hears the whisper of air sanitiser as she approaches the empty smiles at the desk.

The waiting room is packed; this place must be printing money. A woman, camouflaged in beige, hands her a stylus and a glass tablet with a form to fill out. She looks for an empty seat in the crowded room. Mainly couples: some scrubbed-looking and hopeful, some carrying the stale air of defeat, a few pinkly embarrassed, although Kirsten sees no reason to be. As difficult as it is, it's generally accepted that everyone in South Africa is IUPO nowadays: Infertile Until Proven Otherwise. At least Kirsten, and the other people in the room, have the money for treatment—most aren't that lucky, hence the huge skew in the latest population stats.

Some of the patients are wearing SuperBug masks. Kirsten supposes she should be wearing hers too but reckons she has to draw a line somewhere. If she has to choose between wearing a mask over her face every day for the rest of her life or getting sick she'd rather take her chances with The Bug. Besides, the government-issue masks are revolting to look at. Perhaps if she can get hold of one of the designer masks… she's about to sit next to a resigned-looking pair when her name is called.

The gold nameplate on the half-ajar door is blank. The nurse knocks and they enter. *Now or never*. Kirsten takes a deep breath.

The doctor takes the electronic clipboard, dismisses the nurse, and looks with interest at Kirsten over the top of his black-rimmed glasses.

'Miss Lovell?'

His eyes are the palest blue (Quinine) (Arctic Icecaps). They drill through her, make her feel intensely uncomfortable.

'I'm Doctor Van der Heever.'

Kirsten's nerves stretch her smile wide. She feels like running. He motions for her to take a seat and ignores her for the next two minutes while he scans her form, pinching and paging. She focuses on her breathing and casts her eyes around: one side of the office is floor-to-ceiling glass, with an uninspiring view of ChinaCity/Sandton. Glinting certificates take up most of the opposite wall. What kind of specialist feels the need to wallpaper half of his office with certificates? What's he trying to make up for?

'So... you've been trying for around three years?'

Kirsten jumps to attention. 'Three years. Yes.'

He grunts acknowledgement, keeps paging.

'You have children?' she blurts, without really meaning to. She thinks he'll say no, that he's married to his job. There are no framed prints of family on his desk.

He looks up at her, stares. Moistens his lips. 'I do. A boy. Well, he used to be a boy. A grown man, now. A doctor.'

Yuck. 'You must be proud.'

He blinks at her; his eyes magnified by his glasses. 'Your family's medical history –'

'It's patchy. I'm working on getting more information. I'm actually –'

'No matter,' he says, 'we'll do the standard primary diagnostic tests on you and your partner.'

The mention of tests sock Kirsten in the stomach. It's true she doesn't have many memories of her early childhood, but what she does remember is having endless examinations, specialist after specialist, x-rays, MRIs, CAT scans, blood tests. Breathing in gas to trace the blood flow to her brain, a hot flush of an iodine IV to examine her renal system.

It had made her hate her condition. Only once she'd been free of the weekly appointments did she finally start to accept the way she is: regard it as a gift instead of a disability. Now it seems as if it's starting all over again and she is heavy with foreboding.

'What kind of tests?' Kirsten tries to keep her voice even.

'Nothing too invasive, for now. Bloods, HSG, PCT. Then maybe a laparoscopy, hysteroscopy, depending on what we find.'

Using a stylus, he writes something on the glass, then clicks a button to bump the prescription to her watch. Her wrist buzzes as it comes through. A spray of tiny blue polka dots.

'It's a prenatal supplement. Folic acid, DHEA, Pycnogenol, royal jelly, omegas.'

Dr Van der Heever stands up, as if to see her out.

Is that it? Nine thousand rand sure doesn't buy you much specialist.

'Don't look so worried,' he says with a sidelong glance, one Kirsten can't help but to find menacing. 'We'll take good care of you.'

CHAPTER 3

THEY MUST BE PLAYING WITH THE WEATHER AGAIN

JOHANNESBURG, 2021

Everyone holds their breath. The pale, painted puppet-like bodies keep still while the light flashes bright white.

'And it's a wrap,' Kirsten announces, lowering her camera and looking around at her team. The models, tired of holding their stomachs in and being pestered by the make-up artist, pout and blink at her gratefully. She rides her swivel chair to the 24" screen to file her shots.

She's happy with the day's grind. There is a luxury that comes with advertising shoots, compared to the journalistic and proactive stuff she usually does. It makes for an easy day, and she feels good because she knows she's got some excellent cinegraphs. Highly stylised, super slick, this job is definitely going into her portfolio. She feels hopped up, Mint Green.

'Stunning,' her assistant hisses over her shoulder, making her start. She closes the file. 'Seriously, that's some bang tidy work.'

'I'm off,' says Kirsten. 'Will you give the models some of this food?'

Shoots for brands like this are always over-catered. She slips a packet of Blacksalt crisps and a CaraCrunch chocolate bar into her pocket, grabs a bottle of water.

'Tell them to eat something. Models love being told to eat something.'

The sun is sinking behind the jagged downtown skyline when Kirsten walks towards the Gautrain station, and a warm drop of rain on her cheek makes her look up at the sky. She always expects the rain to be perfumed by the data in The Cloud. She imagines all the pictures there, all the poetry and music. Surely the rain should taste of something? Mummatus clouds are gathering in the east. They must be playing with the weather again. It feels wrong to her that the government is allowed to. The country needs rain desperately but influencing the weather just seems wrong. Unnatural.

In her experience, forcing an outcome rarely works. It's one of the reasons she has waited so long to visit a fertility clinic. Surely if it's meant to happen, it would just happen? But it hasn't. So now she guesses she is in the same boat as the weather manipulators.

It's not the first time she's drawn a parallel between the drought and the fertility crisis. Human bodies, after all, are 87% water. Without water there can be no life. Perhaps this is the next step in human evolution—Learnings from Lemmings—our natural resources are coming to an end but instead of diving off cliffs and walking into the sea to control our population, we just became infertile. A neater solution. Civilised.

Although lemming-inspired people still exist on the fringe of society: the suicide stats are soaring. They call it the Suicide Contagion, as if it's infectious. As if you're coasting along nicely, happy with your little patch of life, until the guy in the cubicle next to you decides to take a bottle of TranX to bed with him and the next thing you're contemplating doing it too. Like it never crossed your mind that you could end your life until you hear that someone else has done it. So on your way home from work you buy a bottle of TranX and a box of toaster waffles. You eat the waffles.

Kirsten gets on the train and sits as far away from everyone else as she can so that she can furtively eat her pocket-softened chocolate. The doors slide closed and they start to move. The sugar paints her mouth bright yellow (Cadmium Candy).

The projection looming above her interrupts the 7 o'clock news with snaps of contrived family moments: a father playing soccer with his IVF triplet sons, a mother gardening with her mixed-race daughter, a double amputee with bionic legs graduating from university. Then a slogan in bold typography appears over the picture: "A Future For All!"

It's the global slogan for 2021, but what does it even mean? Kirsten finds it especially ironic given the fertility crisis. She would laugh if it was funny. Ever since The Net shrunk the planet and the rich countries 'adopted' the poor countries, the UN is going around thinking that the Earth is some crazy-quilt version of Shangri-La.

In the meantime South Africa has serious problems; the news broadcast returns to show her cases in point: crippling rolling blackouts for those still stuck on the Eishkom grid; people dying of dehydration, cholera, and the SuperBug; strike after strike in the labour force retarding the already dismal service delivery; townships being razed to the ground to make space for factories and soulless, culture-barren RDP grids; a violent spike in hijackings; and prisoners dying in the Crim Colonies.

The global news: more ocean innocents disappearing on a regular basis, most likely nabbed by Somali pirates. More casualties at Hoover Dam as China continues its invasion of the US in search of water supplies.

Ha-ha, future for all. Kirsten looks down at the wrapper in her hand and realises her chocolate is missing. She checks her lap, her bag, the floor. Surely she hasn't eaten the whole thing?

Now the news shows some square-jawed businessman cutting a shiny blue ribbon, and people flashing their teeth and applauding. His name comes up: Christopher Walden, CEO of Fontus. Airbrushed pictures of Fontus trucks offloading crates of bottled water to impoverished-looking schools and remote villages. Cuts to Walden handing a bottle of Hydra to a lollipop child and showing the cameraman a thumbs-up.

It's good PR, but they don't really need to advertise. Apart from being the largest soda- and water-bottler in the country, Fontus has had the sole government contract to supply subsidised bottled water nationwide since it became unsafe to drink tap water. They practically own the country.

There are portable water purification systems available, towers and billboards and bottles and straws where nanoparticles in the filter remove heavy metals and biohazards, but they are slow and the water still tastes grey. Most homes have them but it's just easier to buy bottled when the world is spinning so fast no one feels they have the time to wait for something as basic and essential as water.

Kirsten and James have recently begun to make a point of drinking Hydra and not the more expensive brands, Tethys, or the luxurious 27-flavoured 'champagne of waters' Anahita, despite their friends' teasing for being 'neo-pinko socialists.' More than the price tag, they reject the notion that water is becoming a status symbol. She would drink tap water if she could, if it was safe. People still do of course, dirt-poor people, and those who shirk the warnings on homescreen and radio, people who believe it is all just a money-making racket, or worse, a post-Illuminati conspiracy. People who consider bottled water as the new Kool-Aid, wear Talking Tees that shout 'Don't Drink the Water!' that make you jump as you walk past.

The thought makes Kirsten feel navy (Blackbeard Blue); she can't wait to get home. She hasn't realised how tired she is, after the demanding shoot and this morning's anxious appointment. She pulls the plaster off the crook of her arm, revealing a light bruise and a blood freckle where the nurse took a sample at inVitro. The train slows to a stop. She surreptitiously drops the plaster and the CaraCrunch wrapper into a litterbin on her way out.

Kirsten loves the flat she shares with James in Illovo. It's an old building with high, ornate pressed ceilings, parquet floors, and decorated in her shabby chic bohemian style, accentuated with knickknacks from their travelling and orphaned props from previous shoots.

It's an old block, aged but sturdy. It has soul, she tells Marmalade, not like those new edge-of-cutting-edge buildings going up in town with their moving walls and pollution-sucking paint. Superglass everywhere so that you are constantly walking into walls. Hundreds of pivoting cameras to catch you walking into said walls. Not a comfortable chair in sight. Fake pebble fireplaces. Not like theirs, which they light with actual matches and feed with solid hunks of wood, and watch the florescent flames slowly work away at the grain.

God knows she likes this brick-and-mortar building, she thinks, punching the worn-out elevator button for the third time, *but this lift could really do with a(nother) service.*

Eventually it cranks into life, something whirrs and settles with a dull thud from above, and it begins its unhurried descent. *Good thing I'm not in a hurry.* The numbers-caught-in-amber buttons light up painfully slowly: 4.

There is another noise, closer, a shuffling behind her and Kirsten whirls around, expecting to see someone, but the lobby is empty. 3.

The overhead lights flicker, and she thinks: just perfect. She is in just the mood to walk up three flights of stairs in the dark. 2.

The lights seem to stabilise, and then they go out. The elevator stops mid-groan. She hopes no one is stuck inside. The auto-generator will kick in any minute but the person trapped might not know it.

She flicks her watch's torch function on and begins climbing the stairs. It's hardly a searchlight, but it will do. She wishes James was home but he touched down in Zimbabwe a few hours ago, to work at the new surgery they've set up there. He has always spent a lot of his time grinding out of the country, but lately it seems he is never home.

They often discuss emigrating: James will be cooking some wholesome dinner while she reads the Echo.news tickertape out to him, and on bad-news days, which seemed more frequent lately, they invariably end up wondering to each other how much worse South Africa can get before they seriously consider moving to a safer place. Sometimes, sitting in the dark of loadshedding, talking by candlelight, eating olive sourdough and cheese, they say all they want is a more efficient place, a country that doesn't seem as inherently broken. And while James is always ready to leave, eager to leave, Kirsten can't bring herself to, as if bound by some stubborn magnetic force.

Kirsten is slightly out of breath when she reaches the third floor (Wheatgrass Shooter). When they first moved in she would say she lived on the green floor, or tell visitors to press the green button in the elevator, and they would think she was crackers. Of course there is no green button, and there is nothing green about the floor on which she lives. Marmalade understands her colours though: If he asks her how many slices of toast she'd like and she answers 'red' he knows that means two. Or yellow: one. Isn't it obvious? No, he says, I'm just used to your type of crazy.

She walks down the dim corridor and fumbles at the door, dropping her access card. Swearing purple (Aubergine Aura), she bends down to pick it up and a dark figure steps towards her.

JOURNAL ENTRY

20 FEBRUARY 1987, WESTVILLE

In the news: *South Africa is reeling in the wake of a grenade attack that killed a number of SADF personnel at Tladi secondary school. A second Unabomber bomb explodes at a Salt Lake City computer store, injuring the owner.*

What I'm listening to: *Slippery When Wet - Bon Jovi!*

What I'm reading: *'Echoes in the Darkness' – non-fiction about the murder of a teacher and the disappearance of her two children. Heartbreaking.*

What I'm watching: *The Bedroom Window. Bow-chicka-wow-wow!*

Can you believe the news? Seems there are bombs going off everywhere.

Today was the worst and most shocking day of my life.

After fainting yesterday in the photocopy room at work, I went to the doctor down the road, at the corner clinic. All the girls here go to him, although I don't know why! He is downright creepy! I won't be going back there again. Told him about the nausea, dizziness etc. Can't keep any food down. Thought I had a tummy bug. Felt like he could see my secret through my skin. He asked me if I was sexually active as he looked at my naked ring finger. SRP. Self-Righteous Prick. And hypocrite. Everyone knows he's been having it off with Susan Beyers since her diagnosis. He's way too young to be such a SRP. Maybe even too young to be a doctor?! He can eat my shorts. Argh, I hate them. Doctors, I mean. They give me the creeps!

So yes, I know you've guessed already. I had too, although I was in serious denial. The nurse phones me today (at work!) and tells me the test was POSITIVE. Not positive, as in, Good News, but positive as in PREGNANT.

I AM PREGNANT (!!!)

I was (am) completely shocked. I'm practically a virgin! Plus P and I have always been so careful. I'm on the pill AND we use condoms. Well, we use condoms most of the time. There was that time at the beach after the concert when we didn't have one. And that once in my Citi Golf when I had that vicious bruise on my left knee from the hand brake and had to wear stockings to work in the middle of summer. Oh, God. Oh God.

A miracle/tragedy. A tragic miracle. Shoot, was all I could say into the phone. Shoot. Shoot. I wanted to say a lot worse!

They wanted me to go in immediately to get prenatal care: vitamins I think. She said something about ultrasounds and folic acid. Acid is right. My life is over! I said I wasn't going back to that clinic and then she tried to refer me to an obstetrician but I just, like, put down the phone. There is NO WAY I can have this baby. P will think I'm trying to trap him. Get him to leave his wife.

P aside, what on earth am I going to do with a baby?!! I'm 24, still kind of new in town, and trying to make a good impression at work and in the neighbourhood. This was supposed to be my new beginning, my Big Break. How am I going to explain being single and knocked up?!

And, more importantly, what about taking care of the little anklebiter? Screaming sprog and dirty nappies? No way, I'm supposed to be a career girl! It's the 80s for God's sake! I left home so that I could make a life for myself, not tie myself down. Not be a gin-swilling housewife. I've dreamt for years of perms and power-suits and matching pumps, and having my own computer. And a telephone that I can dial with the back of my pencil so that I don't ruin my new manicure. Why am I so damned fertile?! It's a curse!

I don't know what to do. Very stressed and there's no one I can tell. Except Becky back home but then she'll think she was right: that the Big City would change me. Oh my God, can you imagine what she'd think of me now? I could never tell her! The girls around the office are great but I'm not close enough to anyone yet. Besides, they all obviously know P and it would be too dangerous. This will make me sound like a hypocrite but I really don't want to hurt P's wife. That would be terrible. I'm a terrible person. This is probably a punishment. As they say, Karma's a bitch.

Also, my family would be totally horrified. I can just imagine the look on Dad's face. He lives in this whacky reality where the 60s didn't happen and we're all still pre-sexual-revolution conservatives. I guess I was, too, until six months ago.

*F*CK! He'll disown me in an instant. And Mom. I'll be an orphan.*

*F*CK F*CK F*CK!!*

It feels like the world is tumbling down around me.

I feel like jumping off a bridge! I may as well! Then at least I could rest. My mind could rest. Who would miss me, anyway?

I feel so sick. Anxiety, guilt, morning sickness: all turning my stomach into a washing machine. I can't eat. I can't sleep. I don't know what to do.

I think I'm going to throw up again.

God help me. I don't deserve it, but please help me anyway!

CHAPTER 4

A BIG RED BLOOM OVER HIS HEART

JOHANNESBURG, 2021

Kirsten gasps, clutches her chest.

'Jesus Christ!'

'I've been called worse,' says the dark figure. The overhead lights flicker back on.

'The fuck are you doing here?'

'*Hai wena.* Is that the way you would greet the son of God Almighty?'

'As far as I know, the son of God doesn't skulk in dark corridors with inflatable motorbike helmets.'

'And how would you know, being the infidel that you are?' asks Kekeletso, arms akimbo. 'And, bless you, *sista,* still such a filthy mouth.'

She holds up a black bag. 'Is it okay if I shoot up in your place?'

Kirsten leans forward and hugs her, smells nutmeg in her cornrows, and warm leather. She loves the way Keke dresses. She seems to pull off a look that is sexy, hardcore, and feminine, all at the same time. Kirsten always feels like a tomboy in her company, in her uniform of tee, denim and kicks. She swipes her card and opens the door.

While Keke is dosing herself with insulin in the lounge, Kirsten opens the door of her antique aqua Smeg and roots around for a couple of craft beers. The idea of needles makes her *gril,* so she's never been able to watch Keke do it. Just hearing the beeping of Keke's SugarApp on her phone makes her shudder. There is the zip of the black bag (Squid Sable), which means she's finished, and when Keke comes through to the kitchen her nano-ink tattoo is already fading. The white ink is sensitive to blood sugar: when Keke's level is normal the tattoo is a faded grey; antique-looking. When she needs a shot it turns white, and the dramatic contrast with her dark skin is quite unsettling.

Kirsten twists off a cap with a hiss and hands the bottle to Keke, who looks like she needs to say something.

'So,' says Kirsten, 'never known you to be lost for words.'

Keke says, 'I think you're going to need something stronger.'

She opens her black leather jacket and slides out a folder, laying it on the kitchen table. Kirsten puts her hand on it. It's warm. Keke moves it away from her.

'Drinks first.'

'At least you've got your priorities straight.' Kirsten forces a smile. The folder burns a slow hole in the kitchen table. Finally, she thinks: finally some explanation, some kind of way forward. She grabs a bottle of Japanese whiskey by its neck, and hooks two crystal tumblers with her fingers. With her free hand she gets some transparent silicone ice cubes from the freezer.

'Do you ever miss real ice?' she asks, 'I mean old-fashioned ice, made out of frozen, you know, water?' She sits down, across from Keke, across from the folder.

'Nope,' says Keke. 'That's like saying you miss coal-powered electricity. Or cables. Or teleconferencing. Or hashtags. Or church. Or Pro-Lifers.'

'Or condoms. Or tanning,' adds Kirsten.

'I wouldn't know,' says Keke.

'I hope you're referring to tanning.'

Keke laughs.

Kirsten says, 'You know what I don't miss? Handshakes. I always hated shaking people's hands. I found it bizarre even before the Bug, before people stopped doing it. It's too... intimate... to do with a stranger. Which is when you usually had to do it. I'm no germophobe, but...'

'I know! You're taught as a kid to catch your sneeze with your hand—'

'—and cover your mouth when you cough—'

'And then the next moment you're shaking everyone in the room's hands.'

They both pull faces at each other.

'Some people still do it, you know.'

'Ja, well, bad habits die hard.'

They drink.

'So,' she says, 'how're you doing?'

It makes Kirsten squirm to talk about herself when she isn't in a good place, when her Black Hole is gaping, trying to swallow her. Who wants to hear about her hollowness? Who wants to be bored with her First World Problems when they have enough of their own? When someone asks her how she is when she feels like this she is always tempted to yell 'Fine!' and change the subject as quickly as possible. But Keke knows her better than that.

The Black Hole is Kirsten's name for the empty space she has always felt deep within herself. She has never known a time without it, only that it shrinks and expands depending on what was happens in her life. When she fell for Marmalade James, for example, it was pocket-sized: a small blushing apricot. When it sunk in that her parents were dead: a brittle plastic vacuum cleaner, emphasis on the vacuum. Not being able to get pregnant is the size of a tightly formed fist, which free-floats around inside her body but is mostly lodged between her ribcage and her heart. Sometimes the hole grows or narrows inexplicably, and makes her wonder if there is another version of her walking around, falling in and out of love and otherwise experiencing the rollercoaster of (a parallel) life. She has always had The Black Hole, it is part of who she is, and it hurts her insides just thinking that she will most likely carry it to her grave.

Keke, sensing her discomfort, says, 'Your plants are doing well.'

'Yes.' Kirsten looks around as if she has forgotten they are there. 'They're happy.'

'Happy may be an understatement. Your flat is a veritable jungle.'

Kirsten laughs. 'It's not.'

'It is! There's a lot of fucking oxygen in here. Do you even remember what colour the walls are?'

'Don't be ridiculous.'

'If I ever run out of news stories I'm going to come back here and do an ultra-reality segment on you. The crazy plant lady. Living in a Jozi Jungle. Madame Green Fingers.'

'Ha,' says Kirsten.

Keke puts on her important-news-headline voice: 'Most lonely women get cats, but Kirsten Lovell is a fan of... flora.'

'Ha. Ha.'

'Most hoarders are content with keeping mountains of old take-away containers, but this woman can't get enough of The Green Stuff.'

'That makes me sound like a blunt-vaper.'

'Her neighbours called the authorities when the vines began creeping through the walls and into their kitchens... it was clear: time for an intervention.'

'Okay, hilarious. You can stop now.'

'Really? I was having fun.'

'I could tell.'

'It started off innocently, you know. A fern here, an orchid there.'

'Ah, yes, those orchids. Gateway plants.'

They smile at each other. Kirsten is surprised at how grateful she is for the company.

'Earl Grey.'

'Er, what?'

'The colour of the walls,' says Kirsten. 'Earl Grey. The colour you get in your head when you taste bergamot.'

'You'd better not say that on camera. They'll cart you off to somewhere you can't hurt yourself.'

'Hm. That doesn't sound too bad.'

Keke leans forward again. Business time. 'So. Is there any news from your side about the... burglary—from the cops? Any leads?'

Kirsten shakes her head. '*Niks nie.*'

God, she hates talking about it, thinking about it. Pictures, unbidden, flash in on her mind. The broken glass and splinters on the floor, the up-ended furniture. Pillows ripped apart. The hungry-looking safe wrenched open and plundered.

The blood was the worst. There wasn't a lot of it—in a kind of detached way she had noticed how little actual blood was spilt—but the vividness of the colour (Fresh Crimson), like leaked oil paint, it was as if it had come alive and advanced on her, misting her vision and strangling her: and that unforgettable assailing metallic smell. An avalanche of a thousand copper spheres.

'Nothing? Not one lead?' presses Keke.

'If they have one, they're not sharing it. All I know is what they said upfront, that it looks like it was a house robbery gone wrong. Looks like it was two guys who broke in. Something about bullet trajectories and blood spatter.'

Keke frowns at her. She knows it must sound bizarre to hear someone talk so technically about the murder of her own parents. But Keke knows that Kirsten doesn't cry. She describes Kirsten as 'immune to face-melting'.

'There will definitely be some kind of... forensic evidence. Crime scenes of botched burglaries are usually teeming with the stuff.'

The bodies had looked like jointed paper dolls, the vintage ones you dress with paper clothes, 2D. Her father's body drawn as if he were a runner in a comic book. A big red bloom over his heart. Her mother, unusually pious, hands secured in prayer position with a bracelet of black cable-tie (Salted Liquorice). A small hole in her forehead. Both lying on their sides, their waxen faces resting on the dull, dirty carpet.

There is a cool palm on Kirsten's arm and she flinches, looks up and blinks past the pictures in her head.

'Are you okay? I'm sure you're still very shaken up, it hasn't even been—'

'I'm fine. I'll be fine.'

'You shouldn't be alone. Where's Marmalade?'

'It's been long enough.'

'Long enough? It hasn't even been a month, Kitty Cat. The last time I saw you was at the funeral, for God's sake.'

They sit in silence. The funeral: twin coffins and the cloying scent of lilies. Pollen stains on white tablecloths. Clammy hugs.

'Zim,' says Kirsten. 'James is in Zimbabwe, at that new clinic.'

'Then who is all this healthy food for?' She motions at the toppling fruit bowl, the mountain of bright green apples, and vegetable stand.

For thirteen years James has tried to stud Kirsten's junk food diet with healthy alternatives. If she is going to eat that CaraCrunch, then she should have a low-fruc Minneola too. *Slap* chips? The mitigating snack is a handful of edamame. He tempts her with fresh chilli gazpachos, honeyed veg-juices spiked with galangal, wild salmon salami. He eats as if he can reverse the diseases he sees in the world.

'He always stocks up the house before he goes, hoping I'll run out of junk and resort to eating some kind of plant matter. He says we should buy shares in Bilchen and then at least we'll have money for the double bypass surgery I'll need one day.'

Bilchen is the Swiss-owned megacorp that produces the majority of processed food in the world: cheap, tasty, and full of unpronounceable ingredients. In addition to their plants in China and Indonesia they own hundreds of factories in SA, producing mountains of consumables, from food to hygiene products to pet snacks.

When James sees her eating something like her staple Tato-Mato crispheres he says to her: 'You know that there is no *actual* food in there, right?' and she laughs her fake laugh to annoy him, licks her fingers, and points at the pictures on the foil packet. 'Tato-Mato, Doctor Killjoy. It's made out of potatoes and tomatoes. *A vegetable and a fruit.* You heard it here first,' and he shakes his head as if Kirsten is beyond help.

Bilchen is perennially in the news for one scandal or another. Anti-freeze contamination in their iguana food, horse-DNA in their schmeat rolls, sweat-shopping kids in Sri Lanka, big bad GMO. They own so many brands they can just kill whichever has caused the controversy and re-label their product, market it as 'new' to hook the early adopters, and deep-discount it to the couponers. The leftovers feed the freegans. *Et Voila*, a new brand is born. P-banners and virtual stickers plead with you to 'vote with your feet' and 'consume consciously': 'Boycott Bilchen' is the new 'Save the Rhino.'

Keke sighs theatrically. 'How lucky does a girl get?'

'Ja, yum, look at all those... shiny green apples.'

'No, I meant Marmalade. Kind, generous, god-like in appearance, saves little children, *and* does the grocery shopping!'

'Well, he gets cars loaned to him all the time, for his job, so it's easier for him.'

'Pssh. There is a Man-Lotto and you won. *uLula.*'

'He also has his faults, you know.'

'Ha! Not likely.'

Kirsten hides her smile.

'Seriously though,' says Keke, 'his parental units did an amazing job.'

'They didn't, actually,' says Kirsten.

'Hai, stoppit.'

'I'm not kidding. His mother was never around and his father is a real nutcase. Horrible guy.'

'I can't imagine that.'

'He left home at fifteen. He just couldn't live with his dad any more. He won't even talk about him. Cut all ties.'

'An evil father… so is that why he keeps trying to save the world?'

'Probably. Good premise for a superhero story, anyway,' says Kirsten.

'It's been done before.'

'What hasn't?'

'Funny you should say that,' says Keke.

'Huh?'

'I have a… story for you.'

'You found something? About my parents?' Kirsten turns the ring on her finger.

'I tried to get something out of the cops, anything, but they completely closed ranks. Even my contact there, in profiling, said only certain creeps are allowed access to the case. Who's that inspector?'

'The thug? Mouton. Marius Mouton.'

'Yes, Mouton is handling the thing, doesn't want too many other creeps involved. Can't have any leaks jeopardising the investigation. Apparently this happens sometimes on high-profile cases, according to my guy, but it's not like your parents were, like, diplomats or anything? But then he said it could be that the criminal is high profile, you know, like a serial killer, or in this case, maybe a terror gang. So maybe they're close to getting someone, and they want the case to be really tight.'

'Ack. We'll never get anything out of Mouton.'

'Ja, we'd have better luck asking a gorilla.'

'The gorilla would have more manners.'

'A better vocabulary.'

'Better teeth. And smell better. A gorilla would smell better.'

'More sex appeal?'

'Okay, I think you just crossed a line there,' laughs Kirsten, 'as in, a legal one.'

'It wouldn't be the first time. Anyway, I don't see us getting much out of them, so I asked my FWB, Hackerboy Genius, to see what he could find, under the radar.'

'Remind me?'

'Friend With Benefits. Marko. The hacktivist.'

Keke is the only person Kirsten knows who's gone bi-curious speed-dating to gather work contacts. The fact that they come in useful for her journalistic grind doesn't mean there is no sex on the table. From Keke's cryptic hints Kirsten gathers there is, indeed, a great deal—and variety—of sex on the table. As well as being 'a raging bisexual,' ('Isn't everyone bi these days?') she is what she likes to call 'ambisextrous'.

'Marko is a very—talented—individual,' she sparkles, sitting up a little straighter.

Uh-huh, Kirsten thinks. 'Speed dating?'

'Yawn! Speed dating is so last season, old lady. How ancient are you? Now it's DNA dating. Very New York.'

Kirsten is glad she doesn't have to date anymore. The dating pool in Joburg makes her think of a tank of Piranhas; Keke loves it.

'Chemically compatible couples, what's not to love? And boy, are we... compatible. You'd never believe it if you met him. Anyway, so he's actually the one who found this for me.' She puts her hand on the folder.

'It's big. Really big. Cosmic. You ready for a mind-fuck?'

Kirsten's fingers tingle. Keke slides it over to her, and she opens it.

JOURNAL ENTRY

3 MARCH 1987, WESTVILLE

In the news: *a guerrilla is shot dead by Gugulethu police after firing at them with an AK47.*

What I'm listening to: *The new Compact Disc (CD) of 'A Hard Day's Night' by the Beatles*

What I'm reading: *'Watchers' by Dean R Koontz. It's about two creatures that emerge from a secret government laboratory, one to spread love, the other doom.*

What I'm watching: *Nightmare on Elm Street 3. Totally gnarly. Usually I enjoy scary movies but I had to walk out of the cinema. Life is grisly enough.*

I went in for my abortion (hate that word!) today. I felt so trapped and alone but it seemed like the only solution. I got up really early, I had to be at the 'family planning clinic' at 7 and after waiting for a while in a grubby room with two other girls with shame-flamed cheeks they gave me a depressing pink gown to change into. Had to take off all make-up and jewellery, even my new nail polish. There was a mirror in the fluorescent room and I just looked at my face and I was so pale and looked so terrible. I kept thinking 'what have I become? What have I become?'

I am NOT the kind of person who sleeps with married men, and definitely not the kind of person who has an abortion! And once these things are done they can never be undone. I will be forever bruised. My soul will be dented. I was looking into that mirror thinking that I didn't even recognise myself, and I just started crying. Weeping, really. That hyperventilating ugly-cry.

Shame, the nurse was so kind to me, she could see that I was really shaken up. She held my hand. Told me if I didn't want the baby then I was doing the right thing. That the world doesn't need another unwanted child. It would be best for everyone, if I was sure that I didn't want it. It's not that I don't 'want it' I wanted to say to her. It's that I can't have it. Look at me, I may be 24 but I'm just a child myself.

So I was on the operating table after taking the pre-med and feeling totally woozy and my legs were in stirrups when something just happened, like a bolt of lightning. All of a sudden the abstract idea of pregnancy became a real idea of a little baby (a little baby!) instead of an 'it,' and the thought was there as clear as day that there was no way I could go through with the termination. Mine and P's baby!! A little pink gurgly precious baby! The anxiety fell away (I blame the drugs) and revealed my true wish, even if it was clouded by conflicted emotions.

I felt so embarrassed telling the doctor but he didn't mind. Usually I absolutely hate doctors but he was really nice: said it was better to be sure, and that I still had another 3 weeks to change my mind if I wanted to, said he'd take care of me. But I won't. Something happened to me on that table and it totally wasn't what I planned.

The nurse squeezed my arm and gave me her number in case I wanted to talk. I started crying again – something about the unexpected kindness of strangers in hard times. Also, the meds! I am going to have to tell P about the baby. I'm sure he will be angry and end things. I will probably have to find a new job, a new town. My parents will, like, never speak to me again! No duh. My life as I know it is over. Never felt so lonely before!

All that said I can't help feeling a tiny jab of excitement (stress?) when I think of the baby. Eeeek! An actual baby. What was I thinking? I'm totally terrified.

Bon Jovi's song is constantly playing on every radio and in my head. I'm living on a prayer!!

CHAPTER 5

TOMMYKNOCKERS

JOHANNESBURG, 2021

Seth sits in the lab. It's late, but he feels as if he's on the point of a breakthrough in the project he's grinding. It's his second-last day at the smart drugs company and he wants to leave with a bang. It will be good for his—already enhanced—ego. He adds another molecule to the compound he's configuring on the screen of his Tile, subtracts one then adds another. It's almost ready.

Seth is the best chemgineer at Pharmax and he knows it. No one can map out new pharmaceuticals like he can. To add to his professional allure-—and to his considerable salary—he is known to be mercurial. No one company can pin him down for more than a year, despite offers of fast-tracking and bonuses. Some colleagues blame his exceptional intelligence, saying he bores easily, others, his drug problem. While both hold some truth, there's a much more pressing reason Seth moves around as often as he does, which he keeps well hidden.

During the short ten months he'd been at the pharmaceutical company he had already composed two first-class psychoactive drugs, and is now on the brink of a third. His biggest hit to date has been named TranX by the resident marketing team. It's a tranquiliser, but modelled in such a way that while it relieves anxiety, it doesn't make you feel detached or drowsy. After the tranquiliser hits your bloodstream, making you feel warm and mellow, it's followed by a sweet and clean kick.

It's all in the delivery system, he told his beady-eyed supervisor and the nodding interns as he showed them the plan. All about levels, layers, the way they interact with each other and the chemicals in the brain. The molecular expression is beautiful, they all agreed.

The drug before that was a painkiller. It doesn't just take away your physiological pain, it takes away *all* your pain: abusive childhood, bad marriage, low self-esteem, you name it. It is one of his favourites, but then he has a soft spot for analgesics. With the drug based on the ever-delicious tramadol, Seth had used the evergreen African pincushion tree for its naturally occurring tramadol-like chemspider, allowing for a rounder, softer, full-body relief, without the miosis or cotton mouth.

Genius, if he doesn't say so himself. The formula isn't perfect though: too much of it is taxing on the liver. And he isn't sure what the long-term effects on the brain might be, but that is for the Food & Safety kids to figure out.

Seth moves to an appliance on the counter, clicks 'print,' and after a rattling he takes out a tray of pills. Shakes them down a plastic funnel and into an empty bottle, catching the last one before it disappears and popping it into his mouth. The bottle makes its way into his inside pocket after he scribbles on it with a pen. These particular pills are green; they look innocuous enough, like chlorophyll supplements, or spirulina. His latest project involves experimenting with salvia, or diviner's sage, as the hippies used to call it. Mexican mint.

On his way out, his tickertape blinks with a news update. A minister has been fired for having a secret swimming pool. The NANC is contrite and apologetic; they don't know how this could have happened. They have hard lines for mouths and use words like 'shocking,' 'unacceptable,' 'unconscionable,' and say they will certainly press charges. The journalist reporting the story looks familiar: a young, uncommonly attractive woman in cornrows and a tank top, leather bottoms. Biker? A white lace tattoo covers her shoulder; she has kohl eyes and an attitude. Just his type.

He thinks of the swimming pool and remembers a sunblock-slathered childhood of running in the sprinklers, drinking from the hose, water fights with pistols and super-soakers. Having long showers and deep bubble baths. Flushing the toilet with drinking water. Chlorine-scented nostalgia: kidney-shaped pools, dive-bombing, playing Marco Polo. The feeling of lying on the hot brick paving to warm up goose-pimpled skin. Then one day they weren't allowed to water the garden, then domestic pools were banned, then all pools were illegal, then, then, then. It had been so long, he'd do anything for a swim. For a tumble-turn in drinking water. How decadent that all seems to him now. The next news story is about a famous pianist found drowned in his bath. Seth switches it off.

He shrugs off his lab-coat, replaces his eyebrow ring and snaps on a silver-spiked leather wrist cuff. He puts on his black hoodie, applies some Smudge to his eyes, ruffles his hair into bed-head, and checks his appearance in the glass door on the way out. His mood starts climbing; he can feel the beginning of the slow-release high.

Thunder in winter, he thinks as he walks outside: they must be playing with the weather again. His superblack jacket renders him almost invisible, and his compact silver-tipped umbrella shields his face from the unseasonal shower. The city street is dark and slick, highlighted only occasionally by pops of lightning and the reflection of neon shop signs on the tar's uneven surface. Algaetrees, green streetlights, flicker on and off as he moves beneath them. There's jubilant shouting in the distance; a wave of music; a car backfires. A building's clockologram blinks an error message.

Jutting edges of the pavement interrupt the man's usually elegant stride: missing bricks, gaping manholes, roots of trees smashing their way through crumbling concrete. Undulating and decorated by shimmering litter, the walkway seems to take on a life of its own.

A group of people is up ahead, walking in his direction. Coal-skinned men dressed in oiled leathers and animal skins. Sandals and scarred faces. He sees their determined foreheads in blasts of light as they pass under the streetlights. *Gadawan Kura.* Ivory bracelets click as they walk.

When they get closer, Seth lifts his chin at the leader. He doesn't step aside, as most people would. Instead he brushes an arm and keeps moving. Once they're clear, one of the men starts shrieking, imitating the hyenas they are known for keeping, and the rest of the men cackle. Seth adjusts his hood and walks on.

A stranger in rags jumps out of a side alley and into his path. A hobo? Impossible. There were no more homeless creeps in the city: they had all been 'enrolled' in the Penal Labour Colonies. The faint whiff of matches and booze. Seth's hand tightens around the gun in his pocket, snicks off the safety. Water droplets glisten on the ragman's dark skin and hair; he pats himself down with twirling hands and a gap-toothed smile to show his tattered pockets are empty. He smells like the street.

'Jog on,' says Seth. 'Scram.'

'Jus' asking for a smoke, *bra.*' One of his eyes is black, bottomless. The other is overcast.

A cigarette? You've got to be kidding. It's 2021 – nobody smokes anymore.

He closes his umbrella.

'Get out of my way.'

A spark of defiance as the obstacle opens his mouth to speak. There's a glint of a blade. Instinctively Seth knees the stranger in the crotch, and when he's off-balance, raps him sideways on the jaw with the handle of the umbrella. The ragman falls backwards onto the shining road, knocked out cold, his trench knife clattering on the pavement beside him.

Seth keeps moving, and the Algaetrees flicker. He turns into a back street scented by tar and trash. A rat scurries out in front of him, but he doesn't flinch, which he takes as a good sign. He expects the drug to peak in two hours, maybe three. Optimism in a bottle. With one click of his earbutton his life has a soundtrack, and he's ready for a bright night.

Once he reaches his block the microchip in his ID card automatically opens the main access gate. A new biomorphic building, cool with smoked emerald glass and metal; glittering charcoal porcelain tiles. Smog-eating exterior paint and a solar Cool Roof with water catchment tanks. It's the ultimate lock-up-and-go: wholescale security, self-regulating, pet-free. He ignores the open mouth of the elevator and runs up the stairs, punches in his code—52Hz—and has his retina scanned to open his front door. The entry panel blinks and the door unlocks. A woman's voice purrs from the speaker above the door in a neutral accent: 'Welcome home, Seth.'

The main lights glow; the temperature is set to 24 degrees. He pops a pill, locks away his gun and checks his Tile for messages. Just as he hoped, the green rabbit blinks on his screen. He has a new job to do. A thrill tugs at his guts. It's his most important post yet. Dangerous. He can't wait to get started.

~

The TommyKnockers club is underground. You have to know a person who knows a person to get in. There isn't any secret code word to gain access; the club is so difficult to find, you either know where it is or you don't. That, and a giant Yoruba bouncer called Rolo, ensure that only the right kind of people get in. As Seth approaches the nondescript front door, Rolo steps into the grey frame and tips his invisible hat to him. Diamond fingers catch the light.

'Mister Denicker,' he says in a voice as deep as a platinum mineshaft.

'Rolo.' Seth nods back. He glances behind him before entering. Despite leaving the ragman in the gutter, he has the distinct feeling that someone is following him.

On the other side of the door is another world. You step from the bleak and broken inner city street into a gaudy 1940s Parisian-style steampunk bordello, replete with scarlet velvet bolted in gold, chain tassels, and oiled men and women wearing very little in the way of clothes and too much eye make-up. The twist comes later: as you move from room to room, and deeper underground, the imagery becomes more exaggerated, bizarre, sinister, as if someone has decided to cross a brothel with a spooky amusement ride. As if TommyKnockers is the representation of someone's erotic dream turning into a nightmare.

The deeper you go, the less mainstream the dancers become, catering to more exotic tastes: a voluptuous woman with three breasts, a freakishly well-endowed man, a heavily inked hermaphrodite with a clock etched into her back. The art on the walls changes from *chat noir* and *Marmorhaus* prints to surreal landscapes, obscured faces, bizarre vintage pornography, disturbing portraits hung at strange angles. Luminous sex toys alongside hallucinogenic shooters at the spinning bars, lit by deranged copper pipe chandeliers. Sex shows featuring Dali-esque hardcore fuckbots.

Seth doesn't usually go further than the first few rooms. He is no prude, enjoys a bit of kink, but his insomnia doesn't need encouragement. He has enough to keep him up at night.

This evening, as soon as he crosses the threshold, he heads directly to an attractive blonde standing against a wall. It's an old tactic, one that frequently pays off. None of that seedy languishing at the bar, surveying all the available meat on offer and later trying to hook up. This technique is cleaner. It shows you are a man who knows what he wants. The woman, caught off guard, invariably accepts the offer of a drink, and from then on it's usually green lights all the way to the bedroom. Or club restroom. Or taxi. Or White Lobster den. Or wherever else they happen to find themselves.

This particular blonde is wearing a belt for a skirt and black boots with heels so high he wonders how she manages to stay vertical. Masses of teased hair, powdered with fine glitter.

'Hello there,' says Seth. Not too friendly, not too distant.

'Er,' she says. Where has he come from?

He looks at the glass in her metallic-taloned hand: 'Campari?'

The rose-coloured sequins above her eyes blink in the uneven light. He has a coldness in his eyes. A hardness. She tries to size him up. A drug dealer? A psychopath? A rufer? Does she, after her countless drinks, even care? She looks him up and down, nods. He leads her to the bar and orders her a double, vodka for himself, and two ShadowShots, which are not, strictly speaking, legal.

The Campari comes on the rocks—it's one of the few clubs that still offer actual ice in drinks—despite the cost, instead of frozen silicone shapes. He grinds a block between his molars; he likes real ice. She purses her lips at the shooters, as if to say he's naughty. He presses one into her hand; they touch glasses and down the drinks. Both feel the rush of the warm spirit as it washes through them.

A man arrives at the bar and pretends to not watch them.

The woman blinks at Seth; sighs as her pupils dilate. With a cool and gentle hand he propels her by her lower back to a more private area, with brocade curtains and oversized couches. An oil painting of a man with a patchwork blazer and rivets for eyes gazes over them.

'Let's get you out of those dreadful shoes.'

~

Kirsten opens the folder while Kekeletso watches her. Inside: her parents' autopsy reports. Keke has removed the photos taken by the forensic team *in situ*. It is enough that Kirsten found them dead, without having to see their death-grimaces again. Not that it makes much difference to Kirsten: a picture on glossy paper won't be much more vivid than the images in her head.

The reports aren't long. Kirsten skims a few pages describing what she already knows: bullet in brain, bullet in heart. .22 calibre Remingtons: one to stop thinking, one to stop feeling. Fired at arm's length distance for her mom, half a room for her dad. Her mother was most likely kneeling there when the killer squeezed a round into her head. Execution style, but face-to-face. The police say it is a botched burglary, but this creep isn't a stranger to murder.

Kirsten scans the medical jargon: entry wound of the mid-forehead; collapsed calvarium with multiple fractures; exit wound of occipital region. Official cause of death: Massive craniocerebral trauma due to gunshot wound.

There are diagrams on one of the final pages, similar to what you might find in a biology textbook: line drawings of people dissected lengthways so that you can see their bones and organs. Kirsten is always better with pictures. She strokes the diagrams with her finger, following the coroner's notes and asides. When she finishes with her father's she starts on her mother's. Immediately something looks wrong.

'Do you see it?' asks Kekeletso. Kirsten has been so absorbed she has almost forgotten Keke is there. She looks up, her finger glued to the illustration of her mother's abdomen. The ceiling rains cerise spirals down on them.

'She had a... hysterectomy?'

'Yes.'

'How come I didn't know that? Did she do it when I was too young to remember?' This is entirely possible given her sketchy childhood memories.

'Turn to the last page. I found it in her private medical file.'

Kirsten locates the last page in the folder and holds it up, pushing the others away. It is a record of an elective surgical procedure undergone by her mother in 1982. A full hysterectomy, five years before Kirsten's birth.

JOURNAL ENTRY

12 MARCH 1987, WESTVILLE

In the news: *Sweden announces a total boycott on trading with South Africa. Les Miserables opens at Broadway.*

What I'm listening to: *The Joshua Tree by U2. Radical.*

What I'm reading: *The scariest book known to man: IT by Stephen King.*

What I'm watching: *Lethal Weapon*

I am, like, the happiest person in the world right now. When I told P about the baby I thought the worst, but I am right to love him because he is the nicest, sweetest, strongest man ever. Okay he was totally shocked but after a few minutes he hugged me so tightly and said that he would take care of the baby and me. I thought that he meant having us holed up somewhere as a secret lover and lovechild (which would have been totally fine by me!) but he is a better man than that. Said he wants to be a good father and you can't do that not living in the same house. He asked me to MARRY HIM!!!

It wasn't, like, the romantic picture I had in my head, the proposal. I guess I thought that when the day arrived it would be all champagne and roses and candlelight. Maybe on a tropical beach somewhere (Mauritius?), or a fancy restaurant. And the man would be taller and have more hair and he'd be rich (and not married!) and I... well, I wouldn't be knocked up. It was more of a discussion than a proposal, and then he, like, blurted it out. Not as a question, but as what we should do, and I agreed.

My mind is swirling right now. I mean I feel bad that he is going to leave his wife, that's so gnarly, but it has been over for a long time and I know that he will take care of her. Still, I feel sick about it. I hope she never finds out the truth. But I'm going to have his child and that is the most important thing right now. I hope that she will forgive him/us one day, and that I will be able to forgive myself. I am going to be a better person. I am going to stop being selfish and be the best wife and mother that I can be. I'm going to make P so happy.

CHAPTER 6

MAD FURNITURE WHISPERER

JOHANNESBURG, 2021

Seeing as James is away in Zimbabwe and Kirsten has no grind planned for the day, she decides it's time to do something she has been putting off for too long. She catches a *boerepunk*-blasting taxi to the south of Johannesburg and takes a long, brooding walk from the bus stop to the storage garages in Ormonde.

As she walks she snaps pictures with her locket. She used to have a superphone with a built-in camera, had a collection of lenses for it, but lugging a phone around when you could snap a Snakewatch on your arm just seems archaic. Now smartwatches are being replaced with Tiles and Tiles are being replaced with Patches. It seemed impossible to keep up.

The LocketCam is tiny, smaller than a matchbox, and is really only a lens and a shutter release. She'll get the pictures later from her SkyBox. It is great for scenes like this: an old bus depot painted white by the ratty pigeons that have adopted it as their home; a mechanic's cheerful advertising mural painted on a brick wall; a poster for a Nigerian doctor with an unpronounceable name who can enlarge your penis, get your ex-lover back, make your breasts grow, make you 'like what you see in the mirror,' vaccinate you against The Bug, and make you rich. *If he had that power, I'm sure he wouldn't be messing around with other men's junk. Or, on second thoughts, maybe he* wanted *to mess around with other men's junk, and that's why he became a junk doctor.*

When she reaches the storage building it looks all closed up. Not very promising. Then she sees their billboard, and the logo: a smiling rhino. Ironic, and sad. Like a dodo giving a thumbs-up, or a winking coelacanth. Who would choose an extinct animal as their mascot?

Once the cops gave her the go-ahead to put her parents' house on the market she paid a company to move all their possessions here. There is no way she could have faced doing it herself. This is the first place she found online, and she doesn't remember the rhino. Now she wonders if her parents' things really are here or if they were on the first truck out to some dodgy location: Alex, Lonehill, Potchefstroom.

There is no bell to ring or reception to visit. When she calls the number on the faded hoarding, a telebot tells her it is no longer valid. She walks around the building and finds a back entrance, a simple fenced gate closed with a heavy padlock. She has been given two keys she at first thought were identical, but she tries one now and the padlock springs open. She steps inside and locks the gate behind her.

The number on the cheap keyring is pink/purple-blue: 64 (Chewed Cherry Gum; Frozen Blueberry). She walks past a xylophone of colours before she finds her lot. The garage door is rusted and needs some persuading to roll up. It screams all the way and the red chevrons the noise causes in her vision momentarily blinds Kirsten. Then, silence: dust glitters in the sunlight.

She stands still, breathing, blinking, trying to cope with the onslaught of smells, colours, feelings, memories whirling around her. The lounge suite is closest to her, and she focuses on that. She lifts the protective sheeting and glimpses the arm, a familiar tattoo of faded chintz. Pictures in her head: her lying on the couch, eating milky cereal while watching TV, one throw-cushion behind her back, another under her knees. The base ragged where their decrepit cat, Mingi, used to sharpen his claws. She lifts a seat cushion and looks at its stained underside where her mother once spilled tomato soup, never to be forgiven by the stubborn fabric.

The coffee table with a small crack in the glass top that had been there for as long as she could remember. The server; the kitchen table; the counter swivel chairs. The buzz in her head dies down. She can do this. Slowly, methodically, she re-acquaints herself with each object. She lays her hand on them as she goes, acknowledging each piece, like some kind of mad furniture-whisperer.

The huge steel angle poise lamp, the bedside tables, the antique oak bookshelf. Box upon box of books and files and folders. Her parental units were academics and personally responsible, she was sure, for razing at least twenty rugby-field-size portions of rainforests each in the amount of paper they used over their lifetimes.

Despite being part of the original e-reader generation, they preferred their reading style old school, and pen and paper to glass or projections. 'It just feels more *real*,' her mother used to say when Kirsten sighed at her for writing down her shopping lists on the back of old receipts. 'Smartphones exist for a reason,' Kirsten would show her over and over how she could have a virtual shopping list, how she could send it to the store and have her groceries picked and delivered for her. Her mother would give her a tight smile, and she would know that she would never win this particular battle. When Cellpurses and then smart watches came on to the market it was just too much for them. They used to wield those old smartphone bricks as if they were something to be proud of, like the burning bras of the 1960s. An image of a particularly ugly bra in flames comes to Kirsten's mind; she doesn't know where it comes from. One of her university courses? An ancient Fair Lady? Picstream? Webpedia? Flittr? Sometimes she feels as though her brain is a giant, multidimensional reflector, filled with the world's random pictures. Where have they come from? A parallel life? A previous life? Someone else's life?

The only exception to her parents' fear of progressive technology was when she had given them a Holograph: a 3D-photo projector loaded with her Somali Pirates pictures. This is before the collection had won any awards. They were so proud of her, kept the projector running on loop, despite its rather macabre content: they had pirates in their lounge for months. The Holograph never moved from the mantelpiece, even when it stopped working.

There, there's a good memory to hold on to, until she remembers that the Holograph was stolen in the burglary, which makes her see the crimson comets again.

She battles to tear open the buff boxtape, cursing herself for not thinking of bringing a pair of scissors, when she finds in the third carton a neat little pocket-knife (Royal Sky). It is, fittingly, a sharp taste, a stab of bitter on her tongue, a hint of cyanide, like chewing an apple seed. She remembers this taste exactly, and gets a poke of nostalgia. Her father would keep this knife in his pocket and bring it out on special occasions: when a bottle of wine needed de-corking at a neighbourhood braai, or a loose thread threatened to unravel a dress. There would always be a calm measured-ness on these occasions. A slow inspection of the problem, a thoughtful diagnosis, and the retrieval of the magical object from the deep recesses of his trousers. A slow opening of the blade, a glint of light when it was revealed, and then at last, the careful incising where it was needed. Never forgetting the cleaning of the tool afterwards, a sleeve-shining of its insignia, and its eventual evaporation. Considered, calculating, careful.

She remembers specifically an occasion when she was battling to free a new baby doll from its suffocating plastic shell. The way he had achingly-slowly dismantled the packaging and kneeled to hand the toy to her. The way he had looked at her, almost with sadness, as if he had some kind of prescience that she wouldn't be able to bear children of her own. The memory, before fond and with pretty edges, now stings her with its poignancy. She swallows the hard stone in her throat.

Kirsten was never allowed to touch the knife, it was forbidden. She flicks it open and starts ripping into the boxes.

~

Seth knows before he opens his eyes that he's late for his grind. He groans and stretches for the Anahita water bottle he keeps next to his swingbed. Switches off his dreamrecorder. A few gulps later he turns on his Sunrise. Throughout the apartment all the curtains open, allowing the morning light to bleach the inside of the rooms, and what feels like the inside of his head. The apartment voice, which he has nicknamed 'Sandy,' wishes him a good morning and proceeds to play his Saturday playlist.

It's his last day at Pharmax so it shouldn't be too much of a problem if he's a few hours late. It takes him a while to remember why his head feels like it had been left on a township soccer field: Salvia pills, cocaine drops, ShadowShots, a beautiful girl with sequins for eyes. Having sex with the shining girl behind one of the curtains in the club, but bringing a different girl home. Rolo calling them a private cab. Long chestnut- and blonde-striped hair, palest skin, beautiful tits, cosmic blowjob. He yawns and rearranges himself, has another sip of water.

Shit, I didn't even check her ID for her Hi-Vax status.

That is dumb, but lately he's done worse. He is either getting less paranoid or more self-destructive. Maybe it's the salvia. Stretching his arms above his head, he makes a verbal note for his Pharmax report. Seth reaches over for his jacket, lying on the floor, and checks the inner pocket. He shakes the white bottle: almost half of the pills gone. He'll need to top up today before he says his goodbyes.

The stripey-haired hook-up wasn't happy when he asked her to leave at around 3AM but that was pretty much the standard reaction. He made the night more than worth her while, so he told her to suck it up as he pushed taxi tokens into her hand and closed the door behind her, opening it again just to turf out a lone red boot that smelled of Givenchy and old carpets.

As always, he is surprised by the hurt expression. *Honestly, how could she expect him to get a decent night's sleep with a total stranger in his bed? Some creeps were Fucked Up.*

He gets up and wraps his raw silk dressing gown around himself. He doesn't like walking around the place naked, even though he lives on his own. He finds people doing mundane things in the nude—like eating breakfast—distasteful. Naked is for showering and sex, for God's sake, not for frying eggs and pressing wapple juice. He switches on the kettle, pours Ethiopian javaberry grounds into his antique espresso maker, and puts it on the gas stove to percolate. While he's waiting he supercharges his Tile, steams some double-cream milk. Makes seedtoast with almond butter and wolfs it down. Makes some more, and takes it to his tablet along with his mug of fragrant coffee. Just as he had hoped, a small green rabbit blinks on his screen. Someone from Alba is online and bumps him. He types in his password to gain access to the thread.

FlowerGrrl> Hey SD. You ready?

He takes a sip of his coffee, dusts crumbs off his fingertips, and types a reply:

SD>> Hello my favourite cyberstalker. Yebo. Starting/F on Monday.

FlowerGrrl> U happy/brief?

SD>> Always.

FlowerGrrl> U did a good job/Pharmax.

SD>> There was nothing 2 do.

. . .

Out of nowhere, his left thumb starts tingling. He examines it, rubs it on the top of his thigh, and carries on typing.

SD>> They had nothing for us.

FlowerGrrl> Clean corporate? Thought those went/way/rhinos.

SD>> Me 2. But they R squeaky. Apart/drugging up country & making lds $$ off vuln & desperate.

FlowerGrrl>Hey, we all need 2 earn/living.

SD>> Sure. Any news re anything else? Heard about/stupid politician/pool?

FlowerGrrl> Criminal.

SD>> :)

FlowerGrrl> Sure there are lots of those at F.

SD>> Criminals or pools?

FlowerGrrl> Both. If u find 1 have/swim for me. Haven't swum since/kid.

SD>> Me neither. Probably have heated springs & shit in there. I'll do/fucking backstroke 4 U. YOLO!

FlowerGrrl> LOLZ! LFD. YOLO FOMO FML.

SD>> Congrats on Tabula Rasa bust. Excellent work. Mind-5.

FlowerGrrl> Going 2 break story next week.

SD>> They'll make good miners/farmers/etc at the PLC.

FlowerGrrl> Ha! Can U imagine? 1 day a botox billionaire, the next you're lubing up a cow.

SD>> Karma's a bitch.

FlowerGrrl> U said it, baby.

SD>> Nice/catch up.

FlowerGrrl> Ja, B careful now.

SD>> Always.

FlowerGrrl> Seriously. Watch yourself.

SD>> I am being serious. I'm paranoid, always careful.

FlowerGrrl> LOL! Funny cos iz true. X

The green rabbit disappears.

~

Kirsten's left thumb is bleeding. She hadn't realised you could get a (double) paper cut from double-walled cardboard. After swearing a great deal in every colour she can think of, she kicks the box that had inflicted the damage. She wants it to go flying, but it's heavy and all she manages to do is nudge it off the pile. It lands with a thud of disappointment on the concrete floor.

The corner of a white card sticks out from underneath the box. She pries it loose. Smaller than the palm of her hand, tacky double-sided tape on the back: it's the kind of card that gets sent with flower deliveries. The illustration is of a lily, printed in sparkling pink ink (Strawberry Spangle), which she bleeds on.

Inside, in a script she doesn't recognise, it says 'CL, yours forever, X, EM.'

Her watch beeps. It's a bump from Keke, wanting to meet up for drinks next week. Says she has something to celebrate. Somewhere dark and clubby, she says.

'Affirmative,' Kirsten replies, 'Congratulations in advance for whatever we're celebrating. Let's bask in our mutual claustrophilia.'

Bumps, or chatmail messages, are getting so short nowadays they can be impossible to textlate. Sometimes Kirsten uses the longest word she can think of, just to rebel against the often ridiculously abbreviated chat language.

She realises that this probably makes her old, and wonders if it is the equivalent of wielding a brick for a cellphone. Even her Snakewatch is now old technology. She doesn't have the energy to upgrade devices every season. Maybe she is more like her mother than she has ever realised.

She flicks the card back into the box and sucks the side of her thumb, where the skin is dual-sliced, and waits for the red to stop. She feels hung over, even though she didn't drink *that* much the night before. Another sign of aging? She sometimes feels like she's ninety. And not today's '90 is the new 40!' but real, steel, brittle ninety. Grey-hair, purple-rinse, hip-replacement ninety.

So far she had flipped through what felt like hundreds of files and documents, most written in jargon that she doesn't understand. She had to page through a library of notes before she found her birth certificate. Onionskin paper, slightly wrinkled, low-resolution print, ugly typography, but there her name was in black and white: Kirsten Lovell; daughter of Sebastian and Carol Lovell. Born on the 6th of December 1988 at the Trinity Clinic in Sandton, Johannesburg.

So she does exist, she thinks, *even though it should seem clear. Cogito ergo fucking sum.*

Perhaps the autopsy report was wrong? They could have mixed up her mother's body with someone else's, easy enough to do when so many people are dying of the Bug. Or the discharge note from the hospital could have been wrong; they got the date of her hysterectomy wrong. A sleep-deprived nurse on her midnight shift could easily have written down the wrong year. Perhaps absent-mindedly thinking of her own surgery, or the birth of one of her own kids.

Getting tired of hunting through the boxes now, she finally finds the one she had come all this way for. It's a bit squashed on the edges, and grubby with handprints. Sealed with three different kinds of tape, it has clearly been opened and closed a number of times over the years. 'PHOTO ALBUMS' is scribbled on the side in her mother's terrible handwriting. When Kirsten catches sight of the scrawl she feels a twinge of tenderness and has to sit down for a breath.

She opens the box with a little more care than she had the others. Twelve hardcover photo albums take up the top half of the box, and the bottom is lined with DVDs. They only started taking digital photos when she was in high school, so it was safe to say what she was looking for would be in one of the paper albums.

There is a specific picture of herself as a baby that she wants to find. She guesses the photo was taken when she was around six months old, somewhere outside in the sun with a tree, or trees, in the background. A silly, fabric-flowered headband decorates her hairless moon of a head. Her back is slightly arched and an arm is outstretched to someone off-camera, a pale pink starfish for a hand.

Slowly she pages through each album, trying to not get caught in the webs of emotion they contain: rhubarb crumble, ash grey, peppermint (the colour, not the taste), coconut sunscreen, soggy egg sandwiches (Sulphurous Sponge), some kind of flat sucker with a milky taste – butterscotch? Butterscotch with beach-sand. Marshmallow mice – available only at a game-hall tuckshop at a family holiday resort in the Drakensberg. Ammonia, baby oil, cherry cigars. Silk carnations, flaking slasto, ants that taste like pepper. She snaps shut the last album and looks for another box of photos.

This can't be all there is. We're missing three years. The first three years.

Kirsten, now driven by a fierce energy, attacks what is left of the boxes. Her mind races with possible explanations. Maybe they didn't own a camera. Maybe they believed it was bad luck to photograph a baby. Maybe the photos were lost, stolen, burnt in a fire. There are no baby clothes either. No baby toys, but she's sure they must have been given away—there were hundreds of orphans in those days—abandoned babies: unheard of today. Wet patches bloom under her arms as she scrabbles through the contents. Her hair begins to bother her and she ties it up roughly into an untidy bun. As the boxes start to run out, her anxiety builds. She finds no more albums, but in the second-last box she opens she discovers some framed photographs. *Of course! It was framed! That's why it's not in an album.* A calming finger on her heart.

And there it is, almost exactly how she remembers it. She clutches it, searching it for detail. The heat of her hands mists the silver frame: heavy, decorative, tasteful, the picture not exactly in focus, but close enough. A blue cotton dress (Robin Egg) puckered by the tanned arm holding her up. She has no aunts, no grandmothers; that must be her mom's arm, although she doesn't recognise it.

She expects the photo to make her feel some kind of relief, but it has the opposite effect. Some small idea is tapping at her, whirring in her brain. Something feels off the mark. She scans the picture again.

What is it? The texture. The texture of the paper is wrong. It isn't printed on glossy or matt photo paper, the way it would have been in 1987. It's grainy, pulpy. Kirsten turns the frame over in her hands and pries loose the back. A quarter of a glamorous cigarette print ad stares back at her, its bright blue slashing her vision.

Kirsten turns it over and over again, battling to understand, not wanting to understand. It's not a photo of her. It's not a photo at all, but a cutting from a magazine. The autopsy diagram flits into her mind with its careless cross over her mother's lower abdomen.

She glances over at the cheap-looking birth certificate then down to the piece of paper she holds. Perhaps her photo was published in the magazine for some reason? Living & Loving, the cutting says, 'New Winter Beauties,' July 1991. She was three years old when this issue was printed.

CHAPTER 7

ORGANIC ARSE CARROTS

JOHANNESBURG, 2021

'Oh,' his new manager says, greeting Seth with an awkward smile, 'I thought you would be wearing a suit.'

At the behemoth reception of Fontus, the walls are covered in digital 4D wallpaper of waterfalls, streams and lakes. White noise gushes through the sound system: water splashing and birds chirping. Seth doesn't shake his proffered hand.

'I don't wear suits.'

Heavy security guards the front door, which is at odds with the holograms of rising mist and darting digital hummingbirds. Men with concealed guns and pepper-spray look serenely on as employees and visitors enter through the metal detectors.

As they make their way through the building, the moving images change according to which section they are in: the waters Anahita, Tethys, Hydra, followed by the carbonated soft drinks. Anahita is platinum and crystal, blond hair, and pale, skeletal models. Diamond drops and sleek splashes of mercury. Tethys is dew on grass, rainforests, intelligent-looking people wearing spectacles, good dentures, hands on chins. Cool, humidified air streams past them as they walk.

Wesley doesn't back down. 'It's company policy.'

Hydra is smiling black children, barefoot, dusty. A gospel choir. Fever trees. Optimistic amateur vegetable gardens. Dry red earth. Seth gets thirsty just looking at them.

'No, it's not,' says Seth. 'I would never have signed the contract.'

There is an awkward silence until they reach the section where he will be grinding: Carbonates. As expected, there are bubbles frothing and fizzing all around them.

Wesley slows to a stop in the red area: CinnaCola. The décor is like a large tin of red paint has exploded.

'It may not be in the *actual* contract...'

'Well, then, there's no problem. Is this my office?' Seth strides in and slips behind the desk, surveying his stationery. Shrugs off his black hoodie and slings it over his chair. He's never had a proper desk job before; he's used to being in a lab of sorts. He uncaps a brand new permanent marker and sniffs it. Wesley looks at Seth swivelling in his chair and purses his lips. Strokes his soul patch with two fingers.

'We have an 8AM meeting every Monday morning to set up our week's goals,' he says.

Yeah, I won't be making those, Seth resists saying.

'A goal not written down is just a dream. What is measured is managed. CinnaCola assembles in the Red Room.'

Seth inspects the contents of his desk drawers. Wesley tries to get his attention.

'But it's not all work-work-work here! On the last Friday of the month, we do a teambuilding activity, where we compete against the other FCs.' Wesley fingers the red lanyard around his neck. 'FC. That's Flavour-Colours,' he says. 'It's teambuilding and fun and all that but it's also a serious competition. It's important that we win. What are you good at? You know, apart from maths? Paintball? Boules? Triathlons? Firewalking? Extreme Frisbee?'

The distaste must have shown on Seth's face because Wesley stops talking and looks uncomfortable. He puffs out his chest and says 'It's compulsory.'

Is it also compulsory to walk around with a carrot shoved up your arse? Do they hand out complimentary organic arse carrots here?

Wesley's cheeks colour, and for a second Seth thinks he said it out loud, but then realises it's because Wesley has caught sight of his sneakers. They're limited edition, by a local graffiti artist, and have the word *Punani* emblazoned on the sides. He guesses they're worth more than Wesley makes in a month. Seth is tempted to put them up on the desk, but then thinks better of it. Best not to push him too far, too soon. Managers are assholes at the best of times and he can't have anyone deliberately obstructing him. As a peace-making concession he takes out his eyebrow-ring and puts it in his pocket. Rubs off some of the Smudge on his eyes. He sees Wesley soften. It works every time.

'Okay, then,' says Seth, pointing at his giant flatscreen Glass, 'I'd better get started.'

Wesley attempts a smile, and looks immediately like a rodent: his nose crinkles up and his lips reveal his large front teeth. Perfect, Wesley the Weasel. At least now he won't forget his name. A welcome pack on his desk contains his access/ID card, to be clipped onto his very own red lanyard, a CinnaCola shirt in his size, complete with animated fizzing logo, and a blue book of Fontus rules of conduct. The Fontus logo is, unimaginatively, a stylised illustration of a fountain, and the word 'Fontus' is set in a handsome font, uppercase. He turfs the lanyard into his drawer and slides the card into his pocket.

'You have to wear it,' says The Weasel. 'The lanyard, and card. It's for ID as much as it's for access.' He points to the camera in the corner of the room. 'Security, you know.'

Seth retrieves the red lanyard and clips his card onto it. Reluctantly puts it around his neck. The Weasel chortles.

'Besides, we can't have those Greens sneaking around the red section, stealing our brand strategies!'

Posters on the walls feature pictures of the Fourteen Wonders of the world on dark blue backgrounds with slogans like: 'It's Not a Problem, it's a Challenge' and 'Opportunities are Everywhere'.

He waits for The Weasel to go before he dumps the rest of the welcome pack into the bin. The shirt continues to fizz. He swivels his ergochair around, stares out of the window. Someone laughs in the corridor. The grounds are immaculate: the lawn grass smooth and green; perfectly tended bright annuals burst with complimentary colours under canopies of handsome indigenous trees. Cheerful employees pass each other with a smile or a wave. The campus is like a hotbed of high spirits, cleanliness, and efficiency, a bright island in the dark fuss that is the rest of the country. Seth pops a pill. Yes, he thinks, there is definitely something very odd going on around here.

JOURNAL ENTRY

28 SEPTEMBER 1987, WESTVILLE

In the news: *Two bombs explode at the Standard Bank Arena in Johannesburg. John McEnroe is fined for his antics at the US Open. Star Trek: The Next Generation debuts on (American!) TV.*

What I'm listening to: *Michael Jackson's Bad album. Superbad!*

What I'm reading: *Misery by Stephen King: injured and drugged, an author is held captive by a psychotic fan. So-o-o creepy. Make P get up to switch the lights off!*

What I'm watching: *Fatal Attraction. Not the best movie to watch in the week before your wedding! Totally scary, I loved it.*

We got married today at a tiny ceremony at Westville Magistrate's Court. P's best man (Whitey) was there, and both of our parents. I totally thought my folks would boycott the wedding but they were troopers. Dad put on a brave face and Mom took turns crying and fussing with my dress in front, as if a piece of fabric could cover my huge pregnant belly. I mean it's totally gigantic! I never thought it was possible to get this big! The ONLY thing that fits me apart from this big meringue of a wedding dress is my old 'Sex Pistols' T-shirt. I practically live in it!

When I wrote to Dad about it (the pregnancy) he was very cross and I didn't hear from him for ages. Mom phoned me and told me to be patient, and that he would come around. If not before the wedding then definitely once the baby was born, she said. His first grandchild! She was right. When I saw him he hugged me (carefully avoiding the bump), and said: "There's nothing to do but to make the best of a bad situation." I wanted to say to him: a lovely baby is not a 'bad situation', but I was so totally grateful to be forgiven and to feel loved that I just kept quiet and kissed him.

The 'wedding photos' are going to be so funny. We got a certificate right away saying that we are husband and wife. Me, a wife?! Ha! I'm so sure! Our wedding song was our favourite song by Bryan Adams: 'Hearts on Fire'. I got quite emotional, think it's the raging hormones. But when I looked at P I could tell that he had a lump in his throat too.

We went to a seafood restaurant afterwards and my dad ordered lots of platters and sparkling wine. I couldn't, like, have seafood or wine in my state but I didn't feel like eating anyway. I toasted our marriage with Grapetizer in a champagne glass. Totally the Best Grapetizer I have ever tasted.

Afterwards, in bed, exhausted but happy, P lay with his hand on my stomach and we could feel the baby moving.

Happiest day of my life, and I can't wait to meet my baby.

CHAPTER 8

MARY CONTRARY

Johannesburg, 2021

Kirsten catches the waiter's attention and motions for another round. She's sitting on her own in Molly Q's, a retro-restaurant, the only one in Johannesburg that still serves molecular cuisine.

It's her best, and James had booked a table for them for his first night back home. Kirsten's favourite gastroventure, she loves the purity of the flavours here; the shapes she sees and feels are so vivid and in focus.

She is drinking their signature cocktail, an unBloody Mary-Contrary. The purest vodka swirled with clear tomato water and essence of pepper. They serve it with a long, slender frozen piece of celery-green glass. Kirsten takes a sip and feels the crystalline shapes appear before her. Not as strong as the first drink, but quite clear nevertheless.

Damn the law of diminishing returns.

They'll get stronger, more palpable, later in the evening; alcohol always makes her synaesthesia more pronounced. Suddenly she feels lips on her forehead, a warm hand on her back, and she blinks past the crystals to see James.

'Kitty! I missed you.'

She springs up to hug him, inhales the tang of his neck. He smells like Zimbabwe: hand sanitiser and aeroplane cabin. Also: miswak chewing gum that has long lost its flavour. They hold onto each other for a while.

'I missed you too.'

Kissing James is always orange: different shades of orange depending on the mood of the kiss. Breakfast kisses are usually a fresh Buttercup Yellow, sex kisses are Burnt-

Sky, with a spectrum in between of, among others, loving, friendly, angry, guilty (Pollen, Polished Pine, Rubber Duck, Turmeric). His energy is warm yellow-orange-ruby, sweet, with a sharp echo. Marmalade James.

They sit down, and Kirsten orders a craft beer for him, a hoppy ale; he doesn't drink cocktails. He always laughs out loud when they watch old movies and James Bond drinks a martini.

'How's the clinic?'

He has a slight tan, despite his usually fanatical compulsion to apply SPF100, and crumpled cotton sleeves. He looks tired, but well.

'Understaffed, underfunded, and bursting with sick people: sick children, sick babies. It was difficult to leave.'

Something small in Kirsten splinters. He grabs her hand.

'Of course, I'd rather be with you than anywhere, but there are just so many—'

'I understand,' she says, looking away. It's easier to be with people you can help.

'So many of the babies there are hungry and neglected. Not like here,' he says.

'Not like here,' she agrees. How can you neglect a baby? How come those creeps are fertile, she thinks, when I'm not?

'I mean I can see how the border-baby trade is thriving. When you see kids like that you get the feeling that their parents would gladly part with them for a couple of hundred thousand rand.'

'Awful,' says Kirsten, pulling a face. 'They should write it into law that you need to qualify for a parenting license before you're allowed to procreate.'

'You don't mean that,' James says, but she kind of does.

They order the set menu, and an *amuse bouche* of wooded chardonnay gelée with pink balsamic caviar arrives, then Asian crudo with a brush of avocado silk, and wasabi sorbet. They keep quiet for the first few bites, allowing Kirsten to appreciate all the shapes, colours and textures of the flavours. The wasabi sorbet in particular sends cool ninja stars into her brain. It feels good.

'How are you?' James asks, 'how have you been holding up?'

'I had a very interesting weekend,' she says, spooning the last of the wasabi into her mouth and feeling the jagged edges of the stars fade away. 'I discovered the reason I'm so, well, fucked up.'

James takes a long, slow sip of his beer. They had been through this so many times before.

One of the problems with long-term mono-relationships, is that listening to the same old issues gets eyeball-bleedingly boring. At least now she has a new angle.

He looks at her, measuring her mood, puts down his glass. She senses him sighing on the inside.

'Kitty, you're not fucked up.'

'I am, a little.'

'Okay, you are, a little, but so is everyone else. You're just more aware of your fucked-up-ness than the average creep, because you're...'

'Special?'

'Not what I was going to say, but let's go with that.'

They smile at each other, and it reminds her of when they started dating in varsity. When things were still shiny.

'Do you mean your synaesthesia?'

'No, the synaesthesia is my light side. I'm talking about my dark side.'

'The Black Hole,' he says. God, how he hates The Black Hole.

As a child she had tried to explain it to her parents, thinking that they had it too, that is was a necessary human condition, but they would get frustrated and lose their patience, just as James does now. Perhaps The Black Hole on its own would have been fine, but with her synaesthesia it seemed too much for them to handle. It caused a rift: a cool, empty space between them that could easily be ignored; not often navigated.

Once, when she was still in primary school, she tried to explain the emptiness to her mother, who became furious and stormed out, leaving her at home alone. When the minutes streamed into hours and the sun started sinking she went to the neighbour's house: a young couple who, nonplussed, plopped her in front of the television. They fed her milky rooibos and stale Marie biscuits while they whispered into the phone. Afterwards, they sat in the living room with her, making awkward conversation, until the glare of her mother's headlights lit up their sitting room, announcing, with bright hostility, her return. It wasn't the first or the last time her mother had left her on her own.

Eventually, a little desperately, her father had produced Mingi: a meowing yin-yang ball of fluff, hoping the kitten would stitch up The Black Hole, but it didn't. She kept quiet about it after that, not wanting to cause them any more worry. Now they were gone and now James was the worrier.

'And?' he prompts, 'what's the reason?'

She smooths out the polka-dotted tablecloth then says the words out loud: slowly, clearly, listening to her own voice. 'I think I was adopted.'

James frowns at her. 'What?'

'Keke visited while you were away. She found out some... well, to cut a long story short, my mother had a hysterectomy before I was born.'

She lets it sink in. James just looks at her.

'And,' she says, taking the birth certificate and magazine clipping out of her bag, 'look at these. Look at this cheap-ass certificate, probably created in CorelDRAW. Do you know that there is not one photo of me as a baby? Not one.'

She flips the imposter-baby picture over to reveal the magazine name and date on the other side. James looks stunned. She doesn't blame him. She doesn't quite believe it yet, either. He grabs the photo from her hand and studies it.

'I know!' she says, 'isn't it crazy? I'm adopted!' The woman at the next table looks over in interest. Kirsten lowers her voice. 'So there is a reason I never felt properly connected to them. Why I always felt like an outsider.'

'Everyone feels like an outsider. It's inherent, the feeling we don't belong. Ironically, the one thing we all have in common.'

'Yes, okay, but... it's crackers, right? Do you realise what this means? I could have a family out there!'

James is quiet, looks worried.

'Well?' she urges him, as if he has some kind of answer for her.

'I'm sorry, I don't know what to say. I mean, it's pretty shocking. If it's true.'

'I need to find them.'

'What do you mean?'

'What the hell do you think I mean? I'm going to find out who my real parents are. And meet them. Have them over for some fucking cake.'

'I don't think it's a good idea.'

'I knew you'd say that.'

'That's unfair.'

'That night… that night they were killed,' says Kirsten.

James puts his hand over hers.

'My mother called me. She said she had to tell me something. That it couldn't wait.'

'Why didn't you... tell me?'

'She was upset, stumbling over her words. Not making sense. I thought she was... having one of her episodes.'

Carol had been showing signs of early-onset Alzheimer's. She hadn't been diagnosed, but the symptoms of dementia had begun presenting themselves the year before, and were increasing in frequency. Kirsten pictured the disease as a whey-coloured cotton wool cloud over her mother's head (Cirrus Nest). As with most issues, her parents hadn't liked to talk about it. James looks into her ever-changing eyes, the sound of the sea.

'Surely you must get it? This is my chance to find my missing part. Besides, it's not just for me; it's for us. To know my biological mother's medical history… it might help us figure out our... fertility issues.'

'I wish that I was enough for you,' he whispers, turmeric in the air. Kisten gives him a segment of a smile. They both know it will never be true.

He takes a gulp of his beer. 'We don't have fertility issues.'

'Are you being serious? We've been trying for years.'

'That's normal, nowadays.'

A frozen veil descends between them.

'I feel the hope too,' says James. 'And the disappointment. I want a baby as much as you do.'

'Bullshit,' she says, although she knows it hurts him.

'Look, the less you worry about it—'

Kirsten curls her hands into fists. 'Less worry is not an option currently on the table. Please choose another fucking option.'

The chicken truffle with cocoa-chilli reduction and green peppercorn brittle arrives. It is beautifully presented but Kirsten is raging inside and can't imagine she can swallow any of it.

'Look,' she says, pushing her chair back. 'I'm meeting Kex for drinks tonight. I'm going to go.'

'Kitty, please don't be like this.'

She stands up. 'I'll see you later.'

~

Seth leaves the Fontus building at 20:30. He is enjoying the actual work of the new job, the flavour-mapping and production process modelling; it's like grinding at Disney World after the serious chemical engineering he did at Pharmax. Plus they have everything you could possibly want on the campus: a gym, a spa, a drycleaner, a download-den, communal bikes, restaurants, a (mostly empty) childcare centre, a virtual bowling alley, a Lixair chamber, SleepPods, all complimentary for staff. They even have wine tasting and book club evenings. Golf days, gaming nights. Infertility support groups. Overnight accommodation. The huge property is not dissimilar to a full-board holiday resort. It's as if they don't want their employees to leave the premises. Seth is surprised they don't run a matchmaking service to keep all the creeps in the family. Or a brothel.

The employees themselves seem to be extremely clean-cut: professionally dressed, well groomed, clear skinned. Not a lot of individual style—no Smudge or ink in sight. Certainly no recreational drugs as far as he can tell.

The Weasel is turning out to be even more of a pesticle than expected, literally leaning over his shoulder as he works. He finds it difficult to be constructive when he's being watched, especially by a bag of dicks. He needs to experiment and play around, and this includes swapping and swerving in between a host of different programs and apps, and you can't do that when you have those watery eyes glued to your screen.

Worse still, it makes it almost impossible to do his real job—his Alba job—the reason he is here is in the first place. Seth feels a hot rush of irritation, almost anger; he needs to blow off some steam. He has a cocaine drop, his third for the day, and decides to head to the SkyBar.

~

Kirsten catches a tuk-tuk for the short ride into the inner city. She has the feeling someone is watching her, and keeps looking over her shoulder for James, that he must have followed her out of Molly Q's, but each time she thinks she hears something, or sees movement out of the corner of her eye, there is no one there. Despite the reassuring company of her fellow passengers, she starts to feel quite spooked.

Kekeletso is already at the bar when Kirsten gets there, and is getting some girl's number. Once she has it, they smile at each other, and the woman kisses Keke's cheek, strokes her arm. Keke is wearing a lacy tank top that shows off her nano-ink tattoo beautifully. It's an antique grey colour now, so Keke must have shot up quite recently.

The SkyBar is on top of the tallest skyscraper in South Africa. It's five hundred floors, and has a glass elevator on either side. They used to have a C-shaped infinity pool outside, running almost all the way around the venue. Now it's dry and filled with exotic-looking plants with larger-than-life leaves and trailing tendrils. The club's main attraction is that there's always an interesting crowd, a good mix of BEE and reverse-BEE millionaires, bohemians, sports celebrities, tourists and race car drivers.

'Hey,' she greets Keke, 'this place is packed! I thought we were only meeting at nine-thirty.'

She waves off the woman. 'I decided to come early, to network.'

'So that's what the kids are calling it nowadays?'

Keke smiles, and Kirsten grabs the still-warm barstool, which is more of a post-modernist statement than an actual chair.

'Seriously, she's a good contact to have. Grinds for the Nancies.'

'Yuck,' says Kirsten, 'and I thought my life was bad.'

'She's clearly a masochist.'

'Those masochists. Handy to have around.'

Keke orders them a couple of beers, hits the 'tip' button twice, and the barman delivers them with a wink in her direction. Her account will be debited with the balance by the KFID system as she leaves.

'So, why are you early? I thought Marmalade was taking you out tonight. What happened, did he stand you up? No petrol in Zim again? No water? No aeroplane stairs?'

'It would have been better if he had.'

'Oh, shit. Sorry. Another fight?'

'Argh... I'm so sick of hearing about my own problems. Fuck it. What are we here to celebrate?'

'Well... can I tell you a secret?' asks Keke, eyes a-sparkle.

'Hello,' says Kirsten, 'who else would you tell?'

'You can't tell anyone, not even Marmalade.'

Won't be the first time. Kirsten nods.

'I'm just about to break this big story. It's huge. I'd love to say that it's been weeks of hard journo-ing but actually it just fell into my lap. All I had to do was fact-check.'

'In other words, all your Friend With Benefits had to do was fact-check.'

'Yeah-bo.'

'Hey? Who did it come from? Why would someone just hand over a story to you? And why you?'

'I don't know. The gods of the fuck-circus that is journalism decided to smile down on me. Why do whistleblowers toot their flutes? Justice? Revenge? It arrived in my SkyBox with no note and no author. Just the picture of a little green rabbit that disappeared as soon as I opened it.'

'Bizarre,' says Kirsten.

'I know already. But listen to this. You know that Slow-Age super-expensive beauty-salon-slash-plastic-surgery clinic in Saxonwold? Tabula Rasa. They were the first spa in SA to have a Lixair—vitamin air—chamber. They made headlines a while ago with their FOXO gene therapy? The one with all-white everything? Like, you get blinded when you go in there?'

'Heard of it. Never been. My freelance salary doesn't stretch that far.'

'Lucky for you. All that white was hiding something very dark indeed.'

'Let me guess. They were exchanging their wrinkled flesh-and-blood clients for smooth-skinned Quinbots?'

'Worse,' says Kekeletso.

'Ha,' says Kirsten. 'What?'

'They were buying *discarded embryos* from dodgy fertility clinics, spinning them for their stem cells, then injecting them into their clients' *faces.*'

Kirsten stops smiling. 'No,' she says.

'That's what I thought. No way it could be true, but this report came from someone who had worked there. Had infiltrated the system and had proof of hundreds of transactions. Pics, video, everything.'

'That is so fucked up. Horrible. I wish you had never told me. I wish it wasn't true.'

'Sorry,' says Keke. 'I had to tell someone. I've been sitting on it for days waiting for all the facts to check out.'

'What kind of world are we living in?' asks Kirsten.

'One where at least there is someone willing to out those bastards. If something like this had happened fifty years ago we wouldn't have had a cooking clue. May The Net bless Truthers everywhere.'

'To Truthers!' says Kirsten, raising her drink. 'Also, ha ha.'

'Huh?'

'Don't you think it's funny? The name? Tabula Rasa means "clean slate", doesn't it? Like, come in all aged and wrinkled and shit and leave with a face like a clean slate.'

'And a brain to go with it,' Keke adds.

'Except now it's going to be revealed as a black clinic.'

'Poetry!'

'You're right, it is funny. Ha!'

'Or would be, if it wasn't so fucked up.'

'Yes,' Keke pulls a face, 'well. You know what they say.'

'Tell me. What do they say?'

'If you don't laugh, you cry.'

'Story of my life. Well, congratulations. That's one big fucking story. I sense some kind of award for journalistic excellence on the horizon. Huzzah!'

'I wish I could take the credit. Oh, Kitty... there's something else,' says Keke, looking hesitant.

'What's up?'

'I found something else. It's something about you. About your parents.' Keke rubs her lips, rings for another round. 'You're not going to like it.'

~

Seth is gliding to electro-house swampo-phonic with a drunk woman in a kimono on the superglass dance-floor. It is easier to dance if you don't look down: five hundred floors up, the vertigo from looking down sucks the rhythm from your feet. Usually he loves the mixed crowd at the SkyBar but he feels off-balance tonight. The drinks don't taste as good; the women aren't as pretty as usual. It's too crowded. He tried taking more coke earlier but it seems like a waste with this mood. Usually he would have already banged this girl in the plant pool, or in the unisex bathroom, but tonight it doesn't feel worth the bother. This makes him feel worse. Is he getting old? Is grinding in a corporate environment leaching him of his personality? What's next? Wearing a suit and tie? A nametag? A hearing aid? Joining the Fontus D&D club? Facebook? Getting married? Viagra? He shivers involuntarily. The sooner he can get his job there done and move on, the better.

He gives up on having a good time, abandons his drink, shrugs off the kimono and goes to get his jacket and gun from the security counter. While he manoeuvres through the warm bodies that block him he inadvertently gets close to the bar. As he's making his way forward he feels a surge, an electric current zip through his body. It shocks him into standing up straight. He is surrounded—touching so many creeps at the same time—and he looks about to see if anyone else felt it, but no one around him registers any kind of surprise.

The fuck was that?

~

Kirsten is doubled over. Keke grabs her arm.

'Are you okay?'

'Christ,' she whispers, 'what the fuck?'

'What?'

'I just had the weirdest feeling.'

'Your synaes-stuff?'

Slowly she starts to straighten, hands on hips. 'Fucking hell. I don't think so. More like getting the electric chair. You didn't feel anything?'

Keke shakes her head.

'I must have touched something.' She looks around for anything that may have shocked her. 'It's so crowded in here, maybe it was just some kind of sensory overload.'

Keke looks unconvinced. 'Good god, woman, the more I get to know you, the stranger you become.'

'It's nothing. I'm okay. Hit me,' she says to Keke. 'I can take it.'

'You weren't adopted,' says Keke.

'What?' says Kirsten, cupping her ear.

'You weren't adopted!' shouts Keke.

'That doesn't make any sense.'

'I know,' says Keke. 'But my FWB knows his stuff and there is no record of your parents adopting you, or of you being put up for adoption. He's the best hacker I know. If Marko didn't find anything, believe me, there is nothing to find.'

Kirsten can't think of anything to say.

'It wasn't easy, either. I did some of the digging myself. Since the last orphanage closed in 2016 it's tricky to get information... enough red tape to strangle all the bureaucrats on the planet. It's as if, now that adoption doesn't happen anymore, it's a closed chapter in SA history.'

'I guess that makes sense. Now that babies are... hard to come by, no one wants to think of a time when there were hundreds of them growing up in nasty institutions.'

'Another legacy of the HI-Vax. No more AIDS orphan babies.'

'And of the fertility crisis. No more babies, full stop.' Pain flashes across Kirsten's face.

'Sorry, I know this must be difficult for you.'

'It's not. I mean, of course it is, but for different reasons. So you're sure? No record of an adoption?'

'Actually, no record of you being born. At all.'

Kirsten had guessed the birth certificate was a fake. She laughs despite herself.

'So, what? You're saying I don't exist? I'm a ghost? No wonder I feel hollow. It's all starting to make sense now!'

'Not quite a ghost, but there's definitely something odd about the way you came into the world. We just need to work out what happened. I mean, if that's what you want. You could just forget about the autopsy report. Go back to living your normal life. It's probably the sensible thing to do.'

'Impossible. Besides, it's never been *normal.* I need to find out the truth.'

Keke downs the last of her drink.

'I was hoping you'd say that.'

~

Seth looks at the clockologram on his bedroom wall for what feels like the hundredth time since getting into bed. Agitated, he wonders if he should get a sleeping pill but he's already had two TranX so another downer would probably be a bad idea, especially on top of everything else he's had today. A rock lyric comes into his head.

'Sandy,' he says to the open room.

'Yes, Seth,' purrs the apartment voice.

'Play the song 'Slumber is For Corpses'.'

Three beats later the song comes onto the sound system.

He closes his eyes and listens for a while, then reaches over for the sleeping pills, taps one into his palm. *Fuck it,* he thinks, and swallows it dry. He feels immensely dissatisfied with life in general. His QOL score was sitting at 32 out of a possible 100.

He logged on to the Alba network when he arrived home to see if there were any messages, but there was no green rabbit. He looked for a chatterbot in the quantum philosophy circuit but didn't find one interesting enough. He watched half an hour of a really bad ultra-reality programme about the Underground Games: NinjaJitsu and Punch-Rugby, before giving up on the day and going to bed. He has been alone for so long, but has never gotten used to the feeling. On nights like this his life gapes before him, one big, empty gash. He is a prime number, and prime numbers are always lonely.

The animated graphic novel on his Tile fails to interest him, and he doesn't feel up to gaming, so he just lies back and watches the red hologram digits click over and over. 00:00. He can't even be bothered to jerk off.

~

They leave the SkyBar at around midnight. Kirsten knows by the look in Keke's eyes that she's on her way to a booty call.

'Watch yourself,' Keke says, strapping her helmet on and inflating it. She flings her leg over her sleek e-motorbike, releases the kickstand, and revs the engine. Kirsten waves as Keke takes off with a roar.

Standing in the monochrome rectangular box of the almost empty, poorly lit parking basement, Kirsten feels restless, cocky, horny, and not at all in the mood to go home. If she were single she'd go back to the bar, pick up some unsuspecting man and show him her talents.

She misses that, sometimes, the thrill of sleeping with someone for the first time. The feeling of a stranger's lips on hers—lips that have nothing to do with love or affection. The first undressing, the first nipple-in-mouth, pulling of hair, and then the heady relief of that first swollen thrust. Just thinking about it, Kirsten feels her breathing deepen, and a general throbbing in the lower half of her body. James is a generous lover, but he doesn't have the same nagging libido she does. Add thirteen years of old-fashioned monogamy to that and it's always tempting on nights like this, with booze in her blood, to accept one of the many advances made to her. After all, no one would have to know, so no one would be hurt. She has never cheated on James, but at times like this, angry with him, angry with the world, she feels a hard, rebellious recklessness, a sharp chipstone in her fist.

The idea of meeting someone new at the bar, someone who doesn't know any of her problems, is tempting. She could pretend to be a different person. Be someone lighter: someone who didn't think as much. Make up a fake name, live one of those parallel lives that loiter in her subconscious, if only for a few hours. Shake some yellow stars of adrenaline into her bloodstream. Have dirty sex.

But she won't do it, wouldn't be able to live with the haunting guilt. Kirsten may have a dozen flaws, but she is not a cheater. Cursed at birth with honesty and loyalty, she's not dissimilar to a Labrador, as Keke likes to say.

All relationships have their rocky roads. She reminds herself to think with her brain, and her heart, and takes a definitive step in the direction of the late-night bus stop.

In the distance a silhouette steps out from behind a car and Kirsten jumps.

Jesus! She scrabbles for her mace.

The figure slowly approaches her and her beer-clumsy fingers can't find the mace so she decides to run. The parking basement, however, is in virtual darkness apart from the exit, and the creep now stands between her and the light. Kirsten squints, shields her eyes, tries to see the face of the stranger.

'Hello?' She pushes her voice deeper, tries to seem strong and confident. The figure slows, but keeps moving towards her, gliding silently, also cautious. With a zinging in her head, Kirsten realises this is the person who has been following her all night. She sweats, feverish with fright.

'Don't be scared,' says a woman with a wobbly voice.

'What do you want?' shouts Kirsten, an edge to her tone. She imagines herself waking up the next morning in a bath of dirty ice, with untidy green stitches (Seaweed Sutures) where her kidneys used to be. But that kind of stuff doesn't happen anymore. They print organs now.

'I have something for you.'

Kirsten can make out her face, cheek-boned but androgynous, with a matching haircut. Skeletal figure hidden in unflattering clothes: mom-cut jeans and a tracksuit top flecked with dog hair. No makeup on her dry lips or darting eyes. Clenched hands.

'Stay away from me!' shouts Kirsten. 'Stay away!'

'I have something for you,' the woman says again.

Jesus Christ. What? A knife? An injection? A cold pad of chloroform to hold to my mouth?

'I'm not here to hurt you,' she says, scuttling up close in dirty sneakers. She has body odour: dried figs and BBQ sauce. The stink smacks Kirsten in the face: it's a giant grey curtain, poised to smother. The woman has some sticky white sleep in her eyes. Kirsten is repelled, nauseated.

'I'm here to warn you.' Her eyes flash from beneath her blunt-cut fringe. 'There are people, people that want to hurt us.'

'Us?'

'You, and me, and the other four.'

'Six people?'

'Seven! Seven! One is dead already!'

Oh boy.

'He was first on the list. He sang a song. Music man. Now he is dead. We were too late. Now I am warning you.'

Kirsten tries to step around her, but she blocks her way.

'I didn't believe it either when she told me,' she rambles, 'but she said I had to find you! Had to warn you. Had to give you the list.'

The woman takes her hand, and the feel of her clammy fingers makes Kirsten cringe. The woman presses a cold object into her palm and closes her fingers over it. A new wave of BBQ BO washes over Kirsten and she almost gags.

'There is real danger. Don't go to the police, they are in on it! They are pawns. Don't tell anyone. Don't trust anyone. Like dominoes we'll fall,' she says, softly clicking her fingers. *Click, click, click*. 'Dominoes.' She clicks seven times. 'Don't trust anyone! Not even the people you love.'

Kirsten's heart bangs, her watch alerts her to a spike in blood pressure. The woman turns and scurries away. After a few steps she turns and whispers, 'Be careful, Kate.'

'My name is Kirsten!'

'Yes,' says the woman. 'Your Kirsten is my Betty, Kate. Betty-Barbara. Kirsten-Kate.'

Kirsten looks down, opening her hand to reveal a small silver key.

'Thank Christ!' says Kirsten as she catches sight of James. Spooked by the delusional woman in the basement, she called and asked him to fetch her, and has been waiting for him in a bright, 24-hour teashop around the corner from the bar. She gets up too quickly to hug him and sends her cup and saucer stuttering to the floor where they crack and break apart in slow motion. They move awkwardly to pick up the pieces.

'I'm sorry,' he says, mid-crouch, eyes on the floor.

'Me too,' she says. 'Well, sorry that we fought, anyway.'

'Yes,' he says.

She's too strung out to catch any kind of public transport, so they walk home. The pavement trips them up, but it's a small price to pay. Kirsten tells him about Keke's latest discovery: that there's no record of her birth.

'That's impossible,' James says. 'There must be. Just because she can't find proof... Look, I got your pills for you.' He takes a plastic bottle of little yellow tablets (Lemon Zest) out of his manbag and hands it to her. After bumping him the prescription from the inVitro offices she has forgotten about it.

'Thanks.'

He stops her, takes her by her elbows. 'Kitty, are you okay?'

'That... that stupid woman in the basement scared me,' she says, childlike, vulnerable.

'Creeps like that should be locked up,' he says, anger grating his voice. 'Instead of, instead of going around... frightening people. We should report her.'

Kirsten knows she shouldn't tell him about the silver key but it's glowing hot in her pocket, in her brain. They are walking over a bridge when she takes it out and shows it to him.

'I know I should get rid of it,' she says, 'but something in me says I should keep it. I mean, I *want* to get rid of it...' She feels silly. 'I don't know.'

'I do,' says James. He grabs the key out of her hand and throws it over the bridge. It glints against the dark sky then is lost forever. Not even a sound as it lands: seconds, metres, storeys, away. Swallowed by the night. Kirsten is shocked by her empty, moon-white palm.

'It's for the best,' James says, and marches on.

JOURNAL ENTRY

10 DECEMBER 1987, WESTVILLE

In the news: *During a police raid on shacks in the Port Elizabeth area, they meet heavy resistance from the residents. The police drive a Casspir over the shack, killing four. Ireland is reeling from the Enniskillen Remembrance Day bombing.*

What I'm listening to: *Faith! By George Michael*

What I'm reading: *Kaleidoscope by Danielle Steele. I needed something light because the only time I have to read is when I'm half asleep and breastfeeding! The story is about three sisters who are separated by fate. I'm hoping they'll be reunited.*

What I'm watching: *3 Men and a Baby. Tom Selleck is gorgeous and hilarious.*

Life keeps surprising me. After 18 hours in labour (an early labour and a very long 18 hours!) Sam Chapman (2.6kg) was born at 8:45. Ten minutes later – surprise! – A little girl arrived too. We have named her Kate (2.2kg).

We were totally shocked but actually my belly had been so big that everyone in shopping malls etc. kept asking if it was twins so we did have some kind of warning. P left the hospital once I fell asleep so that he could go get 'emergency supplies'. It took us months to do up the nursery and here he is, having to double it up in a day!

Sam latched immediately but Kate was too hungry to try—she just screamed!—So P gave her a bottle to get her blood sugar level stable. They are so tiny; the nurses are keeping them in the warming drawers that look like Tupperwares. Pink tummies and tiny little toes that I want to kiss. I am exhausted and sore; all I want to do is hold my babies and sleep. Very tired, and relieved that we are all safe.

CHAPTER 9

SHINING & SLIPPERY WITH SWEAT

Johannesburg, 2021

Seth saunters into the Yellow printer room.

'Oh, hi Fiona.' He smiles at the curly-haired woman and acts surprised, as if he didn't know she was in there. She blushes at him knowing her name. Seth brushes skilfully past her.

'Hi.' She smiles, holding her locket to her lips, warming the silver with her breath. They both watch the printer for a few seconds, as if willing it to print faster. She unconsciously pumps her high heels, as if warming up for a race.

'Our printer's being repaired,' he says. 'It's a dinosaur of a thing: still uses toner. That's why I'm in Yellow.'

'Okey-dokey,' she says.

'Not all bad, though,' he says, 'getting to see you.'

She guffaws. After a while, hand on hip, she says, 'This won't do, you know. I know what you're trying to do.' Her freckles fade against the rose of her cheeks.

'Really?' he says, 'and what is that?'

'Trying to find out Yellow's secrets.'

He moves closer to her. 'Ah, so you *do* have secrets.'

'We do,' she says, 'and we're going to win this quarter.' Her large breasts rise and fall under her unfashionable paisley blouse.

'You don't have a chance,' he says, rubbing his hands together. 'Red is so far ahead, there's no way Yellow can catch up.'

'But you're wrong,' she says in mock-seriousness. 'We were just saving ourselves. We've got something massive planned. It'll sell thousands of units.'

'It'll need to,' says Seth. The printer stops then, as if to flag the end of their conversation.

She gathers up the A4 prints and holds them to her chest, pretending they are top-secret documents, even though Seth knows that they are just her latest holiday snaps: Bali.

'Are you coming to the teambuilding on Friday?' she asks. 'I heard that we're going to go on a 4D-maze tetrick treasure hunt.'

I'd rather stick a fork in my eye.

'Sure,' he says. 'Well, if you're going.'

'Yes! Yes, I'm going.'

'Then I'll be there,' he says.

'Great!'

'Great.' He smiles, almost winking.

He turns to face the printer and presses *print* on his Tile. The printer hums, then starts spitting out pages. She gives him a royal wave and walks away. He waits for a few moments, reading the moronic posters on the wall, then heads back to his office, leaving the blank pages in the printer tray.

~

Betty checks the locks on her door for the fifth time. They're locked, but checking them makes her feel safer. She has to do things that make her feel safer.

She sits in front of her blank homescreen but realises the remote isn't working. Betty shakes the remote around a little, tries again. Then she opens up the back and makes sure the batteries are in place. Takes them out, puts them back in. Still the glass stays clear. Betty gets up to check its connections and sees it's unplugged. She picks up the plug and moves it towards the wall but stops when she reads an orange sticker covering the electricity outlet and switch: 'Don't watch TV.' It's in her handwriting.

Yes, television is not good for me. She should really get rid of the screen, but it was expensive and she abhors waste. The voices are the reason she can't watch any more. They tell her to do things. Soap opera stars, talk show hosts, newsreaders. They tell her that creeps are trying to kill her, blow up her building, decimate the country. They make her write letters to people, telling them that they are in danger. Politicians, local celebrities, airlines.

The police have been here before. They were rough until she showed them the doctor's note she keeps in her bra. The paper is leathery, now. The voices speak directly to her. 'Barbara,' (for they have recently taken to calling her Barbara), 'the next bus you take will be wired with a car-bomb with your name on it.' That's when she stopped taking the bus. The communal taxi and individual cab drivers are also not to be trusted. They could take you anywhere and you'd never be seen again.

Disappear. She clicks her fingers. Just like that. *Click, click*. She has started walking, then running everywhere. She gets to the grind shining and slippery with sweat. She is losing a lot of weight. The running has done it. Also, food is a problem. She can't run with all her groceries so she has to shop every day. She doesn't like shopping: too many people. Her psychologist says to try online shopping. Everyone's doing it, but that will mean giving strangers her address and the hours she will be home. Even if the shop people are harmless, the information could be intercepted.

When she finally builds up supplies she ends up throwing them away. The fridge door looks suspicious: as if someone else has opened it. An intruder. She tries to work out exactly which food they have contaminated but can never stop at one item. Once the pineberry yoghurt has been binned, the cheddar looks suspect, after that, the pawpaw, the black bread, the SoySpread, the feta. The precious, innocent-looking eggs, the vegetarian hotdogs, the green mango atchar, the leftover basmati, until it is all discarded and sealed tightly in a black plastic bag. The dumping of each individual item causes her pain; she so hates to fritter. This happens once a week.

Sometimes she needs to check the cupboards, too. Sometimes it's not just the open things in the fridge that may have been tainted. She'll get an idea, a name, in her head, and those things will have to go too. Last week it was Bilchen—pictures in her head of factorybots polluting the processed food then sealing them in neat little parcels, ready to eat. It is as if someone is shouting at her: Bilchen! Bilchen! Like a branded panic attack. Then she has to check every box and packet in her cupboard and toss everything with the Bilchen logo. Not much is left over.

She chooses a lonely tin of chickpeas, checks the label, and eases it open with an old appliance. She polishes a fork with her tracksuit top and eats directly out of the can. Canned food is relatively safe. She reaches for the kosher salt pebbles, but before she starts grinding it she sees the top is loose. She pictures arsenic, cyanide, a sprinkling of a strain of deadly virus, and puts it back without using it. Washes her hands twice and sprays them with hand sanitiser.

She takes the chickpea can with her and walks around her flat, checking all the windows. She touches the locks as she goes, counting them. Mid-count she hears a noise. A scraping, a whirring. Is someone trying to get in? Is the front door locked? Icy sweat.

There is a high-pitched squeal at her heels and Betty jumps in fright. Her beagle scurries away from her with hurt in her eyes.

'Oh, I'm sorry,' she says, moving to hug and pet her. 'I'm so sorry my girl. There's a good girl, there's a good girl.' The words soothe her.

Sometimes if she talks loudly enough to herself she can drown out the voices. Not in public, though. She shouldn't talk to herself in public. She doesn't like being in public anymore. Sometimes she has to show people the note; she doesn't like that, the look in their eyes.

Squatting on the ground, she feeds the dog some chickpeas. She'll start the counting again.

Outside the door to her apartment, there is humming. A large man in overalls is polishing the parquet corridor.

JOURNAL ENTRY

12 DECEMBER 1987, WESTVILLE

In the news: *A group of police officers is fired upon by freedom fighters from a moving car in Soweto; two police officers are killed and four injured. In Melbourne, Australia, they are attempting to understand the Queen Street Massacre: why 22-year-old Frank Vitkovic killed 8 people in a post office building before jumping from the eleventh floor. Microsoft releases Windows 2.0.*

What I'm listening to: *U2's 'Where the Streets have no Name'*

What I'm reading: *'Tommyknockers' by Stephen King.*

What I'm watching: *Flowers in the Attic. I've read the book before, but now that we have babies we just found it too creepy, P had to turn it off!*

We brought the twins home this week. They keep us very busy but not-busy at the same time. Sometimes when they are both sleeping, P & I just sit in the lounge and wonder what to do. Other times they are both crying at the same time and we feel totally overwhelmed.

P has a pair of red DIY noise-cancelling headphones (that he uses when he does drilling etc.) which have come in very handy at bath-time!

I feel so attached to them that I want to be with them all the time. When we settle them down at night for their longer sleep I don't want to leave the nursery. Once I'm out I feel relieved that I have some time to myself but miss them immediately. Sometimes when I'm not with them I catch myself looking at photos of them. Crazy!

We are totally in survival mode, sleeping when we can, showering IF we can, eating takeaways when we run out of 2-minutes noodles. I feel so consumed by the feeding and caring that I feel like I hardly exist. Or at least, the person I was before, hardly exists. I am just a vessel. A milk machine. As for P and I—we are like ships passing in the night.

We keep the babies next to our bed at night so that I don't have to get up to feed them every 2 hours. Then if they cry I just reach over and pop them in bed with us and snuggle while they feed. I feel very protective of them. Tiger mother.

It's almost Christmas and I think it will be, like, the happiest Christmas ever.

CHAPTER 10

A SWARM, A SMACK

JOHANNESBURG, 2021

The ragged tooth shark swims straight towards her, his dull eyes apparently unseeing in water the colour of an overcast sky. Serrated teeth hang out at all angles, as if he has long given up hunting. Her pulse quickens as he approaches, her finger on the trigger. He glides quickly with little effort. The water is murkier than she had hoped. Kirsten fires away. Just before it reaches her—a severed arm's length away—the shark turns to avoid the tempered glass of the tank. Superglass.

She gets a few shots of his profile: a vast muscle-and-cartilage body wrapped in slate sandpaper. Her head throbbing, she flicks through the thumbnails on the screen of her camera, making sure she has enough that are in sharp focus.

The lighting is tricky because she can't use her flash; it will bounce off the glass. She is shooting in MultiFocus 3D to get more drama out of the looming shark. The shots are certainly dramatic, but shooting in MF3D always gives her a headache.

She sits for a moment, watches the dancing blue light of the water (Aqua Shimmer) paint her arms and hands. The pressure in her head makes her feel as though the silicone-framed glass is going to give way and knock everyone over in a tidal wave of exotic fish, eels, and strangling seaweed.

She has a long gulp of CinnaCola from the can her assistant hands her. She has been at it for ages and she still isn't sure if she had the shot. She powers up her Tile and looks at the pictures in subpixel HR. The pictures she had of the Leafy Sea Dragon, the Blanket Octopus and the Sea Wasp jellyfish are fantastic. The Blanket Octo looks like a silk scarf underwater: a billowing maroon cape. She can watch it for hours.

The Sea Wasp is almost invisible: smoke caught in a bubble underwater, with elegant silver tentacles and enough deadly venom to kill up to sixty humans. If you get stung by this jellyfish in the sea, says the digital projection on the glass, it causes you such intense pain and shock you won't make it to the shore. A group of jellyfish is called a swarm or a smack. Such grace in its movement: hypnotic. She makes a mental note to do a jellyfish project in the future.

Her assistant offers her a ganache-glazed kronut but she, for once, declines. She doesn't feel great. A bit dizzy, nauseated. It had been a long morning and she still has to shoot the model. Her eyes are strained and she's battling to concentrate on the photos, so she closes the window and looks around the aquarium for a moment.

It's deliciously cool and quiet inside; even the children whisper. The cobalt luminescence ripples over the floor and the visitors, making everyone seem calm. It has a clean taste: ice and fresh mint, with a hint of citrus.

Who would have thought an aquarium would work in Jozi? It was an impromptu idea of some BEE-kitten who had more investors than sense. There are so many things up against the project: the water shortage, the protesting fish-hippies, the transport costs. Can you imagine the logistics of trucking sharks, dolphins and other endangered fish from some sleepy coastal town to Johannesburg? It was a joke. Until it wasn't anymore, and now it's AQUASCAPE: a gushing money-spinner, a veritable pot of liquid gold. She looks around at the illuminated faces of the kids and their parental units, and feels a twinge. In drought-blasted South Africa it does feel magical to see so much water. She had always loved water—rivers, lakes, waterfalls, oceans—and swimming. She often wonders why she lived inland. Perhaps one day they can retire to the Cape Republic.

As a teenager she read an article in the New York Times about the 'loneliest whale in the world'. It was about an animal that looked like a whale and sounded like a whale, but her call was slightly off, which meant that even though she called and called, no other whales could hear her.

The people who found her named her 52 Hertz. Her tone was *bassa profunda,* just a notch higher than the lowest note on a tuba, and it became deeper over time. She kept swimming, kept calling, but the entire ocean was dark, cold and deaf to her. *That's me,* Kirsten had thought at the time. *That is the whale version of me.*

Her news tickertape lights up with a fresh story. She clicks it and is taken to page six of Echo.news, the local online newspaper for which she does odd jobs. It's a satirical cartoon of the NANC politician who was caught with a secret pool. He is standing in court with a sheepish smile, dressed in nothing more than soggy grey underpants, with a yellow duck-shaped inflatable tube around his waist. The prosecutor has a whistle around her neck and the judge is sitting on a lifeguard chair, the ones you used to get in public pools. Kirsten moves her cursor to close the window when she spots a headline that draws her in.

WOMAN FOUND DEAD IN BRAAMFONTEIN FLAT.

This has always been a secret fear of Kirsten's: ending up old and alone, slipping in the shower/accidentally electrocuting herself/choking to death on a toaster waffle, only to be found weeks later by the building's rodent-control man. She scans the article to see how ancient this woman was and how exactly she kicked the bucket, so she can at all costs avoid the same sorry end.

But it turns out the woman is precisely Kirsten's age, and it's a suspected suicide. 'Betty Weil's body,' it read, 'was found yesterday by her mental health doctor who had grown concerned when Miss Weil had missed several appointments. She was found in the kitchen where she had died after apparently gassing herself. Miss Weil had a history of mental illness, most notably paranoid schizophrenia.' A little more info on her history follows, and then the usual disclaimer to seek help if needed. Lawsuits are sticky now that suicide is trending. The small black-and-white picture accompanying the article shows a laughing young woman with long dark hair, obviously before her illness took hold of her. Something makes Kirsten look twice. She reads the article again. Betty. It can't be.

Not the mad woman in the parking lot. She had to have been in her forties, at least, and didn't look anything like this photograph. Kirsten puts her fingers over the woman's long hair, giving her a helmet-cut.

Your Kirsten is my Betty.

'Fucking hell,' Kirsten says, speed-dialling Keke.

'I'm busy,' Keke answers, noise and static in the background.

'Where are you?'

'The Gladiator Arena, in Roma. Well, fake Roma, anyway. Roman Rustenburg. Dusty as hell but some fine ass here in gladiator get-up. Skin all bronzed and shit. Failed Amusement Park turned film set for the second instalment of the *Mad Maximus* thrillogy.'

'You do lead a charmed life,' says Kirsten.

'What's up?' asks Keke.

'That mad woman I told you about, the one who stalked me in the basement the other night?'

'Yebo?'

'She's in the paper today.'

'Arrested? Admitted to an asylum? Elected as a minister?'

'Dead.'

'Who wrote the article?'

'What?'

'Which journo wrote that article? Was it from Echo?'

Kirsten scrolls and sees the name of the journalist.

'Echo, yes. Mpumi Dladla.'

'Ha! He's a hack. He probably didn't even investigate. Most likely lifted a police report.'

'Do you have his number?'

'Of course I do.'

~

Fiona's moans, though stifled, are getting louder. Seth cups her mouth with his hand, smudging her lipstick and butting the back of her head up against the gun-metal grey locker door in the stationery room, which makes her groan even more. It started innocently enough, or so she had thought. She was there to pick out some new pens, e-paper and stickernotes for her desk. She had been looking forward to it all week: Fiona Botes had an almost unhealthy love of stationery. It was so old fashioned—romantic, really—to use real pens on real paper.

She had been inspecting the different kinds of yellow pens on offer in anticipation, when Seth strode in and locked the door, startling her. He had used her temporary breathlessness to advance on her. Not a word exchanged, he had put his hand behind her head and kissed her slowly, making sure at every stage that she wanted more. As the kiss grew deeper, she pulled her stomach in as his hand slid over her smooth pink shirt, her generous breasts. Seth used just the right amount of teasing, and the right amount of pressure. He pushed her against the closed door of a locker, trapping her body between the heat of his body and the cool metal. His mouth didn't leave hers as his hand travelled down, lifting her knee-length tweed skirt and stroked her through her panties. At first slowly, in lazy circles, then faster and harder as he felt her grow wet. Her arms, holding the door behind her, became stiff; she stopped groaning, held her breath, and her whole body became rigid before the orgasm took her. He held her up as her knees almost buckled—her entire being felt as if it was buckling—and tears sprang to her eyes.

Fiona Botes has not had many orgasms in her life, and the ones she has never seem quite satisfactory. Her girlfriends tell her that she has to DIY before she can show a man how to do it for her, but she doesn't like thinking about that. It seems smutty. Besides, she believes a man should intuitively know what to do with her parts; she certainly doesn't. Never has Fiona imagined that an orgasm could feel like this. And so quickly! Fully clothed! She is in shock. Intoxicated. What surprises her even more is that she finds herself unbuckling him. This gorgeous, tall man, in the stationery room, with her! She couldn't have dreamt up a better fantasy if she had tried.

~

Kirsten feels a twinge in her abdomen. *Maybe I'm ovulating*. She checks the OvO app on her watch: 36 hours to go, it says. At least she'll get laid this week. She takes the escalator to the second floor of the pastel green art deco building (Pistachio ice cream), where the journalists, editors, copy editors and layout artists buzz around in the open-plan offices of Echo.news like a drone-swarm.

They moved to this downtown building when their original offices in

ChinaCity/Sandton were firebombed a few years ago by a group of Christian extremists called The Resurrectors. Previously infamous for their mission to ban The Net, the group had since taken to terrorising anyone who 'disrespected Jesus'. The newspaper had published a column by a cocky, jaded journo in which he criticised each major religion in turn, and from which could extrapolated that he found anyone of religious persuasion a bit dim-witted. A line about rising-from-the-dead Jesus being a huggable zombie particularly inflamed the group and the next day —*poof!*—the Echo.news building was razed. The Lord doth smite cocky columnists. No one was hurt—how very Christian of them—and because Echo doesn't put out a hard copy, the newspaper business goes on as usual, operating remotely from the employees' individual lounges and tennis courts until this new building is found.

The Resurrectors have also recently taken to threatening fertility doctors, SurroSisters, and bombing IVF clinics. They call fertility treatment 'devil's work,' surrogates 'SurroSluts,' and the resulting embryos—very unimaginatively, in Kirsten's mind—'devil spawn.' They published a piece on FreeSpeech.za outlining their thinking, backing them up with archaic biblical verses. Kirsten tried to hate-read it once, to make fun, but all the exclamation marks had hurt her eyes.

Firebombing the Echo.news building is one thing, but a public outcry follows about their disrespect for the SurroSisters. Without professional surrogates, South Africa's birth rate will be through the floor. Singe fertile women who volunteer to assist infertile couples are afforded special treatment in almost every facet of their lives: free accommodation, travel, medical treatment. Each SurroSis has their own bodyguard, and their own car. Fashion houses dress them, jewellers loan them diamonds, brands nearly trip over themselves to place their products in their hands. They wear 'SS' badges in public so they can be easily identified and shown the proper respect: the opposite of a scarlet letter.

When Kirsten reaches the top of the escalator at the Echo offices, no one takes any notice of her, so she walks up to the closest table and asks where she can find Mpumi. She is directed to the untidiest desk in the place where she casts around for familiar faces but sees no one she recognises. Mpumi is on the phone, and typing at the same time, so she smiles at him and gestures that she'll wait. It's obviously a personal call, because he wraps it up quickly and calls the person on the other side of the line a 'chop'.

'Hi,' she ventures, but he holds up a silencing finger at her and finishes typing his sentence with his other hand. He reads it again, makes an adjustment, makes another adjustment, then smashes the *save* key.

He looks up at her and blinks, as if to clear his head of the previous conversation. Mpumi is super groomed and dressed in 1950s Sophiatown chic. Retrosexual. Kirsten thrusts an extra-large, double-shot cappuccino at him, believing from experience that you couldn't go wrong with that in a news office. He crinkles his nose.

'Sweet, darling, but I don't do caffeine. Or sugar... or moo-milk.'

Kirsten swaps his for hers. He fiddles with his bowtie.

'Half-caff, stevia, soymilk.'

He takes it from her, flips off the plastic top, and takes a small sip.

'So you *are* an angel. I thought so, when you walked in. All fiery-haired and horny and shit, with the light behind you. Are you here for the Feminazi interview?'

'No,' she says. 'I just need five minutes.'

'What can I do for you?'

Kirsten sits on an old, bashed-up office chair, pulls it closer.

'That article of yours on the tickertape this morning...'

'The monkey that they've programmed to talk? My sources swear it's true.'

'No, the woman. The woman that committed suicide.'

'Ah,' he says, 'you a relative? We haven't been able to find any relatives, nor could the cops, so we went ahead and named her. Not a friend or frenemy in sight. If you're—'

'No,' interrupts Kirsten. 'I just have a question, about how she died.'

'Straight up-and-down a suicide, m'lady.'

'You're sure?'

'No sign of forced entry. In fact, the windows and doors were locked from the inside. The super had to get in by smashing a window—the lady had, like, ten different locks on the front door.' He snorts. 'Well, it's ironic, isn't it? Locking the baddies out before you stick your head in the oven.'

'When do you think she died?'

He looks down at the masses of paper spread on his desk and, after a few moments, locates a blue file.

'It's a finely tuned arrangement.' He smiles at her, gesturing at the mess. 'It's the only way I find anything.'

Keke is right: it's a copy of the police file.

He flips through a few pages then stops, pointing to a detail Kirsten can't see. 'Estimated TOD was the evening before.'

'But then how did they find her so quickly?'

'She hadn't been showing up at her shrink's appointments, had been avoiding her calls. It looked like she hadn't left the place in a week.'

'Is there anything else you can tell me?'

His phone rings, but he mutes the tune. 'Not much else to tell. Suicide is contagious now, didn't you know? Bitch went schizo and offed herself. All in a day's grind in this crazy-ass city. Believe me, I've seen worse. A lot worse. In fact, I remember thinking, how considerate of her to take a clean way out.'

'What do you mean?'

'Well, you know, she could have jumped out of the window, slit her wrists, put a shotgun to her head. Can you imagine having to clean that shit up?'

The pictures of her wax doll parents come back to her. Dark red holes, weeping.

'Never thought of it that way.'

'Yeah, well, they're mostly selfish bastards, Suiciders. We used to call them suicide victims but, ha! Hardly. Men are the worst, always the messiest. Pigs. They seem to like the drama of leaving blood and bits behind. Leave their mark, like a dog pissing on a tree. Women are more considerate. Usually do it with more grace: pills, asphyxiation, walking into rivers.'

'But she *was* a victim,' says Kirsten. 'I mean, she was ill... she couldn't help it.'

He purses his lips to show that he doesn't agree. His phone rings again.

'Anything else I can help you with? I have a 6pm deadline and I don't have any of my facts checked yet.'

She gets up to leave, binning her coffee cup. Caffeine dulls her synaesthesia, so it feels as if she is moving in monochrome. She still can't believe normal people see the world this way. Flat.

'Was there anything weird about it? Anything that you thought was strange?'

He uses the back of a pencil to scratch his scalp. Shakes his head, but then stops, narrows his eyes. 'There was one thing... I wanted to put it into the article but Ed said it was unnecessary. He didn't want it to sound like we were making fun of the lady.'

'What was it?'

'It was something the shrink said to the cops. I didn't interview her personally but she said that the woman had out-of-control paranoid delusions. She heard voices talking to her and telling her to do shit. But she also had this idea that she had been microchipped, I don't know, by aliens or Illuminati or something. She had a lump on the back of her neck—had it for as long as she could remember—and she started to believe that it was a tracking chip. Thought someone was monitoring her. Maybe she watched too many nineties movies. But it's cool, you know, in a way, that's why I wanted to put it in the article. I mean they say they want more readers but I had to pull the most interesting part. Ed can be a bastard.'

'So what you're saying is that she really was crackers, and she really did kill herself.'

'Yes, ma'am. Oh, and one other thing...'

Cheeky shit, calling her 'ma'am' as if she is twice his age. 'Yes?'

'There were dog bowls—and dog hair—but no dog food, and, well... no dog.'

She stares at him. His outfit is now desaturated of colour. She snaps a pic of him with her locket.

'You look like you stepped out of a fifties Drum magazine cover. I like your style. Thanks for your help.'

'You're Kirsten Lovell, aren't you?'

She is surprised, and nods.

'I've just recognised you. I loved your photo essay on Somali pirates. It was really cool. Bang tidy work. Epic stuff.'

That was years ago, how could he know it is hers? The essay is from a time when she had been young and irresponsible, doing dangerous work to try to fill The Black Hole. It hadn't worked, but she won some awards. It advanced her career, made her semi-famous in the journo circuit.

'You a freelancer now?' he asks.

She nods. 'Now I have the flexibility to panic about my job insecurity at any time.'

It's an old joke. He smiles, holds up the coffee cup in thanks and farewell.

~

He waits until he sees the escalator swallow her then dials a number. 'She came.'

He doesn't know why the cop wants to know this, but that is the deal, in exchange for a copy of the police report. Mouton is a cop, after all, Mpumi reasons, trying to assuage his guilt. It's not like he's a psychopath.

~

Seth is reading the news while he waits for The Weasel to go to lunch. A headline about a woman committing suicide catches his eye. So young, so alone. He feels a jab. He knows better than to think it's compassion; it's just his own mortality raising its head to give him a nudge. *That could be you, dying alone in your apartment. Not suicide, never suicide, but people die all the time, and you could be next. Freak accidents, dehydration, murder. And who would miss you?*

The Weasel leaves his desk at 1pm every day, on the dot, and goes downstairs to the American-styled health diner. He has a cheese fauxburger, which is less delicious than it sounds, and certainly not anything vaguely sexual, which is what Seth first thinks when he overhears Wesley's order and almost chokes to death on his whole-wheat carob-chip doughnut. Choking, falling, earthquake. No one would miss him.

The Fauxburger is a shamwich: the diner's healthy take on the old classic, with a full-grain rye roll, cottage cheese, masses of micro-greens and sprouts, a black bean and wild mushroom schmeat patty, topped with a black tomato-chilli salsa, and sweet potato wedges on the side. Since meat and fish have become so expensive, many sheeple have switched to meat alternatives. Not before, not to save massacring animals, or to spare thousands of cows/pigs/chickens their sorry battery lives, but when steaks start to cost a week's wage. Enter the age of carnaphobia. Then all of a sudden soya loses its bland taste; vegetarianism becomes mainstream and schmeat steaks and Portobello burgers become the food of choice to bring to Saturday braais. Hairy men snapping their tongs and discussing the merits of citrus versus balsamic marinades over their fire-warmed tins of lager.

Seth still eats steak—ostrich, duck, venison, or any GMO version thereof. His favourite is still real beefsteak, AKA cow-meat, bovine oblivion. Medium rare: he likes it a little bloody. It's not that he doesn't have empathy for the animals. He just believes humans are top of the food chain. You don't see a leopard crying over its prey.

After The Weasel eats his sad burger, wipes his too-full lips with the old-school red-and-white checked linen napkin, he goes to the bathroom, presumably to wash his hands. Then he opens the communal drinks fridge and gets himself a CinnaCola, which sits on his desk for the rest of the afternoon. Seth has never seen Weasel drink the stuff—after all, he would know what's in it—but there it is, every day, sweating on his desk at 1:30 sharp. Seth no longer takes lunch breaks because it's the only time he can escape his manager's beady eyes. He uses this time very carefully.

JOURNAL ENTRY

JANUARY 24TH, 1988, WESTVILLE

In the news: ***6*** *African National Congress guerrillas are injured in a car bomb explosion in Bulawayo, Zimbabwe.*

What I'm listening to: *Johnny Cash is Coming to Town*

What I'm reading: Dr Spock's *The Common Sense Book of Baby and Child Care*

What I'm watching: *Good Morning Vietnam*

P loves the babies so much. He is good at comforting them. He sings in a really deep voice—these silly made-up songs—and makes these funny faces and then they stop fussing and laugh. Sometimes they laugh at the same time and that's the funniest thing, then we all laugh together.

CHAPTER 11

CORPSE FINGERS STROKE HER NECK

JOHANNESBURG, 2021

Kirsten watches Keke pull into her building's entrance in a wide arc and is reminded why she has so many suitors of both genders: her punk hairstyles, roaring bike, deep, easy laugh and fuck-you fashion. It's a hot little package.

'Sorry I'm late.' She deflates her helmet and hugs Kirsten. Keke smells like leather and something more feminine. Hair product? Little violet shiny balls float in the air around them.

'No problem. It's probably my punctuality karma finally burning my ass.' Kirsten had, herself, been twenty minutes late.

'There was a breaking story and I was five minutes away so I had to pop in.'

'Anything interesting?'

'Not really. Just a little shoot-out between the AfriNazis and the Panthers. Some scratches, some crocodile tears, no fatalities.'

'Oh my God, *racism*. It's so 2016.'

The two groups were extreme right and left wings, white and black respectively. No one took them too seriously; in a nation that is now indifferent to skin colour, their bizarre antics leave everyone shaking their frowns.

'Just some punks looking for an excuse to spill blood.'

'Too many video games.'

'I blame hip hop. No, *marabi*.'

'I blame sugar. And processed food.'

'Hyperconnectivity.'

'The Net.'

'GMO produce.'

'ADHD.'

'Neglectful parental units.'

'Lack of corporal punishment in schools.'

'Boredom. There's nothing to rebel against anymore! We're a nanny state and it's a very gentle, easy-going nanny, with no tattoos or inappropriate piercings.'

'Although she must have a very high libido.'

'Ha!' laughs Keke. 'This nanny likes to screw!'

'And get screwed,' adds Kirsten. 'It's a mutual arrangement. And also: polyamorous.'

'Hey,' says Keke. 'Don't knock polyamory. It's the way of the future.'

Inside Kekeletso's Braamfontein apartment, the door automatically locks behind them.

'Too early for wine?' asks Keke, glancing at the clock on the wall. 12:55. A giant Elvis Presley poster looks down at them.

'I don't understand the question,' says Kirsten.

Keke smiles and grabs a bottle of Coffeeberry Verdant-Pino. Two glasses. Kirsten instinctively reaches for a nearby empty Tethys bottle, fills it up with grey water from the waterbank (Liquid Smoke), and goes around watering Keke's sad-looking houseplants. Using her father's pocketknife, which she now always keeps handy, she snips a few dead leaves off the aspidistra on the lounge coffee table and sends them down the communal compost chute.

'It's not that I don't love them, you know.' (That's what she always says.) 'It's just that I'm never home.'

After binning a long-dead and crumbling plant a year before, Kirsten had suggested keeping succulents instead as they wouldn't need as much care, but Keke said she had read somewhere that thorns were bad for your sex life. 'Feng Shui or some shit. What is it with you and plants, anyway?'

Kirsten had shrugged: 'I don't know. I just like looking after them.'

Keke had pulled a 'you're sad!' face, and Kirsten had thrown something at her.

'If you knew how amazing they were, you wouldn't perpetuate mass murder against them like you do.' This is her pet hate. Her mother had been just as bad. Her teenhood had been strewn with dead chrysanthemums. 'Besides the whole filters-the-air-we-breathe thing, do you know that there is a flower that turns red when it grows over landmines?'

'Okay Miss Greenfingers.' Keke had sighed. 'I get it, no more needless slaughter of our plant-friends.'

'If you're like this with plants I'd hate to imagine you being responsible for something with actual feelings. Ever consider getting a pet?'

Keke had almost choked. 'No!'

'Good.'

'So, what's the emergency?' Kirsten commandeers the bottle and passes Keke a glass of wine, who in turn opens a packet of chilli-salted beetroot chips and empties them into a bowl, which may have needed a bit of a wipe beforehand. The shape of their taste is unusual: spinning flat discs, like frisbees, but not as rigid. Rubber. Quite uniform, earthy, with little spikes of salt and a halo of warmth from the chilli.

'Something came for you today, through The Office.'

This isn't unusual. Keke and Kirsten office-share in the same building in the CBD. As card-carrying members, or colloquially: 'Nomadders,' they are allowed unlimited access to everything they might possibly need in an office environment, from receptionists, couriers, IT support, boardrooms, carpooling and bad filter coffee to 4D scanner/printers. A steady stream of people is always coming and going, as well as a 24/7 cleaning team to make sure that each new client gets a sparkling office. They charge by the hour, but the longer you stay, the better the rate. They even have a (legendary) annual end-of-year office party.

Keke knows someone at The Desk who keeps a premium office free for her when he can, at no extra cost. It is one of the few with a fridge and a concealed safe where she can keep some of her grind paraphernalia and clean underwear without having to drag it around town on her bike. It also has a dry shower and a SleePod.

'Through The Office?'

Kirsten thinks it must be something she ordered online and had since forgotten. New lenses for her camera? Prickly-Pear Verjuice? Sex toy? Bulk box of pregnancy test strips?

Keke produces a small white envelope that looks a bit worse for wear.

'That's it?'

'Yip. Isn't it wonderful?'

Kirsten takes it from Keke's hands and examines it. The address is scratched on, as if the penman-or-woman was in a hurry. She doesn't recognise the handwriting. Two colourful stamps are glued on the front: an illustration of the president wearing too much lipstick, and an extinct fish. The post office stamp obscures both of the pouting images. No return address.

'I mean,' says Keke, 'when is the last time you saw an actual letter? In the—you know—the post! In an envelope! It has stamps and everything.'

Kirsten uses her pocketknife to slit open the envelope. She takes out the note, and as she does so a key drops into her lap. She picks it up and inspects it, recognises it; feels corpse fingers stroke her neck. Hands it to Keke.

'It's the same one,' she says. 'The same one James threw over the bridge that night...'

'It's a wafer-key,' says Keke. 'For a safety deposit box. This part,' she says, touching the head, 'contains some kind of circuit, to allow access. So, for example, the wafer will get you into the bank and into the safety deposit box room. Then the key itself is used to unlock the box.'

Kirsten opens the note and sees more of the scrawl: DOOMSDAY.

'The fuck?' Keke comes around to read it over her shoulder.

'Who's it from?' she asks.

Kirsten studies the signature. 'A ghost.'

~

At exactly 1pm Seth watches The Weasel make his way down to the Fontus diner. Seth waits five minutes. In that time, three different sheeple stop outside his office to say hi and ask how he is. He recognises the same vacant look in their eyes as the employees he sees around the campus: scoffing ultrabran muffins, playing squash, jogging, waiting for the decaffee to percolate. Staring, expressionless, as if a zombie had eaten their brains. And then as soon as they register him (eyebrow ring, Smudged eyes, faux-hawk, hoodie) they snap to attention and greet him effusively. Their smiles become wide and full of white teeth, but it never reaches their eyes.

Once the coast is clear, he slips into the filing room, which is really just a giant computer in the middle of the room full of whirring fans. He's not allowed access to this room but the door is sometimes left ajar. There are clearly people in the world less paranoid than him. Ribbons in different shades of blue are tied to the fan skeletons, giving the feeling that the room is some kind of stage design for a scene out of Atlantis, or an experiential advert for Aquascape.

He closes the door and sits backwards on the swivel chair, starts to work on the machine. The security on the files he wants to look at is ironclad. There will be a chink, there always is, but as he looks around he realises that it will take him months to hack. He smacks the side of the flatscreen.

'Fuck a monkey,' he says.

'Excuse me?'

Seth spins around. Weasel.

'Oh,' says Seth. *Fuck!*

With all the white noise of the fans he hasn't heard Wesley come in. He quickly uses a shortcut to close his windows. Has The Weasel left this door open on purpose: a test?

'This is a limited-access room,' says Weasel, 'you're not allowed in here.'

'I didn't know,' says Seth.

'It was in your Fontus Welcome Pack,' says Wesley.

Seth gives him a blank look. 'I needed to find something.' It wasn't a lie.

'Look,' starts Wesley, rubbing his beard and drumming his fingers on his chin.

'I'm going to have to report this... incident. They're not gonna like it. They're not gonna like it one bit. We're talking a warning, or a disciplinary meeting at best. You'd better come in tomorrow wearing that suit I've been asking you about.'

'Are you kidding?' asks Seth.

The Weasel starts guffawing. Seth looks on in astonishment.

'Of course I am, Mr Maths!' he snorts, whacking Seth on the back. 'You genius-types sure lack a sense of humour. Ha! Ha!' He steers Seth out of the room with a firm hand and makes sure he closes the door behind him. It beeps twice to signal that it's locked.

'Beep-beep!' says Wesley, and guffaws again.

~

Kirsten reads the letter out to Keke:

KIRSTEN/KATE—

I know you didn't believe me when we spoke. Am sending you extra keys. THEY ARE WATCHING YOU. DO NOT LET ANYONE TAKE THEM FROM YOU. Take care of yourself. Do it for your mother. Despite this mess, the list is proof that she loved you.

DOOMSDAY is the key. God help the Taken Ones if you don't get this. ACT NOW. B/B

Keke lets out a loud wolf whistle. 'No prize for guessing which particular delusional schizophrenic sent this.'

Kirsten replays their interaction in her head: the shadows in the basement, the shock, the foetid warning, James throwing the key off the bridge.

'I guess sometimes it pays to be paranoid,' says Keke.

'What do you mean?' asks Kirsten, dry-mouthed.

'Well, just that, you know, she knew you wouldn't keep the first key.'

'She said keys. She said I'm sending you extra keys, plural.' She shakes the envelope even though she knows it's empty.

'Maybe she didn't get around to sending the other one,' reasons Keke, 'you know, before she stuck her head in the oven.'

'I don't understand,' says Kirsten.

'I'll explain it to you,' says Keke, taking the letter to the compost chute. 'This lunatic lady didn't know fantasy from reality, and she for some reason decided to drag you into it.' She is about to throw the note away when Kirsten jumps up.

'Don't you dare,' she says, snatching it away.

'Listen, Cat. She was a delusional schizophrenic. She killed herself. Surely that's the end of this conversation?'

'Not necessarily.'

'You have got to be joking. They're watching you? *Dooms*day?'

Kirsten thought Keke understood her Black Hole but clearly she doesn't.

'She is dead, Keke. She said that they would kill her, and now she's dead. She believed in this enough to track me down. Approach me. She wasn't even leaving her flat to see her shrink anymore, but she came to see me. I think I at least owe it to her to see whatever this key unlocks.'

Out of the corner of her eye, she sees a familiar blue-and-white striped jersey (Cobalt & Cream). It doesn't make any sense to her. It takes her a few moments to catch on. That's James's jersey. It should be on James, or at home. Their home. She walks towards it, picks it up, smells it. Marmalade.

'What is this doing here?'

'Kitty,' says Keke, 'I was going to tell you. I just wanted to give you the letter first.'

'Fine, then, I have the letter.'

'James was here last night.'

'What?'

'He's worried about you.'

'Why? What is there to worry about?' She knows the question is disingenuous.

'He says that you've been having a rough time. Obsessing about your parents—'

'He used the word 'obsessing'?'

'Said you're not sleeping. That you haven't been feeling well. Haven't been yourself. In denial about all of the above.'

'What did he want you to do about it?'

'He asked me to keep an eye on you. He said he knows you tell me things that you don't tell him.'

'He wants you to spy on me? Tell him what I tell you?'

'He wants me to make sure you're okay.'

'Make sure I don't stick my head in an oven too?'

'Well, yes. I guess that would be first prize. And he asked me to... discourage... you, from investigating any of this... what-what. Your parents. The crazy lady. He just wants what's best for you. You guys have been together for what? Eleven years?'

'Thirteen.'

'A lifetime. He said you're pushing him away. And he's worried that you might do something... risky.'

'Fuck.' She sighs. 'Am I out of control? I don't feel out of control.'

'That's what you said when you went off chasing pirates.'

'Which I won awards for. Which launched my career.'

'Kitty, no one respects you as a photojournalist more than I do. No one. That story was cosmic. You deserved every award you got. But you almost died.'

'Well, that's an exaggeration.'

'Cat, you almost *died*.'

'Okay, but that was different. I was young. Reckless.'

'So you're less reckless now?' Keke laughs.

'Hello? Yes! I'm practically a housewife. I mean, look at me.'

'The day you become anything close to a housewife I will personally deliver you to the Somalis.'

'Keke, I have a fucking OvO app on my watch. I can tell you the actual minute that I ovulate.'

'Marmalade is right, you *are* out of control. What's next? Hosting crafternoons?'

'Ha,' says Kirsten.

'Look, lady, I told your better half I'd watch over you, and I will. But I'm behind you all the way with finding out about your parents.' Keke opens the freezer and brings out the bright red box that she keeps as a staple especially for Kirsten. She pops some waffles into the toaster and pushes down the lever.

'So, what do we do next?'

JOURNAL ENTRY

27 JANUARY 1988, WESTVILLE

In the news: *Guerrillas open fire on a police vehicle in Soweto and injure three policemen and a civilian. The first reviews are in for Andrew Lloyd Webber's musical 'The Phantom of the Opera' which debuted last night on Broadway.*

What I'm listening to: *Pop Goes the World (the babies like it!) Men Without Hats*

What I'm reading: *Bill Cosby's 'Fatherhood'—hilarious.*

What I'm watching: *The Running Man with Arnold Schwarzenegger*

P went to the nursery today and bought us a few trees and plants. He's trying to make the house as homely as possible for us. I hope he is not missing his old life (his wife).

I've never really been interested in gardening but we worked a bit together today—I just planted some flowers and watered, really—and I enjoyed it. (Petunias? Pansies?) I think I'll spend some more time in the garden. It's a nice break from taking care of the twins.

They are doing really well. Me, less so. In the beginning I didn't mind the sleep deprivation too much but I think it's building up now. It is starting to impact on my mood, and my memory. And my day-to-day functioning: I do ridiculous things like put the teabag canister in the fridge. The other day I answered the front door with my shirt unbuttoned! I don't know who was more embarrassed, me or the neighbour! My God I would do anything for a full night's sleep. Amazing what we take for granted! Sometimes I just get one of the twins to sleep and the other one starts crying and wakes up the other, then the other way around, and I just want to sink to the floor and cry.

They are both good eaters. Thank God. Sometimes I feel like I'm a walking, talking (leaking!) boob. Sam is a frowny, focused feeder, who goes in with closed eyes and gets the job done. Kate, always hungry, starts off quickly but then takes her time. She stares at me with her big slate-grey eyes and I hope that she can feel how much I love her.

They have very distinct personalities, even at this age. Sam is serious and independent and seems to always be thinking about something, working something out in his head. I'd love to know what babies think about. And Kate is always smiling and likes being with people. They seem to get on with each other, too, which is great. Hope it carries on that way!

Sometimes strangers stop us to look at the babies, say how cute they are, ask who is the 'oldest', say they look like me, or if P is with us, that they look like him.

I tell myself every day how lucky I am. I look in the mirror, at my pale skin and the dark circles under my eyes, and smile. I've learned to put on a good smile.

CHAPTER 12

A GOOD VIEW, TOO

JOHANNESBURG, 2021

Seth is sipping a coffeeberry shot at his local barista when an Echo.news story flickers on his tickertape. He clicks to listen to the audio version, which automatically streams to his earbuttons.

In breaking news, William Soraya, South Africa's gold medallist sprinter and media darling was this morning severely injured in a skycar accident. Soraya, known as 'Bad Bill,' who is no stranger to adrenaline pursuits (or front-page news), was flying the new Volantor StreetLegal plug-in hybrid car as a publicity stunt for the corporate, who are 'deeply distressed' about the accident, and have begun an intensive investigation.

'We have tested and re-tested this new model and were 100% certain that it was safe to fly. We have no idea what could have gone wrong, but we will find the reason behind this terrible tragedy,' said Volantor spokesperson Mohale Mhleka.

Despite the low number of uptake, the fatalities due to skycars and hover-cars are numerous and on the rise. Various groups are lobbying for the skycar to be banned, including a 2 000-strong protest outside the Union Buildings this morning, with a further 6 000 citizens adding their presence online.

'Look, it's something we're going to have to get right,' said Minister of Transport Solly Ngubane. 'We mustn't shy away from technology. We must embrace progress. When motorcars were first introduced there were also a great deal of accidents. This episode was unfortunate. We have to take a hard lesson from this, look forward and make this mode of transport the safest we possibly can.' In the mean time, Ngubane has promised a task team to launch an official enquiry, and committed to flying his own Volantor every day for a month, to prove his faith in the product.

'Last year Soraya made news for breaking the national record for both the 100m and 200m

sprint, as well as for his notorious partying, womanising, and more than one incident of road rage. He was also accused of 'resping' or 'respirocyting': injecting robotic red blood cells to improve his performance, but was cleared of the charge after undergoing vigorous testing. Ironically, he may now undergo respirocyte treatment in order to speed up his healing.

Soraya is in the ICU of an undisclosed private hospital. He has broken bones, including both tibulae or shin-bones, and internal bleeding; his spinal cord is swollen, but intact. His PR manager says that his condition is serious, but stable. As the minister said today: 'The hearts and minds of South Africans everywhere are with William Soraya, and we wish him a speedy recovery'.

Fuck, thinks Seth. He had always kind of identified with Soraya. They were the same age. They lived a similar lifestyle, although Seth preferred the shadows to the limelight. He gets that fluttering cold feeling again, almost like a premonition that a similar fate awaits him. He shakes himself out of it. He has got to pull himself together, up his game. Put his plan on fast-forward. He sends Fiona a bump. Acts cooler than he feels.

SD> What are you wearing?

FB>> LOL! Naughty. *blush*

SD> Send me a pic.

FB>> NO!!

SD> I want 2CU.

FB>> In meeting, in meetings all day. Yawnerz!

SD> Take 1 under the table. No 1 will eva know.

If he can get prudish Fiona to sext him it will be a very good sign. It would mean that —apart from getting to see her knickers—she is, to a certain extent, under his spell.

FB>> LOL I can't!! Very NB meeting. Boss is presenting w/Serious Face.

SD> Killing me.

She goes quiet for a while, and he thinks she's probably put her phone away to concentrate on the meeting. He pictures her, sitting up straight, blushing slightly, just-sharpened pencil at the ready, nodding sagely at her fellow colleagues. But he's wrong, and his Tile buzzes with an image.

Yes please, he thinks, picking it up and sitting back into his chair, admiring it. A chocolate brown lace affair. Teal trimmings. Excellent. A good view, too: she would've had to open her legs wide to take it. Despite not finding her particularly attractive, he feels a twinge in his pants and moves to adjust himself.

Thundercats are go.

~

Kirsten is at her apartment, touching up the aquarium pictures, when James comes home. She is relieved to have a break; her eyes feel scratchy, overworked. She saves the huge 4DHD RAW TIFF file that she has been working on and is about to shut down when she feels a warm hand on her back, then another on her chest. She looks up, smiling, but the smile is wasted on James.

His mouth is on hers; he snaps the cover of her Tile down. His hand moves to her right breast; her nipples harden. She begins to stand, but he puts his arms underneath her and picks her up, carries her to bed. Throws her down. She laughs, reaches to unbutton him, but he stops her, pushes her back. She can tell he is angry with her. There is rare passion in his face, but it's shadowed with anger. This is going to be bossy sex, one of her favourites.

He looks at her while he takes off his belt, as if he is going to spank her with it, but then lets it drop to the floor. Kirsten feels heat trickling inside her thighs, her stomach. Her hand travels to her open zip to touch herself but James bats it away. He wants to do all the work. He pushes up her shirt and guzzles the tops of her breasts, above her bra, then yanks the lace down and sucks her erect nipples. She feels his teeth, his hot mouth on her skin, closes her eyes, groans as the warmth builds.

He pulls off her jeans, her white cotton panties. She wants him to lick her, would do anything for him to put his warm tongue on her, knows she would come in a second if he did. But, no, this is her punishment, and he is showing her who's boss. He grabs her around the waist and turns her around, so that she is on her knees, facing away from him.

She wants him inside her so badly that she wants to shout, but holds it in. Agony, bliss. He slaps her butt, gently, then harder, sending orange vibrations (Sunset Sex) through her pelvis. She almost comes, but he stops in time. She wants to beg, but doesn't. The cresting becomes unbearable. A whimper. She bites her own shoulder.

James, relenting, enters her from behind. She comes immediately, her spine curling, her muscles contracting around him. Feels as though the bed is swallowing her. Before she finishes he begins thrusting into her spasms and she cries out, her body half crumpled. He grunts, breathes deeply, thrusts harder, deeper. Put his hands on her. Again her body is seized, stiff and then soft, as she melts into the next rolling orgasm.

~

FB>> Hey, good news.

It was a bump from Fiona.

SD> All yr meetings hve been called off & U free 2C me?

FB>> LOL, no, been promoted.

Seth smiles. Just as planned, but it feels good that everything is on track.

SD> See? U shld send me pics more often. Promoted 2 what?

FB>> Head/Marketing at Waters. Hydra. Eeeeek!!

SD> Wow. Well done, sexy thing. Mind-5.

FB>> Sooooo happy.

SD> Meet me in the red stationery room in 10min 2 celebrate?

FB>> *blush*

SD> I'll make it worth your while.

A moment's silence.

FB>> CU in 5.

Afterwards, Kirsten still tingling with pleasure, they spoon, naked, on their bed. She sighs. It's not often she feels sated like this. He rubs her neck, her back, her waist. His hands tell her that the anger is gone and now there is only tenderness. God, in this moment she feels so connected to him. Nothing else matters but his warm hands on her, the damp bedclothes, their nestled feet. If only the moment could last forever.

JOURNAL ENTRY

3 FEBRUARY 1988, WESTVILLE

In the news: *I don't know. When I look at P's newspaper the words all swim before me.*

Not watching, reading or listening to anything. Have the concentration span of a gnat. When will the babies sleep through the night?!

Need. To. Sleep.

But now there is more than just sleep deprivation. There is a darkness.

A nothingness. Am being swallowed whole.

CHAPTER 13

MESSIAH MAGIC

JOHANNESBURG, 2021

Kirsten waits for James to leave for the paediatric clinic in Alexandra before she pulls out the envelope from Betty/Barbara. While he tries to save the world she'll try to, well, save herself. She flattens out the note on the desk in front of her and tries to decipher it.

Doomsday. D-day. Apocalypse. Armageddon. End-of-the-world. She's never been good at this hellfire-and-brimstone thing. While everyone else in the classroom was learning about the cheerful trio of Christ, Mohammed and Buddha, she had been staring out of the window, wondering why no one else saw what she saw, felt what she felt.

A school religious counsellor once tried to tell her that her Black Hole was the absence of Jesus's light, God's love, and if she were to take the righteous steps and be saved then it would disappear, just like that. Messiah Magic.

Kirsten's eyes had rolled so far back in her head she almost lost them completely. Later, with his warm hand on her back, he had instructed her to stay behind after class, with a look in his eyes that told her that if she did her life would never be the same. His handprint still tingling on her skin, she had been first out the door when the bell rang.

She holds the note to the light, hoping to find a clue. Turns it over and over in her hands. Suddenly she feels ridiculous, trying to make sense of a demented woman's ramblings. She looks at her Tile. Her Echo.news tickertape flashes with new stories. A man gunned down fellow shoppers in a Boksburg mall, killing five people and injuring three. A(nother) municipal worker strike, as if our streets don't stink enough.

The usual spate of muggings and hijackings, some fatal, some just inconvenient. A flaming crucifixion in Sandton Square, courtesy of The Resurrectors. Funny, that they call themselves that, when they do the opposite. Jesus's light, my foot. They also cover the small spat that Keke told her about the day before, exaggerated by graphic pictures of gaping knife wounds, and a convicted rapist taking the government to the Constitutional Court for 'enrolling' him in a Crim Colony, or PLC.

When the government instituted the Penal Labour Camps the rest of the world was horrified. *Concentration camps for criminals!* Shouted the international headlines. *New Apartheid for SA!* and *Underground Crim Colonies!* It was in the beginning of the New ANC rule—when they still had balls—and they were dead-set on implementing the programme despite the international pressure not to.

They move prisoners from their crowded, dirty cells to various high-security farms and mines throughout the country where they set them to grind. They learn skills and earn wages, with which they pay their food and board, and have mandatory saving schemes that will be released to them, with interest, at the end of their sentences. The money that is saved by emptying the prisons go to prisoner rehabilitation and university fees.

Crime stats are down and all in all it is a neat move; the conviction rates are still low, but at least the captured criminals are in some way paying their debt to society. The then-defunct 'reclaimed' farms have been revived and South Africa has reverted to being a mass exporter of goods. The general public is still divided on the matter, but the initial outrage seems to have dissipated, along with the trade deficit.

Kirsten scrolls down. Thabile Siceka, the health minister, is in Sweden to receive some kind of award. South Africa has had some pretty dodgy health ministers in the past, including HIV-denialists who promised that a beetroot and olive oil salsa would cure even the direst case of Aids. Siceka doesn't have to excel at her job to be the best minister to date, but excel she has.

It is well known that she had a tough start in life. Both her parents and her grandparents died of Aids, and she had to leave school at eleven to look after her younger siblings. When the HI-Vax was in development she pushed it through every stumbling block. She raised funds when they were needed, flew in experts, sped up the testing phase. The vaccine could have taken twenty years to get into public circulation; Siceka had it out in four. She took HIV/Aids from being the Africa's biggest killer—apart from mosquitoes—to being as easy to avoid as MMR.

The Nancies do have some strong ministers, but as a whole their leadership just doesn't stand up to the pressures of the country. Too many poor people, poor for too long, too few rich people, and a wide, painful gap in between. Add to the mix deficient service delivery, economy-crippling strikes, the panic of the water shortage and relentless violent crime and it's no wonder that creeps are ready to pull out an AK47 at any asshole who says the wrong thing. South Africans are frustrated, and it is erupting in every facet of life. Clearly she is not the only one with a hollow where her heart should be. Where is the Messiah Magic when you need it?

JOURNAL ENTRY

13 FEBRUARY 1988, WESTVILLE

In the news: --- *I don't care.*

Something strange is happening to me. A twisting inside. I have everything I want, a wonderful husband, a nice home, two precious little babies, but I have this weird feeling of dread and sadness. When I wake up in the morning I don't want to get out of bed. I'm exhausted and just want to sleep all day. When I do get up I am like a zombie. Sometimes P gets home and I'm sitting in front of the TV in my sweaty pyjamas, not even watching, not really, and the kids are screaming from their room. He gets angry with me but he tries not to show it, tries to be understanding. When he is angry like that he doesn't talk to me. Doesn't want to show his feelings. In this terrible stony silence he fixes the babies up, changes them, feeds them, finishes the ironing. I should care more, but there is something wrong with me.

He doesn't understand. The days are just too long.

I've lost my appetite, no food seems appealing anymore. I exist on endless cups of tea. Tea sometimes makes me feel better. Not sure if it's the actual tea or if it's just something to look forward to: a treat, to break up the day yawning ahead of me. And biscuits, if there are. A hot mug of tea and a biscuit—like a little steaming beacon of hope. If there is a (rare) moment in the day that I have my hands free, the first thing I do, instead of doing the washing or cleaning the kitchen, is have a cup of tea.

There is no energy for anything that is not completely vital: Washing my hair seems an insurmountable task. The thought of lifting my arms for that long just seems exhausting.

P hugs me and tells me that he loves me, but that I need to 'snap out of it', for the babies. Doesn't he know that if I could, I would? Does he think I WANT to be like this?

I feel like nothing matters anymore. Don't see the point in anything. Overwhelmed.

Maybe I am being punished for breaking up P's marriage. Devastation wreaks devastation. Only myself to blame.

Sometimes I find myself wishing that we had never had the twins. They are so dear, they truly are, and I love them with my entire being but sometimes I just resent their existence. Wish we could go back in time when it was just P and me, and we went out to concerts and dinners, and sleep and sex came so easily. Sometimes when the babies are being demanding I want to pinch them. Hard, so it leaves a mark. Or just smack them when they won't stop crying. I picture the welt my hand would leave behind on their pale thighs. Of course I don't ever hurt them, won't ever. But these dark thoughts smear my soul. Make me feel so terrible. Terrible mother.

Being washed away by despair.

The flowers I planted are dead. They were violas.

CHAPTER 14

TEAMBUILDING

JOHANNESBURG, 2021

Fiona and Seth lie naked in their hotel bed. They are on their backs, gazing at the ceiling, allowing the air conditioner to cool their pink skin. It's a Friday afternoon and they're supposed to be at teambuilding, but instead they're at the third hotel on their list: The Five-Leafed Clover. They have decided to try out all the top hotels in Jo'burg; they have thirty-six to go.

Fiona loves hotels. She likes to arrive at the concierge, hot, breathless, and get a room for an hour, or an afternoon. She likes leaving the room a tangled, stained mess, steal the stationery, and flounce out of the entrance a few hours later, flashing the eyes of a woman clearly satisfied.

Seth expected her to be the opposite: shy of checking in, sure to make the bed before they left, straightening towels on her way out, but she has surprised him, and herself. She giggles, mid-strip, and says things like 'Goodness, what has happened to me?' or, more specifically, 'What have you done to me?'

She still wears polka dot silk blouses, but underneath she has exchanged her practical undies for the expensive lingerie Seth buys her, or she now buys herself. She still has the innocent freckles and the easy-blush cheeks but she won't hesitate to go down on him in his office, as long as the door is locked and the camera cloaked.

Seth holds her hand, which is wrapped around the locket she always wears. Lockets are back in style; even some forward-fashion men wear them, but Seth gets the feeling Fiona has been wearing hers long before they started trending again.

'What's in the locket?' he asks. They are used for so many purposes nowadays: pills, flash drives, patches, pedometers, mirrors, cameras, keys, IDs, phones.

'It's a vintage one,' she says, 'just holds a couple of pictures.'

'Let me see,' he says, peeling her fingers back.

'No!'

'Why not? What are you hiding?'

Fiona giggles. 'Nothing.'

'You are,' he says, kissing her nose. 'What is it? A photo of your ex? Your KGB files? Your real identity?'

She laughs some more. 'No, silly.'

She relents and lets him open the locket. Two cats stare back at him.

'That's Khaleesi.' She points. 'And that's Killmouski. I have a third one now, but I don't have his photo in here.'

'Kevin?' he asks. She smacks him, laughs, kisses him. He closes the locket and lays it back down to rest just above her cleavage.

'Lucky kitties,' he says, resisting a dirtier phrase.

She smiles at him. He thinks: *I've got you.*

'Although,' she starts.

'Mmm?' he murmurs.

'Talking about spies... I'm sure it's nothing... I don't want to talk... but when I was looking at the composition reports, just as a matter of interest, 'cos I'm trying to learn everything there is to know about the Waters, I saw that this month's Hydra reading was exactly the same as last month's, and as the month before. I mean, I know nothing about science...'

Seth lifts his head, acting interested, but not too interested. 'Isn't that normal?' This was just the pillow talk he was hoping for. 'I mean, it's supposed to remain stable.'

'Relatively stable, yes, but these reports are carbon copies of each other! As if someone in the lab is too lazy to test the sample and is just copying the exact same data every month. I mean, if I was too lazy to do the readings then I would just tweak them slightly month to month.'

'And the others?'

'Tethys and Anahita have fewer samples, fewer readings, but their reports vary slightly. You know, January magnesium 3.13, February it's 3.11. It just doesn't make any sense.'

'Strange, indeed,' Seth says, moving onto his side to face her, stroking her stomach. 'I think you'd better investigate.'

Fiona scoffs. 'Yeah, right, little Fiona Botes against the megacorp that is Fontus.'

Seth's hand moves down to stroke her, and she stops laughing. 'It's probably nothing.'

She inhales. 'An admin error.' She feels the blood rush away from her head: no more talking shop now.

'Yes,' agrees Seth, 'probably.' He shifts his body down; she opens her legs.

Maybe she would just check it out.

CHAPTER 15

EVERY PERFECT BONE

JOHANNESBURG, 2021

An attractive platinum-haired woman sits on a park bench at a children's playground in uptown ChinaCity/ Sandton. You can see that she is wealthy. She's laser-tanned, wearing SaSirro top to bottom, some understated white gold jewellery, and has a smooth, unworried forehead, but that's not what gives her wealth away. She is watching the ultimate status symbol: her white-ponytailed son, playing in the sandpit next to the jungle gym. He holds a dirty grey bunny—a stuffed animal—under one arm as he builds a sandcastle with the other. The toy clearly goes everywhere with the boy.

The perfectly made-up woman may look like a bored, stay-at-home mother, but in fact she is on her office lunch break. She was top of her class every year at Stellenbosch University and was fluent in 26 languages by the time she was twenty-one. She didn't finish her degree: she was poached by the top legal attorney firm eight months before she graduated, won over by a huge salary and the promise that she would make partner by twenty-five, which she did.

She opens her handbag, takes out a pill, pops it into her mouth and washes it down with a gulp of Anahita, saying a silent prayer for whichever drug company it is that makes TranX. She should know the name—she can tell you the capital city, currency and political state of nearly every country in the world—but today she can't picture the label on the box of capsules in her head. She wonders if she is burnt out; she definitely feels it.

Her son begins a tentative conversation with another little boy in the sandbox. Always the charmer. Her heart contracts; she loves him fiercely, every square millimetre of his skin, every pale hair, every perfect bone, she loves. The scent of his little-boy skin. His cow-licked crown. She has such dreams for him, wonders what he will be like at ten, sixteen, thirty. She never thought she'd feel this way about another person. She'd grown up feeling aloof, alone, her parents blaming it on her stellar IQ, but when her son was born that sad bubble burst. It hasn't taken away her anxiety or depression, but it has given her quiet, exquisite moments of joy she hadn't before imagined possible.

Satisfied that her son is playing happily, she opens her lunchbox. She takes home 14 million rand a year but she still packs her own lunch every day. Today it is a mango, pepper leaf and coriander salad, humble edamame with pink Maldon salt, and a goose carpaccio and kale poppy-seed bagel.

She takes a few bites of the bagel, enjoying the texture of the expensive meat, the tingling of the mustard. Soon there is a slight tickling at the back of her throat. She tries to swallow the irritation but it lingers. Trying to stay calm, she opens her bagel and inspects the contents, assuring herself that she had personally made the sandwich, there is no place for contamination, but the itch becomes stronger, furring over her tongue too.

She drops the bagel, starts to hyperventilate, presses the panic button on her locket. It sends a request for a heli-vac and a record of her medical history, including her severe peanut allergy, to the nearest hospital. Her airways are closing now and she clutches her throat, desperate to keep it open. She searches for her EpiPen, but when she can't see it, looks for a straw, a ballpoint, anything she can force down her throat to keep breathing, but her hands are shaking too much and she loses control over her fingers.

She stands up, lurches forward, waves blindly trying to attract someone's attention. Her vision becomes patchy; there are sparks and smoke clouds blotting out her son. She tries to call him, tries to call anyone for help, but it's too late for that. One arm outstretched towards her son, she sinks to her knees on the grass, then, blue-faced, topples over.

A woman's gasp rings out, and concerned strangers come to surround her. Ambulances are called, CPR is administered, but the woman dies within the minute. A white-haired toddler is held back, not kicking and screaming as you'd expect, but dumb with shock.

The strangers stand distraught, arms by their sides, not knowing what to do next. Just terrible. What a tragedy. They begin framing the story in their minds, to tell spouses and friends later. They think of how to word it in their respective status updates. Where is the ambulance? They have children to mind, places to be. One of the bystanders, a large man with a scarred arm, gives up on finding a pulse and walks away. Furtively, he strokes the soft stuffed rabbit he has hidden under his jacket. He retrieves his dog, a beagle, whose lead he tied to a swing post moments earlier, and ambles off. Chopping of the sky can be heard in the distance: the heli-vac approaching. It forms the intro to the song that starts in his head. He hums along—Pink Floyd?—and doesn't look back.

~

Fiona is on top of a cliff, ready to tumble. She holds back her curls with one hand, breathes hard, feels all her muscles contract, is paralysed, and then she topples. She flies through the air, through warm air, sultry water, then lands, is laid down, her blood turned to syrup. Seth comes with her, gasps with her then holds her until she stops twitching.

They lie clutching each other on the floor of the Fontus recreational cloakroom. They've been playing lasertag. Down to her last life, her nerves on edge, she screamed into her mask as someone in the shadows tackled her to the floor and dragged her into the cloakroom.

She knew it was him, knows the feeling of his hands on her. He zipped her out of the body-hugging suit, out of her clothes, and took her roughly against one of the dressing room tables, watched her body spasm in the reflection of the mirror.

'This is becoming a bad habit,' she says.

'I find that this kind of teambuilding is right up my alley.'

Fiona giggles. She can feel his gaze on her. She opens her eyes, self-conscious at his staring. Covers up her still-hard nipples.

'You're not going to spoil the moment, are you? By confessing how you really feel about me?' She is half-joking, half-pleading. *Please God, tell me you're falling in love with me.*

He laughs, a low bark, says, 'That's the last thing you need to worry about.'

While Fiona showers, Seth pulls on his clothes and adjusts his hair.

'I'm heading off,' he calls through the half-open shower door.

'Okey dokey, pig-in-a-pokey,' she sings. 'See you later!'

On his way out, Seth pockets her Fontus access card.

JOURNAL ENTRY

29 MARCH 1988, WESTVILLE

In the news: --- *Something about an ANC rep being assassinated in Paris. Not sure, just heard something about it on the radio.*

After staying in bed for three (?) days, P showered me (washed my hair, tenderly), dressed me, and hauled me off to a shrink. After an hour or so of talking she explained to P & I that it looks like I have something called Post Partum Depression - PPD. I knew about Baby Blues—most women feel some kind of down after giving birth (hormone crash, exhaustion, disillusionment, etc.) but this is different.

Just admitting the terrible thoughts I have been having (only when P was out of the room) helped me. Judy (the shrink) asked me lots of questions and we went through a checklist of symptoms. Just knowing the symptoms exist on a piece of paper made me feel slightly better – definitely less guilty. Other mothers also feel this way? It was like a huge raven that had been sitting on my shoulder shook his feathers and flew away.

She gave me some pills and I need to go back to see her a few times a week until I'm better. Before the session I had so little energy that I felt like I didn't even care about getting better anymore. Now I feel like I would do anything to feel better. P kept glancing over at me on the way home, not sure if it was because he was worried or relieved.

CHAPTER 16

HELLO, PRETTIES

JOHANNESBURG, 2021

Fiona jumps out of the communal taxi with a skip in her step. She has ordered lingerie online and the nondescript parcel has been delivered to her at work. It has burnt a hole in her desk drawer the whole afternoon. She hasn't been this excited to open a package since she won a stationery extravaganza basket a few years ago. At five o'clock she grabbed it and ran to catch a lift home.

She opens the door to her flat and her three cats rush to trip her.

'Hello, pretties,' she says, and they meow back at her. She stumbles in, looking for a place to put down her parcel while trying not to step on any of the cats.

In her bedroom she opens the box and spends time admiring the silk and satin. She can feel the excitement build in her pelvis. A hum, a zing. She strips down in front of her full-length mirror. The sun is setting and the light coming through the window bronzes her body. She touches her nipples. She takes the first set, an ivory satin push-up bra ribbed with black lace, and small matching panties, and puts them on. In her mind, the bra makes her cleavage look like a swimsuit model's.

She stands and admires her reflection, moves to see the different angles. She runs her fingers over the softness of the material, over the bra then over the panties. Her fingers trace her buttocks and the triangle of her front. She feels swollen from the afternoon of anticipation. She touches herself, hesitantly at first, but as she feels the pleasure build she lies down on her bed and lets her hand take over.

Afterwards, she lies in the light of dusk, listening to her pounding heart and enjoying the full body tingle that she had before only associated with sex with Seth. It's dark when she hears a noise in the front of the house. She grips the bed. It must be one of the cats, she thinks, but hurries to put her dressing gown on. She would investigate, to put her mind at rest. Chide the cats for giving her a heart attack. But then she hears something else, something like slow footsteps, and knows that there is a stranger in her house.

CHAPTER 17

SUB ROSA

JOHANNESBURG, 2021

KL> I found it.

Kirsten bumps Keke.

KK>> God? Jesus? Yourself? The Meaning/Life?

KL> No, asshole. Doomsday.

KK>> Intriguing. Let's say our final g-byes & go.

KL> Too far to drive on your bike. Limpopo. Comm taxi? I can get away by 1.

KK>> Sure. Meet u at Malema rank/town? Can lock up there.

~

Seth is busy with a taste diagram of CinnaCola. Each taste has a specific shape, made up of how each of its flavours hits certain zones on your palate and nose. CinnaCola, for instance, has a complex, multi-layered flavour repertoire, so the diagram is very much 3D, with spikes on certain levels and rounded notes on others.

This isn't dissimilar to the grind he did at Pharmax. There he would map out the delivery system of the drugs he created, making sure that the hits and the mellows were in the right place, conveying the best possible high and softest downer he could. Fizzy drinks aren't all that different. Apart from the aromas, you also have to map the fizz, the refreshment factor, and the sugar-and-caffeine buzz.

He's almost finished, and it's looking good, if he doesn't say so himself. It'll make a good abstract artwork for the red boardroom. Tomorrow he'll work on variations, ideas of how to 'up the feel-good factor', and 'maximise the full-palate experience' in

CinnaCola-speak. It's only 2pm but he feels as if he's done enough grind for the day. He stands up, bracing himself for Wesley's disappointed expression, but realises he's not in.

He glances both ways down the passage, as if to cross the road, then enters his manager's office, closing the door behind him with a soft click. He swoops behind the desk, smacks a few keys, checks the projection. Checks the desk drawers. They are clean, tidy, disturbingly organised, apart from one item of contraband: a rogue packet of Bilchen BlackSalt. Nothing how an office desk drawer should look. No expired snack bars, Scotch hipflasks or decade-old packets of cigarettes. Also, nothing to help his mission.

The computer asks for a password. Seth tries the Weasel's wife's name, the kids, the pet dachshund. Their birthdays. The date of their wedding anniversary. Access denied. Out of frustration he tries 'fauxburger'. Denied. It was worth a try. He walks down to the Waters section, where Fiona now works. He circumvents her office and gets to the elevator, presses the button for the labs. Stepping inside the silver room, he takes off his red lanyard and stuffs it in his pocket. Puts Fiona's new blue one on. Tries to not look suspicious as he exits the lift and holds Fiona's access card up to the Lab entrance.

The Laboratory is a huge, glass-walled warehouse filled with an army of white-coated nerds. Transparent doors lead to the adjacent factory, giving the impression that it is one huge—busy—hall of glass. He has his own lab coat on, so blends in to a certain degree, but still feels as if there is a brightly lit, candy-coloured Las Vegas-style arrow hanging above his head, pointing out his intruder status.

He grabs a mask and sprays on some insta-gloves. He puts his head down and walks towards the back of the hall, taking mental notes as he goes. There are floating graphs in the air: 3D liquid displays, animated spinning cheese-wheel pie charts, shivering towers of calcium versus magnesium. Infographic heaven.

The other activities surrounding him are UV sterilisation, water ozonation, deionization, reverse osmosis, water softening, and blow moulding of the superglass bottles. A ticking banner overhead informs him that this plant produces a hundred thousand litres of water per hour. He needs to get a sample, which means he needs to get into the factory. He doesn't know if Fiona's access card is authorised but he knows he may not get another opportunity to try it. He holds the card up to the glass door—

The building's alarm goes off, high volume, as if it's right in his head. *Fuck!* He swings around, expecting to see security guards with handcuffs, ready to cart him to the Red Jail. He wouldn't be surprised if they had cheerful, colour-coded cells in the bowels of this building.

He hurriedly makes his way back to the lab entrance, but the white ants follow him. Looking over his shoulder, he sees masked faces and blank eyes, looking in his direction. He rushes out, trying to escape them, pulls off his own mask so that he can breathe. Gets to the elevator and pushes the button over and over, looks for stairs and takes them. Whips off Fiona's lanyard.

He runs up the three flights to the Colours' offices, steps into the corridor and starts to head in the direction of the building's main exit. Sweating, breathing hard, he wonders if he'll make it before being shot with one of the guards' stun guns. All of a sudden there is the chaos of people going in the opposite direction to him, as if choreographed.

For once, the Reds, Yellows, Greens and Blues mix madly and without prejudice. Like vibrating atoms threatening to spill out of the building. As if the building is going to spew this multi-coloured mess onto its perfect pavements. *Rainbow Vomit,* thinks Seth, surprised by the strange phrase. The workers seem puzzled that he is walking against the flow. A worker bee flying in the wrong direction. Then, a firm hand on his back, and he turns around, expecting to see a guard, but it's Wesley, smiling from ear to ear in all his fat-lipped glory.

'Seth!' he says, rosy cheeks aglow.

'I was just on my way—' Seth says, motioning vaguely.

'No, no,' laughs The Weasel, still holding onto him tightly, 'you're going the wrong way. That wasn't a *fire* alarm, it was a *gala* alarm.'

Seth has no idea what he means, but allows Wesley to steer him into the stream of Fontus employees. The swarm seems excited. They gather in the main boardroom, a massive space filled with glass screens, holograms, cascading AVs, stocked fridges. People hand out drinks to their colleagues, joking about catching Yellow team members drinking Green drinks, and vice versa. The only cross-product consumption allowed is water: everyone is authorised to drink any of the waters, guilt-free. There is animated murmuring and smiling, a sea of expectant faces.

As a rule, public gatherings make Seth uncomfortable. It makes him feel as if he is buying into something, an automatic victim of groupthink, a forced Kool-Aid enema. A (black) sheeple. Now, especially on edge, perspiring, he manoeuvres himself into a corner and swallows a TranX.

He tries to spot Fiona but can't see her. Didn't see her yesterday, either. The crowd peels away from a tall, handsome man striding in, like Moses parting the sea. Everyone falls silent. He is wearing a sharp black suit—expensive—and just-greying beard and hair. The shoulders-waist ratio of a superhero.

Seth recognises him immediately from the Alba brief: Christopher Walden, founder and CEO of Fontus, one of the richest men in South Africa, and general do-gooder. Like a politician, he has the knack of getting good deeds in the media at every opportunity.

'Good afternoon, my favourite employees.' He beams. His white teeth are a spotlight on the tittering crowd. Given his appearance, you almost expect him to talk in a broad American accent, but his delivery is Joburg Private School. He cues his assistant, who presses a button on a remote control. Images of an informal settlement come up on the scattered screens: a Mexican wave of blue skies and tin roofs. They are the usual images used to manipulate: dry-skinned, snot-crusted toddlers, skinny-ribbed dogs, litter bunting on wilting fences.

'This is a suburb in Thembalihle, just forty kilometres away from here. These people are in dire need of our help. They can hardly afford staples like water, bread and maize. It came to my attention yesterday that a couple staying there had been trying for five years to have a child. Finally, they were granted their miracle.' He pauses and the picture of a sunny baby comes up on the main projection. The infant's petroleum-jellied dimples elicit a chorus of coos.

'This is Lerato. She was hospitalised yesterday with cholera symptoms. I don't need to tell you how dangerous cholera is for a small child. It happened after the mother mixed her formula with grey water, from the tap.'

The crowd shakes its head, clicks its tongue.

'She was desperate. She had run out of money for food. It was her only option.' He pauses to let his employees feel the weight of it. 'But we're not going to stand around and let this happen!' he says. 'There are buses downstairs, waiting for you. We're off to visit Lerato's neighbourhood to deliver care packages. Food, paraffin, blankets, and water!' The room erupts into applause and cheering.

'Are you ready, Fontus?' he shouts. There is a ripple of affirmation. Walden's eyes glitter.

'I didn't hear you! I said, are you ready, Fontus?'

The room shouts 'Yes!'

'Go Fontus!' he yells, fist in the air.

'Go-o-o-o-o Fontus!' the room yells back, and everyone starts moving out.

~

Kirsten had brought them cold-pressed coffeeberry juices, cream-caff for her, to dull her synaesthesia for the trip in the communal taxi: black double-caff, extra stevia for Keke. Two vanilla-bean xylitol kronuts the size of saucers.

'Okay, lady, spill.' Keke says, once they are squashed in at the front. 'Where are we going and how did you find it?'

'How does our generation find any wisdom of great substance and worth?'

'Er... Google?'

'Yebo.'

They are stuck in traffic. Nowadays this is unusual, but still seems to happen to Kirsten when she is in a rush to get somewhere. She sticks her head out the window to glimpse of what is causing the delay. A line of obedient vehicles snakes ahead of them.

'It couldn't have been easy, with all the doomsday prophets around, promising that every day is our last. The Suiciders, the Rapture kids, the Resurrectors.'

'I've never understood the whole "The End is Near" crowd,' says Kirsten, sitting back down.

'I know,' says Keke. 'You hate it when people state the obvious.'

'Exactly. Of course the end is near! As soon as there is a beginning the end is near.'

'I hope that coffee of yours is full-caff. You need a cup of optimism.'

'I don't mean it in a macabre way,' says Kirsten.

'Is there another way?'

'Yes! I mean it in a... I don't know, a Zen way. All beginnings have ends and that's the circle of life.'

'So what's your point?'

'I don't have a point. All I'm saying is that it's ironic. Life is really short and the creeps going around with their shouty-shirts telling you "The End is Near" are wasting their time.'

'Got you. Really they should listen to their own message and get a life. Literally.'

'Exactly.'

'So there were hundreds of silly results for "Doomsday"?'

'Thousands! So I ended up Googling *her* instead: the deranged lady.'

The driver enjoys pumping the pedals. The combi pitches forward, then stops dead, pitches forward, in an awkward dance of accelerator and brake. He speaks at volume to no one in particular. The passenger next to Keke is wearing a bad weave and singing along to the punk-gospel in her diamanté earbuttons, flashing a gold front tooth. They have to talk over her vibrato. Despite Kirsten's dulled senses, all the stimulation around her is disorientating. Finally they see the reason for the gridlock: a red-light brigade dominating the highway.

'Someone should tell them that this is supposed to be the fast lane,' mumbles Kirsten, and gets a dirty look from a fellow passenger. The red-lights signal it is a SurroSis and her entourage, and are to be respected at all costs and inconvenience. The driver touches his hat and then his heart, and they finally nudge past.

'She may have been schizo, but she was also, well... gifted.'

Keke shoots her a look of thinly veiled patience.

'Seriously, she had what they called "advanced intelligence".'

'Who called it that?'

'Her colleagues, at Propag8—where we're going. She ran the whole project. She was a bio-what? A biohorticulturist.'

Keke takes the straw out of her mouth, frowns. 'Propag8 sounds familiar.'

'It's a seed sanctuary bank in an old sandstone quarry. Like Svalbard on Spitsbergen, but a local, more indigenous version. They nicknamed it The Doomsday Vault.'

'Doomsday. Ha.'

'Vavilov built the first one. A botanist-geneticist in the 1930s, he grew up poor and hungry, so became obsessed with ending famine. The seeds even survived the Siege of Leningrad. And Hitler. Although not all the guards did.'

'Starved to death surrounded by edible seeds?' says Keke.

'Clearly better people than you or I.'

'And Vavilov? Became a rich and famous hero?'

'*Nyet.* He died in prison.'

'Hitler?'

'Stalin.'

'Jesus.'

'Are we just saying names out loud now?'

Keke cackles.

'What about your coco-loco lady?'

'According to her colleagues, she was the best in her field, some kind of genetic genius. She was no garage genome-hacker; she invented all kinds of disease- and pest-resistant crops. Got a 99 million-rand grant for her work on revolutionising vertical farming. Contributed to amazing brainswarming sessions when she open-sourced her ideas for cheap, organic biofuel and designs for living buildings. And she was ambitious. I mean, Propag8 was her idea. She was guarding against Doomsday.'

They travel for a while in silence.

'So her paranoia worked for her, to a certain degree.'

Kirsten shrugs. 'Maybe it used to, anyway.'

They disembark ten kilometres south of Bela-Bela. A local cab drives them from their stop on the main road along the dusty way to the slick exterior of the Propag8 building.

The design of the sandstone façade looks sunken into the ground, giving the idea that half of its face is under the earth. It's the same colour as the surrounding sand and rocks, which makes it blend into the landscape, despite it being the only building on the horizon.

It reminds Kirsten of Shelley's poem *Ozymandias*, and it makes her smile. Doomsday, and '*Nothing beside remains.*' The architect obviously had a sense of humour.

Keke moves to ring the bell but the smoked glass doors slide open before she touches the button. The inside is huge, cavernous, bare. There is a figure eight in the floor mosaic; Kirsten realises that it's an infinity sign. The only colour is a row of what must be a hundred different succulents in African clay pots along the dark glass front.

The receptionist looks up, ready to help them, but Keke motions that they've got it, and subtly moves Kirsten towards the large stainless steel door at the opposite side of the expanse. As they get to within two meters of it, the light on the doorway switches from red to green with a beep (Cashmere Cherry to Spring Leaf) and they hear the mechanism on the other side unlocking. The heavy doors glide open, revealing a high-tech elevator with confusing buttons. Instead of a neat ladder of floors, one on top of the other, they are set out in a complicated 3D diagram in the shape of a lotus flower.

'Lotus flower?' says Keke. 'Was she some kind of yogi?'

'Lotus seeds are viable for a thousand years,' says Kirsten. She had read it while researching the vault on The Net.

Fifty-two stops to choose from, and they are clueless. Keke pushes the stud closest to her. They start as the elevator moves sideways. When the doors open again, it's into a dark corridor. They step out, and the light above them flickers on. Keke does a quick dance, *Caipoera*-style, and more lights come on. Kirsten considers the whole seed bank in utter darkness, apart from this little cell of light.

There is another door across the passage. Kirsten steps towards it and holds up her key. The light stays red, and the door locked. They step back into the elevator and study the plan etched into its wall.

'Do you remember anything else from what you read about her work here?'

Kirsten racks her brain, tries to use Google on her watch, but there is no signal. She moves closer to the map and one of the buttons automatically lights up. Sub Rosa, it says, floor 36. She opens her hand to look at the key. The doors close and this time they move downwards, into the depths of the old mine.

When the door clicks open they enter a space that would look like a bank deposit box room if it weren't for the floor-to-ceiling animated wallpaper. Huge rose buds and blooms (Rusted Carmine) caress the walls, as if alive. Kirsten tries to take a photo with her locket but it's blocked. It feels as if she is looking through pink mist. She should have doubled the caff in her coffee.

Keke takes the key from her and approaches the wall of safety deposit boxes. It does its now familiar magic trick and a box on the right, just below eye-level, shows a blue light. Keke pushes it in, and it slides out like a drawer, the size of a shoebox. Inside is another box, with a keyhole, which Keke unlocks.

'It's like pass-the-parcel,' whispers Keke.

'Pass the what?'

'Oh,' says Keke, 'Never mind.' They both peer into the box, wary, as if something could jump out and bite their fingers.

'It's empty,' says Kirsten.

As an act of desperation, she puts her whole hand into the box and rummages around, just so that she would have no doubt in her mind that the box is definitely, absolutely, 100% empty. But it isn't.

'Hey,' she says. The far side feels different. Not textured metal, but plastic. She gets her fingernails underneath the corner and rips it off, bringing it out of the box and into view. It's a small plastic bag, like a sandwich bag, but four-ply and heat-sealed.

. . .

On the way home, a white minivan comes into view, then disappears, then appears again. It looks like another communal taxi, but without the trappings: no dents or scratches, no eccentric bumper stickers, furry steering wheel or hula-girl hanging from the rear-view mirror. Instead: clean paintwork, tinted windows. Something about it bothers Kirsten.

'I know I sound crackers but... is that van... following us?' Kirsten frowns.

'Please don't start,' says Keke.

'Seriously,' says Kirsten. 'They've been behind us for the last ten minutes.'

Keke looks over at the vehicle, then turns back around and plays on her phone. The white minibus weaves aggressively and gets too close to the taxi. Kirsten starts to panic.

'They know we have it. They're trying to stop us.'

'Stop it,' growls Keke, but as her eyes go back to her screen their taxi is knocked sideways. The minivan swerves away then back to hit them again, causing the passengers to scream and the driver to grab his hat, fling it down, concentrate on keeping the vehicle on the road.

Metal screeches as the van pushes hard against the taxi, trying to force it into the guardrails. The taxi driver keeps his head, accelerates, takes back the road. Keke pushes Kirsten down and covers her. They are smashed again, harder, and they veer off the road, onto the shoulder. Their driver steers hard to not go over the rails, then overcorrects and crashes into a bakkie, almost rolls the vehicle.

They sway on two wheels, then land safely back on the tarmac. The white minivan speeds off. Cars all around swerve and hoot, people shout. Inside the taxi: silence, the caustic smell of burning brakes. Broken glass glitters.

JOURNAL ENTRY

15 APRIL 1988, WESTVILLE

In the news: *A bomb explodes prematurely outside Pretoria's Sterland cinema killing the carrier and injuring a bystander. The passengers of plane-jacked Kuwait Airways Flight 422 are still being held as hostages – it's been 11 days – the Lebanese guerrillas are demanding the release of 17 Shi'ite Muslim bombers being held by Kuwait.*

What I'm listening to: *Chalk Mark in a Rainstorm – Joni Mitchell*

What I'm reading: *Margaret Atwood's 'The Handmaid's Tale' – I feel like this book is speaking directly to me, making me question my life.*

What I'm watching: *Beetlejuice*

My shrink says that it's good to write my feelings down so here I go: the ugly truth. I don't think the pills are helping. I love the babies more than life itself. I do, honestly, it's like they are physically connected to my heart. I can't imagine life without them.

But I also feel trapped. Isolated. I'm so young and here I am washing and cleaning and changing nappies while I should be out in the world, making friends and money and just LIVING. I feel like I am stuck in a life – that sometimes feels like a living hell of pee and poo and vomit – that I didn't choose.

I miss home and my family, even though we don't get on that well. I'm sad that they haven't come to visit the babies. I love P. Sometimes I think that he must regret marrying me; I can't imagine how he finds me attractive when I am such a stretch-marked baggy-eyed zombie. Other times I think, I am so pretty and young (on the inside!), I should be out there dating a whole lot of different men, be taken to new restaurants and getting flowers and goodnight kisses.

I don't want to eat because eating binds you to this earth in some way and I want to be free. I can see my clothes hanging off my body and it feels good to have an outward expression of the way I'm feeling inside.

I feel like I have wasted my life, that there is nothing to live for. Even though I know it's not true, that is how I feel, and that's why it's so difficult to get up in the mornings. And then when I do get up the babies cry and cry and I just feel like jumping out of a window.

The sticky love for the twins is push-pull: sometimes I'll be holding one of them and swaying and they'll melt into me and I think that the moment couldn't be more perfect. In the next minute something will happen: I'll slip on spilled milk, the washing machine will pack up, Kate will vomit on my clean top, Sam will start screaming, then they'll both be screaming and the kitchen will flood and I'll realise we're out of breakfast cereal and I can't stand it so my mind just floats away.

On these days I have the urge to just run away. To leave P and the twins. Not to be a coward, but to be brave, to save my life. I get anxious in the car on these days because my body and mind want to push that accelerator as far as it will go and just go anywhere that isn't here. Another province. Another country. Or even into the side of a bridge. But then I pull over and breathe and try to listen to my heart, which is connected to the babies, the sweet babies, my beautiful Sam and Kate, and it tells me to stay.

CHAPTER 18

BORROWED SCRUBS

JOHANNESBURG, 2021

The man dressed as a nurse puts his latex-covered fingers on William Soraya's wrist, feels his pulse. It is slow and steady. There is no need to do it: the athlete is hooked up to all kinds of monitoring equipment. He fusses about the room, rearranging giant bouquets of flowers and baskets of fruit and candy. He admires the medal—Soraya's first Olympic gold—on the bedside table. Its placement seems a desperate plea: *You were once the fastest man in the world, you can beat this. Please wake up.*

The nurse takes what looks like a pen out of his pocket, clicks it as if he is about to write on Soraya's chart, and spikes the tube of the IV with it. It is slow-acting enough to give him the ninety seconds he will need to leave the hospital. No alarms will go off while he is still here. He takes the medal and slips it into his trouser pocket as he moves. It is cold against his thigh.

It's a bitterbright feeling for him, leaving while his mark is still breathing. Doesn't feel right, especially after the accident he engineered hasn't proved to be fatal. Still, there will be others. He walks down the passage as quickly as he can without alerting anyone. He breathes hot air into his medimask, requisite for any doctor, nurse, patient or visitor in the hospital. It's large and covers most of his face, which is most fortunate. Hospitals are one of the easiest places to kill people. His borrowed scrubs cover his other distinguishing characteristics, apart from his generous build, and height. But no one will say: there was a nurse in there with a burnt arm.

CHAPTER 19
PIRANHAS

JOHANNESBURG, 2021

Seth gets home at midnight. He'd been drinking at TommyKnockers and is a bit unsteady on his feet. A cab dropped him off, courtesy of Rolo. Upstairs on the 17th floor, he punches in the code—52Hz—and his retina unlocks his front door. It clicks open, and Sandy greets him. He shows the speaker his middle finger. He checks all the security screens, sees the place is empty.

Knowing he's had too much to drink, he shrugs, pours a few fingers of vodka into a tumbler with ice. Takes it to his Tile to check for messages. He's been checking throughout the day to see if Fiona tried to get hold of him, but *nada.*

All he sees is update after update about William Soraya's death in hospital. He tries to block the story in his feed but it keeps on coming up on his screen, as if to haunt him, as if to say: this could have been you. You think you're indestructible; so did Soraya. Now he's lying on a slab with multiple organ failure, because that's what happens to people like you.

Not being able to get hold of Fiona adds to his anxiety. He doesn't know where she lives, doesn't know who her friends and family are, which makes it impossible to get hold of her if she doesn't come to work, and doesn't answer her phone. It nags at him: Fiona isn't the kind of girl to screen calls or not come to the grind for two days in row. He takes her Fontus access card out of his hoodie pocket, looks at it. His guilt accentuates her clear blue eyes, the salmon of her cheeks. No one has mentioned her absence at work. Piranhas.

He turns on the Tile, takes a slug of vodka. The green rabbit flashes; FlowerGrrl bumped him earlier in the evening.

. . .

FlowerGrrl>Hey SD, what's/hold-up? Thought u'd hve Fontus in bag by now.

He knows she's kidding, but feels the pressure nonetheless. He's been there for weeks without much progress. He'd figured Fiona would be his ticket, but she's gone MIA. His drinking tonight has had a purpose: to wipe out any inclination that he is worried about her. It hasn't worked. The more he drinks, the more it becomes clear that, for the first time in his life, he cares about someone else.

He replies to FlowerGrrl:

SD>> Making headway, shld hve s/thing soon.

Without washing his face or brushing his teeth, and still in his jacket, he gets into bed with his slippery glass of vodka. Takes a bottle of pills from the pocket, pops two, washes them down with the spirit. Spreads a throw untidily over his body, and falls asleep with the lights on.

Outside the building, a large man is walking his dog. The dog pauses to sniff the innards of a pothole. The man uses the time to look at the entrance of the building, get an idea of the security system. Backs up, looks up to the corner apartment of the 17th floor where a light is still on. Having seen enough, he makes a kissing noise: pulls the protesting beagle along, firmly, but not unkindly.

~

Kirsten's watch rings; it's Marmalade. Oh shit, she thinks, looking at the time, then at the two empty bottles of wine on Keke's desk. The clockologram clicks in disapproval. She touches her earbutton to answer the call.

'Hi, sorry I'm late,' she says, her voice gruff. Gives Keke the grimace of a schoolgirl in trouble.

'And you haven't called,' he says.

'And I haven't called. Sorry.'

'I was worried about you.'

'Sorry.'

'When are you coming home? I made dinner. Four hours ago.'

'Ah, sorry! I didn't know. You should have told me.' She stands up, throws two empty sauce-stained Styrofoam shamburger clamshells in the bin.

'I wanted to surprise you. Do something nice for you.'

'I'm really sorry. I'm with Kex.'

Keke gives her a soft kick in the shins.

She winces and hops up and down. 'At The Office. We're working on a... story.'

'Well, wake me when you get home.'

'It'll be late.'

'Wake me, Kitty. I miss you.'

He ends the call. They never say 'I Love You.' They agreed long ago that that the phrase is overused and trite. They won't reduce their relationship to a cliché. What they have is deeper.

'How much trouble are in you in?' asks Keke.

'He cooked dinner for me: a surprise.'

Keke looks at the time on her phone. 'Ouch.'

'He wanted to do something nice for me.'

'Double-ouch.'

'So where were we?' Kirsten asks, but Keke is looking at her strangely.

'What?'

'Since when do you lie to James?'

'What? I didn't. I don't.'

'We're working on a "story"?'

'Well,' says Kirsten, 'we are, kind of. Aren't we?'

Keke pouts, not convinced.

'You're the one that says everyone has a story. Maybe this is mine. And, believe me, the less James knows, the better.'

They go back to solving the puzzle they have been working on all night: trying to make sense of the code that is in the plastic envelope they found in the seed bank. It is a list of barcodes that, when scanned, are numbers, 18 digits to a line.

100380199121808891

104140199171209891

20290199142117891

20201199161408891

101250199160217891

201250199160217891

1010199112016891

They all start with either 10 or 20, all contain the numbers 1991 in the same position near the middle, and end in 891. The more wine Kirsten drinks, the more the numbers glow with their colours. It is distracting. For this reason, she has never been good at maths.

'I don't know how much longer I can look at this,' she says, rubbing her neck, which is tender from the car accident. 'Are you sure you don't know any maths-geniuses-code-crackers?'

Keke shakes her head. 'Nope.'

They have tried everything they can think of, from simple alphabet a=1 algorithms to squares and prime numbers, and all the search engines they can think of. Kirsten is playing with Keke's Beckoning Cat. If you push its belly-button its USB port comes out the other side, like a stunted tail. A secret porthole of information.

Maneki Neko, she thinks*: Japanese Lucky Cat. Brings good fortune to owners.* She gives the hard plastic a squeeze, puts it back on Keke's desk.

'Look, we've had a hectic day and we're not getting anywhere tonight.' Keke sighs, standing up. 'Why don't you go home to Marmalade and make up?'

Kirsten starts to protest but Keke is right.

'Besides,' says Keke, putting on her leather jacket. 'I need to get laid.'

~

As soon as Kirsten opens the front door she smells roast chicken, her favourite. James had left a plate for her on the kitchen counter: a succulent thigh, butter-roast potatoes, candied golden beetroot. She peels the cling wrap away and starts to eat the chicken with her fingers. It is exactly right, the taste: an undulating curve with a few small points bouncing off it, finishing in a wavering line. She's exhausted; it feels like more than just tiredness. Deathargy.

Her body is cold when she climbs in next to James, and she's unsure of whether to wake him. She moves closer to him, barely spoons him, trying to gauge how lightly he is sleeping.

'Thank you,' she whispers, 'the potatoes were perfect.'

He grunts, turns around, pulls her towards him in a full-body hug. A warm, sleepy hand slides under her pyjama top, rubbing her back, then settles under her panties, on the arch of her hip. She moves against his hand, slowly, rhythmically, but stops when she realises he is asleep.

A few hours later Kirsten wakes with a start. Colours swirl in her head: green, grey, brown, yellow. 7891. She knows the colour combination so well, but where from? Pine Tree, Ash, Polished Meranti, English Mustard. Somehow she knows it's part of her. Then she gets it. She bumps Keke, even though it's past 2am:

KD> The colours are backwards!

. . .

Surprisingly, or not, Keke responds.

KK>> Wot R U doing? LSD?

KD> It should be yellow/brown/grey/green.

KK>> U need to be institutionalised. Good night & good luck.

KD> Not 7891, but 1987, the year I was born. Think the whole sequence is backwards. It says 60217891, that's my birthdate, backwards. 6 December 1987. It features twice in the list, 5th and 6th lines. It must mean something. I knew the colours but it was hard to see when they were backwards.

KK>> What about the other numbers?

KD> No idea.

KD> Yet.

CHAPTER 20

TOY CHASE

JOHANNESBURG, 2021

Despite a late night, Seth is in the office early. In theory he is trying to tweak his 3D mathematical model animation of the CinnaCola taste experience, but his head is pounding and Fiona's pass is burning a hole in his pocket. He gulps down his anxiety with a few pills and leaves his office, heads towards the Waters wing of the building. He walks past Fiona's office and does a double take as he sees her sitting at her desk. Relief like a splash of water on his face.

'Fiona!' he says.

The brunette at the desk looks up at him, puzzled. 'Hello?'

It's not Fiona. Similar looking, thinner, more attractive.

'Oh,' says Seth, taking a step back and looking at the new name on the door. 'Do you know where Fiona is?'

'I don't know a Fiona,' the usurper says, mechanical smile, cherry red lipstick, and a whiff of Stepford. 'Can I help you with something?' She is being super polite: she wants him to leave.

'This is her office,' Seth says, incredulous.

She blinks at him, stops smiling. 'Not anymore.'

Despite Seth's better judgment he strides up to the main reception. The receptionist looks alarmed.

'Fiona Botes,' he says, 'she's been away from the grind, and I was wondering if you knew where she was.'

The man fingers his hair, taps on his tablet, looks cheerfully confused.

'No record of a Fiona working here,' he says.

Seth wants to pull him by his effeminate tie, punch him in the face. He does everything in his power to keep calm. He shouldn't be here asking questions, calling attention to himself.

'Check again,' he says.

The man taps a bit more then patches the HR infobot on his earbutton. 'Botes,' he says, 'Fiona.' After a moment he ends the call. 'It appears that Ms Botes is on a business trip. Asia. She's not expected back any time soon.'

'Asia?' mumbles Seth, 'Is that the best you can do?'

At the look in Seth's eyes, the receptionist takes a step back, despite the counter separating them. His eyes dart to the army of security guards. Seth retreats. He has five, maybe ten minutes before someone with clout realises he needs to be taken care of.

He runs to the Waters wing and uses Fiona's access card to get into the lab, hurries to put on a mask. Once he gets into the factory it's easy to disappear between the giant vessels of water, darting between gauges, graphs, clicking dials. Fiona had told him that the tap at the end of all the barrels and valves, just before the bottling, is where the sample test tubes are filled.

Seth removes the test sample of Anahita, replacing it with a virgin tube, and slips the sample into his pocket. Then he walks over to the Tethys section, and the Hydra section, and does the same there. Cameras are everywhere.

Once he is out of the lab he bins his mask, runs up the stairs, towards his office to grab his Tile, but immediately feels as if someone is following him. He picks up his pace. As he's about to turn into his office he sees them: three security guards armed to the max, ready to pounce. Dobermans with a rabbit in their sights. Just before they grab him, The Weasel steps in their way.

'No, no,' he's saying. 'I'm telling you there has been a mistake.'

Hurting an innocent Fontus employee would have consequences.

'On whose orders?' Weasel's demanding, the back of his white-collared shirt straining, struggling with the mountainous men as they try to reach around him, but Seth is just out of their grasp.

He darts into his office and locks the door. Grabs his backpack and jumps out of the window, onto the narrow balcony. Sprints towards the back of the building and runs down the perforated metal stairs of the fire escape. Once he hits the grass, he hijacks a CinnaCola golf cart, floors it, mows through a gazebo, sending trays of breakfast hors d'oevres and flutes of Buck's Fizz flying. A waiter in a tux stands frozen, open-jawed. Seth swerves and narrowly misses the corner of the squash courts.

He can hear them behind him now, in turbo-carts with flashing lights. They motor past the swimming pool, a strip of restaurants, a mini touch-rugby field. It's like playing cops and robbers in Toyland. He can see the exit, but at the speed they're approaching they'll be able to stop him before he reaches it. A bullet zings past his head. Another hits his cart. Toy chase, but real guns, real bullets.

A small bang and his cart spins and tumbles, rolling over itself and throwing Seth out. He stands, re-orients himself, notices his head is bleeding. Feels for the test samples to make sure they're not broken. The three guards are out of their vehicle and pointing their weapons at him with practised aims. A trio of testosterone. More guards will be on their way. Seth doesn't have a choice: he reaches to his ankle holster and pulls out his gun. They all begin to shout orders at him, drowning each other out.

'Put down your weapon!' yells the one with the blond crew cut.

'You put your fucking weapons down!' shouts Seth, flicking off the safety catch. No one moves.

'I am warning you, Mister Denicker, we will use force against you if you don't come with us.'

'We just want to talk,' pipes the other one.

Seth walks backwards, towards the exit. The men stiffen their arms, each one wanting to take the shot. Frustrated wannabes with itchy fingers: dangerous.

'You have families, children,' he shouts at them. 'I have fuck-all. No one. Nothing. You've got the most to lose.' They keep their sights trained on him. Then, slowly, the youngest of the three lowers his gun. The crew cut shouts at him, swears, but the man slides his gun back into his hip holster, backs away.

'You two: you're ready to widow your wives over fucking bottled water?'

They don't say anything but keep advancing while he inches closer to the exit. Seth has no choice: he squeezes the trigger and puts a bullet in crew cut's leg. The man lets out a shocked noise, falls to the floor, lifts his gun at Seth, pulls the trigger, misses, and misses again. Now empty, the felled man's gun clicks impotently in Seth's direction, and he roars in frustration. Specks of saliva in the sunlight. The other man doesn't know what to do. He appears shocked by the blood and doesn't seem to want to shoot or be shot. His gun is still raised but it's at an unconvincing angle.

'Tell them to open the exit,' says Seth.

'No!' shouts the crew cut, his arms out at his side as if to hold back the other man. Seth points his gun at the uninjured man's thigh.

'Wait!' shouts the man, 'wait,' and he throws his weapon forward, onto the grass, and speaks into the crackle of his radio.

'We have the suspect in hand. Call off back-up and open exits. Repeat: suspect is apprehended, all clear.' An acknowledgement sputters back.

Seth collects the abandoned gun. 'Give me your access card,' he says, and the man does so. He wonders what in particular this man has to live for.

Thirty seconds later Seth walks out of the Fontus grounds and the colourful throngs of morning tuk-tuk and taxi traffic swallow him up. Until now he hasn't been convinced that Fontus had something to hide.

CHAPTER 21

RED FINGERPRINTS

JOHANNESBURG, 2021

Kirsten takes her eyes off her screen to think, and sees the file she has been keeping on her mother. Opens it, looks through the morbid illustrations, the pricked paper dolls, the onion-skin birth certificate, sees the colours. She thinks that's the end of the file but then she sees the magazine cutting again, the one she found framed in storage. Cute baby, but not her. The date on the back says 1991.

She puts away the file and Googles the year 1991. She searches South African pages: South African cricket was unsanctioned, political violence continued, Nadine Gordimer won the Nobel Prize for literature. 1991: Yellow, brown, brown, yellow. Not a nicely coloured year at all. She can't imagine it being a very happy year for anyone.

The birth dates, if that's what they are, thinks Kirsten, are all around the same time. From 1986 to 1988: a year or two apart at most. So that's seven people, born around similar dates. Then the other set of dates all contained 1991. Her watch rings, making her jump. She turns on her TileCam and answers the call.

'Hi,' she smiles, happy to see Keke, but Keke doesn't return it.

'Listen, you're in trouble.'

'What?'

'You should leave your house.'

'Now who's paranoid?' Kirsten laughs.

'As soon as you can, Cat. The list, it's a... kind of a... poisoned chain letter. It's not just a list. It's a hitlist.'

'Slow down, Keke. You look manic. Too much caffeine?'

'I'm not fucking around, Kirsten, you need to listen to me. It's a *hitlist*. You are *on it*.'

'Seriously, you need to calm down.'

'Someone wants you dead. You need to leave your apartment.'

'You're not making any sense. Why would anyone want to kill *me*?'

'Marko... he came up with this mad algorithm and matched the birthdates with recently dead people. As in, the last few weeks, days. The people born in those years, the numbers at the end of the lines, they're dead. One, two, three, four, they're all dead, in that order. The schizo was number three. William Soraya was second. Before him, a musician in the bath.'

Panic reaches for her: serpentine plumes of yellow smoke (Sick Leaf). Betty/Barbara had said something about a music man.

'A musician, in the bath?' she asks.

'He was drowned.'

'In the *bath?*'

'Oh, for Christ's sake!' screams Keke. 'Just leave the fucking house already!'

'But you're not making any sense!'

'Listen to me, Kitty. Number four, a woman in a park. Dead. You're number five. You're next on the list.'

'I'm next on the list.'

'You or the other person with your birthdate. You're five or six.'

'Wait, you're saying that the crazy lady was right?'

'We don't have time to talk about it now. Go to a police station. I'll meet you there.'

'Okay.'

'Okay?'

'Wait. No. She said no cops, Betty/Barbara said no cops.'

'Well then just get out of there. They know where you live. Two of them were killed in their own homes. Get out and go somewhere public.'

'But you said... number four was killed in a park?'

'Jesus Christ, Kitty, I'm about to strangle you myself.'

'Okay. Okay. I'll go somewhere safe.' Even if this is some stupid misunderstanding. It doesn't matter. Even if it is just to prevent Keke from having a heart attack.

'Okay,' she says, 'I'm leaving.'

As she stands, a thought almost knocks her over.

'What about the chip?' she whispers.

'What?'

'The microchip. The crazy lady said she had a tracker chip in her head.'

A recent trend had been that overprotective mothers had them implanted in their children's necks, but it had only became legal a few years ago. Kirsten's hands fly up to her head. She tries to search her scalp but her hair gets in the way.

'A tracker? That's impossible, right?'

'No. I don't know. I just want you to get out of there.'

'But if you're right about the list, then Betty/Barbara was right, and she told me about the chip. Which means that they'll find me wherever I am. I'm not safe anywhere.'

'Yes,' says Keke, 'if she was right.'

'But you're saying she *was* right.'

'I don't know what I'm saying!'

'Holy fuck, Keke!'

'A chip is implausible, but even if it's true... So there's a chip in your head. What could you do about it anyway?'

'Hold on,' Kirsten says, and runs to the bathroom cupboard. Grabs James's hair clippers. She sits in front of her screen and sweeps the zinging shaver from the base of her neck all the way to her forehead. Keke lets out a sound of shock: an almost-sob. Masses of red hair fall to the wooden floor as Kirsten finishes the job. The buzzing stops, and Kirsten is bald. She tries again, palpating her scalp to feel for anything strange.

'Those things can... move,' says Keke, emotional, 'it could be anywhere.'

Kirsten's fingers freeze at the back of her head. Just lower than halfway down is a thickness, a form. She gulps. She didn't believe it existed until this moment. Now there it is, under her finger.

'I think I found it. Now what?'

Keke looks at her with plates for eyes. They both know the answer.

'Let me phone James,' says Keke, 'let him do it for you. He'll have the right... instruments.'

'Do you honestly think he is going to believe any of this?' shouts Kirsten. 'That I'm on a hitlist and have a fucking tracker in my head? I need to get it out *now*. Now!'

She runs to the spare room and starts to search through James's things. It's the room they use to store her camera equipment and his medical gear and its suitably messy. She doesn't find a scalpel.

As she's raiding, a white envelope falls out of a back pocket of his doctor's bag. At first she ignores it, focused on the search, but then she sees the envelope has her name on it, and her address. This apartment's address. She remembers now a day not so long ago when she had walked in on him in here. He had jumped.

'You gave me a fright,' he said, tucking a white piece of paper into his doctor's bag.

'Sorry,' she said, lifting a lens off the windowsill. 'Just wanted to get this.'

She hasn't given the interaction a second thought, except maybe to observe that they were being overly polite to each other: never a good sign for a relationship.

She pockets the envelope and keeps looking for something sharp until she had gone through every satchel. Then she remembers the pocketknife in her handbag. She speeds back to her desk, brings it out, flicks open the glint.

'No!' whispers Keke, covering her eyes, 'you can't!'

Kirsten grabs a bottle of vodka and some surgical cotton wool. She wipes down the blade and the back of her head. Brings the knife up to her shorn skull, feels for the lump, takes a breath. She chickens out, puts the knife down and has a large mouthful of vodka, then another one, and tries again. This time she draws blood, splitting the skin just above the thing. She waits until the cut is finished before she shouts in pain. Keke is covering her eyes but shouts in sympathy. Kirsten tries to get it out but her fingers are shaking and greasy with blood. She gives up, wipes them on her jeans.

'Tweezers!' says Keke.

Despite tears in her eyes, Kirsten finds a pair in her make-up bag, douses them, and starts to root around in the wound. Every movement of the sharp metal in the gash sends bright orange currents of pain down her neck, down her spine. She feels all the blood drain from her head, as if she's about to faint, but then she gets a grip on what she hopes is the chip and pulls it out. She holds the tweezers up to the camera, and there, in its sticky grasp, is a tiny microchip in a glass capsule. A treacherous grain of rice. Warm liquid runs down Kirsten's neck, between her shoulder blades. She is swaying in her chair. She holds the cotton wool up to the wound to staunch the bleeding, then rips open a platelet-plaster and sticks it onto the wound.

'Have some more vodka,' says Keke, but Kirsten feels too dizzy, wants to keep her head.

'I found this,' says Kirsten, her speech slurred by shock and spirits. The envelope is stamped with red fingerprints. She tries to open it with her stuttering hands. Gives up. 'I don't know where to go.'

'Go anywhere, just get out of there!'

'I need to warn the other people on the list.'

JOURNAL ENTRY

2 JULY 1988, WESTVILLE

In the news: A car bomb explodes near the gate of Ellis Park stadium in Johannesburg. Two people are killed and 37 injured. Bombs, bombs, bombs. What kind of world have we brought the twins into?

What I'm listening to: *Tracy Chapman. Fell for her after watching a bootleg VHS of her amazing performance at the Nelson Mandela 70th birthday celebration concert at Wembley Stadium. Talkin' about a Revolution!*

What I'm reading: *'Radical Gardening: Politics, Idealism and Rebellion in the Garden (George McKay).*

What I'm watching: *Who Framed Roger Rabbit?*

I don't know if it's the pills or the sessions with my shrink or just the fact that the twins are sleeping through the night but I feel SO MUCH BETTER! I feel almost like myself again. It is like coming up for air after a long, deep dive in some cold black lake.

P hired a domestic worker / nanny to help me with the kids. She comes in on Tuesdays and Thursdays and does all the washing and cleaning (usually with one of the twins strapped to her back!) It gives me time and space to just 'be.' Who knew you needed time for that? But I do. I work in the garden and read books and then I feel ready to be a mom again. I no longer feel as though I am being consumed.

I feel better, I look better, I even put on a new dress the other day and took the kids for a walk. I am hungry again and it feels good to cook and eat.

P is so happy he is spoiling me. Buying me clothes and a nice necklace, and we even got a babysitter the other night and went to dinner like we used to. I had a sirloin and a baked potato with sour cream and P just watched me eat as if he had never seen anyone eat steak before.

My shrink says I'll have good days and bad days while I'm getting better and soon the good days will outnumber the bad days. I think that is starting to happen.

I planted some new flowers – arums this time – they flower beautifully in winter instead of dying like some other annuals. Also planted some other things. P says I've got green fingers now. I laughed. It felt good.

CHAPTER 22

TSOTSI

JOHANNESBURG, 2021

Seth is in a communal taxi heading towards his apartment. His fellow passengers give him a wide berth as he tries to stem the flow of blood from his forehead. He is lucky the driver let him on. A pearl-clutcher wearing thick glasses clicks her tongue at him and calls him a *tsotsi* under her breath. He bumps Alba.

SD> In some trouble here, position at F compromised.

FlowerGrrl>> What do u need?

SD> Security check & bugsweep ASAP at my place. I'll remotely disable my BM-retina access.

FlowerGrrl>> Motioned, will contact u when it's confirmed clean. You need a bodyguard?

SD> Ha. Since when does Alba hve budget 4 bodyguards?

FlowerGrrl>> Worried about u. It can b arranged.

SD> I'll b fine.

FlowerGrrl>> Famous last words.

SD> Hopefully not LAST words.

FlowerGrrl>> ROFLZ! Danger suits you. Never knew u had/sense/humour.

SD> Funny. Also, I'll need someone/labs, I'll b bringing in samples.

FlowerGrrl>> Excellent. Will have someone here ASAP.

. . .

Seth's head stops bleeding.

~

Kirsten's head stops bleeding. She switches on the shower and doesn't wait for the water to get warm before she blasts her face, neck and back, then quickly towels off, leaving a Pollock of red and pink behind (Blood Marble). She throws on some fresh clothes: black, and steps into her dark trainers. Grabs her bag but leaves her Tile behind. Just as she is out the door she remembers the envelope and goes to fetch it, stuffs it in her bag along with a clean plaster and the pocketknife. She doesn't have time to think, she just moves.

CHAPTER 23

HER ABDUCTOR'S HANDWRITING

JOHANNESBURG, 2021

Kirsten puts her watch up to the screen so the ATM can scan it. She draws her daily limit of ten thousand rand, hoping it will keep her going for the next few days. The machine thanks her for her business and ejects 20 perfumed five hundred rand notes. The cash is bulky but she can't leave a credit trail. She checks over her shoulder for anything suspicious but everyone seems to be going about their regular lives without a clue of what hers has become.

She catches a communal taxi to Mbali Mall in Hyde Park. She can't think of anywhere safe to go but when the taxi driver stops outside the shopping centre for another passenger, Kirsten jumps out, leaving the microchip hidden in the fold of the seat.

Usually she hates malls, but for now the soulless space and dazzling lights seem like a good idea. Polished floors, store staff too tired to smile and shopzombies bleached by the artificial light. The killer wouldn't pump her full of bullets in front of all these people, will he? Still, she is cautious, keeps her head down and walks along the shop fronts, gazing at the window displays without seeing anything. She grabs a mask off a rotating display and uses it to cover her face.

~

Seth is walking, to kill time and get some air, and is twenty minutes away from home. Tuk-tuks and bike-cabs hoot at him as they pass, offering him a ride. Alba had just confirmed that their bugsweep has entered his apartment, so by the time he gets there it should have been given the all clear. It is just a precaution: so far as he is aware, no one at Fontus knows his address, but he was born with a healthy sense of paranoia and it has kept him alive and (relatively) unscathed up until now. What the fuck is going on at Fontus that they would remove Fiona and set armed security guards on him? Numbers stream through his head as he thinks of the files he had accessed there, the graphs, the summaries, all seemingly in order. What is it that they're so desperate to hide? He will find out soon enough: he needs to get the samples to Alba HQ.

~

Her adrenaline flagging, Kirsten looks for a place to sit but is accosted by a Quinbot, AKA Stepford Wife. Despite her side-stepping it, the mannequinbot sidles up to her.

'Hello *Kirsten*,' it says. 'How are you? Isn't it a wonderful day?'

'Jesus,' says Kirsten into her mask. 'Really?'

'I'm sorry. Hello *Jesus*. How are you? Isn't it a wonderful day?'

'Leave me alone,' says Kirsten.

'Jesus, would you like to try on this SaSirro alpha-cut dress? It has a built-in corset that will accentuate your lovely body shape.'

'No.'

'The shimmer in the hemline adds grace to your movement, and—'

'No, thank you, not interested.'

'Jesus, if you look at the detail, you'll see—'

'Stop calling me Jesus.'

'I have scanned your measurements. You have a lovely body shape. This is how the dress would look on you.'

The Stepford Wife grows a little taller, her bust shrinks by a cup, and her waist grows by a few centimetres. Her abs get softer, and her calves become more pronounced. Her hair is reeled into her scalp. Kirsten picks up her pace, but the bot keeps up.

'Leave me alone,' she says. 'Scram.' She looks around to see who is watching.

'It has a built-in corset that will—'

'Fuck off!' she shouts, causing some nearby shopzombies to look at her. The bot stops and reverses. Its wide lipstick-smile doesn't falter.

'Thank you for your time,' says the bot. 'It's always lovely to see you.'

'Fucking bots,' mutters Kirsten, jogging away. The last thing she needs is to cause a scene.

'Don't be a stranger!' it calls out after her.

Mannequinbots are always getting abused: fondled, defaced, hacked, taken for trolley rides that invariably end up in some kind of accident, shoved into garbage removal chutes, stolen, decapitated. Kirsten has little sympathy.

She finds a hoverbench outside a Talking Tees shop. It seems to be a politically themed store; usually they're more light-hearted. The four shirts in the window tell her, via rather basic animations, to 'Beware The Net,' 'Boycott Bilchen,' 'Ban the SkyCar,' and 'Pray for Peace in Palestine.' She prefers the more light-hearted shirts, ones with beautiful, evolving illustrations, and ones that tell you jokes. The problem with the joke-shirts, though, is that you have to walk past the person before you hear the punchline.

She opens the letter she found in James's case. Her name is scrawled on the outside of the envelope.

Dear Kirsten, it says, in her abductor's handwriting. *When you find out the truth you won't believe that we loved you, but we did, in our own way. It's terrible to want to tell you the truth, because it puts you in danger, but the truth will out, I can feel it bleeding out of me already, and it's better if you are warned. Your foster father, my pretend-husband of thirty years, heard us talking on the phone just now and—*

Maybe he thinks they'll spare him, but I know differently—

I don't have long—I know they'll be here any minute—who is to say no one else has confessed... I can't be the only one who feels like this. Festering, about to burst.

The details aren't important. Please know we truly believed we were doing the right thing.

This is important: What you must know is that I have now compromised the cell and if you don't move now you will be removed from the programme—killed.

My God, what have we done?

Once you are safe, contact ED MILLER in Melville. He is my life partner & soulmate. We've been together for 26 years. He doesn't know anything about GP, I spared him that much, but has a packet of info for you. Everything you need to know about why you were taken. You need to read this to understand why we did what we did.

You need to get rid of the tracking microchip (embedded in your scalp). You need to move countries. Just get on a plane, fly anywhere, for now. You need to do this without letting the police know. And you need to do this immediately. They will eliminate everyone in our cell, all seven children that were taken. Enclosed is a list of the others. I am sending this and a duplicate to the only other person I (shouldn't but do) know in the programme, Betty Weil (Barbara). I have given her your address. You can't trust anyone in the GP, but I had to take the chance. Warn them too, if you can.

Kirsten, one of them is your twin brother.

I'm sorry. Truly. We chose you because you were special. You were all special. God forgive me, and God help you. RUN.

Kirsten's brain stumbles. All she can see on the page are the words 'taken,' 'twin brother,' and 'RUN.' Kirsten's watch rings, snapping her out of her shock. It's Keke.

'Hey Cat,' she says, 'how are you doing? Hey, never mind. You're alive. That's the most important thing.'

'Yes,' says Kirsten, lowering her mask. 'I guess so. I'm inside—'

'Whoah! Don't tell me where you are.'

'Of course. I'll buy a 'sposie.'

'Good.'

'You got anything for me?'

'Ready for your rather interesting day to get a bit more... interesting?'

'Impossible.'

'What?' says Keke.

'What?' says Kirsten.

'What do you know?' she asks.

'I need a moment,' says Kirsten, trying to think straight. 'You go first.'

'So FWB Hackerboy Genius found the other person on the list.'

'Where is he? Joburg? Do you have an address?'

'How did you know it was a he? And get this, you were right, he was born at the same clinic as you.'

'I know,' says Kirsten.

'Wait, what?'

'Just carry on,' says Kirsten.

'While Marko was hacking into some illegal tax shit to find his address, I checked the other names on the list and they—you—were all born at the same clinic.'

'What kind of clinic was this?'

'That's exactly what I thought, so I looked into it, and according to Google and the National Health Authority it never *existed*.'

'It never existed.'

'Correct.'

'So... I was born to a mother without a uterus in a clinic that never existed.'

'Er... correct,' says Keke. 'In other words—'

'In other words,' says Kirsten, 'she was not my mother and that is not my real birth certificate.'

'It looks like it, yes.'

'I was kidnapped,' Kirsten finally whispers. Snatched. Abducted.

Keke is talking again; Kirsten tries to tune in.

'... but I have a feeling this is just the beginning. It's clear that someone will do anything to keep whatever this is, a secret. Get that disposable phone and we can meet up. We can look for this guy together.'

Seven people on the list, all with forged birth certificates. The first four on the list: dead. Five, six, seven alive: orange, pink, green (Grapefruit Skin, Baby Toe Pink, Camouflage).

'Kitty Cat? Hello?'

'No, it's too dangerous. Stay where you are and keep looking.'

'Will you at least phone James? I'd feel much better if he was with you.' James hid the letter from her. Kirsten ignores the question. 'You'll bump me this guy's co-ordinates?'

'Yebo. Watch yourself!'

For a moment the danger fades and the realisation glitters before her: She has a twin. Unbelievable. But hadn't a small, lonely part of her known all along? 'RUN' the letter says. *Fuck. Fuck running away.* She is going to find her twin.

~

Seth hasn't received anything from Alba, so he waits outside, sure he'll get the go-ahead soon. He still has a few bullets left in his gun, which is cold but reassuring against his palm. He keeps his head down, his hood up. Slips into the camouflage of pedestrian traffic, but the creep is headed straight in his direction.

He feigns nonchalance, flicks off his safety. The person is getting closer, closer, and Seth's finger travels to the trigger. When the person is a metre away Seth finally looks up and is ready to fire.

There is a blast of light, and his mind scrambles to work out what has just happened. Has he been shot? Has he shot? He doesn't remember pulling the trigger. But no one is hurt and there is a shock of a beautiful woman in front of him: a haunted look and a shaved head.

'Seth Denicker?' she says, breathless.

'Who are you?' They've never met but he feels as if he knows her. Kirsten's body is vibrating. This man's face, his presence, shakes her, she feels like she's touched a live wire. There's an immediate electric psychic connection.

Seth is paralysed by the magnetic field of this familiar stranger.

'I'm...' she starts. Could it really be true? But she knew it was, without a doubt. Every bit of her could see it, taste it, feel it.

You are my parallel life, she wants to say. *I have always felt your existence echo in mine.*

She pulls off her face mask.

'I'm your twin sister.'

JOURNAL ENTRY

6 DECEMBER 1988, WESTVILLE

In the news: *A limpet mine explodes in at the Department of Home Affairs in Brakpan. Bangladesh is devastated after the cyclone of December 2 – 5 million homeless and thousands dead.*

What I'm listening to: *Patti Smith's Dream of Life.*

What I'm reading: *Keith Kirsten's South African Gardening Manual*

What I'm watching: *Die Hard. I love Bruce Willis!*

The garden is absolutely exploding with colour. P says he can't believe it's the same garden. I'm so proud of it. Durban weather is the best: heat to get things growing and blooming, and lots of rain to keep it going. Allamanda, Bougainvillea, Mandevilla, Plumbago. Now I understand the saying 'riot of colour'. The babies and I spend some time in it every single day.

But besides the garden, there was a big celebration today! The twins turned ONE! We took them to Mike's Kitchen and they both had a free 'kids meal' – a vienna and some chips with tomato sauce and then an upside-down ice-cream cone with a clown's face on it. Kate has such a sweet tooth and loves ice cream so that was her favourite part. She said 'green, green' (even though the ice cream was white). The waiters sang happy birthday to them and gave them red balloons with ribbons (which Sam promptly popped with his teeth). It was so cute, he had this shocked look and he looked at us, not sure if he wanted to laugh or cry.

It was a wonderful day. While the kids were eating P put his hand over mine and gave me this searching look, as if to see where that awful vacant person is, and I smiled back as brightly as I could. That part of me is pushed deep inside and I'll do whatever it takes to keep it there.

CHAPTER 24

A LITTLE LESS CONVERSATION

JOHANNESBURG, 2021

Seth scrubs his scalp with his knuckles. It is obvious that this woman is insane, you can tell at a glance: head shorn, blood-stained. Of course, his head has been bleeding too, but... that wild look in her eyes. She does seem eerily familiar. No, not familiar, but similar. Looking into her flecked irises is like looking through a mirror into some parallel universe.

'You what?'

'Your sister. Twin. I think.'

'You *think?*'

'This is also new to me. I still don't know what happened to us or what is going on, but I know that we're both in danger.'

'Look, lady...' He puts his hand up and takes a step back.

'I know! I know that I sound crackers. That's what I thought about the woman who warned me, but then she turned up dead.'

'Who's dead?'

'It's not important. What you have to know is that there is a... list... and the people on the list are being killed, in order, and we are next.'

Too many teenage summer horror movies.

'Bullshit,' he says, and then, 'by who?'

Kirsten takes the piece of paper out of her bag, hands it to Seth, who makes sure their hands don't touch. Looks down, looks at her.

'Lotto ticket?'

'They're barcodes. Of people. Look at five and six. That's us—see our birth date? Everyone above us on this list has been murdered.'

'What happened in 1991?'

'I don't know yet.'

'Where on the list is the woman, the one that approached you?

'Number four.'

'So then I am five and you are six?'

'So you believe me?'

'No, but I'm naturally paranoid and I like patterns, and when I hear that someone is trying to kill me I pay attention.'

Seth's rational side knows the story is far-fetched, but what if this is really his twin? His flesh-and-blood sister? Standing here with her feels right. There is an unmistakable connection. Against his better judgment he flicks the safety back on.

Kirsten looks at his face, wants to touch it, but all of a sudden he grabs her arms and throws her to the ground. As she opens her eyes a body crashes down onto the pavement next to her, where she was standing. In slow motion she watches black oil spread towards her, and just before it reaches her, Seth pulls her away from it and to her feet.

The dead man on the ground is young, twenty-something, black-clad with waxed spiky hair and smudged eyes. He lies with his mouth open towards the sky, a leg bent at an awkward angle. Seth bends over the warm body and searches his pockets. Kirsten wants to ask him what he is doing but her voice doesn't seem to be working. Seth doesn't find a wallet. He sees the glint of a locket, and looks inside: the smallest green rabbit glows at him.

'Fuck,' he says, 'fuck!' He rips off the locket, pockets it, grabs Kirsten's hand, and they peel off into a charcoal alley.

A few blocks south, out-of-breath Kirsten manages to flag a cab. Before they get into the car, Seth makes a point of checking the cab driver's licence.

'You're good at it,' puffs Kirsten as they climb inside.

'Good at what?'

'Being paranoid.'

'Ha.'

Kirsten gives the driver the address of The Office.

'I wouldn't have—' She motions to the driver. 'checked.'

'Ja, well, it comes naturally.'

'Being paranoid comes naturally?'

'Yip.'

'Bad childhood?'

'Is any childhood not bad?'

Kirsten hesitates. 'I'd like to think so.'

'Yours?' he asks.

'Actually, to be honest, I don't remember a lot of my childhood, especially early on.'

'Me neither. Our brains are programmed to forget bad stuff.'

'So you're a glass-half-empty kind of guy.'

He shrugs. 'Depends what's in the glass.'

Kirsten fidgets, plays with the ring on her finger, desperate to tell him about the microchip, knowing that every minute it stays in his head is a minute's advantage they've lost, but she has to weigh up the consequences. *Just another half hour, till I can show him some proof. Till then I need him to stick around.* Instead she tells him about Keke.

Seth watches Kirsten talk, recognises himself in the anxious motions of her hands, the spinning of the ring on her finger. He feels impelled to do the same, but denies the urge. He pops a pill instead. She watches him do this, and without thinking, reaches for her own pills. She keeps forgetting to take them. She snaps the cap off the bottle, but before she can take one he grabs it out of her hand.

'What is this?' he demands.

She is shocked. 'Um,' she says, 'a prenatal supplement.'

Seth studies the label: *Dr Van der Heever,* it says, *PN supp 1 per day.*

'Prenatal?' he asks, 'so, you're...'

'Yes. Well, no. Been trying for a long time. No dice.'

'Where did you get this from?'

'Take it easy,' she says, 'my boyfriend filled it for me. He's a doctor.'

'I hate doctors,' says Seth.

'So do I. Ironically.'

Seth pockets the pills. Kirsten lets him.

'How long have you known this guy?'

'James?' She laughs. 'Forever.'

'How long?'

'Thirteen years longer than I've known you.'

Betty/Barbara said to not trust even the people you love. And James hid the letter from her. She doesn't know what it means, and she wishes Marmalade is with them, but there was a little tapping, a little whirring in her brain, warning her to be careful.

They arrive at The Office and take the stairs to stay out of view. Kirsten leads Seth to Keke's regular office.

'Keke!' she shouts, glancing around. The room doesn't look right: it's in its normal mess but it doesn't have the right colour. It feels like cold water is rushing over her body.

'Has someone been here?' Seth frowns at the open drawers and floor white with paper.

'It's difficult to say. It is usually—messy—but something doesn't taste right.'

'Excuse me?'

Kirsten checks the safe; it's empty. Keke's Tile is gone.

'Maybe something spooked her and she ran for it,' says Kirsten, more to reassure herself than anything else. 'Maybe she's hiding out, waiting for to hear from us.'

She dials Keke's number, and they both jump when a disembodied voice starts singing from underneath the desk. Elvis Presley: *A Little Less Conversation*. Kirsten scrabbles around on the floor, and she finds Keke's phone.

'Fuck,' she says again. Keke would leave a lot of things behind in a hurry, but never her phone. 'They've taken her.'

All her contacts. More importantly: her SugarApp.

Seth scrunches up his face. 'Elvis? Really?'

While she is on the floor she spots the Beckoning Cat flash drive. Thank God. They don't know it is a drive. She holds it up to Seth, pushes its belly to reveal the tail. 'They left her flash drive.'

He takes it from her, plugs it into his Tile.

Kirsten uses her pocketknife to unlock the fridge. As soon as she opens the door, she sees Keke's insulin kit and there is another wave of cold water. She shuts her eyelids against the glow of the refrigerator, wishing the insulin away, but it's there again when she opens them. She puts it on the desk in front of Seth.

'We've got seven hours to find her.'

'Hey?'

'Seven hours to go,' she says, 'before Keke... gets really sick without her insulin.' She says 'really sick' but what she means is: 'die'—she just can't say it out loud.

'She's diabetic?' he asks.

Kirsten doesn't answer. She sits back down on the floor and closes her eyes for a while. After a few minutes Seth is kneeling in front of her. He touches her gently on the shoulder.

'Kirsten?' I think we've got something.'

CHAPTER 25

THE SEVEN THAT WERE TAKEN

JOHANNESBURG, 2021

There are two folders on Keke's *Maneki Neko* flash drive. The first one is called 'The Seven That Were Taken' and has seven old, scanned and archived newspaper articles, dated from 1991. The second folder—'RIP'—contains four recent PDFs from Echo.news.

They start with the folder called RIP. Kirsten recognises the first article immediately. She read it a week or so before, at her shoot at the aquarium, about Betty/Barbara being found dead in her flat.

'This is—was—her,' says Kirsten. 'The crazy woman who gave me the key.'

'The key?' asks Seth.

'The key that opened the safety deposit box at the seed bank that had the list in it. Look at the date of her birth, the colours are backwards.'

Seth frowns at her. 'You are truly odd.'

'Look,' she says, and shows him that Betty/Barbara's date of birth is backwards in the third line of numbers on the list.

'So the one date is our birth date,' he says. 'What is the other?'

They open the next article. It's about a well-known composer, found dead in his bathtub, by his lover. Seth frowns.

'I remember this story from a couple of days ago.'

Drowned, it says, apparent suicide, or accident, although the lover wouldn't accept it, said they had everything to live for. They were about to be garried: a trip to Paris planned for spring, after an intimate wedding in Paternoster. On finding the blue body, the lover smashed up the apartment, destroying any evidence that may have existed. He swore foul play: Blanco's most prized possession is missing: an antique ivory piano key from a Roger Williams piano. It was his proposal gift. The lover required sedation, and was not being treated as a suspect. The musician is dead, their future washed away in a few inches of waxy grey liquid (Cold Dishwater).

'It could have been suicide,' says Seth.

'He was first on the list.'

Seth hesitates then opens the next document. A picture of a blond woman laughing into the camera comes up on screen. *Top executive dies in front of toddler son.* The story is about a high-flier corporate who accidentally ingested peanut matter—the source unknown—and went into anaphylactic shock and died in the kids' park down the road from her office. The people at the park had tried to resuscitate her but her airways were swollen closed and CPR wasn't successful. The white-haired child was first taken in by the paramedics, then the policewoman on the case, and eventually collected by the husband who had unplugged on the golf course and had heard about his wife's death on the radio on the way home from the pub. The fourth article was Soraya's organ failure. He had felt a connection to Soraya. Coincidence?

They move on to the second folder; there is a picture of an awkward little boy, a toddler, dressed in a brown suit, sitting on a piano stool in front of a baby grand. *Baby Beethoven kidnapped,* reads the headline.

'The drowned composer,' says Kirsten.

Seth opens the other archived articles: they are all stories of abduction. *Toddler missing,* about a too-blond two-year-old who can speak four different languages. The executive.

Has anyone seen Betty Schoeman? A mug shot of a not-pretty baby dressed in old-fashioned clothes, frowning at the camera. Betty/Barbara.

Child abducted from nursery school, reads another, about Jeremy Bond, a two-year-old snatched from a crèche playground just minutes before his parents arrive to collect him.

Seth reads the fifth one:

Saturday Star, July 1991

Toddler kidnapped while father shops

Tragedy struck in the friendly city today in the unlikeliest of places. Young Ben Jacobz (14 months old) escaped his pram in a department store at Green Acres Mall, Port Elizabeth. 'He was always so fast,' his mother told us, unable to keep from crying. 'He started crawling at eight months, was walking by ten. He would just tear around the place like the Duracell bunny.'

Baby Ben managed to toddle out of the store while his father was standing in the queue to pay for some clothes for him. 'It happened all the time,' says Mrs Jacobz, 'his uncle used to call him Now-You. Now you see him, now you don't.'

'We even tried one of those terrible things,' said Mr Jacobz. 'Those toddler leashes, but he would [...] throw a tantrum. He hated it.'

As soon as the boy's father spotted the empty pram he left the queue and started looking for him. 'I wasn't too worried yet,' he said, 'Ben did it all the time and we always found him.' But then he saw a strange woman outside the entrance of the store pick the baby up. 'I started shouting at her, and at Ben, but she didn't look at me and hurried off [...] and disappeared into the crowd. I started running after them, and that's when the guards tackled me.' Mr Jacobz was unknowingly still holding store merchandise when he ran out of the door, setting the alarm off. The security guards, not aware of the kidnapping, saw him 'make a run for it' and apprehended him. When he could finally explain the situation the baby was gone.

The police have launched an extensive search. They ask that the public keep a look out for anything suspicious.

'We're sure they'll find him and bring him home,' said Mrs Jacobz. It was then Mr Jacobz broke down weeping.

That must be William Soraya. Ben/Bill. They open the last PDF.

The Observer, 21 May 1991

Snatched

Twin tragedy hits small Durban suburb

After a gruelling 48-hour search in uncharacteristically cold weather for the missing Chapman toddlers of Westville, KZN, the South African Police called off the operation as of 2 AM.. Brown-eyed twins Samuel and Kate (3) were last seen in the front garden of their parents' home before Mrs Anne Chapman moved inside to answer a telemarketing phone call on the landline. Less than a minute later the children had, according to their mother, 'vanished'.

The search party combed the area, as well as a nearby river where Mrs Chapman purportedly used to take the children to swim and picnic. Anne Chapman, having a record of PPD or post-partum depression, is being questioned despite the divers not finding anything incriminating. Mr Patrick Chapman is standing by his wife, stating they are both 'extremely anxious' to find the twins. In a strained voice, on camera, he urged anyone with information to come forward. The SAP, faced with a dearth of any kind of evidence and an already-cold trail, promised they would keep looking, but don't seem to hold out much hope of finding the children, dead or alive.

Kirsten and Seth stand pale under the fluorescent light in the office, looking at each other, speaking aloud as they process the jolt of information.

'Holy fuck,' they say at the same time.

'Samuel and Kate,' says Kirsten. 'The mad woman—Betty/Barbara—called me Kate.'

'Samuel and Kate, abducted at three, become Seth and Kirsten.'

'Moved to a different province, and split up.'

Kirsten shakes her head. It doesn't make any sense.

'Wait, it says 'brown-eyed.' She looks into Seth's blue-green eyes that mirror hers (Sound of the Sea).

'They must have had our irises lasered. Strōma'd the brown out. It's easy enough to do.'

She thinks of her biological parents, the Chapmans, and feels overwhelmed. What they must have gone through. What she and Seth must have gone through. There is an extreme feeling of loss for the life she should have had, the life that was taken from her, and here he is now, standing in front of her: the missing piece of her puzzle.

'The Black Hole,' she says. 'It finally makes sense.'

He blinks at her. She has the feeling he understands; maybe he feels The Black Hole too but has filled it with other things.

'I was always—disconnected—with my father,' he says. 'Never met my mother. Never felt he really wanted me around, didn't understand why they had me in the first place.'

'Exactly,' says Kirsten. 'But why abduct a child you don't want? Surely a creep so desperate for a baby would, I don't know, love the child more?'

Seth is silent.

'It doesn't add up,' says Kirsten. 'It's too much to take in. I don't have the mental bandwidth to cope with this.' She moves to run her hands through her hair but feels her prickly scalp instead, the plaster on the back of her head. Realises she's been holding the knife all along and puts it on the desk. He glances at it and narrows his eyes.

'Whose knife is that?' he asks.

'This?' she says, 'It was my father's—well, whoever he was—the man who pretended to be my father for twenty-eight years. Why? What's wrong? Why are you freaking out?'

'Who was your father? What did he do?'

'Who was my father? I don't know. He was a research guy, a lab guy, a grindaholic who ignored his wife and daughter to read a lot of scientific literature. I still don't actually know what he *did.* Will you please tell me why you are getting so freaked out by the knife?'

'You're not quite Nancy Drew, huh?'

'What?'

'Did you even think to look up that insignia?'

'No. Why would I? And who the fuck is Nancy Drew? I'm a fucking photographer, not a member of the Hawks. All this—' She motions around her. '—this fuck-circus, is new to me, okay?'

He stares at her, then scans the insignia of the pocketknife and does an image-match search. Nothing comes up.

'You recognise it, the logo, I can see.'

'Yes, I recognise it,' says Seth. 'But... it's impossible. An urban legend, a myth. It's not supposed to exist.'

'I don't understand.'

Seth points at the diamond-shaped insignia. He traces an angular 'G' in the left of the diamond and a 'P' in the right.

'The guys at Alba are going to flip out when I show this to them.'

Kirsten looks at the knife, looks at him. She sees him smile for the first time.

'GP,' he says. 'It's the fucking Genesis Project.'

CHAPTER 26

NON-LIZARDS

JOHANNESBURG, 2021

'Okay,' says Kirsten, 'there's no easy way to say this, so, well, here goes: I need to cut a microchip out of the back of your head.'

'Wow,' says Seth, 'just as I was beginning to think we were getting on.'

'The crazy lady—'

'Now you're speaking about yourself in the third person.'

'The *other* crazy lady, Betty/Barbara, said she knew they were tracking her because she could feel the microchip in her head. And the killer—killers—whoever is trying to kill us, knows where we live. Knew that lady who took her toddler to that park.'

'Look,' says Seth, shaking his head, 'that just can't be true. Technology for trackers didn't even exist when we were kids. Wait, is that why the back of your head was bleeding? You tried to look for a fucking microchip?'

'Not tried, I found it!'

'Show me,' he says.

'I planted it in a taxi. It could be anywhere.'

He looks around the office, rolling glassy eyes. She's known all along he won't believe her.

'Next you'll be telling me to wear a tinfoil hat.'

'Actually, that's probably not a bad idea.'

'Ha,' he says.

'I'm not fucking with you.'

'Okay, but you're not cutting it out with that thing. I know someone.'

'We don't have time to fuck around!' shouts Kirsten.

'Look,' he says, 'I need to go to Alba. That is not negotiable. They'll be able to remove the chip. Analyse it. Then we need to get bullets, and get you a weapon.'

'What the hell is Alba? What about Keke?'

'We can only find your friend when we have more information. The chip is the only thing we have at the moment.'

A thought strikes Kirsten.

'Hackerboy Genius,' she says. 'Keke's contact. His number will be on her phone. He can get into anything: it's how we found you.'

'You think he'll know something?'

'He'll know more than what's on this drive,' says Kirsten. 'She asked him to dig.'

Seth shoves his Tile into his backpack.

'We'll call him on the way.'

'What is the Genesis Project?' asks Kirsten as they head down the fire escape stairs, towards the basement.

Seth shakes his head. 'There's not a lot to tell. I mean, there have been rumours for years, but I don't think anyone actually believed them.'

Kirsten thinks of her father: heavy, steel-framed glasses, dulled by time. Big hands, badly tailored trousers, egg-yolk stains on his ties. She finds it difficult to imagine that he was involved in any kind of covert movement. *Unless he was good, unless he was very, very good.*

'It's a bit like The Singularity – never gonna happen, but still as scary as shit.' He shoots a glance at Kirsten, as if to size her up, as if to see if he can trust her. 'When I started at Alba—'

'You still haven't told me what that is.'

He stops on the sixth landing. The caged light next to his head flickers, a loose connection.

'Alba is a bit like *Fight Club*. The first rule of Alba is: never talk about Alba.'

'Fight Club?'

'Have you *ever* read a book? Do you know that inquisitive mice grow more neurons?'

The only book she has ever read cover to cover is the collector's edition of *Hansel & Gretel* that James gave her. The cruel coincidence is not lost on her.

'Besides, we're probably going to die tonight,' says Kirsten, 'I'm thinking all rules are off.'

'Well, ja, that's the second rule.'

'Ha.'

'Seriously,' he says, holding her arm, 'no one is allowed to know, do you understand?'

They start moving again.

'Alba is a crowdfunded underground organisation: a rogue group of engineers, scientists, biologists, geneticists... We experiment with biotechnology, but mostly we investigate others that do the same thing.'

'You're a biopunk?'

'Technically I'm a chemgineer, but, yes, biohacker, biopunk, hacktivist... basically we're high-tech Truthers.'

'You uncover stuff.'

Seth nods. 'We're a technoprogressive movement that advocates open access to genetic information. We play around with DNA—only in a clean way—but our aim, the reason we exist, is to infiltrate and expose what we call black clinics—megacorps who use biotech in an uncool way.'

'Like?'

'We look for anything dodgy: any way the company might be ethically dubious, illegally practising, or trying to exercise any kind of social control.'

'That plastic surgery place—in Saxonwold. Tabula Rasa.'

'They were buying discarded embryos from fertility clinics, injecting the stem cells into people's faces.'

'You exposed them?'

'Alba did. A colleague—she had to suck fat out of housewives' thighs for a year before she was allowed near their faces. It took her another year to uncover the black market stem cells. We also exposed the Ribber Ranch, XmonkeyD and Slimonade.'

Kirsten had heard about all of them over the last few years: their nasty secrets being revealed and those involved being strung out during the subsequent trials.

'The thing about amazing runaway technology,' says Seth, 'is that it makes it easier to be evil. Government can't legislate fast enough to keep up. Alba is the self-appointed, independent watch dog.'

They quicken their pace down the stairs.

'So, there has always been talk about the Genesis Project. It's seen as, like, the ultimate black clinic. Like a human version of Reptilians: a huge clandestine society that actually controls the world. They're supposedly everywhere, especially in leadership positions.'

'The Queen-is-a-lizard theory, but no, well, lizards.'

'And local. It's a South African group.'

'So the Nancies are probably lizards. Or, whatever, non-lizards. You know what I mean.'

'According to the rumours, there would be a few strategically placed Genesis Project members in key political positions.'

'The president?'

'I've always thought she looked a little reptilian.'

They get to the parking basement, and Keke's motorbike is parked in its usual place. Kirsten opens the storage space at the back of the bike, takes out the inflatable helmet and key, and packs the insulin kit and Seth's backpack. She offers Seth the helmet but he waves it away. She puts it on, wincing as it inflates, and fastens the strap underneath her chin.

'But you don't believe it? I thought you'd like the conspiracy element, given your predilection for paranoia.'

'I don't know. Before today, I thought that if it existed, we would have some kind of proof by now.'

'Now we have the knife.'

In the corner of the parking basement, a car comes to life. Kirsten and Seth move quickly into the shadow of a pillar. It revs, its tyres squeal on the smooth concrete. It blasts warm air on them as it rushes past. Tinted windows. Kirsten releases her grip of Seth's arm.

'GP could mean anything,' he says. 'It could be from your dad's local bar. GastroPub. Gin Party. Geriatric Pints.'

'Getting Pissed.'

'Gone Phishing.'

'Green Phingers.'

'Gay Pride?'

'He wasn't stylish enough.'

They get on Keke's bike, and Kirsten starts the engine, revs. She accelerates gently, trying to get a feel for the machine thrumming between her thighs.

'Except that I've seen that insignia before, that diamond.'

'What do you think?'

'I think it's the only lead we've got.'

CHAPTER 27

CRACKED COBALT

JOHANNESBURG, 2021

There is a loud bang, as if someone had shunted a wheel, and the bike goes skidding, screeching off the road, and slams into a stationary 4X4. Spinning colours, heat and tar, tumbling, until they are still. Kirsten's left arm sparks with pain. She touches it gingerly with her other hand. Blue gleam (Cracked Cobalt). Broken.

Seth isn't wearing a helmet.

'Oh my God,' she says, trying to turn to see him, but he's also pinned to the tar. 'Oh my God. Seth? Seth?' She doesn't recognise the sound of her own voice. She tries to wriggle out from the bike, but only manages an inch. She looks around for help, but the street is dead. Seth groans, brings his hands up to his head.

'Are you okay?' she asks in the stranger's high-pitched voice.

He doesn't say anything for a while.

'Depends on your definition of okay.'

Kirsten sighs loudly, lies down. 'You can talk, which means you have a pulse. That's something.'

He gets up, tries to find his balance, staggers on the spot for a while before realising Kirsten is trapped under the bike. He comes over to her side, releases her. Once she rolls clear, he lets the bike crash down again.

'Something happened,' he says, 'to the bike. I heard it.'

He kneels to get a closer look, tries to spot any signs of sabotage, but he doesn't know what he's looking for. He always liked the idea of a bike, but liked the idea of being alive more.

'Donorcycles,' says Kirsten, wincing. 'That's what James says they call them in the ER.'

'Cute,' says Seth.

Using one hand, Kirsten deflates her helmet, opens the compartment at the back of the bike, retrieves their things. She checks Keke's insulin pack. Three out of the five vials are broken.

'Let's try get a cab,' she says, limping in the direction of the main road. The left leg of her jeans is hanging on at the knee by a thread, her calf is bloody and gravel-bejewelled. Her shorn head is bruised and dirty; she supports her injured arm as she walks.

'You look like you're straight off the set of *Terminator 8*,' says Seth.

'You don't look too bad yourself,' she says, gesturing at his newly bleeding forehead. There are sparks in her arm. She eases off her shirt, revealing a tank top, and ties it into a sling. Seth hands her his hoodie to wear.

'Is your arm broken?'

'I don't know. Think so. Never broken an arm before.'

Seth can't say the same.

'The pain is blue. Different shades. Right now it's Cyan Effervescence. I think that means broken.'

'You're one of those people,' says Seth. 'Those points-on-the-chicken people.'

She looks sideways at him.

'Those people that taste shapes,' he says.

'Taste shapes, feel flavours, smell words, hear colours, see sound... yes. My wires are crossed. I have no walls between my senses.'

'So that's why they wanted you,' he says.

'Hey?'

'All the kids that were abducted had some kind of talent, some aptitude, something that set them apart. Musical genius, edgy horticulturalist, uber-athlete, super-linguist...'

'What's yours?' she asks. 'What's your super power?'

'Maths.'

'Yuck,' Kirsten says. 'Sorry for you. You must have drawn the short straw.'

'Maths is the language of the universe.'

She looks at him with his fauxhawk, smudged eyes and eyebrow ring.

'Seriously.'

There are no cabs, so they catch a communal taxi instead. The passengers inside move up quickly when they see the state of the new fares. Even the driver seems concerned. Kirsten pays him double to expedite the journey and he takes the cash with an upward nod. It's a quiet trip. Kirsten can feel the glares cutting into her body, as if it isn't lacerated enough. A few passengers are exchanged en route: they swap a sweating businessman for a woman with blond dreadlocks and a see-through blouse, a couple of floral aunties clutching an over-iced cake inch their way out and in jumps a metal-mouthed schoolgirl in a uniform (Dried Cornflower). Kirsten catches the girl staring at her, so she smiles, but the girl quickly looks away.

It takes them fifteen long minutes to reach Parkview and they jump out when they get to Tyrone Avenue. There seems to be some kind of afternoon street party going on: the road is strewn with streamers, and paper lanterns float above them on invisible wires. Small crowds are milling about, drinking craft beer and warm cider in dripping plastic tumblers. A food truck hands out hot crêpes and galettes. Warm air, acoustic tunes on the speakers, and the laughter of strangers. The cafés and restaurants spill their swaying customers out onto the pavements. Despite the sunshine, empty wine bottles act as candleholders, growing capes of white wax. As they pass the tables, someone says a toast and glasses are chinked.

'This is it,' says Seth, motioning to a florist with street art for signage that reads "Pollen&Pistils." Inside a petite girl with a beehive, her back turned, is wrapping a fresh arrangement of hybrid green arums (Neon Cream). They enter the shop, a bell jingles, and immediately her eyes shoot up to the back wall strip mirror, where she sees Seth's reflection.

'And in come the walking dead,' she says, spinning around with a giant pair of scissors in her hands. She is wearing glam 1950s make-up: dramatic eyeliner, striking red lips, beauty spot on powder-pale skin.

'Well,' says Kirsten, 'I know we're not looking our very best.'

The different colours and fragrances in the small room swirl around and Kirsten has to blink through them and step slowly to make sure she doesn't walk into anything. The back wall is a painted mural, graffiti-style, of an outdoor flower market, and this also affects her depth perception.

'I didn't mean that, honey,' she says, 'I'm talking about when You-Know-Who finds out you Called A Friend.'

'I didn't have a choice,' says Seth.

The girl palm-weighs the scissors, purses her ruby lips.

'Seriously,' he says, 'there's a lot more going on than you know. The bugsweep you sent...'

Her wide eyes flicker.

'I'm sorry,' he says, handing her the dead boy's locket.

She looks down and wipes the blades of the scissors on her red-and-white damask apron, leaving sharp lines of bright green (Cut Grass) that cut across her torso.

'Your current assignment?' she asks.

'We seem to have a bigger problem.'

She puts down the scissors, closes and locks the front door of the shop and turns the 'closed' sign to face the street. Automatic blinds shudder across the glass façade. Once the blinds are in place, she claps and they all disappear into darkness. She hits a button hidden from view under the counter, and a portion of the mural on the back wall starts rolling up.

They follow her down a tapering passage that leads to a security gate where she punches in a complicated code then has to stand on her toes to look into the small screen above the number pad. A red laser scans her retina and it clicks.

The door opens up into a large bleached-looking room with a few shoulder-height cubicles. Bright lights, chipboard ceiling boards and cheap wooden veneer desks: not what Kirsten expects a rebellious cult's underground HQ to look like at all. A few people are dotted around, grinding quietly at their desks. They look up unseeingly as the three enter, then return to their screens. A few of them lift their chins at Seth.

They approach the back corner, where a typical office kitchen is attached: a basic sink, bar fridge, and coffee machine. A man springs up from a small Formica table tucked around the corner and Kirsten and Seth both jump.

'Sorry!' he says, 'I didn't mean to startle you.' He is a wiry man with a nervous demeanour and a pale moustache. 'I shouldn't have jumped up like that. I guess I'm a jumper. I think I'm just a little nervous. Very nervous. I wasn't thinking. Sorry.'

The flower girl doesn't make introductions and no one shakes hands.

'I'm the Lab Man,' he says, rubbing his palms on the back of his trousers. 'I'm the one who will be looking at your samples.' He speaks too quickly and finishes his sentences by putting his index finger to his lips, as if to stop himself from saying more. Seth takes the still-intact Fontus samples out of his bag and hands them over, along with Kirsten's bottle of pills. The florist raises her eyebrows at the pills but doesn't ask any questions.

'There's something else,' says Seth. 'I know it sounds insane, but I think I may have a chip, a microchip,' he rubs the back of his head, 'and I need it destroyed. We think it has some kind of tracker system...'

The man's eyes grow wide; he holds the samples to his chest, as if to protect them.

The florist bangs shut a drawer and glares at Seth. 'So not only do you bring a civilian in, but you send the target our fucking GPS co-ordinates?'

'I'm sorry. I didn't have a choice. The chip is the only clue we have. They'll find the shop, they won't be able to get in here.'

She stalks out, head down, speed dialling.

'So the chip,' says the man, 'the microchip, it's still in your... actual head?'

As opposed to his non-actual head? His theoretical head?

'Yes,' says Seth. 'You have a scalpel?'

The man gulps. 'I can't take it out. I don't do blood. I faint when I see blood. I'm haemophobic. Once, in high school, I fainted on the stairs because there was this big poster with a cartoon vampire on it, a blood donation drive. It was this big friendly kind of looking vampire, kind of like a Nosferatu-looking vampire, not a contemporary kind of sparkly good-looking vampire, but friendly, with a big toothy smile, and fangs. He had a cartoon speech bubble and it said "I vant to suck your blood." And I just fainted. There, on the stairs. Fainted, bam, just like that.' Then he remembers his finger and puts it to his lips.

Seth rummages noisily through the drawers but finds nothing with which he'd be happy to cut open his head. He sighs, rubs his eyes. 'Fine,' he says to Kirsten. 'Fine,' he says again, more firmly, motioning to her bag.

She takes out the pocketknife.

'Do you have any alcohol?' she asks the Lab Man.

He shakes his head. As if on cue, the faux-florist comes back with a first aid kit, a half-empty bottle of whisky and some toasted sandwiches.

'Thanks,' says Seth, and she winks at him without smiling. Kirsten wolfs down half a sandwich, its gooey melted cheese golden lava on her tongue. It's one of the best things she's tasted in years. She feels a rolling brown spiral mow towards her, and just before it touches her it disappears. She gingerly washes her hands, uses hand sanitizer, and swabs the knife and the back of Seth's head with the booze. Her injury slows her down. Seth sits at the table and the man turns away, busying himself with the lab kit he has brought with him.

With her good arm, Kirsten begins to touch Seth's scalp. At first they both flinch at the feeling: it's too intimate an act for strangers. But we're not strangers, they both tell themselves. A slight sensation remains where they connect.

'So, what made you get into biopunking?' asks Kirsten. She's trying to distract him and he feels like telling her to just get on with it; he's not a child. He feels the cold blade against his skin.

'In high school I saw a YouTube video of the LSD experiments they did on British soldiers in the early 60s. It's hilarious. Ever see those?'

Kirsten is concentrating too much to answer but the Lab Man starts giggling.

'I've seen it, I've seen it.' He smiles, nodding at them, then immediately looks away. 'LSD-25,' he says. 'Acid. Soldiers be trippin'.'

Seth smiles, despite himself. 'They were considering using it as part of their chemical warfare, to incapacitate the enemy, so they tried it out on the men. They go from these upright marching men with machine guns to complete jokers. They can't read the map and get lost even though the hill they need to find is right in front of them. They just walk around in circles and hose themselves. One guy climbs a tree to feed the birds.'

Kirsten finds the small thickening and quickly excises it, squeezing the chip out. Seth doesn't flinch; his only movement is to spin his ring. It's a much neater procedure than hers.

'The troop commander eventually gives up, and falls on the floor laughing.'

After applying pressure to stem the bleeding, she sprays it and covers it with the extra plaster she brought with her. Kirsten rinses the chip under the tap then hands it to Seth, who stares at it.

I didn't believe it until I saw mine, either.

'It was so powerful. A simple drug changed men trained to kill into fools. Affectionate fools. Imagine the lives that could have been spared in our wars. It kind of hit me in the face. That's what made me want to become a chemical engineer.' He hands it over to the Lab Man, who hesitates before taking it.

He holds it up to the light, taps its glass capsule with his fingernail then holds it close to his eye, looking at it through a magnifying glass.

'Very scientific methods,' murmurs Seth in Kirsten's ear, causing her to almost choke on the last bite of her sandwich. He takes a swig of whisky then offers it to her. She doesn't wipe the mouth of the bottle: they are double-blood-siblings now.

The Lab Man puts the chip on the tiled floor and steps on it. It doesn't break, so he steps on it again, this time putting more weight on it, and still it doesn't break.

'Very interesting,' he says, causing Seth to snuffle. He turns around, unsure of why they are laughing, then turns back to the chip. 'Superglass,' he mumbles. 'Super. Glass. Hmm.'

'Why is that interesting?' asks Kirsten.

'Because superglass was only put on the market in 2019,' says Seth.

'Yet I'd guess that the chip itself,' says the man, 'was created in the early nineties. But tracking biochips were only invented in 2007, so this isn't making sense. It's not making sense at all.'

'It must be, like, an early prototype,' says Seth. 'The guys who made it were obviously far ahead of the crowd, but didn't share it. Technology wasn't as open source back then.'

'There is a code on here,' the Lab Man says, 'which could link back to the manufacturer.' He scans in the miniature barcode on the chip and reads out the numbers. Kirsten knows the colours by heart now, recognises Seth's numbers from the list.

'GeniX, it says.'

The Lab Man hands the chip back to Seth.

'Excuse me,' Seth says, holding up the chip, 'I need to go to the little boys' room.' Within a moment of him leaving, they hear the gush of water through pipes in the wall. *Good riddance.*

Seth comes back, and the flower girl sidles in.

'I've evacuated the office, and we now have security outside. Hopefully they'll be able to stop anyone from coming in.'

She gives Seth a hard look, and there's something close to an apology in his eyes.

'I'll let you know the results as they come in,' she says, stepping aside so that they can leave. They nod at the Lab Man and make their way outside, where there are still many noon-drunk creeps wandering around on the chunky pavements, enjoying the music and the open air. Seth and Kirsten survey the faces of the people around them. A man leaning against a broken algaetree streetlight acknowledges them with the slightest movement of his head. Kirsten hopes he is the security post.

A cab rolls to a stop in front of them, and the leaning man motions for them to get in. They hesitate, but then the driver flashes a card at them: a green rabbit. It happens so quickly Kirsten wonders if she imagined it.

They climb inside, and Seth gives the driver the address of TommyKnockers. Kirsten feels every bump of the drive; every pothole sends more blue sparks flying up her arm. She needs to talk to distract herself from the pain.

'Why the green bunny?' she asks. 'Seems a bit, I don't know, too fun and quirky for what you guys do.'

'No science journals lurking in your house, I can tell.'

'You don't have to be snarky. I prefer pictures. It doesn't make me dumb. It's how I see the world, in thousands and thousands of photos. Pictures fly at my brain all the time as if I'm some kind of five-dimensional dual projector. From reality, hyper-memory, from my senses... books are just too much of an assault... you wouldn't want to be in my head.'

'Mine neither,' says Seth. 'I see formulae and patterns and equations in everything. Sounds like a similar affliction.'

We're similar, in some ways, he thinks.

'We're similar,' she says, 'of course we are. We're twins.' It sounds strange to say it out loud. He finds it strange to hear it.

'Ever heard of the Fibonacci sequence? The Golden Ratio?' he asks.

'Of course. It's that pattern that keeps appearing in nature. And in beautiful things. Didn't know the Fibonacci part.'

'He was a mathematician. He discovered it by theoretically breeding rabbits.'

'*Theoretically* breeding? That doesn't sound like much fun.'

'I don't want to bore you.'

The nerves in Kirsten's broken arm hum.

'Tell me. I'm interested.'

'So in theory you'd start with one pair of baby rabbits. When they mature at two months, they have their own pair of baby rabbits. So it's just one pair for the first and second month, then an additional pair in the third month. How many pairs? Zero, one, one, two Then the parents have another pair. 3. By then, the first babies are mature enough to breed, and they have a pair, along with the parents. 5. Then 8, 13, 21, 34, 55... etc. In a year you'll have 144 rabbits.'

'So you just add the number to the number before it to get the next number.'

'If you wanted to suck all the beauty out of the equation then yes, I guess you could say that. So the sequence is fn equals fn minus 1 plus fn minus 2 where n is greater than 3 or n is equal to 3'

'Okay, you just lost me.'

'It's not important. I get carried away. The cool thing is that the ratio plays itself out in nature. Pinecones, pineapples, sunflowers, petals, the human body, DNA molecules. Like, a double helix is twenty-one angstroms wide and thirty-four long in each cycle. It's also in lots of different algorithms. So, handy in... software and stuff.'

'Hacking?'

'In theory.'

'You smartypantses like your theories.'

'Goes with the territory. Science, and all.'

'Ooh, "science",' she mocks, smiling. 'Using a strange and beautiful ratio to bring down the baddies. A green bunny.'

'It's the symbolism, more than anything.'

'I like it.'

'Any reason you chose bright green? The green number is three, so that kind of makes sense.'

'It's a nod at bioartist Eduardo Kac. He created artwork based on a transgenic albino green fluorescent rabbit called Alba. They bonded. Once he had finished his research, the corporation he was grinding for went back on their word and didn't let him take her home, and she died in the lab. It was sad. They were attached, after all that time. The corp became, like, the epitome of bio-bullies, and she's kind of our mascot.'

'Poor Alba,' says Kirsten. 'What did they splice her with, you know, to make her glow?'

'GFP of a jellyfish gene.'

Kirsten thinks of the beautiful jellyfish she saw at the aquarium, when she

learned of Betty/Barbara's death.

'I don't know, it seems wrong to me.'

'That's the whole point. He used transgenic art to spark debate on important social issues surrounding genetics, and how they are affecting and will affect generations to come. It was ground breaking, for its time.'

'And poor Alba lives and dies in a lab.'

'Yes.'

'Not cool.'

'Not cool.'

'And so... Fibbonacci, Kac... you pretty much have an obsession with bunnies?'

'Science does. Theoretical bunnies, anyway.'

The car stops, the driver cuts the engine. Seth looks past Kirsten, out of the car window, and says, 'We're here.'

She moves, but he puts his hand on her shoulder. Still, a kind of vibration.

'Stay here, this will just take a minute.'

Kirsten watches him disappear down an alley, then lies down on the back seat, cradles her arm, and closes her eyes. *Keke, we are on our way. Keep breathing, keep breathing.*

Rolo sees Seth coming and begins to lift the red rope to allow him access into the club. Seth gestures to show he's not going in, and Rolo clicks it back into place.

'Mister Denicker,' he says in a low rumble, 'what can I do for you?'

'Good to see you, my man,' says Seth, and they click their fingers together, leaving two five hundred rand notes in the giant Yoruba man's palm. 'I need to see your—associates—again. The ones you introduced me to a few years ago.'

'You wish to make another purchase?' he enquires.

'I do.'

'The people themselves change. They have various addresses, and various contact numbers. Are you looking for heat, or spike?'

'Heat.'

'In that case, I suggest you contact Abejide.' He takes out his handset, which looks like a toy in his huge hands, and pushes a button. Seth's Tile pulsates. 'Tell him I sent you.'

Seth turns to go, when Rolo says, 'I gather you know, Mister Denicker, that you are being followed?'

CHAPTER 28

LITTLE LAGOS

JOHANNESBURG, 2021

Seth spins around, hand in pocket, but he can't see anyone in the alleyway. Rolo motions with his eyebrows that the interloper is ahead of them, around the corner to the right, effectively blocking his way out. He motions for a bouncer stationed inside to watch the door, and jerks his head for Seth to follow.

They enter the club and walk through the velvet curtains and over the plush carpet towards the restrooms. It feels like midnight inside. A woman in a snakeskin bikini dances lazily around a pole. Guests, swirling the ice in their drinks, nod at Rolo as he passes. The restroom is large and spacious, tastefully decorated in comparison to the club's gaudy interior. A man is swaying at one of the urinals.

They walk to the last stall on the left, which is always closed. Rolo takes a bunch of keys out of his pocket, squints at them, locates the correct key and unlocks the door, revealing another door in the wall where the toilet should be. He hefts his bulk through the narrow stall door and unlocks the next door, which swings out into the darkness of the back street of the club.

'Good evening to you sir,' he says, as if nothing was out of the ordinary.

'Good evening, Rolo.'

Seth glides in the shadows along the buildings until he reaches the car. He sneaks up to it and is about to jump in when he sees that the car is empty. He stays down, crouching next to it, pulls out his gun. As he moves forward, he looks into the car and sees that it is not in fact empty, but that the driver's body has listed to the side, a bullet hole in his temple. He glances around, but the evening is silent around him.

'Kirsten?' he says, knowing if the killer is near he will be giving his position away, but in the moment not caring. 'Kirsten?'

A hand shoots out from under the car, grabbing his ankle, and he yells with fright, pointing his gun at it. He realises a split-second before he pulls the trigger that he recognises the hand—it's the female version of his own.

'Kirsten!' he whispers. She starts crawling out; he tries to help her. She's ivory-skinned and beaded with sweat. He sweeps her into his arms for a moment then opens the driver's door and pushes the dead man out onto the street. He looks for a wallet but the driver's pockets are empty. Kirsten clambers into the passenger side, feels the warm blood seep into the seat of her jeans. Seth jumps in, locks the doors, and presses the ignition button. It's been a while since he has driven.

'Put your safety belt on,' he says, but Kirsten's numb fingers can't follow the instruction. He doesn't flick on the headlights until they reach a main road, and keeps checking for a tail in his rear view mirror.

'What happened?' he asks, keeping his eyes on the road.

'What happened? A boy with a nice face falls out of a window and then a man's brain is blown out of his skull.'

'Did you see who did it?'

'No. He saw something—'

'Who?'

'The driver. Saw something or heard something. He told me to hide. There wasn't any time. He would have seen me run. I rolled under the car. Then I just heard the shot and there were yellow stars everywhere. I saw his feet. The killer. Big. Black boots, like... workman boots. He circled the car, so slowly. I was trying not to breathe. Then he walked in the direction you disappeared.'

'One guy?'

'Yes. I think so.'

'He must have followed us from the flower shop.'

Kirsten keeps quiet, looks ahead.

'He was waiting for me, in the alley. Hopefully we're a little ahead of him now.' He fiddles with the air conditioning dial. It's not cold in the car but Kirsten is shaking. They travel in silence for a while.

Kirsten scrolls through Keke's drop-down list of contacts, looking for Marko. He isn't listed by name, so she looks for FWB, but doesn't find it. Most of the contacts seem to be in codes and nicknames. LoungeLizard; Open SAUCE; hotelbarsuperstar. Then she sees HBG and clicks on it. Hackerboy Genius.

KK> HBG, Kirsten here. You there?

HBG>> Whre is Keke, wth u?

KK> Missing. We need your help.

. . .

He takes a while to reply.

HBG>> Anything. For her.

KK> Is there any new info you have, that you hadn't shared with her yet? I have her FD.

HBG>> Not / lot. Ths fckers knw hw 2 cover thr trax.

KK> Chips were made by GeniX. Capsule was superglass.

HBG>> Ahead / thr time.

KK> Can you find out who had access to that kind of tech / early 90s?

HBG>> Short answer = no1, but let me look.

Kirsten looks across at Seth, who is concentrating on navigating the narrow roads crowded with pedestrians.

'Anything?' asks Seth.

'He's looking. He'll let us know as soon as he finds something.'

The roads are crammed with communal taxis of all different colours and states of disrepair. Reading the bumper stickers, Kirsten thinks she should photograph them some time and have an exhibition of taxi décor in Jozi. She considers all the mini-disco-balls, the hula girls, the fuzzy dice hanging on rear view mirrors she has snapped over the years. A cut-out picture of a car radio face Prestik-ed to the dash; a makeshift beverage holder made from an old plastic Castle lager beaker, held in place with an artfully manipulated coat-hanger wire; a handheld fan taped to the windscreen and wired into the cigarette lighter power source; a dog-eared picture, stuck in the sun-shield flap, of a young bride, perspiring in a synthetic fibre dress. *They all tell their own stories.*

People swarm around their car. Drivers steer one-handed, leaning on their hooters, heads out of their windows. A scuffle takes place a few metres away from them.

'Welcome to *Gadawan Kura* territory: Little Lagos,' he says.

'You aren't supposed to call it Little Lagos,' says Kirsten. 'It's un-PC.'

'Fuck PC,' says Seth. 'It has the highest concentration of Nigerians—and hyenas—outside of Nigeria.'

'And Malawians. And Zimbos.'

'Those guys don't count,' he says, 'too quiet.'

'African Slum of Nations.'

'That's more PC. More representative. Good one.'

They haven't moved for a while, so Seth parks with the intention that they walk the rest of the way.

'It's nothing short of insane to walk around here, but if we sit in this gridlock your friend's had it.'

Kirsten grabs the insulin kit, slings the handle over her arm and keeps it pinned to her chest as they manoeuvre their way through the throngs of people. Seth presses the button to lock the car and set the alarm, but has little hope for it to be there when they return. There are a few other white creeps around who look like locals—poor whites, thinks Kirsten—who don't stand out as much as she does with her new apocalyptic hairstyle, and Seth's smudged eyes and piercings. Having grown up in a virtually colour-blind society, it's a novel feeling to be so aware of the tint of her skin; she feels the glances from everywhere. They pass an informal marketplace, a few stalls on the side of the road that seem to be doing a great deal of business. Airtime; doorstops of white bread; *amaskopas*; paraffin sold in re-purposed, scuffed plastic soda bottles; yellow boxes of Lion matches; half-jacks of cheap brandy-flavoured spirits; spotted bananas. Leathery R50 notes travel from palm to palm and change is slipped deftly into warm pockets, never counted. They weave in and out of the streams of people, Kirsten shielding her broken arm, till Seth turns into a road without a name.

They make a few more turns, passing a house in mourning with a SuperBug warning on the door. The occupants' wailing sends streamers of powder blue out of the house and Kirsten tries to dodge them. Seth almost trips over a blind beggar with grey milk for eyes, and the stench of open sewers makes Kirsten retch in the direction of a greasy, defaced wall.

'Almost there,' he says, checking his Tile and grabbing her hand when she straightens. She lets him lead her further into the jutting maze.

When they arrive at the destination, it's not at all what Seth expected. A 1950s style brick-and-mortar house stands defiantly among its corrugated-iron shack neighbours. Chipped steps lead up to a small burgundy veranda: sun-brittle plastic chairs and a blue front door. Cracked black windows like broken teeth in the grimy façade.

'I expected... more of a... security system in place,' says Kirsten, 'taking their particular business into account.'

'They move around a lot. I guess there's not always time to put up an electric fence.'

They walk up the steps and are startled when something with matted brindle fur bolts straight for them, screeching, yellow fangs bared (Rotten Egg Yolk). They both jump. The animal gets to within a metre of them but is yanked back by its chain. A monkey.

'Jesus Christ,' says Kirsten, hand to hammering heart.

Despite the limitation of being chained to a pillar, it still tries to get at them, chattering and screaming in frustration. There is a raw patch of skin around his neck where the collar chafes; it seems there are frequent visitors to this house.

'There's your security system,' says Seth.

They knock on the door. Kirsten has the urge to wash her hands and wonders if the house has running water. And if they have running water, would it be acceptable for her to ask if she could use it? She isn't sure what kind of etiquette is expected in this kind of situation. She will smile and ask nicely, and hope to not offend protocol. Footsteps sound behind the door and a masculine voice says, 'Yes?'

'I'm looking for Abejide,' says Seth. 'Abejide.' The door opens, but there is no light on inside, and no one says a word. They take it as a sign to enter, and as soon as they step across the threshold, the door is slammed shut behind them and they are pressed against the wall, smoke-fragrant hands over their mouths, gunmetal clicks to their heads.

CHAPTER 29

YIP, YIP, YIP.

JOHANNESBURG, 2021

Someone flips the light switch and the image of the room jumps out at Kirsten. Cadmium blazes around five glistening, tight-muscled men; dark, oily, like sealskin. They wear layers of light, dusty clothes, wildlife-fur armbands, leather trinkets, and carry the biggest automatic weapons Kirsten has ever seen. Only two aim their guns at them; Kirsten guesses two AK47s are enough.

The youngest of the five pats them down, takes Seth's gun off him. Looks embarrassed when he finds blood on Kirsten's jeans. She has the unreasonable urge to tell him it's not hers, but has a hand over her mouth. He snatches the insulin kit from her hand, sniffs it, and drops it on the floor. She protests and the muzzle of the gun gets pushed right into her ribs. Seth strains a little against the man holding him down. Not too much to warrant being shot, not too little to show he's not a pushover.

'What do we have here?' the man says.

'A couple of white maggots,' another says. He pronounces it mag-GOTS.

'You a cop?' he asks Seth, taking his hand away in order to let him speak. The animal teeth on his leather necklace click together, sending little circles towards Kirsten. Seth laughs.

'I think that everyone knows that cops don't come into Little Lagos.'

The man lets out three bars of a laugh, looks around at his colleagues. They flash their teeth. The moment is short lived; as soon as he stops smiling the others do too.

'Then who the fuckayou?' he asks.

'A punk,' says one of the other men. 'A fuckin' punk come to make trouble for us.'

Seth can see he is the dangerous one: hopped up on something—tik? Nyaope? White Lobster?—and unable to contain his jerky movements. Not a quality you want in a man pointing a large gun at your face. Kirsten senses that he has killed a lot of people. *Bloodthirsty,* she thinks. She can almost smell the warm red metal on him.

The man with the tooth necklace, possibly the leader, narrows his gaze at Seth. He takes a hunting knife out of its casing on his thigh and runs it along Seth's face, his neck, then uses it to inspect his clothing.

'I think we should skin him,' says the aggro one, hopping on the spot. 'Skin him and feed him to the fuckin' hyenas.'

The other one chips in, 'They're hungry. They didn't get their chickens this week.'

'You know what that means?' he asks Kirsten, licking his lips, 'It means they'll eat your bones too. Crunch-crunch!'

Kirsten glares at him.

'And what's in this pretty little box?' the man who is gagging her asks, kicking the insulin across the room. The other man stops it with his foot as if it's a soccer ball. Again she objects but she's beginning to feel dizzy and the smell of the man's hand right up against her nostrils is distorting her vision.

'I'll tell you what it is,' says the mad one, lifting his foot. Seth tries to step forward but is thrown back against the wall. The man jumps on the bag with all his weight. 'It's broken!' He laughs.

A gushing of saliva in Kirsten's mouth. She tries to warn him but it's too late, and soon hot vomit is spraying through her guard's fingers, through her nose, and she is doubled over.

The man looks at her, horrified, and backs away.

'You have the Bug.'

'No, no,' she says, shaking her head, 'I don't,' and she retches again.

The other men also take a quick step back.

'You brought bad juju into this house,' he says. The others look worried, their fingers dance on the triggers.

Kirsten gets angry. She wipes her mouth with the back of her hand. '*I* brought bad juju into this house? Have you even looked in a mirror lately? You reek of death. You want to *skin us* but you say *I* brought bad juju into the house? Fuck you!' Then she turns to the others, 'and fuck you all too!'

They look at her and each other, not certain of what to do. She swallows and looks down at the wet stain on the floor.

'And I'm washing my hands now,' she growls, moving towards the kitchen sink, 'just try to stop me.'

She finds a hard bar of soap with which to scrub her hands. The tap spits water at her and the pipes groan overhead. Once her hands are clean, she splashes water on her face and neck. When she walks the few steps back into the open-plan lounge no one has said a word. She collects the kit and stands away from the spill of puke on the thin, cigarette-burn-patterned carpet, hoping to not get sick again. The man washes his hands too.

'Look,' says Seth, 'Rolo sent me. He said I should ask for Abejide.'

'Rolo sent you?' the leader asks.

'It's the first thing I would have told you if you hadn't jumped us.'

'Give me your phone,' he says.

'I don't have a phone,' says Seth. 'I wear a patch.'

'Smart man, hey? Then give me your tablet.'

Seth hands over his Tile. He pushes a few buttons, checks his bump history for Rolo's message thread, then gives it back to Seth, motioning for the others to lower their weapons, says something, perhaps in vernacular, that Seth doesn't catch. The aggressive man looks annoyed, probably on behalf of the hungry hyenas.

'I need bullets, and we need something for her, something easy to handle.'

'We don't sell lady-guns,' he spits.

'Good thing I'm not a lady, then,' says Kirsten.

He looks at her then laughs his strange, three-bar laugh again.

'Okay,' he says, and nods at the others. Seth expects them to print some guns in front of them, or have some printed already, but instead two of the men scrape the coffee table towards the side of the room and roll up the lounge carpet to reveal a huge trapdoor. It takes some effort to lift the piece of wood, and buried below it is a pile of all kinds of different guns in what appears to be no particular order.

Less like a gun store, more like a wartime weapons cache, thinks Kirsten, an old *uMkhonto Sizwe* stash. She is half expecting the man's arm to be blown off by a rogue landmine when he dips his hands in. He motions for Seth's gun and it is thrown to him; he catches it with one hand and inspects it.

'Z88?' he asks.

'Yes,' says Seth.

The man locates the correct ammo and passes a few boxes up.

'More,' says Seth.

He passes two more.

'Another one.'

The man shrugs and passes up another one. 'You taking on an army?' he asks, making the other guys chuckle.

'Could be,' replies Seth, serious.

'And for you?' he says, looking up at Kirsten.

'Do you have a compact semi-automatic?' asks Seth, 'like a CS45 or something like that?' The man shakes his head. He starts sorting through the pile to look for something suitable.

'Give her an AK,' says the one, and the others cackle again.

'What about this one? You like this one?' he asks, showing her a big silver revolver: a Ruger. She frowns at it.

'Does it work?' she asks.

'It works,' he says.

'Then I like it.'

'We only sell guns that work,' he says, passing her bullets. 'We like—what is it called? —return customers.'

'You could have fooled me,' mumbles Seth.

'Abejide is very good with faces,' says one of the men. Kirsten thinks this is his way of saying their next purchase will run more smoothly, but then he adds a sinister, 'Never forgets a face,' and it sounds more like a threat than anything else.

'What are those things?' She points towards what looks like second-hand lipsticks.

'You won't like those,' he says, 'they for ladies.' He picks one up, twists the cap off, and pretends to apply lipstick in a wide circle around his mouth. Pouts and bats his eyelashes. Snickering in the background.

'They are magic wands,' he says. 'You didn't know we could do magic here?'

'How does it work?' she asks.

'Come with me,' the leader says, 'I'll show you.'

She's sorry she asked, doesn't want to go with him, doesn't want to know.

'Come,' he commands, and she follows, Seth right behind her. They walk down a passage and into another room with a crumbling back door. He opens it and they see reflective eyes looking back at them (Glowing Green). The outside light comes on automatically and there is loud laughing and yipping. Five, six, seven beasts trawling around in the patchy grass, scratching and sniffing, pink tongues lolling.

'Holy Hades,' says Seth. 'They weren't kidding about the hyenas.'

Yip, yip, yip, the animals say. Abejide calls one of them by name: an older female who has the lope and old eyes of a war vet. He whistles: six high-pitched calling sounds, and she comes forward, ribs patterning her side: perhaps hoping to be fed. Kirsten's stomach seizes.

Abejide points the magic wand at the animal and presses a button, sending a long blue thread of electric current into her body, whipping her up into the air with a surprised yelp then dropping her, in slow motion, onto the sandy ground, where she lies motionless. The other hyenas panic and try to run, but they are ringed in and bounce off the garden fence, shrieking all the while. The man laughs, and Kirsten feels ill again.

'See?' he says, 'I told you it works.'

The animal lies twitching on the ground.

'Did you kill her?' she asks, 'is she dead?'

'Na,' he says, 'she is a tough one. Survivor. Like you.'

They take the guns, the ammo and the lipstick-taser, pay cash: a fat roll of R500 notes. It's all the cash Seth has, and it's triple the amount the weapons are worth. They go through Kirsten's slimpurse and take all her money too. No one says thank you. After all, it is more like a hijacking than a business transaction.

They've only been inside the house for an hour but it feels like days when they exit the front door. Dodging the rabid monkey, running down the steps, they both breathe the polluted air deep into their lungs. It's warm, and Kirsten gives Seth his hooded jacket back, bunches her new gun and taser into her bag. Her arm jars, but the adrenaline in her system dulls the pain.

The streets are quieter on their way back; most of the market stalls have been packed up and moved to another location, as if they never existed. It takes them a while to find the car and they both think the worst until they see it, abandoned-looking, on a road in which they don't remember parking.

They do a quick inspection: all four tyres are still attached, the engine and battery seem to be in place, and there is no pool of brake fluid under the car. Kirsten opens the crushed kit and finds one vial of insulin that survived the attack. She shows it to Seth, kisses it, then eases it carefully back into its pouch.

One, we've got one, Kirsten thinks.

One is all she needs, thinks Seth.

Kirsten sees a bump from Marko to check her chatmail.

HBG> Hey, hve something 4 u.

CHAPTER 30

CAPITAL FUCKING F

JOHANNESBURG, 2021

KK>> Sorry only replying now, we were held up.

HBG> Ws worried.

KK>> What do you have?

HBG> Sending u a pic.

An image pops up on her screen: a picture of three young students sitting on a grassy knoll. They look like students in every way: casual, hippie-style clothes, relaxed faces, a slight air of the arrogance of youth. Two leggy white men in stovepipe trousers, one in thick black-rimmed glasses, and a young dark-skinned woman gazing distantly at the camera. In the background, some kind of university insignia. A badge. They look vaguely familiar—has she seen this before?—but Kirsten can't place their faces at all.

KK>> Got it. University students, circa 1970s?

HBG> Yebo. Thr is a spec search u can do 2 look esp 4 files and images / hve bn deleted ovr & ovr again over time. This pic has been deleted ovr 6K times. Some1 doesn't want it on Net.

KK> Relevance?

HBG>> Kex didn't give me much 2 go on. I ws searching 4biddn files / 'Trinity'. These 3 known as The Trinity when they studied together. WITS. Tag keeps comng up.

KK> Trinity? As in Trinity Clinic?

HBG>> Looks like it. Then superglass & Fontus unrelated on paper apart from / obvious business relat, but dig deeper & c they r both subsids along / 100s other companies under holding company GeniX, trading as GNX Enterprises.

KK> All owned by the same creep?

HBG>> Same creeps. 3 creeps.

KK> Trinity.

HBG>> Registerd GeniX when thy wre still / varsity.

KK> What's / connection 2 Keke?

HBG>> You.

KK> ??

HBG>> Kex starts digging / keywords / threaten the company. My guess / thy hve hackbots automonitoring 4 anything like that, & find source & quash it.

KK> But Keke didn't have any of this info, only the list of barcodes.

HBG>> Et voila.

KK> So the barcodes threaten them. The list of abducted kids threaten them.

HBG>> Yebo, hence your hitlist, + any1 else who gets in / way.

KK>> We wouldn't have known there was a connection if they didn't react to Keke.

HBG>> Thy were too careful.

KK> Who R people in the photo / Trinity?

HBG>> I'm running thr faces / my FusiformG now. Will have a match in hour/so.

KK> An HOUR? Keke's SugarApp says only 5 hours left.

HBG>> It's going as fast as it can.

KK> Can we come over?

HBG>> Who is 'we'?

KK> Seth (no.5) and I?

HBG>> I dn't allow visitors. Esp 1s assoc / kidnapping & grim reaper.

KK> We hve nowhere else 2 go.

HBG>> Police?

KK> No police.

HBG>> Cape Town Republic? Mexico? Bali?

He is quiet for a while.

. . .

KK> Just till we can work out who the Trinity are / how 2 find Keke.

HBG>> U being follwed?

KK> Don't think so.

HBG>> Dn't think so? Tht's reassuring.

Kirsten logs out and gets Marko's GPS co-ordinates; directs Seth out of Little Lagos in between telling him about GeniX. When she tells him about Fontus, he hits the top of the steering wheel.

'*Shut* the front door,' he says. He has the face of someone who has just won the Lotto. Or found Jesus. 'I knew it!'

'You knew that the creeps responsible for abducting us are the same creeps you were grinding for?'

'No. I just knew they were dirty. I knew that they were fuckers. Fucking fuckers. Capital fucking F.'

'Look, that sentence didn't even make sense.'

'Fucking Fontus.' He exhales, shaking his head.

'Do you still think that the Genesis Project is a myth?'

Seth's mouth twitches, but he doesn't answer. He takes his bottle of pills out of his pocket, is about to take one, then throws them out of the car window.

~

Marko is drumming his fingers on his knees, then his desk, then his knees again. Hundreds of thousands of faces are flying through his FusiformG software, trying to recognise a pattern. He can't sit still. He stuffs a doughnut past his lips, but his mouth is so dry he chokes. He looks around his room, picks up a vinyl toy and pretends to shoot another toy with it. He makes laser sound effects then kicks the other toy over. In his head, crowds cheer.

The computer chirrups: it has matched one of the three faces. Marko looks at the screen and drops the rest of the doughnut.

'Go home FusiformG,' he says, 'you're drunk.'

~

Marko's place is more of a bunker than a house. *Fort Knox would have been more welcoming.* Kirsten studies the giant gate and 8m walls frosted with the glitter of electrified barbed wire. The kinesecurity cameras follow their movements to the gate. She buzzes the intercom but there is no answer. She buzzes again.

'You think he changed his mind?' she asks Seth. 'He really didn't want us to come.'

Seth is inspecting the gate. He pushes on it, as if to test the lock, and it swings open. Kirsten's glad—now they can get in!—but then her heart sinks. *Oh. Oh, this is bad.*

'It's impossible,' she says. 'It's impossible that they found him. That they got here before us. I was online with him fifteen minutes ago.'

'You sure it was him?'

They look around, notice some broken glass on the driveway, some damaged plants. Seth heads back to the car, unlocks it.

'What are you doing?' she says.

'Getting the hell out of here.'

'We have to go inside,' she says, 'it's the only way.'

'It's a bad idea,' he says, but closes the car door anyway. Once they step inside the property and are halfway to the house, the gate swings closed, and the lock mechanism clicks into place. The electric wire that circles the property like a malevolent halo begins to hum. They hear vicious dogs barking, but there is nowhere to run.

'It's a trap.'

CHAPTER 31

THE UNHOLY TRINITY

JOHANNESBURG, 2021

The dogs' barking is deafening now, but there's not a dog in sight. White spikes etch into Kirsten's vision and she has to close her eyes.

'It was him online, I was sure!'

'Maybe it was him, but with a gun to his head.'

Seth realises that the sound is a recording, playing on loop. There must be speakers hidden in the unkempt garden. The front door opens, the security gate is unlocked in three different places, and out walks a chubby young cappuccino-skinned man with tinted spectacles. He pushes them up on his nose and squints at his guests. He's carrying a game console that he touches, and the barking stops. Another button turns on calming white noise: a waterfall, birds, a rumble of thunder.

'Hello,' he says, 'sorry about the dogs, and the gate. I programmed it myself and I'm still ironing out some of the kinks. Or, I was. I'm a procrastinator. A paranoid procrastinator.' When they still don't move or talk, he comes out further along the driveway, looking left to right as if to cross the road. His hands remain on the console.

'I'm Marko,' he says to Kirsten, then blushes. 'Obviously.'

He's wearing a Talking Tee shirt a size too small that stretches over his doughy belly. It has a simple animation of a panting Chihuahua and says: 'My favourite frequency is 50,000 Hz'. When he turns around to lead them inside the back of the shirt says: 'You've probably never heard it before.'

'Come in,' he says. 'I've got something to show you.'

His room—the basement—is wall-to-wall glass screens, blinking projector lights, drives, processors, constant white noise, and the smell of powdered sugar. The walls are papered with posters of T-Rex jokes, incomprehensible maths formulae, and one with a picture of a pretty planet. It says: 'God created Saturn and he liked it, so he put a ring on it.'

Nerdgasm, thinks Kirsten, nudging Seth.

'Your kind of guy.'

He makes a ha-ha face. She spots a brooding woman on the wall, black and white, thinks she kind of recognises her.

'Vintage movie star?' she asks Marko. He momentarily stops smashing his keyboard with his stubby fingers.

'That,' he says, 'is Hedy Lemarr.'

Her face is blank.

'Lemarr was a remarkable woman and I will love her forever.'

Okay, that's not weird.

'She was the most beautiful woman in Europe in the forties, starred in thirty-five films, one of which was the first portrayal of a female orgasm ever, and a math genius. She invented frequency hopping spread!'

'That's Wi-Fi,' says Seth. 'Wireless internet.'

'Never heard of it,' Kirsten says, but is impressed nonetheless, specifically at the intensity of his geekdom. She is surprised he doesn't have a neckbeard, or giant gaming thumbs.

'So your timing is excellent,' he says, using his handset as a wireless pointer to open a browser on the main projection, revealing the photo of the college students and allowing the programme to run, showing which facial features were isolated to run a match.

'This FusiformG has the most amazing features baked in. You won't believe the results. Who the creeps are, in the photo, I mean.' He pushes his glasses up again. 'It's huge. It's, like, cosmic. No wonder they're trying to cover it up.'

'Marko?' comes a feminine, distinctly Hindi voice from the top of the stairs. Marko rolls his eyes.

'Not now, Ma!' he says. 'I'm having a meeting!'

'Marko?' she calls, closer now.

'Ma!' he says, 'I'm busy!'

Gold-trimmed indigo erupts at the bottom of the stairs.

'I *thought* I heard voices!' She beams—a handsome woman in a sari bright enough to spike your eyes out, holding a silver tray full of deep-fried goodness. Smoky ribbons of scent: cumin, turmeric, cardamom billow towards them. Kirsten blinks, wonders briefly if she is hallucinating. Her arm seems swollen now.

'Marko, you should have told me you were expecting visitors. I would have cooked *dosa!*'

He blushes, stalks up to her, takes the tray, bangs it down on a crowded desk. A designer toy—a Murakami—falls over. Kirsten gently rights it.

'Thank you,' she says, 'I'm starving.'

'It's just a little plate of eats, nothing special.' The woman smiles.

'Thanks, Ma,' Marko mutters, steering her towards the stairs. 'I'll see you later, okay?'

'You're too skinny!' she says, pointing at Seth. 'I'm making beans, if you want to stay for dinner.'

Once Seth sees samoosas on the platter, he laughs out loud. It is refreshing to see an old cultural stereotype played out in real life. South Africa has become so cosmopolitan that it is rare to see, say, an Afrikaner farmer in a two-tone shirt wearing a comb in his khaki socks, or a coloured fisherman missing his front teeth. He celebrates this by eating a samoosa that burns his mouth. *Excellent.*

'As I was saying.' Marko sighs, then looks excited again: 'Cosmic.'

FusiformG automatically opens browsers on three of the other screens, one for each of the faces, and the first two identities are revealed: *blip, blip*. The software is still searching for the third face. Cross-referenced with hundreds of televised interviews, PR shots and virtual news articles. Kirsten and Seth stare at the matches.

'Shut the front door,' whispers Kirsten.

The first man, good looking, smiles back at them with his perfect teeth.

'This is—' begins Marko.

'Christopher Walden,' says Seth. 'Founder and CEO of Fontus.'

'Then,' continues Marko, 'Thabile Siceka, the Minister of Health.'

'No,' says Kirsten, in disbelief.

'The third face is taking a while... could be that the third person isn't as well known or photographed as much as the first two. Maybe the shy one, staying out of the limelight.'

'So, we have the CEO of one of the biggest, most successful corporates in the country, and the minister of fucking health. Industry, government, and what we can probably guess is some kind of academic, doctor or scientist. Reach and power to do anything. The Trinity.'

'The Holy Trinity,' says Marko.

'More like the Fucking Unholy Trinity,' says Kirsten.

'But we still don't know *why*. Why the kidnappings, why the murders,' says Seth, 'and why now?'

'We need to focus on finding Keke. She's got,' Kirsten looks at her watch, 'maybe three hours left before she—'

'That's if they haven't killed her already,' says Seth, and they both glare at him. He spins the ring on his finger. 'Where do we even start?'

The room is quiet.

'Marko?' comes his mother's voice from up the stairs again. 'Marko? Would your friends like a mango lassi?'

~

'There's one person that can help us find the Trinity HQ,' says Kirsten, as they jog to the car. 'Someone that's not involved in the Genesis Project. Someone who would want justice done.'

The gate opens and the barking starts again. Once they're on the road, Kirsten takes her mother's letter out of her pocket and reads it to Seth.

'Ed Miller is his name. There's an address. Melville. He has the packet of information. Everything we need to know about what the Genesis Project is and why we were taken.'

The car is redolent with curried potato and coriander. Marko's mother wouldn't let them leave empty-handed and packed them a Tupperware take-away, along with some gold-coloured paper serviettes, despite her son's embarrassed protestations.

Kirsten is quiet, anxious they won't find Keke in time, or, as Seth had said, worried that the worst had already happened. Tears sting her eyes but she blinks them away, opens the window to get some fresh air. It's a strange sensation to her: tears. Little lines like pins dance in the top half of her vision. She doesn't remember the last time she cried. Has she ever cried? She breathes in deeply, swallows the warm lead in her throat and looks out the window at the ChinaCity/Sandton skyline. Seth catches himself thinking about the future. He won't be able to go back to his ordinary life after this. What will he do? What will it be like?

That's if we survive today, thinks Kirsten, *which is looking increasingly unlikely.*

They stop at a red light in the middle of the CBD. A man dressed in filth appears out of nowhere and peers into the passenger side, giving Kirsten a shock.

'Jesus,' she says, in fright, 'I'm not used to seeing beggars anymore.' A gun appears in the ragman's hand.

Oh.

His wrist is inked with prison scrawls. A Crim Colony graduate. In other words: an ex-con, or in this case: a con.

'Out,' he barks, shaking the weapon at her. She tries to go for her handbag, reach for her own gun, but the man loads the mechanism and something tells her he won't hesitate to put a bullet in her brain. She puts her hands up.

'You have got to be kidding me!' shouts Seth, flames in his cheeks. 'Not today!' he shouts at the hijacker, 'not today! You can fucking *have* the car tomorrow, but not today!'

'Out,' says the man, his voice iced with violence.

'Fuck!' shouts Seth, hitting the steering wheel, 'Fuck you!' He gets out, slams the door, sending a lightning bolt of silver through Kirsten. Kicks the car door, kicks the tyre.

'I need my handbag,' says Kirsten to the hijacker, 'and that other bag. It's medicine. I'm keeping both bags, you take the car.'

The man is annoyed, looks around: this is taking too much time. Kirsten unzips the insulin, shows him, but he searches her handbag himself, takes her Ruger with a loud whistle, and her empty slimpurse. He throws both bags onto the road and Kirsten scoops them up off the tar, picking up the lipstick taser and keeping it hidden in her palm. The hijacker loses focus for a moment as he tries to start the car, lowers his gun-hand. Kirsten tasers him and is surprised by the force of the current. A thin blue line connects them for a second (Electric Sapphire then he slumps back.

'Holy fuck!' she says.

His gun clatters onto the road, his eyes roll back.

'Is he dead?' she asks.

Seth opens the car door, pulls the slack body out and leaves him on the shoulder of the road. It doesn't escape his attention that this is the second time he has pulled a limp body out of a car during the past six hours. He inspects the man's gun, a semi-automatic, and finds it empty. Throws it into the car. Passes Kirsten her Ruger.

'I don't know, don't care,' he says. 'Let's go find Ed Miller.'

CHAPTER 32
CHEERIOS

JOHANNESBURG, 2021

Kirsten presses the red button (Faded Flag) and a doorbell rings out, jarring in its cheer. Static. It's an old Melville house, with chunky whitewashed walls and a green tin roof. It has the look of an artist's residence: slightly run down, a little messy, decorated in a quirky way. The house number is a mosaic. If you look through the pedestrian gate you see a goat, made out of wire and beads, grazing in the garden. The rusted arms of an Adventure Golf windmill inch around. The black-spotted roses need pruning.

She presses the doorbell again, holds it down for longer. More static then they hear the phone being picked up. Crackling on the other end.

'Hello?' says Kirsten. 'Ed Miller? I'm Kirsten Lovell. You knew my mother?'

There is a pause then the gate buzzes. He opens the front door, cautious, sees her, and relaxes. When he sees Seth he looks nervous again.

'You can trust him,' she says.

'How do you know?' says the man she assumes is Ed Miller.

'He's blood of my blood.'

Miller stares at them for a while. He is wearing a creased Hawaiian shirt and ill-fitting chinos. Horrendous tan pleather sandals. He has a full head of snow-white hair that moves when he nods. He comes out to make sure the security gate is closed behind them, sweeps his gaze left and right on the street before he clangs it shut. Kirsten studies him. Can't imagine her mother dating a hippie.

'You have something for us?' she asks.

'It's not here,' he says. 'Too risky. They're everywhere. I put it somewhere safe.'

Kirsten closes her eyes, hears the ticking of time she doesn't have.

'It's close,' he says, 'I'll take you.'

His aftershave smells like something with a ship on the label. Small crunchy loops the shape of Cheerios float around him. He shrugs on a light jacket and takes a set of keys off the hook by the door. Seth grabs them out of his hand, startling him.

'I'll drive,' he says.

They climb into the beetle of a car. Miller seems too tall for it and hunches over in the front. Kirsten wonders what kind of person buys a car that is so obviously too small for them.

'Oh, wait,' he says, tapping his temple with the side of his index finger. He gets out of the car, walks to the garden shed. Ducks under the door and disappears into darkness. Kirsten and Seth look at each other. They don't have to say it out loud. They are both thinking: *Fuck.*

Miller steps out of the shed, back into the sunlight. He is holding a couple of shovels. He holds them above his head and shakes them, as if he has won a race.

'My mother said we could trust him,' Kirsten says.

'By 'mother', you mean, 'kidnapper'?'

She pulls a face at him. What choice do they have?

He returns to the car, folds the passenger seat forward and takes in Kirsten's long legs.

'Move up, honey,' he says, dumping the shovels next to her. He winks at her before he slams the chair back in place and climbs in. She kicks the back of his seat.

Seth starts the car. It's a prehistoric thing, and chokes twice before it comes to life. Miller smacks the dashboard twice.

'Good girl!' he shouts, making them both jump.

Kirsten is still staring at him, trying to imagine what on earth they had to talk about. She had thought of her 'mother' as a dry, sexless, beige, irritated woman. She can't imagine the two of them having a conversation, never mind a twenty-six-year-long affair.

'Which one to open the garage door?' asks Seth, looking at the rubber buttons on the ancient remote.

'Uh, the blue one,' he says, but nothing happens.

Pins of dread on Kirsten's skin. Seth is slowly reaching for his gun.

'I mean, the orange one. Sorry.' He laughs. 'Nervous.'

Seth clicks the orange button and the garage motor heaves up the door. They all exhale. Four and five, thinks Kirsten, easy enough to mix up.

The man beats a melody on his khaki-clad thigh.

'Left,' he says.

'Where are we going?' asks Seth.

'To the hidey-hole I came up with. Genius, if I don't say so myself.'

'Where?' asks Kirsten. 'We don't have much time.'

'We'll be there in twenty minutes,' he says.

Kirsten looks at her watch, feels the adrenaline pulling at her stomach. This had better pay off, or Keke is dead. Seth puts down his foot.

They pull up at a small flower farm on the outskirts of the city. The guard seems to recognise Ed and drags the gate open for them. The metal catches on the hard sand. Miller directs them along the powder dirt road, and they drive until it comes to an abrupt end. Seth, driving too fast, slams on the brakes and they skid a little, landing in some wild grass. They look around, as if wondering how they got there, sitting in a vast field of flowers.

Kirsten is exhausted, nervous, dirty, and hurt, surrounded by blue skies and blooms. The prettiness around her is not making sense.

'I don't understand,' she says, 'why here?'

'Why else? Your mother loved flowers,' he says.

'Loved killing flowers, more like,' she says. 'She killed every plant we ever had.'

'Okay,' he says, 'correction: loved *cut* flowers. I sent her some every year on her birthday. Lilies—' He sniffs. '—were her favourite.'

Kirsten remembers the huge flower arrangements arriving once a year. She had always assumed they were from her father, but realises now that would have been out of character for their relationship: there hadn't been a flicker of romance in it. She doesn't remember ever seeing them touch. She hadn't realised that holding hands was a thing couples did until she saw someone else's parents do it.

When the bouquets arrived her father would complain of hay fever. He'd throw out the flowers as soon as a single petal turned brown; inspected them daily until he found one.

'It's buried under that tree,' he says, pointing at a leopard tree a hundred metres away. Kirsten and Seth each grab a shovel, swing them over their shoulders. They must look daunting in their ripped clothes, their skin bruised with black blood.

'Whoah,' says Miller, feigning surrender. 'Settle down there, puppies.'

'Let's get a move on,' says Seth. The sun is sinking fast.

'Seriously, whoah,' says Miller. 'I'm gonna need to pat you down, cowboy.'

'No need,' says Seth, taking his gun out of its holster. 'I'm packing. So?'

'Well, will you be kind enough to leave it in the car, please?'

'Why?'

'Son, no offence meant,' he says, hand on hips, Hawaiian shirt restless in the breeze. 'But I don't know you, I can't trust you. A couple of weeks ago the love of my life was murdered for a reason I'll never understand. Then you two show up in your punk clothes saying you're the people Carol told me to expect. I'm hoping for the best, but I will not walk into a field in the middle of nowhere with a bunch of strangers with a gun. I am not armed. I think it's fair to ask you to leave your weapon in the car.'

Seth thinks about it, then shrugs: 'Fair enough.' He walks towards the boot but Miller stops him, putting his hand on the warm metal.

'It's broken,' he says. 'Hasn't sprung open in years. Just put it in the cubbyhole.'

He does what Miller says, gives Kirsten a quick questioning look. She barely nods. They rush to the tree. Miller falls behind.

'Which side?' Kirsten yells from under the canopy.

'Where you're standing!' yells Miller. The twins begin to dig. Kirsten struggles with one arm, but is able to use her foot for leverage. It hurts like hell. The ground is baked clay. Keke's phone beeps with a SugarApp warning. Code orange: three hours left.

'Are you sure?' asks Seth, swiping his brow. 'You sure it's here?'

They both look up at the same time, and find themselves staring up the barrel of his gun.

'You have got to be fucking kidding,' says Kirsten.

'We are who we say we are,' says Seth. 'We're the good guys.'

'I know,' he says, 'Keep digging.'

They know he means for their graves.

CHAPTER 33

BABY STARTER KIT

JOHANNESBURG 2021

The heavy-set man, clad in charcoal jeans and polished workman boots, looks completely out of place in bright and bonny BabyCo. He is standing before a twirling display of sippy cups that plays a childish song and ends in a forced giggle. He wishes there are more customers so he can at least attempt to blend in. The cheerful products on the shelves seemed to age right in front of him. It is like browsing in a pastel-shaded ghost town.

He is excellent at his job, but this isn't his job; this is the antithesis of his job. If a polar opposite exists of what he was good at, this is it. But he is not one to shirk orders.

He grabs a blue silicone beaker with an animation of a sniggering snowman on it and slings it into his basket. He hopes no one he knows will see him in here. It will be difficult to explain. Another reason he gave in motivating for ordering this all online, but The Doctor said no. It is urgent, he said, and he doesn't want any kind of paper trail. Moving towards a new aisle, he jumps when a BabyCo-bot surprises him on the corner. The bot is clown-themed: wide eyes, red nose—grotesque, painted-on smile. A uniform of bright, clashing colours and a *hyuck-hyuck-hyuck* chuckle. Scary as hell. No wonder this shop is a graveyard.

'Congratulations!' effuses the robotic shop assistant. 'May I give you a hug?'

'Not unless you want your arm broken,' the man says.

'Pregnancy is such a special time. You and your baby deserve the very best!'

The man tries to walk past the bot, but it blocks his way.

'What can I help you with?' the clown says, glowing and *hyuck*-ing at him.

The man growls.

'We have great specials on disposable nappies!' shrieks the machine, lighting up. 'A pack of forty newborn-sized diapers for only nine hundred and ninety-nine rand! Get two packs for one thousand and seven-fifty!'

It assaults his ears with a tune.

The man pushes up his sleeves, cracks his knuckles. Moves his head from side to side. Indulges in a quickie fantasy where he snaps the bot's neck with a flick of his wrist, and drags its body to the stuffed toy section, to later frighten some kids.

The daydream perks him up. He takes a deep breath.

'I need a...' What does he need? If he knew, he wouldn't be standing around here like a gimp.

'Yes?' says the bot, desperate to help.

The man realises his scarred arm is showing, and pulls his sleeves down. A scar like that has no place in BabyCo.

'I need a... starter kit. For babies.'

'Can you repeat that please?'

'A starter kit.'

'I'm sorry, I didn't get that.'

'Everything you need when you're... you know. Expecting.'

'You need everything?' the bot asks. 'I can help you with that!'

It spins around and starts taking products off shelves, scanning the barcodes on its chest as it goes. A packet of glow-in-the-dark dummies, an Insta-Ice teething ring, a self-regulating temperature taglet. A swaddling blanket puffed up with clouds and zooming with planes. The BabyCo-bot stops and its head swivels around to look at the man.

'You're going to need a bigger basket.'

CHAPTER 34
UNLUCKY FIREFIGHTER

JOHANNESBURG 2021

'You fucking viper,' says Kirsten, thinking of the twenty-six years of lies.

'Au contraire,' says Miller. 'I'm one of the most loyal members of the Genesis Project. Was born into it. Not a bit of traitor in my blood.'

'Did my mother know?' she asks.

Miller looks as if he is going to say something, then shakes his head. 'It's complicated.'

Seth spreads his feet, wields his shovel like a sword.

'Don't get uppity, whippersnapper,' says Miller. 'Dig.'

'Fuck you,' the twins say, at the same time.

The gun glints in the late afternoon sun.

'Where's the packet?' asks Kirsten.

Miller pats his pocket.

'You never gonna get it, sweetheart. It's over.'

To illustrate his point, he zips his pocket open and takes out a plastic wallet. He opens the wallet and pulls out what looks like a notebook full of bookmarks and stickies. It is wrapped up with an old fashioned flash-disk on a lanyard, like a retro ribbon.

'Inside this book is everything you need to know to bring down the GP,' he says. 'Do you think I would hand it over to you punks?'

The combustible smell of paraffin wafts towards them. Petrol-green pinstripes. He has pre-doused it. Turned it from a book, a holy grail, a weapon, into an unlucky firelighter. Kirsten imagines the pages and pages of handwritten details. Blue ink on oily paper. Who their real parents are, the Chapmans; what happened in 1991. Who their abductors really are. Why they were killed. And why she and Seth, and the other five children, were taken.

He throws it on the ground, among the wildflowers. Takes a matchbox out of his top pocket, lights a match, and drops it towards the book. The match moves towards the ground in slow motion.

'No!' shouts Kirsten, starting to run towards it. Miller shoots the ground next to her foot and she freezes. Puts her arm up in surrender. The match lands, nothing changes, then the front cover begins to slowly curl, pulled by an invisible flame. The fire gains momentum, and is soon hungry and crackling. They stand in silence, watching it burn, scorching the surrounding flowers. Kirsten feels as she is burning along with it.

'Get on your knees,' Miller says. 'Hands behind your heads.'

They fall on to their knees, their faces masks. Seth puts his hands behind his head but Kirsten is in pain. Miller allows her to cradle her broken arm. He walks behind them.

'You don't have to do this,' says Seth.

'Actually, I do,' says Miller, gripping the butt of his gun, placing his finger on the trigger. 'Doctor's orders.'

The colours of the sunset tinge the flowers orange and pink (End of the Rose). There is some poetry in being surrounded by wildflowers, and death at dusk.

Miller takes aim. Kirsten reaches into her makeshift sling, grabs her revolver, turns in a smooth arc and shoots Miller in the shoulder, sending him listing backwards. Shocked, he tries to regain his footing, aims the gun at her again, but she is faster than him and she gets another bullet into his torso. He begins to stumble, still trying to shoot her, but not able to lift his arm high enough.

Seth jumps up, grabs a shovel, and smashes the gun out of his hand. He falls forward, onto his hands and knees. Blood spreads over the flowers on his shirt and the ones under his body. He grunts from the pain then pulls himself up so he is kneeling in the flowers. He notes the irony of his position.

'Where are they?' demands Kirsten, gun cocked.

He laughs. 'And why would I tell you? An extra bullet isn't going to make a difference. In fact, you'd be doing me a favour. Go ahead, do it.'

She lowers the Ruger, kicks him in the stomach. He moans. She kicks him again. He falls onto his back and lets out a long, terrible sound. Seth wields his shovel as if to brain him.

'Tell us!' she screams, stamping on his crotch. He cries out, tries to protect himself, so she stamps on his broken hand too.

Seth waits for him to stop screaming, and says, 'We can draw this out for hours.'

'I have a knife in the car,' says Kirsten. 'A Genesis Project pocketknife.'

'Think of what that would feel like, punk,' says Seth. 'Death by pocketknife.'

Miller mumbles something.

'What?' says Kirsten.

'Okay,' says Miller, 'okay.' Blood is running out of his mouth now. 'You'll never be able to get in, anyway.'

'Where are they?' she asks again.

'ChinaCity/Sandton. A round building made out of glass. Called inVitro.'

Kirsten kicks him again. 'You think we're stupid? You think we're going to believe that?'

'Believe what you want. It doesn't matter. Your friend's probably dead by now. And, anyway, you'll never get inside. You need a member with you to bypass the biometric access. Every member has their own access code, and it has to be combined with that member's fingerprint. Impossible—' He coughs scarlet. '—to hack.'

'Then you're coming with us,' says Kirsten.

Miller spits rubies on the grass, shakes his head. 'You kids have no idea who you are dealing with here.'

Miller's whole shirt is red now; his eyes are getting glassy.

'I don't think he'll last the trip,' says Kirsten.

'Me neither,' says Seth, 'and he'll slow us down.'

Miller watches the darkening sky as Seth fetches the car and drives it over the flowers; they lever him into the back seat. His breathing is laboured, and there is a bubbling sound. Kirsten finds some cable ties in the cubbyhole and Seth ties Miller's wrists together, then his ankles. Kirsten hands Seth his gun back, returns hers to her sling.

'Big mistake, *honey*,' she says to Miller, 'thinking a woman wouldn't be armed.'

Miller gets paler as they get closer to the clinic. His eyes are closed, skin waxen. His Cheerios are fading. Kirsten is sitting in the back with him, Ruger pointed at his stomach, safety catch off. *He will die today. I have killed someone. I'll never be able to eat cereal again.*

Seth is driving as fast as the car will go. 'We won't be able to get in.'

Kirsten looks out of the window, as if searching the sky for an idea. With a sudden grunt, Miller launches himself at Seth, throws his arms over his head and hooks his ligatured wrists across Seth's throat. The cable tie cuts off all his oxygen. Miller's body is taut and his veins like ropes with the effort of the strangulation. His jaw muscles ripple, his teeth melded together with pressure and pink spit. Seth, purple-faced, takes his hands off the wheel and immediately loses control of the car. Kirsten screams and grapples for the gun and shoots in the direction of Miller once, twice, three times. The sound of the gunshots and the ricocheting is blinding. *Did she hit him?*

She can't see past the noise of the gunpowder blasts. The car is off the road now. Seth manages to wrench the noose away from his neck for a gasp of breath, then tries to force the car back onto the road, but it's too late. It veers wildly and they hit something and fly through the air. Airborne, she feels her cheeks lift, her arm spark. The weightlessness is terrifying, and then there's an ear-splitting almighty crash, her brain short-circuits, and everything goes black.

The twins regain consciousness at the same time. The front of the car is smoking; the boot has sprung open. Miller lies dead in the road in front of them, his bare skin lacerated by the broken windscreen. The smashed insulin kit lies beside him. Kirsten and Seth don't talk. They reach out for each other, touch hands. Kirsten can hear herself blink.

She starts scanning her body for injuries: wiggles her toes, pumps her legs, palpates her ribs. Apart from the pain in her already-broken arm she feels fine; or as fine as numb can feel. Seth is holding his neck. He gives it a few squeezes, then kicks at the door. It takes three hard kicks to swing it open. He gets out and wrenches open Kirsten's door, helps her out.

They mumble worried phrases at each other, touch each other's grazes with furrowed brows. Satisfied that they are not too badly injured, they go over to inspect Miller, to make sure he is dead. He is a red spectre: his skull is crushed and he has five bullet holes that they can see. His skin is etched with a patina of blood. There is no life in him. His Cheerios are gone.

Kirsten picks up the bag of insulin. Despite being atheist, she crosses her heart and says a quick prayer to The Net and any god that will listen. She goes to the boot and heaves when she sees the contents. Motions for Seth to come over. Seth doesn't seem surprised. He leans in closer, to get a better look at the day-old corpse's face. A battered face and a body dressed in a Hawaiian shirt and chinos. Some fingernails are missing.

The real Ed Miller.

When Kirsten checks the insulin kit she discovers that the only remaining vial is broken. The bag is wet with the precious liquid. No insulin remains for Keke. No medicine to stop her from going into hypoglycaemic shock, stop her from going into a sugar coma and dying.

How strange, thinks Kirsten absent-mindedly, *how sugar and death can be so closely linked.* She bites down hard to stop herself from crying.

The car is un-driveable. They try to hitch but no one will pick them up looking the way they do, so the pair give up and sit on the kerb, facing the road, wobbling knees pointing to the sky. Seth puts his arm around Kirsten.

'James,' she says.

'What?'

'James can come get us. He has a car.'

For some reason this fills Seth with dread.

'James might have insulin.'

Kirsten sends James their co-ordinates in tracking mode.

'Let's walk so long. It's not too far from here. Five or six kilometres?'

Kirsten checks Keke's phone. Her diabetes app timer says thirty-four minutes.

'Keke doesn't have that long.'

'Can you run? With your arm, I mean?'

Even if they do run, they wouldn't make it to the clinic in time. If they make it to the clinic in time, they won't be able to get in.

'I can try.'

'Good girl.'

They stand up and start jogging. Seth tries to flag down cars as they go. Kirsten is dizzy, and she feels every footfall deep in her broken bone. The jagged pain mounts and mounts, until the blue light blots out her vision and she has to stop and throw up into a patch of roadside ivy. A plague of rats scurries away. She wipes her mouth and starts to run again, almost falls. Tries again.

'Stop.' Seth catches her. 'Stop.'

She tries to wriggle free, tries to keep running, but he grabs her again, just in time, and she faints into his arms.

When Kirsten comes to, it takes her a second to remember where she is.

'Keke?' she asks, but Seth shakes his head. Twenty-one minutes left on the SugarApp. When it reaches twenty minutes it begins flashing a red light.

'You've done everything you can,' he says.

She stands up, trembling. 'No.'

As if on some otherworldly cue, a white van appears on the road and drives in their direction. Seth starts yelling, waving his arms, like an island castaway trying to signal a rescue chopper. Kirsten blinks at it, trying to figure out if it is real, or some kind of desperate inner-city mirage. The car drives right up to them and stops on the shoulder of the road. The driver gets out and Kirsten's knees almost buckle again.

'Kirsten!' shouts James, running towards her.

'James,' she says, 'James.'

'Where have you been? I've been looking everywhere!' He seems agitated, but becomes gentle when he takes in Kirsten's shorn scalp and make-shift sling. He hugs her gently on her right side, kisses her forehead, her cheeks, her shorn head.

'What have they done to you?' he asks, 'What have they done?'

Who? thinks Seth. *What have* who *done?*

'I'm okay. But... Keke...'

Seth steps forward. 'We need to leave right now.'

James looks at him, the shock clear on his face. He doesn't say anything.

'This is Seth. He's been helping me,' says Kirsten. 'I'll explain everything later. We need to find Keke. Immediately. She needs insulin. Do you have any?'

James releases her. 'We'll get some.'

He jogs over to the van and opens the sliding door. It is dark inside the back, and there is a silhouette of someone, sitting in the front passenger seat: a large man. Both Seth and Kirsten stop.

'Come on,' says James, beckoning.

There is a flash of light in Kirsten's mind that bleaches her vision. Some kind of terror, some kind of dreadful *déjà vu,* roots each to the spot. Seth shakes his head, wants to hold Kirsten back. Kirsten's whole body is telling her not to get into the car, but she reasons with herself: *Must Save Keke.* Also: *this is James; Sweet Marmalade.* James beckons again, and this time Kirsten obeys: head bowed, like a shy little girl. Seth swears under his breath and climbs in next to her.

James slams the door closed and gets into the driver's seat. The passenger is looking out of the window and doesn't acknowledge them. The car has a chemical smell to it, rectangular in shape. Dry cleaning? New plastic? No, neither shape is right. And then she gets it: paint. A new paint job. Just as James is about to start the car, she gives him the clinic's address. James and the passenger look at each other. He stops for a moment, as if he can't decide whether to press the ignition button.

The man scowls at him, and only then does Kirsten recognise him.

'Inspector Mouton!' she says, not understanding the connection. He purses his lips, gives a nod in her general direction. Has James been so worried about her that he called the cops? Has Mouton agreed to help him find her?

The engine starts; the doors all lock automatically. She tries to open her door, but it won't budge, as she has known it won't. Child-lock. There is the distinct aroma of turmeric in the air.

Seth's Tile vibrates with a bump.

FlowerGrrl> Hey, hope u OK. Hope you get this. Results in. Ramifications huge. Hve already called emergency meeting with YKW. Hero u. Biggest bust in Alba's history.

Fontus going down in big way. All yr previous fuck-ups forgiven. U officially now Rock Star. Whn can u come in? We hve a few bottles / Moët wth yr name on.

SD>> Results?

FlowerGrrl> Oh, U R there! Alive. :) Sending report now. Come in ASAP!

Two separate PDFs come through. The first is the report on the Fontus samples: Anahita and Tethys clear, Hydra with lots of red tabs, showing irregularities. Seth recognises the main chemicals: ethinyl estradiol; norgestrel; drospirenone; mestranol; ethynodiol—the same active ingredients you'd find in a contraceptive pill. James casts a backward glance, but keeps driving.

The next PDF is the analysis of Kirsten's yellow pills, and he sees some more red tabs. Confused for a second, he checks that he is looking at the right report and not the Hydra analysis, but it's the correct one. The red tabs highlight various chemicals, all of which Seth recognises from his time at Pharmax. Diazepam, Sertraline, Doxepin. *The fuck?* It's a zombie pill. He starts as he remembers James is the one who fills her prescription for her.

James speeds up and weaves through the traffic, causing them to sway in their seats at the back. He swears under his breath and skips red lights. Smacks the steering wheel with his palm.

Seth bumps Kirsten.

SD>> Who's the beefcake?

KD> Cop. Mouton. He worked my parents' case.

SD>> WTF?

KD> ??

SD>> U know those pills u had?

KD> Yebo?

SD>> Tranquilisers.

KD> No way. I got them from James.

Kirsten digs in her handbag for her lipstick magic wand, and slips it into her pocket, along with her pocketknife. When the front entrance of the clinic is in view, Inspector Mouton pulls off his long sleeve shirt. Kirsten's eye is drawn to the skin on his arm. It's marbled, shiny. Burn scar?

They pull into the parking space closest to the giant glass entrance, and James and the inspector get out. Kirsten tries her door again, but it's still locked. She jimmies the handle, knocks on the window.

'James!' she calls. 'It's on child-lock!'

The realisation hits Seth just before it does Kirsten, and he puts his forehead in his hands. She doesn't understand his reaction, and then all of a sudden she does.

The memory comes back to her like a swift punch to the stomach, slams her back into her seat, takes all the air out of her lungs. She sees it as if she is back in that moment, that terrible moment, when the light went out of her life. A moment so long buried in her subconscious she'd think it would be decayed in some way, but it's not. It's cruelly vivid and so clear Kirsten can taste the colours.

She is playing a game with her twin brother on an emerald lawn in the front garden of a pretty little house. She remembers the building: rough ivory paint that scratches your skin if you brush up against it, curlicue burglar bars in the windows, cracked slasto leading up to a light blue (lemongrass-smelling?) front door. A brittle little letterbox on a pole with two red numbers on it (Lollipop)... red means two, so maybe it is twenty-two? The garden is bursting with colour, enough to make Kirsten giddy.

The sun is shining brightly but it is uncharacteristically cold that day, and they are dressed in warm boots and brightly coloured jackets: peppermint for Sam and mandarin for her. Her mother—her real mother—is leaning on the doorframe, watching them. She is pale and slim in a charcoal polo neck. She has on her gardening apron, and dirty gloves. A smear of soil on her cheek. Young, beautiful, with a long, thick braid of red hair. Kirsten gives her a toothy grin, and she responds with a smile and a thumbs-up. The phone rings from inside the house, and her mother peels off her gloves and goes to answer it.

Despite the warmth of the jacket, the skin on her hands is red when she looks down at them. Sam passes her something: a toy horse. No, a little pony, pink with a grubby white mane and tail. One of his action figures astride. A Thundercat. She zooms the pony over the grass and makes the appropriate sound effects, laughs. Sam doesn't smile. Something has caught his attention in the street and he looks past her, frowning. He stands up on his chubby legs, toy still in hand, held against his round stomach.

A black kombi has pulled up and all of a sudden there is a blond-haired little boy right there, on their pavement. He seems only slightly older than they are. He beckons to them with his hands, his sweet face promising something fun and exciting. She babbles excitedly, starts to go towards him, but Sam puts his hand on her shoulder, wanting to hold her back. He looks at the boy then back at the house, for his mother, but the doorframe is empty. Kirsten keeps walking and is soon beside the rosy-cheeked stranger. Sam calls out: 'Kitty!' and runs to catch up with her.

As he reaches the walkway beside the kombi, the door slides open and a giant man swoops over them and there are meaty forearms squeezing the air out of them. Before they know what has happened, they are struggling in the car. The other boy, stricken, is shouted at and jumps in last, and the door is slammed shut. From light to darkness, like that. Like that, the light in her heart went out. Nothing but darkness and a shocked wail in her ears. She realises the wailing is coming from her. In the dim interior she sees the blond-haired beckoner also crying, his face contorted with silent tears.

The face she knows so well. James.

CHAPTER 35

THE ULTIMATE BLOODLESS REVOLUTION

JOHANNESBURG, 2021

James opens the sliding door, flooding the car with light. Dust motes dance in the white air. Inspector Mouton stands beside him, gun drawn and pointed at the twins.

'Is that necessary?' James demands, anger gravelling his voice.

Mouton ignores him.

'Come with us,' Mouton says to Kirsten and Seth. 'Come quietly and no one gets hurt.'

'Fuck you,' the twins say in unison. Kirsten can't even look in James's direction. She sees where the car's paintwork has been touched up. James is the one who tried to run them off the road on the way back from the seed bank. James hid the letter from her mother. James tried to incapacitate her with pills.

Her heart is in shock, as if she has just been stung by a jellyfish. A swarm, a smack. His betrayal is a deep blue venom spreading throughout her body.

'Your friend is very sick,' says Mouton. 'You don't have much time. If you come with us, we'll give you the medicine she needs.'

'Go!' Kirsten says to Seth, 'I'll see to Keke. You get out of here.'

'No way,' he says. 'I've only just found you.'

'The deal is for both of you,' says Mouton. 'Just one of you is useless to me.'

Keke's phone starts vibrating and wailing, the SugarApp counter is at 0: 'DANGER ZONE.'

'Fine,' says Kirsten, 'we're wasting time. Let's go!'

Mouton halts them, pats them both down, takes their guns, including the sling-smuggled Ruger. He finds the pocketknife and magic wand. Puts the knife in his pocket and looks at the lipstick, undecided. He's about to inspect it when James makes an agitated sound.

'Come on,' he says, 'we need to move.'

Mouton hands the tube back to Kirsten. 'Go.'

He pushes the pair in front of him. They walk into the main entrance, which the regular security detail has deserted, and head to the elevator. James tries to take Kirsten's hand but she stands as far away from him as she can, squashing herself into the cool corner. The mirror, meant to make the small space seem bigger, reflects their taut faces and the result is claustrophobic.

Worried that she will get sick again, Kirsten closes her eyes and breathes into her corner, resting her forehead on the mirror. Her breath and sweat mist up the glass, veiling her reflection. Mouton inserts a wafer-key and they start moving down—past ground level and two levels of basement parking listed as the bottom floors—and still further, until they are deep in the ground and Seth can almost feel the weight of the earth above them.

'Kitty,' says James.

Shut the fuck up, she wants to say. *Your words are poison darts.*

'Let me explain.'

'There is not an explanation that would make this okay.'

'Van der Heever said to bring you in or he'd kill you.'

'And you believed him?'

'I know what he is capable of.'

'And yet you are delivering us to him.'

'Don't you see? I didn't have a choice.'

Kirsten sneers at him. 'I can't believe I ever let you touch me.'

'How long have you worked for the Genesis Project?' asks Seth.

'It's not like that,' answers James. 'That day, in 1988, when you were taken—'

'You mean when you took us,' says Kirsten.

'Just like you did today,' says Seth. 'Deja-fucking-vu.'

'After that day,' says James, 'I kept tabs on you. I made sure you were okay. I watched you from afar. Watched you grow up, as I grew up. I loved you—I did, I loved you—from the very beginning. We were meant to be together. Don't you see? We're a family. A different kind of family... that day we met—'

'Oh my God,' says Kirsten, '*everything* was a lie.'

They step out of the lift and stand before a massive security door, like something out of a high tech bank. It reminds Kirsten of the Doomsday Vault. Mouton keys in a five-digit code and puts his thumb to the scanner pad, two green lights glow (Serpent Eyes) and the door unlocks with a decisive pop. Kirsten lifts her hand to her face and narrows her eyes to cope with the intense light.

Everything is white: a passage with many inter-leading doors is made up of clean white floor tiles, white painted walls, a whitewashed cement ceiling. They walk along the passage and make a few turns. Every corner looks the same and Kirsten wonders how they'll ever find their way out again. They are rats in a 4D maze. She takes as many photos as she can with her locket. Some of the doors seem to lead to more passages; others open up to deserted labs. Huge machines whirr away. Ivory Bead. Wet Sugar. Coconut Treat. A hundred shades of white. Stuttering holograms of static. Glass upon glass upon glass.

The employees seem to have left in a hurry: Seth sees half-drunk cups of tea, open desk drawers, an out-of-joint stapler, an abandoned cardigan. Air sanitiser streams in through the air vents, sounding like the sea. It reminds Kirsten of being on one of the ghost ships floating endlessly on the Indian Ocean, many of which she explored and looted. Why had she been so captivated by stories of the Somali pirates? Because she had known all along, had a deeply buried awareness, that she, herself, had been kidnapped. Her life had been seized, snatched, carried off. It left her an empty vessel, unmoored. Haunted.

'That book I gave you,' says James, 'The fairy tale. "Hansel and Gretel". I gave it to you for a reason. Do you understand, Kitty? It was for a reason. I have a file on your real parents. I've tried to give it to you a thousand times, but every time I... I knew if I gave it to you we'd end up here.'

At the end of a nondescript passage Mouton pushes them into a room. The sound of a dog barking shocks them. A beagle rushes to Mouton and nuzzles his shin with a low whine and a wet nose. Mouton opens a drawer, takes out a treat, and feeds it to the hound. Gives her a cursory pat on the head, gives her loose skin a gentle shake. Locks Seth's and Kirsten's guns away in a safe full of meticulously arranged weapons.

Kirsten recalls the image of dog hair on Betty/Barbara's jersey, remembers the journo telling her that Betty/Barbara's flat had dog food bowls, but no dog. Seth looks up, at the opposite wall, and Kirsten raises her eyes too. They stand and stare.

Pinned, stapled, and tied to the vast wall are hundreds of objects. Rings, coins, photographs, pieces of jewellery, dead flowers, frayed ribbons, candy, baby shoes, old toys. Like a vast artwork, a collage of found objects, except they know as they are looking that these objects were not found, but taken. Special things stolen from the people he has killed. *Objets d'amour.* Not just a regular serial killer's bounty of murder mementoes. Not just a random hairclip or sweater or cufflink, but tokens of genuine affection. Layer upon layer of love, lost.

A love letter engraved on an antique piano key. A muddied toy rabbit. An Olympic gold medal. She sees the holograph photo-projector she gave to her parents. Both feel their rage build. The beagle barks. Mouton ushers them out of the room and raps loudly on the adjacent double door. A voice inside instructs him to enter, and they tumble in.

The room can't be more different than the bleached Matrix of the way in: soft light, warm colours, wood and gold, linen, organic textures. It's someone's office. No, more intimate than that: someone's den. Keke is lying on the couch, as pale as Kirsten has ever seen her. She runs over, puts her hand over her mouth to see if she is still breathing, and she is, but the movements are shallow. How long has she been unconscious? Her nano-ink tattoo is so vivid it looks as if it is embossed, and her body is slick with perspiration. James hands her a black clamshell kit (New Tyre) that she unzips. Three brand new vials of insulin stare back at her. Kirsten fumbles with the case with shaking hands, can't seem to co-ordinate her fingers. Eventually she gets a vial out, then looks for syringes, needles, but can't find them. She hadn't even considered this part: that she would have to load the syringe and inject her friend. Her trembling hands are all but useless.

'Let me do it,' says James. He finds something that looks like a pen in the side pouch, snaps the vial of insulin into it, and presses it against Keke's thigh. He clicks a button and Kirsten hears the hiss of the jab, watches as the vial empties. He puts the back of his hand to her forehead then measures her blood sugar, pressure and pulse with his phone.

'She's going to be okay,' he says.

Kirsten pushes him out of the way and grabs Keke's hand, bunches it into a tight fist around the magic wand, and covers it with a blanket.

'We wouldn't have let her die,' comes a voice from behind the mahogany desk. Dr Van der Heever swirls around in his chair and Kirsten recognises the icy irises behind his black-rimmed glasses (Wet Pebble).

'You,' says Kirsten. The word comes out the colour of trailing seaweed.

The doctor nods at Mouton, who forces Seth's hands behind his body and clicks handcuffs on him. James takes Kirsten's arm out of her sling to handcuff her. He does it as gently as possible, trying not to hurt her. She winces and squirms at his touch, as if his skin burns hers. There is a neat, metallic click, a perfect aqua-coloured square. She doesn't see the second click, the bracelet for her injured arm, and James squeezes that same hand. She glares at him and he looks away. Slowly she tests the cuffs, and it's true: he has left one open.

The doctor notices her hostility.

'Dear Kate, don't blame James,' he says. 'He had no choice but to bring you in.'

'There's always a choice,' says Kirsten.

'True. His options were: find a way of bringing you two in, or see you die. He has seen Inspector Mouton's... convincing... work. He chose to bring you in.'

'Mouton has been the one killing for you? A policeman?' she asks the doctor. Then, to Mouton: 'You killed those people? A sick woman, a young mother?'

'He was simply following orders. He is extremely good at his line of work.'

'Plus he gets to clean up the mess when he walks in as an inspector. I bet he's really good at covering his tracks,' says Seth.

'Just one of his many talents,' says the doctor.

'Why?' asks Kirsten, 'Why the list, why the murders?'

Doctor Van der Heever pauses, as if considering whether to answer.

'It's complicated,' he says, pushing his glasses up the bridge of his nose.

Keke's breathing seems to get deeper; her sheen is disappearing.

'The truth is,' says the doctor, 'the truth is that deletion is always a last resort. We did everything we could to stop it from getting to this stage. Unfortunately, people don't always know what is good for them. Or their daughters.'

'You mean my parents? My so-called parents?'

'Your—adoptive—mother. After being loyal for over thirty years she suddenly decided that she wanted to tell you about your past. She was a brilliant scientist, a real asset to the Project. Her decline was most unfortunate. If she had just been quiet, as she had been all these years... so many lives could have been spared.'

'Including hers?'

'Including hers. Your father's. And your cell's.'

'What? Cell?'

'Your mother deciding to tell you about the Genesis Project compromised the cell. We don't take chances. Compromised cells are closed down, their members removed from the programme.'

'Killed,' says Seth.

'Deleted is our preferred term.'

'I'm sure it is,' says Kirsten.

'Every generation,' says the doctor, interlacing his fingers in front of him on the desk, 'the Genesis Project selects seven very special infants to join the programme. We are very rigorous when it comes to this selection and hundreds of babies all over the country are considered. They need to match certain—strict—criteria. They must be absolutely healthy, highly intelligent, and have some special talent or gift. Also, during their gestation, their parents must have at some time seriously considered family planning—'

Kirsten: 'Family planning while pregnant? You mean... abortion?'

'Abortion, or adoption. They must have gone as far as signing the papers: a demonstration that they were not 100% committed to raising the child themselves for whatever reason.'

This stings Kirsten and Seth equally: they were not wanted in the first place anyway. When they discovered they had been abducted a little flame had ignited in their hearts: they were once loved, once cherished, before they were stolen away. Now that flame is snuffed out. Not one, but two sets of parents who didn't truly want them. Kirsten knows she shouldn't be surprised. After all, in the original story, Hansel and Gretel's parents lost them in the woods on purpose.

'Why?' asks Kirsten, 'why would the Genesis Project steal children?'

'The Project is concerned with far more than seven little children. In fact, the clonotype programme was really just a small hobby of mine in which the others indulged me. Our vision is far more all-encompassing than that.'

'You wanted to clone us?' asks Seth.

'Not clone you as such... more like, try to isolate the genes you carry that makes you... different. Special. Then we could recreate those genes in a lab and, well, graft them into new babies being born. Can you imagine?' His eyes sparkle. 'Can you imagine what our country could be if all our citizens were healthy, clever, strong, creative?'

'So that's what the Fontus thing is about,' says Seth.

The doctor throws him a sharp glance.

'GeniX. Eugenics. You audacious motherfucker.'

Van der Heever shifts in his chair. 'The word *eugenics* has become unpopular of late.'

'Perhaps because it's an archaic, racist, ethically reprehensible practice,' says Kirsten.

'What we do isn't racist,' he says.

'Really?' asks Kirsten. 'Is that why you are using the country's drinking water to practically wipe out South Africa's black population?'

'No,' says the doctor, 'not the *black* population. The *poor, uneducated* population.'

'This is post-apartheid South Africa. Most of the poor people *are* black.'

'Merely coincidence.' The doctor shrugs. 'Many non-whites are rich. In fact, very rich, not so?'

'Coincidence?' says Seth. 'We have that fucked-up legacy because of people like you who dabble in social engineering.'

James manages to get Kirsten's attention.

'Listen,' Dr Van der Heever says. 'Fertility rates are plummeting the world over. It's a well-known fact that in first world countries infertility is most prevalent in the educated and employed strata—we may even go as far as to say—the intelligentsia. The higher IQs go, the less chance of procreation. We also have the Childfree Movement: Ambitious couples are choosing to prioritise their careers and lifestyles over starting families. And yet the world's population is still mushrooming out of control. People with limited resources, limited faculties, are reproducing, putting a huge strain on the world's—finite—reserves.'

James wiggles his finger to draw her eye down, then, barely moving, he points at his shirt, the couch, his jacket, then touches his hair.

'It's a catastrophe waiting to happen,' says the doctor. 'So, the three of us—'

'The Trinity.' says Seth.

'The Trinity.'

Kirsten, frustrated, looks away, but James keeps staring at her. When she looks at him again he does the exact same thing. Shirt, couch, jacket, hair. He actually points twice at the couch, which she missed the first time around.

'We met in varsity,' says the doctor, 'took the same ethics class in first year. The debate question was: should South African citizens be required to obtain a permit before they procreate? This is, after all, what people do in Europe and other such countries, when they want to adopt a pet, an animal. There is a battery of psychological tests, a home screening. The system works well. The whole class was in an uproar: of course not! everyone yelled. What about human rights? The constitution! But the three of us argued in favour of the hypothesis. Human rights on the one hand, quality of human life on the other.'

Shirt, couch, couch, jacket, hair.

Seth wonders how many times the doctor has given this impassioned speech, how often he rehearses it in the shower, or while shaving.

'When tap water became undrinkable, it came to us. It was such an elegant solution. Dose only the state-subsidised drinking water, and leave the more expensive waters pure. If the privileged citizens drink Hydra for whatever reason, and find they have problems conceiving, they have the means to get help. Fertility clinics abound.'

'It's cruel. Barbaric.'

'Nature is cruel, Miss Lovell. Do you know that the embryos of sand tiger sharks kill and eat their siblings in utero? It's the epitome of survival of the fittest. You can't fight evolution.'

'Children may be the only gifts a poor family has.'

The doctor laughs. 'Ah, now you're being sentimental. What about the burden those 'gifts' cause the family, and the country? The planet? What about those children who have to be brought up in dire circumstances? They fall through the cracks. Before we started implementing The Programme the situation was reaching breaking point. Hundreds of babies being born every day and South Africa's education system was broken.

'Do you know what a broken education system does? It puts people on the street. Criminals. Beggars. Infants were being hired for the day by professional street beggars to garner more sympathy from drivers. There were newborns for sale, advertised in the online classifieds! Other babies were lost on crowded beaches never to be claimed, left in dumpsters, or worse.

'In May, 2013, I was having a personal crisis. Wondering if my work would ever make a real difference. In that month two abandoned babies were found: one wrapped in a plastic bag, burnt. The other was stuck in a sewage pipe—his mother had tried to flush him down the toilet. A healthy newborn! And you talk to me of barbarians. The bottom line was that children were too easy to come by, often unwanted, abused, neglected. The Trinity vowed to take a stand against their suffering. It was—is—incredibly personal. We all have our own stories. Christopher Walden was brutally sodomised—raped—by his priest at a church camp. He managed to escape to a nearby house and use their telephone to call his parents. You know what they did? Told him to stop making up stories and go back to camp. Then they called the priest and told him where he was.'

The doctor walks over to Mouton.

'Mouton,' he says, now with compassion in his voice. 'Show them your arm.'

For the first time, Mouton is hesitant to obey orders.

'Show them,' says the doctor. 'Help them to understand the work we are doing here.'

Mouton sets his jaw and lifts the sleeve of his shirt to reveal the entire burn scar. It travels from his wrist to his armpit. A swirling motif of shining vandalism.

'That's not one burn. It's not from a once-off childhood accident. Marius's father used to hold his arm over a flame for punishment every time he cried, because "Men Don't Cry". A candle, the gas stove, a cigarette lighter, whatever was handy at the time. It started on his first birthday.'

Mouton pulls his sleeve back down. Shirks his shirt into place.

'My scars aren't so obvious,' says Van der Heever, 'my father preferred the crunch of breaking bones. That, and psychological abuse. Once, my dog, the only friend I had, followed a farmworker home. My father was furious. That night I put out extra food for him, for when he came home. The next morning, when he returned, galloping and barking and happy to see us all, my father shot him in the head. The dog had been disloyal, he said. It was to teach me the value of loyalty. I was six years old.'

He takes a breath, lifts his glasses then rubs the bridge of his nose.

'I'm sure you can't imagine that now. It was before your time. Babies were seen as... expendable. Too many to go around, and most born to undeserving parents. Abuse was inevitable. Unchecked procreation was a scourge on our society. I knew when I heard that story about the baby being flushed down the toilet... I knew then that my work was vital.'

Shirt, couch, couch, jacket, hair. Blue, brown, brown, grey, yellow.

'Don't you see?' he asks, 'what we planned so long ago, what we have been working towards, is finally starting to come to fruition. Peace and purity. By tamping off the birth rate we have solved a host of societal ills. There are no more abandoned babies. Schools now have enough books and tablets and teachers and space for their learners, and children are looked after and cherished. Fewer uneducated people means less unemployment, less crime, less social grants. More tax money to invest in the future of the country. Better infrastructure, better schooling, better healthcare.'

Blue, brown, brown, grey, yellow, thinks Kirsten. *49981.* It's the code, she realises: the code to get out.

'Don't you see?' he says again, this time more urgently, pride like fever in his face. 'We did it! We are responsible for the ultimate bloodless revolution!'

CHAPTER 36

NEXT STOP: CYBORGS

JOHANNESBURG, 2021

Keke stirs on the couch, but settles down again. Van der Heever is tireless.

'If you put your emotions aside for just a moment and look at the results, morally and ethically speaking, it's accepted that the welfare of the many should take precedence over the welfare of the few, and as such, sacrifices needed to be made. We were not, contrary to what you may think, barbarous about it, as many eugenicists have been before us... unwitting patients waking up, in pain, only to realise that their uteri had been removed. Our solution was much more humane. Cleaner. In fact, we believe that once it becomes clear what has happened here, other countries will follow suit, and soon we'll have a global population that is both under control and more efficient.'

'Next stop: cyborgs,' says Seth. 'That's not a world I want to live in.'

'Dear boy, if the population of the rest of the world keeps growing as it is, there will no longer be a world to live in. We are safeguarding the future for all.'

'For some. For those you deem fit. Others you deny a future altogether. How many cells are there?' asks Kirsten. 'How many people's lives have you stolen?'

'A dozen, maybe more. An infinitesimal portion of the population. Genesis members, however, are in the thousands. They're in every strata of South African life.' He lifts his palms to the ceiling, as if he is some kind of prophet. 'How else would we be able to pull this off?'

'I still don't understand,' says Seth, perhaps trying to buy more time, 'the point of the clone project. So you isolated some interesting genes. Then what?'

'You wouldn't believe me if I told you.'

'Try me. What was the point? To splice a little army for yourself? Take over the world?'

'The point was to create a superior race.'

'So not unlike Hitler, then,' says Kirsten.

'To the contrary, dear Kate. It was never about me, never about power. I've never liked the limelight. A superior race would get ill less often, work harder, be more intelligent, less violent, have more talents, and lead more fulfilling lives. It was to make the world a better place.'

'But how would it work,' asks Seth, 'in your sad, imaginary world? Deserving parents would get their license and then come along to you for a designer embryo? You harvest their eggs and sperm and make a few little tweaks, remove any genetic abnormalities, add some extra brains or blue eyes. Ask them if they'd prefer a boy or a girl. It's bespoke IVF. You're fooling yourself. You're not making the world a better place. You're in the designer baby business, a fertility quack. There is nothing new or noble about that.'

'You don't understand how far technology has come.' The doctor smiles.

'Okay, you straight-out clone them, then.'

'Cloning is now old tech. It was never very successful. The ratio of live births wasn't good at all. We started with cloning because it was the best technology we had at the time, but now... now we have other means. Besides, cloning is still dependent on the pregnancy and birth being successful. There are just too many things that can go wrong. Too many variables we can't control. So... we cut out the gestation period.'

'Wait,' says Kirsten, 'what?'

'You've cut out the gestation?' says Seth. 'As in, you grow them in artificial wombs, in the lab?'

Kirsten pictures a room filled with transparent silicone wombs and feels like throwing up again.

'We experimented with that, but it wasn't a viable solution in the end. It was difficult to get the exact... nuances of the environment right.'

'Right,' says Seth. He is genuinely interested now. 'Okay, now you have to tell me.'

Dr Van der Heever's lips curl up into a smile; there is a snap in his eyes.

'We print them,' he says, not being able to keep the pride out of his voice. 'We print babies.'

CHAPTER 37

THAT'S WHAT FRANKENSTEIN SAID

JOHANNESBURG, 2021

'You print babies,' repeats Seth. It's not sinking in.

'That's impossible,' says Kirsten.

'Oh believe me,' Van der Heever says, 'it is.'

The doctor gets up from his chair and motions for them to follow him. He activates a door hidden in his bookshelf, which swings open, and he steps through. Mouton pushes them forward from behind, leaving Keke on the couch in the den. Soon they are standing in the white cube of a pristine lab (Immaculate Conception), the brightness highlighting the dirt and blood on their clothes and skin, adding to the surreal quality of the moment.

Kirsten looks down at her hands, fingernails black with grime, but is distracted by a small cry in the corner. She studies the row of incubators against the wall: a stack of empty Tupperwares. Has she imagined the sound? Is she imagining this whole thing? Is she lying unconscious somewhere, at the scene of the earlier car accident, or in hospital, having this bizarre dream?

A nearby machine, monochrome, spins. It looks like some kind of body scanner.

'We were already printing fully functional organs in 2010. It was the natural progression to print a whole body. All you really need is good software and some DNA. And stem cells, obviously, which there's no shortage of in our game. We've printed over a thousand healthy babies, and we have a 100% success rate. No more failed fertility treatments. No more mothers dying in labour, no more birth injuries or foetal abnormalities. Just screaming healthy newborns with 10 out of 10 Apgars, every time.'

'But you can't print a beating heart,' says Kirsten.

'Ah, that was one of the most challenging parts,' says Van der Heever, touching his chest, 'but a quick current to those heart cells and off they go—galloping along. It's a beautiful thing to behold.'

Seth says, 'I think that's what Frankenstein said.'

The doctor indulges Seth with a smile.

'Where are they, then? The babies?' asks Kirsten.

'A lot of them have been adopted out. As you know, the demand for healthy babies nowadays is astronomical.'

'You sold them?'

'In a manner of speaking.'

'So you cause a nation-wide fertility crisis and then set up a designer baby factory,' says Seth. 'Genius.'

'What about the rest?' asks Kirsten.

'We evacuated them when we got confirmation that you were coming in.'

'You evacuated the whole building,' says Kirsten.

The doctor nods. 'I couldn't take the chance you'd not... co-operate with us.'

'I wouldn't "co-operate" with you if my life depended on it.'

'That's what I thought you'd say.'

Another soft sound from the corner: a cooing. Transparent bubbles float playfully towards her. Kirsten blinks forcefully to wipe them out of her vision.

'That's why,' says Van der Heever, 'I had to up the stakes.'

He walks to the corner incubator, opens the top, and gently lifts a newborn out from inside. He carries the baby back to them like a proud relative. It's swaddled in a blanket embellished with planes and clouds that float in the sky. The baby squirms, tries to break free, shouts, and then fixes Kirsten with an intense stare. She knows she should feel revulsion. The doctor can barely contain his excitement. He raises the baby up, like a trophy, like the prize he'll never get from his peers.

It looks... It looks just like—

'James, Kirsten, meet your progeny. Congratulations. It's a baby boy.'

CHAPTER 38

WHITE HOLE

JOHANNESBURG, 2021

'No,' says James, breaking his silence. 'It can't be.'

'What have you done?' whispers Kirsten.

'You came to me for help,' Van der Heever says, 'you wanted to have a baby.'

'Not like this,' she says.

'I know it's still a novel idea to you, but this is how *all* babies will be made in the future.'

'No,' says Kirsten, shaking her head.

'There's nothing wrong with him. He's a perfectly healthy baby!'

'You're saying he's ours? Mine and Kirsten's? You used our DNA?' asks James.

'That's what I've been telling you! All your best traits, with none of your problematic genes. We switched off two for cancer, and one for dementia, I believe. He'll have Kirsten's hair, your eyes. Your fine motor skills, and Kirsten's artistic talent.'

The baby starts fussing, his skin blooms pink. The doctor motions for James to take off Kirsten's handcuffs, and as he does so, she feels his fingers slip into the back pocket of her wrecked jeans. A set of small keys: for Seth's handcuffs, she guesses. She takes the baby from Van der Heever without thinking, just scoops him up with her un-broken arm and rocks him, inhales the warmth of his skin, kisses his forehead. The baby calms, gazes up at her, barely blinking. She can feel him, smell him, and in that moment she knows acutely this is no dream. This baby—her baby—is real. Her whole body stupidly longs for the bundle in her arms.

'Why did you do this?' Kirsten keeps her voice low. 'Why bring us in and tell us everything? Why didn't you just have us killed, like the rest?'

The doctor puts his hands behind his back, strolls towards the empty incubators, leans against one of them.

'I'm getting older now. Softer? My health isn't what it used to be. It's too late to switch off the genes that are causing my heart to fail. My career has always been all consuming. I'll continue working but it's time for me to start taking some time off. Play golf. Travel. Watch my grandson grow up.'

'You can't be serious,' says James. 'You think we can just forget all this and play Happy Families?'

'Grandson?' says Kirsten.

Van der Heever's eyebrows shoot up. 'You haven't told her?'

'Why would I tell her?' demands James. 'Why would I tell anyone?'

His words hang in the air: the outburst makes Kirsten's head spin.

'Father?' She looks at James. 'He's your *father?'*

'Not by choice,' spits James. 'I broke all ties with him as soon as I had an idea about what he was doing. But this... my imagination didn't go this far.'

'Not your choice,' says the doctor. 'Indeed. It was *my* choice.'

'What?'

'My choice, to be your father. You were the first of the 1991 seven to be chosen to be incorporated into the clonotype programme. You were the first to be... taken.'

Kirsten thinks of the list, pictures it in her mind, sees the code of the last person on the list: number seven. Sees the colours, and recognises Marmalade's date of birth. So he was also abducted, she realises, was also a victim. Abducted then used to lure the rest of us. Bait. A toddler version of Stockholm syndrome.

James blinks.

'I am one of the seven?' he asks, amazed. 'I am not biologically tied to you? We don't share the same blood?' Something dark and heavy lifts off his shoulders; a shadow escapes his face.

'I did... care for you,' says Van der Heever. 'I didn't make the same mistakes my father made, with me. You were always well cared for.'

'You abused me,' says James.

'I never lifted a hand to you.'

'You used me as a lure,' says James. 'I was a child.'

Kirsten gazes at the baby who has now fallen asleep in her arms. His energy, like James's, is orange (Candied Minneola). Fresh, tangy, sweet. Mini-Marmalade. She feels a rush of tenderness.

'So, you now have a choice,' says the doctor. 'You can take your baby, walk out the door, and never look back. As long as you keep the Genesis Project a secret, no harm will come to the three of you. We will be watching over you—'

'Surveilling us,' says James.

'Yes, surveilling you. And making sure you are safe and that life is... easy.'

'What's the catch?' asks Kirsten.

'No catch, if you are willing to co operate.'

'And if we aren't?'

'Then we'll take the baby back.'

'Like you took us,' says Kirsten.

'Like we took you. For the greater good.'

'I have a hard time believing that you're just going to let us walk out of here,' says Seth. 'What are you not telling us?'

'I said I would let Kirsten and James go, with the baby. You, on the other hand, we can't release. With your history, your contacts at Alba... we just can't take the chance. I'm sure you understand.'

Seth nods.

'No,' says Kirsten.

'It's a good deal,' says Seth. 'If I were you, I'd take it.'

'No way,' she says.

'It's not like it would be the end for you, Mr Denicker. You would work for us,' he says to Seth. 'A chemgineer of your ability would be a great asset to The Project. You would choose your hours; we'd pay you handsomely. Not that you'd need the money. Everything down here is complimentary. And you'll have an extremely beautiful companion in that journalist who also needs to stay.'

'But I have to live... underground—literally—for the rest of my life?'

'For the foreseeable future, yes. Until people come to understand and accept our work. It's not as dreary as it sounds. Think of it as... living in a high-end hotel with every one of your needs met.'

The doctor takes a clicker out of his lab-coat pocket and switches on a hologram in front of them. It's like a hotel brochure in 4D: there is a picture of a beautiful suite, impeccably furnished, followed by other images the doctor clicks through.

'We have a heated swimming pool, sunlight rooms, halls of trees for nature walks. Movies, games, room service 24/7. As a bonus, you'll have a personal assistant who will make sure that your every need is fulfilled. Mouton, remind me, what is the young lady's name again?'

'Fiona,' says Mouton. 'Fiona Botes.'

Seth's face flushes.

'The finer details will all become clear once you settle in.'

The doctor switches off the projection.

'You'll also have access to all of this,' he says, gesturing at the lab equipment. 'Everything you need. We have equipment you wouldn't believe exists.'

'But I'll be your prisoner.'

'That's looking at the cloud, instead of the—rather significant—silver lining. I'm giving you—giving all of you—a way out. A unique mercy. I'd advise you to give it some serious consideration.'

'Five-star prison, with benefits, or death,' says Seth. 'I guess I'll take prison and see how it works out.'

'You can't work for them!' says Kirsten. 'They represent everything you hate.'

'Did you not hear the options presented?' asks Seth. 'You'd prefer me dead?'

'Of course not. I just thought... I just think you'd prefer it, over this. Over them.'

'Then you overestimate my moral compass. Or underestimate my will to stay alive.'

As they re-enter the den Kirsten sees Keke's eyes flutter closed. Without warning, James leaps at Mouton, tries to bring him down, scrabbles for the gun in his hand. Mouton roars. Kirsten whisks the baby onto the couch, needing both hands free to unlock Seth's cuffs. The doctor, now behind his desk, calmly opens a drawer, takes out a shiny pistol, snicks off the safety mechanism. Mouton, outraged to see that Kirsten had Seth's keys, aims his gun at her and fires.

The shot knocks her to the ground and she feels a sudden heaviness in her chest, and a sick warmth spreading. Her hearing is muted but she can hear the baby crying, as if he is behind a wall. She can't see, can't breathe. Her breastbone is on fire. A mint-coloured lightness; a searing sadness. The baby—her baby—wails.

This is what it feels like to die.

She expected relief, if anything. Instead it feels as if her heart is being stretched, shredded. She tries to reach for her child but she can't move. She waits for the eventual blackness, blankness of death, but it doesn't come.

She senses movement through her closed lids and opens them. Her vision is blurry: the animated shapes of James and Mouton are still struggling in silent slow motion, the white figure of the doctor has his pistol pointed at them. Keke on the couch.

She can't see Seth. Where is Seth? She feels her heart beating, so she knows she is still alive. Things are coming into focus. She's pinned to the floor. She tries to move again and that's when she sees him: her brother, slack-mouthed, white-skinned, lying on top of her.

'Seth?' she says, but can't hear herself. 'Seth?' but he doesn't move, and then she knows that the warmth and the crushing weight is his. Knows that he had jumped in front of the bullet meant for her heart and had trapped it in his own instead. She shuffles under him, uses her good arm to try to ease his body off hers, tries to get free. Her sense of hearing starts to return and the baby's screaming slashes her vision. She hunches over Seth, tries to find his pulse, but there is too much noise and too much yellow adrenaline singing through her body, numbing the pads of her fingers. She begins CPR, just as James had taught her.

1 and 2 and 3, she says to herself. *1 and 2 and 3.*

Blue sparks travel up her injured arm and lodge in her clavicle, shock her jawbone. She continues the compressions: wave after wave of jagged Pollen Yellow and Traffic Light Red and Fresh Sage Leaf Green. Van der Heever keeps his gun aimed at Mouton and James as they struggle.

'Stop it!' shouts van der Heever. 'Stop it immediately!' but the men carry on their clumsy wrestling. 'This has been my life's work. It cannot end today!'

No one pays any attention to the flailing doctor.

'This lab will self-destruct as soon as my heart stops beating. Do you understand that? Do you realise what is at stake?'

Kirsten looks up momentarily, sees his face is taut with anguish, and feels nothing for him. She turns her attention back to Seth, only then realising that there is no blood. She sticks her finger into the bullet-hole and finds it dry. Kevlarskin. Tries for a pulse again, and finds it. Out cold, but alive. The baby screams and screams from the couch. Mouton is eventually able to throw James to the ground. He stops resisting when he looks up into the barrel of Mouton's gun.

'Let me reiterate,' says the doctor, taking a calming breath, 'If I die, we all die. There are explosives in every room that were designed specifically to blow this place to dust. We cannot risk anyone finding any evidence here. I have a one-of-a-kind pacemaker in my heart: if it stops beating, the pacemaker sends a signal to the bomb and detonates it.'

This seems to calm the room. Kirsten crawls over to the baby, gathers him up, tries to comfort him. Puts a pants-polished knuckle into his mouth to suck on. Van der Heever follows her with his pistol. James moves to stand up and go towards her, but Mouton shakes his gun and says 'Uh-uh,' motioning for him to stay where he is.

'You said you wouldn't harm her if I brought her in! I had to believe you. I'm asking you as the person you raised as your son...'

'You were never my son,' says the doctor, giving Mouton the signal to shoot them both. Mouton takes aim at James, and Kirsten shouts 'No!'

Before Mouton squeezes the trigger, Keke presses the button on the magic wand that Kirsten had tucked into her fist earlier and tasers him in the back. He yells out, his body convulsing with the current, letting off a few shots into the ceiling then into the wall.

She tasers him again, knocking him off his feet, unconscious. The doctor fires at Kirsten but she ducks, and the bullets land in the gilded frame of an oil painting.

Keke points the lipstick at Van der Heever. Just as James gets Mouton's gun out of his hand and points it at the doctor, the doctor turns his pistol on him.

'If I die,' he says again, 'we all die.'

Keke hesitates, perhaps not sure what the taser would do to the incendiary pacemaker. Kirsten cries out as the doctor shoots James in the shoulder. James clenches his jaw and pulls the trigger, twice, and Kirsten sees two black apertures appear in the doctor's white coat. The force of the shot pushes him back a few steps, and he looks at James in astonishment.

'You were never my father,' says James.

Somehow, the doctor has enough strength to grasp his trigger, and he shoots James again, this time in the chest, causing his body to fall backwards and collapse at an awkward angle. Now, battling to stand, Van der Heever aims at Kirsten and the baby, but Keke moves quickly and tasers him before he has the chance to fire, and he falls down onto his knees, then onto his front. Kirsten crouches over James.

'It wasn't your fault,' she says, putting pressure on his wound. 'It wasn't your fault. You were four years old.'

James's face crumples.

'You were four!' Her hands, slippery with blood, slide off his torso. 'Hold on,' she says, putting them back in place. 'Just hang on,' she says.

She tears open his shirt, front and back, grabs his medical bag, claws it open, empties the contents onto the floor beside her. She finds some Platelet-Plasters, rips the backing off with her teeth, and sticks them onto the entry wound. She knows it won't help.

'Kitty, you know your Black Hole?' he says, 'That cold... emptiness...'

'Don't talk,' says Kirsten.

'You have always been the opposite of that, to me.'

'Sssshhh.'

'Whatever the opposite of a black hole is. A white hole?'

'Yes, a white hole,' whispers Kirsten past the stone in her throat.

A white hole: the opposite of a vacuum. The opposite of nothing.

The ability to escape.

Kirsten realises they're sitting in a pool of red. Sees he's fading. James puts one hand on her arm, the other on the baby.

'You were always that. You were everything,' he says, and the light goes out of his eyes. She shakes him, tries to wake him, but he is gone. She doesn't say that white holes don't exist.

'I love you too,' she says to his still body, 'I love you too,' and for the first time in her life that she can remember, huge sobs crash out of her mouth and she is wailing, tears mixing with blood.

A shrill siren stings their ears.

'We need to go,' Seth says to Kirsten, grabbing her arm, lifting her off the floor, away from James's still body.

'We can't leave him here!'

'This building is going to blow up,' says Seth. 'We won't get out in time if we take him.' Kirsten looks at Keke, sees how grey she still is, feels her own strength leaking out of her body. Despite losing so much, she still wants to live. They leave the office, but stop almost immediately when faced with the colourless maze of passages and rooms.

'I don't know where to go,' whispers Keke. 'I was carried in. I was barely conscious.'

Kirsten looks at the photos she took with her locket. The pictures get them halfway but then they are lost. The siren blares. She looks around, tries to think, but all she can see are the bombs in the walls. She looks down at the ground.

'Can you see that?' she asks Keke, pointing at the floor tiles (Toaster Waffles).

'What?'

'Scuffmarks.'

'It doesn't mean anything,' says Seth.

'Breadcrumbs.'

'What?'

'Hansel and Gretel. It's a trail of breadcrumbs. There weren't any marks coming in,' says Kirsten. 'Marmalade... was walking behind us. He marked it for us.'

They follow the grey marks on the floor, turn a few corners, and find the exit: the huge vault-like door. It's locked. Keke, panting, sinks to the floor. She is perspiring heavily again.

Shirt, couch, couch, jacket, hair, thinks Kirsten, and punches 49981 into the number pad. One of the two red lights turns green, and the door remains locked. They both see the small biometric scanpad at the same time, know that it's for a thumbprint.

Inky dread, mixed with neon nerves: Kirsten hands the baby to Seth, tells him to wait with Keke. She follows the scuffmarks back to the den. She doesn't look around at the devastation, the bodies, tries to remain clear and focused. She leans over Mouton's vast torso, finds her pocketknife in his jeans.

As she pulls the knife free his bear claw grabs her wrist. She screams white bolts, and knees him as hard as she can, landing a good one in his stomach, but he hardly flinches. He grunts and starts pulling her body towards him—a meaty tug-of-war. She screams, kicks. The siren screeches zigzags.

She uses her fractured arm to elbow him in the face, breaking his nose so that he can't see. They cry out at the same time and he loosens his grip. Kirsten launches forward, scooping Mouton's gun off the floor and turning on her back, taking aim from between her knees. He roars and lunges at her, but she is quicker than him and gets two shots in and rolls out of the way before he crashes down next to her. She shoots him again, and again, until she has emptied the magazine; until she has no doubt that he is dead.

How much time does she have left? She has no idea. She is hyperventilating, trying not to shake. Picks up the pocketknife again and springs the blade.

Kirsten starts to cut off James's thumb. She can't saw through the long bone, she doesn't have the strength or the time, so instead she cuts deep around the bigger knuckle until the joint is exposed, then digs the knife into the joint and pops the thumb out. The horror of what she is doing does not escape her, but she can't afford to think about it now. She files it away somewhere close and dark. She grabs the digit and runs. She doesn't think of the mutilated hand left behind, the body, the face, the lips. She thinks about getting to Keke, to Seth and her baby, and getting out in time. Staying alive.

The alarm increases in intensity; she is sure only seconds remain. Kirsten flies out of the room, intent on the exit, but halfway down the first corridor she hears something that stops her. Barking. Then beneath the siren: a snuffle, a whine, a whimper. She takes a few more steps. There is no time to save the dog. If she goes back for the beagle they would probably all burn. The dog scratches and whines. All the swearwords Kirsten knows explode in her head, splattering the inside of her skull. She turns around, runs back to Mouton's memento room, and gathers up the dog that is sitting waiting for her as if she knew she would come.

With the dog in her arms she hurtles back down the corridor, reaches the security door where Keke is lying on the floor. She holds the thumb to the scanner while she punches in James's code again. Both lights turn green and the door jolts open.

She puts down the dog and levers Keke up, supports some of her weight with her good shoulder and gets her through the door. Seth carries the baby, and a gun. The elevator is disabled, so they jog up the stairs, losing count of the flights—flights and flights of stairs—going as fast as they can, the dog at their heels.

They all lose the rhythm at different times, causing them to stumble, waste split seconds. Keke stops with only a few more steps to go, sways and falls, causing her and Kirsten to tumble down half a flight, sending the dog into a flurry of barking. Keke doesn't get up. Seth passes Kirsten the baby, picks up Keke and throws her limp body over his shoulder for the last few stairs.

They trip out of the front door. Kirsten glances down at the baby to see if he is okay. He frowns back. She tucks him further into her body to protect him. The blue gleam from her broken arm is gone. They get to barely a hundred metres away from the building before an ear-splitting roar occurs behind them that hurls them up into the air and crashes them down again onto hard concrete. The baby wails.

JOURNAL ENTRY

12 MAY 1989, WESTVILLE

In the news: *I am happy. Truly, wonderfully happy.*

What I'm listening to: Madonna's 'Like A Prayer'

What I'm reading: 'The Alchemist' by Coelho. Don't really get it. Sure I'm missing something.

What I'm watching: Rain Man

Today P and the kids 'surprised' me with breakfast in bed for Mothers Day. At 'terrible two' they are a handful—I call them my adorable monsters—but on days like this I could just eat them up, they are so cute and charming, on their best behaviour. Sam had made me a 'card'—a fingerpainting of our family standing outside our house—and Kate gave me a necklace she had made by stringing dried pasta shapes together. I stuck the painting up on the fridge and wore the necklace the whole day.

P went around the garden cutting some of my favourite flowers and put a big bunch in a vase for me. (Poor garden!) It was very sweet.

I love watching the kids learn and try out new things. I love it when they say new words. They really are a handful—you can't leave them alone for a second (just this week: Sam dropped my brand new hand-held vacuum cleaner into a bucket of water, and Kate climbed INTO the fridge and closed the door. Last week Kate cut up a dress of mine to make 'ribbons!' and Sam jumped out of his pram and smacked his forehead on the tarmac. One of them flushed a plastic car down the loo and flooded the bathroom). Some days—most days—I just collapse on the couch after getting them into bed.

I have started taking them to the river every now and then, for swims. I take snacks like Provitas and little cubes of cheese, and some CapriSuns and then we call it a picnic. It is a great way to get rid of all their extra energy so that they are tired and calm when P gets home from work, and they adore it. Especially Kate—she is such a waterbaby! I really have to keep an eye on her. They have matching costumes and these bright orange inflatable armbands and they love to splash. Sam is very protective, always keeping an eye on his 'little' sister. He gets this worried frown when he thinks she is floating too far away and when we call her ('Kitty! Kitty!' he says) then she'll turn back, smiling her funny, naughty little smile. God, my heart bursts. I love them.

My shrink says that we can probably start weaning me off the anti-depressants. I'm not in a hurry. I never want to go back to that dark place again.

Oh! I almost forgot. The strangest thing happened yesterday. I was grocery shopping with the little ones—NOT the easiest thing in the world—but they were on their best behaviour and sitting nicely together in the trolley while I passed them things (not eggs, from experience). A woman who was walking past us looked intently at me and I smiled back. I thought, we must look funny. Like I had gone shopping and taken two toddlers off the shelf and put them in my trolley. Imagine it was that easy: you just go to a shop and choose which adorable monsters you want. 'Hmm, yes, I'll take this one and this one.' They would need barcodes! And what would the return policy be?

But then later I realised that she had smiled at me because she had recognised me—she was the nurse at that family planning clinic that was so kind to me and held my hand! I wonder what she must have thought, seeing us together. I wonder how it made her feel.

EPILOGUE: SIX MONTHS LATER

A DIFFERENT KIND OF FAMILY

WESTVILLE, KZN, 2022

Kate sits in her hired car, parked a little way away from the river, under the glittering dappled shade of willow trees. She takes off her safety belt, adjusts her tender back in the chair. Her left arm is slightly paler and thinner than her right, still recovering from being in the exoskeletal cast she had to wear for months.

She breathes in the muddy green smell of the river (Wilted Waterlily): a smooth, undulating smell. Balmy Verdant. Rolling Hills.

Keke urged her—citing her 'condition'—to take the isiPhapha speed train from Joburg to Durban, but she wanted to drive, to take her time, to think. To appreciate the journey.

Keke has just won another journalism award for her coverage of the Genesis Project. She always tells people she doesn't deserve them, that Alba deserves all the credit, but they just call her 'humble' and love her all the more. She's getting job offers from all over the world: most notably, Sweden, where they have offered her an eight-figure retainer for a year's contract. She and Marko are considering it, but only when she is fully recovered. In the meantime she gets weekly Tupperware takeaways from Marko's mother, who insists that good Indian food, specifically *dosa,* can cure any affliction. Keke is sure she'll hate the cold, and Kate knows it will be difficult for Keke to leave her post of Godmother to Baby Marmalade. She doesn't want to give up her partial custody of Betty/Barbara the Beagle, either.

God, Kate has missed driving, the freedom of the open road to the thrumming soundtrack of your choice. Stopping for a hydrogen refuel—not as pungent a memory as petrol—and greasy toasted cheese in a wax paper envelope. Flimsy paper serviette. Vanilla whipped Soy-Ice in a hard chocolate coating that you get to crack open with your teeth. Noticing, inside the store, that all the Fontus fridges are gone.

Kirsten imagines them yawning in recycle tips, stripped of any valuable metal, or re-purposed as beds or dining-room tables in townships. Most likely, though, they have just been bleached and re-branded with S/LAKE decals: Bilchen's "100% pure" bottled water, Hydra's supposedly incorrupt replacement.

Alba's secret underground identity has been blown wide open since they disclosed the information they had on Walden and his company. They are instant heroes, and the logo of the green rabbit silhouette has gone viral. True to hypothetical bunny breeding, they have multiplied overnight. Virtual stickers, 3D wallpaper, hoverboard art, graffiti stencils, and playful holograms: Alba is everywhere.

They receive offers of funding from various (apparently non-evil) corporates. Keke has heard rumours of a splinter group forming, with new 'unknowns': a secret faction that can still do the same job without worrying that their mugs are splashed on every news tickertape (and Talking Tee) in the country.

Kate winds her window down further, allowing more of the clear air into the car. After tossing out the air-freshener at the car rental agency (Retching Pink) she had driven the first hour with all the windows down to try to flush out the fragrance. Artificial roses: the too-sweet scent painted thick vertical lines in her vision. Her sense of smell seems to be in overdrive lately, and the shapes more vivid than ever.

It is a superb day: warm, the humidity mitigated by a cool breeze, and the sky brighter than she has ever remembered seeing it. The branches of the weeping willows stroke the ground, whispering, as if to soothe it. She can smell a hundred different shades of green in the motion of leaves.

A woman pops up in the distance, walking towards the river. She has handsome silver hair, a thick mass of it, twisted up and fixed in place with a clip and a fresh flower. A stained wicker picnic basket in her hand. She is tall and moves in elegant strides: not rushing, nor dawdling, her sense of purpose clear. She doesn't look around for a good spot; she knows exactly where the good spot is.

She sets down her basket, lays out the picnic blanket, smoothes it down in a practised movement. Once she has removed her shoes she sits with her legs out in front of her, crossed at the knees, leaning back on her hands with her eyes closed and her face to the sky.

The woman takes her clip out and lets her hair tumble down like mercury. Kate unthinkingly touches her own short hair, rakes her fingers though the awkward length of re-growth. The woman relaxes like that for a while, then sits up and opens her basket, bringing out a plastic plate and knife, a packet of crackers, cheese triangles. A small yellow juicebox.

Kate snaps a photo of her with her LocketCam, then retrieves the cooler-box from the back seat that she had packed that morning. She takes out a dripping bottle of iced tea, a packet of Blacksalt crisps, and a CaraCrunch chocolate bar. Watching the woman by the river, she opens the foil packet and starts to eat; then she remembers the bright green apple in her bag (Granny Smith), and eats that too.

So this is what her real mother looks like. Not just her non-abductor mother, more than just her biological mother, but her real mother. She can feel it. She sees Seth/Sam in her body language, her straight nose. But the hair and the eyes are hers.

She looks at her reflection in the rear-view mirror, touches the new streak of grey at her temple (Silver Floss).

'We have the same hair, and eyes,' she whispers to herself.

She feels a welling up in her chest, an inflating of her ribcage, and breathes deeply to stay calm. Warm tears rush down her face; she is used to the feeling now, even welcomes the release. During the past few months she has made up for a lifetime of not crying.

The woman looks so peaceful, so at ease with the world: a trait Kate hasn't been lucky enough to inherit, but she hasn't always been like this; she has also had her dark days.

James kept an eye on the Chapmans during the past twenty years, even kept a file, which he had left in his SkyBox for Kate. She found the access code in the "Hansel and Gretel" book he had bought for her a lifetime ago. It had been there all along. The file contained a comprehensive log of the Chapmans' lives: the different jobs they held, the close friends they had, and the holidays they went on. The grief counsellor they consulted. They never moved house—they still live at 22 Hibiscus Road—as if they thought if they moved, they would lose all hope of the twins finding their way home.

Anne Chapman still visits the river almost every day, the spot where she used to sit in the shade while the twins splashed around, and then later, their subsequent children: another son and daughter, born five years after Kate and Sam, spaced three years apart. The children, now grown, visit often, and the family looks like any normal, happy, loving family. It would be difficult, seeing them laughing and joking at family dinners, to guess at their sad and fragmented past.

Kate's yearning crowds the car. How she would love to meet her mother, grasp her hand, taste her cooking, ask her about the years before the kidnapping, and after. But looking at her, seeing how content she is, how restful her spirit seems, she knows she can't do it. It would be like smashing a shattered mirror that has taken decades to put together. Its hold is tenuous, gossamer, and she won't be the one to re-splinter it.

No fresh heartbreak.

She has a new life, thinks Kate, like I do now. She thinks of Seth at home in Illovo with Baby Marmalade: how good he is with him, how gentle. Seth who wants to keep his Genesis name, instead of 'Sam,' says it doesn't suit him, and he is right.

He has a new life too, despite not changing his name. She pictures what she guesses they are doing now, sitting on the couch in front of the homescreen, Baby Marmalade asleep in his arms, Betty/Barbara the Beagle snoring in her usual spot, her snout on Seth's lap. The wooden floor littered with nappies and wipes and teething rings and toys.

A different kind of family, James said.

An unusual family, but a family nonetheless: waiting for her to return home, and anticipating its new addition.

She thinks of her Black Hole, which is still there but has been sewn up to the size of her skin-warm silver locket. It's the smallest she can ever remember it being, but it yawns when she thinks of James.

She watches her mother pack up, shake the blanket, fold it and put it away, then start walking back in the direction from which she came. Kate reaches for the door handle then stops herself.

No. No. But when that feels too harsh, she allows herself a concession, thinks: *At least: not today. Maybe tomorrow, but not today.*

After a few steps, her mother turns, looks directly at the car in the distance. Kate can't see her expression. A moment goes by; she turns back and continues her walk home.

Kate takes a few breaths with her head back and her eyes closed then snicks her safety belt in and starts the car, swinging it into reverse. Her back is aching again, her ankles puffy. She adjusts her position, rubs her swollen belly.

'Time to get you back home, little one.'

Born seven months apart, her babies will be almost like twins. A different kind of twin.

She pops the car into drive, and puts her foot down.

HOW WE FOUND YOU

BOOK 2

WHEN TOMORROW CALLS BOOK TWO

HOW WE FOUND YOU

JT LAWRENCE

PART 1

CHAPTER 1

THEY NEVER FOUND THE BODIES

Johannesburg, 2024

Kate looks up from her holoscreen and blinks hard. How long has she been online? She only meant to look up a recipe for a quick dinner but has fallen into a rabbit hole quilled with xlinks. The open tab leaves all nipping for attention. Animated 4DHD in hypercolour floating before her – or as Seth calls it: Rainbow Crack.

The twins are far too quiet. They must be getting up to something. Defacing the walls with chocolate glitter? Baking their Lego cake in the real oven? Kate sighs, rubs her eyes and lets her warm hands rest on her neck. She pictures the multicoloured plastic blocks sagging through the metal grid. Caramelised Lego lava. She hopes the smell of burning plastic is a figment of her synaesthesia.

"Silver?" she calls. "Mally?"

No answer.

"Silver?"

Part of her wants to pretend she doesn't notice the quiet. Peace is difficult to come by when you're the single mother of four-year-old twins. Well, not quite a single mother, and not quite twins. Not quite four years old yet, either, but this is how life is: a series of not-quites and half-broken dreams.

The silence hovers around her like a fresh white cloud (Bleached Bliss).

"Mally?"

She unclips her feet from the pedals and climbs off her cycling desk. The holo leaves wink out, making the silence seem somehow louder. She calls again. "Silver?"

Maybe they're watching something with their earbuttons in. She checks the games room. An animated film is playing silently on the cinewall, but no eyes are watching it. The bedroom floor is an obstacle course of discarded toys and clothes. She picks up Alba, Silver's cuddle-bunny, and lays it gently on her pillow. The HappyHammox are empty, although Mally's is swinging slightly, as if someone has just brushed past it. Kate stops its motion with her hand.

There is a mewling from the corner. She spins around and dread tingles in her stomach. Another sad cry escapes from a heap of teddies and trucks. Kate tip-toes over to the wailing pile and picks her way through it, discovering a Bébébot of Silver's. Registering that its been picked up, the playbot stops crying and blinks at her.

"Mama," it says. "Mama."

The infant's silicone limbs are warm to the touch. Its lips open and close, looking for its pacifier. Kate has never liked the soft robotics doll. It's not the toy's fault; something in her is just revolted by its similarity. Uncanny valley, they call it, when a robot bears a resemblance too striking for comfort.

"Mama," it says again then roots for something to suck.

Kate turns the doll around, unbuttons the cotton onesie and lifts up the fabric to reveal the switch on its back. A shot of yellow adrenaline spikes her blood. It's already off.

"Mama."

Kate almost drops the thing. She toggles the switch on and off again, turns the doll around. It blinks at her.

Faulty wiring. Her heart is hammering. She takes a step and cobalt stars rip into her foot. She looks down to see that she's stood on a toy Volanter. Curses crowd her head and she shakes them away.

She calls louder now, in a voice that's not quite hers. "Silver?"

At least we're in a high-rise. A nice safe apartment instead of a house on a road that can coax the kids away with the promise of adventure. Then again, scores of other people live in the block, and in her experience, people are far more dangerous than roads.

Kate hurries to the front door, checks the locks. Seth promised her that his new Safeguard, state-of-the-art security system is "bullet-proof" but she made him install some old-fashioned locks just in case. She doesn't trust a retina scanner. Tech is wonderful until it stops working. She won't settle for anything less than an old-school door chain, a deadbolt and panic hardware. Her synaesthesia interprets the sounds of the mechanisms locking as reassuring blocks of grey stacked on top of each other. *Click, click, click.* Not that it helps her sleep at night.

"Kids? Where are you?"

She scans the lounge, the kitchen, the study, the kids' bathroom.

"Don't panic," she says, but the shooting neon yellow is back.

She checks Seth's room, her bedroom, her bathroom. The shower door is closed. Did she close it? Is there something behind the frosted glass? A shadow? Her breath catches, heart-in-throat. Kate reaches for the retraction button, but hesitates. Her outstretched fingers tremble.

They never found the bodies.

Shut up. Just shut up.

She could fetch her gun from the safe in her bedroom cupboard but decides against it. Kate presses the retraction button and the superglass partition slides into the wall to reveal an empty cubicle of porcelain tiles.

A spray of relief that the shower is intruder-free. Terror that the twins aren't in it.

Interwoven with the ribbons of fear is the scent of almond soap. Bad thoughts swarm Kate's brain. She tries to keep them out but there are too many of them – in her head and in her throat, threatening to cut off her oxygen.

It's happened again, the voices in her head say. *Just like you knew it would.*

"Shut up." The cold mist of fear rustles on her skin.

They're gone. They've been taken.

CHAPTER 2

A QUICK CONTAGION

Kate, fright-frozen, hears knocking at the front door. It's enough to propel her out of her paralysis. Another knock, and her brother's muffled voice calls her name. Her fingers, confused by her racing thoughts, fumble with the locks.

"Kate? What's wrong? Are you okay?"

Finally she manages to open the door. Seth takes a step back when he sees her pale face. "Whoah. What's happened?"

"The twins!" Kate shouts. "I'm calling SafeGuard. And the police."

Seth's face is marble, his jaw set, and his mouth is a hard, white line. Fear is a quick contagion. "What do you mean? Where are they?"

"They're gone!"

"They can't just be 'gone'." He gestures at the motley collection of locks on the door. "They can't get out. They're here somewhere."

"I've looked for them everywhere."

Seth starts to search. Kate follows him, almost tripping on his heels. Echoing her, he calls out the kids' names over and over. He turns the corner in his room and a squeal makes them both jump. Betty/Barbara the beagle gives him a hurt look.

"Sorry, old girl," says Seth. "I didn't see you there."

Kate starts to feel faint. There's snowy static behind her eyes.

"I've looked there," she said. "I've looked everywhere."

"Silver?" calls Seth.

Quiet.

"I'm calling 911." Kate touches the Patch behind her ear.

"Hang on." Seth puts a finger to his lips then he puckers up and whistles, a clean, clear strain that severs the tense silence.

An electronic beeping comes from the next room. They dash towards the kids' bathroom, crowded with robofish and rubber dux, and Seth whistles again. The laundry basket emits a cheerful beep. Slowly, slowly, he lifts the lid of the hamper to reveal two bobbing heads of white-blonde hair. Mally shrieks in excitement; Silver giggles.

"You found us!" shouts Mally. He holds up the arm with his watch on it, light flashing. He doesn't seem to mind that the FindMe app betrayed his hiding place.

Warm blood returns to Kate's face; her heartbeat still thuds in her ears.

Seth hauls Mally out of the basket, zooms him around then pretends to gobble his stomach. "You rascals! You little *skelms.*"

"I'm not a *skelm,*" says Silver.

Kate picks her up, hugs her. The girl's innocent limbs wrap around her waist. Kate sniffs her skin, her hair. Grips her tighter.

"Ow, Mom. Not so hard."

Seth puts on a serious face. "You guys gave your mom such a fright. You mustn't do that again." The colour is returning to his cheeks too.

"We were only playing. Hide and seek."

"I don't like that game," says Kate.

"But I'm good at it," says the little boy.

"I don't care." There's an edge to Kate's voice. She doesn't want to cry in front of the kids again.

"But – " says Mally.

"I don't care," she says. "I don't want you playing it anymore."

The children's faces contract with dismay. Kate puts Silver down and leaves the bathroom.

CHAPTER 3

A BLACK WHISPER IN HER BRAIN

"What's wrong with Mom?" she hears Mally asking. "Was it my fault?"

"No," says Seth. "Not your fault."

"It's 'cos we were playing," says Silver.

"It's because she got a fright. She couldn't find you and she got worried."

"It's 'cos I'm so good at the game," says Mally.

"It's because she loves you so much."

"Too much?" asks Silver.

Seth clicks the bath icon and warm grey water rushes into the tub: four fingers of murk. The kids jump around and peel off their clothes. They don't mind the cloudy water, they don't know any better.

Kate hears the splashing as the twins climb into the bath and she starts to cry. Relief, anger, and the not-yet-dissipated fear are a hot whirlwind in her chest. She should be happy, she thinks. The kids are safe. But she cries in hard gasps.

Seth comes through and sees that she is weeping. His arms fall to his side.

"Hey," he says, gently. "They're okay. Everything's okay."

"It's not, though," says Kate, rubbing her swollen eyes. "You know it's not."

"It's just a difficult time."

He tries to hug her but she pushes him away. She hasn't showered today.

"Where were you?" she demands.

"What do you mean, where was I? I was at work."

"You were supposed to be home an hour ago."

Seth looks at Kate with narrowed eyes. "I didn't realise I had a curfew."

"You don't have to be an asshole."

"I'm not the one being an asshole."

Kate cries some more, and blows her nose.

"Come on," he says. "You've had a fright. Let me make you some tea."

"I don't want tea."

Seth switches the instakettle on and the water bubbles and steams. He'll make some anyway. A big mug for her, a double-walled glass for him.

"You're still in your pyjamas," he says.

"They're comfortable."

Recently she's been reluctant to wear her regular clothes. She can't find anything in her cupboard that doesn't appear full of irritating seams and prickly textures. Too colourful. Too constricting. It's hard enough as it is to breathe.

"It's not a criticism," Seth smiles at her. "I like you in pyjamas."

"Shut up," she says, but she feels better.

He passes her the mug. It's the bespoke blend he has made up especially: red nettle and *rooibos*, or something like that. She pours half of it down the sink, gets a bottle of whisky out of the cupboard and tops it up, then offers it to Seth. He hesitates, but then does the same thing. They clink their drinks together while they listen to the kids chattering like monkeys in the bath.

Later, once the twins are safely in bed, Kate collapses on the couch in front of the homescreen. She's about to turn it on, but Seth catches her wrist and takes the remote from her.

"We need to talk." Seth sits on the couch next to her.

"Uh oh," says Kate. "You can't break up with me, you know. I'm your sister."

"I don't want to break up with you."

Betty/Barbara the beagle snores from the other side of the lounge.

"I know what you're going to say."

"No, you don't."

"You've had enough of the kids. Of me. You want us to move out."

"No, Kate. No."

A warm wave of relief brings more tears.

"I couldn't love those kids any more if they were my own. You know that."

"You're so good. You're so good with them."

The children love Seth as surely as they love each other.

"I'd say that they love you like a father, but we both know that means nothing."

Kate and Seth's adoptive fathers had both been cold. When they finally met their biological father they were in their mid-thirties and too grown up to experience that all-encompassing love a small child receives from a tender-hearted parent. It was part of their twin tragedy.

"I need to go on a trip," says Seth.

"You're leaving us?"

"Just for a little while."

Kate's inside is dyed with dread.

"I won't cope without you."

"You'll be fine."

"I won't."

"Kirsten – "

Her desperation mounts.

"Don't call me that!"

"Sorry."

"I hate it when you call me that."

"I didn't do it on purpose."

"I left that all behind."

They both know it's not true.

"Kate. You're the strongest woman I know. You're the strongest *person* I know."

"I'm not. I'm a mess. I'm a fucking disaster," she plucks at her pyjamas. "Can't you see it?"

"You know I wouldn't go if it wasn't important. I won't be gone for long."

"Please don't leave. I have a bad feeling."

"You'll have Sebongile. I've already asked her if she can work more hours. She'll dress the twins in the morning, take them to school. She can work evenings, too. Cook the kids' dinner. She said it's fine. It might even free you up a bit. You can have some time to yourself."

The last thing Kate wants is time to herself. Being left alone with her thoughts is a dangerous thing.

"Maybe you could – I don't know – take your old camera out for a day. Or you can take up your shooting practice again. You were saying the other day that you wanted to -"

"What if you're not here when I need your help?"

"I told you, the nanny will be here."

"No, I mean -"

"What?"

"What if someone comes to take the children?"

Seth moves closer to her, takes her hands.

"Kate," he says, looking into her eyes. "No one is going to take the children."

She starts crying again. She can't help it. The tears embarrass her, make her feel weak.

"It's over," he says. "What happened to us was terrible but now it's over. It was four years ago. You need to move on."

"I know," she cries. "I mean, I know. But I have this ... feeling."

"They're dead, Kate. Van der Heever. Mouton – "

"They never found the bodies," she says, without meaning to. The thought goes around and around in her head when she has a panic attack. A black whisper in her brain.

"Of course they never found the bodies. They were blown to pieces."

"We can't be certain," says Kate.

"Of course we can. We were there. They were dead before the building blew up."

CHAPTER 4

BITTER CARAMEL SKIN

Kekeletso shifts in her seat. Taps her feet. She's not used to sitting for long periods. Most days, her job as a freelance journalist keeps her running. She thinks of all the stories she's missing and her mouth goes dry. Keke motions for a glass of water from the banker sitting next to her.

At least she thinks he's a banker. He could be a trader. A businessman. A pimp of any kind. He's successful: She can pretty much smell the money on him. What is his story? That sharp suit could be hiding anything.

He pours her a glass out of the sweating S/LAKE bottle on the counter in front of them, and their fingers touch when he hands it over. After a curt nod in thanks, she lifts her mask and takes a gulp without inspecting the drink, which is a good sign. It means she's becoming less paranoid about The Water Thing. The Fontus Thing. Genesis: the story that almost killed her. The story that's made her so famous she hasn't been able to go anywhere for years without a face mask.

The face masks were at first a burden, a grudge accessory, but she's become so used to wearing them they've joined her trademark antique leather jacket as part of her look. Like tinted windows and sunglasses, face masks allow her a degree of separation from the frenetic place her world has become.

Since American scientists finally discovered how to defeat the SuperBug – using a compound found in an Antarctic sea sponge – people binned their masks with glee, but Keke kept hers on. The designer face mask business moved to China and she's been able to buy scores of remaindered stock for next to nothing. Add to that her intricate cornrows, white lace shoulder tattoo and ice-blue eye contacts – arresting in their contrast to her bitter-caramel skin – it's no wonder strange bankers stare. She takes off the mask, crumples it into her pocket.

"What?" she silently mouths to the man.

He shakes his head in apology. He hadn't even realised he was looking.

"Pay attention," she whispers, pretending to scold him, pointing to the front of the court house.

The suit gives her a wry smile. Keke spends a moment looking at his hands – he has nice hands; is he good with them? – then tunes back into the court proceedings.

This isn't the first time she's been in court – as a journalist, she's followed a slew of cases – but it's the first time she's ever been on the juror's bench. She's considered trying to dodge jury duty, but something told her to go through with it. Maybe it's a sense of civil responsibility, or maybe it'll make a good story. Either way, she doesn't regret the decision.

The accused – the father of the victim – is told to take the stand. He stumbles as he reaches the bench and almost trips, and the woman beside Keke gasps and jumps involuntarily, as if to catch him before he falls. Keke doesn't blame her for wanting to help him. He's a husk of a man. Whatever will he had to live has been stripped from him like skin. A terrible thing, to lose your child, especially one so young. There's nothing worse, she's sure, apart from this – being charged with his murder.

The defendant eventually sits. He rubs the bridge of his nose, an old habit from when he used to wear glasses, Keke guesses. Not many people wear specs anymore, now that bio lens technology has become so affordable. Her own BLs cost a fortune, but that's because they're medicated. They monitor her blood sugar levels via her tears and dispense insulin as needed. The blue tint is just for fun.

The man on the stand is shaking. He doesn't look nervous; his face is waxen and loose. Keke glances at his wife, who is trying to catch his eye, maybe to reassure him, but his gaze is downcast. The wife looks just as desperate in her ivory suit, matching face and freshly shampooed hair. She was told to wash it, Keke's sure. She's watched the woman's hair get greasier and greasier as the trial wore on. Who can blame her? In her position, hair-washing must seem utterly insignificant, but they're reaching the end of proceedings now, and it's important to keep up appearances. The expensive clothes, the powdered face: maybe if she acts the part of good wife and mother instead of the mess she has become, the jury will be influenced in her husband's favour. Think of them as a respectable family. Or maybe not. Maybe dirty hair might have won her more sympathy.

Impossible to say which way it'll go – clean hair or not – impossible to know what Keke's fellow jurors are thinking. The suit thinks he's guilty, the woman on her right is sure he's innocent. Keke can't be sure. She has to know more. The prosecutor begins his last examination.

CHAPTER 5

'D' FOR DICKWEASEL

Seth swings his backpack into the cab and climbs in after it, careful to not spill his street-bought coffeeberry freezo.

"Hello Cabbie," he says. The car takes a few seconds to read Seth's Patch.

"Good morning, Mister Denicker." The engine ignites with a purr, and the system adjusts the air-conditioning and window-tint to Seth's preferred settings. "Please choose a destination."

This particular cab's voice reminds him of the one he used to have in his apartment before Kate moved in. Urbane, sexy, almost devoid of accent. Her name was Sandy and she'd known him so well. She'd remind him to drink electrolytes before going to bed after a late night out at Tommyknockers then stall his artificial sunrise the morning after.

"The airport," he says. "Lanseria."

He checks his hair in the mirror. It's blue black, freshly dyed, and it matches the smudge on his eyes.

"Calculating route to Lenasia."

"Not Lenasia. Lanseria. The airport."

"Calculating route to Lenasia."

"Oh, for fuck's sake," says Seth, leaning forwards and flicking the rear-view mirror into smartscreen mode. He types 'LANSERIA AIRPORT' and smacks the 'enter' button.

"Calculating route to Lanseria."

"Thank you," mutters Seth under his breath.

"You are most welcome," says the car and takes off a little more quickly than usual, pushing Seth back into his seat.

"You're a feisty one," he says.

"I'm sorry. I didn't get that. Could you please repeat it?"

"Never mind," says Seth, mopping coffee frost off his jeans. Luckily they're dirt-repellant or he'd be walking into his new job with stained pants.

The solarplane's hull is made of seamless superglass, allowing the passengers an almost 360-degree view while they're up in the air. There's a special cabin at the back for people who are afraid of flying, replete with white noise, liquid-weighted jumpsuits and virtual reality sets that allow them to believe they're safely on the ground. They can choose between options of virtual Tropical, Urban or Alpine settings and even get breakfast to match, if they've booked ahead. Tranquili-tea comes standard.

Seth's eating a buttermilk waffle snackwich with morellos and chia cream. He was going to choose the healthy option – scrambled tofu with allium micro-greens – but he's feeling in need of some comfort. Either that or Kate's junk-eating habits have been rubbing off on him.

Life used to be a lot easier before they were reunited. He had his high-tech apartment to himself, an interesting nightlife, and as many women as he wanted. Sure, it was a kind of shallow, superficial existence, but it was one that he had carefully created for himself. It was neat, and it had suited him. Fast forward four years, and his routine is unrecognisable. His days of recreational drugs, ShadowShots and unprotected sex are far behind him, replaced by loud 4D cartoons and edible wax crayons. Scrawls of beginner alphabets on his climachange walls: A is for apple, app-app-apple. Peanut butter stains on white pine-leather designer couches, animated stickers on his Punani sneakers, stray cereal crunching underfoot.

His place, previously a handsome and sophisticated bachelor pad, now resembles a toddler zoo.

Of course, he wouldn't choose to go back to how it was. His current life, in all its chaos, is more rewarding now than it's ever been. He's found some kind of meaning – a deep connection he never had before. The kids teach him a lot. In some ways, ankle-biters know a lot more than adults do. Still, a break from them is great, he thinks, as he stretches out his legs. He had made sure to choose a kid-free flight.

The stewardbot cycles noiselessly down the aisle, collecting empty trays and handing out steaming hotwipes. He's sure the robot is more efficient than a human counterpart but he misses the eye candy, the days of red-lipped beauties breathing over you as they served pink gin and tonics. Lean arms and pert tits. As if, as a precursor to being hired as a stewardess, you had to be at least a runner-up in those strange competitions they used to have. What were they called? Beauty pageants. Before the world realised what a fucked-up thing it was to parade women around in bikinis and high heels for satin sashes. Pipe dreams of 'world peace': what a crock of shit. Still, he considers as he downs his vitadrink, it's nice to be in the presence of beauty, no matter how shallow. There's not enough of it in the world. Not enough to counteract the dark stuff.

He rubs his face, leans back into the reclining chair. They'll be touching down soon.

This trip will be good for him. Sure, it's for grind, but it's exciting work, and any time he's away from Mally and Silver it feels like a holiday. He closes his eyes; maybe he'll have a nano-nap. He tries to empty his mind, but there's a nagging thought that won't go away, no matter how much he ignores it. He takes a deep breath then imagines he's sitting in the back section, VR set on, lying on the beach and listening to the waves lapping. Wind rustling the leaves of palm trees. Still the thought is there.

It's not the twins he needs a break from; the kids are not the problem.

A young man in row D takes a hotwipe and smacks the stewardbot with it. It's the same creep who tried to trip the robot while it was handing out breadrolls earlier. 'D' for dick. Dickweasel. Douchebag.

"I don't want it," the creep says. The wipe hangs onto the side of the bot's head for a moment then drops to the floor. The man laughs, and his cohorts around him laugh too. Students. Seth takes in their athleisure wear and lazy body language. Too much testosterone and too many beers. The robot, confused, picks up the cloth and drops it into the cache on his back. He produces a new wipe and tries again to hand it to the jock.

"I said I don't want it," says the creep, this time with anger.

The robot's code obviously doesn't allow for dick passengers. Seth shakes his head. This is a glaring mistake. When the stewardbot doesn't move away, the jock kicks it. The robot's head spins around in alarm. The gang laughs again. Seth unfastens his safety harness.

Some of the passengers frown at the student, and make clicking sounds with their tongues to show their disapproval, as if he had kicked a puppy. He's about to kick it again when Seth stands up and walks over. Bot or not, he won't stand for bullying.

"Leave it alone," he says.

The jock is still smiling. He looks around at his friends for support, but they look away, so his cockiness fades. Seth can read his thought process through his facial expressions. He's wondering if it's worth the fight. He thinks he might be able to beat Seth, but will it be worth being arrested at the airport? Missing his bro-moon with his mates? Being drafted into a Crim Colony?

The robot whirrs away down the aisle.

"Okay, man," the jock says, throwing his hands up in jokey surrender. "Chill."

The overhead icons light up, showing a Quinbot buckling up. Seth returns to his seat just in time for the plane to descend.

CHAPTER 6
FOUR FINGERS

Kate's walking down an alley that smells of urine and ash. The sun is just setting and it coats the grimy city walls with shades of candied blood orange. A drone buzzes overhead and she wants to swat it away. She wants to be like that giant woman in the 1950s movie posters. Attack of the Fifty Foot Woman. She wants to swat that drone away like a fly and crunch cars and smash buildings. And she wants to roar while she's doing it.

But she's not a giant. She's the small one. The ant underfoot. The skyscrapers loom over her as if to assert their phallic concrete-metal-glass. The buildings – palisade spikes and buzzing neon lights – crowd around her like schoolyard bullies.

She's hurrying now. She can smell the danger in the dusk. She doesn't know what she's running from. No matter how many times she tries to change direction, the littered street seems to snake its way further and further into the black heart of the city.

She has no option but to follow it. There's someone chasing her. He thinks he's well hidden but she can hear his footsteps behind her, feel his eyes on her body. She imagines his breath on her neck. When she looks back all she sees is a dirty, deserted lane. Is the threat in her mind? She knows how paranoid she's become but it doesn't stop the red flags shooting up in her brain. Imaginary or not, she has to keep moving. The sky is completely dark now. Algae street lights flicker on and off. She has to get somewhere before it's too late. Is it Keke? Is she sick? Kate's not sure. She hears hyenas growling and yipping. Then she remembers why she's hurrying. The twins. She left them somewhere. How could she leave them alone in this terrible place? They'd be so scared. They'd be beside themselves. Crying for her. What has she done? The guilt hacks at her like a *panga,* splitting her back open, letting her blood run and mix with the ink of the midnight air.

She runs, her soles hit the tarmac, she passes graffitti'd walls, but she doesn't get anywhere. It's like she's stuck in some kind of monochrome Möbius strip. An animated Escher painting. Her breath is barbed, and the energy drains out of her. She stops for a moment, gasping, hands on knees.

It's a mistake.

The stranger grabs her from behind. Two hot hands: one on her stomach, one on her throat. She screams and tries to dislodge his grip on her. One of his hands goes to her mouth to stop the sound from coming out.

"Ssh," he says. "Keep quiet, or they'll hear you."

Kate cries and thrashes, trying to get him off her.

"Kitty, shush," he says again. There is a sprinkle of turmeric in the air. Her hand goes up to the one covering her mouth. She wants to dislodge it, wants to shout for help. The skin on the attacker's hand is smooth to the touch – too smooth – shiny and marbled. It's been burnt. She recoils and gags. It only has four fingers.

Kate wakes up screaming, her hands at her throat. There are stars in her vision and her white cotton sheets are wet with perspiration. In her pitch black room, she fumbles for the Sunrise switch and smacks it hard. The curtains sway open and pretty pink and yellow light hits the walls. Birds flutter and tweet on the sound system.

It's okay, she tells herself. *It's okay. You're okay. It was just a dream.*

The block-out blinds are still in place. The artificial dawn is cool and gentle, not like a real South African sunrise that has you sweating by 8AM. With these floor-to-ceiling windows, if she opened the block-out the room would be bleached and baking in seconds. She tries to slow her speeding pulse; tries to even her breath. It takes her a full minute to adjust properly to her reality. She's home. She's safe. The kids are safe.

Are the kids safe?

"Mally?" she calls. Without waiting for an answer she jumps out of bed. She needs to see the twins. Touch their sleep-scented skin. Hug their little bodies. Kate needs to feel the realness of their warm bodies to ground her spinning mind. "Silver?"

A note on the kitchen table stops her from going to their room. It's in Sebongile's handwriting, saying that she's taken the kids to school. Kate didn't even know that it was a school day. It means that the nanny woke, fed and dressed the twins and walked them to school all before Kate had even woken up. She had also cleaned the place. The apartment was spotless apart from some half-eaten apples, and cereal bowls on the table.

It's eerily quiet. Kate taps the countertop, unsure of what to do. She pushes the memory of the nightmare away and thinks of the children. They'd be home in a few hours and everything would be fine. Goosebumps needle up her spine, making her whole body shudder. She blames it on her damp pyjamas making her cold, pulls them off, and gets into the shower.

CHAPTER 7

POPGRAINS AND SEX

Marko is in his man cave. That's what Keke calls it, anyway. It's his hoffice, his happy place, the room in which he keeps all his electronics. It's dim, apart from various LEDs and alphalights blinking. The cinewall, while state of the art, remains largely mute, apart from a weekly Hedy Lamarr film they watch together. The room always smells of popgrains and sex the day after.

He never thought he'd move out of his mother's house, where he had the whole basement to himself and authentic Indian food on demand, but then his mom decided to travel through India, and, well, Keke is a uniquely persuasive woman. Just last night she was persuading him of the benefits of a walking desk. He knows he's sitting too much, eating too many stevia-laced kronuts. None of his favourite shirts fit him anymore. His fan-shirts look like crop tops on him. He'd turfed his Talking Tees years ago, when the fad had ended, and now he wishes he hadn't. He's sure at least some of them would fit him now. He hates the idea of a walking desk. He helps himself to a NutNut cookie. He can always order more shirts online. Bigger shirts. It will be nice to have something new.

Marko spins around on his chair, dusts buttery crumbs off his fingers. Keke's heart is beating, slow and steady, through his Soulm8 Ring, and it reassures him. Whenever he feels a stab of anxiety, he closes his eyes and concentrates on her real-time pulse. Eventually he drags his attention away from the image of Keke's heart beating under her beautiful chest, and gets back to work. More than twenty leaves are open in front of him. He checks his international bank account and is pleased with what he sees. Last month he'd designed a hack to beat an online casino in Thailand. It was just a trickle of Baht, but a trickle is all he needs. A trickle stays under the radar and pays his modest bills. It's the greedy bank-gamers and clickjackers who get caught. His low-grade ambition serves him well. Still, he can't become complacent. He'll shut it down soon, before they are any the wiser.

Marko wheels himself away from the desk and all the leaves wink out, leaving the room considerably darker. He'll need a new strategy for the next stream of income, but not the same-old – not just anything. This time he wants to try something more exciting.

CHAPTER 8
THE CHEERFUL PSYCHOPATH

It's the second day of the accused, Mack Lundy, being up on the stand. Every part of him looks worn out and weary, as if he's aged a decade during the past few weeks, as if his will to live has been siphoned out of him. Everything about him is grey. Keke can't look away.

Lundy has been asked over and over again about the events of the night his young son died. The prosecutor is trying to catch him out.

"It's not going to change." Lundy rubs his face. Maybe he thinks that if he rubs hard enough he can erase himself altogether.

"What's not going to change?" The prosecutor has beady eyes and a sharp nose. She's like a crow: peck, peck, pecking at his testimony.

"What happened that night," says Lundy. "It's not going to change what happened that night."

"You mean *your version* of what happened that night," says the crow.

"It's the truth."

The prosecutor looks up at the three judges. "Your Honours, will you please instruct the accused to answer the question?"

The junior judge is about to talk when the head judge interjects.

"It would please the court," says the old man in a gentle Greek accent, "if you would answer the question."

"Chief Justice," complains Rabinowitz, Lundy's lawyer. "My client has given his version of events over and over again. Can we please move on for the sake of everyone in the house?"

Rabinowitz gives the jury a look that says 'Am I right?' Some subtle nodding happens around Keke. It's a good tactic to win favour with the audience and get Lundy off the stand. Two birds with one stone. The crow narrows her little black eyes at the defence attorney, and he keeps his face neutral. Are they sleeping together?

"Your Honour?"

"Mister Lundy, please answer the question."

The man sighs, takes a moment to gather himself. "Justin – " His lips pull momentarily to the side. A sad tic. Just saying his dead son's name is almost too much to bear. You can't fake that, can you?

Lundy swallows hard. "Justin was watching something on the homescreen when – "

"What was he watching?"

"Does it matter?" asks Rabinowitz.

"Details matter," counters the prosecutor.

Rabinowitz gives her a subtle nod and motions for Lundy to answer the question.

"It was that dog programme. That robotic dog."

"RoboPup?"

"Yes. That's it."

"I was cooking. I told him to get into the bath."

"What were you cooking?"

"Excuse me?" says Lundy.

"Relevance, your Honour?" says Rabinowitz.

"If you could stop interjecting," says the prosecutor, looking at the jury, "this won't go on longer than it needs to."

It's almost time to break for lunch. Everyone is hangry. No one wants this testimony to go on for a minute longer than it has to.

"It was stir-fry." Lundy seems puzzled by his own answer. It's probably because he can't imagine his previous life being so mundane, so simple. His main concern that night was probably getting dinner on the table and his son bathed and in his pyjamasuit before his wife came home. Now he's facing losing everything and spending a lifetime in the Crim Colony. He wilts in his chair. His lawyer gets his attention and signs something to Lundy. Something to wake him up.

All of a sudden he shifts gear, sits up straight. Blinks to clear his eyes. This is his last chance to convince the court that he's innocent. He swallows hard.

"Asian-style stir-fry, with water chestnuts," he says. "Butternut noodles. I even had those edible chopstix, you know. I thought Justin would think it was fun."

This is a glimpse of what Lundy was like before he lost his son: happy, hopeful. His wife holds a trembling, crumpled tissue to her eyes.

"I had to nag him to get into the bath. He loves that show."

The court is absolutely silent.

"Loved," says Lundy, clearing his throat. "He loved that show."

"Did you get angry with him?" asks the prosecutor.

"Angry? No."

"Are you sure?"

"Yes?"

"You don't sound certain."

"I wasn't angry with him."

"But he wasn't listening to you."

"Ja, but..."

"But?"

"Small kids are like that, you know."

"Like what?"

"You have to ask them a few times to do something. They're not robots."

"How many times did you have to ask him?"

"How many times? I don't know. Sometimes it's three times, sometimes it's ten."

"But that night. How many times?"

"I honestly don't know."

"If you had to give an answer."

"I don't know. Five times? Six?"

"So he was being disobedient."

"Not disobedient. Not really."

"He wasn't listening to you. And you got angry."

"That's not what happened."

"Do you have a temper, Mister Lundy?"

Lundy falters. He looks down. The answer is clear.

"Do you have a temper?" the prosecutor asks again.

"I..."

All three judges are looking at Lundy.

"Your Honour, will you please instruct the accused to – "

Lundy whispers something into his chest.

"Could you please repeat that?" says the crow.

"I have a temper."

"Louder, please?"

"I have a temper," he says.

The audience murmurs.

The prosecutor is filled with a new resolve. She strides across the room to address Lundy. "On the night of the fifteenth of August you lost your temper, didn't you?"

"Objection," says Rabinowitz.

"No," says Lundy, shaking his head, "No, I didn't."

"You got angry and you slammed your child's head against the lip of the bath."

"Objection!" shouts Lundy's lawyer.

People gasp at the idea, as if this is the first time they've heard it.

"The blow was enough to knock him out, and you left him to drown, face-down, in the water."

There is an uproar. Emotion propels onlookers from their benches, shock bleaches others' cheeks. Both lawyers shout over each other and all three judges bang their gavels for silence.

"I didn't," Lundy says, wilting again, and weeping. "I didn't. I would never."

"So?" says Keke. "Did he do it?"

She looks out onto the cityscape and takes a huge bite of her shamwich. Lab-fab ham and cashewmilk cheddar.

"How's your fake ham?" the suit asks.

His skin looks really good in the early afternoon light. Good lips, too.

"You're avoiding the question," she says. "And it's not 'fake'. It's lab-fab."

"That's what I said."

"Laboratory-fabricated meat has the identical chemical makeup of biological meat. It's not like it's…counterfeit," says Keke. "Molecule for molecule, it's exactly the same thing."

"But it's not, is it?"

"Not for the pig."

He laughs then covers his mouth, as if the joke has caught him off-guard. "Anyway. I'd rather be vegan than eat that modified shit."

"This *is* vegan," says Keke. "Kind of."

"You know what I mean."

"Cute."

"What's cute?"

"You. In your fifty-thousand rand suit. With principles and everything."

"You think I can't have principles just because I dress well?"

"I never said you dress well. I said you're wearing a fifty-thousand rand suit."

Keke sits back, puts her lace-up, knee-high boots on the seat of an empty chair, chugs half a bottle of coconut water then holds it to her chest. "Do you think he's guilty?"

"Lundy?"

"Who else?"

"I don't think the boy's death was an accident."

"Really? I've been thinking this whole time that he's innocent."

"That's exactly what he wants you to think. What his lawyer wants you to think. Lundy's a psychopath, and not in a good way."

"You get psychopaths…in a good way?"

"You know. World leaders. CEOs. Olympians."

"What makes them good?"

"Focus. Drive. Commitment. And that they don't kill anyone."

"He doesn't seem like a psycho."

"They never do."

"Well, some of them do."

"Which ones?"

"I don't know," she says. "The cheerful ones."

The man laughs. "The cheerful psychopath. That does sound ominous."

"Who are you?" asks Keke. "What's your name? Why the snappy suit? What are you doing here?"

"You'd make a good lawyer." He folds his ricepaper plate in on itself then rubs his fingerprints off the table top with his serviette.

"So would you. You're really good at avoiding questions."

CHAPTER 9

GRAM BY GRAM

Kate should be doing the laundry, or at the very least, switching on the hoover bot. Even clearing the breakfast plates would be a good start, but she doesn't have the energy. Since she's become a mom and stopped taking photo assignments, she's been at home, but she's resisted the slow suck of domestic duties. Kate is sure that if you hung enough washing or mopped enough floors, the job of housekeeping would vacuum out your brain entirely.

Of course, what she's doing now is on the same scale of zombie activity. Every muscle is at rest, apart from the hand she's using to shovel pretzel stix into her mouth and toggle the remote to switch streams. She's hardly blinking, either, as she scans the homescreen in front of her. It's the last episode of a series she's been binge-watching, and when the credits roll she's besieged by a roving purple haze. What will she watch now? It sends her into a kind of shallow mourning for the characters. She'll miss them.

A thought occurs to her, but she rejects it.

God, what has happened to you?

She scrolls along the streams to find something decent to watch. AI Olympics; underwater laser tag; reality porn.

Your life is fucking pathetic.

Kate pushes it away, but the seed of dissatisfaction has been planted.

She thinks back to when she was a photographer made reckless by ambition, travelling the world, chasing stories, winning awards. How she was creating content instead of this: this endless consumption of brain-atrophying bullshit. Consumption used to be the name of an illness. Was it TB? Something to do with breathing: gram by gram, a disease that slowly consumed you. Consumption is a different kind of sickness, now.

The disgust she feels for herself isn't, however, enough to lever her off the couch or to switch off the projection. Instead she just surfs with more fervour. She can, at the very least, find something edifying to watch.

There is a programme about a new kind of self-driving taxi. Still in beta testing, it's called a listening cab, nicknamed 'Turing', and there are only a few of them on the streets as part of a pilot programme. The cars eavesdrop on their passengers' conversations — not just their driving instructions — and learn the art of human interaction. They are taught the difference between just following orders and AE, or applied empathy. Kate watches with a mixture of fascination and dread. Keke and Seth make fun of her for being a technosaur but she's not, really. She's just slower to adopt certain technologies than they are. They were the first to run out and buy a SnapTile as soon as they became available in South Africa, while Kate is still happy with her Helix, despite its slowtech and diminishing battery life.

Artificial intelligence is a whole different enchilada. She's not one of those Chicken Littles who go around tweeting that the robots are going to kill us all, but at the same time, some of the stories she hears make her blood chink with ice-cubes. Just last week there was that game where the intelligence went rogue and built its own weapons — more sophisticated weapons than the programmers designed — and starting hunting down the players and killing them. Sure, it's only a game, but it's enough to make you wonder if real-life intelligence would ever do the same thing.

She's not the only one with reservations: the Gordhan Hospital started using AI surgeons and nursebots last year, and when an old pocket granny with advanced liver disease died on the table, people went crackers. Seth had said that "rednecked backwads" — fuck, she misses him already — throw their hands up when a robotic surgeon kills someone, but they don't take into account the number of human-led surgery deaths, which usually outnumber the former, and it's true. Those deaths don't make headlines.

Everyone's obsessed with AI nowadays. Even the nature broadcast stream is showing a documentary about that robotic rhino they're trialling in the Kruger National Park. He's a handsome beast, like some kind of animé version of a rhinoceros. The voiceover says that the technology was donated by China as reparation, and now the Nancies are cloning the real thing back from extinction, and the robot is tracking and protecting them from poachers. Kate yawns without covering her mouth and keeps scrolling.

She stops on *Channe! Woke*. Usually the programming is so crunchy it's practically granola: how to grow your own hydroponic organic sprouts from empty eggshells, how to make sun tea, ten different ways to compost — that kind of thing. But Maistre Lumin is on, and the show is called IN THE HOT SEAT so she puts down the remote and starts eating pretzel stix again.

"Maistre Lumin," says the interviewer. "With all due respect — "

Kate immediately sides with Lumin. She hates it when people use the phrase 'with all due respect'. A person who says 'with all due respect' inevitably says something offensive, so why the fraudulent warning?

"You can't honestly tell me that you think we shouldn't make use of the technology we have to stamp out diseases like cancer."

Lumin, as ever, is serene and cheerful. He's known as the white Xhosa-speaking spiritual sweetheart of South Africa and lives up to his reputation as being perennially unruffled. Kate's not interested in his spiritual shit, but she loves watching his gardening programme. She misses the urban jungle she used to have in her old flat in Illovo and watching Lumin double-dig and compost and prune is balm for her weary soul. The drought seems to have killed most of the country's roses, but Lumin designed his own water harvesters and has the lushest garden on the continent. He's always banging on about permaculture and how everyone should be growing something edible, even if it's just a pot of catnip on your windowsill. He's especially good with roses, and he has more than six hundred varietals in his elaborate rose maze at the Luminary. He has hounds and geese and rabbits and these golden secateurs that are his trademark in the celebrity gardening circuit; he says in every show how important it is to keep them super sharp. But this isn't his gardening show. It's some kind of debate with a man in a suit and bespoke tie. God, how Kate hates the bespoke tie fashion. Especially when those damn yuccies dye their beards to match.

The man continues, "We've managed to get rid of malaria, zika, lyme disease and HIV. We've decimated Rift Valley fever. Why do you think we should stop at cancer? We've been trying to find this cure for hundreds of years, and now that we have it, you don't want us to use it?"

Lumin smiles at the debater. "I have no problem with cures. I am happy about the cures."

"Forgive me, Maistre, but that doesn't seem to be the case."

"A vaccine that prevents the disease in the first place is excellent," Lumin says. "A cure is almost as good. But this gene drive tech is not that. Cancer crisping is a different thing, entirely."

"The chairman of the Bioethics Committee has expressed his support for the technology."

"Of course he has." His eyes twinkle.

Kate straightens her back and turns up the volume.

"Would you like to elaborate on that?"

There is a moment of hesitation. "No." Lumin laughs.

The host isn't sure what to say. He fingers his awful tie. "Please, help me to understand."

Lumin claps his hands in front of his chest. "It's as complicated and as simple as this: Gene drive technology is interfering with God's work."

Okay, you've just lost me there. Kate likes the man, but to bring a topic as old and dead as religion into this debate seems nonsensical. Besides, crisping has been around for a decade already. You could go to an underground black clinic and get your DNA segments hijacked for various outcomes.

"When you take human genes," says Lumin, sketching an invisible double-helix in the air with his strong hands, "and you edit out a small part of it — " He plucks out the imaginary piece. "That part is gone forever. Every subsequent generation will be missing that part. You can never put it back. *You can never put it back.* Do you understand the ramifications of that?"

The man hesitates, then gives a half-shrug. "No."

"Exactly," says Lumin, his eyes alight. "Nor do I! And that is my point. No one does."

"Then I assume that you are not a fan of AI." He smiles at the camera. It's kind of a joke. He's trying to lighten up the interview. There is a moment of silence.

"I beg your pardon?" says Lumin.

The host chuckles awkwardly. "I just meant… You're obviously not a fan of skinbots. Humanoids. Anthrobots."

Despite the man's obvious attempt at humour, Lumin's eye-sparkle falters for a moment. Then he zips on a matching fake smile, slaps the tops of his thighs, and chuckles.

"Well! That's a conversation for another day!"

CHAPTER 10

THE LOST ART OF SWIMMING

The Cape Republic, 2024

The self-driving taxi drops Seth off at the entrance to Nautilus.

"Thanks, Cabbie," he says, climbing out and closing the door after him. A ping in his Patch-ear lets him know that he's been billed for the ride. He'd love a coffee before the meeting, but he doesn't have time. He taps out some Snaffeine on his knuckle and snorts it instead. He can almost feel his pupils contracting.

Seth walks to the jetty at the water's edge where he spends a minute admiring the vast ocean. Was it the Atlantic, or the Indian? He can never remember. He's a city dweller, and the Cape Republic had never been more than a holiday destination to him. Or at least, the idea of someone else's holiday destination. Seth doesn't take holidays, and he hates beaches. He doesn't see the appeal of a day out to garner skin cancer. He finds the sand irritating, the water unpredictable. The snakewatch and locket footage of the Indo tsunami of 2022 was surely enough to put off even the most intrepid beach-goer. With all the weather tech that's available, you'd think the experts would have been able predict a wave gigantic enough to wash away entire islands and kill twenty-two thousand people. By the time the warning bumps were sent out, it was too late. There was nowhere to go. What were the Indonesian weather technicians doing? Playing Pachydon, perhaps, or watching the pirates that always hovered on their horizon.

The memory of the disaster unsettles him. He doesn't mind the idea of dying too much, but the kids are another story. They're small. They can't swim – who can, nowadays? There's something sad about that. The lost art of swimming. What bothers Seth is the idea of the helplessness he would feel with that wave coming, blasting everything in its path, when he has the twins with him. It's impossible to swim, holding a child. And even if he could, he'd have to choose one over the other.

This water is cold. You can tell by the surfers who are wearing their full climasuits. Cold water means hypothermia and Great Whites. The suits and smart surfboards repel the sharks now, but that is no reason to venture in.

Seagulls flap and cry above him. The air tastes like salt.

The Whale Coast, they call this strip. He thinks of Kate and the sad whale. 52Hz: No other whale can hear his frequency. For all he knows he's all alone in the deep dark sea.

Does everything always have to lead back to Kate? Is that what being a twin is about? Being trussed to another person for life just because you're almost identical, genetically-speaking? Usually their connection makes him feel secure; less alone in a lonely life. Fills up the space, as Kate likes to say, where his heart should be.

"Mister Denicker," says a clipped British voice behind him. Female and as smart as the Union Jack.

Seth turns around, and an astonishingly attractive woman smiles at him. Clear skin and eyes; her hair is a hundred shades of blue. He wonders if she is the kind of mermaid that lures sailors to their deaths. She's wearing a tailored lab coat with barnacles for studs, and a silver charm – a seahorse with an extravagant tail – around her neck. Seapunk.

"I'm so glad you could make it. Thank you for coming. I'm Arronax." Her accent is as sexy as hell.

"I'm still not exactly sure – " he starts, but she puts her hand on his arm and leads him towards the access path. Nautilus has, in the past, proven impossible to investigate. The hacktivist Truther organisation he used to belong to tried for years to infiltrate the place, but without an invitation from the head of the corp it was clear that no one was getting in.

"The entrance is this way," she says. "I'm sure you'll find the work very exciting."

CHAPTER 11
ESCAPE

The jurors are led out of the main court house and into the adjoining admin building. It's time to examine the proof. The suit sticks close to Keke: a self-appointed companion, an undercover bodyguard. Keke doesn't dislike it.

They are briefed on what to expect from the virtual reality evidence experience then, one by one, they're called by their numbers to go through to the Immersion Room. Some jurors opt out of the experience. It will no doubt be traumatic and barbed with triggers. She is called last, and the administrator hands Keke a pair of visigogs which she puts on. They ping as they sync with her Patch. The administrator vanishes and she finds herself transported back in time: standing in a family bathroom while a toddler pours grey soapy water from one jug to another. He has hazelnut hair, matching eyes. He's talking to himself and playing so sweetly that Keke can't imagine him being disobedient. There's a large mirror on the wall, but when Keke looks at it, her reflection is not there.

She can smell cooking, hear the hiss of frying next door. When she pops her head around the door she sees Lundy standing at the stove, humming to the neoclassical music and shaking a wok of sizzling vegetables. The instakettle tweets. As Keke steps back into the bathroom, the boy is trying to climb out. He has one foot on the lip of the bath and a jug in each hand, so when he slips, he can't grasp onto anything to break his fall, and he bangs his head on the way down, toppling face-forward and unconscious into the shallow water. The sounds from the kitchen mask the sound of his tumble. His last breath bubbles up in the murky water, and his small body is still. Keke knows it's a simulation, but she steps forward to save him, anyway. When she reaches to pull him out of the water her hand just disappears. She tries again and the same thing happens.

There is a buzzing and the bathroom vanishes, as if she has messed up her part and someone has yelled 'cut!'. She pulls off the goggles. The administrator comes back into sight.

"Are you okay?" he asks.

"I'm sorry," says Keke. "I know it's not real, but — "

She feels off-balance.

"Just because it's virtual, doesn't mean it's not real," says the man, tucking a lock of hair behind his ear. She can tell he's a complete VXR-head. Perfect person for the job.

"I know I'm not supposed to...participate," she says.

"It's not a problem. Homocide first-timers *always* try to save the vic. It would be weird if you didn't."

She looks around at the blank room.

"Only one juror today didn't try to save the boy. Suffice to say, I wouldn't want to be stuck with *him* in a dark alley, if you know what I mean."

Keke's mouth is dry.

"You can still opt out," he says, "if it's too much for you."

"No. I'm fine. I'm ready to go back in." She puts her gogs back on.

"The next scenario is a lot more disturbing," he says. "You don't have to do it."

Keke takes a breath. "I'll do it."

Once again, Keke is in the bathroom. The toddler is in his own world, splashing and chirupping to himself. Again, she looks in the mirror which is empty of her reflection. She smells and hears the cooking. But this time, when she looks around the corner, Lundy throws down his utensil and storms right towards her, his face red with rage. He walks right through her and stops on the wet bathmat.

"Damn it, Justin," he says through gritted teeth. "I've told you five times already to get out of the bath!"

The boy, startled, looks up at him, drops his jugs in fright.

"Look at all this water on the floor! You *know* you're not supposed to wet the floor!"

"Sorry, Daddy," says the pale-lipped boy. He starts to get up, but Lundy smacks him hard across the face. The boy spins, falls, and the father stalks out, not seeing the boy hit his head on the top of the bath and end up in the water. Lundy switches off the stove and slumps at the kitchen table. Puts his face in his hands, tries to gather himself. Talks himself down from his fury; he spends a minute cooling down while his son drowns in the next room.

"Escape," says Keke, and the simulscene disappears.

Admin is there, in his empty room. "You okay?"

Keke nods.

"So those were the two scenarios. You get to decide which you think is true, or more true, anyway, than the other."

She nods again.

"Now you'll go back one more time, but to the empty house, *post event*. The crime scene. You get to poke around."

"Okay," says Keke.

"You'll see some transparent icons on the side of your vision. If you want to listen to any of the testimony again, just tap in."

With a ping, Keke is back at the house. This is how it looked when the police arrived. Dinner still on the stove, congealed and long cold. Four fingers of water still in the bath. A puddle on the floor. Keke walks around, not sure what to look for. The victim's pyjamas — RoboDog — sit neatly on a chair, never again to be filled with a small boy's just-bathed body.

"Shit," she says under her breath. "Shit." She'll never, ever get that image out of her head.

Keke goes back to the bathroom. How is she supposed to know which scenario holds more truth? She taps on the icons and they zoom into a window on her main visual: clips of the testimony, still pictures, objects of interest.

She taps on video clips and listens to Lundy's wife, sobbing at the stand.

"He would never, he would *never*," she's saying, overwrought with emotion.

She clicks on the nanny, Mirriam Maila, who has maintained throughout the trial that Lundy was nothing but a dedicated and loving father to his son. When asked about his temper, she seems surprised. Raises her eyebrows at the camera, shows us her generous brown eyes: "I've never seen him angry. Not even once."

There are hours and hours of Lundy's testimony. Keke scrolls through to the most recent clips.

"Let us talk for a moment about negligence," says the prosecutor.

"Negligence?" says Lundy.

"The fact that you left your child in the bath on his own."

"He's almost four years old," says Lundy. "I was cooking dinner."

"The WHCP recommends you supervise bathing children at all times. Children under seven."

"I know, but — "

"Justin was a toddler."

"It was so shallow, it was safe — "

"And yet he drowned," says the prosecutor. She's off-camera. Keke still imagines her as a crow.

"It was a freak accident," says Lundy. "Never in a million years would I — "

"Ah," she says. "So you admit that the chances of a child slipping and drowning in ten centimetres of water is extremely unlikely."

"Well — "

"So, basically, the scenario proposed by your defence attorney is virtually impossible."

Lundy stutters an unintelligible reply.

Keke scrubs through the next fifteen minutes.

"If it pleases the court, the prosecutor would like to admit the following document into evidence."

The judges nod, call the crow up to the bench. An icon pulsates — a document — so Keke taps it and it opens in a new leaf adjacent to the video clip. It's a hospital record. She swipes through it. Pictures of bruises, stitched-up skin and an arm in plaster.

"2022. A dislocated collarbone. 2023. A fractured wrist. Lacerated forehead. 2024: twenty-fourth of January — just a few months ago — a broken arm, two fractured ribs, and a contusion to the head."

"I know how it looks, but he was an energetic boy. He was always in the wars."

"He only seemed to be 'in the wars' when he was under your care."

"I didn't wrap him up in cottonwool. I didn't coddle him. Although, now — " His voice breaks.

"Cottonwool is one thing. But a broken arm? Ribs?"

Lundy clears his throat, tries to pull himself together. "He fell off the roof."

"He fell off the *roof?*"

"His bedroom is upstairs. The attic. I don't know how he got out of that window."

"Ah. *Another* freak accident."

"It was burglar-proofed, for Net's sake."

Lundy's lawyer rises. "Objection. Relevance, your Honours?"

"Mister Lundy is clearly a negligent parent!"

"Mister Lundy is not on trial for negligence."

"The hospital record goes to prove that the man is not the careful, loving father that he or his wife makes him out to be." The pitch of the crow's caw rises. "In addition, he has admitted that he has a temper, and that the scenario set out by his defence team is implausible."

Keke scrolls to the end and closes the clip. Opens the nanny's testimony again.

"I've never seen him angry," Mirriam says. Keke thinks she's telling the truth.

"I would've heard him if he was shouting," she says. "It was my night off, but I was right next door."

This clip isn't from the courtroom. It's inside the Lundy home. The lounge, the night of the incident.

"You're a live-in nanny, correct?" asks the off-camera investigator.

"Yes. My room is right there," she says, gesturing. She keeps rubbing her wrist. A nervous tic. "There was no shouting. Not until he found — " Tears cut off her sentence. She holds the back of her hand to her nose.

"Excuse me!" she cries. "I just need a minute." She gets up off the couch, and the camera cuts. According to the timestamp, she's back a few moments later, eyes swollen. She has a box of tissues.

Keke stops the video, pushes its icon back to the sidebar. She looks around the bathroom again. Checks the depth of the water. The towels on the rail are skew. She averts her eyes from the pyjamas. There is a metallic glimmer on the floor, next to the bath mat. She tries to focus on it to see what it is, but can't make it out. Goes closer, bends down, gets on her knees, but it disappears. She gets up again, takes a step back, and there it is again, but she can't see what it is. Probably nothing. Probably a glitch in the VR, but she'll ask about it, anyway.

CHAPTER 12

THE SOUND OF THE SEA

Kate's waiting for the kids to come home from school. It makes her nervous, not having them within touching distance. The clockologram ticks slowly. She'll have to do something while she waits, something constructive, to stop herself from going mad. It's always a push-pull instinct with the kids. When they're here and being cretinous she looks for ways to outsource them – get them away from her and out of the house. Yet, as soon as they're gone, the house is too quiet, and she has this unsettling feeling of them not existing at all, and has this desperate need to get them back.

Maybe she'll cook dinner. She opens the door to the fridge but it's close to empty. She has a flashback of James, five years ago, walking into their old flat in Illovo, groceries toppling from his synthetic burlap bags. Fresh fruit and vegetables, seedbread, beetroot jam, almond butter. She'd kiss him and call him Marmalade. Kiss his beautiful SPF100 skin. He was so goddamn wholesome – too good to be true. And, of course, in the end, it *was* too good to be true. He had been haunted by his demons just like everybody else; he'd just been better at hiding them.

Kate shakes him out of her head and closes the fridge door. She'll order something for dinner. It's so old-fashioned now, anyway, to cook anything from scratch. Who is she, to buck the trend? She is perfectly happy with mass-produced meals drone-delivered from Bilchen. They taste great and contain the perfect amount of nutrients and kilojoules, which she can't always claim as true for the food she cooks. If she lived alone she'd have toaster waffles for dinner six nights a week. She taps the screen on her fridge to order. The Bilchen face smiles and bats eyelashes at her. Kate chooses between Italian, Indian, Greek, South African, or Japanese cuisine. Then she chooses her protein and her carb. The app knows her body type and height, her ideal weight, and the amount of exercise she's done today by syncing with her Helix. It portions accordingly. The same goes for the kids and Sebongile. What Kate really feels like eating is a tub of proper cane-sugar Darkoco ice cream, but she wouldn't know where to begin tracking it down. Sugar has been semi-banned for almost two years now, much to her chagrin. Fizzy drinks were the first to go. Blunt in, sugar out. How the tables have turned. At least the toking fringe-dwellers are happy.

She does have a small stash of chocolate bars left over from before the sucrose ban, but she only dips into it in emergencies. Does her current state of mind warrant a CaraCrunch chocolate bar? They're getting old now, and the chocolate is developing a white patina, so she shouldn't really leave them for too much longer. She turns to walk to her bedroom, but hears something, and stops.

A sound coming from the kids' room, even though they're not yet home from school. Remembering that she needs to take the batteries out of Silver's haunted Bébébot, Kate gets the screwdriver case from the top cupboard in the scullery. She lingers over the toolbox and has a flash of a memory: James with a nail between his lips, hammering another one into the wall. Using his old tools always makes her feel purple. She closes the lid and makes her way to the twins' room. She's sure that she must look deranged, standing at the doorway, head cocked, with a sharp tool in her hand. A scary silhouette, waiting for the baby to cry.

It doesn't make her wait long.

"Mama," comes a wail from Silver's side of the room, then a sad whimpering. It sounds so real. It sends her tumbling back in time to when she was trapped in the Genesis clinic at the mercy of the doctor. When the psychopath had handed a baby to her. Their baby. Not of her womb, but of her and Marmalade's blood. Their DNA-printed boy. Their Mally.

Damn it. Damn it, Kate. You've got to pull yourself out of that toxic memory fog. You need to get over it and if you can't do it for yourself then do it for the kids.

"Mama," comes a voice from behind her, and she almost jumps through the roof in fright. It's Mally, with his big green-blue eyes. Her eyes. The sound of the sea.

"Jesus," she says, screwdriver flattened to her heart. "You scared me."

"Who's Jesus?" pipes Silver, trailing in after her brother. Her not-quite brother.

They're still wearing their character-themed backpax: blue RoboPup for Mally and pink KittyBot for Silver. The nanny is right behind them, laden with their artwork and baking projects, and she smiles when she sees Kate. She seems happy to see her awake and showered but then she registers the screwdriver at her chest and looks puzzled. Kate quickly whips it behind her back and grins, realising as she does so that it must make her look more suspicious, not less.

"How was school?"

"Mally's teacher wants to know why he insists on learning his numbers in colours. Says it's confusing the other kids."

"Er – "

"And they said to not send Silver to school when she has a runny nose."

On cue, Silver sniffs and wipes her nose with the back of her hand.

"Last week they complained that she was absent too often and risked falling behind. Can you believe it? She's three. Have you ever heard of a three-year-old falling behind?"

The nanny shrugs. "Don't shoot the postman."

"Who *is* Jesus?" asks Mally.

"That's a conversation for another day," says Sebongile, pulling a funny face at Kate. She puts her hands on their shoulders and steers them gently towards the bathroom. Bongi is fastidious about hand washing. Silver, who was conceived and born biologically, catches colds regardless. Mally has never been sick in his life.

Kate resisted hiring a nanny for the first two years of the twins' lives. She had suffered for so long with infertility that she couldn't imagine getting someone else to look after them. She wanted to experience every first moment: words, steps, bites. She wanted to be there for all of it. She stopped working and immersed herself completely in motherhood. Part of it was her way of withdrawing from the world; a product of her PTSD. Back then there was no way she'd trust her kids with a stranger, not after what happened to her.

But it hadn't been good for her. Slowly, Seth had introduced the idea. Sebongile used to be a SurroSister: a young, single woman who volunteered to assist infertile couples to have children when South Africa's fertility crisis was at its worst. Without them, the country's birthrate would have cliffed to zero. When the crisis ended, the demand for surrogates dropped off, the baby boom exploded, and the need for nannies ramped up. It was a natural conclusion that the discarded SurroSisters would become nannies. Not just any nannies, but the very best nannies you could get: pre-approved in every category: criminal; medical; psychological. The surrogate badges gave way to small legacy 'SS' brooches: copper pins they would wear over their hearts.

At first they just hired Sebongile to look after the toddlers for an hour while they went for a coffeeberry freezo in the resident restaurant, three storeys below, and watched her via the multiple Gimlet nanny cams. Soon it became clear that the perennially sunny Sebongile was good for everyone, and so she became a regular babysitter, then a live-out nanny, then, last year, she moved into the nannypad next door. Now she is the twins' best friend, and Kate can't imagine life without her. Every now and then Kate is tempted to ask her about her surrogate experiences, but Bongi is a private person, so she respects that.

The Bilchen drone hums outside the delivery window in the lounge. It lands expertly on its platform and sounds its greeting. Kate opens the latch and takes the food, and her ear pings with the receipt. She feels foolish for always instinctively wanting to say thank you to the machine, or give it a tip. Old habits die hard. One day soon the kids will be rolling their eyes at how very old-tech their mother is. Until then, she'll try to at least act cool.

"Can we get a dog?" Mally asks this every day, without fail.

They're all at the table, eating black mushroom burgers, with sides of sweet potato chips and deep-fried broccoli stalks.

"We've got a dog," says Kate. "Betty/Barbara."

Mally screws up his nose. "She's old. And snorey."

"And stinky," says Silver, making them both giggle. It's true. Betty/Barbara does have a particularly fierce flatulence problem.

"So what?" says Kate. "Are you going to want to replace me too? When I'm old and stinky?"

Mally laughs with his mouth open, showing Kate his half-chewed food. Silver's smile has vanished. Perhaps it's never occurred to her that Kate will be gone one day.

Mally, on the other hand, is not put off. "A robotic dog doesn't stink and you don't have to feed him and he doesn't need to be walked and no vet's bills."

But then what's the point?

"And he doesn't poo," says Mally.

"Well." Kate takes a sip of her wine. "There is that."

"When's Seth coming home?" asks Silver. She separates all the elements of food on her plate before she starts to eat. She doesn't like the flavours to touch.

"I don't know," says Kate. "Soon."

"I miss him," says Mally.

"So do I," says Kate. "But he won't be gone long."

The nanny pats Silver on the hand, winks at her. Kate's sure Silver is her favourite, although she's careful to not let it show.

"My favourite colour is orange juice," announces Mally.

Silver puts her white serviette over her head.

"I'm a gho-o-o-st," she says. "I'm a gho-o-o-o-st."

She does it every night, but it still makes them laugh.

"Mom," says Mally. "Tell me something I used to do as a baby."

"What? Why?"

"Just because."

"Have the other kids been saying something to you?"

"What?"

"Have they been saying something about you…when you were a baby?"

Sebongile looks away, as if she's not listening to the conversation. As if it's too personal.

Mally frowns.

"Okay," says Kate. "As a baby you used to… I don't know. You walked at nine months. Which is really early for a baby."

"That's nice."

"You talked early too. You did everything early."

Silver looks put out. Already, she knows she is the weaker of the two.

"It's 'cos I'm older than Silver," he says. He's eaten everything but the broccoli.

"Not by much," says Kate. "A few months."

"Am I always going to be bigger than Silver?"

"No," says Kate.

Silver cheers up.

Mally stares at her. "Not unless you eat your vegetables."

Suddenly her Patch starts pinging wildly and the Helix on her wrist buzzes. Three bumps in a row from three different news agencies. Something big has happened.

CHAPTER 13

FAHRENHEIT451

Marko's leaves fade to draw his attention to his beeping main screen. He guesses it's his health monitor telling him it's time to take a break: to stand up and walk around for a few minutes, but instead, when he reads the tickertape, it's a big news story. Where is Keke? She'll be so bleak to miss out on this.

The screen cleaves to show him different videos of what's being reported. He taps on one and sees a man in a black hooded robe and a Jesus Christ mask shooting at people outside a building. He has some kind of automatic shotgun. Russian? It looks like it could be a sawn-off Saiga. Marko's knowledge of weaponry is mostly gleaned from his gaming, so he's never quite sure if the guns exist IRL. Not unlike his games, the screen is a mess of screaming and blood spatter – a violent animation replete with motion capture and breathing arcs. Only it's not a game.

The terrorist's not acting alone: Marko watches the other witnesses' clips and recognises the robed attackers as they enter the clinic and mow down patients and medical staff. A pregnant woman is dragged away by her hair.

TERROR ATTACK, shout the headlines. FAMILY PLANNING CLINIC RAZED BY RESURRECTORS. Over thirty people killed, scores injured: doctors, nurses, patients.

The distinctive JC face masks and flowing hooded robes of superblack arachnasilk make the terrorists easy to identify and almost impossible to kill. The synthetic silk is produced by splicing the spider silk gene into silkworms, resulting in a thread tougher than steel and more flexible than kevlar. The masks have built-in night vision. The terrorists also have animarks – moving tattoos – of a revolving crucifix on their necks. A bold symbol of their commitment to their cause.

The Resurrectors started making news around seven years ago, but they've never been this brazen or bloodthirsty before. They began as a Christian extremist group, firebombing any individual or organisation that 'disrespected Jesus' in any way. Keke had almost been killed when they blew up the Echo.news building. She had been freelancing for them at the time, working late one night, and had missed the blast by minutes. The chief editor at the time knew it would be a risk to run the satirical cartoon about a zombie Jesus (raised from the dead, eating communion flesh) but he did it anyway. He had been a Hebdo fan. *Je suis Charlie.*

The Resurrectors' love of violence soon overtook their love of their God, and they were no longer guided by the Old Testament but by their paranoid delusions of "Rapture" and "Doomsday". They began to use any excuse to terrorise South Africans. No one called them extremist Christians anymore, despite their spinning cross logo. They just became The Resurrectors, terrorists, feared by all.

And they were gaining momentum: Last week they burned down the Sandton Library because it refused to remove the books that the group had asked them to. *Harry Potter, The Perks of Being a Wallflower* and *The Satanic Verses* were just some of the titles they believed were corrupting peoples' minds. When they were refused, they planted a practically invisible incendiary device in seven different books for the seven different storeys and set them off that evening while the restaurant patrons at the square below watched in horror. The bombs lit up the sky and not a book was saved.

As a complete Bradbury fanboy, Marko had decided then that he wanted to do something to stop them. He'd never stand up to them in real life, of course. They are mostly tall, vicious, highly trained people, and he is, well, he's cuddly around the middle and generally soft-spoken. But his anonymity as a hacker is ironclad. He's so anonymous, he brags to Keke, that it would take the CCU nothing less than a year to find him, by which time he'd be eighteen months ahead of them, having revolved his online identity hundreds of thousands of times. So while he'll never dream of approaching a Resurrector in person, he's certain he can do a significant amount of damage from the safety of his dim room.

He sends a bump to FlowerGrrl, Seth's contact at F0X, the hacktivist Alba splinter group.

Fahrenheit451 > Seen the news? They're getting out of control. I'm ready to do something. I'm officially checking in for duty.

CHAPTER 14

A SKELETON OF GOLD

The Cape Republic, 2024

They make their way to the entrance of Nautilus. The spiral seashell-shaped sandy building blends in with the surrounding dunes and black rocks, and is surrounded by inviswall. The security guards are wearing the same colour, and Seth jolts when one of them breaks his camouflage to open the gate for them. Once they're in the lobby, a female guard guides Seth to the X-ray machine to check that he's not carrying a weapon or any kind of recording device. She shines a little torch into each eye, then with an expert move, clicks his SnapTile off his wrist and places it in a safe.

"I need that," he says.

"You'll get it back." She doesn't smile.

His host, along with a barrel-chested ginger-bearded guard called Carson, leads him to the glass elevator. The touchscreen offers them the choice of ten floors, except that they're not called 'floors' but 'leagues', and are numbered 0 to 10,000. A moving graphic of a Kraken – the mythical giant octopus-like sea monster – reaches out to touch the ten buttons with its tentacles. It's a beautiful, nuanced piece of Japanimation. The elevator shuttles towards the ocean then falls quickly to their selected league: 4,000, and they are indeed beneath the sea. The view of the water on the other side of the superglass turns from cerulean to midnight blue.

So, it's true.

He's heard rumours of Nautilus being an underwater sea lab, but none of his research could confirm it. For all anyone knows, it was just a high-tech house built on the rocky dunes. His stomach falls along with the elevator, then the doors slide, soundlessly, open.

The lab is cavernous, all white and glass and water. For a second it reminds him of the underground Genesis lab and the hairs on the back of his neck stand up. A school of silver fish swims by the ocean wall. They dart in synchronised bursts. Carson stands at the door while Arronax uses a spray to sanitise her hands, then motions for Seth to take a seat at the infinity table.

A robotic salamander the size of a domesticated cat crawls past.

"That's Meadon," says Arronax, smoothing her purple-blue-aqua hair down and away from her face. "One of our first successful builds. He's our mascot."

"He's old," says Seth, inspecting the creature's 3D printed bones, electrical circuit, and motorised joints.

"We became quite attached. Couldn't bear the thought of killing him just because the tech advanced."

"Hello, Meadon," says Seth.

The creature slinks over to a nearby tank and slides in, swimming away effortlessly.

"We created him when we were studying vertebral columns and spinal cords. He informed a lot of our work on cyprosthetics."

"He likes swimming," says Seth, amused.

"Yes. So…it's not a lost art for everyone."

Seth stares at her.

"You were – " he starts.

"I was reading your thoughts when you were out there. I apologise. It's my psychic-switch. It's part of our security procedure."

"But…how?"

"It's not something I can discuss. Not yet, anyway. I'm sorry about the intrusion. I'm sure you're aware of how careful we have to be. I've deactivated it now."

"How do I know that's true?"

Her lips twitch. "You don't."

Seth crosses his arms.

"We're under a constant threat here, as you can imagine," she says. "The programmes we run: they're ahead of even the most cutting-edge research out there. Some of them can be seen as…controversial."

Seth knows. That's why he agreed to come.

"I'll get straight to the point. We need your expertise on a specific project." She places her hands on the white table that separates them. "There's an extremely small pool of specialists on our Trust List and you came the most highly recommended."

This doesn't surprise Seth. He's the best chemgineer in the country.

Meadon hops out of the water on the other side of the lab and hunkers down on a terrycloth bed.

"He's like a dog," says Seth.

"Better than a dog," says Arronax. "Less mess. But if you're a dog-person – " Her nose wrinkles at this. "I must show you our latest K9000. It is an extraordinary animal. We developed it for the veterinary science institutions so that the students could practise their surgeries, but everyone involved in the pilot programme fell in love with the things and wanted to adopt them."

Mally would go nuts for a K9000. He'd pretty much been nagging for a petbot since he was born. Well, not *born*. Since he was –

Arronax blinks at him, and he stops himself from thinking of the kids. "So that's what you guys do? Robotic animals?"

"Bionicreatures are just an offshoot of our main work."

"Which is?"

She smiles. "Perhaps, Mister Denicker – "

"Call me Seth."

"Perhaps we can have a comprehensive briefing in the future, but for now, let's stick to the project we asked you here to assist with. We're on a hard deadline."

They've certainly paid him enough. Business-class flights and one hundred thousand Blox for a 24-hour contract. Seth puts his elbows on the table and leans in. "I'm all ears."

A keyboard of sorts appears in front of Arronax – a few buttons of blue light. She taps one to bring up a 3D hologram and a jellyfish appears, swimming with stilted movements. Something about it is odd.

"2010. Our first robotic jellyfish." She taps another button and the jellyfish morphs into a small transparent sea animal following a flashing light through water. It's the size of a ten rand coin and flashes something metallic at them.

"2016. A biohybrid sting-ray."

"Biohybrid? Like, cyborg?"

"Essentially, yes, but technically it's the other way around. While a cyborg is smartificial – an animal with a bionic adaptation – a biohybrid is a synthesised animal with a biological addition."

"Biotech, brought to life. Artificial life."

"Layers of soft silicone printed with cardiomyocytes – mouse heart cells – in a serpentine pattern. The cells are genetically engineered to contract when light hits them – "

"Which propels the ray forward."

"Yes."

"Is that a – " Seth pinches the screen open, zooming in. " – metallic spine?"

"A skeleton of gold. Elastic gold. It stores energy."

Seth looks at her. A gold skeleton? Why does that sound familiar? Where has he heard that before? It nags at the edge of his thoughts. He sits back in his chair. "It's very pretty, but what's the endgame?"

She seems pleased he's asked. "That's why you're here."

Another button, another image fades over. It's an invisible heart, and then it all makes sense.

"You're engineering tissue," says Seth. "Human hearts."

"We're almost at the finish line. It's taken sixteen years, and we're on track to push this to market by December."

"Just in time for the Christmas rush."

Arronax ignores his flippancy. "That is, on track, apart from one thing, which I'm hoping you can help us with."

"Push it to market? So, you're going to sell them?"

"Of course we're going to sell them. There's a huge demand. The infertility epidemic wiped out a whole potential generation of young, healthy organ donors."

"Why a synthetic heart? You can get those bacon hearts nowadays, can't you? Those human hearts grown in pig chimeras."

Oinkubators, the press liked to call them.

"Epi-hearts are not acceptable to everyone. A biohybrid heart arrives at the patient brand new, with no history. No baggage. It's seen as an upgrade, instead of a leftover. This is more pleasing to our clientele."

"Your wealthy clientele."

"Nautilus is a business, Mister Denicker."

"Sure." Seth stretches his arms above his head. Of course it is. He didn't think it wasn't, not when they're paying him so much bank – money that he hasn't refused or donated to charity. He just misses Alba. Misses biopunking. Doing grind that matters.

"This work matters," she says. "You'll be saving lives."

"You said you turned the psychic-switch off."

"Sorry," she says.

Seth can tell she's not in the least bit sorry. He needs to be careful of what he thinks in front of her. Already he's given too much away.

"Okay," he says. "Tell me what I need to do."

CHAPTER 15

THE DANDY LION

Johannesburg, 2024

Kate sits down at The Six Leafed Clover. The table is some kind of scrubbed timber and the couch feels like it's made from mushroom leather. It always makes her think of that dumb old joke.

Why did the mushroom get invited to all the parties?

Because he's a fungi!

Her Patch tells her that Keke is right behind her – or rather, just below her – parking her e-bike in the revolving parking lot. The Clover is a new concept bistro that serves edible weeds. Organic, aeroponic, self-sustaining, zero-import, carbon-negative, vertical-farming weeds. The idea doesn't appeal to Kate at all but Keke wants to try it, perhaps write a story on it, so she's agreed. Kate won't say this out loud, but it seems Kekeletso had lost her appetite for more substantial stories since Genesis. In a way it makes her feel better – less weak? – that she isn't the only one to have lost her nerve.

The waitbot scurries over to her, but doesn't slow down in time, and knocks the table, causing the bottle of miso to fall over and stain the hemp tablecloth. Kate waits for it to apologise, but then realises it's a mute. Some servbots are programmed to talk, but it opens up a slew of complications when people assume the machine can understand any command just because it can act on simple verbal instructions. The robot reverses a safe distance from the table and projects its holoscreen menu at her. At least there are pictures of what the dishes look like, or she'd have no idea what she's ordering. The pack shots are vivid: 4D and revolving, as if you can just pluck one of the plates off the hologram and put it on the table. She swipes over to the drinks menu. Twenty different kinds of weed coolteas and shakes. God, she hopes there is alcohol available. She swipes to the next page and finds it – elderflower wine, Chickweed Chaser, a shooter called The Wild Amaranth. She decides on the house cocktail, and taps the picture of the Dandy Lion, twice. The bot spins around and heads to the bar to collect them.

"Kitty!" shouts Keke from the other side of the restaurant, causing patrons to turn around and look at her. She has never been good at volume control. Some of the people look away again, some don't. They're both used to the stares. Kate stands, hugs her friend. Kisses her on the cheek. Warm leather and spice and all things nice. They didn't see each other as often as they would like, but when they do, it's as if they've never parted ways.

"I can't believe you made me come here," says Kate. "They do literally only serve weeds."

"Ha! What did you expect?"

"I don't know. A few wild daisies as garnishes. A clover salad."

"No such luck," she says, and sits down. "But please tell me they're licensed?"

As if in response, the waitbot zooms over with their cocktails.

A few drinks later, they're giggling like schoolgirls.

"This weed booze is crack," says Keke. "I'll be back here tomorrow."

"I won't!" says Kate. She had the Wakame noodles with deep-fried crickets and it almost made her hurl. The texture of both foods sent her synaesthesia into overdrive; it was like trying to swallow an animated cactus. Keke, on the other hand, was more adventurous and ordered steamed larvae dumplings with purslane pesto. The pesto was delicious.

"But, yes," Kate says. "The elderberry gin is especially good."

They chink glasses.

"You're feeling better?" asks Keke.

"Not really."

"Still having the panic attacks?"

"Panic attacks. Insomnia. Nightmares. And you know what my nightmares are like. Hyper-realistic."

"They have drugs for that, you know."

"I know! Seth keeps trying to push them on me. Drugs to stop you dreaming. What next?"

Keke seems amused. "Well, if there's anyone who knows his spike, it's Seth." She gets a kind of warm, sexy look in her eyes when she talks about him. Kate's not sure she likes it.

"It's not so much that I can't sleep. It's more that I...don't want to sleep."

"You're still having those bad dreams about James?"

"About James, about Van der Heever. That man who tried to bury us at the flower farm. The one we – " She gulps down the rest of the sentence as she's assailed by the memory of his face skinned by the broken glass. "And… Mouton."

Keke shudders, touches Kate's arm.

"I don't know what's wrong with me."

Kate feels sweaty under Keke's scrutiny. She takes away her arm, swats perspiration from her lip, her eyebrows.

"There's nothing wrong with you."

"There is. How come *you* don't have PTSD? What they did to you was just as bad as what they did to me. You almost *died.*"

"We *all* almost died."

"Why, then? Why don't you get the panic attacks?"

Keke takes a sip of her drink, shrugs. "I don't know. I was semi-conscious when the bad shit went down. I couldn't take it all in. Not like you. You experience everything in scented super-def hypercolour. I mean, a walk down the road must be traumatic for you."

Kate blinks at her. It's not untrue.

Her Helix buzzes and Keke's eyebrows shoot up.

"It's not what you're thinking," says Kate.

"Damn. Thought you may be getting a booty call."

"Hell, no. Those days are over."

"Those days are over? My God, woman, no wonder you're depressed. Who on earth is bumping you at this time of night, then? The nanny?"

"It's not a bump. It's my phone telling me that I'm over the limit."

"Then your phone kind of is your nanny."

"Ja. Good point."

Keke tops up her glass. "What are you going to do?"

"Switch it off."

"So, talking of sexy time -" says Kate, ordering another bottle. "How's Marko?"

Keke licks her teeth. "As good as ever."

"How is his cyber-what-what working out?" Kate points vaguely to her eyes to show what she means.

"He loves it, I hate it."

"Why?"

"His lens isn't like mine, you know. It's not a simple BioLens, it's cybernetic. It's permanent. It's connected."

"So what does that mean?"

"It means a lot of things, right? Cool things. Like he can search The Net for anything at any time. He can type out shit and order groceries while he's in the shower."

"That *is* handy. What's not to like?"

"He's perennially distracted! It's like he's never just *there* with me. Like we're never alone. I'll be talking to him about Nina and he'll be nodding, but I can see he's not really listening. But the thing that bothers me the most – "

"Yes?"

"Let me put it this way. I make him cover it up when we do the diggety."

"Because it takes pictures?"

"Because it records everything."

"But it's not like anyone can download it."

"I don't care."

"But – "

"I don't care. You know how these things work. One day you're the only one with access to it and the next day it's on Reverber8.tv for the world to see."

"You have a point."

"I'm not going to be *that* person. That gets famous from a kinky sex clip."

"You're famous already. Wait... You could always wear one of your face masks. While you – "

"I think I'm done with the masks."

"Really? What happened?"

"A guy I met. At the trial."

"You're still polyamorous? I thought you and Marko – "

"Marko knows that the day I have to be monogamous is the day I kick my own bucket."

"Fair enough," says Kate.

"That said, I'm not shagging the new guy."

"Not yet," says Kate.

"I actually thought of introducing him to *you*."

"Oh, no." Kate shakes her head. "No thanks. Not interested."

"He's as handsome as fuck," says Keke. "Intelligent. Funny. Rich."

"Still not interested. I can't even deal with myself at the moment, never mind someone else."

"Maybe he can help you with that. Sex is extremely therapeutic, you know. There have been studies."

Kate sighs, wonders if the bags under her eyes look as heavy as they feel.

"You don't even have to date him. Or talk to him. You could just have sex."

"Charming."

"What?"

"It's not going to happen."

Kate leans on the table, hand on forehead.

"So…you make Marko cover his eyes when you have sex?"

"Just the one."

"Just the one? Like, an eye patch? That *is* kinky."

"It's like making love to a pirate."

"Aaarr," growls Kate.

The servbot presents the bill on its holodash. Kate taps 'pay' and her Patch beeps with the receipt.

"You wanted to tell me something," she says.

Keke pulls on her jacket. Musk. A soft breeze of brown hide. Tan Billow.

"Did I?"

"I got the idea it was about the trial. You said you had just adjourned for the day when you called – "

"Right," she says. "Look, I'll tell you straight up you're not going to like this idea."

"But…you're going to tell me anyway."

"But I'm going to tell you anyway."

They leave the restaurant and head towards the street.

"Share a cab?" says Kate.

"No way I'm taking Nina out after drinking that weed booze."

Keke has taken to calling her bike Nina for no apparent reason. They pour themselves into the backseat of a nearby cab that reads their codes.

"Good evening, Miss Lovell, Miss Msibi," says the cab. "Please choose a destination."

"Let's drop you off, first," says Keke. "You need to get back to the rug-rats."

"Thanks," says Kate. "Take me home, please, Cabbie." She has already bumped the location to the Cabbie app.

Keke giggles. "That's so analogue."

"What?"

"You know that you don't have to say 'please', right?"

"It's good manners!"

"It's an automaton."

"So?"

"So, you're like that story of that grandmother who used to type 'please' when she Googled something."

"Rubbish."

"Not rubbish. I was at Echo when that story ran. 2016."

"I mean, rubbish that I'm like that grandmother."

"Really? When's the last time you immersed?"

"You know that I don't like VR."

"See? Old lady."

"It's not about being a technophobe – "

"Although clearly you are. Kittysaurus."

"Ha."

"For instance: you still carry cash."

"You never know when you're going to need cash."

"Really? When's the last time you needed cash? 2019?"

"I still use it for some things."

"Like what?"

"Okay, that's a lie. I tried to tip someone the other day and they pretty much threw it back at me."

The real reason she keeps cash is because she's paranoid. Who knows when something catastrophic might happen and all the virtual money just blips out of existence? You can't eat Blox.

"And look at that dress you're wearing."

Kate looks down. "What? I happen to like this dress. I thought you'd appreciate me showing up in something that wasn't jeans. Or pyjamas."

"You've been wearing that old thing since I've known you. Ten years?"

"Hang on, we're not that old. Are we? Besides, I don't have time to shop. I've got toddlers."

"You don't need to shop! You've got that mode printer at home. You know how many people would kill for that machine?"

"I think the shape scanner is broken."

Keke rolls her eyes. Neither of them say: the shape scanner is not the thing that's broken.

"Fine, but about the VR – "

"Virtual reality really fucks with my synaesthesia."

"Oh," says Keke, sitting back into the carseat. "Well, that's different. I didn't know that."

"Seth always has the latest kit, he's forever buying new headsets and body sensors. He's given up asking me to join him. Silver is his gaming partner, now. She's as addicted as he is. The other day she beat him at that Medieval war one."

"DarkAges."

"That's it. Seth says she's a regular Robin Hood."

"Okay, well, then what I wanted to talk to you about is a no-go."

"Just tell me."

The car swerves to avoid hitting a pothole, and the women hold on to avoid being thrown around inside the cabin.

"So, you know I'm on jury duty, right?"

"Yes! How is that going? What's the case about?"

Keke hesitates. Kate can tell she doesn't want to discuss it.

"It's *sub judice*. I'll tell you all about it once we've wrapped."

Kate knows that Keke doesn't give a hot damn about *'sub judice'*. Something else is up.

"So we were being taken through the evidence, right? And instead of just showing us photos of the crime scene, they took us through the actual crime scene."

"Hey?"

"Well, I mean, the virtual crime scene. An exact replica. We could look around properly. Get a feel for the room. See everything, not just what the forensic photographer thought was relevant."

"Wow. Didn't it freak you out?"

"Of course it freaked me out. The victim was a – " She catches herself just in time. "But it made me think. So VXR is everywhere and it has a million different applications."

"I'm not interested in V-XXX-R, if that's where you're going with this."

"It's not about virtual sex, I promise. Although it's not a bad idea – "

They are a street away from Seth's apartment.

"I thought you should maybe try immersion therapy."

"Ugh!"

"I knew you were going to say that, but – "

"That's like taking two concepts I loathe and, like, monster-hybridising them. Then super-sizing them."

"I know. I know, my friend, but think about it. I heard it can be really, really effective. Especially for PTSD. There's this clinic called SecondLife – "

"Yuck."

The car slows to a stop. "We have reached your destination."

"Just think about it."

Kate's passenger door clicks open.

"Okay. There. I've thought about it. The answer is thanks, but no thanks."

"Can't blame a friend for trying," says Keke, shrugging. "See you on the flip-side."

As soon as Kate opens the front door she goes straight to the children's room, where she finds two sweet warm bodies ensconced in their hammox. She touches them to make sure they are there, and real. She kisses Mally's cheek and strokes snoring Silver's hair out of her face.

God, she loves them. Sometimes she's completely overwhelmed by the feeling. She stays for a minute, drunkenly gazing at their cherubic faces. At times like this it can be so intense, like a punch to the stomach: Sometimes she feels bent double by affection.

"How were they tonight?" Kate whispers, trying to not breathe her weed-booze-breath in the nanny's direction.

"They were good, they were good." Sebongile never has a bad thing to say about them. She lets herself out and, as Kate hears her enter the nannypad next door, she triple-locks the door behind her. Kate swallows two SoberUp!s, chases them with a large beaker of water, and falls into bed.

CHAPTER 16

HAUNTED MANSION OF EMPTY TANKS

Kate's at Aquascape, the massive, nonsensical, wildly successful landlocked aquarium that was closed down by an animal rights group a few years ago. A corporate snatched up the prime real estate but they haven't yet razed the mammoth-sized building. It's a haunted mansion of empty tanks. Squatters have moved in, dismantling what they can to sell or build make-shift kennels in which to sleep. Petty criminals have stripped the building of anything valuable: superglass, candy-coloured fibre cables, glitter-white mosaic tiles. As Kate walks through, she remembers what it used to be like: the blue reflection of the water dancing on the walls. A miracle of water in a city plagued by drought. The inverse of an island. Now it's more like a sun-bleached whale skeleton. Sad, pale, dry.

Kate's nervous. Is it the squatters she's afraid of? There are none in sight, but the floor is spotted with burn marks and human stains: vomit and blood. Why is she barefoot? There is broken glass everywhere.

Her limbs are shaking. Fear, or cold? She can't tell. Both, perhaps. She can't think why she's here. A photography assignment, perhaps. She has a memory of shooting a great white shark here. Skew teeth and sandpaper skin. She remembers especially the jellyfish: a swarm, a smack. Electric green venom. A model in a shimmering mermaid costume. The memory is bright and joyful and full of colour – not like this: this eviscerated cave of a place.

Is she looking for someone? There is a shadow in the distance. Someone running? Nerves claw at her bowels. She needs to get out of here. This place is not for her. The empty tanks take on a menacing appearance: gaping mouths of black. Broken tiles crunch under her tender feet and smoky smells make it difficult to breathe. She needs to get out. She starts to run, to look for the exit, but it's not where she remembers it being. If she doesn't get outside and get some air, her head will explode.

An object glints from the floor. Her instinct is to pick it up. It's her gun. How did her gun get on the floor? Kate is about to holster it, when she sees that shadow again. It's someone who wants to hurt her. She pushes herself up against the wall and flicks off the safety catch.

It's Mouton. Who else would it be? She's sure she killed him at the Genesis lab, remembers the fleshy shock of his large body slamming into hers when they were wrestling for their lives. His gorilla hands on her. She emptied her magazine into his torso. She killed him. Didn't she? They never found his body.

She has her gun now, and she refuses to be his victim. She'll kill him again. She'll wreck the sonofabitch.

The shadow flickers. Hide and seek.

The smell of him inflames her terror. Kate points the firearm out towards the darkness, ready to fire. She can't hear anything over her own breathing. Her finger trembles over the trigger. The darkness penetrates her brain, her body. It's going to take her over.

Kate gets a firmer grip on the trigger. She's ready to shoot, but the smell again – the smell is wrong. It's not Mouton. It's citrus peel in a fire. It's –

A hand is on her shoulder and she spins around to shoot. A bolt of orange.

"James?"

"What are you doing?" asks James, worried. He looks so young, so innocent, as if he's just woken.

Kate starts crying. Her voice cracks. "James?"

There's a flash of light. The gutted aquarium is illuminated, but it's not the aquarium anymore, it's her bedroom. And it's not James she's pointing her gun at. It's Mally.

CHAPTER 17

EMPTY PYJAMAS

"There's something about this case that's bothering me," says Keke.

They're on the roof again, her and the suit. It's where they go to escape the rest of the jurors. She's had enough of the whole thing. Keke's tired of being a spectator. She needs to work, to feel useful. She wants the trial to end but she can't let go of the niggling feeling she has that she – that everyone – is missing something. Above all, Keke can't forget the VXR image of the boy in the bath. The empty pyjamas haunt her.

"What?" The suit's in the shade: leaning up against a huge water harvesting tank, one of hundreds on this roof alone. One of millions when you look out at the city. The roof's swivelcam follows her as she moves closer to him.

She still hasn't asked his name.

"I'm Kekeletso," she says.

"I know," he says. "My FusiformG recognised you as soon as you took your mask off."

Face radar apps are ridiculously expensive. Keke would have one if she could afford it.

"Have we met before?"

"You don't remember."

"Sorry. I don't get exposed to many bankers. I didn't think we knew each other."

What she really means is, she's sure she'd remember someone with a face like his. Best to not be too forthcoming, though. She doesn't know if this man can be trusted.

"I'm not a banker."

"Trader, then."

"Nope."

"Financial consultant. Bloxchain advisor. General mafioso."

"No, no, and no."

"What then?"

"I'm a suicide expert."

"Ha," says Keke.

They trade amused expressions.

"You think it's funny?"

"It's a strange job title, that's all. Like, if you were an expert on suicide then you probably wouldn't be…alive?"

"Very funny," he says, smoothing down his silk tie.

"So, suicide seems to be a lucrative business, then."

"It is. The prevention part is, anyway, but that's not why I do it."

"Amazing. I would not have guessed that the Suicide Contagion would be a money spinner."

"Anything that involves corporates and The Grim Reaper is a money spinner."

"That's probably true."

"Believe me, it's true."

"So it's the big corporates that use your services?"

"Mostly. Their attrition rate is sky high. I'm brought in to appraise risk and recommend therapy."

"You're telling me that big corporates care whether their employees snuff themselves?"

"They do. It's very expensive to hire new people and train them."

They look out at the city. A blue haze tints the air.

"So, we've met before?" asks Keke.

He purses his lips. He's got great lips.

"I'm Zack," he says. "Zachary."

Zack. A name that sounds like onomatopoeia. Whack! Crack! A lightning bolt.

Her Patch pings. She looks at her wrist; it's a bump from Marko.

Darko > Lo beautiful.

Kex >> *Aweh* my bling-bling.

Darko > You left without saying goodbye.

Kex >> Sorry. Early start. Trial's wrapping up.

Darko > So, soon I'll have you back?

Keke hesitates, doesn't want to be rude. Zack motions for her to carry on, disappears deeper into the shadows with a wave.

Kex >> You never lost me.

Darko > You wanted me to find something for you m'lady?

Kex >> If you don't mind.

Darko > Anything for you.

Kex >> I hope you don't think I'm just using you for your superlative hacking skills?

Darko > I wouldn't mind if you were.

Kex >> …

Darko > As long as you're using me, I'm happy.

Kex >> …

Darko > …

Kex >> I don't know exactly what I'm looking for.

Darko > Is it about the trial?

Kex >> Yebo. Something just feels off.

Darko > ??

Kex >> …

Darko > You've got good instincts. You're probably on to something.

Kex >> I don't know where to start. It's all under wraps.

Darko > LOLZ

Kex >> What?

Darko > Nothing is under wraps. EIH.

Kex >> ?

Darko > Everything Is Hackable.

Kex >> But I don't even know what to ask you.

Darko > Ask me what I'm wearing.

Kex >> *Wena.* I'm being serious!

Darko > Sorry.

Kex >> …

Darko > Just give me one thing. Off the top of your head. One thing to work with, and I'll go from there.

Kex >> Okay. Maybe just look for similar cases. In Jozi, in the past year.

Darko > Similar cases to a father drowning his toddler?

Kex > Yes. No. Suspicious toddler deaths.

Darko >> That's bleak.

Kex > I know. Sorry. Won't be easy.

Darko >> Consider it done.

Kex > Thank you.

Darko >> …

Kex > Hey.

Darko >> ?

Kex > What are you wearing?

CHAPTER 18

SECONDLIFE

Kate's sitting across the room from the psychiatrist. The space is nondescript and monochrome, giving her a break from her synaesthesia, apart from a small revolving sphere hovering near her head. It's a secret clinic. Some may even call it a black clinic, which is ironic, given the fact that Seth's Alba grind used to close down places like this. But you get illegal clinics and then you get morally bankrupt illegal clinics, and Kate believes – or hopes – that SecondLife belongs to the former category. Alba shut down, among others, Tabula Rasa, a slow-age beauty spa that was buying discarded embryos from dodgy fertility clinics, spinning them to harvest their stem cells, then injecting them into their patients' faces. Kate's cheeks tingled just thinking about it. Then, of course there was Genesis, the black clinic to rival all black clinics. The clinic that killed Marmalade and almost killed her.

Kekeletso booked this appointment. Underground treatment facilities like these only accept patients from referrals and are usually booked up months in advance, so she's not sure how Keke pulled it off.

Doctor Voges is empty-handed, there's no notepad or Tile in sight. Some other kind of recording device must be out of view. Voges is dressed in squid-ink grey from head to toe, as if she's an extension of the slate room. Her face is powdered to perfection. Kate has always hated doctors: she was poked and prodded her whole childhood: blood, urine, DNA tests. X-rays, MRIs, CAT scans. It made her resent her condition instead of embracing it for what it was: a gift. She had her own augmented reality before VR even existed.

"What do you know about Immersion Therapy?" asks Doctor Voges. "Or VXR?"

"Not much," says Kate, biting her lip. "I've tried to stay away from it, to be honest."

"Why?"

"I don't know. It doesn't appeal to me the way it does to other people. I guess I've got enough going on my head without it."

The doctor gazes at her. "That's understandable. So why, then, are you here today?"

Kate gulps. Where to start?

That she can't trust her own body anymore?

That alarm sirens are the soundtrack to her everyday reality?

That she craves physical nurturing but can't stand to be touched?

Of course, all of that is secondary. The reason she's here is because of what happened last night.

The doctor sees her hesitate and offers a way in.

"You consider yourself a threat." she says.

"Not 'consider'," says Kate. "I am a threat."

"To yourself?"

"To myself. More importantly, to my kids."

"Tell me about your traumatic episode."

Kate barks a laugh. "Which one?"

CHAPTER 19
DEATH IN MID-AIR

The Cape Republic, 2024

Seth slams his fist against the counter of the standing desk, making Carson jump. With the help of Snaffeine he's pulled an all-nighter, trying every mathematical sequence and pattern he knows, but it's still not working. The cardiomyocytes on the biohybrid stingray have been printed in a serpentine pattern – easy enough to do on a shape as simple as a ray – but a human heart is a different creature entirely. He's watched footage of a live heart beating over and over, frame by frame, at every angle, and tried to copy it exactly, but there are obviously nuances that he is just not getting. His silicone heart prototype is clumsy. The transparent 4D animation floats in front of him, his 263rd version, taunting him with its graceless beating. Seth deletes his latest algorithm and the heart freezes. Death in mid-air.

A hand touches his shoulder and he jumps.

"Sorry," says Arronax. "I didn't mean to scare you."

She's wearing hermit crab shell earrings, and pieces of polished mother-of-pearl sewn into the shoulder panels of her lab coat catch the cold light.

"You didn't," he says. "I was just…thinking."

How does she get her hair like that?

"I see you haven't made much progress," she says. "We had hoped it would be solved by now."

"It's proving to be more challenging than I predicted."

What he really wants to say is: I've tried every equation I know. Nothing has worked. I'm out of options. He sniffs, rubs his nose. He definitely overdid the Snaffeine.

"Let me help you," she says.

A mermaid-glimmer of hope.

"That would be great," says Seth, knuckle-scrubbing his faux-hawk. "Which area of maths do you specialise in?"

"I don't," she says. "I don't specialise in maths. There are other ways I can help you."

She motions at Carson to close the door, and he does so. If the guard wonders why, his face doesn't show it.

Seth looks at Arronax, really looks at her, as she takes his hand and places it on her breasts. Waits for his reaction. Her lab coat is open just enough for him to feel the warm silk of her skin on his fingertips. The seahorse pendant shimmers.

"You're tense," she says, stroking his shoulders. "Your brain can't function optimally when your stress levels are high."

At first Seth resists. His nervous system is galloping on the caffeine he snarfed and it always makes him paranoid. What is she doing? Why is she doing it? The deep blue of the ocean outside paints her chest cerulean. It's like some kind of ocean-themed hallucination.

Her hand travels down to his jeans, unzips him. "You need to decrease your level of cortisol."

She's so fucking beautiful and her hair smells like seawater. He decides to just go with it.

"I love a woman who talks dirty."

She's got his pants open and starts to lower herself, but he stops her, pulls her up again. Slams his counter down to hip-level and picks Arronax up, putting her onto the ledge. Standing desks are so versatile.

He eases up, then, and they kiss as strangers do: feeling each other out, trying to gauge what the other person likes. It's an exercise in erotic discovery more than blinding passion. He feels himself swell, senses the hard restriction of denim.

Seth disengages, slowly, from her lips, and moves down to her lily throat. The faintest hint of perfume and salt. Down to her chest. She runs a hand through his hair, then presses a button on her SnapTile and the lab door locks: the LED goes from green to red. The lights dim. The corner camera clicks off.

"We've got six minutes," she says.

Seth unbuttons the rest of her blouse, discovers her beautiful breasts cupped in aqua padding and lace. He pops open the back strap of her bra and pushes up the front to reveal the palest, softest tits he's ever seen. He buries his face in them, luxuriates in them. God, it's been a long time. Too long. Takes a small brown nipple in his mouth and sucks hard, massages the other breast in his hand. Arronax straightens her back and sighs in pleasure. Seth's mind flashes with images of cornrows and caramel. Hot leather. She pulls his head even deeper inside the crispness of her lab coat.

Reminded of where he is, he sweeps up her skirt, and she opens her legs. He accepts her invitation and pulls down her panties. Kisses her again. Uses licked fingers to tease her clit before penetrating her with them. Slowly at first, just the fingertips, until she pushes her hips forward to get more of him inside. Seth goes deeper, deeper, and Arronax revolves her hips and breathes in mounting waves. Arronax groans. She's close to coming so he slows down, eases off, but never lets her go. Seth pulls down his pants, gets himself ready. He wants her to come when he is inside her, not before. Arronax drags his head up from her breasts; her breathing is ragged. Her body is stronger than it looks. He wants her to bite him.

"Hurry up," she says, her lips touching his ear. "I want you right now."

He enters her, and groans when he feels how wet and swollen she is. She groans too: a gasp; a growl. He goes all the way in, then doesn't move for a moment. They hold each other, breathe each other's air. It feels too good. His mind is clear of everything except what is happening right then, and he wants to stay there. Stop the clocks. But their bodies have a different idea and a will of their own. Slowly, they start moving together, easing into a steady rhythm, a rocking. His hands on her hips, hers in his hair. Her muscles clench around him. Seth tries to slow down again but they've created a momentum now that can't be stopped. He starts to thrust into her and she groans louder and louder. He thrusts harder and faster and their energies build together until he is soaring and it feels as if she is too. She bites his neck and they both come with a big, loud, bang. Arronax shouts. Seth lets out a rolling moan. A different kind of death in mid-air.

When their breathing finally returns to normal, they're still clutching each other. Arronax's face is resting on Seth's chest.

"Holy shit," they both say, at the same time, and the lights power up again.

CHAPTER 20

THE MAN WHO PERFORATES HER DREAMS

Johannesburg, 2024

"VXR can be extremely disconcerting, to begin with," says the slate-grey psychiatrist, adjusting Kate's wide-view visigogs. "Some of my patients refer to Virtual Explicit Reality as 'VR on steroids'."

Kate's standing in the middle of the room with her haptic liquisuit on, and she's already feeling claustrophobic. Her instinct is to run, but she has to do this thing. If this therapy doesn't work –

Her ear Patch beeps as it syncs with the immersion equipment. The blank room disappears and she finds herself at home. Not Seth's super-contemporary apartment with its breathing walls and artificial sunrises, but her old flat. The pressed-ceilinged, wooden-floored, plant-filled place in Illovo she shared with James before –

"How?" she says. "How could the machine know what my home looked like?"

"It's not the machine," says the doctor, who is now in her home with her. Sitting at the kitchen table. A bowl of green Granny Smith apples appears and the woman picks one up, takes a bite. "It's your brain that does all the work. It's not a simulation, it's a manipulation…of your mind. That's why everything seems so real. You are the operating system."

Kate looks around. It's exactly the same. It's perfect. Nostalgia peels her heart.

"It's like…" she says. "It's like Marmalade is going to just walk through that door."

"Do you want him to walk through the door?"

Yes. No. She doesn't know. Which James will it be? The one she loved for thirteen years before she learned the truth? The one who betrayed her, who killed a small part of her, the one she loved so hard, regardless?

"He's dead. I need to accept that."

"What do you need to experience in order to accept that?"

"I don't know. I don't want to look back. I don't want to have to experience that moment again. When I had to – "

"We don't have to jump in. Let's just take it slowly. Let's go back to your first childhood memory."

"I don't have a lot of those."

"Let's see what your brain comes up with."

A clear blue sky replaces Kate's Illovo flat. She's in shallow water. Warm. There's a baby boy, wearing an identical floating device to hers: an orange lycra tube vest. Sam. His name was Sam. Now it's Seth. The Bad Men named him Seth. A woman with a mass of red hair spins her around slowly in the water. Gentle laughter.

"I know this place," Kate says. "The river. My mother – my biological mother – used to take us to picnic and swim here."

"It's a happy memory." Dr Voges is standing on the riverbank, arms by her side. Her tailored suit seems out of place.

"Yes. I loved the water. I've always loved water."

"You were loved."

"I can't remember that part."

"But you can feel it?"

Kate looks at her mother. The reflection of the river sparkles in her eyes. She gives Kate a smile so tender and unguarded it makes her want to cry.

"I can feel it," she says. Tears sting her eyes.

"You were loved," the doctor says.

Now the river disappears and she's sitting on a front lawn. The leaves spike her soft toddler-skin.

"Oh," she says.

"Where are you now?"

Kate looks up, sees Voges standing in the road, watching her.

"This is when it happened."

"When what happened?"

"When they took us."

"Who took you?"

"The Bad Men."

A phone rings. Kate pictures an old set with a rotary dial and an elastic spiral cord.

Seth looks up. How old is he? How old are they? Two? Then looks back down at his Thundercats figurine. It's riding a My Little Pony. He's wearing a jacket. Peppermint. Hers is Mandarin.

Her mother, who is leaning on the doorframe (Lemongrass Lazuli), flicks off her gardening gloves and goes inside to answer the phone.

No, she wants to say. No, Mom, don't go, The Bad Men are coming. But the doorframe is already empty.

Despite the warmth of the jacket, the skin on her hands is red when she looks down at them. Her brother passes her the pony – perfumed plastic – the Thundercat astride. Cheetara. She zooms the pony over the grass. Sam doesn't smile. Something has caught his attention in the street and he looks past her, frowning. He stands up on his chubby legs, toy still in hand, held against his round stomach.

"Move out the way," she says to the psychiatrist who is still standing in the street. "They're coming." Just in time, the woman in grey steps out of the road.

A black Kombi pulls up and all of a sudden there is a blonde-haired little boy right there, on their pavement. He's only slightly older than they are. He beckons to them with his hands, his sweet face full of promise. Sam looks at the boy then back at the house, for his mother, but the doorframe is still empty. Kate finds herself beside the rosy-cheeked stranger.

Sam calls out: "Kitty!" and runs to catch up with her.

As they reach the walkway beside the van, the door slides open and a giant man swoops over them, and meaty forearms squeeze the air out of her lungs. Kate chokes. Before they know what's happened they're struggling in the car. The other boy, the blonde boy, is stricken. He's shouted at and jumps in, and the rolling door is slammed shut. From light to darkness, just like that.

Like that, the light in her heart goes out. Nothing but darkness and a shocked wail in her ears. The wailing is coming from her. Kate knows now that she won't see her mother again, her father. Not like this, anyway, not for thirty-two years. In the dim interior the blonde-haired beckoner's face contorts with silent tears.

The face she knows so well.

Mom, it hurts so much.

Her Marmalade. Her James.

Kate is doubled over. The grief is still fresh after all these years.

"Would you like to take a break?" asks the grey doctor.

"No," says Kate. "No."

This is torture. She wants to get it over with. Tears are streaming out of her nose, and she grasps blindly for a tissue. Dr Voges hands her one.

"Is it real?" she asks, meaning the tissue.

"It's all real," says the doctor.

"He was just a child. As innocent as we were."

"What did they do to him?"

"Used him as bait."

"I'm sorry that happened."

She chokes again, tries to not vomit. Wrenches the goggles off just in case.

"I'm sorry it happened to both of you."

"It happened to hundreds of us."

"It's in the past, now."

Kate swallows over and over, trying to keep the bile down. "How do you get over something like that?"

"It's possible."

"I lost both my parents and my twin brother in a split second."

"It was a terrible thing that they did, kidnapping you."

"I walked towards them."

"You were two years old."

"I walked towards them. And Sam followed me."

The doctor passes her a glass of water. "You got them back," she says. "Your parents. Eventually."

"It was too late."

"They'll always be your parents."

"It doesn't feel like it. It was too late to fill the black hole."

"It's natural to be paranoid about your own kids when you experienced what you did."

"I keep thinking." Kate gulps. "I keep thinking that someone is going to take them."

"Of course you do."

"It's stupid. I can't get it out of my head. Who would want to take them?"

"It's not stupid."

The doctor gives Kate a few minutes to gather herself. "Is this the trauma that haunts you?"

"This, and others."

"Which is the worst? Which is the one that caused you to aim a loaded gun at your son?"

Kate hasn't told her that. Keke must have, in order to get the emergency appointment. The words hang in the air, hurting her.

"Tell me what happened."

"It was four years ago, at the Genesis Clinic."

There is a multi-flashback, like vintage camera globes going off: bang, bang bang. Kate sees her abductor parents lying dead on the family room floor, shot execution-style. A comet-shaped bloodstain on the beige carpet. She feels the hard tumble of the accident on Keke's motorbike, when she thought she and Seth, after just having found each other, were going to die. Then the Alba driver being shot in the head, right in front of her, close enough so that she was misted with his blood. A rabid monkey on a chain. The Nigerian gang hurting an old, loping hyena. Jumping around, crazed by Nyaope or White Lobster, licking dirty teeth, placing a revolver in her hands. She sees the man posing as Ed Miller, sees his dead face skinned by the car's front windshield. The real Ed Miller's broken body revealed when the vehicle's boot sprang open.

Then Mouton. The assassin with the burnt arm. The man who perforates her dreams.

CHAPTER 21

BABY BLANKET

Marko checks his Thai casino winnings and his Ontario clickjacking farm, then follows up on the leads he acquired during the past hour. The first thing he did was to put out feelers on the suspect – Lundy – accused of killing his son. If the man's got any secrets, he'll be able to find them.

There's nothing so far. No documented history of violence or abuse. No criminal record apart from a campus police report from twenty years ago. A minor incident concerning the vandalism of a university statue – some kind of political protest. The institution didn't press charges, and even if they had, his record would have been expunged by now. Apart from that, Mack Lundy seemed like an extremely boring individual. An average student, he went into an unremarkable career in data sales, married his childhood sweetheart, and had a child. His Flittr profile paints the same picture: a Springbok supporter with a beer *boep* who plays action cricket every Wednesday and surfs vanilla porn on weekends. A walking cliché.

Keke thinks he's innocent, and Marko tends to agree. Although it's possible the man has an undiagnosed mental illness: something that could cause him to just snap. Marko gets the feeling it isn't the case. No priors involving violence, no social media trolling.

It could have been an accident. The Net knows accidents happen all the time. There have been more than a hundred thousand Volanter deaths alone this year. That's what happens when people don't trust the self-flying tech and think they can do a better job.

Satisfied that he has cleared Lundy, Marko rotates on his swivel chair and lets the holo leaves wink out behind him. As he practises typing with his eyeborg, new leaves pop up. He disables the visuals in his search results. No way he wants to see crime scene pictures for this.

During 2019, the Nancies implemented a very basic web censorship – dubbed 'The Baby Blanket' by those who knew about it – that suppresses the results of anything they deem 'difficult' for the citizens to handle. It includes news of service delivery protests, criticism of the government, and anything with obvious triggers: murder, rape, suicide. There is still bad news, but it's now seen as 'better' news. Their private emails congratulate each other for the initiative's success, citing stats that proves it's good for the general morale of the country. They refuse to acknowledge it as censorship. After all, they don't block the bad news, they just manipulate the search result algorithms to make it more difficult to find. Hacktivists and news agencies in the know are always trying to 'lift the Blanket' with varying degrees of success. There's never been a more exciting time to be a Truther.

It's not a difficult hack. Toddlers dying under suspicious circumstances – or any circumstances – would be instantly classified as a trigger. Marko just needs to get under the Blanket. He can't help being reminded of four years ago when Keke asked him to investigate the mystery surrounding Kate's childhood. He uncovered not only her abduction as a small child, but the kidnapping of six other kids too. The seven who were taken. It feels like *deja vu*. A bad omen that burns in his stomach.

He scrolls past headlines he'd rather not be reading.

Three-year-old girl falls down elevator shaft;

Toddler (2) killed in cab accident;

Mother arrested for drowning child (3) in lake.

Pages and pages of results of accidental and not-so-accidental child deaths. Accidents happen, but surely this is too much? The articles create a buzzing in his head. He can't help picturing Silver or Mally in dangerous situations. No wonder they've hidden this.

Four-year-old swallows battery.

He knows he's naturally paranoid, but how do parents sleep at night?

Boy (2) drinks pesticide.

How does anyone sleep at night? Have kids also caught the Suicide Contagion? Is that even possible?

His Patch tells him that it may be time to take a break: his heart rate is up. It asks if he'd like to do a breathing exercise to calm down. He closes the message. Something is going on here, and he's going to find out what.

CHAPTER 22

EYES THE COLOUR OF AN OLD BRUISE

"You up for a trip?" asks Keke.

Zack looks up from his SnapTile. "Sure. After court today?"

"I was thinking of going now."

"It's 10am."

"We can take a couple of hours of personal leave. We're entitled to it. Besides, we'll be back after lunch."

"I don't know. The trial – "

"This is about the trial. It's more important than sitting here, listening to the same thing over and over again. And we can catch whatever we've missed later on the refresh immersion."

"Are we going on a joyride?"

"Have you ever been on a Tesla e-Max motorbike?"

"No."

"Then, yes, we're going on a joyride."

Keke auto-inflates her helmet, plus a spare for Zack. She puts on her tinted eye-mask as a special precaution to protect her BioLenses then folds down her visor, straddles the bike. Zack hesitates, then climbs on the seat behind her.

"Ready?" she asks.

They roar off and zoom through the city, dodging cabs, pedestrians and shabby tuk-tuks. Keke has been driving Nina for so long now the machine is an extension of her body. She doesn't have to think; she clasps the humming seat between her thighs and the rest is instinct. Smoke and pollution mixes with the heat coming off the road and makes the air choke-worthy, but once they're out of the chaos of the CBD and the air clears, Zack's body relaxes against hers. The problem with riding a bike is that once you've experienced the open road this way, it's difficult to go back to the claustrophobic confines of a car cabin.

Twenty minutes later, Keke pulls to a stop outside the Carbon Factory. It's the Crim Colony in the south of Johannesburg. She shows the guard at the entrance her press ID and mumbles someone's name. Usually, visiting here as a journalist, she has to supply her DNA Profile Code and verify it with her fingerprint, retina scan and a cheek swab, but for some reason they're going easy on her today. Maybe her contact – the one whose name she mentioned to the guard – holds more sway than she realises. They're allowed access and shown where to park; Keke grabs a spot under the solar trees. It seems so quiet after having the engine rumble in their ears.

"I wasn't expecting this." Zack motions at the charcoal-tinted building. The structure was designed by a tenderpreneurial trust fund kid with more cheek than sense. After it was built, it came to light that his architectural degree wasn't worth the paper it was printed on. He paid a cheapjack college for his 'qualifications' and paid an equally dodgy designer to draw up the plans. All in all it cost him a few hours of expensive lunches and easy bribes, and he made more than twelve million rand.

Not bad going, making a million rand an hour. Viva corruption and bribery.

"It's quite a thing, isn't it?" says Zack, looking up at it while shading his eyes from the sun. "I've never seen it in real life."

The draughtsman had "taken inspiration" from the Suprematist influence of old Soviet architecture – he basically plagiarised a drawing he found online and mixed it up a little – and the result was a peri-modern brutalist building with an expressionist leaning and a lunar edge. It left most conservative South Africans puzzled at best and besieged by inarticulate fury at worst. Despite its corrupt beginnings, Keke liked it.

"I was here in '19, when they cut the ribbon. I was covering the story. There was still a lot of criticism back then."

They skip up the concrete steps.

"I remember that. The architect. Some kind of greasy deal."

"Not just that."

Just the idea of having penal labour camps made a lot of people uncomfortable. The Nancies had tested it in various provinces, moving convicts out of overcrowded prisons to live and grind in underground platinum mines and vertical cannabis farms, and found that it worked well. The crims learned skills and earned wages, with which they paid for their food and board, and had mandatory saving schemes. Within a few years the convicts, instead of being a drain on taxpayers' money, were turning a profit for the SACS.

Human rights organisations and the international press had a field day, saying that South Africa was up to its usual terrible tricks, and accused the president of furthering a neo-Apartheid agenda. Colonisation, even of dangerous criminals, was very much frowned upon. The outrage hadn't lasted long. Europe had its refugee problems to deal with, China was invested in space mining above all else, and America was at bio-war with Russia, so after some mean headlines the outrage, and the journos, moved on.

They approach the building's front entrance where men in full riot gear stand guard. Whole-face visors, batons, tasers. Kevlarskin overlaid with exoscales, and not a smile in sight. Glass doors slide open, and they let the pair through without even glancing at them. Next they're in the X-ray box which beeps its approval of their unarmed status, and a woman wearing a bulletproof skinny-onesie pats them down. She clicks a torch on, next to her head like a stopwatch, and looks in their mouths too.

"So much for going easy on us," says Keke, as they catch the conveyer belt to the convicts' res. They're accompanied by two guards: one in front, one at the back.

"I guess they need to be careful. Don't want their cash cows breaking out."

They scoot past what looks like a warehouse and then, behind an impossibly high glass wall: a barn of workers with face-masks and protective glasses on. Busy with assembling something directly in front of them, they don't look up. Their hands are like synchronised swimmers, dipping in and out of whatever it is that they're putting together. By appearances, it seems to be an extremely well-oiled machine. The belt takes them further into the factory, and they pass more barns of workers, and more armed guards. Misters spray the air with sanitiser in scheduled bursts, and security cameras follow their progress with red LEDs.

"Imagine," Keke says under her breath, as they go deeper into the bowels of the building "if they decide to keep us in here. We'd never be able to get out."

Zack pulls a startled face at her.

The factory's business is carbon capture. Gigantic pumps suck CO2 out of the surrounding atmosphere and converts it into useful products: pre-fab rock brix, graphite pencils, compressed carbonites, and they spill the leftover O2 into the air. By 2026 they'll be able to package and sell the oxygen, too. Asia can't get enough of the stuff. Fresh mountain air is the most popular, and most expensive. Switzerland exports bags of it to Taiwan. Factory oxygen doesn't quite have the same appeal, so they're working on ways of making it novel. They're putting their money on flavoured oxygen, and are currently experimenting with ice cream flavours: Cara/Choc/Mint; Hazelnut Brown-butter Swirl, and of course, Nostalgic Neapolitan, which sounds like one of Kate's paint colours.

"Are you going to tell me what we're doing here?" says Zack.

They get a private room for the interview. As they sit down on plastic chairs, the corner cameras swivel in their direction. Zack is about to say something when they lead the convict into the room. She has circles under her eyes the colour of an old bruise. Melange overalls held together by stitched-on patches, and a strange haircut. Keke thinks that the woman must cut her own hair; must sew her own clothes. Maybe they all do.

She stands up. The noise the chair makes scraping the cold concrete floor makes them all cringe. The crim has stooped shoulders and stares down at her bound wrists.

"Mrs Nash," says Keke. "Thank you for agreeing to speak to us."

The woman looks up at her. There is no life in her eyes.

"Does she have to wear those?" Kekeletso says to the guard. "Those cuffs? They look uncomfortable."

The man doesn't answer her.

"I mean, she's an accountant, for Net's sake. Not a gang leader."

They're new-tech handcuffs and look like something out of a steampunk movie. Designed to administer behaviour-correcting pulses of either shock treatment or medication. They haven't had a riot in this wing since they switched to these smart copper bracelets. The less dangerous crims wear them around a single ankle. The powers that be can drop the entire prisoner population with one button if it comes to it; paralytics are handy like that. But by the look of Helena Nash, Keke guesses they use her cuffs to administer psychotropics: mood stabilisers, maybe, or anti-psychotics. Seth would be able to tell her.

"I told them I didn't want to see any more reporters," she says, eyeing Keke's press ID.

"I know. I'm sorry for what you've been through."

"No more journalists, I said." She keeps tucking her hair behind her ear, despite it not being out of place.

"I know, they told me, but that's not why I'm here. This isn't for a story."

"Ha," she says. Bitter smile. Dry lips. "You think I'm stupid."

She slumps into her seat.

"I believe you're innocent," says Keke. Zack sits up a little straighter, leans in.

"No one believes I'm innocent," she says. "Didn't you see how quickly they sped through my trial? I didn't even have a chance to explain myself. Not properly. They were in such a hurry to just lock me up and throw away the key."

"It did seem like an especially short trial," says Keke.

"What do you know about it? Were you there? Weren't you one of the bloodhounds in the courtroom who were baying for blood?"

"No," says Keke. "I wasn't there. All I know about your case is the file I have on my Tile."

"Liar," Nash says.

"What?"

"You're a liar. No way you have that file. It's buried as deep as a dungeon floor. All our files are," she gestures as if there are hundreds of other convicts in the room and she is the nominated spokesperson. "Don't you know? Don't you know that the government hides all this shit?"

"We do know that," says Zack.

"We can't go around upsetting the general fucking public, can we?" she says in a shrill, put-on, voice. "We can't let them know that there is this dark underbelly of putrid shit underneath everything good. One day the whole city – the whole country – will just sink into it. Sink into the muddy, shitty lava that is our shadow side."

"I – " starts Keke, but the woman interrupts her with sour breath.

"You just go along with your life and think everything is okay. You in your designer leggings and your fancy jacket. Drinking overpriced coffee and thinking everything is just fucking dandy. You think the crime stats are down. You think all the bad people are locked up in mineshafts and factories. It is not the case, let me tell you. It is not the case, even though the government wants you to believe it. The stories in here," she says, "the stories I can tell you."

"I'm very interested in the stories," says Keke. "I want to hear them, if you're willing to talk."

"Ah. What's the point?" Nash says, tucking her hair in, "what's the point? They'll just lose your articles just like they lose everything else that's not sunshine and fucking roses."

"I'd like to hear them anyway," says Keke. "But today I need to ask you about something else. Something specific."

The woman cocks her head to one side, blinks. The temperature in the room seems to drop.

"You want to talk about Erin?" she says. "I can't talk about Erin."

CHAPTER 23

A HEART. A CLOCK

The Cape Republic, 2024

Seth is eating lunch. Prawn-flavoured coleslaw in a salmon-swiped wasabi wrap. He holds the food in one hand and jots down his free-flow ideas with the other: blue and red markers on recycled sheets of paper. Food at the Nautilus, while excellent quality, leaves a little to be desired in the inspiration department. He can't help but see the parallel in his own work. Mathematically sound, but ultimately insipid.

That said, the motivational session with Arronax this morning shifted something in his thinking. He realised, as he was holding her, that he has to go back to basics. Skin on skin, that is the thing, especially when you're dealing with something like the human heart. He closed down all his predictive algorithms, let his holos wink out, turned off the transparent heart that had been floating before him, taunting him with its clumsy, lumbering rhythm. He grabbed an A0 notepad and markers and set to work, starting from scratch, writing down every formula, equation, and pattern he could think of that could spark the solution.

He's thirty-three pages in, now, and something is happening. He's still miles from the final pattern, but at least now he is on the right track. Every page edges him nearer to the answer.

He looks up at the clockologram: it's 12:38. The Powers That Be wanted this work by noon yesterday. They extended his contract for another 24 hours. So he's late for his already-extended deadline. Is that why he's nervous? He's not used to the feeling. He likes to think that anxiety is for other people. A problem he has solved on multiple occasions with his pharmadesign. Has a corporate deadline ever scratched at his nerves? He doesn't think so. Something else is going on. 12:40. What is he missing? And then the picture of Kate pops into his head. Kate. The kids. Has something happened? Surely he would know? He'll call her to check on her, as soon as he's finished with this page.

12:43. He can feel the tentacles of the solution reaching for him. Without taking his eyes off the page, he discards what is left of the wrap. Numbers at the periphery of his brain, like words on a tip of a tongue. It's no use trying to grab them: that makes them disappear. He knows he needs to coax them out. He keeps scribbling. Swaps colours when a new concept emerges. 12:45.

His eyes keep going back to the clock, as if he's late for something. He thinks of Arronax's lips, her inner thighs. Stop the clocks, he had thought when he was with her. He looks at the clockologram again. Is it the numbers? 1245? Almost Fibonacci. Almost the golden sequence, but not quite. 11235 is the beginning of the Golden Ratio. No, it's not the time on the clock that's got his attention, it's the clock, itself.

A heart. A clock. What is a heart, but a clock? And like every clock, a heart has a finite number of ticks in it. The maths behind the twenty-four hour, sixty-minute, sixty-second day won't help him, so what other patterns are there? Seth senses the beginning of relief. He can feel the answer is finally in his head, he just needs to find it.

~

Seth is in the middle of the lab, on the ground, surrounded by paper sheets and scrawls when Arronax arrives. He holds a marker to his lips. His hands and arms are tattooed with marker dye. He writes a few more fraction sequences down, numbers that are illegible to anyone but him. He changes the colour of his pen and, starting from the top sequence on the page and working down, he draws a complicated spiral that joins the lines of every fraction. It grows to take up the whole bottom of the page: an inverted hurricane. He snaps the lid back onto the marker and then looks up at her.

"I need my Tile back," he says.

"Of course." She nods at Carson, who leaves to get it.

"I still need to test it, but …"

"But you've got it," she says. "I can see it."

He stands, puts his inked-up hands on his hips.

It's 12:59.

"I've got it."

"So," says Seth, explaining the equation to Arronax as he types furiously on the holopad, mapping out pinpricks on the model heart of where the cardiomyocytes should be printed, "clockmakers – old school clockmakers – used to rely on the Stern-Brocot tree."

She blinks at him.

"It's like Fibonacci, but super-sized," he says, still typing. "Or, rather, super-deep."

"How long will it take you to upload the sequence?"

"Not long. It's self-perpetuating, so the machine can take care of it after the first few lines."

Arronax brings up another holopad on the counter and begins typing too. She brings up the 4D model between them and watches his progress as tiny dots start appearing on the organ.

"Who is she?" she asks.

"What?" says Seth, "Who?"

"That woman you keep thinking about?"

Seth stops working, scratches his scalp with the back of a pen.

"You've got to stop doing that," he says, then continues to work.

"I can't help it. You have an extremely…interesting mind."

"Isn't it against your Nautilus ethics or something?"

"Desire pays little attention to ethics."

Seth remembers a specific moment from the day before and there is a rush of warmth to his equipment. He clears his throat. Does this woman want him to finish the job or not?

"Keep working," she says.

"Easy for you to say," he says, adjusting himself. "Do you use your psychic-switch on all of your conquests?"

Her laugh sounds good.

"You were not a conquest. I was doing what I had to, to move the project along."

"I feel completely used," he says.

Arronax laughs again. "No, you don't."

"No," he says, trying not to smile. "I don't."

"Believe me, you want the switch on. Why do you think it was so good?"

"Yes, I thought that might have something to do with it."

The artificial heart beats once, twice, then shudders to a stop.

"It would be even better if we were both wearing one," he says.

Arronax bites her lip, says: "Absolutely not, Mister Denicker," but then she writes out on a piece of paper in front of him: *Perhaps that can be arranged.*

The heart starts again, this time beating three times before stalling.

"What do you think?" she asks.

"I think that sounds bloody marvellous."

CHAPTER 24

A RED STAMP ON THE TILES

Johannesburg, 2024

"Please," says Keke again. "I think you're innocent."

Helena Nash looks down at her lap.

"Are you innocent?" asks Zack.

The convict swallows hard, tidies her hair. The cuffs glint in the harsh fluorescent light.

"No one is innocent," she says. "Not really. That's what I've learnt in here."

"But you're innocent, of what you were charged with."

"I've learned that luck is everything," says Nash. "Have you ever heard of moral luck?"

Keke shakes her head. Maybe she's wrong about this one. She seems unhinged. Maybe she *did* do it.

"Moral luck," she says. "Some people are in here because they were unlucky. Simple as that. Here's an example. My father was a terrible drunk. Terrible! I mean – " She puts her bound wrists on the table in front of her. "We won't get into it. But he was a bad man. And he never spent a day in jail."

"And you," says Keke. "You were a 'good' drunk?"

"So you did read my file."

"A friend of mine got hold of it for me. He's good at that kind of thing."

"I never hurt anyone."

"If that's true – "

"It's true. I never hurt anyone and I've got five years in here."

"Then I'll do what I can to get you an appeal."

"I don't have any money left. It all went to legal fees. I don't make much bank in here, and they only give us twenty per cent to spend."

"Don't worry about the money," says Zack.

She looks at him as if for the first time. Her gaze rests on his bespoke tie.

"You just need to tell us what you know."

"That's the problem," says Helena. "That's why I had no defence. Not really. I can't really remember much about that night."

"You drank too much?"

"No more than usual. I had a bottle of wine. And only after I tucked Erin in for the night."

"What happened?"

"I fell asleep – I passed out – on the couch. Usually I can drink a bottle, no problem, but it was as if I had been drugged."

"You think there was something in the wine?"

"No one believes me. I understand that. Why believe an alcoholic? Especially one that you think killed her baby daughter."

Keke checks her SnapTile to make sure it's still recording.

"When did you find her? Erin?"

"I woke up in the middle of the night. Disorientated. The house was completely dark. I felt woozy. I thought: I mustn't go upstairs. It would be dangerous, in my condition. My co-ordination was off. Mouth was dry." She licks her lips, as if the memory has made her thirsty. "I turned on the lounge light and there she was, on the floor. There was hardly any blood. Just a red stamp on the tiles. Her body was already cold."

"I'm so sorry." Zack takes her hand, but the CrimCol guard notices and gestures that he should let go.

"She had a big – " Helena gestures at the back of her head. " – a big … Her skull was smashed in, at the back here. When I lifted her up, and touched it … It was … soft."

"That's terrible," says Keke.

"I thought it was a dream, you know? A nightmare. Because my head was still all mixed up. It can't be true, I kept telling myself. It can't be true. But then, I still think that. I thought that during the trial and I think it now. How could I have lost my little girl? There should be a name for people like us, who have lost their children. Kids who lose their parents are called orphans. There should be a name like that for us, because that's how I felt. That's how I feel."

Her eyes turn red, but they are dry, as if no more tears are left.

"She was probably looking for me, you know? If she woke up at night she'd come across to my bedroom, but I wasn't there, so she tried to come down the stairs to look for me. She was probably calling for me."

"And the stair gate wasn't latched?"

"I latched that gate. I know I did. I did it every night for three years. She must have, I don't know, unlatched it. Or climbed over it."

Keke's wrong about the tears. They stream down Nash's face. She ignores them.

"You didn't hear her fall down the stairs."

Keke and Zack, late for the second part of the day's proceedings in court, jump on the bike and race off. They chat via the helmet connection.

"That was so creepy," says Zack.

"Nash?"

"Nash was creepy, but I meant the factory. It was like, I don't know. The convicts seemed like automatons."

Keke dodges a slow cab and gives him the finger.

"I don't understand the connection," says Zack. "Apart from the obvious – that Lundy and Nash both lost a young child – but how does Nash's story have any bearing on Lundy's trial?"

"I asked Marko to look into any similar cases. I just have a feeling that there's something…"

"Who's Marko?"

It's always difficult to describe her relationship to Marko. He's her boyfriend, her partner, her non-exclusive lover. He's the one she wants to climb into bed with at night, and wake up with the next morning.

"He's the best hacker I know."

Keke smoothly dodges a pedestrian walking a pack of small yapping dogs.

"So you think they're connected, somehow?"

"We'll never know if we don't look."

Keke and Zack's Patches buzz at the same time. It's court. They're twenty minutes late.

"Marko also checked Lundy out. Top to bottom. No secrets."

"Everyone has secrets."

Zack holds Keke a little tighter as they take the offramp, exiting the highway and heading into town.

PART 2

CHAPTER 25

COPPER SQUARED

Johannesburg, 2024

"Damn it, Mally!" shouts Kate. "I asked you to put your shoes on!"

Mally throws his head back and wails. Silver sees her brother crying and joins in. Snot flows down her face. Kate wipes it away, causing the girl to cry harder and launch into a coughing fit. Why is she always sick? Damn it. How is it that they've found a way to cure cancer but not the common cold?

"We have to leave now or we'll miss the show!"

The twins' crying sends bright green spirals drilling into her skull (Forest Fright) and she can't see past the noise. Her head is going to explode. She steps on something cold and slimy that makes her whole body shimmer-cringe. It's half a peeled banana. She scrapes the sticky slug off her bare foot and as she looks up she catches her reflection in their funhouse mirror. She hasn't had time to shower or get dressed yet and she looks a hundred years old.

"Stop crying," she says, wanting to cry, herself. "Please stop crying, both of you!" But they carry on as if they've both lost an arm. She jams Mally's foot into a boot. The zip jams and it tears off the front part of Kate's nail. She swears under her breath.

"It's too tight!" he cries. "Too t-i-i-i-i-i-ight!"

She wrenches it off again, throws it across the room. Goes to the kids' cupboard to hunt for another option. Her face is hot. What is she thinking, trying to get the kids ready on her own? She searches for another pair, but can only find single shoes. Bloody hell, it's infuriating. Why do toddler shoes always separate from their mates? They are the opposite of swans. Thankfully, the kids have stopped bawling. She hears their clumsy footfalls on the other side of the wall.

She finds a pair. They're slightly too big, but they'll do. Why hasn't someone invented children's shoes that grow with the kids' feet? And that stay together when they're not in use? How difficult can it be? Grasping the sandals to her dressing gown, she returns to the lounge, and sees why the twins are quiet. They've stripped off all the clothes Kate has just dressed them in, and are dancing, naked, on top of them. Grinning at her like mad gremlins.

She smiles at them, but she's crying inside. She can't do this. She gives up. Is it too early to drink? She looks at her Helix: 2PM. Pity.

"Mom?" says Silver. "Mom?" Her face is a glazed doughnut.

Kate sighs with her whole body.

"Yes?"

"Are we going to the show now?"

Mally stops dancing. Hops over. "Are we? Are we going now?" Tiny perfect white teeth like pearls in his mouth.

"No," says Kate.

"But you promised!" says Silver. "You promised we'd go to the show!"

"I know. But look at you two."

They look each other up and down, then back at her. They don't see the problem.

"I like being in the naked," says Mally.

"I know, my boy, but I can't take you out in your birthday suits, and I'm too tired to dress you again. It's already two o'clock and the show starts at half past. We won't make it."

"I'll dress myself!" says Silver. Mally repeats after her. Silver pulls her socks onto her hands like gloves and wears her pants on her head. Mally laughs and helps her put her T-shirt on around her legs like a skirt. They both look up at Kate and giggle.

Doctor Voges had recommended she take the twins on an outing. She hoped that a successful excursion would work towards quelling her paranoia of the kids getting snatched. Mally had been nagging for weeks to see the RoboPup holo show, so when the street pole ad offered her tickets on the way home, she bought them. They're sitting in her Helix now, ticking away to the show's start time. Tick, tick, tick.

"You are SUCH *skelms,*" says Kate.

Who is she kidding? They're never going to get out of the house, never mind get to the show on time. How can she break it to them, without unleashing that godawful racket? She's barely recovered from the last outpouring of grief. She dreads an afternoon cooped up at home with them.

"Silver, Mally, I need to tell you something." They look up at her with expectant faces. She can just see them thinking: *are we going now? Are we going now?*

Net help her.

Just then, there's a sound at the front door. Her heart lifts. Seth? He hadn't told her he'd left the Cape Republic. Maybe he wanted to surprise her. She goes to the door and looks at the monitor. Sebongile stands there in a starched uniform and a shining face.

"I thought it was your day off?" says Kate, after opening up.

"It is, but I heard you," she says, gesturing at the wall they share, "and I thought that you'd need help today."

She must give Sebongile a raise. A large one. Immediately.

"Thank you," says Kate, and hugs her. A sharp jab in her chest. A bright orange star, a fizz of firework. "Ouch," she says, pulling away, rubbing the pricked skin.

"Oh, sorry," says Sebongile, looking down. She adjusts her SurroSis pin.

"Don't worry," says Kate. "It's nothing."

A bead of blood forms on her chest. She wipes it off with the pad of her middle finger and puts it in her mouth. Copper squared. The kids come running and throw their naked bodies at the nanny's legs.

"Bongi! Bongi!" they shout while they scrum.

"Jump in the shower, Ma," says Sebongile. "I'll get the twins ready." She tickles their bare skin and they shriek.

"Bless you, Bongi."

Sebongile points at Kate's Helix, gesturing for her to hand it over. Kate looks down at it and sees the low battery light flashing and swears inwardly at the self-charge function that hadn't been working lately.

"I'll plug it in for you," says the nanny, shooing her into the shower.

CHAPTER 26

FLICKER OF WHISKER

The Cape Republic, 2024

Now that Seth is so very close to the end of the job, his resistance rears up like a mean cobra. This is by far the easiest part, but his brain blanks. He's tired of the vacant walls, white noise and bland food. He needs something with a bit of colour or grit or stink to get going again. A sanity break. Seth steps away from his desk, rubs his face, and is reminded by doing so that he needs a shave. Maybe he'll just go outside for a few minutes; breathe some salty air. He takes his Tile with him.

The lab door senses his objective and slides open, and the camera's eye swivels after him. Where is Carson? He makes his way towards the glass elevator but a movement at the end of the passage catches his eye.

"Hello?" he says, hoping it's Arronax. The Nautilus building is spooky in the way that although he knows there are over a hundred people working here, he never sees anyone. There's another flicker in the corner of his eye. Is he imagining it?

"Hello?" he says. Now there's a sound: a scampering. Seth follows, turning the corner, and jumps when he sees the synth salamander at his feet.

"Jesus, Meadon."

He laughs, but his humour is cut short when he looks up from the lizard to see that a lab door is open. This is not the kind of facility that leaves lab doors open.

He steps inside, knowing he shouldn't, but not being able to resist. It would go against his nature to walk away. In his experience – and he's had a lot of experience hacking laboratories – an open door like this is a highly unlikely bit of luck. As he enters, he expects some kind of alarm to sound, and gets his excuse clear in his head: *I took the wrong turn; I was looking for the bathroom; I was following Meadon and he led me in here.*

It's a huge barn of a room, and mostly dark, and seemingly empty, apart from a large machine at the back. There're no cameras in here, or at least, none that he can see. Something about the behemoth appliance spikes his blood with adrenaline as he approaches it with measured steps. His pulse accelerates as an idea forms. An idea, or a memory? A thought that inks his outlook with dread. What is this thing? Its exterior is twin doors of polished metal, like a giant-sized fridge/freezer. Like a futuristic time-journey chamber, or a travel pod. When he touches the panel on the right the machine beeps and makes a whirring sound. Then a mechanism unlocks and there's hissing as the doors glide open and fold around the sides to reveal a complicated dashboard of buttons, LEDs, dials and toggles. Beyond the dashboard is an empty glass shell. Seth looks over his shoulder, expecting a security guard to run in and tackle him, but when that doesn't happen, he pushes a button and the whole thing lights up like a December tree, including an overhead fluorescent that makes the shell radiate white light. The machine casts a glow on the whole room.

Seth looks more closely at the dash and that thought is knocking at his brain again. Has he seen this thing before? Then he spies a button with one word on it that causes the memory to come smashing in on him.

'PRINT' it says, and all of a sudden, Seth knows. He'd seen a more sophisticated version of this thing four years ago in the Genesis building. It was the machine that had printed Mally as a newborn, and a hundred other babies. Flesh and bone and blood babies.

He taps the screen: an origami-style picture of a rodent. Four crane-like arms descend on the platform of the shell and begin printing.

It starts with the skeleton: a shiny white paste that dries on contact. Once the spinal column is formed, the tiny organs appear, then the printing arms sweep out in elegant arcs to form the ribs, as if it's stitching the air with liquid ivory. Seth is mesmerised. The muscles are next, and the ribbons of tendons, and on top of that, creamy membranes and spongey pink meat. The skin prints the fastest, the fur, the longest. The final touches are the eyes, tiny liquid-filled beads, and long, impossibly thin whiskers.

Within a minute there is a white rat centre-stage. It's perfectly formed down to its tender-looking feet, but its eyes are closed, and there's no movement. When Seth presses another button a zap of electricity, like a lightning bolt, knocks the rat onto its back. If it wasn't alive before, it certainly looks dead now. The violence of the electrocution disturbs Seth. Of course he's seen his fair share of lab animal cruelty – the prevention of it was one of the reasons he'd joined Alba in the first place – but he's never been the one with his finger on the trigger.

He steps up onto the platform and the glass doors lift and open, like a transparent flower blooming. His sneakers appear dirty against the backdrop of glowing white. Gently, Seth picks up the rat with one hand and and lays it in the palm of the other. He shouldn't feel anything for it, but there's a gleam of something in his conscience, some small spark of regret. What will he do with this tiny corpse? Is it even a corpse, if it never lived? But then a whisker moves, and then a pink toe. Then nothing. Has he imagined it? Seth looks harder, and the rodent is still. Then there's another flicker of whisker and the rat is bicycling in the air, trying to get on his feet. It startles Seth and he drops the thing, which squeaks like a bouncy ball as it hits the floor then scuttles away into the shadows.

He should try to catch it. Better yet, he should leave this room, but the screen on the machine has so many options he finds he can't just walk away. Along with the icons of insects and rodents and marsupials there is an emblem of a human which he absolutely must not press.

His job here is important; he can't fuck it up.

So many lives at stake. Seth stands in front of the machine and tells himself to go back to his work station, but then his hand is out and he's tapping the human button, and the machine starts calibrating. It beeps, asking him for a dynap code.

"No way," he says under his breath. His fingers are tingling. Does he give his own DNA Profile? He takes out his SnapTile. Alongside his profile he has Kate's, and the kids'. Surely it wouldn't work, would it? Without stopping to think, he sends the machine Mally's code.

CHAPTER 27

HACKMAGG0T PENTESTER

Johannesburg, 2024

Marko's sweating. He's spent the past eighteen hours designing the hack to end all hacks. A biblical hack in magnitude and theme. He took inspiration from the ten plagues of Egypt. He's about to hit the Resurrectors' vital system files with wave after wave of afflictions. First: Blood. An injection attack that will flow into their SQL database. Next, Frogs, Lice, Flies. He's especially proud of the HackMagg0t pentester he's ready to sprinkle all over their firewall. His network-sniffing locusts will eat everything in their path. His boils are symlink attacks that will climb and corrupt. The grand finale: Death of the Firstborn: a shell-scripting masterpiece that will divert all their traffic to his deep server while poisoning their cache, spreading and replicating from one DNS server to the next, blighting everything in its path. It's fitting, elegant and masterful, if he doesn't say so himself. He feels like a demigod, finger poised, ready to unleash his fury and damnation.

"You wanted Doomsday, you motherfuckers. Here it comes."

Do demigods sweat? Do their stomachs rumble with trepidation? Why is he so damned nervous? Sure, the Resurrectors are reckless, cold-blooded killers, which would give anyone pause to reflect before pissing them off in such a cosmic way. But his methods are untraceable. He's tested and re-tested his entry points, tweaked the shit out of them. If the technophiliac Thai mafia can't locate him, how would the Resurrectors do it? They wouldn't. They couldn't.

He gets ready to click again, this time with more confidence. His finger hardly has time to hover before his Patch rings and shoots him out of his chair.

"Kaiser Soze," he says. His eyeborg shows him a picture of Keke.

"What's wrong with you?" she demands.

"What do you mean? Nothing."

He dusts biscuit crumbs off his chin.

"You're whiter than an ill Englishman."

"Am I?"

"You've got a sheen."

"A what?"

"A sheen, all over your face. Perspiration. Are you doing something bad?"

"Nope." Marko wipes away the sweat. "No. Not bad. Well. A little bit bad."

Keke narrows her eyes at him. "I can't wait to hear all about it."

"You're calling about the toddler thing?" Marko asks. "I've got something, I think."

Keke's face is alight. "Why didn't you call me, you bastard?"

He loves it when she calls him that.

"I've been hectic on a job. A big job."

"I knew you were up to something. What is it?" she asks.

"I'll fill you in later."

Suspense always makes Keke horny. God, he loves the woman. He's never actually told her. The concept of love is such a cliché, right? They've been together for almost four years now, surely she knows? He's exhilarated. Should he say something now?

"Tell me," she says.

His mind goes blank. How the –

"Wh-what?" he stutters.

"Tell me what you found out! Quickly, I need to go. I'm late."

"Okay. Right. So, the Lundy case."

"You found something on him?"

"No. There's nothing, but – "

"We went to see Helena Nash, as you suggested. She seems clean too. I mean, she's an alcoholic, and she's an asshole, but apart from that, I'm not sure why she's doing time. Both deaths look like accidents to me. What am I missing?"

"This is going to sound extremely paranoid, right?" says Marko.

"I expect nothing less."

Marko swivels around and taps some tabs in his holosphere. "Hang on. There's more stuff coming in." The leaves start multiplying. "Holy Hedy Lemarr."

"What?"

Those kids weren't ordinary toddlers.

"This is," he says, "this is ... bad."

"Fuck's sake, Marko, tell me what's going on!"

"You need to call Kate right now."

CHAPTER 28

RUFF-RUFF ROBOPUP

They arrive at the RoboPup show twenty minutes late. Luckily it seems that the organisers, knowing that the majority of the audience will be small children and their perennially stressed parents, built in some warm-up acts to buffer the disappointment of late-comers. They're at Soccer City, the stadium built to host the Johannesburg games in the 2010 World Cup. It's only sixteen years old but the building is a scarred husk of what it used to be. It reminds Kate of the pictures of the crumbling arenas in Italy, but dirtier, and with more graffiti. Still, there's enough space for the five thousand ticket holders and everyone looks cheerful enough. She needs to shake the dark clouds out of her head and try to enjoy the experience.

Kate's never been good with crowds. All the smells and sounds assail her synaesthesia until she feels that the horde is climbing on top of her and she can't breathe anymore. She knew it would be like this, so she's come prepared: she glugs down a TranX with her complimentary bottle of Bilchen water. It'll take the edge off. She says a little nonsense-prayer to the sky in Seth's direction. He has his faults, but he sure knows how to design good pharma. Before they're let into the main area, the kids are given a temporary wrist tattoo: a Z-code containing all their information, in case they're in an accident or they get lost.

A blue man on stilts walks past them, throwing pink popcorn about like confetti. Kite-drones the colours of candy floss hover around them like jellyfish. Kate hears the familiar theme music, and electronic barking, in the distance. They get stuck behind a family testing out their new Sunbrella. They smile and make funny faces as the SPF umbrella takes selfies of them.

Mally pulls on Kate's hand.

"It's starting!" he says, eyes as wide as fifty-rand coins. They pick up their pace towards the stage. Silver is skipping and her white-blonde hair glints in the sunlight. Kate feels bad, seeing how excited they are. She should really take them out more. It's not fair on them to keep them away from events like this just because she has issues. A deep breath of the afternoon-warmed air and her shoulders relax. There's a spilling of wellness inside her chest and Sebongile catches her eye and smiles at her. Kate smiles back. Yes, she thinks, the shrink was right, she'll definitely start taking the twins out more.

Kate buys the twins GlitterCola and a packet of Crispheres each. Sebongile purses her lips at the junk, averts her eyes as she drinks her water. SurroSis nannies – always beyond reproach. She shakes her head at the persistent hat hawker, but then changes her mind and buys blue dog-eared and pink cat-eared hats for Mally and Silver respectively.

There's more robotic barking and some miaowing now too. The tix on Kate's Helix directs her to their standing space. Hundreds of small children are jumping up and down. Some are dressed as RoboPup, some as KittyBot. She could have brought the kids dressed in their pyjamas, after all. The young audience starts shouting at the empty stage: *Where are you, RoboPup? Come out, RoboPup! Woof-woof, we're waiting for you!*

Some of the parents join in, and Kate looks around and starts to feel uncomfortable again. There is too much same-ness going on. Too many kids dressed the same, too many adults with the same blank faces. Despite the tranquilliser dissolving in her stomach, her anxiety starts to climb.

"Stay close, kids," she says.

"Keep an eye on Silver," says Bongi to Mally. She's always telling Mally he needs to protect his sister. He nods, and they both smile at the nanny; excitement shines their eyes.

She does a quick head-count, one-two, then breathes in and out, slowly, to keep her nerves under control. Next time she'll bring more pills. Next time she'll choose a less popular event, and it won't be Ruff-ruff RoboPup. It's not that she doesn't like the character, or the show, she just disagrees with its politics. RoboPup is the first kids' homescreen show that's completely written and produced by artificial intelligence. The machines were taught the principles of a good story and given thousands of examples, then instructed to replicate it. After a few bad shows that needed course-correcting, they came up with RoboPup. Most kids love it; Mally is obsessed with it. Eighteen months in and it's the most profitable show in the history of animated television. No writers, actors or artists needed: the AI just churns episodes out into the Stream and it's gobbled up by mesmerised kids the world over. Each episode has a moral, of course: Be Kind; Sharing is Caring; Respect Your Parent/s; Take Care of the Earth; Save Water. It's a show without boundaries: the same intelligence that creates the programme also translates it into a hundred different languages. At first she boycotted the series, but when she saw how much the twins loved the characters her need to please them outweighed her moral position.

The crowd starts to get antsy. Kate and Sebongile are pushed from behind. Kate holds Mally's hand more firmly and makes sure Silver is holding the nanny's. *Breathe. Breathe.* Perfume and holiday-scented sunblock and some sweet, sticky smell. Kids yelling, Mally jumping up and down and pulling on her arm. A nearby drone hot air balloon floating over the crowd explodes with a loud bang and showers the cheering audience with glitter-strips and Stevia Pops. It sends Kate's pulse racing.

"Mom, can I have some of that?" Silver is looking at her neighbour's freshly bought ice shavings.

"No," says Kate. "You've already had something and the show's about to start."

"Please, Mom? Please?" She has the same sweet tooth as her mother. "I want some. I've never had some before."

Kate looks around her. It will take forever to get out of this crowd now and get back here.

"I'll take her," says Sebongile. "I don't mind."

"I don't know if it's a good idea."

"Please, Mom."

She remembers her earlier commitment to have more fun and let the kids try new things. It's good for their development. She needs to relax, to stop being so over-protective, to let the kids be kids.

"Let me take her," says the nanny, hoisting Silver up on her generous hip. "No problem."

Okay. Why not? Kate nods for them to go. She bumps Sebongile's bank for two servings so that Mally can have some too. The crowd swallows the two of them up. Mally lets go of her hand.

"Don't let go," she says, "I don't want to lose you."

"Your hand's sweaty," he says, rubbing his palm on his shirt. "I don't want to hold it."

Kate's eyes find the sky. Where are those toddler leashes when you need them? She grasps his shoulder, instead.

Finally, the show starts. Kate looks over her shoulder for Sebongile but she can't spot her. White-and-blue vapour surges from the smoke machines and overflows onto the audience. Kate's Patch rings with an incoming call. She checks her Helix: it's Keke. She silences the call. No way she'll be able to hear anything above this throng of chattering kids.

A show-branded Volanter approaches, slicing up the blue horizon. It hovers over the stage then lowers a giant pimped-out dog kennel. There's more smoke, and more glitter, and RoboPup jumps out: a twenty-foot tall robot puppy hologram that can smile and stand on his hind legs. The small children scream serrated shapes (Shrill Stab).

"Ruff-ruff everybody!" he barks.

The kids all shout back: *Ruff-ruff RoboPup!*

"Thanks so much for coming today," he says. "It's really nice to see you!"

Fuck, the inanity. How is she going to get through an hour of this?

Pop-pop-pop-pop-pop go the lights. The theme music starts in earnest and everyone sings along. The same lyrics that are a constant earworm to thousands of people all over the world. Kate finds the words slipping into her head even though she resists them. Her Patch rings. It's Keke, again. Kate looks backwards to try to spot Bongi. All she sees are a sea of hypnotised faces singing the stupid song. Her earlier feeling of wellbeing curdles into dread. 14:53. They should have been back by now.

CHAPTER 29

STICKY CHEEK

It's 14:58 when the sirens sound so loudly that Kate can't see what's in front of her. She lets go of Mally's shoulder and shields her ears. Sharp objects embed themselves in her vision like ninja stars. The crowd around them are shocked into silence. Is this part of the show? But the RoboPup hologram evaporates into pixels and the smoke machines are turned off.

"The fuck?" says the man standing next to her with his toddler on his shoulders. His partner smacks his arm for swearing in front of their spawn. Another man shrugs. The woman in front of her stands on her tip-toes, trying to understand what is going on. The siren continues to saw through Kate's brain.

"What's happening, Mom? Mom? Mom?" says Mally, but she can't see him through the noise. She grabs his hand.

"It's a bomb!" shouts someone, stunning the crowd. "Bomb!" "Bomb!" people start yelling. Yelling and running, but everyone's packed so tightly it's difficult to move anywhere in a hurry. "Get out!" screams a woman in Kate's face. "They're going to blow this place up!"

A new hologram flickers on, above the stage. It's the Soccer City Stadium mascot, a giant yellow *vuvuzela* with eyes like rolling footballs and a Zulu accent.

"Please, remain calm," he says. "Exit in an orderly manner. Exit as quickly as you can. Do not panic."

Kate looks for Silver. Where the hell are they? Will they exit from where they are, or come here to find her, first? People are jostling her, holding onto their kids as if they are licenses to shove other people out the way.

"Please, remain calm," says the vuvuzela. Kate and Mally are getting swept up in the tide of panic. They've already been displaced twenty feet. She tries to phone Bongi but there are too many signals and the call won't start. How will she find them? Coconut sunblock, agave flatdrinks, soydogs. Does she try to fight her way back to her original position, or go with the flow? It looks like she doesn't have a choice. They lose another metre, then another. Kate's heart is hammering away, but she wills herself to stay calm for the sake of the kids. A glitter-cannon misfires, making the crowd scream. Some people tuck and roll, others double their efforts to push out of the park. The grass beneath them is littered with dropped snax and forgotten cardigans. They have to get out of here.

"Mom!"

There are hundreds of children around them, all confused and crying, but Kate recognises Silver's voice instantly.

"Mom!"

"Silver!" she shouts, catching sight of her. Silver is perched on Sebongile's hip, and they all wave madly at each other. The siren is still distorting Kate's vision but she can see her daughter and the relief paints her heart green. Sebongile and Kate fight their way through the crowd, towards each other. Finally they touch. Kate wants to hug Silver but when she leans forward to take her from the nanny's embrace, Silver's face turns white; etched with shock.

"Where's Mally?"

Kate's confused. What does she mean? Mally's right here, holding her hand. Kate looks down as if to show her, and it's like she's just touched a live electric wire. She whips her hand away from the strange boy who's standing there. Mally's height, Mally's RoboPup hat, what felt like Mally's soft warm hand, but not Mally. Just then the boy realises he's lost. He opens his mouth in a silent cry, his face flushes with fear, and he just stands there, frozen to the spot, bright-blood skin and streaming snot: a monument to lost children.

"Oh my God," says Kate. "Oh my God." When did she lose him? How far could he have gone? She tears her eyes off the little boy and scans the crowd around her. He's under this sea of people. All the little boys look the same from this angle – all metallic blue dog ears. How will she ever find him? She starts shouting his name over and over again. Sebongile joins in. Kate expects Silver to start bawling but she remains eerily calm.

"Don't panic!" Kate says to the nanny, but more to herself. Her heart has gone back to knocking around so hard she feels it may eject itself right out of her chest. Kate grabs Silver, needs to feel her small limbs around her. Sebongile tries to comfort the strange boy but he won't have it, so instead, she tries to shield him from the rush of people so he doesn't get trampled.

Kate has the irrational urge to whistle, so that she can find Mally via the FindMe app on his watch, but of course it would never work in this noise.

There's a buzzing sound; Kate shakes her head to get rid of it. Every second that passes could mean he's getting further away. She shouts his name again. The buzzing gets louder. In the distance she sees where it's coming from: a massive cloud of brown and green is swarming towards them. The bomb squad has arrived and has released the Pavlocs. The bomb-sniffing locusts move in the air like a flock of swallows. Sebongile screams when she sees them.

"Don't worry," Kate says. "They're here to help us."

The locusts blind the blue of the sky, making it feel like sudden evening. The LEDs on their thoraxes are go-robot green, which bodes well. Once their hijacked antennae sense anything incendiary the electrode in their brains will register the electrical activity and the light will flick to red.

Kate tries to ignore the buzzing and flitting. Jettisoned wings rain over them like floating ash. In the artificial dusk it'll be even more difficult to spot Mally. She tries to shout for him again but her voice is hoarse.

"Mally is in danger," says Silver, as calm as Kate has ever seen her.

"What?" croaks Kate. "What did you say?"

Silver's eyes are filled with light, despite the darkness that surrounds them. "We need to find him, now."

"What do you mean?" she shouts. "What are you talking about?"

People are still pushing past but the crowd is thinning now: Kate and Sebongile are no longer at risk of being swept away. Kate coughs into her arm, clears her throat, trying to get her voice back, but it just makes it worse. She casts around for Mally. He's here somewhere! The vuvuzela mascot is repeating his mantra, advising everyone to be calm and move as quickly as possible to the emergency exits. "For ease of exit," he says, football eyes rolling, "the Z-code barrier has been temporarily disabled."

No!

She wants to scream. The Z-code tattoo the kids get on their way in is linked to her Patch which means they can't leave the ground with anyone but the guardian they came in with. It's the one thing that has been stopping Kate from full-blown panic. Now anyone can snatch him.

The Pavlocs continue their swarming, sniffing, looking for a bomb. Their built-in sensors are more sensitive than anything a human can manufacture. They've been trained to seek explosives to receive their reward, and they are kept hungry.

"He's going out of the stadium," says Silver. "Mally's leaving."

"Where?" says Kate, "Can you see him?"

Silver nods. "Number green-red," she says.

Kate looks around, frantic. She can't see exit 49 from here, how can Silver?

"Green-red," she says again. "They're leaving.

Kate's blood runs cold. "Who is 'they'?"

Silver just blinks at her. Kate leaves Bongi to sort out the imposter child and runs towards gate 49. Bodies are everywhere, blocking her way, just as desperate as her to get out. They don't understand the real danger. Green-orange, green-grey, green-purple. Finally they get to green-red. Luckily it's a less popular exit, and there are fewer people with whom to wrestle.

"Mally!" she shouts, but it comes out a whisper. She runs up to a security guard who is shepherding the crowd out. "Have you seen a little boy?"

The man purses his lips at her. They are surrounded by hordes of little boys. She shows him a photo on her Helix: a picture of Mally's face. He looks at it but shrugs again; he's seen a thousand faces today. Kate's phone keeps ringing. She's so scared and frustrated and full of vile yellow adrenaline that she wants to pull out her hair. Silver's eyes light up again as she looks through the fence to the people outside. She lifts her arm and points, like an arrow poised to let fly.

"There," she says, but she doesn't have to. Her finger has found her brother, who is being led away by the silhouette of a woman. Kate yells his name over and over, breaking her already broken voice. Free of the crowd, the strange woman and her son are walking at a steady pace, while Kate is stuck behind a herd of babbling idiots.

"Mally!" she shouts, fighting her way through the crowd. The guard, formerly indifferent, sees what is happening and tries to create a path for her: he holds some cursing people back to give Kate room to run. Eventually she breaks free of the maddening throng and sprints up to her son, grabbing him from behind and breaking the stranger's hold on him. The woman, head-to-toe in yummy-mummy gear, black tights and jacket, designer scarf and fully made-up face, does not seem startled at all by Kate's feverish appearance.

The split-second before Kate grabs him she imagines she has it wrong, that this isn't her son and the moment she touches him he'll turn around, startled, and his face will not be Mally's. And it would be embarrassing; a terrible misunderstanding. But of course it's her son, a mother knows how her children look from every angle, how they walk, and here is Mally, here he is, she has found him.

She rips off his hat and throws it to the ground, pulls his face towards hers, feels his sticky cheek. Tear-stained and hot. She's found him, she's found him, Jesus Christ, she'd almost lost him.

"I was looking for security," says the ruby-lipped woman. "I didn't know who to report him to."

Kate stands up and looks at her; brown eyes devoid of kindness. Two raisins on a plate.

"You were walking towards the parking lot." Kate looks back at the security guard but he is busy with someone else. "Security is that way," she says, thumb pointing back towards the stadium gates. Silver stares at the petite woman in black.

"There was so much confusion," says the woman. "I thought it was best to move away from the bomb threat." She's not backing down. She smiles too much. A practised smile, a smile honed to make you want to trust her, but Kate knows better than that. It's too wide, and it doesn't reach her dead-grape eyes.

"The lady was helping me," says Mally. "She scanned my code. She tried phoning you."

Kate lifts her shaking arm to look at her Helix and sees twelve missed calls.

"Who are you?" Kate tries to sound strong but her voice is shredded by the shouting and the fright, and there is a high note to it that she doesn't recognise.

"I'm no one," says the woman. "Goodbye, Mally." She ruffles his hair.

Kate pulls him away from her. The woman puts her sunglasses back on and walks away, the tail of her scarf floating behind her.

Kate falls onto her knees. She looks Mally in the eyes, searching for damage, but there is none. People continue to stream past them, not paying them any mind. They are flotsam stuck in a river. She hugs both twins, head bowed, in a huddle, as if they are saying a prayer.

CHAPTER 30

SWITCH BLADE

The Cape Republic, 2024

The printing arms set to soundless work and Seth instantly regrets it. He taps the 'CANCEL' button over and over but the machine has other ideas. He looks for somewhere to switch it off but it seems to be self-powered.

"Shit." He says, "Shit," as he tries to cancel it again, but the printer is already well on its way, with 04:16 to go on its completion timer. He sits on the floor and, with his hands covering his mouth and nose, watches the printer work as it builds Mally up from scratch, layer by layer. Ivory, cream, pink.

Horrifying.

Fascinating.

What has he done?

When the machine is finished, an age-correct, near-perfect copy of Mally stands within the glass shell, naked and vulnerable. Seth climbs up onto the platform again and opens the doors. He approaches the print-out with caution, examines his skin – too clean – and his hair. Touches his shoulder, which feels so life-like his fingers automatically spring away. The boy even has the scar from his newborn vaccinations – the ones for which Seth had taken him to the baby clinic, and had left an angry red nub for weeks afterwards. Seth didn't realise those records were embedded in his dynap code too. The anthrobot's eyelids are closed, so Seth uses his thumb to half-open his left eye and he peers in closely. They're the same as Mally's, the same as Kate's. Exactly the same, but –

Both of the eyes spring open, and Seth jumps a foot in the air. His heart sprints. He stumbles backwards, almost falls, then scrambles down from the machine, and ends up face to face with a ginger beard.

"Carson," he says, but the man doesn't reply.

"Seth," comes the voice of Arronax from the dark corner of the room. The overhead lights brighten by a fraction, revealing her sitting there comfortably, long legs crossed. Has she been sitting there all along?

"Sometimes I like to come in here and just look at the machine. I've been working on it for over a decade."

"It's impressive," says Seth.

"And yet you don't seem impressed."

"Don't take it personally. It's just that I've seen a – "

"You've seen a more sophisticated version of it. I know. We know. Why do you think we brought you here?"

"I know nothing about printing living things. Unless you need something chemgineered, or a mathematical sequence, I'm not your man."

"You're more useful than you know."

Seth's body is on high alert. His instinct is to flee, but he has questions. "The synthetic heart was a ruse?"

"Not at all. That heart is the key to everything."

Seth shakes his head.

"Here, let me show you." She steps up to the printer and her finger hovers over the button that shocked the mouse. That brought the mouse to life.

"No!" says Seth. "Don't. Please."

She ignores him and there is a bolt of electricity that cuts through the chamber and knocks the anthrobot Mally off his feet. The body jitters with the after-effects.

"Damn it! What are you doing?"

He rushes back up the platform and opens the glass doors. Arronax shouts "Don't!" but he touches the naked body and a flash of energy blazes up his arm and throws him backwards. The breath is knocked out of him, and he stays where he is, watching the boy in horror.

"See?" she says. "The ignition command doesn't work on him. It doesn't work on humanoid prints. That's why we need the heart. The heart you're working on."

"You said it was for people who needed heart transplants."

"That's a fortunate side business. Good for PR, and for cash injections."

"I won't do it."

"You already have," she says.

"I haven't finished. I won't."

"Think of all the lives you'll save."

"I don't give a fuck."

Arronax pauses, pouts. "You can't stop progress, you know."

There's a bitter taste in his mouth. He gestures to the small naked body sprawled on the platform. "This isn't *progress.*"

"You're taking this too personally. That's not him, you know. That's not Mally."

"Obviously."

"But what I mean is, that thing's not human. At all. We print with synth-cells – for now. There are more meat-cells in a Bilchen burger than there are in that body."

"But it looks – "

So real? So lifelike?

"Thank you," she says.

"That was not meant as a compliment."

"I'll take it as one, anyway," she says.

Seth stands up. "I'm out."

"You can't leave."

"Yes," Seth says, "I can."

"You're on contract."

"I don't give a fuck about a contract."

She takes a step forward. "We'll pay you double. Triple."

"I'm leaving." Seth tries to walk past her but Arronax stands in his way – she's flustered – she looks around the room, perhaps for another angle to sell him on.

"But it's not real, don't you understand? If you cut it, it won't bleed. Here," she says, rummaging in her lab coat pocket until she pulls out a plastic-capped scalpel. A scientist's version of a switch blade. She approaches the body on the stage.

"Don't," says Seth. "Put that away."

"I just want to show you – "

"Put that away!"

Arronax fixes him with her crystalline eyes and the frantic energy in the room slows. She puts her trembling hand on his chest.

"You think I don't know how you feel about that boy? About Mally? About both of them?"

The psychic switch obviously relays more than simple thoughts. Seth pictures the Genesis Clinic's printer clearly in his mind, then she takes her hand off his chest.

"Then you'll know why I can't do this."

There is a movement near the passage, and the rat scuttles across the doorway. Without hesitating, Carson stomps on it. A final half-squeak as the rodent is flattened, and Carson lifts up his boot. There is no blood.

CHAPTER 31

RUBBER BONES AND HAPPY HEARTS

Johannesburg, 2024

Kate arrives home, grasping the shoulders of both children as if she'll never let them go again.

"Ow, Mom," says Mally. Kate is hardly sorry.

She's about to place her finger on the biometric pad to open the front door when Sebongile puts up her hand and whispers "Wait."

Kate is so exhausted and relieved to get home she hasn't been processing the clues: The pad's LED flashing red; the disabled security alarm; the gate bent ever so slightly; the front door one click away from being properly closed.

"Fuck!" she whispers, grabbing the kids and pulling them even closer. She hits the panic button on her Helix, triggering the silent sting and alerting the security company. Of course, SafeGuard already know about it, and they're on their way. She just hasn't seen their bump on her phone.

"You said a bad w– " says Silver, but Kate slaps her palm against the girl's mouth to silence her. They pick up a child each and run back towards the elevator. It's still there, open-mouthed, after delivering them ten seconds earlier. They slide in and Kate presses the 'close' button over and over until they're safely shut inside.

"What's going on, Mom?" says Mally. Silver says the same thing at almost the exact same time.

"Something looked funny," says Kate, stroking Mally's hair with a flat hand. She sees a hundred versions of herself in the mirror, life-size to miniature, and they all look sick.

In her house? They're in her house?

"Funny?" says Silver.

They know where we live.

"I want to go home," says Mally.

Sebongile looks ill too.

"I've just asked SafeGuard to check it for us, before we go in. Nothing to worry about." Kate kisses his head. "Just being careful, that's all."

Kate installs the nanny and the kids in a private booth in the resident restaurant, orders them fauxburgers and fries and promises them malt soyshakes if they're really quiet. She finds the manager's office and asks him for the room, and he takes one look at her feral eyes and agrees, gives her the bottle of water he was just about to drink. Closing the door after him, she dials Seth, but it just rings. She phones the emergency number he left for her and someone strange answers, telling her to speak up, but she can't. Eventually she gets the message across. Next SafeGuard is on the line and Kate tells them she needs a security escort. Within minutes, two guards arrive. One of the burly men gives her the safeword – 52Hz – to assure her that he can be trusted. It's a paid-for extra, just like the night beams, the rapid/stealth motion sensors, the steel-reinforced door of the panic room. You can never be too careful, the sign-up guy had said. Seth had called him paranoid, pushy, but Kate liked him then, and she likes him even more now.

She watches the kids slurp up the last of their shakes and for a moment it's like they're in some kind of crazy surrealist show. Toasted marshmallow flavour. How can they just sit there, swinging their skinny legs, chatting to Bongi, as if it's an ordinary day?

She's reminded of the resilience of kids. Rubber bones and happy hearts. Up to a point, of course. Everyone has their line in the sand.

The guards are wearing the latest in protective gear: Kevlarskin onesies and Russian automatics. They wait patiently for Kate and Sebongile to put the kids' shoes back on and wipe their faces, then they travel up in the elevator. The space inside the lift, usually generous, seems packed, and sends Kate's exhausted synapses into overdrive. The mere size of the men who take up so much air-space, the children smelling like spiky tomato sauce and grime. Sebongile smells like cheap soap, and Kate can smell herself too: wilted perfume over body odour and SPF. There's not a litre of breathable air in the confined space, just a soupy brown mess of colours and textures that brings Kate's saliva rushing into her mouth. She holds one hand to her lips, the other against the wall of the elevator, and wills herself to not vomit. When the doors slide open she's the first person out.

The biometric pad has been dusted for prints. Kate doesn't stop to inspect it: she needs a shower and a whisky, not necessarily in that order. She needs the kids to be safe in their kid-cocoons. She'll sleep in their room tonight. When she pushes the door open every single light is on.

"Hello?" She takes a few steps inside and cries out when she sees the unconscious body in the hallway.

CHAPTER 32
HACKSPIDER

"Oh shit," says Marko to himself. "Oh shit, oh shit, oh shit."

He's busy executing his fourth plague on the Resurrectors' system files when something appears on his screen that shouldn't be there. Something he's only ever heard about but never seen before. It's a hackspider: code injected into his hard drive that tangles things up, with a vicious virtual bite that can be fatal to his OS. It's already confused his running system, corrupted important files. His SQL database is reeling.

"Son of a bitch," he says, typing frantically on his holopad. "Who sent you?"

Marko knows his system is basically impenetrable. Or at least, he thought it was, until now. He tries to catch the spider, tries to squash it, but it's a slippery thing that is always just out of his grasp. A long minute passes as he chases the autohacker and sees it wreak havoc. He can't catch it, and he can't risk it biting, so he executes an emergency shut down. He force quits the entire system, which he's never done before and unplugs every cable. He's sweating: he doesn't know if it'll ever come alive again. He sits in the dark, silent room, thoughts buzzing around his head like flies. He needs to go to the bathroom urgently, but he can't move. Who sent the spider? Who has access to such advanced tech? Someone with a lot of clout knows who he is, and where he is.

CHAPTER 33

MORE LIVES THAN A CAT

"Betty!" Kate cries, running over to the beagle. She crouches next to the dog and puts her hands on her head and flank. Inspects her for injuries. Betty/Barbara's mouth trembles. She squeaks and her eyes roll back.

"What have they done to you?" she cries, "What have they done?" She strokes the dog's paralysed body.

A man comes over to her. He's not wearing a bulletproof onesie, and his SafeGuard e-badge reads: 'Assessor'.

She hears the twins come in from behind her. Tries to cover up the beagle but it's too late: they've both seen her and their mouths drop open. They're too shocked to cry. Sebongile sees the dog last and her mouth turns down. They got on well, the two of them. The nanny pulls the kids into the bathroom; there is the sound of water running as she draws their bath.

Kate crouches even further down, kisses the dog on her head, lays an ear on her side, closes her eyes.

"She's not dead," says the Assessor, offering her a hand up.

Kate's eyes flit open. "Do you mean not dead *yet?*"

"Not dead at all."

Kate looks at Betty/Barbara, then up at the man again, this huge stranger in her home. He helps her up.

"Now," he says. "You've had a shock."

He doesn't know the least of it.

"Come and sit at the table and I'll take you through what we found."

"My dog," says Kate.

"She'll be fine," says the man, leading her to a seat.

"Not poisoned?"

"Just drugged. Diazepam is my guess."

She wants to run and tell the children, but her body doesn't move from the chair. She doesn't think she'll ever move from the chair. *That dog has more lives than a cat.*

A mug of tea is placed in front of her. With shaking hands she takes a sip, but looks longingly at the booze cabinet. The same man who made her tea fetches a blanket from the lounge and places it over the beagle, tells the nanny and kids that the dog will be okay. She wants to hug him. He's the Comforter. She'll never complain about the high cost of this security company ever again.

"I think it would be prudent, if you agree, to station two of my men outside your apartment 24/7 until the threat has passed."

"Yes." Kate nods. "Yes, please."

"I would also like to stay until things are settled. Are you okay with this?"

She knows what he's doing. After any kind of breach in security, the victim feels out of control. By asking her at every turn if she agrees, it gives her some sense of restored power.

"Yes," she says. "That will be fine. Thank you."

The kids are fighting in the bath. Bongi scolds them gently and they seem to simmer down. The Assessor takes her through the intrusion, point by point. Their first assumption is that it was most likely two professional thieves, the way the system was disarmed.

"It's quite a thing," he says, shaking his head, "six years since we've had this particular technology and I've never seen it circumvented." He tells her that a few drawers had been turned out, some furniture up-ended. The company had tidied what they could to lessen the trauma and sent their report to the insurance company. Indeed, looking around the place, you'd never say that it has just been burgled. The police force has been notified, although they don't expect anyone to turn up; they hardly ever do. It's why security companies like SafeGuard are such a profitable business. They are there for every facet of house invasion, he says. Their job is to make it as hassle-free as possible.

She finishes the tea (Chamomile Dream) and excuses herself to take a shower. God, she needs a shower. She's covered in dust and dry fear-sweat.

"We thought it was a burglary, but then – "

Kate stares at him.

He clears his throat. "Then someone showed up and briefed us on – "

"What?" says Kate.

"She said that there is another element at play. She needs to meet with you, urgently, regarding the safety of your children."

Kate looks around. She's already refused his offer of complimentary counselling. Has she missed someone sitting here? But the couches and chairs are empty. She's confused.

"Who? A colleague of yours?"

He shakes his head. "We've never met."

"But you let her into my house?" Perhaps SafeGuard isn't as professional as she had previously believed.

"It's a mandate," he says. "She's on the PreApp security list. She's allowed anywhere, any time."

"Bullshit. This is a private residence and we don't have anyone on our pre-approved list."

"Not your personal list. It's the national PreApp list."

The national list? Only uber-VIPs are on there. Venerated, squeaky clean, public figures. Why would someone like that be in her flat?

"I'm sure she'll explain everything."

He stands up, and she follows suit. She puts her head around the door of the bathroom and sees Bongi vigorously towelling off the twins, as if they've been swimming in the ocean instead of sitting in ten centimetres of bathwater. The kids notice her and look up, grinning, and she has never seen them looking so clean. The nanny reaches for Mally's pyjamas – RoboPup, of course – and just seeing the animated dog again fills her with dread. She can't believe how close she came to losing him today. The Assessor leads her to the panic room, as if it is his house, instead of hers. The door is only just ajar. She opens it wider, and steps inside.

A mature woman with long, straight, light grey hair is sitting in the lazy chair. She's wearing a simple white shift robe, and would blend into the white interior if she didn't have a distinct glow about her. Kate guesses she doesn't blend in anywhere she goes. The picture of her sitting there, surrounded by white, gives the impression of a pale-petalled lotus, her glowing face the centre of the flower. The image reminds her of when she visited the seed bank – the Doomsday Vault – and she had learnt that lotus seeds can keep their promise for hundreds of years.

"Solonne," says Kate.

The woman seems pleased. "You know who I am," she says. "That makes things easier."

Kate can smell the sandalwood beads around the woman's neck. Treebark. Cinnamon.

"Of course I know who you are."

Solonne is the closest South Africa has to a holy matriarx. She's the head of the SurroTribe. Outwardly chilled and bohemian looking, she has a fierce moral imperative and a titanium spine. The discarded SurroSisters, who live together in a gated community, have to be beyond reproach in every way or they are stripped of their pins. She doesn't allow them idle hands, either. If they're between jobs they have a strict schedule of extra-murals to stick to, including, among others, horseback riding, coding, language acquisition, and archery.

Solonne looks like a new-age hippie but she's marketing savvy enough to know how important brands are, and she won't stand for anyone tarnishing hers.

"I'm here to help you," she says.

"Help me? Why?"

The woman sighs through her nose, then steeples her fingers.

"Kate, you must know. Your son is in much danger."

CHAPTER 34
ASYLUM

"She's right," comes a voice from behind Kate, and she jumps. Kekeletso. "Sorry, I didn't mean to scare you."

Kate holds a fist to her heart. "Come in. Join us. Have you met Solonne?"

They say hello and exchange tight smiles. Keke grabs a chair. "I'd kill for a beer. Does this pad come with room service?"

"Kind of," says Kate, and presses on a shiny cabinet door near her head. A tidy liquor cabinet is revealed.

"Magical," says Keke. "Why have I never been in here before?"

Kate tries to slow her breathing. The whiteness of the panic room is balm to her ragged nerves. No shapes to jump out at her, no clouds of colour to billow over her brain. She opens a bottle of red without looking at the label and, with trembling hands, pours them each a glass. She expects Solonne to refuse it, ask for water, but instead she sticks her nose right into the glass, (Berry Bouquet), and takes a sip.

Kate checks the dashboard, inspects the footage of the interior of the house. The Assessor is sitting at the kitchen table, filling out what she guesses is a case report on his Tile. The Comforter has picked Betty/Barbara off the floor and is sitting with her on his lap, in the lounge, stroking her shivering head, and Bongi is tucking the twins into their cocoons, storybooks at the ready. Seth's room is dark and empty. He'll be home soon, then things will be back to normal. Solonne casts a glance at her. Well, not *normal* normal.

They sit in a triangle. Keke's dusty cowboy boots, Kate's old sneakers, Solonne's gladiator sandals.

"Tell me everything. I want to know everything."

The two women start talking at the same time, then Solonne gestures that Keke should go on.

"The court case I've been grinding. I didn't want to tell you the details because I knew you'd find them upsetting – hell, I find them upsetting – but now I have to. Marko found something that you need to know."

"I'm not some tragic fragile female figure, you know," says Kate, flushing. "I don't need to be protected."

"You're nothing close to fragile," says Keke, "I know. But the last few years – since the thing, since Genesis – have been tough on you. Of course they have. It was a terrible thing you had to do."

Kate closes her eyes, rubs her face.

"No one blames you for not, I don't know, for not keeping it together all the time."

"Well, that's nice to know." She smells bitterness, like tar.

"A lesser person would be in straightjacket; would be in an asylum somewhere."

"Right now that sounds very appealing," says Kate. The Net knows she's tempted by the idea of constant white walls and TranX and a view of a meadow. But then she thinks of the field of flowers, the farm to which the Ed Miller impersonator took her and Seth, tricked them into digging their own graves, and her anxiety shoots right up again. The inside of her mouth is powder dry. Her glass of wine remains untouched.

"I didn't want to tell you because I didn't want you to worry unnecessarily. The case had nothing to do with you, until – "

"Until?"

"Well, until it did."

"You should have told me immediately."

"I am telling you immediately. When I couldn't get hold of you, I got here as soon as I could."

"And?"

"And, I didn't want you to be on your own when you heard it."

"You do think I'm weak. That I've become weak."

"No," says Keke, shaking her head. "But it's about the kids. The twins. And they're like your Kryptonite."

Kate's stomach simmers.

"Tell her about Lundy," says Solonne. "Tell her about Nash."

Keke gives Solonne a strange look. She puts down her wine glass and looks Kate in the eyes.

"The trial will be over in the next few days. The accused is a man named Mack Lundy, who's going to be found guilty of killing his son – his toddler – in the bath."

In the bath? The case reminds Kate of Blanco, the assassinated pianist, and she shudders. The Bride in the Bath. No wonder she's hankering after an asylum with all these memories beating her up inside her head.

"Did he do it?" asks Kate.

"No," say Keke and Solonne, at the same time.

"It was an accident?"

"Well – " says Keke.

"No," says Solonne, with decided finality. "It was certainly not an accident."

"Maybe you should be telling the story," says Keke.

Solonne shakes her head. "It's better if Kate hears it from you."

"So we did some research," she says. "Well, by that I mean that I asked Marko to do some research. And it turns out that there's a kind of phenomenon happening, this terrible thing – "

"Yes?" says Kate.

"I'm sorry, Kitty. There's this thing happening, under the Blanket, and we don't know yet what's causing it – "

Solonne cuts in. "Toddlers are being targeted."

Kate swallows hard. "What?"

"A wave of small children," says Keke. "Kids the twins' ages. Countrywide."

"What?" says Kate. "That doesn't make any sense. What do you mean?"

"Lundy swears it was an accident. Thinks his son must have slipped and hit his head."

"Ha!" says Solonne, but she's not laughing.

"The other one? Nash?"

"Helena Nash is serving time for the murder of her daughter, who she says fell down the stairs."

"Not an accident?"

"Not an accident."

"Am I missing something?"

"That's exactly how I feel," says Keke. "It doesn't make sense. Yet."

"So…this feeling I have, that they're in danger. It's true."

"It's never been more true," says Solonne. "At least, for one of them."

"Mally," says Kate, because she just knows. She can feel it. Has always felt it.

"Yes," says Solonne. "Mally."

Kate stands up again, checks the dash, sees that the twins are safely ensconced in their HappyHammox while Sebongile reads to them. Checks the front door, which is armed by the two strapping men who escorted them from the restaurant. She can't see their fingers, but imagines them resting gently on their respective triggers.

"Why?" asks Kate.

"Marko said… Marko worked out some algorithm. Found a pattern to the deaths. It's the Genesis Generation they're killing."

"No," says Kate. "Impossible."

"Not *killing*," says Solonne. "Killed. They're all dead. Apart from – "

"But no one knows who the printed babies are. Apart from the parents, I mean. All their identities were protected."

"The Genesis Project knows."

The mention of the GP kicks Kate in the stomach. "It's not the Genesis Project," she says. It can't be. "They're dead. They're all dead, aren't they?"

"Van der Heever is dead. Mouton. Marmalade. But they may have just been the tip of the iceberg. Who knows how many agents are still out there. All those people who evacuated the building before – "

"No," says Kate. "No. I can't deal with this." She tries to take a sip of wine but is surprised by the suddenly empty glass in her hand. She puts it on the table. There would be a list of the printed babies. Of course there would be a list.

"As far as I know, the Genesis Project has been dissolved. It became too dangerous for them to operate once the story of the clinic hit. They've gone underground. I don't think we'll be hearing from them any time soon."

"Besides," says Keke, "why would they kill the generation they fought so hard to create? The DNA-printed babies were their vision for the future."

"A stalled vision," says the matriarx.

"Then who?" says Kate. "Who would kill *toddlers?*"

"I have a theory," says Solonne. "But you're not going to like it."

CHAPTER 35
THE LAST ONE

Solonne drains her glass, sets it on the table in front of her, and clasps her hands together. "I have reason to believe that the people behind the killings are the Resurrectors."

Kate's brain whirrs.

"I know it seems odd," Solonne says, "especially as they're always going on about the innocence of children – "

"And gunning down doctors at family planning clinics," interjects Keke.

"But we have … informers … that have intimated that it's the Resurrectors that are behind the hits."

"You have informers inside the Resurrectors?"

"It's not something we discuss."

"But you trust your source?"

Solonne shakes her head. "I don't even know who the source is. This information comes trickling through what is a very shaky – and barbed – grapevine."

"It does make sense though," says Keke. "Remember how they reacted when the Genesis Generation story hit the news? They said that the printed babies were an abomination. An insult to God. And they seem to have no problem with killing children."

Kate nods. "Look at what happened today. At the stadium. Half that audience were kids."

"It was just a bomb threat. The Pavlov Locusts stayed green. No bomb. We don't even know if the Resurrectors were behind it."

"Of course they were behind it. It was all engineered to distract you."

Kate stares at her. "A bomb threat that cleared an entire stadium…to distract *me*?"

"Well, it worked, didn't it? You lost Mally."

"What?" says Keke.

Kate, having started to relax in the company of the women, feels her terror rise again and wrap around her throat. "Surely not," she says. "Surely they wouldn't."

She pictures the woman with the scarf leading Mally away, her dazzling fake smile outlined in red.

"But why go to such lengths, for a little boy?"

"Because it has to look random. It has to look like bad luck. It's too controversial, otherwise. They can't risk their members or crowdfunders turning away from them."

"Who are they?" says Keke. "Who are the Resurrectors?"

"That's what we need to find out."

Kate stares at the empty bottle of wine. She can't help but to think of the biblical water-into-wine story. It would be nice if the religious fundamentalists took something like that up, for their cause. Be kind to your neighbour, make wine, be a good samaritan. If they took those to heart, and applied the same extreme energy, instead of mowing innocent people down at clinics and going after little children the world would be a better place, for sure. In the mean time, she's going to do anything – everything – it takes to keep Mally safe.

"They're getting desperate," says Solonne. "Our canary broke protocol to contact me when she found out they need the Genesis Generation gone by midnight tomorrow. They have some kind of – I don't know – some prophecy, some deadline, or the world falls apart."

Kate blinks at them, brain spinning. "Surely there are others. Other Genesis children, out there."

Solonne's lips turn into a small, hard line.

"No, dear," she says quietly. "Not anymore. Mally is the last one."

Kate storms out of the panic room. The Assessor jumps up, asks her what's wrong. She ignores him and marches into the kids' room, claps on the light.

"Wake up!" she shouts at them. "Wake up!"

Silver continues to snore. Mally frowns in his sleep.

"Wake up!" she yells again.

Sebongile jumps up. "What is it?" she asks, eyes wedged wide in alarm. "Ma?"

Kate goes to the hammox and shakes the twins by their shoulders. Slaps Mally softly on the cheek.

"Please," says the nanny, hovering over her shoulder, "leave them. They're sleeping. It's been a long day. Tell me what's wrong."

Mally sits up, blinking blindly. Silver, cradling her cuddle-bunny, starts crying in her sleep.

"Wake up, guys. I need to speak to you. Get up."

"Let it wait till the morning, Ma," says Sebongile. "They're exhausted."

Kate ignores the nanny and hauls the children out of their cocoons. Parks their warm, sleepy bodies on top of one of their toy trunks.

"What's wrong, Mom?" asks Mally.

Silver is still whining, her long hair tousled, obscuring most of her face.

"Silver!" she shouts, and Silver jumps, finally opens her eyes. Sebongile reaches out to comfort her but Kate holds up a hand to stop her. "Wake up. I have something important to say."

They sit, bleary-eyed, mouths pouted by sleepiness.

"You are *never,* and I mean *never, never ever* allowed to go with a stranger. Do you understand me?"

They both nod.

"We know that rule," whines Mally.

"But you still went with that woman today!" Kate's voice has an ugly edge to it.

"She was a nice lady," says Mally. "She was going to help me find you."

"Listen very carefully, Mally. Are you listening?"

His whole body sways backwards and forwards with his nodding.

"The rule isn't that you mustn't go with strangers who look bad. The rule is you don't go with *anyone* you don't know. *Ever.*"

"Why?"

"Because some people look very nice on the outside, but they're not nice inside."

Silver has fallen back to sleep, and her body lists against the wall.

"Okay," he says. "Okay Mama."

"Okay," says Kate. She bundles him up in her arms and slots him back into the cocoon inside his hammock, claps so that the light switches off again. Sebongile tucks a sleeping Silver in.

"Thank you, Bongi," she says. "You can go home now."

"No way I'm going home!" she says. "I'm staying right here."

By the time Kate kisses Mally's forehead and squeezes his hand, he's also drifted off. She nudges the hammock anyway, and it sways him gently in the dark.

Keke is waiting in the lounge for her.

"Don't look at me like that," Kate says.

"I'm not looking at you like anything."

"He went off with that woman today, you know. Willingly. Despite me telling them all the time that they aren't allowed to do that."

"I know. I've heard you tell them."

"I've drilled it into them! It's the most important rule!"

"I know," says Keke.

The real or imagined danger of the twins being kidnapped looms – mostly unspoken – in every exchange between the friends, so much so that Marko has taught the kids how hack self-driving cabs. They can catch a lift from anywhere on their own, without a credit card or an adult dynap code. Seth showed them some self-defence moves, Keke taught them how to scream. Kate's told them, over and over again, to never go with anyone they don't know.

"Fuck's sake," she says, holding her shaking hand against her forehead.

"It wasn't your fault."

"There he was, holding her hand, strolling along. She could have killed him!"

"She would have killed him. Or taken him to someone who would."

"She would have done it herself. I saw it in her eyes."

"We'll protect them," says Keke, pulling Kate towards her in a hug. "Don't worry."

Kate breathes in her scent, nutmeg and leather, is comforted by a cloak of familiarity.

"You can't protect him," says Solonne from behind them.

The Assessor joins in the conversation. "Of course we can. We're the top personal security company in the country. You know that," he says to Solonne, "we guard all the country's top VIPs. The president, the ministers, even the Luminary."

"You're on Lumin's detail?" asks Keke. "Why would Maistre Lumin need protecting?"

He shrugs. "He's important. He has opinions. And it's a dangerous world."

"Christ on a cracker," says Keke. "You're telling me."

"Why do you say that?" Kate asks the matriarx. "Why do you say that we can't protect Mally?"

"Because in the Resurrectors' minds, the only thing that stands between them and the end of the world is your boy."

"You can't be serious," says the Assessor.

"How many of them are there?" she asks the man. "How many Resurrectors?"

"Fifty?" he says. "A hundred. That we know of."

"An army of a hundred brainwashed religious fundamentalists want your child dead. As far as they're concerned, they've got twenty-four hours to stop the apocalypse. How are you going to protect him?"

"W-we have the guards," Kate stammers. "At the front door."

"You have two guards at the front door. Really? You're really going to be able to sleep tonight because you have two men standing guard and two hundred on their way?"

"I never said anything about sleep," says Kate. She's sure she'll never sleep again.

CHAPTER 36

A HOWL IN THE DISTANCE

Marko sits in his dim office. All his equipment is off. It's a novel feeling. If it weren't for his eyeborg, he'd be completely cut off from the world. He unscrews the lid of his bottle of saline and dispenses a few drops into his eye. He isn't sure his eye needs it, but it's something to do. He taps on the desk. Plays an imaginary piano. Maybe he should turn on a light. Or open the curtains. Who knows what's behind those; they haven't been moved in years. Maybe a large window, looking out into the wild garden beyond. Maybe a brick wall covered in a lunatic's scribbles, or a genius's workings. Maybe a painting worth nothing, or a painting worth everything. He sits still, lost in thought. He doesn't open the curtains.

Soft footsteps sound at the back of the house. Keke, at last. He's been missing her these past weeks. They've both been so busy. He takes her for granted. Decides to do something nice for her. Take her out to dinner, or something. Maybe they can even go for a walk; she'd like that. It would be good for him too. Some natural light, some exercise. It feels to him, with all his machines off, that he is kind of waking up. He blinks into the darkness, resists the urge to turn on his Lens. His finger hovers over the switch on his old SnapTile. More footsteps. Why hasn't she come in yet?

"Keke?" Marko angles backward on his chair. "I'm in here!"

It is a stupid thing to say, really, because where else would he be? Maybe he should stand for a change, and go and greet her. That would be nice, instead of just sitting here and mumbling at her with donut-dusted lips when she comes in.

"Kex?" He gets up, then stays frozen in the middle of the room. He can hear himself breathing. It seems quicker than usual. Marko imagines the hackspider in his head, tangling his brains, poised to sink its teeth into his brain. He tries to calm himself. Wipes the sweat from his upper lip. There's no way they've found him. His TCX trail leads to eighty-three different locations all over the world before coming back here. Even if they had the means to find him, it would take weeks.

Surely it would take weeks?

There's movement at the entrance to the room. He squints into the low light. The next sound he hears sends him into a cold sweat. Unmistakable, that sound, and immediately familiar to any gamer worth his salt. A sword being unsheathed.

He dives under his desk. He has nothing with which to defend himself. He closes his eyes and says a silent prayer to Hedy Lamarr, then taps his 911 button, which auto-selects 'POLICE' and 'AMBUDRONE'. His Lens sends his details and location to the relevant departments. His blood pressure spikes, sending his Patch into worried chirrupping. It's outwardly silent, but it deafens him to the intruder's movements. He tries to mute the function, but the default setting for health alerts means it can't be silenced. The warning beeps get louder as his heart races. He rips off his Patch, taking some scalp with it, and swallows his exclamation of pain. Finally free of the pinging, he locates the housebreaker, who is prowling around the room. Marko holds his breath as the black boots walk right past his face. What are the chances that he didn't hear Marko call out, like an idiot, when he first broke in? What are the chances he'll just have a look around and not notice Marko under the desk? His heart is banging madly. It's so loud he imagines it filling the room with its galloping. How can the man not hear it? But then the boots reach the other side of the room, and turn towards him. He can see the silhouette, a body and a handsome sword, hanging casually by its side, but can't make out a face. The body isn't especially muscle-bound; he's not a brawny thug. Small, athletic. Whoever sent someone to knock him off didn't send their biggest killer.

And then it makes sense: the man is petite because he's Thai. The Thai mafia have tracked him down.

Oh shit oh shit oh fuck-me shit.

Marko fantasises about springing up, knocking the table over and using it as a shield while he pumps the trespasser full of lead from imaginary automatic weapons in either hand. He fantasises about sweeping the assassin off his feet with a well-timed ninja kick, then karate-chopping him till he loses consciousness. A light sabre –

The boots start walking towards him. His blood pressure is so high he thinks he'll pass out. At least it will be a peaceful way to go. Instead of … What? Instead of what this person has in store for him. Where are the cops? Are they at least on their way? He has no way of knowing. The boots come closer and closer. Marko holds his breath. It's not the way he pictured himself dying. He hopes there's not too much pain.

The prowler stands before his desk now. The sword is held with more purpose. Marko wishes he has time to tap out a quick bump to Keke, telling her that he loves her. That he loved her.

The silhouette lifts a leg and kicks over the desk, sending Marko's machines flying, and exposing him lying on the floor: a tortoise without a shell. Fear jams his eyes shut.

A howl in the distance. Police sirens. They'll be minutes too late. Marko pictures

Keke in his mind. This is the last thing he wants to see. But his eyes won't stay closed; his panic forces them open like matchsticks.

A sword is lifted in slow motion and aimed at his chest. He looks straight into his murderer's eyes, and is surprised by what he sees. It's not a Thai, and it's not a man.

CHAPTER 37

LIKE DOMINOES THEY FALL

Kate turns on Solonne. "I don't understand why you're here."

"I came to warn you, and to offer help," she says. "We have a prophecy of our own."

"What's that?" says Keke.

"It's not for civilians to know, but suffice to say we need your son to live."

Civilians? Kate has had enough crazy for one day. "Look, I don't know what you're up to. I don't know what your endgame is, but I want you to leave Mally out of it."

"You don't understand," says Solonne. "We can't."

"Who is 'we'?"

She looks surprised. "The SurroTribe, of course."

"I think it's time for you to leave."

"Wait," she says. "Please. You need to hear what I have to say."

"If you can't tell me what you need my son for, then I'm not interested."

"It's…complicated."

"Then un-complicate it for us," says Keke.

"Let us help you," says Solonne. "Let us look after Mally."

"What do you mean? Look after him?"

"Let him come and stay with us, at the compound."

"No!" says Kate. "No way. Are you insane? After what happened today?"

"*Because* of what happened today! He'll be safer with us than anywhere else. It's the reason I'm here."

"There is no way I'm letting him out of my sight. And you're mad for thinking I would."

The matriarx is getting frustrated. She tries to not show it but her eyes are jumpy. "Don't you see? It's the best way to protect him!"

The Assessor chirps in again: "It's a good idea, Miss Lovell. They wouldn't look for him there."

Solonne takes a calming breath. "It's the only way to keep him safe. To keep you *all* safe."

Kate's mind is a tumbling mass of broken boxes: half-formed ideas and fears and stories without endings. How is she supposed to think with all of this going on inside her head? The Assessor and Solonne look at her expectantly.

I can't, she wants to say. *We can't be separated.* But the alternative is unthinkable.

"If you can't tell me why you need him alive," she says to Solonne, "then he's not coming with you."

Kate thinks of Betty/Barbara, the beagle's namesake and previous owner. The first and only time Kate met her, in a dark parking basement, B/B warned her about people wanting them dead. *Click, click, click,* she had said, clicking her fingers in Kate's ear. *Like dominoes they fall.* Betty/Barbara had also been a couple of straws short of a haystack, but she had been right. Kate and Seth would both be dead without her.

Keke's face suddenly knits together, her skin tints.

"What is it?" asks Kate. "Keke?"

Keke puts her fingertips on her Soulm8 ring. Feels it. Looks more worried, takes it off, shakes it next to her ear, puts it back on again.

"What?" demands Kate.

Keke looks as though she's just seen a ghost.

"It's Marko," she says. Dry lips. "His heart just stopped."

CHAPTER 38

EMPTY OF A HEARTBEAT

Keke grabs her bag and shakes on her jacket while Kate auto-inflates her helmet for her, trembling in empathy.

"Where are you going?"

Keke checks her SnapTile. A bump from Marko's medical aid to her as his ICE number: a notification that he is being medevac-ed to The Gordhan in ChinaCity/Sandton.

"They sent a defib-drone to our place but it wasn't activated." Nerves pull at her lips. "He's on his way to hospital," she says, "that's a good sign, right?"

"Yes?" Kate gulps. "Did they say what happened?"

Keke doesn't answer. Perhaps her nerves are jangling so loud she can't hear anything else. She feels the ring again, closes her eyes to concentrate, but it's empty of a heartbeat.

"You shouldn't take Nina," says Kate. "You're in shock. Take a cab."

Keke grabs the helmet from Kate's hand.

"I know you need me," Keke says. "I'll be back."

Keke rides her motorbike hard through the dark and glittering city streets. More than one self-driving cab pulls to the side of the road when it registers her speed. Nina scolds her for speeding via her helmet speaker, and then again when she skips a red light just outside the hospital.

"That was a red light," says the electronic voice. "You should stop at red lights."

Keke races into the boomed area, parks right next to the accident and emergency entrance. Runs up to the counter where a bored-looking resident snaps to attention.

She shows him the bump she received from Marko's health plan company and he taps a few keys on a fossil of a keyboard. It's cream-coloured, has actual keys grubby with fingerprints, and makes crunching sounds as he types.

The Gordhan is the best hospital in Africa. It's not one of those quiet five-star boutique medical centres that has only the latest equipment. Instead, it's a bustling medical metropolis: a wide spectrum of patients and top doctors. Surgeons from all over the world come to teach and practise here; the experience looks good on their portfolios. While it's semi-privatised and well-funded by the Nancies through the NHP, there always seems to be more investment needed, as evidenced by the crunching keyboard.

"He's just come through, from the drone pad," the man says, pointing upstairs. He has a Nigerian accent. "Going straight into surgery."

Keke doesn't wait for him to finish. She ignores the gaping mouth of the elevator, runs up the stairs instead.

"You can't go up there!" he shouts after her, but stays behind the counter.

When she reaches the top her lungs burn. She's stopped by a barrage of patients coming in via air. The flapping rubber doors leading in from the drone pad on the roof is like an old dinosaur mouth vomiting out gurney after gurney into the hallways, pushed by shouting medics holding IV bags and adrenaline shots.

Knife-wound! Overdose! Gunshot trauma! Skull fracture!

Has there been some kind of attack, again?

"What's happened?" Keke asks one of the medics, still breathless. She can hear the traffic outside. Chopping and whirring and yelping sirens.

He frowns at her. "What do you mean?"

"Has there been another attack?"

"What?"

"A terrorist attack?"

He shakes his head. "Just another Saturday night."

He pushes past her, followed by another rattling bed, and another, and another. Warm air streams in from the black night outside, diluting the smell of antiseptic. How is this not making headlines? It's like a war zone. Thank The Net for robot surgeons. Humans would never be able to keep up with this intake. She'll come back for the story next time.

Her ring pulses. Hope punches her in the chest. She waits for the next vibration, and just before she gives up, it pulses again. She runs towards the east wing. A number of staff members half-heartedly try to stop her as she runs past them, but they're either too busy or too indifferent to take chase. Or maybe they just see the look on Keke's face, and know that there would be no stopping her.

She reaches the double doors of OR1, looks in, sees an old man having his leg worked on by a machine that looks like a titanium building crane. OR2 and OR3 don't have Marko either. Eventually, in OR6, Keke recognises the limp body on the operating table.

"Marko!" she shouts, her lungs still blazing, but no one hears her. Seeing him lying like that, a dead weight on a slab, almost doubles her over. He has human doctors attending to him. They're covered head-to-toe in surgery scrubs as they lean over him, their hands inside his chest cavity. She tries to make out what they're saying. The door filters it into dull monotone, but their body language spells out despair.

"This isn't happening," Keke says, both hands on the door, eyes on the slack body she knows so well. Her own heart aches; her stomach is a mess of liquid nerves. "This isn't happening!"

"Clear," says the surgeon, and the other two lift their bloodied latex hands. There is a dull thump of a current and Marko's body jumps. Keke's ring vibrates. She pulls herself away from the small screen of reinforced glass and sits on the floor. Her whole body is focused on the ring on her finger.

"Come on, Marko," she says to the ring.

But the ring doesn't pulse again.

CHAPTER 39

SCENTLESS

It could have been minutes or hours later when the steel gurney slams the double doors open and they wheel Marko's body out of the operating room. Keke looks up with swollen eyes, as if waking from a dream. She doesn't hurry to stand up. She's in no rush to see Marko's corpse. The three surgeons walk out, weary and blood-spattered, their white butcher gumboots squeaking on the hospital floor. The nurse pushing the bed looks at Keke in surprise.

"Oh," she says. Even her shoes are covered in blue paper.

Keke thinks the young woman will chase her away but all she says is: "I'm not used to seeing people out here. Visitors, I mean." Her subtle Zulu accent gives Keke a small measure of comfort. She steps closer to the body lying still on the bed. Takes his cold hand. Doesn't understand why he still has an oxygen tube jammed down his throat.

The nurse's shoulders relax. Her ID badge introduces her as 'Nursing Intern: Themba'.

"Are you coming?"

"To the – " starts Keke. She can't say the word out loud. To the dead place? *Mortuary.*

"To ICU."

"ICU?" says Keke.

"Oh!" says the nurse again. "You thought he had – "

"His heart stopped beating," says Keke.

"Yes."

"It didn't start again."

"No. They tried to get it to work again. Put a stent in. But it didn't work."

"I know."

"Look," she says. "I'm just an intern. You should be downstairs. Talking to the Patient Resources person. They know the right things to say."

"You're saying the right things," says Keke. "You're taking him to Intensive Care. That means – "

"He's alive," says the intern.

"What?"

The woman looks both ways down the corridor, as if waiting for someone to come along and yell at her.

"He's alive," the nurse says again. "Only just. I mean, we're not sure if he'll make it through the night."

"He's alive?" A loud sob gets stuck in Keke's throat. Suddenly there are tears everywhere.

"Marko?" she says, looking at him properly for the first time since he was wheeled out.

"He's…comatose," says the intern.

Keke touches his face: as pale as milk. She lowers the sheet that was pulled up to his chin to reveal his battered chest: bruises leaking from under the waterproof whitecell dressing. She sobs again. There is a backpack on the bed, one that she doesn't recognise, and a ziplock of personal items. The backpack is connected to Marko by a red tube.

"Come on," says the nurse, pulling the sheet back up and pushing the gurney slowly, taking Keke with. "Let's get to the ICU and get him plugged in. It looks like you could do with a cup of tea."

Once the nurse has installed Marko in a private ICU ward, Keke is allowed to stay, as long as she *'hambas'* if any doctors come around. Themba makes sure Marko has everything he needs: oxygen, painkillers, saline, catheter. She plugs the backpack into the wall, so it looks as though Marko is inadvertently plugged in, too. Keke wishes it could be that easy – to recharge someone back to life.

Then the nurse comes back, scrubs discarded, with a cup of tea for both of them. "Don't tell anyone." She winks.

The tea is in a heavy old mug with the Gordhan logo stamped on the side. It's one of the heat-sensitive ones that show the temperature of the drink by changing colour. Hers is a gradient of orange. Themba's is already fading to yellow. The tea is Earl Grey, which makes her think of Kirsten, before she changed her name back to Kate. A previous life: when things still made sense. Or at least, when things had appeared to make sense.

"What is it?" asks Keke, motioning at the backpack.

"It's his new heart."

Her brain scrambles to understand.

"What?"

"It's not a permanent solution, obviously, but his heart was so badly damaged. The waiting list for donor hearts is miles long. It's a synthetic heart – a Cardiocirc – basically, a machine that circulates his blood. And of course, we're resping him. That's when we inject robotic red blood cells to – "

"I know what resping is. It'll keep him alive till he can get a new heart?"

"Hopefully."

"Hopefully?"

Themba sighs, scratches her leg. "You know I always hate it when the doctors say this, because it seems contradictory, but…his condition is critical, but stable."

Keke swallows hard, watches Marko's corpse-still face.

"Don't think of the coma as a bad thing. It's helping him. It'll be very good if he makes it through the night. It's the new heart we need to think about. You don't know anyone in high-up places, do you?"

Keke blinks at the nurse. Themba is joking. Kind of.

The intern's shift ends, and she leaves Keke by Marko's side. To pass the time, Keke sorts through his personal effects. He didn't have much on him when he was medevac-ed. His clothes had been cut off in the OR, his shoes were lost, but Keke holds his SnapTile – the device he used to call for help. She checks his 'sent' items and sees his 911-bump. Then she sees a message in his draft folder, written at around the same time as the emergency message but not yet sent. A bump addressed to her, but it never made it. That was when he had his heart attack, thinks Keke. 20:16. That is when his heart flew out the window. Keke opens the message. He had typed the beginning of a note to her, knowing he was dying, and all he had managed was one letter before he lost consciousness. "L".

She doesn't know what to think of it, and is too tired to try to figure it out. Instead, she gets up onto the hospital bed and squashes in, next to him. She's scared to put an arm over the train tracks on his chest; scared she'll hurt him, even though he's deeply unconscious, so instead she nestles her face right into his neck and breathes him in. She can just get his scent from under the medical smells on his skin and body. This body that was so close to death a few hours earlier, and then that smell would have been gone forever. Scentless. She inhales as much of him as she can.

The sun rises slowly in the east, painting the hospital window gold.

"I've got you," she says. "I've got you."

CHAPTER 40

ORPHAN ON A TRAIN

Seth carries Silver's and Sebongile's suitcases, while Kate walks hand in hand with the twins, who are still in their pyjamas and dressing gowns. Two armed guards follow on a beat behind them. It's just after five and the sun is just beginning to rise. Neither Seth nor Kate have had any sleep: Seth's plane landed at 11pm, and once he got home, he and Kate stayed up all night discussing what was to be done. They're too early for the isiPhapha, so they get a booth in the 24-hour tea shop with the vintage newspapers on the walls. Two extra-large double-caff flats, they order from the servbot, and red cappuccinos for Bongi and the kids. The guards shake off Seth's offer of coffee like a bad idea.

Seth taps the tabletop as they wait in silence for the drinks to arrive. Kate's eyes are rimmed with red. Blinking Pink. She wants to hold Seth's hand, stop it from tapping little circles into her head, but she doesn't. Sebongile seems miles away, perhaps worried about Mally, perhaps upset that she is being sent away. The twins notice the cake display box and rush over to it, breathing all over the glass and fogging it up. Then, using their fingers, they draw pictures in the condensation. A star, a house. Usually Kate would make a fuss, tell them to stand away from the glass and wipe their handprints away with an apologetic glance at the manager. Today she just sits quietly and watches them play.

"Can we have cake?" asks Silver. Usually the answer would be 'no', but this time Kate looks at Seth, who shrugs.

"Only if you say the magic word." Kate wants to smile at the kids, be warm and cheerful, but her face is tight with emotion and raw nerves.

The twins cheer with their good fortune: an early morning adventure *and* cake. The servbot is back, wanting to know how many blackchoc cupcakes to bring. Kate can't stomach the idea. Her mouth is so dry she doesn't think she'll be able to swallow even a bite. Sebongile takes the kids to the bathroom to wash their hands.

One of the guards goes with them. The other stays behind, scanning the empty platform.

"I keep changing my mind," says Kate. "Is it really the best thing to do?"

"Yes," says Seth. "It'll be easier to keep Mally safe."

She knows. They've said the same thing over and over, but the decision still nags at her. It's not too late to change her mind. As if Seth can read her thoughts, he touches her arm and says: "She'll be fine. We need to focus on Mally. He's the one in trouble."

"I'm worried that she'll think we're sending her away. An orphan on a train. Like those horrible stories in our history lessons at school."

"It's hardly the same thing. It's sunny Durban, not World War Three. Besides, Silver absolutely loves Mom and Dad. She'll have a great time. Think of all the ice cream they'll feed her."

"It'll probably be good for her," says Kate, more to convince herself than anything else, "to have all the attention, for once."

Kate's bio parents had jumped at the chance to have Silver and Bongi come to stay. They don't understand why Mally isn't coming, too, or why they were sending Silver escorted by a nanny *and* a bodyguard, but Kate said she'd explain later, in a couple of days, when they would come to collect her.

It's the right decision. It's the right thing to do, but still there is that magenta spiral turning in her brain, roiling in her gut. She drains her coffee and orders another one.

Half an hour later Kate is hugging Silver so hard the little girl complains. After such a big dose of caffeine, Kate's synaesthesia fades; her senses are numbed. It's like eating a rice cake, seeing the world in dry grayscale.

"Be good for your gran," she says, passing Silver her cuddle-bunny and tapping her pink backpack. Seth tells Sebongile to make sure Silver eats some healthy food and brushes her teeth. Bongi nods. The unlikely trio of guard, nanny and girl-child step up onto the speed train and go into the first cabin where they find a window from which to wave. There is the sound on the tracks: an unclamping, and a pressure building. The bells chime their warning that the doors will be closing. Kate feels like jumping on and grabbing Silver, taking her home, but instead she stands frozen by grey heartache on the empty platform. Silver seems happy, excited, even, until the doors close and the train starts moving. Then her eyes grow into saucers and she starts crying, setting Mally off too, and then they're both wailing their heads off. Seth pulls Mally towards him, holds the little boy's shoulder while he reaches out for his sister and cries. Sebongile tries to comfort Silver, who is now hysterical, and trying to climb through the closed window. Kate covers her face with her hands, swallows her tears. She doesn't want either of the kids to see how upset she is. The train rolls away slowly, slowly, then gathers momentum and shoots away with a hiss. Kate watches it turn into the size of a toy then disappear into the black cave of a tunnel. Seth gathers a sobbing Mally up into his arms and makes comforting sounds, wipes away his tears and spit. How did Seth learn to be such a good father, when he had no role model, growing up? She feels a rush of gratitude for him, and she joins the embrace. She can no longer hear the train.

CHAPTER 41

FLINTY STONE

All morning, strange nurses drift in and out of the room to monitor Marko. Keke waits for one of them to ask her to leave, but they pretend she's not there, even though she's lying right next to him, eyes closed but unable to sleep. Their kindness renders her invisible. She has this idea that if she's touching him, if she can keep him warm with her body heat, then he'll stand a better chance of surviving. When his breakfast arrives, in the form of a creamy white IV bag, the muscles she didn't even realise were tense finally relax. He has made it through the night.

Keke gets up, goes to the small white basin, and washes her hands with pink liquid soap. She rinses her face too, and gulps filtered water straight from the tap. She drinks and drinks until the flinty stone she has stuck in her throat softens a little. There's no time wasted looking at her reflection in the mirror; she knows she looks like a wreck, and she doesn't give a shit.

Despite giving her underarms a quick scrub too, Keke can smell yesterday's panic. There's no deodorant in sight, although she's sure they'll have downstairs at the pharmacy. She tries to keep her arms close to her body to limit the stink but knows she's going to have to go home to pick up clean clothes. Her SnapTile had been buzzing all night with messages, probably from Kate. She should go and see her, find out if she's okay, if Mally's okay.

She should be in court today. She should be with Kate. She should be at home, in the shower. But how can she leave Marko? She sweeps his fringe out of his eyes: a maternal gesture. Probably her first, most likely her last. Her Tile buzzes again.

ZikZak > You have 2 come / court today.

Kex >> Um. RU fucking mad? Did U not get my message?

ZikZak > I know U want 2 be there with M but it's the last day of Jduty.

Kex > I don't care.

ZikZak >> Yes U do.

Kex > I need 2 be here.

ZikZak >> Marko's in / coma. He doesn't need you.

Kex > And U do?

ZikZak >> Lundy does.

Kex > I have nothing 4 Lundy.

ZikZak >> U know he's innocent.

Kex > It's just a theory.

ZikZak >> The prosecutor also just has a theory. One that will send him away 4 life.

Kex > I can't help Lundy. Or Nash. I don't know anything.

ZikZak >> You do. You just haven't realised it yet.

Kex > I don't know what U want from me.

ZikZak >> Yes U do. See U in court.

CHAPTER 42

MOM

"You can't just come in here," says the psychiatrist, still wearing slate. Grey face, grey clothes, and eyebrows as stern as any Kate has ever seen. "I'm busy with another patient. You need to make an appointment."

Kate, panting, looks from the doctor to the patient, whom she hasn't even realised is there. The man looks sheepish, as if Kate has caught him out in the middle of an embarrassing confession.

"It's an emergency." Kate gulps. "It's my last chance."

"Your last chance? At what?"

Kate takes the VXR gogs from the patient's hands. "You can come back, right?" says Kate.

He nods at her.

"This is entirely inappropriate," says Voges, arms crossed.

"Let me have this session and I'll never bother you again."

The doctor wavers, scratches her cheek. The man doesn't talk, he just takes off the rest of his gear and hands it to Kate with downcast eyes.

"This is a professional practice," says the woman. "That patient waited for over four months for this appointment. I'll not stand for this."

"It'll never happen again."

The woman looks doubtful.

"I promise you that it'll never happen again. Can we get started? I don't have much time and my family is in trouble."

The doctor blinks at her, straightens her back, clears her throat. Her frown softens. Perhaps she's trying to get back into caring mode. Kate pulls on the kit.

"Okay. Tell me why you're here."

"Something has happened," says Kate.

"Would you like to talk about it?"

"No. But I need to get better. I need your help."

The woman looks at her, irritated, clicks her stylus on her Tile.

"I need to speak to Marmalade," she says.

Voges shakes her head.

"You know that immersion therapy doesn't work like that. We don't talk to...dead people."

"My family," says Kate. "I need to protect them. And I can't protect them if I can't think straight. I have to get rid of this...this fog that comes with my PTSD. These... slippery thoughts. I need to get over it. I can't risk pulling a gun in my sleep or letting go of my son's hand in a crowd."

The therapist sucks at her bottom lip.

"You know that it's not really James you'll be talking to. It'll be your brain's version of him. What you know of him, what you expect of his responses."

"Of course. Yes."

She checks Kate's gear then sits and smoothes down her hair, as if to unruffle her grey feathers.

"Alright," she says, tapping a button on her holopad. "Let's see what we can do."

"Let's start with a happy memory," the psychiatrist says.

"I don't have time for happy memories."

"It will work better if we do it this way. We need to fool your brain into believing we're back there and that things are good."

"Honestly, I don't have time. Can we just – "

"Miss Lovell. Would you like this to work, or not?"

Kate takes a deep breath, counts to purple, and then lets it out.

"Back where?"

"What is your most poignant memory? A happy one."

Kate has to think. It's been a while since she was happy.

"Giving birth to Silver."

"Let's start with that."

The room around Kate changes into what looks like a hotel room. She's in the bath, wearing a bikini top but no bottoms. Her belly is huge, her fingertips are wrinkled from the water. The contractions are all-consuming. The pain takes over her whole body in waves and she can't help but to groan and pant. The doula tells her she's doing a good job.

"Just a few more pushes," she says.

Kate is light-headed. The labour – eight long hours of it – has already taken all the energy she has, and she has no more to give. She feels like she's going to pass out. She should have listened to Keke when she said to have a C-Section.

The doula sees the look on her face and squeezes her shoulder. "You can do it."

Kate is really not convinced that she can.

Her mother crouches down next to the birthing pool and clutches Kate's forearm.

"Mom," says Kate. She had never called her that before. When they were finally reunited a few months before, it had been like meeting a stranger. Yes, they have the same hair, the same chin, but they were separated by thirty years, childhood memory loss, and Kate's gnawing black hole – the one she can't remember ever not having.

The word makes tears spring to her mother's eyes. Emotions swirl around the room like Holi powder in a breeze.

"Mom," she says again, and her mother cries openly, touches her head to Kate's. "My beautiful Kate," she cries. "My beautiful girl."

"Get ready to push," says the doula.

"I don't know if I can. I'm finished. I don't have anything left."

"You can," says her mother. "You can. You're the only one who can get this baby out. We're almost there."

Kate resumes her breathing. The next tide of contractions catch her off-guard. It's sooner than she expects and double the pain of the previous one.

"Push," says the doula. "Everything you have."

Kate screams and pushes, and it does feel like she's giving everything she has, like she'll be empty and broken after this. She'll never be the same. She pushes harder, bears down, and just as she thinks she is literally dying, the room explodes with light and colour. There's an intense sting as the head crowns, then the baby slips out, and she catches it, underwater. Her screaming gives way to happy sobbing as she clutches the waxy baby girl to her chest. The warm, slippery weight of her daughter on her breasts moves her, irreversibly. There are no words in her head anymore, just a ferocious glow.

She doesn't feel broken anymore.

CHAPTER 43

FILM OF FEAR AND DREAD

Keke can't sit in the jury room smelling like she's run a marathon on *tik* – which is pretty much the idea that comes to mind when she lifts her arms – so she zooms home on Nina. The shower washes away the film of fear and dread and heartache that's covering her body like a membrane. The three-minute timer rings but she stays inside, under the water, not giving a damn about the water restrictions. Not today. She'll eat a carbon-negative lunch to make up for it, or something. Not that she has an appetite, but she hasn't eaten in twelve hours and that's asking for trouble, given her condition.

She pulls on some kevlarskin steampunk-print leggings and a tight red shirt. Swaps her moo-leather jacket for something less bloodstained; chooses her new pine-leather wrapper. She's not sure how it'll hold up in a motorbike accident but there's only one way to find out. Her fashion sense is almost entirely dictated by Nina. She likes it that way.

She packs some things for Marko: his sonic toothbrush, laser-razor, solar multi-charger, a set of clean clothes. As she zips up the bag she feels foolish. He doesn't need any of this stuff, but she'll take it anyway, because if nothing else it will make her feel better. As she's rushing out the front door, another item occurs to her: she's sure he'd like his noise-control headphones. He practically lives in the things and everyone knows hospital noises are the worst. She opens the door again and runs to his man cave. The scene that greets her sucks the air out of her lungs. Not only is his desk lying on its side, like some kind of dead animal with rigor mortis, but his machines are lying all over the floor, smashed to oblivion. His data lockers have been levered open and plundered.

Her brain stops working for a moment, like a GPS that is re-calculating. She doesn't understand what she's seeing. So, Marko had a heart attack. The most destruction she expected to see – apart from the ravaging inside his chest cavity – is a coffee cup spilt on the table. Perhaps, at most, his chair knocked over. But this isn't that, this is a vicious onslaught.

Keke tries to switch on a few pieces of equipment but they either don't turn on at all, or they make dangerous electric sounds, as if ready to shock in retaliation for the prior abuse. Keke's Patch keeps beeping, letting her know that she is already half an hour late for court.

She doesn't stop to put on gloves. The South African Police are notoriously crap at their jobs and even if they do arrive to take fingerprints, Keke guesses the scans will go straight into some docket in the Cloud, never to be seen again. Most crims are convicted only if the victims, or friends and family of victims, are willing to pay for their own private C&P. Capture and Prosecution teams are big business.

Zack bumps her, knocking her thought processes sideways. They're just about to decide on Lundy's fate. She needs to go. She'll deal with this shit-show later. Keke grabs the headphones and crams them into her bag. Underneath them is Marko's Tile. Cracked, but perhaps not entirely broken. When she switches it on, to see if it works, she notices on the desktop a single file called LUNDY.

She arrives at the court building with a roar from Nina. Runs into the jury room and ignores the knives of disapproval shot into her torso by the other members. Out of breath, she sits huffing next to Zack, who has saved her a seat and a smile. The juror who was talking when Keke scrambled in gives her a pointed look, and continues with her speech about why she thinks Lundy is guilty. Keke's body tingles with the new evidence; she can't sit still until she gets it off her chest. The others want to talk about timeframe and psychological reports and prior accidents, and Keke wants to shout that it doesn't matter. None of it matters, because she has found something on Marko's Tile that swipes all of it away.

CHAPTER 44

A BLUE BREEZE BLOWS IN

"Are you ready to see James?" asks Doctor Voges.

Kate takes a deep breath. She's still recovering from the re-imagined birth. She's warm in bed, cuddling a five-month-old Mally while the swaddled newborn with a wisp of silver hair is sleeping in Seth's tattooed arms.

Look at us. Our funny little family. She's overwhelmed by love and an intense feeling of gratitude. It's such a warm, safe space, she doesn't want to leave, but then she remembers what's at stake.

"Yes," she says the to the therapist. "I'm ready."

She moves from memory to imagination. She's in their old flat, in Illovo. Her forest of plants are flourishing, and every surface is coated in nostalgia. She's sitting at the kitchen table, the book collector's edition of *Hansel & Gretel,* James's gift, in front of her, symbolic of so many things. Bergamot scents the air.

All of a sudden he's sitting right across from her. He looks so real he takes Kate's breath away.

"Marmalade," she whispers.

He smiles at her, eyes twinkling, as if he's alive and well and they never had to go through the terrible time they did. A furtive glance down at his hands reveals all ten fingers. Relief. She wants to touch him.

"Kitty," he says, "God, I miss you."

Kate's chest contracts, her sinuses sting. "I miss you. I miss you so much. You took such a big part of me with you, when you – "

The rest of the sentence catches in her throat.

"You look beautiful."

"No, I'm a mess."

"You're absolutely beautiful. Motherhood suits you."

Tears run down her cheeks. "I don't know about that."

"It's your eyes," he says. "Something's changed."

She smoothes down her hair self-consciously, then she remembers it's virtual reality. The 5D image is super-realistic, but there are little clues that it's not real. The fridge keeps disappearing, and her clothes change without warning.

"Everything's changed," she says.

"Tell me about them," says James. "Our kids."

The question makes her ribs ache. She has never truly accepted that the twins will never know their biological father. She clears her throat, tries to swallow her sorrow. "They're like you," she says. "Like us."

A blue breeze blows in. Now it's James's turn to blink away tears.

Kate watches the fridge flicker. Her shirt changes from white to blue then back again.

"Why did you need to see me?" he asks.

"Our boy's in trouble."

"You named him after me. Marmalade."

"It was a mistake."

A ripple of hurt on his face.

"It used to hurt too much. I couldn't bear it. A child shouldn't see pain on his mother's face when she says his name. Now we call him Mally."

"Your mother's maiden name."

"Yes."

"What do you need from me?"

"I need you to tell me what to do."

"No one's ever told you what to do."

"I need guidance. To keep him safe. Shall I send him to live with the SurroTribe?"

"What do you think?"

"I think he may be safe there, but how do I know? How do I know who to trust?"

"Wait," he says. "Where are the kids now?"

The pattern on the pressed ceilings swirl.

"They're safe."

"Where are they?"

Kate's insides turn to cold metal.

"They've both got bodyguards," says Kate, more to reassure herself than anything else. "Silver's in Durban, with my parents. Mally's at home, with Seth."

"Kitty," he says, his face flushed now, and grim. "What was the biggest thing, the most important thing I taught you? The lesson that almost tore you in half."

She looks at him blankly, then she gets it and can hardly hear herself for the whirring of panic in her brain. Kate feels the blood drain out of her face.

Never trust anyone.

CHAPTER 45

HANGMAN

Keke puts her hand up. "I have something to say."

"You'll need to wait your turn," says the head juror, who is overseeing this final meeting. He's an especially large man, full of meat and sighs and heaviness, as if weighed down by metaphysical rocks in his pockets.

"You don't understand," says Keke. "I have new information."

The man scoffs under a bent finger. "No, Miss Msibi, I don't think *you* understand."

"You can't make this decision without what I have," says Keke.

"There is a time and a place for evidence, and this is not it."

"I'm telling you that I have evidence that will exonerate the accused and you're not even curious?"

"We've heard the evidence at the trial." The man's cheeks are beginning to colour with either embarrassment or anger.

"I'd like to see it," says Zack.

"Me, too," says the woman next to whom Keke has sat for most of the trial. She shoots Keke a strained smile.

"Your job is that of a juror," says the large man. "Not to prove anything. Not to influence the judgment. We have a procedure to follow." He speaks in a breathless way, as if his bulk is pressing in on his lungs.

"You're okay with sending an innocent man to a crim colony for the rest of his life, for the sake of correct procedure?"

He ignores her.

"All of those in agreement that the accused, Mack Lundy, is innocent of murder, please register your vote now."

The jurors all look down at the remotes in their hands and tap buttons. Four spinning green votes go up on the holoscreen.

"And those who agree that he is guilty, please vote now."

Five red points on the board.

"That's five votes guilty to four innocent. As you know, we need at least a two-point difference in order to convict or acquit. For those who didn't vote, please reconsider your position."

The people toggle their remotes again, and Keke can't help thinking it's like an obscure analogue video game of hangman. This time there are five red and five green. Two people still haven't voted.

"This is ridiculous!" Keke stands up.

"This is a warning, Miss Msibi. If you try to swing the vote you'll be expelled from these proceedings."

"You may as well hang him right now with all the red tape you have in this room!"

The head juror sends her a look that could freeze fire.

They vote again. Five to five.

The man sighs deeply, as if he has the world on his shoulders. "I'll open the floor to discussion, now. Please remember," he says, making eyes at Keke, "it is for discussion and questions only. Anyone trying to convince anyone else of a verdict will be asked to leave."

"I have a question," says Keke.

He looks skywards. "Why am I not surprised?"

"Why is the nanny not on trial?"

"That is not a valid question."

"Of course it's a valid question," says Zack.

"You said to not influence the jury regarding Lundy's guilt. I won't even mention him. I want to discuss the nanny."

"Let her talk," says someone of the other side of the room – a woman with great boobs in an extravagant silk dress. "We all want to hear it, don't we?"

There is nodding, murmuring. The head juror purses his lips and gestures for Keke to continue.

"I have evidence …" She hauls out the cracked Tile. "… that the nanny wanted the boy dead."

Exclamations ring out.

"That's preposterous," says the big man, pretending to laugh.

"Why is it preposterous that a nanny would hurt a child? You think the own child's father is more capable of killing him than a stranger?"

"Miss Msibi. It is common knowledge that SurroSisters are beyond reproach. They are tested and prevaluated for every kind of physical and moral defect. Only the very best specimens pass the rigorous screening." His double chin quivers. "It's no coincidence that a SurroSis has never seen the inside of this courthouse."

"That's going to change." Keke clicks 'play' on the Tile and it projects onto the verdict voting board. The image shakes a bit, probably due to the damaged device. The point of view is that of a low-flying camera travelling through a suburban area: green trees, solar roofs, puckered roads like metal zips. Old swimming pools turned into rock gardens and skating rinks, and emerald astroturf lawns. A few people are busy with daily chores, a domestic assistant is hanging out washing, a child kicks a ball, a woman in heels jumps into a cab. It's date-stamped the 24th of January 2024.

"What is this?" he asks.

"Drone footage," says Keke, "of a pharmacy wasp delivering medicine."

"Where did you get it?"

"Does it matter?"

"Drones aren't allowed to record their journeys," he says. "It's in part three of the 2018 almanac of domestic and personal privacy regulations of non-passenger air-vehicles."

"It's not for viewing," says Keke, then corrects herself. "What I mean is, it's not for broadcast. It's not for anyone's eyes apart from the security detail of the owner of the drone, which is allowed, under section C of that almanac."

Thank you Marko.

He'd made this note on the video for her. She wouldn't have had a cooking clue what the legislation was.

"People steal drones all the time," says Zack. "This was probably a live-stream feed back to the owner of the drone. Kind of like a FindMyDrone."

"Okay," says the heavy man. "So what?"

Keke scrubs ahead to the relevant part of the clip. The jurors sit up and pay attention.

"This is Abercorn avenue, where the Lundys live."

She has to zoom in, which makes the picture fuzzy, but you can still get a reasonable idea of what's going on. As the camera flies by a double-storey house with maroon cladding, a small boy is visible, standing on the very edge of the roof, just a step away from an open attic window. His knees are slightly bent, and he's looking down to the synthetic grass below, as if gathering the courage to jump.

"Watch now," Keke says. "If you blink you'll miss it."

Like a lightning flash, an adult's arm shoots out of the window and pushes the child off the roof. The drone passes the house before you are able to see what becomes of the fallen boy.

The jury titters in excitement and dismay. Keke rewinds and plays it again, slo-mo. Although you can't see whose arm it is, it is distinctly female, and clearly not Mack Lundy's.

CHAPTER 46
COSMIC CREAM

"Drive faster, for fuck's sake!" Kate yells at the cab.

"This is an eighty-kilometre-per-hour zone. We are travelling at eighty kilometres."

Kate clenches her teeth and kicks the chair.

"Please refrain from abuse. Abuse will result in Cabbie pulling over."

"Just go faster!" She knows the cab is programmed to adhere to all the rules of the road but she can't help shouting at it.

The cab accelerates to overtake a donkey of a tuk-tuk, but then slows down again, back to eighty. She looks out of the tinted window, tries to distract herself from the yellow epinephrine pushing through her veins (Yelling Yellow), making her skin hot and clammy. She tries to focus her mind. She has to keep a clear head to keep her babies safe. That's what the VXR therapy was all about. She mustn't let the panic make her spin. She wipes her sweating hands on her jeans. Ramping up her stress levels by trying to make the car go faster isn't going to have any effect on the car; it'll only go as fast as it can go. Kate needs to spend the time calming down. She breathes and watches the sky, still dry, and realises how thirsty she is. She seems to always be thirsty. Was it like this, before the water shortages, before the drought? Just the idea of the Vaal dam being at twelve per cent makes her tongue swell.

Kate had taken the risk of leaving Mally at home so she could get the help she needed to sort out her head, but if anything, it's made her feel more mixed up. Wouldn't it be ironic if the measure she took to help herself, so that she could be wholly present to protect the kids, turned out to be the thing that jeopardised their lives? Her stomach roils. Seth's not answering his phone. She hadn't even really considered it a risk when she left this morning. Not really. It's Seth, for Net's sake, plus the security guards. Surely he's safer there, than anywhere else?

He's safe, she says to herself as they pass sunbaked buildings and cyclists with tadpole-shaped helmets. He's safe.

They stop at a red light and a billboard starts talking to them.

"Have you tried our new Cosmic Cream?" the advert asks.

Kate snarks. She looks up at the projection and sees a whirlpool of white liquid splashing into someone's cereal. It's full of sparks and glints and is really pretty but Kate imagines it can't be very nice to eat. All those little metallic starry explosions and planet dust in your mouth. But then she thinks maybe the creaminess takes the edge off the snapping sensation and in that case it may be quite nice. The next cut shows a woman adding the cream to her coffee and laughing as it sparkles. Kate rolls her eyes and looks away. Maistre Lumin's voice comes on through the cab's sound system. She'd far rather listen to what he has to say over crap advertising for (perhaps) an even crapper product. He looks at Kate from the cab's smart mirror dash, and it's like he's in the car with her, with all his trademark impish charm. Kate turns off the sounds from outside and further darkens the windows.

Lumin's face glows, and his voice is so calming; it always makes her think of getting into a bed with freshly laundered sheets. She likes listening to him speak in his vernacular, even though she understands very little of it; she has always loved the sound of the clicks and pops of *isiXhosa.* She's never had a word for the soothing sensation it creates in her, but from now on she'll call it Cosmic Cream, short for Cosmic Cream Without the Crap.

"Can you imagine a world," he says, his generous smile ever-present,"free of anxiety?"

One of the things she likes about these in-cab messages is that it always feels like Lumin is speaking directly to her. She doesn't know how they get that right. As if the car reads her emotional status on her Patch and gives her the message that is most appropriate. On the days she doesn't leave the house – which have started to outnumber the days she does – he manages to find her anyway, on the homescreen or her news tickertape. He seems to know when she needs him.

"It may seem impossible to you," he says, "but anxiety serves no one. Anxiety is just a byproduct of overthinking. *Hai wena,* that sounds too easy, hey? You need to stop thinking!" Clearly amused by the idea, he starts chuckling. "In order to cut anxiety out of your life, you need to realise that our souls are here for our own joy. Not just to go shopping. Not to grind. Not to pay debt. But for joy. Did you hear that?" he says playfully, eyes sparkling, "JOY!"

"Easy for you to say," mumbles Kate. "You just sit on your gold throne all day and your minions bring you nice things to eat."

That isn't, strictly speaking, fair or true, although Lumin does have a reputation for having a sweet-tooth. He's known for often misquoting Julia Child, saying "life without a cake is just a meeting".

Lumin is frequently spotted digging community gardens for permaculture programmes in shack-towns and rural areas. He is forever backing previously disadvantaged communities with cheap green tech that improves their lives, like showing them how to make home-made refrigerators, sky-lights, and natural air-conditioning from sawn-off water bottles. He doesn't have a PR firm working for the Luminary. Instead, civilians armed with their pointers and Tiles will record him and his people doing these things and plaster them all over social media. Perhaps it is their way of reassuring themselves there is still good in the world.

"So little time," he says. "Look at me, I'm almost eighty years old, and I feel like a small boy." He makes the hand gesture of all fingertips touching and pointing to the heavens, usually used, in African culture, to denote the height of a child. "Believe me now. One day you're going to look up from all your anxious thoughts that you call your life and realise that it's over. That it's already over! Like a party when you are too busy thinking about the snax and the small talk to just let go and enjoy."

Every time Kate brings him up in conversation with Seth he gives her the cynical look he usually reserves for people who still smoke. He likes to say that he's allergic to KoolAid.

"How can you be suspicious of permaculture? It doesn't make sense."

"It's not the permaculture, you know that." (Seth has never grown a thing in his life, unless you include the clean-meat lab turkey he designed for Bilchen ten years ago).

"It's the monastery itself?" Kate asked. "The Luminary? The gold paint?"

"Yes. It's the gold paint. I mean, the man dresses like a monk who works in a 1940s flour mill, so what's with the bling?"

"He likes the colour!"

He looked at her as if she was crackers.

"It's a cheerful colour. He's a cheerful chap. It brings him joy. Besides," Kate said. "The man's allowed to have some kind of shortcoming. He'd be too perfect, otherwise."

Seth put his hands up. "Look, I'm not saying he's a bad person. I'm just saying that he's probably not the saint that everyone thinks he is."

"You think he has some deep, dark secret?"

"I'd put serious bank on it. That man has skeletons in his closet."

"Doesn't everyone?"

"Not like his."

Kate had laughed, and pictured a gold skeleton falling out of a creaking cupboard.

She thinks she knows what really bothers him, though. The Luminary published what they had called *The Celestia Prophecies* a few years ago. Really batshit biblical sounding things like "the sea will rise up and kill masses of men, women and children without discrimination". Crazy until it happened: The 2022 Indo Tsunami wiped out thousands of people, including an old colleague of Seth's who was workvaccing there. At least twelve of the hundred prophecies have so far come true.

"Coincidence," Seth insists, but she isn't so sure.

The cab pulls to a stop and the windows un-tint to reveal they're already outside the apartment building. She rushes in. Her body is scrambling, but her mind is working in slow motion, as if Lumin has mesmerised her into a calm state of mind. Kate has the clarity now that she was after. When she reaches the front door nothing seems out of place. The guards greet her and open up to let her in.

"Mally?" she calls, checking his room. "Seth?"

No answer. This time she doesn't panic, but instead calmly lopes from room to room, looking for her son. When the troubling emotions begin to rise, she pushes them down. Despite this, sweat breaks out on her upper lip. Where are they? Why aren't they answering her? Then she thinks of the guards. Are they the same men who were there when she left, this morning? She doesn't know. She didn't look at them properly, their faces partly obscured with those turtle-shell shaped helmets and purple visors they wear. They could be anyone.

Then again, anyone could be anyone.

Just because they grind for a security company doesn't mean they're good people.

Anxiety serves no one, says Lumin in her head. Stop thinking.

She sees, out of the corner of her eye, that the delivery drone-pad window is open.

Mally's body would fit through there.

She walks up to it and pulls the window closed, latches it. Swallows her electric blue agitation.

They'll be in the panic room. They'll be in the panic room, but then why aren't they answering her?

She walks over and opens the panic room door, revealing chaos: the floor is littered with train tracks, snack bar wrappers and spilled popgrains. Mally sits on Seth's cross-legged lap, on the floor. They both have headphones on and are twiddling game remotes with their thumbs, eyes fixed on the cinescreen.

Kate lets out a long breath of relief. Waves at them. They're so engrossed by the game they hardly acknowledge her. She hugs them anyway.

CHAPTER 47

ORGANIC MARTINIS AND WILD SEX

"Good God," says the woman next to Keke. "Are you saying that's the nanny's arm?"

The room buzzes with questions.

"Mrs Lundy was at work that day, that was verified during the trial."

"Are you saying that the Lundy boy was murdered? Premeditated?"

"That after he survived this fall, he was killed in the bath?"

"That doesn't make any sense."

"Why would a nanny kill her charge? She'd be out of a job, for one thing."

"I'm not saying anything," says Keke, looking at the head juror. "I wouldn't want to sway your vote."

Everyone talks at the same time.

"Okay, okay," says the man. "Settle down, everyone, please. Settle down. I don't know how I'm going to explain this to the judges, but...what else do you have?"

Keke makes to put the Tile away in her bag but the HJ waggles his fingers at her and takes the device. His security guard brings him a green plastic envelope and he deposits the Tile inside and zips it up. Stamps the outside, signs it.

Keke's not finished. "When I saw this video for the first time, it made me think of the interview with Maila, the nanny. When the cops spoke to her, that night, after the boy was found dead. It was part of the virtual reality evidence room."

"Yes?" The man is suddenly very interested in what Keke has to say.

"Well, when I was looking in the bathroom, there was something on the floor, by the bathmat. Like, a sparkle. But then when I tried to inspect it, close up, it disappeared. I spoke to the VR facilitator about it and he said that it's possible that they captured the floor last."

"So, in other words," The HJ says to the others, "there was something on the floor when they began recording the crime scene but it disappeared before they finished."

"Exactly."

"You're saying that the crime scene was compromised."

"But no one was allowed in there, apart from the forensic capture specialist."

"Well..." The man with the world on his shoulders sighs. "Unfortunately...knowing what I know about the police force...it's not entirely impossible that someone slipped in there and removed whatever it was you saw."

"But what was it?" asks the woman in the silk dress.

"In the beginning of questioning the nanny," says Keke, "on the video, with the cops. She wasn't wearing her SurroSis pin."

There is a hush.

"Then she takes a break, and when she comes back on, she's wearing it."

The HJ orders someone to fetch the footage, and they play it on the scoreboard holoscreen. There she is, the nanny, without the pin, and after the break, it appears.

"You see how she keeps touching her wrists, too?" says Keke. "Pulling her sleeves down to cover them."

"She's just doing that to wipe away her tears," says someone.

"Maybe," she says. "Or maybe there was a struggle in the bathroom when she was drowning the boy, and he managed to dislodge her pin and bruise or scratch her wrist."

"The father would have heard a struggle," says someone else.

"Not necessarily. He was cooking stir-fry. When I was in the VR kitchen, I couldn't hear anything over the frying."

"There was music, too," says Zack. "He had classical piano playing on the sound system."

"Blanco," says the woman in silk. "I'd know Edward Blanco's Aparello symphony anywhere."

Blanco. What are the chances? She takes it as a sign that the universe is telling her that she's on the right path.

"Well," says the head juror, clasping his hands together. "This is an interesting turn of events."

The jurors are excused until further notice. Keke is sure the HJ is glad to see the back of her, but then he surprises her by calling her over the din of dismissal and saying 'Good job' and that he'll 'be in touch'.

The jurors take their time in leaving. They don't want to go without knowing What Happens Next. Will Lundy be let off? Will Maila be arrested? Most of all, Keke guesses, they want to know why on earth a nanny would kill a child.

"I guess it's goodbye, then." Zack's looking especially dapper today in a pink silk tie.

"Not so fast," says Keke. "You've got the rest of the day off, don't you, now that we've been excused?"

"What do you have in mind? Organic martinis and wild sex?"

"I was thinking coffee."

They grab a table at an Italian deli down the road from the courthouse. It's called ProntoPrint and, as the name suggests, you don't need to wait for the kitchen to make your food. Instead, it's printed right in front of you. Great for quick lunches for important attorneys. Not great for your bank balance. Keke's eyes widen at the menuscreen. R368 for a bullet coffee?

"I retract my offer," she jokes.

"Of wild sex?"

"I wasn't the one who offered wild sex," she says, "I meant, the offer to pay for coffee."

Zack adds on a chocroissant for each of them and Keke checks the time on her SnapTile. There's a message from the police, updating her on their progress, which is, unsurprisingly, zero.

"You need to be somewhere else?"

"Yes. The hospital."

"Oh, shit." Zack's face falls. "I completely forgot. Sorry. How's he doing?"

"He made it through the night. That's what they keep telling me, as if I wasn't there, checking on his breathing every five minutes."

"I'm really sorry. Is there anything I can do?"

"You're doing it." Keke takes the last bite of her croissant.

"More than coffee, I mean."

"I need to talk it out. The Lundy case."

"You solved it. You're amazing."

"Shut up."

"Seriously. What's to talk about?"

"Why would a nanny kill a child?"

"Who knows. Does it matter?"

The expensive coffee sparks an idea in Keke's head. Helena Nash had accused them of *'drinking overpriced coffee and thinking that everything is just fucking dandy'*.

"Helena Nash. She was an accountant, right?"

"Yes?" says Zack.

"She had a full-time job. So..."

"So?"

"So, it's likely that she had a nanny too. What are the chances it was the same woman?"

"Holy shit," says Zack.

Keke places a call to the Carbon Factory. She spends five minutes convincing the operator to let her speak to Nash, and finally the convict is on the line. Zack looks uncomfortable. Keke puts her on speaker then grimaces as Nash clears her throat right into the receiver.

"Yup?"

"Did you have a nanny?" asks Keke.

"What?"

"Did you have a nanny, for your little girl?"

"Is this that journalist speaking? Kakky?"

"The nanny was on duty? That night?"

"No."

"Are you sure?"

"She didn't work nights."

"But was she there?" whispers Zack.

"Was she in the house?" Keke asks Nash.

"Is there someone else there? Who is it? What's going on?"

"Helena. Please. Was the nanny in the house on the night your daughter fell down the stairs?"

"Yes," says Nash. "Yes. She was always there. She was live-in. Her room was upstairs."

"Was she around, you know, when you poured your drink that night?"

There's a brief silence.

"Hello?" says Keke. "Are you still there?"

"Jesus Christ," says Nash. "Are you saying what I think you're saying?"

CHAPTER 48

HARD PEARL

"Kate, Kate," says Keke through the line. There's static and other noise. Buzzing. Zooming. She must be calling from her helmet.

Kate's heart jumps. Her gaze falls, unseeingly, on Mally, who's playing with his cars on the carpet.

"Keke? Oh no. I've been trying to get hold of you. Don't tell me – "

"Marko's alive."

"Oh, thank goodness."

"I need to talk to you. Tell you something."

The last time she heard those words from Keke it had forced her to run, and the information had saved her life.

"I'm listening."

She leaves the panic room to get a better connection.

"Where is Mally?" asks Keke. "Please tell me you're with him?"

"I'm with him. And Seth's here. And a bodyguard. We're safe."

"Marko left me a couple of things on his old..."

"What?" says Kate.

"...dead..."

Keke's voice crackles like foil packaging.

"What?"

"It's why I called...found out...Lundy's nanny..."

"I'm losing you." Kate strains to hear.

The line is so bad Kate can only hear snatches.

"...It's the...tribe that is...toddlers. The nannies..." and the line cuts out.

"Keke?"

Kate tries to call her back, but it won't go through. The doorbell rings.

Kate opens the door, and Solonne sashays in. The guard gives her a curt nod and closes the door again, and she locks all three bolts.

Solonnne's robe is white, lustrous. A hard pearl in Kate's mouth. "I wanted to thank you, for the warning."

"And what is the point?" says Solonne, tight-faced, "of being warned, when you are doing nothing about it?"

"We've got security. We're – "

Solonne looks around. "Where is the boy?"

Kate frowns at her. "What's wrong? What's going on?"

"I thought I had made that very clear."

"Why are you back? What are you doing here?"

Solonne starts looking for Mally. She checks his room, then the bathroom.

"He's in the panic room with Seth," says Kate, following her. "He's fine."

She beelines to the white room and swings open the door. Mally looks up, mid-car-crash, and smiles.

"Hello Solonne," he says.

CHAPTER 49

A TERRIBLE MISTAKE

What? thinks Kate. *How does he know her name?*

"Mally," Solonne says, warmly.

Seth looks as confused as Kate feels.

"How do you know Solonne?" Kate tries to keep her voice light despite the lead in her stomach.

"Solonne's my special friend." He zooms a car up Seth's denim leg. Seth grabs him and hoists him up, on to his lap, puts protective arms around him.

"What's going on here?"

Solonne uncaps her lip balm and runs it over her lips. "My only vice," she says, holding it up to them, eyes crinkled with a smile. "I'm addicted to the stuff." It looks like she is gearing up for something. Kate smells artificial fruit (Cheap Cherries).

What had Keke said? Something about nannies, and the SurroTribe.

"I think you should leave," says Kate.

"I will," says Solonne. "But I need to take the boy."

"Fuck that," says Seth, tightening his grip. Mally pretends to be alarmed by the swear word and makes a gaping fish-face at them.

"The boy has a name," says Kate, "and we've been over this. You're not taking him anywhere."

"I wanted to give you one last chance to do what's right," says Solonne. "To save your son."

Mally squirms out of Seth's grip. "It's okay, Mom," he says. "I want to go."

"What?"

He screws up his eyes and parrots a line: *"There will come a day when the last boy goes to the sun and that's how he saves the world."*

"What? What is that? Where did you hear that?"

"It's the prophecy," he says. His eyes pierce Kate's. For a second Kate sees him as an Other, as a Something Else, not quite human, and it's like someone is holding an ice cube against her spine. Then the moment passes and she sees her son again, her flesh-and-blood boy.

"Come along, then," Solonne says to Mally, and puts her hand out. Mally takes it without hesitation.

"Leave him alone," growls Seth, standing up, and grabbing Mally's hand from out of the matriarx's.

It looks like Solonne wants to snatch him back, but she knows she won't win the fight. Not here. Not today.

~

Two minutes after Solonne leaves, shaking her frown, Keke shows up.

"Solonne was just here," says Kate, and Keke freezes.

"Please tell me – "

"I didn't let him go with her."

She clutches her chest. "I was worried I'd be too late."

"Too late for what?"

"It's the nannies," Keke says, panting. "But I don't know why."

"What?"

"The nanny killed the Lundy kid. The Nash kid. The printed kids. All dead."

Kate's head spins. "What?"

"It's the Surro-nannies," says Keke. "They're the ones killing the Genesis kids."

Kate's Patch rings. She checks her Helix, sees that it's her mother, and taps to take it.

"It's my mother," she mouths to Keke. "Mom, how are you? Everything okay?"

"Darling, have I got the wrong day?"

Kate's mouth dries up instantly. Lemon Pith.

"What do you mean?"

"I'm at the speedtrain station. I thought you said they'd be on the DBN930? Did they miss it?"

Kate checks the time. It's 10:15.

"They were on the 9:30. I personally put them on the 9:30. They should have arrived in Durban at half past nine."

"They're not here, dear. I checked the cabin myself. Completely empty."

"Please check again. They must be there."

"It's gone. It left fifteen minutes ago. Back to Joburg."

Curses explode in Kate's head, like paintball guns of night-glo colour.

"Oh no," she says. "Oh no no no no."

There is a smashing sound. She looks down and sees a mug she doesn't even remember holding, shattered on the floor. Seth comes running with Mally in his arms, greeting Keke with raised eyebrows.

"Hello?" says Kate's mother. "Kate?" but Kate can't talk. Anne's disembodied voice keeps on: "Shall I wait here? I'm not sure what to do. Have you tried calling that bodyguard, or the nanny?"

Kate ends the call. Seth looks worried. "Who was that? What's wrong?"

"You're as white as a sheet."

Kate looks at Seth. She chokes on the words. "We made a terrible mistake." She feels the ground falling away from her and puts hand on the table to steady herself.

Seth puts Mally down. "Fuck's sake, Kate, what's happened?"

His Patch rings, and without looking who it is, he mutes the call.

"Take it." Kate can see he doesn't want to. "Take it!"

He taps his Patch, barks out a terse "Hello." He must have double-tapped by accident, because a small hologram of the SafeGuard Assessor appears.

"Mister Denicker," he says. "We have some upsetting news."

"Go to your room," says Kate to Mally.

"I don't want to!"

"Go to your room and put your earbuttons in."

It looks like he'll resist, but he appears to think better of it and walks towards his bedroom.

"What is it?" Seth asks the SafeGuard man, who clears his throat.

"Perhaps you should sit down."

"You've lost Silver," he says.

"Our man accompanying your daughter was found dead at the next station. His chip stopped travelling at Rivonia. His body was just discovered in the public restroom. Garrotted. Our on-site coroner says it happened a couple of hours ago."

Seth puts his hands up to his face. Kicks a kitchen chair over. It bangs hard on the tiles.

"What about Silver?"

"Missing."

Kate shouts at the hologram. "What?!"

"We're doing what we can to find them."

"No," says Kate. "This can't be happening. I don't understand. They're supposed to be after Mally. Mally is the one in danger."

The SafeGuard man's face flickers with anxiety.

Kate gulps down rising bile. "There's something you're not telling us."

"Well," he begins, then stops.

"Tell us."

"We found Silver's luggage too. A plush rabbit, and a pink backpack with her name on it, abandoned in the toilet stall."

The extrapolation of this doubles Kate over. She puts her hands on her knees and tries to breathe.

"You're sure?" says Seth. "That there are no other...bodies there?"

"We did an extensive sweep. To be frank, we were expecting the nanny's body to show up, but nothing so far."

"You won't find it," says Kate, horror rising like smoke inside her. "You won't find the nanny's body. Because she's the one who took Silver."

Kate feels like she's on one of those old school fun fair rides, where you get spun around so hard that the g-force keeps you pinned to the wall while the floor drops away. Candy cane stripes and stale popcorn and teeth sticky with toffee apple, and children, shrieking children, until she retches, hard, right there on the kitchen floor.

"Let's sit down," Seth tries to lever her on to a chair.

"No," says Kate, pushing them both away. "I'm not sitting anywhere. We need to go. We need to find Silver."

Kate can't believe she's saying the words out loud. It's like she's always known something like this would happen. She put it down to her past trauma – the gold-edged paranoia that flaps around her like a death's head butterfly – but deep down she always knew that this would happen.

"There's something else," says Keke, biting her lip.

Kate and Seth zero in on her.

"I wasn't sure it was relevant, but now I...I don't know. I think it might be."

"About the trial?" asks Seth.

"About Marko."

Kate's finding it difficult to concentrate on the conversation. She wants to know what Keke has to say but it's like her mind is split into two windows: one showing what is happening here, in the kitchen, and one picturing her little girl being afraid, or alone, or…worse. The idea of Silver being hurt…she can't stand it. Acid green betrayal corrodes her insides. She thinks of all the times Sebongile fed the kids, played games with them, laughed with them, hugged them. She thinks of her own affection for the woman who had, millimetre by millimetre, insinuated herself into the nucleus of her family. In her mind she pictures Bongi's black tentacles coiling around her heart, poised for a slow strangle.

CHAPTER 50

TESTIMONY FROM THE GRAVE

The nursing intern puts down her cold tea and greets Keke like an old friend.

"You brought reinforcements," Themba says, looking at the untidy troupe of Keke, Kate, Seth and a monkey-like Mally, clinging to Seth's leg. The bodyguard fades into the background. The boy has never been to a hospital before but something about it scares him immediately.

"I don't like it here," he keeps saying.

"No one likes hospitals." Seth's jaw is tight. It must be the visual of Marko lying in bed, as pale as a dead body. Kate knew he was gravely ill, toppling on the verge of nothingness, but seeing him looking like a corpse is difficult to bear.

"What's the 411?" Keke asks the nurse. She walks up to the bed, holds Marko's hand. He has new wires and tubes trespassing all over his body. Sticker sensors beep reassuringly.

"You should probably wait to ask the doctor that."

Seth sits in the corner, away from everyone, concentrating on his SnapTile.

"I want your opinion," says Keke. "You're the one who's watching him."

Themba smoothes down her nurse uniform. "He's not doing as well as we'd hoped."

Kate is irritated by a tear spilling down her cheek. She wipes it away and blows air upwards to evaporate the rest. It's a tic that is not in the least effective.

"We expected some kind of increase in independent activity by now."

"Waking up?" asks Keke.

The nurse nods. "Or, at least signs of beginning to wake up. But, if anything, he seems – "

"He seems deeper," says Keke. "More deeply unconscious."

"Yes."

To mask her emotion, Keke keeps her hands busy. She gets a blanket out of the cupboard and lays it over Marko, cracks open the window and raids his bar fridge for drinks. Seth is tapping away at his screen. Everyone is acting oddly, as if there is a strange new filter on their reality. Kate is stuck in a strange limbo: desperate to search for Silver but stuck in this slow-motion in-between of Not Knowing. She keeps checking her Helix for a message from the kidnappers, but the tab remains empty.

A man appears at the door. He has long black hair that rests on his shoulder in a thick braid. It's held together with decorative steel clips that match his other piercings: brow, nose, lip. His clothes match his hair, and he doesn't look anything like a doctor but has the medical professional visitor security tag clipped to his shirt.

"My, my," he says, surveying the room. His voice is deep and resonant. A purring black sports car.

"Doc," says Kekeletso. "Thank you so much for coming." She introduces the others, but Seth hardly looks up from what he's doing. Mally peers out from his hiding place, underneath the blood pressure monitor.

"This is the man who's going to help us find Silver."

Seth looks up, frowning.

"I'm sorry that we're meeting again under such sad circumstances." Dark Doc approaches Marko's still body and looks him over. "What can I do?"

"We need to access the footage from Marko's cyberlens."

The doctor is calm, measured. "You know that we don't allow for that. We discussed it prior to the lens surgery."

"I know what we discussed, but this is an emergency."

"Marko's vision is entirely private. There is no recording device outside of the body. It's a strict policy we have for various legal reasons."

"I know, but – "

"But?"

"I was reading something. About a murder trial in the US, a landmark case. Testimony from the grave – "

Dark Doc holds up a hand. It's a canvas for ultra-delicate black ink tattoos.

"I know what you're going to say. The Radford case. Melissa Radford, who was shot by her partner."

Keke turns to Kate. "They used the film from the victim's cybernetic lens – she had one like Marko's – as evidence to convict the perpetrator."

"So it's not impossible," says Kate. "To access the footage. You just don't allow for it in your policy."

"It's fraught with legal repercussions," says the doctor. "But that isn't why we can't do it." He looks at Keke with affection. Says in a low tone: "You know I'd do anything for you."

"We need the film to find out who did this to him. To protect him from further attack."

"We think that it was the same people who kidnapped my daughter," says Kate. "It's life or death."

"You see, that's why I can't do it," he says. "The reason the team in the States could retrieve the Radford recording was because...well, the victim. She was dead. Her death terminated the privacy agreement she had with the surgical tech company that implanted her lens. The strings were cut, and it was no longer a morally ambiguous decision."

"I don't give a fuck about the privacy agreement," says Kate. "My little girl is missing."

"Look, I told you before...I'm less concerned with the legal standpoint, and more concerned with – "

"With?"

"Well, with Marko. I've been briefed on his status. His condition is precarious."

"What does that have to do with anything?"

"To get the recording, we'd need to – "

"Operate?"

"Remember," the doctor says. "The implant is permanent. It's literally part of his eye. It's not removable."

"Oh," says Kate, beginning to understand.

Keke freezes.

"To access the footage," says Dark Doc, "we'll need to remove his eye."

CHAPTER 51
NUCLEAR GHOST TOWN

"We're wrong about the SurroTribe," says Seth, standing up from his makeshift desk of the hospital bed food tray in the corner. "It's not them that's behind it."

"How do you know?"

"I ran a photo of Sebongile through my FusiformG to get her facemap. Then I uploaded the map to the list of SurroSisters."

"Where did you get the list?"

"On the official Surro site. It's a matter of public record."

"No match?" asks Keke.

"No match," says Seth.

Kate is cold. An ice cube on her neck. How could she have been so careless?

"But we made sure she was legit, didn't we?" says Kate. "When she was first recommended to us? We checked her out."

"Of course we did," says Seth. "I'm assuming whoever planted her in our lives created some kind of sophisticated mask over the Surro site. Temporarily superimposed a fake list for us to check."

"And we fell for it? How can we be so fucking stupid?"

"We fell for it, as did every single other parent who is now mourning their child."

"Don't say that," says Kate, her eyes burning. "Don't talk about mourning."

Marko lies motionless.

"We need to be sure," says Keke. "Facemaps aren't 100% accurate. Run her dynap code."

"We don't have it," says Seth. "Do we?"

"I have it," says Kate. "I have it. I needed it to register her for tax."

Kate sends Seth the nanny's DNA profile code, and again, there is no match on the Surro site.

Themba checks on Marko, then coaxes Mally out from under the equipment with a packet of Holee Molees.

"Wait," says Keke. "What about the blacklisted Surros?"

Any SurroSister who breaks the code of Surro ethics gets stripped of her pin and placed on a blacklist. Some of the women, the ones who lived and breathed their purpose as surrogates, take the seemingly callous casting aside to heart. They're the ones who ended up as spike addicts, or prostitutes, or victims of the suicide contagion. The blacklist is a slow-growing directory that floats in the tide of the darkweb. Seth runs Sebongile's dynap, but again, there is no match, like she never existed.

Kate looks at the doctor. "Do it."

"Are you insane?" says Keke. "Remove his *eye*?"

"It's the only way."

"It's his eye, for Christ's sake!"

"Think about Silver. Think of how scared she must be. Do you know how many kids these people have killed?"

"We don't know that. We don't know if it's the same people."

"Of course it's the same fucking people! Marko was perfectly safe until he found out about the Genesis kids being murdered."

"Don't argue," says the doctor in his deep, listless voice. He shows them his etched palms. "There's no point in arguing. I won't perform the surgery and nor will anybody else." He prepares to leave.

"That's not true," says Kate. "There's always somebody else.

"Keke, please," says Kate, desperation pulling at her face. "Please. We need to know. We need to know!"

"You can't put her in that position," says Seth in a low voice. "It's an impossible position. It's not fair."

"There is no position!" shouts Kate. "There is no fairness in this situation! These people have our daughter and we need to go and find her. That is all there is."

"I can't," Keke says, shaking her head. "I can't do that to Marko. I'm sorry."

Kate's body stiffens. Her hands are fists. "You don't even know if he's going to wake up."

The words taste terrible in her mouth. Bitter and sharp. A burnt blade.

Kate realises her face is dripping. And she swipes the tears away. She doesn't have time for emotion. Seth moves closer to her, pulls her into an embrace. She relaxes into him, and sobs into his shoulder, and asks the same question over and over again. "How can this be happening?"

Keke's face is a long, dark veil of pain.

Kate's Patch pings, snapping her mind back to the present moment. It's an unknown number.

Unknown > We have your daughter.

Kate shows Seth her Helix screen with shaking hands.

"Ask them what they want from us," says Seth.

"I already know what they want from us."

KittyKate >> What do you want?

They stare at the screen in silence and dread.

Unknown > A meeting.

The Unknown contact sends a GPS marker for a location in Springs, forty kilometres east of Johannesburg. 5pm, it says. A sun emoti hologram rises and smiles rays of sunshine at them. It's branded SOLAR CITY.

"Springs?" says Kate. "We can't go there. It's still red-bordered. It's a fucking nuclear ghost town."

Since the nuclear power plant accident razed the place, the land is no longer fit for human habitation. They can't farm or mine. The government bought the whole tract and began to turn it into Africa's largest solar farm.

"They've re-opened parts of it," says Seth. "To workers."

The journalists who were brave and/or stupid enough to break in to document the devastation during the first few years after the accident sent back images worthy of a sci-fi film: thousands of glinting solar panels in a deserted radiation wasteland.

"I've seen the pictures. Those guys work in hazmats and gas masks."

Grocery stores, hotels and personal homes left exactly the way they were on the day of the disaster, like a museum of misfortune. Cereal aisles in perfect order apart from one box dropped on the floor and never picked up. A skew-sitting doily on an abandoned tea tray, only a black stain left in the milk jug. Not a living plant for miles. Everything covered with a thick layer of dust and devastation.

"The radiation is still very dangerous there," says the nurse. "We sometimes have people trying to seek treatment here, but we have to turn them away. It's too dangerous for the other patients. It's the Zama-zamas. They think if they come to Jozi they can fence the merch. But the stuff's old, and practically glowing with radiation."

"Zama-zamas?"

"Chancers," says Keke. "They go in to loot the empty shopping malls."

"But they either die in there or come out poisoned, and we can't treat them. No one can."

"We can't go there," says Kate. "Can we?"

Seth rubs his eyes."I don't think we have a choice."

Unknown > 5pm. No cops, no guards, no games.

"That's in two hours' time. It'll take us almost an hour to get there. We'd better leave now."

Unknown > Bring Mally.

"Of course," says Kate. "Of course."

"What?"

"They want us to bring Mally."

The boy looks up from his snack. "What Mom? What?"

"Nothing, Sausage," says Kate.

Seth speaks through gritted teeth: "We are not fucking taking Mally."

"Silver is their bargaining chip."

Of course they can't, they won't, take Mally. It would be like signing his death warrant.

Unknown > Bring Mally, or Silver dies.

CHAPTER 52

SHRIEKING LIMPET

Mally's screaming sends shards of mirror into Kate's vision. He's attached himself to her leg and refuses to let go. A shrieking limpet.

"Let go, Mally, for Christ's sake," says Seth, trying to wrench him off. His screams just get louder. Themba looks concerned at the noise, worried about her other patients. She waves another snack at Mally but his eyes are winched shut so tightly he can't see her or her bag of treats.

"We'll be back," says Kate, combing his hair with her fingers. "We just need to go and see someone and then we'll be right back and everything will be fine. You'll see."

Seth shoots her a look. So it is a lie, but what else can she say?

"I want to come with!" he squalls. "I hate it here!"

"Let go."

More crying and gnashing of teeth.

"We need to leave right now," says Seth, checking his SnapTile. There is a bump from Arronax: a copy of a signed waybill that confirms a delivery from Nautilus to his apartment.

"Excellent," he says, but no one hears him above the din.

The nurse pops out of the room and is back a minute later with a small nebuliser. She turns it on and the candy-floss pink mask hisses. The aroma of artificial vanilla drifts in the air. She places the neb over Mally's nose and mouth. At first he fights it but when he smells the sweet gas he lets go. Within ten seconds he's out.

"What the hell is that?" asks Seth, lifting the boy's limp body.

"A sedative. Creme Soda flavour. He'll have a nice sleep, now."

TranX Junior, thinks Seth. The chemgineer in him wants to inspect the product, see what the active ingredient is. The uncle in him wants to be in the car already, on the way to get Silver.

"You go. We'll look after him," says Keke.

Kate seems conflicted. She doesn't want to let Mally out of her sight.

"We'll take him with," says Seth.

Kate stops what she's doing and stares at Seth. She has an image flash in her mind: a picture of Mally, in the nuked shell of a Red Zone shopping mall, standing at the bottom of a long-abandoned escalator. Lost.

"I'll explain to you when we're in the car." He looks down at Mally's peaceful, sleeping face, then up at the nurse. "We're going to need some things."

PART 3

CHAPTER 53

SHARK FINS AND LIGHTNING

Seth and Kate are outside their apartment building where they had to pick up supplies. They sling their backpax into the cab and climb in, panting. Seth bumps the GPS co-ordinates of Solar City, and the car beeps an error message.

"That is a restricted area," says the car. "I cannot drive you to that location."

"Just get us as close as you can."

"I will need to file a report on your illegal request."

"Fine," says Seth. The dashboard chimes.

"Report filed. You may receive a visit from the police force regarding your request."

"*Ja*, right," says Kate. As if they've got the time.

"I am only kidding," says the cab.

Kate and Seth frown at each other. Since when does AI have a sense of humour?

They pull into the hooting city traffic and are immediately stuck behind an old bus – not a straddlebus – which they can't drive under. The cab waits patiently, then they crawl a metre forward. Kate wonders if it's a Turing: a beta listening cab. She taps her foot, runs her fingers through her hair. An ancient tuk-tuk that looks like it's held together with sticky tape and string passes them, almost knocking off their side mirror.

"Come on," she says. "We need to go faster. Is there a way we can go faster?"

"We are gridlocked," says the cab. "Peak hour traffic."

"Listen to me," says Kate. "My daughter is in danger, and I need to get there as soon as I can. Do you understand?"

The car hesitates to respond.

"Do you understand?" she says again.

"That must be difficult for you?" ventures the car.

"*Now* can you drive faster?"

"Re-calculating route," says the cab. The smart mirror animates with green lines and arrows. All of a sudden the car reverses, almost knocking over a cyclist who yells and hits the roof of the car, then it turns a sharp left into a side road and whizzes down an alley that is clearly marked 'NO THOROUGHFARE'. It sends a rubbish bin flying and takes out a low-slung washing line. Windscreen wipers drag a shirt off the front glass.

"This isn't a road," says Seth, hanging on the side of the door's interior. A pedestrian jumps out of their way, then shouts at them, shaking a fist in the air. Turing doesn't respond. It makes a hard right into the next road and travels the wrong way up a one-way street. All the other self-driving cabs freeze when faced with such erratic driving from a fellow vehicle, and allow it to pass. They take a few more dangerous turns, and before they know it, they're coasting on the highway, in the emergency shoulder, at 164km per hour.

"I like you, Turing," says Seth. "Can I keep you?"

The car's response system whirs. It doesn't understand, and it doesn't have an answer, but it sounds happy enough. They sit back into their seats for the first time since climbing in.

"Thank you," says Kate, looking at Seth.

"For what?"

"You're always there. Even when you're not."

"That doesn't even makes sense."

"I wouldn't be able to do this on my own."

"Yes, you would," says Seth.

"No. You're my better half."

Seth looks out the window. Holoboards and oak tree canopies rush by.

"No," he says. "You've always been the better half."

They hug – an awkward gesture, with the small body in-between them – and Kate thinks, not for the first time, that Seth smells of bright rebellion. Zig-zags. Shark fins and lightning.

"I can't believe we're doing this," Kate says, adjusting Mally's outfit.

Seth squeezes her hand. "What choice do we have?"

CHAPTER 54

THE PERFECT PLACE TO HIDE

The Red Zone, 2024

When they arrive at the red border they expect the cab to stop, but instead it takes the right fork and follows a dirt road along the barricade for a few kilometres. Sentries armed with automatic rifles and faces of stone watch them clip along. Massive billboards warn them to not enter: 'Out of Bounds', 'No Entry', 'Hazardous Materials'. 4D icons of gas-masks and radiation hover above the angry-looking palisade fence.

"Cabbie?" she says, but it doesn't respond. They slow down to avoid dead trees that have fallen in the way – long, brittle-barked skeletons. Martian dunes. Not a green leaf in sight. Once they've made it through the dead forest, the car races along the perimeter again until it gets to a spot marked at its base by an old water bottle: a secret sign that's almost impossible to see from the road unless you know exactly what you're looking for. The car brakes abruptly and the wheels lock, causing them to slide a few metres forward and spin ninety degrees before they come to a stop up against a soil bank. In the still car they listen to each other's hard breathing. Once their seat belts decide it's safe to disembark, the obligatory thirty seconds post-collision, they click open. They get out and inspect the red zone barrier for an entry point. Up close, they see that a portion – the size of a car – has been cut out and then put back again, on barely visible hinges, turning it into a swing gate. Their eyes meet to acknowledge their good fortune, but there is a hint of apple seed too (Sour Cyanide), because being handed a key to kill yourself is bittersweet, even if it's a key you went looking for.

The cab kicks up the soft sand in getting through, and the steel swords of palisade trail along the exterior with a crowd of shrieking that sends voodoo pins into Kate's eyeballs. The clockologram says it's ten to five: if they survive the evening, which has never seemed very likely, they'll have this cab to thank. They're already wearing the hospital hazmats Themba gave them; all they need to do before they get out of the car is put their full headmasks on. They were able to fashion a child-sized hazardous material suit from an adult 'small' by using biostitches and medical tape. Kate expected the protective gear to be the colour of radiation, which in her mind is glow-in-the-dark orange, but instead they're a fresh chewing-gum colour. Ice blue-green. Medical Mint.

The car sprays more sand as it guns for the exact location of the co-ordinates. They pass the outlying houses: shax and RDP housing, mansions and huts. Windows, front doors, and roofs broken or hanging at oblique angles. Gardens flattened. Cars corroded so badly they look melted into the ground. The shops here, so close to the border, are the ones hit hardest by the Zama-zamas: not a window remains in place. They drive on a tarred road now, wide and empty, and pass a playground with rusted primary colours. The motionless swings are eerie. Were there children here when the accident happened?

Five minutes to go.

"Are we close?"

Seth checks their co-ordinates against the clock. "Yes."

The stunted suburbs morph into an industrial area. The buildings here are also stripped: the open mouths of stolen glazing gape at them as they pass by. The monochrome landscape is easy on Kate's synaesthesia: muddy browns and charcoal hues soothe her manic thoughts. She pats the holster against her ribcage for the tenth time to reassure herself that she has her gun. It's over her kevlarskin but beneath the hazmat material. A sandwich of borrowed outfits: one that will either save her life or robe her corpse.

They pull to a stop outside a water-processing plant. The adjacent dam is sludge. Mud mousse. The perfect place to hide bodies. They're not planning on opening this area for the next three years, and when they do, it will be to government-contracted Chinese corps who will demolish anything standing to make space for the solar stalks. It's what they did in the north of the red zone. So far the giant solar farm is an incredible success, and the Nancies' PR firm won't let the civilians forget it. They never mention the actual accident, unless you count the one day of the year they reluctantly lower the flag to commemorate the victims. Every other day is fair game for the spin doctors to celebrate Solar City and their resulting carbon deficit. Kate pictures hungry machines, like giant lawnmowers, sweeping over everything in sight, ploughing the empty structures and play-sets into the earth.

"Ready?" says Seth.

Kate nods and puts on her headgear. It's claustrophobic and she has to stop herself from immediately wrenching it off. Once she's a bit more used to it, the mask further dulls her senses. Her shapes feel far away.

"Ready."

They climb out of the car. Seth carries the small, mint-coloured body in his arms.

CHAPTER 55

CRASH CART

Johannesburg, 2024

Keke jerks when she hears the shrieking. The machine against the wall, the one that monitors Marko's synthetic heart, is screaming blue murder. She rushes up to Marko, as pale as ever, and puts her hands on him. Presses the emergency button and keeps pressing. The room is crowded with the din of the flatline. Keke refuses to believe they've lost the battle. She zips open his heartpack and looks inside, but knows – knew before she opened it – there's nothing she can do.

The double doors are smashed open by a casualty team with a crash cart. Keke lets go of Marko and leaps out of the way. They shout at each other above the noise, nonsensical phrases like "jump the cardio" and "shake his coronaries" as if he is in some kind of cutting-edge fitness class, instead of what he is. Dead. For the second time in three days.

As the team works on Marko, Keke's panic subsides. It's out of her hands. It's always been out of her hands. Her fright fades and it's replaced by a flaring anger. Who did this to him? Who the fuck did this to him, to them, to Kitty and Silver? There's nothing she can do to save Marko, but she can damn well do whatever she can to save Silver. There's only one thing left to do. She taps a contact on her SnapTile.

"I told you, I'm not doing it," says the Dark Doc as soon as he answers.

"Things have changed," says Keke.

CHAPTER 56

ELEGANT SURRENDER

The Red Zone, 2024

The building itself is menacing. A tall, smog-eating silo etched with spiderwebs of cracks. Too much concrete, not enough windows, not enough air. Not that you can breathe this air, anyway. Not without getting really sick, not without turning your organs into radioactive lightbulbs.

Lots of pipes too, plugging into the adjoining locked-up block-shaped building that houses the processors. Giant waterpipes empty of the very thing that is the reason for their existence. Kate can feel the dryness of this place inside her body, as if the scorch has travelled into her bones. She trips over a piece of sunburnt rubber – made clumsy by her protective boots – and Seth catches her arm before she tips forward into the sand.

"You okay?"

She nods and lets go of his arm. She's breathing hard. Despite the filter over her nose and mouth, Kate can smell the ashy decay.

They make their way up the front steps and into the black innards of the silo, and blink, waiting for their eyes to adjust to the low light. It's quiet. Too quiet. She looks at the time on her Helix: 17:04.

"There's nobody here." Kate's voice would echo if she weren't wearing a mask.

They step away from the stream of afternoon light that is like a golden laser coming from a crack in the exterior wall. It's safer in the shadows.

Seth needs his hands free, and the small, unconscious body cannot stand. Kate collects some offscourings from around her and packs it close together to form a small bank against the wall: a nest of detritus. A legless chair, a planter, a few bricks.

There is nothing soft. Seth lays the mini hazmat suit bundle down inside the shallow cardboard box on the top. Mally's little body looks so lonely; vulnerable. Kate forces her thoughts to Silver.

The silence is heavy on her ears, as if she's underwater, and everything is greyscale. It feels like a dream, but Kate can tell from the bubbling in her stomach it's not. She looks at Seth and the sleeping boy. The cool mint of their suits pops against the charcoal surroundings. Will this be their last hour?

The deep quiet gives way to a faraway buzzing, like a swarm of bees, in the distance. A few seconds later it becomes clear that it's a Volanter, and that its on its way to them. They creep along the silo wall to look outside and watch it approach, and the elegant chopper whips up red sand as it lands. Rich sunshine glints off the Volanter's black carapace. The engine whines as it shuts down, causing Kate's insides to contract. She's as ready as she's ever going to be. She reaches for her gun.

A man opens the horizontal-hinged door of the craft and jumps out. He's freakishly tall, wearing a foil space-suit, replete with bubble mask. He extends his arm towards the hatch. A woman, wearing the same uniform, takes his hand and pounces onto the wasted ground. The pilot stays inside, seemingly ready to take off again. Kate can't see Silver. Is she in the aircraft? It's a scene from Mars, with the shimmering hot red soil – bad and barren. As they lope towards the silo, Kate recognises the confident gait of the woman. Despite her bubble helmet, it's clearly the same person who led Mally away at the RoboPup show. She's wearing the same bright red lipstick as before, but she's not smiling today. Kate's grasp tightens on her revolver. She wishes she had the foresight to apply some sweat-ex on her palms. Her latex gloves are already slippery on the inside.

The silver-suited couple comes through the entrance and the pair blinks into the darkness, then their eyes rest on Kate and Seth's guns, which are pointed right at them. The woman lifts her palms to them in elegant surrender. And there it is, thinks Kate, as the woman's lips curl into her trademark smile. Unholy Ruby. As if she is constantly amused by the havoc she wreaks. Kate's trigger-finger tingles with fury. How she'd like to just blow a hole in that space-suit, the closer to that smile, the better. In between the eyes would be a good start. Or, more fittingly, a good ending.

"You can put those down," the woman says, motioning at the weapons. Her helmet has some kind of speaker that amplifies her voice, making it crisp and clear, not like their chunky hospital hazmat masks that swallow their words.

"Why would we do that?" asks Seth.

"A gesture of good faith," she says. "We are not armed."

They won't fall for that one again.

"Not going to happen," says Seth.

If she's put out by his refusal, she doesn't show it.

"Mister Denicker. Staring down a barrel of a gun is not a good way to begin our…negotiations."

Kate judders her gun at her. "What is there to negotiate?"

"You've got something we want – "

"Not something. Not some-*thing*," says Kate. "He's my son. He's a fucking human being."

"In your eyes, perhaps," she says.

"The fuck does that mean?"

"He's a Genesis Baby, Kate." The woman slants her head, shrinks her smile. Kate hates the way her name sounds when it comes from this cretin's mouth. "*Silver* is your real child. Silver is the one you're here to save. Mally is nothing but a…a science experiment."

"How dare you?"

"An ill-advised experiment. Ethically wrong, and morally reprehensible. It should never have happened, but God is a forgiving master, and He knows that we are correcting the mistake. When we are finished here, he will forgive you too."

"Mally is not a 'mistake'."

"Naturally you're attached to him. That's understandable. You've been brainwashed, after all."

"We're not the ones who've been brainwashed," says Seth.

"We can help you to see the Truth."

Kate's trigger finger is burning now, crackling with heat. She has to keep calm. She has to keep calm if she wants to ever see Silver again.

"You're the one killing people – killing children! – to appease an imaginary god, and you think *Mally's* an abomination?" Kate's anger shakes her voice.

"Where is he?" the woman in foil says, casting her gaze around the darkness. "I hope you've not wasted our time. I hope you've not been stupid." But then her eyes zero in on the contents of the box and her smile returns.

"Oh, how perfect," she says, taking a step forward and craning her neck. "You've packed him for us, all ready to go. Is he sleeping?"

"Don't you come any closer," says Seth, stepping in the way.

"Where's Silver?"

"Silver is safe. For now."

"You said that if we brought Mally, you'd give us our daughter back."

"And we will."

"*Now,*" says Seth. "Give her back now, or the deal is off."

Ruby lipstick produces a sword from a hidden sheath on her thigh. The steel had been camouflaged by the colour of the suit. A glinting magic trick. She tosses it from hand to hand and swirls it in quick circles in front of her chest. The swordplay gets faster and faster until the blade becomes a blur. Her partner, still and silent until now, pulls out his gun with a practised motion. No showmanship, no noise, just steady confidence. How many people has he killed?

CHAPTER 57

FOILS VS MINTS

They stand there in the dark silo, facing each other. Two foils versus two mints, armed and poised to fight.

"Give him to me," says Ruby.

"Who are you working for?" asks Kate. "Solonne?"

Kate wants to wipe the amused look off her face for good.

"Solonne?" She smirks. "No."

"Who, then?"

"I answer to God," she says.

"The Resurrectors," says Seth.

The man takes aim at Seth, who returns the favour.

"Of course, the Resurrectors," the woman says. "Always the Resurrectors. We are the militant arm of God. We are God's Army."

"You're nothing but bloodthirsty terrorists."

"Sometimes God needs terrorists."

Kate points her gun at the woman's head, puts some pressure on the trigger. A dark part of her wants to blow her brains into that bubble mask.

"I'm not leaving here without him," she says.

"Then you're not leaving here," says Kate.

She looks directly at Kate. Growls at her. "Give the boy to me or I'll come and get him."

"Then come and get him," says Seth, sweeping his barrel from the man to the woman and shooting her in the chest. The sound of the shot rings out through the silo and echoes wildly, crashing Kate's vision. She expects the woman to fall, but the shot just knocks her back a few paces. Everyone in the silo knows that bullets are no match for arachnasilk. She's breathing loudly: the shot struck the air out of her. She spins her sword again and advances on Seth. He shoots at her again, but this time she jumps away from the blast. Once Kate can see past the noise of the second shot, she aims her revolver at the woman, to back up Seth, but the tin-suited man has her in his gun's sights. The second it takes to switch targets is the second he uses to pull his own trigger, and she's flattened by a hard, hot bullet to the shoulder. She's splayed onto the dusty floor, and her senses explode with electric blue. Her revolver skates away from her, into the shadows.

"Kate!" shouts Seth, looking at her. The woman takes advantage of the distraction and with one quick motion she shears his hazmat suit wide open. He grabs the cut sides of the yawning suit with one hand and forces them together. Kate pictures the invisible radiation seeping in like mustard gas. Ruby advances on him again, swishes her blade, but he ducks out of the way.

Kate's shoulder is on fire. She can't tell yet if the bullet pierced the kevlar, but the neon zinging in her head tells her damage has certainly been done. The man is standing over her, his face expressionless, awaiting Ruby's order to finish her off. Kate scrambles backwards on her hands and butt, the pain zipping through her whole body. A glance over at Seth tells her they're now in full combat mode: she's swerving away from his bullets, bouncing and slicing, and he's doing what he can to dodge her keen blade.

When will he begin to get sick? When will she? There's a hole in her suit too.

Her attacker follows her progress calmly through the sight of his weapon; he knows he's won this battle. She keeps scrambling, and he keeps following. She's a metre away from her gun. What is he waiting for? But she knows the answer.

"Get the boy!" shouts Ruby.

The man finally looks away from her, and she is able to grab her revolver and fire at him. Bang! Bang! Bang! She gets three shots off before he's even noticed. One bullet misses and ricochets off the wall. One is embedded in the man's suit, and one smashes his bubble mask. He steps back, in surprise, and Kate jumps up and high-kicks him in the chest. She expects it to hurt her shoulder like hell but the yellow adrenaline is painting over the blue and she feels as if she can walk over coals if it would mean defeating these terrible people and getting her daughter back.

The man can't see properly through his silver-shattered mask and he stumbles forward, trying to cover the hole with one hand and aim his gun with the other.

"Get the boy!" Ruby shouts again, as Seth manages to grab hold of her sword. She doesn't let go and they wrestle for it. The man stumbles again, gun swinging from side to side, trying to see past his frosted visor. At that moment, the boy sits up in the box, his bespoke hazmat gear a beacon against the shadow wall, and the man lifts his gun and shoots, riddling the small body with bullets.

CHAPTER 58

A NEW KIND OF SMILE

The man empties his magazine into the small body. The slugs are hollow-pointed, designed to cause maximum damage, and they tear into the torso and face, blasting it back into the cardboard cot, out of sight.

"You bastard!" shouts Kate, emptying her own bullets into the Resurrector. This time she aims them all at his head, hoping to crack his mask completely and open the suit up to the radioactive gas that surrounds them. The superglass holds around the original hole, but his mask is now opaque with the scars. A face cataract.

Seth and the woman are still fighting over the sword. Kate aims her revolver at her, but they're moving too quickly and her hands are slippery from the sweat inside her gloves. The only vulnerability of the space-suit, as far as she can see, is the throat area, but she doesn't have the confidence to shoot and not hit Seth.

"Is the boy dead?" The woman is panting. The man doesn't answer. "Is he dead?"

Kate wonders if he talks at all. Maybe his microphone is broken.

"Get him," Ruby lipstick says. "As proof. Bring a part of him." She's Snow White's evil stepmother, demanding the hunter bring back her heart.

The man staggers unseeingly, and Kate sticks her foot out to trip him. He pitches forward, tries to steady himself, but fails. As soon as his weapon-holding hand clatters to the floor Kate jumps on it, forcing him to bellow and release the gun, which she grabs. She aims both of them at the woman, but it's no use, because it's not safe for Seth. The man roars in outrage and frustration at not being able to see, and he wrests his bubble helmet off his head, and takes a deep breath of the toxic air.

Seth pries the sword from Ruby's hands, and she dashes away from him, towards the torn-up body. Just as he brandishes the blade, he doubles over, opens his breathing filter, and splashes vomit on the ground.

The tall man tries to stand up but he's disorientated, and he falls back down again. His nose gushes, staining the floor with red spatter. Seth heaves again, then loses his balance. They've got to get out of there. Get to hospital. But if they let the Resurrectors go, how will they find Silver?

Kate grabs the sword from Seth and goes after the woman, but she's too late. She reaches her just as she's lifting the maimed body out of the box with a horrified expression on her face. A leg dangles, semi-detached. Ruby realises then that the small body is not Mally, but his printed body double.

She throws down the shredded silicone, her cheeks flush with fury.

Kate lifts the sword and cuts the woman's throat. Crimson blood, made luminous by the sunset, spills out of the gash. A new kind of smile. The woman grabs her wounded neck with both hands, and the red liquid peaks through her fingers. Her eyes are on fire.

Kate, shocked by what she's done, drops the sword, and the woman grabs it almost before it hits the floor. She backs away from Kate, reverses to exit. Blood streams from the long gash. Her partner, his face now the colour of the concrete floor, sees her leaving and puts out his hand for help. She can't take both him and the sword; she chooses the sword. As she trips out into the dusk outside, the beetle-black Volanter starts up again, its blades chopping up the evening air.

Kate wants to go after her. She's overcome with violent urges to hurt those who are hurting her family. She wants to tackle her, slam her to the ground, pin her down with her knees and jam a gun into her cheek. Force the truth out of her. Force her to tell her where Silver is.

There's a sagging sound behind her that jerks her thoughts back to Seth. He has slumped to the ground; his light has gone out. Kate looks again at the Volanter: the woman is helped aboard by the pilot. It's Kate's last chance to go after them, to find Silver. Seth's body spills over the floor. He'll die if she leaves him here.

CHAPTER 59

DANGEROUS CHEEKBONES

Kate drags Seth's unconscious body out of the silo to the soundtrack of the vanishing Volanter. Despite them being twins and having very similar builds, he seems to weigh double, and her injured shoulder doesn't make the job any easier. He's groaning, as if he's trying to wake, trying to break through the veil of sleep, but this just causes him to vomit more, and Kate worries he'll choke or drown. She's out of shape, and there's limited oxygen in the suit, so she has to take breaks every few metres. The slow progress is maddening. Every extra minute she takes is a minute that Seth gets sicker, and that Silver seems more lost to them.

Eventually she makes it to the car, panting and coughing, and uses the last of her energy to lever him, with a groan, into the back seat. She gets in after him and closes the door. The cab purrs with ignition.

"Turing – " She huffs, so relieved to be back inside the cabin. It's like the embrace of a friend.

"I am at your service."

"Get out of here," she says. "Get out of this place."

The car reverses on its tracks. "What is your required destination?"

But Kate doesn't know. Back to the hospital? Themba made it clear that anyone with radiation poisoning is turned away. But if not them, then who? It was risky, it would take an hour, and looking at Seth's vitals on his SnapTile, they don't have that much time.

"Where do you take the Zama-zamas?"

"I'm sorry, I didn't catch that," says the car. "Where can I take you?"

Kate pulls off her protective mask."The people you bring here."

"I don't bring people here. The Red Zone is off limits."

The self-driving taxis are linked to the same network; they 'talk' to each other.

"What about other Cabbies?"

The car hesitates. She's wasting her time. Zama-zamas wouldn't take cabs, they'd have their own cars, old communal mini-bus taxis with their seats sawn off with angle-grinders and plenty of space to pack their loot.

"Where do they take them afterwards? What is the most common route from this spot – this hole in the palisade – to somewhere nearby. A shacktown, maybe."

"Gugulethu/Everest is an informal settlement," says the car. "There is a common route recorded on hijacked cabs to the business premises of a Mister Zeebee."

"Mister Zeebee?" What's that? An arcade, maybe. Or a dumping site. The place they go to before they get arrested. Self-driving cab companies take the theft of their vehicles seriously. Kate starts stripping down. "Let's go."

While the cab drives, Kate asks her Helix to talk her through how to care for someone with radiation sickness.

"Start by removing all contaminated garments," it says.

Kate peels Seth's hazmat and bullet-proof suits off him and throws them out the window. She does the same to her own clothes, wincing as she pulls her Kevlarskin off her injured shoulder. The bastards shot her in the same arm she'd broken during the motorbike accident four years ago. Same arm, same electric blue pain. The car's air-conditioning is cold against her bare, goose-pimpled skin. She pulls on a jacket from her backpack.

"Thoroughly wash the patient's skin and hair," says her Patch.

She uses the baby wipes she always carries to clean as much of his skin as possible. She's dubious as to whether it's been at all effective, but it's the best she can do, for now. The teddybear on the packaging taunts her with its baby button eyes.

"Take the patient to a medical care facility as quickly as possible. If it is available to you, give the patient diethylenetriamine pentaacetic acid."

Kate settles for a bottle of water from the cab's cooler. Her Patch pings with the purchase. She tries to rouse Seth enough to drink, but he fights her off.

They enter the township, and it's not a shacktown at all, but a neat suburb. What's left of the sunset renders the modest RDP houses in romantic light, with scruffy dogs running in the road and a child taking down dry laundry from a smiling washing line. More children shout happily, racing each other on their bikes, while others run alongside them. Young fruit trees leap out of tidy succulent gardens.

Informal shops are closing their doors for the day, hawkers are packing up their bruised fruit and junk chips. One of the hawkers juggles *naartjies* for the kids, then finishes the act by lobbing three of them into the small crowd as prizes.

It's getting dark, those kids should be at home. Kate's chest tightens with the thought of Silver and Mally. She'll do anything to have them safely at home. How could she not have seen every ordinary day with them as the miraculous thing that it was? Because motherhood doesn't work like that. Miraculous, yes. Easy, no. The hard parts can cast long shadows.

Five minutes later, in a slightly darker part of the burb behind the cheerful façade, there are lurkers and prostitutes drinking on street corners. A woman in a glossy black trench with popped collars stares at the cab as it cruises past. She's wearing only lingerie underneath. Matching hot pink mesh with futile suspenders that bounce off her ebony thighs.

Turing pulls up at a disused carwash. There is a hand-painted sign on the building that says "Zee Bee's Carwash". The walls are unevenly checkered where the glossy white tiles have fallen away, and the mechanical mops wilt in sad obsolescence. As Kate gets out the car, she can't help noticing the similarity of her outfit – underwear and a long jacket – to the prostitute's down the block. She won't be surprised if the woman comes after her, and tries to scratch her eyes out for being on her turf. Competition in the sex trade is hard enough, with virtual reality porn hubs popping up next to every Adult Planet store. Erotic theatre and V-XXX-R, robo-hoes and sexbots. Gradually, human doxies, with their real skin and the mess that come with it, have become less appealing. Although there are still – will always be, Kate guesses – those who think that no immersive experience, no matter how tailored to your tastes, will ever replace real, warm, flawed flesh.

As if reading her thoughts, there's a clear wolf whistle from inside the building. She pulls her jacket together, zips it up to her throat. Now it's more like a body-hugging minidress. She watches the dark interior of the broken-down premises, and as a man steps out, the Apollo lights all ignite with bangs, and they are bathed in white light.

"Halala," he says, dreadlox bouncing. "Who is this angel I see before me?"

What the hell was she was thinking, coming here? Why did she choose a carwash over a hospital?

"I need help," she says. "Can you help me?"

The man is tall – abnormally so – and cable-thin. His cheekbones are sharp enough to break through his skin. Looking at them make Kate's sinuses ache. Despite the dull evening air he's wearing sunglasses and a wide smile. He reminds Kate of the cheese chip man. Nostalgic Naks.

"For a pussycat like you," he says, two long fingers on his bottom lip, "I'd do anything."

Kate is uneasy, and grateful. She starts to pull Seth out of the car. She can feel her jacket riding up, exposing her panties. The backs of her thighs must be made lunar by the bright street lights.

"Hang on, hang on, hang on," says Mister Zeebee.

Kate stops, turns around, and pulls her jacket down. Of course. That was just too easy.

"I said I'd do anything," he says, dreads springing off his shoulders, "but of course…it will come at a price."

Revulsion pulls at her stomach, stings her throat. Her body is revolted by the idea of what he may request as payment. She swallows the acid broth and looks at Seth's face, so like her own. "Of course. How much?"

"Let's not talk numbers, sweet thing. It's bad for my appetite."

Green dye rises within her and splays over her cheeks (Bitter Bile). It may be the after-effects of the radiation exposure, but it's more likely the thought that she may have to touch this man in some kind of flesh barter if she wants to save Seth's life. "Please." She gestures towards Seth. "We need to hurry."

The man peers over her and his lip twitches as he takes in the pale, unconscious body. "Boyfriend?"

"Brother," she says, an edge of hysteria, now, to her voice. She's about to say 'twin', but thinks better of it, thinks somehow that may give him more power over her.

He takes a deep breath, chews his yellow teeth. Kaiser Chiefs. Focused eyes like a jaguar on the prowl. Those dangerous cheekbones. Seth groans and retches.

"Please," says Kate, desperation pulling at her lips. "I'll do anything."

CHAPTER 60

A CARWASH CRUCIFIXION

Gugulethu/Everest, 2024

Mister ZeeBee can see Kate means it, and looks satisfied. He puts his bony fingers back to his lips and whistles again, loudly, and two men step out of the dark innards of the gutted building. Black skin against black clothes against the blackness of the smoked brix. Triple deck. He motions for them to come over.

He speaks *scamto* to them, of which Kate only understands a few words. They're going to wash Seth, give him medicine. They nod – they've done this before – then look at Kate. At her pale skin, smudged make-up, strange outfit, matted hair. What about her, they ask, in their innovative mash-up of vernac.

"I'll take care of her," says the man.

The dark footmen snap on gloves, haul Seth out of the car and carry his dead weight towards the old washing bay. One holds his body up to a metal T-frame while the other lashes him to it with a frayed red tow rope. A carwash crucifixion. Except that instead of killing him, they are bringing him back to life. What is the opposite of an unholy execution?

They turn on the stiff rubber hosepipe – also a relic from the pre-drought days – and begin power-spraying him all over. Next they mix up some shampoo foam in a sun-brittled bucket and use odd implements – giant sponges on broom handles – to wash every inch of his skin. They wash his hair too, from a distance, till his limp body is snowed over with suds. One of the men rinses him with the power hose, and repeats the exercise, while the other begins mixing some concoction in an old CinnaCola bottle. ZeeBee pulls Kate inside with his long, cold fingers.

He leads her along a short corridor, the light from the Apollos outside flashing in on them through the broken windows as they go. Kate's body is stiff with resistance. She reclaims her hand when they step inside the office at the end of the passage. He closes the door behind them then shores it up with a chair under the handle. The room smells of oil and cheap liquor, dust and drywalling. He doesn't take his eyes off her as he sinks down into his wasted leather chair. She feels like a little girl who is prescient of her guardian's aim to abuse her. So far she's been one of the lucky ones; she's never been coerced into sex. An unusual gift to have, in this country. She returns his gaze; she needs to regain some measure of control.

"How much do you want?" she asks him. "I have a hundred thousand Blox limit on my Patch transfer. You can have it. Give me your code and I'll send it right now."

An answer plays on his lips, but he's enjoying watching her. Takes pleasure in her squirm.

"It's not enough," he says.

"I'll send you more tomorrow. The same amount. And the same the next day."

"We don't accept transfers," he says. "Traceable. Besides, I don't need more bank. I have enough."

The walls are grubby, covered with grime, torn posters, and old Prestik stains. A 2019 wall calendar hangs askew, giving the impression that the August feature – a Porsche Ventrillo – is driving up into the sky.

"Someone like you never has enough bank," says Kate.

He laughs. "Someone 'like me'? And what is that? 'Someone like me'?"

"Someone who has henchmen," she says. "Someone who packs an automatic."

She doesn't say: you reek of bad things, with your sour breath and old prison tattoos.

"Someone who likes to scare women."

She wishes he'd stop staring at her. His gaze is a laser on her exposed skin. His nicotine eyes scan her constantly, making her feel dirty.

"Are you scared?" he asks.

She doesn't see the point in answering.

"Come here." He adjusts his crotch.

Every fibre of her being shouts NO. The bile rises again and she swallows to keep it down. The thugs outside might be finished treating Seth by now. Would she be able to run for it? But how would she get him into the car, if indeed, the car is still there?

"Come here," he says again. "You said you'd do anything. I want you to come here."

She gulps again. Takes a step forward, but can't take another. He looks on, expectantly.

"Don't make me ask again," he says, now with a spark of anger. She takes another step towards him, and he adjusts his position in the chair. His tongue peeks out from his lips. She's about to take another step, but she knows that she can't do it. Not to save Seth's life, not even to save her own life.

The man slams the desk with his hand, making Kate jump. Temper ignited, he shoots up like a piston, and she backs away from him, not taking her eyes off his. He advances on her, jaw set, fingers curled into sharp-knuckled fists. She reverses into the wall, into the corner, looks at the window that's been painted shut. His tall frame blocks the path to the door. The fore-knowledge of what's about to happen is like a hot poker in her bowels. Window. Door. There is no way to escape him.

"You could have made this easy," he says. "Now it won't be easy. Not for you."

He reaches down to his belt, begins to unbuckle it.

"Please," says Kate. "Don't do it."

This is happening. This is going to happen. Could she somehow leave her body, go somewhere else in her head, to lessen the trauma of what he's about to do to her? She closes her eyes and tries to float away, to leave this dingy office and terrible thing behind her, or below her, but he comes closer, and the meat-heat of him brings her back into her body with a jolt.

He's right up in her face now. His belt is off, jeans unbuttoned. She can smell his dreadlox, his sullied clothes, his evil tang. Underneath his dangerous stink, she can smell her own fear.

ZeeBee traces her cheek with his amber snuff-nail. She can't help recoiling. He slowly zips open her jacket, revealing her bare skin underneath, her scant underwear. She moves to pull the jacket together, to cover herself, but he stops her. Without thinking, she lashes out at him – an automatic response – but he catches her arm and squeezes it so hard she thinks she'll faint.

"The more you fight," he says, his face so close to her that all she can see is the pores in his skin, "the more it will hurt."

CHAPTER 61

A BLUNT NURSE IN HOT PINK

Kate casts around for a weapon, any kind of object she can use to defend herself: a ticket spike, a desk lamp, a staple gun, but there is nothing. She has her own nails, her fists and knees, but ZeeBee is armed with a semi-automatic she's certain he won't hesitate to use. The seconds trundle. This is the last moment she will have of being unstained.

He takes his time, unzipping and leering, and Kate is sure this will be a prolonged torture. His left hand travels up to and around her neck, and he applies pressure, as if he's measuring how hard he can squeeze before he cuts off her oxygen altogether. His other hand works its way down her bare belly to her panties, where he hooks the top elastic with his fingertip. She's lightheaded, thinks she might fall, or be sick, or both.

A sudden, loud banging on the door makes them both jump. It's like the rest of the world had fallen away when they were locked in their terrible dance, but now it reasserts itself, and they are just two people in a room, instead of what they were before. What they were about to be.

There is more banging, and a woman starts yelling through the cheap masonite. She jiggles the handle, but the chair keeps the door shut.

"Zeebee!" she shouts. "Zeebee!" then follows it up with a long strain of angry *ringas* with clicks and pops that are launched at the door like a spray of ball ammunition. "You open this door right now."

"I'm busy," says Zeebee, eyes trailing Kate's body once again. "Leave me alone."

This makes the woman even more angry. The banging changes into a heavy whole-body thump. She's trying to knock down the door. After the third thump, the chair is dislodged, and with the next thrust she comes flying into the room, a hot mess of braids and cerise lipgloss. Kate's never been so happy to see a prostitute in her life.

Zeebee whirls away from Kate, but this doesn't save him from a torrent of abuse. When she decides that a verbal bollocksing isn't enough, she smacks him too. Her flat hands whack him on the back of the neck and around the ears. He's so tall she needs to jump to reach – no mean feat in electric pink stilettos – with her wobbling breasts and springing suspenders. He curses her as he tries to defend himself, tries to swat her away, but this just makes her angrier, and she whacks him some more, shouting all the while.

Kate takes the gap and tries to exit the room, but the woman grabs her hand. They make eye contact. The prostitute's eyes are zinging with fury, and Kate wonders if she's going to get *klapped* too, but then the woman squeezes her hand.

"*Mara wena*," she says, "are you okay?"

The woman gives Zeebee one last hard push so that he falls backwards, against the desk, and pulls Kate out of the awful room, the broken building, out into the blazing artificial light.

Once illuminated, she gives Kate a quick once-over. Grabs her jaw and turns it to the side to check her bruised neck, confirms that her underwear has not been damaged. A blunt nurse in hot pink lingerie. When she's satisfied Kate hasn't been attacked, she nods and Kate zips up her jacket again. Such a simple thing, the zip's tiny metal teeth closing ranks, but it almost makes her cry with relief.

"*N-n-ngiyabonga*," she stutters, "Thank you," but the woman doesn't reply.

She raises her arm and shouts at the two men, something about hurrying up with the job, she's got other grind for them to do. Kate realises that they are, in fact, *her* henchmen, and not Mister Zeebee's. Seth is sitting up against the wall now, but he seems to be floating in and out of consciousness. He doesn't acknowledge her presence. There's a parcel of old clothes beside him. A faded Iron Maiden shirt, with a hole at the neck, and shiny black slaxuit pants. She wants to leave immediately, but they are still busy treating him. Feeding him some blue gruel with a spoon, like a baby. As she looks more closely, he chokes and splatters the floor with teal. For Kate, it's the colour of hissing, and it's cold.

"What are you doing to him?"

"Muti," says the one. "It takes away the poison from the rays."

Not convinced, she looks up at the woman, who nods at her. They spoon the last of the mixture in, wipe his mouth, and are instructed to help him to the car. They throw the clothes in after him.

"I don't know how to thank you," Kate says.

The woman dispatches the men in the direction of Zeebee, then extends her palm to Kate.

"Twenty thousand," she says.

"Oh," says Kate. "Of course."

Is she the prostitute, thinks Kate, or is she the pimp? She rummages in the car and pulls out all the cash she has, and hands it over. The woman counts it, her blinging false nails glittering in the bright light.

Definitely the pimp.

The woman folds twenty thousand away into her trenchcoat pocket and gives Kate five thousand back. Kate gestures for her to keep it, but she refuses, and jams it back into her hands. Seth seems to be gaining a better grasp on his consciousness.

"Kitty," he slurs. "Silver."

"Please choose a destination," says the cheerful cab, as if this is an ordinary night and they're going out for dinner. The woman stands, arms akimbo, waiting for them to leave. But where will they go? Where is her daughter?

Behind her, Kate sees for the first time a faded mural on the outside of the carwash building. It's an ostrich with a trash can. "Zap It" says the banner above the bird, but she can't read the rest of it. It's lost to solar bleach and grime.

"Where would you like to go?" says the cab.

Kate doesn't have an answer. The woman closes her car door and gives her a stern, flat-handed wave through the tinted glass. Turing locks all the doors and pulls off. Only then does Kate start really shaking, and she can't stop.

CHAPTER 62

ONE AND A HALF FEET IN THE GRAVE

Johannesburg, 2024

Themba finishes with her checking up on Marko, with her adjusting of tubes and wires, her emptying of his entero-purse and catheter bladder, and snaps off her purple latex gloves. Keke looks up at her, for an opinion on how he's doing, but the nurse tightens her lips and leaves the room. She's not talking to Keke anymore, not since she brought the dodgy techdoctor in from the black clinic in Fourways. Not since she gave the instruction for the man to remove Marko's eyeborg.

Marko lies dormant, as before, but he now has a white patch and bandage over his left eye.

His left eye-socket, she corrects herself. Eye-socket. Because the eye is gone.

The nurse shouldn't be so damn self-righteous. She doesn't know what the stakes are. It had been an impossible decision to make, but in the end she couldn't ignore the fact that Marko, her beloved, her lover, is already one and a half feet in the grave, and dearest Silver, her fairy god-daughter, has her whole life ahead of her.

If she's still alive, Keke thinks, looking over at the sweet-sleeping Mally, curled up on the lazy chair under a blanket. If she's still alive.

Keke's Patch buzzes, making her sit up.

DarkDoc > Have uploaded the footage we found. Use this link. Password is x0PeNx. I think you'll find it extremely interesting.

Keke hits the darkweb link on her SnapTile and taps in the password. While she waits for it to authenticate she sees she has a bump from Zack.

. . .

ZikZak > How is / patient?

Kex >> Same. Worse.

ZikZak > Sorry.

Kex >> He'll die if / doesn't get / new heart.

ZikZak > Not many of those around, nowadays.

Kex >> No. I've been searching for one on / Net. Strange thing 2 look for.

ZikZak > ...

Kex >> Found some bizarre things on Marxet. BIZARRE.

ZikZak > Can imagine.

Kex >> Only bacon hearts available.

ZikZak > ??

Kex >> Cardiologist says he's not strong enough. If we suppress his immune system he'll die. If we don't suppress it his body will reject it.

ZikZak > Anything I can do?

Kex >> ...

Keke is tempted to tell him about the man in the grey suit who came to see her earlier. The one with the emergency medevac ambudrone invoice and the hospital bills. The ones she couldn't pay. Marko's private medical aid will pay for half of it, but that's still twenty-one million rand she doesn't have in the bank. The man said that if she's unable to raise the cash they'll have to move Marko to another hospital – an NHP centre – and that will surely be a death sentence. Keke's been in far too many of those institutions for her job and the stories are always bleak. Not enough doctors, not enough nurses. Black bloodstains on the corridor floors, because there's no cleaner, no mop, no fucking bleach. Women giving birth in waiting rooms and public toilets and standing up because no beds are available and the floor's too dirty. People complain they don't like the smell of hospitals: privileged people who sniff at the antiseptic air and wrinkle their noses, but they don't have a clue. She's been there and experienced the opposite, and she'll take the smell of disinfectant over disease any day.

Something's happened to Marko's bank balance too. Some kind of blip in the bitcoin system. All six of his Blox accounts are showing a negative balance. Unless someone has managed to hack his personal –

ZikZak > U name it.

. . .

She can't ask him for bank. Or can she? Marko lies, unmoving. She'll find a way to pay him back.

Kex >> I'm FUBAR.

ZikZak > I'll come over.

She should say no. She should say she's fine, or lie that she needs to be on her own. But the truth is that with Marko in this terrible way, and her best friends in danger, she's never felt this lonely. She touches the skin on her arm, on her stomach, it's some kind of tactile reminder that she is alive and warm in this hard, dangerous place the world has become.

The footage becomes available to view. There are hundreds of separate files, and she scrolls past all of them till she gets to the very last one. Her stomach is a knot as she taps the 'play' button. The hologram spins open in front of her.

It's dark, and difficult to see what's going on. The red recording button glows. Keke realises Marko is under the desk. Hiding? Legs walk by. She gasps, even though she knows Marko was attacked, and should not be surprised by the sight of an intruder in their home. She gasps again, and realises it's not a gasp of surprise but that she's crying. Her chest is one big ache; she feels Marko's pain; that he had to go through this terror. She wipes away the tears, tries to clear her eyes so she can watch the clip. A vibrating icon comes up, 911. With one click he had used his panic button, called emergency services, and given them his co-ordinates. But not soon enough.

Give me something. Give me something to make this risk worthwhile.

The intruder stops right next to Marko. He looks at the stationary boots. There is a period of complete dark – he must have closed his eyes to the horror – and then they open again when the attacker kicks over the table, exposing him completely. The eyeborg auto-focuses on the sword-bearer's face, and automatically adjusts the dim light so Keke can take in her pale cheeks and vulgar smirk.

The face shocks her; she almost drops the tile. This is it. *This is it.* She scrubs backwards to see the attacker's face again and takes a screenshot.

Got you.

Keke sends the pic to her FusiformG app and it starts cycling it through its recognition system. While she waits for the results, she resists watching the very end of the eyeborg clip, can't stand the idea of Marko being so scared, especially when he's lying here on this hospital bed, right next to her, unable to even breathe on his own. With five seconds left of the video she's about to click off when a yellow sticky note appears on the screen. It forces her to keep watching. Four seconds, three seconds. Is it a note for her? It remains blank. Two seconds. Then a second away from the end – when Marko loses consciousness – a single letter appears on the note, and then there's nothing.

CHAPTER 63

MISTRESS CATFISH

There's a knock at the door of the private ward. It must be the man in the grey suit again, here to throw them out of the hospital, but a friendly face pops around the door. Keke's eyes sting with tears of exhaustion and gratitude.

"Look at you." Zack has a beribboned white card box in his hands, which he puts down on the side table so he can give her a tender hug.

"Not looking my best?" she jokes, pulling away, even though she doesn't want to.

"Quite the opposite," he says. "You look positively angelic, sitting there, surrounded by hospital white. Like some kind of angel. Or saint."

"Believe me, I'm neither of those things."

"They say that a saint is just a sinner who keeps trying."

"Ja, well…I'm not even trying."

"I know," he says. "That's why I like you."

They stand apart, looking at each other. Keke tries to sniff away her tears.

"Besides," she says, "Saints don't come in my colour."

"And they are all the poorer for it."

She imagines herself as a cocoa-skinned saint, then thinks of what she has done to Marko, and her ring of light buzzes out like a bulb in a brownout. The vision reminds her that she hasn't slept in days, hasn't eaten properly. She's so hungry it feels as if her stomach is eating itself. No wonder she is hallucinating.

"For you," says Zack, handing her the white box.

She puts down the tile she's been clutching for the past hour and takes the box, pulls the ribbon off and opens the lid. Her sleep-deprived mind pictures different scenarios of the contents of the box, before she looks inside. First, a flock of finches bursts out and scatters throughout the room, leaving small multi-coloured feathers floating in the air. Next, a foil balloon with a nonsensical congratulatory message: "It's a BOY!", and after that, a bomb that explodes as soon as the lid is opened half-way. The explosion ignites the room, the corridor, the whole wing, and the entire hospital building falls in a atom-bomb cloud of fire and dust.

"Go on," says Zack. "It won't bite."

She opens the box properly. Choxolate brownies, crowded with pecans.

"Now who's the saint?" she says. If her stomach could leap out of her body and into the box, it would.

He holds up his other hand, in which he's holding a brown bag. "I brought real food too."

They sit on the other side of the room from a curled-up Mally, so as to not wake him with their words. Over facon, rocket pesto and cashew-cream wraps, and in a low voice, Keke fills Zack in. If he thinks badly of her for choosing to retrieve the footage then he doesn't show it. When she's finished, he sighs and rubs his face in empathy for her.

"You've really been through the mill," he says, eating his ricepaper plate. "I want to help. What can I do?"

Keke fixes her bright biolenses on him.

"Who are you?"

He laughs. "You know who I am."

"You're too good to be true," she says. "And in my experience, that's bad news."

"I'm not going to try to convince you that we're on the same side. It sounds like we don't have time to waste. Either I stay, and try to help you however I can, or I leave. It's up to you."

"Why are you helping me?"

"Isn't it obvious?"

"No."

"Because I can. And because it's the right thing to do."

"That isn't what I thought you were going to say."

He winks. "There are other reasons too."

"Tell me how we know each other. From before, I mean."

"I will. When the time is right."

"Tell me now."

"We have more important things to do. That little girl – "

"Silver."

"Silver. We need to figure this out. Find her while she's still – "

They stare at each other over the plastic table.

"While she's still alive."

"If she's still alive. We need to do what we can to find her."

Keke bumps the eyeborg footage to Zack, along with the picture of the attacker and the face-mapping results.

"L?" says Zack. "Some kind of code between you two?"

Keke shakes her head.

"L?" he says again.

Keke's eyes are sandpaper. She fishes for her eyedrops in her bag.

"What about this assassin? What do you know about her?" asks Zack.

Keke hands him a steaming cup of the awful instant coffee they keep at the nurses' station. It's the kind of stuff her parents used to drink in the 1970s, made of soluble granules of a chicory mix. It has hardly any caffeine in it, which doesn't make any sense for a nurses' station.

"Absolutely nothing. That's the problem. It's like she came out of nowhere."

They have a sip each, and their faces simultaneously reflect their distaste. Keke takes back his mug and pours the contents of both down the drain of the small hand-washing basin next to the hospital bed, then offers him a tray of caffeine gum instead. He shakes his head.

"Take me through the FusiformG results."

Keke snaps the last two out of the foil backing and pops them into her mouth. Without caffeine she would have melted into the floor by now.

"There were fifty-three different matches."

Leaf after leaf shows the same woman with different names, and different wigs, shades and scarves, but the same painted pouty lips. Mistress Catfish.

"Face-mapping is one thing, but what we really need is her DNA profile code," says Keke. "I bet you she has a hundred fake identities. We'll need her dynap code to isolate her real dossier."

"Not much chance of that."

Keke agrees.

"Unless she left some kind of bio evidence at your place. Did the detectives check?"

"I'd be surprised if they did. You know what they're like. Besides, I don't think this woman is in the habit of leaving evidence around."

"It only has to be one hair, you know. It's possible."

Keke thinks of Marko's man cave and pulls a face. She can count the number of times he's cleaned it on one hand. In fact, she can count the humber of times he's cleaned it on one finger. There's probably enough DNA in there to identify hordes of his RPG friends, none of whom would appreciate being flagged.

"It'll take too long," says Keke. "We need it now. There are only a few hours left until – "

She looks over at Mally and hopes the effects of that gas will keep him asleep till the morning. It will be easier to cope with the results – whatever they may be – when the danger has passed and the sun is up.

Zack stands up. "Let me see what I can do with that pic. I'll try everything I can to fetch her file. I'll let you know if I find anything."

CHAPTER 64

CALAMINE ICE

"Kitty," says Keke. "Thank The Net. You're alive."

"Am I?" says the blipping Helix hologram. "God, it's been a dream. A fucking bad dream."

"What happened?"

"I'll fill you in later. Suffice to say I've got enough nightmare fuel for the rest of my life."

"God. Sorry. But you're okay."

"I'm alive, anyway."

"And Silver?"

Kate's voice catches. "We don't have her."

"What?" Keke's whole body goes cold. What does she mean, they don't have her? Where is she?

"They didn't bring her."

"Those motherfuckers."

Keke pictures the little girl all alone. Scared.

"Oh, Kate – "

"Tell me that Mally's still safe, with you?"

"Of course. He's right here. Still sleeping. Snoring, actually, with his mouth open." When Kate doesn't reply, she adds, "I need to get myself some of that gas. Ha."

Kate starts crying.

"Sorry. It's not funny. None of this is funny. I'm totally tripping on sleep-dep."

"I'm just so relieved, that's all. At least one of them – "

Keke knows what she means. At least one of them is safe. It's not enough, but it's something.

"And Seth?"

"He's recovering."

"From what?"

Kate hesitates. Too emotional.

"I'll tell you everything when I see you."

She turns away from Mally and lowers her voice. "Where're you now?"

"We need to find Silver, but I'm all out. I don't know where to go."

They're both quiet for a moment. Urgent thoughts jostle to be spilled.

"I think – " says Keke, but Kate interrupts.

"I killed someone."

"I would have done the same thing."

"Would you have?"

"Hell, yes. I'd kill them right now for you, if I had the chance. Kill every last one of them."

She's looking at Marko, and it's as if Kate reads her mind.

"How's Marko?"

"The machines are doing all the work. It doesn't look like he's going to – "

The words hang in the air.

"Oh, Kex, I don't know what to say. I'm sorry. I'm so – "

"So I figured, if he's gone already – because he is, really – then we may as well retrieve the footage."

"Retrieve the – "

"Kate, I watched it. I watched the attack. And I think I've got something for you."

A pause as it sinks in.

"I'm sorry. That must have been so hard."

"I processed her face," says Keke. "The woman who attacked Marko."

"What? Are you sure?"

"A hundred per cent. I think she's our biggest lead. And I think I know where you'll find Silver."

~

"Instruct your car to head north east."

Kate drags her gaze away from the projection and instructs the cab.

"Of course," says Turing. "Redirecting."

"Now here are the co-ordinates. Ready?"

"Ready."

"Pink, khaki, dot, purple, brown, purple, dark green, 'S'."

Kate is about to ask why Keke is talking colours then realises the phone call is most likely being monitored. She needs to watch what she says. She taps the numbers manually into the cab's dashboard. 25.8084° S.

"Pink, purple, dot, grey, brown, purple, cyan, 'E'."

28.7081° E.

Kate's desperate to ask where she's sending them but of course she can't. Not if the enemy is listening.

"You got this from Marko's eye? "

"We got a picture of the person who attacked Marko from his eyeborg, yes. Then a friend helped me to ID her. And this is where she's most likely to be."

"And we'll find Silver there?"

"It's our best bet. Do you want the long version or shall I cut to the chase?"

Turing chimes in: "We will reach our destination in thirty-four minutes."

"Then I'll take the long version. Information is ammunition, right? Besides, Seth's still out cold and I need some company for the ride or my brain will implode."

Kate sits back. It's a welcome tide of relief as they allow themselves to lapse into the comforts of their friendship, even if it's only for a short while.

"I found out that you and Marko's attacker have something in common."

"I doubt that very much."

"You were both taken away from your parents when you were kids."

"She was a...was she a Genesis abductee? She can't have been."

"Nothing like that. Welfare nabbed her."

"Welfare?"

"I'm sending you the report right now," says Keke.

Kate's Helix pings.

"It says it's sealed."

"Don't worry, I unsealed it."

"How?"

"A fellow juror – the one I told you about – he came to visit, and he helped me. It turns out that because of his job he has special privileges when it comes to certain personal information."

Kate's not surprised that Keke has this kind of contact. Her career has been built on giving and getting favours. She realised before anyone else that information would be the currency of the future and she's been building her database for decades.

"I gave him the footage and he – "

Kate's heart skips when she opens the file and sees the computer-generated 4D mugshot.

"It's the same woman!"

"What?"

"It's the Resurrector. The woman who we've just been fighting. The one who tried to take Mally at the show. You found her!"

"Well, Marko found her."

What they don't say is: And then, unfortunately, she found Marko.

Kate starts reading the file and sees that the woman's name is Rosalind Jackson. A jarringly pretty name for such a work of evil.

"Her parents were nutters. Crunchies."

Kate scrolls down and sees another head-shot; this time it's a photo of a scrawny little girl with knotted pigtails. Her raisin eyes and mean mouth give her a feral appearance. Small bubbles of scar tissue on her cheeks and neck.

"What now?"

"You know the type. Anti-GMO, artisanal vegan, carbon negative, home-schooling, communal-living crazies. They took her away when she was six years old."

In her mind's eye, Kate sees the little girl with a slit throat, sees the stained sword in her own hand. It makes her feel ill. She refuses to feel guilty, but, still, there is a hint of blood-copper on her tongue. What happened to this child to turn her into the killer she is? The same question can be asked of herself, although she knows the answer all too well.

"You can't take someone's child just because they're fringe dwellers."

"It wasn't because of the home-made muesli. The girl almost died."

"Abused?"

"You could say that. One of the crunchy hippies called it in. A neighbour. Saw how sick and weak the girl looked, then stopped seeing her altogether. Questioned the parents but they said that they believed in meditation over medicine. Ha!"

Emotion has pushed up Keke's volume. She tones it down again. "Can you believe that?"

"They were anti-vax," says Kate. It's not a question.

"Of course they were anti-vax. Rosalind would have died if it weren't for the nosy neighbour. She was practically dead when the ambulance collected her from those bat-shit crazies."

"Diagnosed with Varicella, VZV. What's that?"

"Chickenpox."

"You can die from chickenpox?"

"You can die from complications from chickenpox. Inflammation of the brain membranes. Meningitis."

"The crackers parents didn't treat her at all? Even when she was clearly ill?"

"They treated her with their own homegrown hoodoo-voodoo shit. Calamine ice. Organic cannabistea compresses."

Kate can almost feel the cool trail of calamine on her skin. Can taste the dusty pink. "That sounds quite good, actually. I mean, as a name of a colour."

"I thought that too. I thought: I could do with some cannabistea right now."

"You and your weed booze." Kate almost smiles. "Okay. Rosalind Jackson. So the Nanny State takes custody. Then what?"

"So because of the infertility crisis, some of the orphanages were already closing down then. Plus she stayed sick for a long time. Turns out no one wants to foster a sick six-year-old with dead grapes for eyes."

"What about the parents? Didn't they appeal?"

"No record of appeal. They were probably all, like, *if it's meant to happen it will happen.*"

"*Everything happens for a reason.*"

"Morons."

"Weasels."

"Managed to spawn a right fucker of a daughter too."

"She broke out of the institution they put her in. Can't blame her, really. You know what those places are like."

Kate shivers. The mention of any kind of institution makes the hairs on the back of her neck turn into exclamation marks. As if the calamine ice cube has travelled into her backbone and lodged itself inside there.

"She broke out. Lived on the streets."

"A rat hunter," says Kate.

"A what-now?"

"A rat hunter. That's what Seth calls them. The street urchins. Says he hates to see them because it lends credence to Doctor Van der Heever's uGeniX scheme."

"What can I say? He has a point."

"Yuck."

"I know. I despise that man as much as it's possible to despise a corpse – "

Kate scrolls through the leaves of the dossier as she listens to Keke. She sees the charge table and interrupts her. "Arrested for petty crimes: shoplifting, pick-pocketing, vandalism of a Bilchen Burger vending machine. Nothing violent. It looks like she was just doing what she could to feed herself."

"I also would have broken into a burger vending machine if I had grown up with… what did you call them? Artisanal-vegan parents. I don't even know what that means."

"I know, right? Shudder."

"So, she was a little girl on the streets. Pretty much the most vulnerable thing you could be. I'm guessing that someone came along and took advantage of her."

"You couldn't be more spot-on if you tried. You ready for the reveal?"

"Born ready."

"The Good Samaritan took her in. Do you remember him?"

"No."

"The bearded guy. The loin-cloth guy. He used to make the news when we were kids."

"I have a vague recollection. You know me and my childhood memory blank."

"The Good Samaritan gave up his life as a high-flying corporate something-something to be a better person. He donated all his cash and possessions, including a Maserati, to the needy and roamed the streets, surviving on 'the milk of human kindness'."

"I'm surprised he didn't starve altogether," murmurs Kate.

"He even gave up his name. Was always telling the people who interviewed him that he's never been happier. I always found it hard to believe."

"The Good Samaritan took her in? Into what? His cardboard box in a dirty alley?"

"Ja. And soon he had an entire collection of rat hunters," says Keke. "Very Dickensian."

"Very what?"

"Oliver Twist, you know?" says Keke. "Fagan? Never mind. I always forget that you don't read and then I wonder how we can possibly be friends."

"You know why I don't read."

The car takes an exit off the highway.

"So. In an ironic twist, people were so enamoured by The Good Samaritan's renunciation of materialism that they started throwing cash at him. Someone opened an NPO bank account on his behalf and all of a sudden he's a multi-millionaire again. He realised that he'd never be able to escape his wealth – "

"Ah, well, we all have our cross to bear."

"And decided to keep the bank. Do something worthwhile with it. He built a –"

The cab disappears into a tunnel, cutting off her signal.

CHAPTER 65

COLD LULLABY

Keke tries to call Kate again, but she can't get through. Themba arrives, and Keke steels herself for the frown she knows she is going to receive from the nurse, but it doesn't happen. Instead, she hands Keke a mug of tea. She's brought another packet of Holee Molees too, for Mally, who is still sleeping on the lazy chair.

"You're not angry with me anymore?" Keke asks.

"I wasn't angry with you," says the intern, avoiding eye contact.

"You're a bad liar."

"Okay. I was, but I felt bad for him. For Marko. He's my priority, you know."

"He's my priority too," says Keke. "You just don't understand the stakes."

She starts to say something in rebuttal but then puts a finger to her lips. "You're right. I don't know the whole story."

"What changed your mind?"

"About what?"

"About you being cross with me."

"Well. You were very generous. Too generous. And then I felt bad."

"What?"

"I've never received a tip that big before. I mean, sometimes patients leave their leftover baskets of stale muffins for us, or wilting flowers, but...well, thank you. It was very generous of you."

She gives Keke a shy smile then disappears out of the room.

Zack. Keke checks the Gordhan invoice total on her live statement for Marko's medical account. At first she's confused. Has the amount owing doubled? But then she sees the minus mark in front of the total. It's all paid off, and more. It's an eye-watering forty million in credit. The man in the grey suit must be grinning from ear to ear. She doesn't even know what to think about Zack. Why is he helping her? She's learned some hard lessons in the journo trade: there's no such thing as a free lunch, but what could Zack want from her? She doubts it's anything as prosaic as sex. Hell, she'd shag him right here on this hard hospital counter if she thought it would mean getting to keep Marko in this ICU, and she doesn't care what that says about her.

They won't kick us out. She has a sip of tea and leans her head back, massages her neck muscles. She starts to yawn, stretches her arms above her head then hugs herself. Her body is absolutely finished: stiff, sore, on the brink of getting sick. Keke can't remember the last time she slept and feels ready to collapse. She climbs onto the hospital bed, next to Marko, and cuddles into him. Slings her arm over his battered chest, puts her warm hand over his cool one. She'll just close her eyes for a moment. She won't sleep. She can't. How long has it been? 48 hours? 72? Keke tries to count back to a time when things were normal but the numbers tumble down around her. Slumber swirls in and inks her temples. The medical equipment beeps a cold lullaby.

CHAPTER 66

DINNER FOR ONE

Keke drifts up from her dreamless slumber. She's still in exactly the same position in which she dozed off, spooning Marko's sleeping slab of a body. She doesn't want to wake, doesn't want to open her eyes and face the world since it has been turned inside out. Even in her semi-conscious state she longs for a rewind button – just a week – if they could go back just a week then she could have Marko back, and the twins would be safe. Now a bitter new reality awaits her. She wants to float back down again, into the peaceful shallows, but someone is calling her name. Has something happened? She opens her irritated eyes – her BioLenses need replacing – but her sleep deprivation closes them again. She's drunk on delicious sleep, and wants to keep drinking. Has she ever felt this tired? The person is calling her again.

"Kekeletso," says the woman. "There are some people here."

Keke grunts.

"They need to speak to you."

She opens her eyes again, blinking into the harsh fluorescent light. Why do they make hospitals so damn bright?

"Who?" Her mouth is stuck together, so she has to say it again for it to be heard. "Who?"

Themba's face comes into view. "There are some men here, looking for you."

She sits up and tries to blink away the bleariness. Her brain is still half asleep. "What?"

"They said they need to speak to you urgently."

"Is it about the hospital bill? It's been paid."

"It's not about the hospital bill."

Keke sighs, puts the pads of her fingers on her closed eyes to try to reduce the swelling then gets up off Marko's bed.

Why is the nurse looking sheepish? Or is it apologetic? What has she done? She opens the door and three uniformed police officers stride into the room. Keke's brain can't make sense of their presence. Have they tracked down that woman – Jackson? – who did this to Marko? But it must be more than that. Why would they go to the trouble of finding her in a private ward in a hospital?

"Good evening," says the one who takes centre stage. The other two stand at the door.

Keke glances out the window: a shallow pane of darkness. What time is it?

"I'm detective Ramphele, with the SAPS."

Alarm bells go off in Keke's head. This isn't making sense. "How do I know?" she asks.

He moves his legs so that his knees bandy back and forth, as if he's warming up for a race. "How do you know what?"

"That you're with the police?"

"It's not important. We're here to ask you some questions."

"Has something come up?"

"I beg your pardon?"

They look entirely out of place in their new police uniforms. Black spines and kevlar scales, as if they're preparing to go into battle, instead of questioning an exhausted woman with swollen eyes who barely has the energy to stand there in front of them.

"Would you like to…sit down?" Awkward.

"We won't be here that long."

Keke wants to pour herself a glass of water but she feels as though she is stuck in the officers' sights, and that any sudden moves would be risky.

"Have you found something?"

The police officer's eyebrows knit together. "Could you be more clear?"

Keke fights the urge to roll her eyes. Could the South African Police Service be any more incompetent? She's reported on so many cases where important evidence has fallen through the cracks because of corruption and badly trained cops. Now it seems like it's her turn to experience it for herself.

"Why are you here?" she says, unsuccessfully keeping the irritation from her voice. "Have you found something, some evidence? Have you caught the person who did this to Marko?"

The men's faces mirror her confusion.

"The break-in at my place," says Keke. "The attack."

"We're not here about that," says Ramphele. "We don't know anything about that."

Of course you don't, she wants to say. *Because you're fucking useless.*

The men have been here for about two minutes but the confusion and dead-end questions make it stretch before her: an hour stuck in Kafka spiderweb. Keke doesn't have the emotional bandwidth to deal with this. She closes her eyes, breathes, then opens them again.

"Can you please just tell me what's going on?"

Ramphele clears his throat. He's stopped warming up for his imaginary race, now. "We have it on record that you visited a Ms Helena Nash a couple of days ago, in the Carbon Factory Penal Colony."

Keke frowns. "Yes?"

"Why was that?"

Keke's head spins. "What is this about?"

"Just answer the question," pipes one of the men at the door.

"We saw Nash because we had a theory about a case we were working on."

"You were working on a case?"

"Not officially."

Ramphele taps his foot.

"I was on jury duty, and then I had an idea. So we tracked down Nash."

"You had an idea?"

"You're amused that I had an idea?" she snarks. "Why is that? Because I'm not a cop, or because I'm a woman?"

"It was just the way you said it."

"I didn't realise there was a more serious way of putting it."

"No offence meant. You made it sound… frivolous."

"Fuck you."

"Now listen here, Ms – "

"Don't tell me to 'listen here'. Look around you. Look at this man who's a whisper away from dying. Does any of this look 'frivolous' to you?"

Ramphele exhales out of his nostrils, puts a hand up in apology.

There's a tense silence. The machines breathe and beep.

"Let's just get to the answers," he says, "then we'll be out of your way."

"Fine."

"You went to see Nash. On a...hunch?"

"Yes."

"What transpired?"

"It's complicated."

"Believe me," says the detective. "It's a lot more complicated than you think."

"What's that supposed to mean?"

"Who were you with, when you visited the convict?"

"A fellow juror."

"Why?"

"Why? I don't know. Because we both had the same hunch? Because it was nice to have company?"

"Was the man Zachary Girdler?"

"Yes?"

"You're not sure?"

"I know him as 'Zack'."

"You were together."

"Yes," says Keke, "but you knew that already. It's not like you can just walk into a crim colony. They have a biometric record of us being there."

"That's the funny part," says Ramphele.

"There's a funny part?"

"In a manner of speaking."

"Tell me."

"It seems that after your visit to the Factory there was some kind of surveillance breach. None of the twenty-three cameras that should have recorded your visit had any footage of Mister Girdler."

"What? That's peculiar. Are you sure?"

"We wouldn't be here if we weren't sure."

"Well, I can tell you that we were definitely there."

Ramphele takes a glass Tile out of his chest pocket. He taps on it and a hologram swirls out above it. It's a security video of the Carbon Factory. Keke sees herself walk into the building, thumb-scan, and endure the frisking for weapons.

"Zack came into the building with me. We walked to the interview room together."

"Not according to this," says Ramphele, clicking on another clip. It shows Keke walking on the conveyor belt, alone, apparently talking to herself.

"I don't know what to say." Keke's head is spinning.

"Are you working with Mister Girdler?"

"I've told you already. Zack and I were on jury duty together. We sleuthed a case together. If that counts as working together then, yes, we worked together."

"He paid you for this work?"

Keke laughs. "Of course not." Then she thinks of the hospital bill and her stomach becomes a tightly coiled rope.

"The BSS has no record of Girdler's presence at the Carbon Factory."

"I'm telling you, that's impossible, okay?"

"You said you were on jury duty together?"

"Yes. The Lundy case. Judges Mbete, Rens, and Vlok."

"You see." Ramphele smiles. "That's where this thing gets funny again. There's no record of him there, either. He's not on the jury list. Not on any of the paperwork."

"He was there. I sat next to him. That's how I met him."

"He's not even on the security footage. Again."

Ramphele shows another clip of Keke on the roof of the courthouse building. She's sitting, eating lunch alone.

Seeing herself eating gives her an idea. She goes to the bin next to the hospital bed and roots for the brown paper bag with the leftover packaging of the dinner they shared.

"What are you doing?" asks the cop.

"He brought me dinner," she says. "We ate together. If he brought me dinner then there'll be evidence of him in this bag." An extra plate, cutlery, serviettes.

She finds the bag and tears it open. Inside is one lonely, crumpled-up serviette, and a sauce-smeared paper plate. The branding on the bag is the Gordhan deli logo, and it's clearly labelled as *Dinner For One.*

She remembers Zack wiping his fingerprints off the table. Folding up and eating the rice-paper plate.

"Themba!" she shouts. "Themba!" The nurse must have been listening at the door because she nearly falls into the room.

"Themba. Was there a man in here earlier?"

The nurse shakes her head.

"Good looking. Expensive suit," prompts Keke.

"No," she says. "I didn't see anyone here, and I've been on duty all night."

"I...imagined him?" Keke asks the detective. "This whole time?"

Memories of her conversations with Zack now take on a surreal quality. She imagines herself on her own, now, driving her bike to the Carbon Factory, getting a coffee at ProntoPrint. Imagines herself sitting in the corner, laughing at an invisible person's jokes. Has this all been a dream?

"I'm...delusional," she says, not believing it. Although she's pretty sure that does not count in her favour.

The detective shakes his head. "No."

"I am. I'm going insane, aren't I? You're here to...take me away. Lock me up in some padded cell."

"No," he says again, this time with some compassion in his voice.

"Then, what? What the fuck is going on?"

Is the cop gaslighting her?

"Zachary Girdler is the slipperiest person of interest I've ever encountered."

"Never," grumbles one of the cops at the door.

"Alright," he says. "That I've *never* encountered."

Keke remembers her first impression on hearing his name. Onomatopoeia. Zack! Crack! Crash! She feels for a chair.

"Are you okay?" asks Ramphele.

Keke nods, but in truth she feels like she is falling sideways.

"You're not the first person he's done this to."

Done what to? It's not like he's taken any kind of advantage of her. He was a friend. A sidekick. She and Marko would be out on the street if it weren't for him footing the medical bills. Kate wouldn't have the GPS co-ordinates to find Silver. But why? What is his end game?

"Are you aware," asks Ramphele, his badge glinting in the too-bright artificial light that is now not only hurting Keke's dry eyes but also her brain, "that Helena Nash is dead?"

It takes Keke a few seconds to register what he's just said.

"What?"

The cops look dubious. "You really don't know?"

"No," says Keke. "What happened to her?"

People hardly ever died in the PLCs now, not like the overcrowded prisons that South Africa used to have, where you'd be shivved for your dirty pillow. The penal workers have excellent security and medical care. Plus they have to wear those terrible new-tech smart copper handcuffs when they aren't actively working. Terrible, but safe. The Nancies are forever bragging about how they are able to keep their prisoners alive and well, but of course they do what they can to keep them breathing. It's a significant part of the country's workforce.

"She committed suicide."

"No," says Keke. "That can't be. We were in the process of getting her guilty verdict overturned."

"Did she know that?"

"She knew we were working on it. That was the reason we went to see her."

"She left a letter and everything. Said without her kid or her freedom she had nothing to live for."

"But I thought that PLCs were suicide-proof."

"They are. Unless someone on the outside helps."

"Who?"

The police officers all glare at her. She laughs. She can't help it. "Me? Really? That's why you're here?"

Ramphele watches her face closely. "She couldn't have received the kill pill from anyone else. She'd never even had a visitor before you two traipsed in there."

Keke blanches at the mention of the lethal pill.

"And now her body's in a cooler."

"Do I need a lawyer?"

"I don't know. Do you?"

"I haven't done anything wrong."

"You aided and abetted a known serial killer."

There is noise in her head, now, a clunking, and her legs feel weak. She can't get any words out; it's like her cerebrum is choking.

"Zack," she finally gets out. "Is not a serial killer."

"Really?" says Ramphele. "You said yourself that you hardly know him. You only met him a few days ago."

"But I would know," she says. "Don't you think I would know if I was spending time with a psycho?"

Ramphele taps his Tile again and pictures of dead people float in the air between them. An old man in a standing wheelchair, a young woman, a couple holding hands. A teenage boy in a Mars-themed bed.

"Ted Simmons, dead. Neo Kodwa, mother of two, dead. Tracy and Charlie Fenton, twins, dead. Cindi Page, about to graduate from high school, dead."

Keke closes her eyes, waves the holograms away as if to make them disappear. As if she hasn't seen enough dead people during the past week.

"They all supposedly took their own lives, but in each case there's been a common denominator: a visit from Zachary Girdler."

A moment of quiet follows.

Slowly, she opens her eyes. "He told me he was a Suicide Expert."

The detective taps out, and the pictures twist away.

"Well, that part seems to be true."

Keke needs to sit. She looks for a seat, and her eyes automatically skitter over to the lazy chair, which is empty. Her stomach plummets.

"Mally?" She checks under the bed. Did he get scared of the cops in their crazy get-up and hide in a cupboard? "Mally?"

Ramphele looks at her as if she's lost it.

"Did you see a little boy in here?" asks Keke. "A little boy? He was sleeping on the chair!"

The officers all shake their heads. "That chair's been empty since we arrived," says Ramphele.

"No," says Keke. "No, no, no," as she checks the cupboards and the bathroom. She hasn't seen him since she woke. He must have stolen away when she was asleep. Keke jams on her boots, ready to run outside to look for him, but a solid arm across her chest stops her from leaving the room.

"Let me go!" she says, trying to push past him. "I need to find Mally!"

"We can't let you leave," says the cop. They scuffle some more.

"I have to find him. He's three years old! He's in danger!"

Ramphele walks over to her, and she stops squirming. "You're not going anywhere," he says, and before she has time to register, she looks down to see that he's clicked copper cuffs on her.

CHAPTER 67

RE-BREAK THE BONE

"Wake up," says Kate, shaking Seth. She has let him sleep for as long as possible, to recover, but she needs him now. His lips are still blue from the medicine Zeebee's men forced down his throat.

"Yes," he says, swiping his mouth for drool and sitting up. "Yes, I'm awake." He looks out of the tinted windows, into the darkness.

"I've been out for hours," he says, knuckling his hair, as if she doesn't already know. As if she hasn't been counting the minutes till she can rouse him.

"Are you okay?" she asks. "How do you feel?"

"I'll live."

"Well. That's good news. I wasn't convinced of that an hour ago."

"I know. I'm better now."

"What was that blue stuff?"

"Blue stuff?"

"What's the last thing you remember?"

He looks at her suspiciously. Looks down at his mostly naked body. "Why? What happened?"

"I had to take you to these men, to help you…oh, never mind. It was awful. But we're okay now. Right?"

"Blue stuff?"

"Like…paint. They called it *muti.* Poured it down your throat."

"Prussian Blue," says Seth, wiping his mouth again.

"Yes. That's it. I mean, I don't know what that is but it tastes exactly right."

"It's a dye. It binds with radiation molecules so it gets them out of your system. Wait. You didn't know what it was but you let them administer it to me?"

"I would have let them force-feed you wet cement if they'd suggested it. I was desperate, and they're the ones who know their stuff. They've been helping the Zama-zamas for years."

She hands him the old clothes. He holds up the faded Iron Maiden shirt and nods in approval, then climbs into the soft, smoke-fragrant garments.

"What happened to you?" he asks.

"What do you mean?"

"You look different. Did something happen?"

She swallows hard and looks away. "No," she says, feeling Zeebee's hot breath on her cheek. "Nothing happened."

She can tell he wants to ask again, but he keeps quiet. There's not a lot of time to talk.

"Where are we?"

"Keke gave me the co-ordinates but before she could tell me where we were going we got cut off. I tried to call back but she's not answering."

"You don't know where we're going?"

"It's a long story."

"Tell me the short version."

"Keke. She did it for us."

"Did what?"

"She got that doctor to…to hack Marko's eyeborg."

"Jesus." He holds his eyebrows with his fingertips.

"She found out where Silver is."

Kate's Helix rings. Keke's smiling icon appears and Kate answers the call.

"Kex," she says. "You're on speaker."

"Is that Kate?" says a burly male voice.

Her stomach lurches. "Where's Keke? What have you done to Keke?"

"This is detective Ramphele of Rosebank Murder & Robbery."

"No," says Kate, thinking the worst. "She's not. She's not dead."

"She's not dead," he says.

Oh, thank the Net. The relief is so palpable it feels liquid.

"Why are you calling me?"

"We've had to confiscate her device, but as a once-off favour, I agreed to call you to deliver some important information."

Now Kate can hear Keke yelling in the background. She tries to make out what she's saying. Something about –

"Miss Msibi would like me to tell you that your son is gone."

"Gone?" says Kate. "What do you mean, 'gone'?"

Keke is still shouting.

"She woke up and he was gone. I've notified the force. They'll be on the lookout for him."

Keke yells something else.

"She's saying that he must have heard your last conversation."

"What?"

"When she gave you the co-ordinates – "

"Fuck!" shouts Keke. Kate can hear her struggle.

"She thinks he's on his way to that destination."

Seth is pale again.

Kate imagines all the kinds of people who would open their car door to a little lost boy late at night. She sees the moon shining on his blonde hair just before someone grabs him roughly by the arm and makes him disappear forever.

"This can't be happening." It's too much. Silver in the hands of the enemy and now Mally is on his way there too.

"Look, lady," says Ramphele. "I'll dispatch a team to help you find him."

Muffled conversation follows.

"I've already got people looking for your boy on the streets. Send me a recent photo to distribute, and his dynap code."

"No," says Kate.

"No?"

"Don't go near my children. They said if we got cops involved they'd kill her."

"Kill *her?* I thought – "

"Let me speak to Keke," says Kate.

The man's sigh drifts through like grey smoke down the line.

"Please."

"Okay," he says. "You've got one minute."

Keke comes into view. Her eyes are bloodshot. She opens her mouth to talk but Kate doesn't hear anything except for the loudest bang she's ever experienced in her life as the cab is shunted by an unseen vehicle and the superglass all around them explodes into flying crystals. They are weightless for a second before they spin 360 degrees and the siliconeskin airbags blow up into their faces, punching them backwards into their seats as the car revolves again then slows down to a sudden stop as they crash into something stationary. Kate gets a sniff of burnt rubber and metal sparks over the new-plastic smell but then liquid gushes out of her nose and sprays the airbag with crimson. She wants to scream but there is no breath in her lungs. She holds a hand up to her nose, not quite believing that all that red paint could be coming from her. Beyond the deafening ringing in her ears and the spirals of blue that scribble across her vision, Kate can hear her name being called, as if she is dreaming and someone is trying to wake her up.

"Kate! Kate!" comes the muted voice then she realises it's Seth calling her, and she turns her head to look at him, her hand still covering her spurting nose. "Are you okay?"

"I think so," she says, but she can't hear her own voice over the screeching in her head. It hurts her neck to nod, but she does so anyway. She can feel the blood running down her throat so she tries to spit it out, knows that ingesting blood can make you sick, and that she can't afford to feel ill when her life is imploding right in front of her like the inside of this car.

"It seems that we have had an accident," warbles Turing. "I have sent our location to Emergency Services. Please stay still and calm while we wait for someone to arrive."

Kate wants to obey, wants to sit back under the reassuring pressure of the airbag on her chest but she looks out of the shattered window and sees black boots approaching the car. For a millisecond she thinks, thank goodness, they're already here to help us, but then she sees the glint of gunmetal against the night sky. Realises that these people caused the accident. Silhouettes with AK47s. Someone smashes in the crystallised window next to her and the superglass peels down like a flayed pelt. Two automatic weapons are pointed at her head while the man in black pulls her from the wreckage, shearing her torso on the broken glass.

"Fuck!" Kate exclaims as it razors ribbons into her skin. One of the other shadows pulls Seth from the wreckage. The man's grip is so strong it makes her arm buzz with blue, warning her that more pressure might re-break the bone.

CHAPTER 68

SCENTED WITH GUNPOWDER

The men in hooded robes and JC face masks drag Kate and Seth away from the smoking car and towards their multi-van, which is matte black against the tar of the street, against the pitch of the night. Black on black on black, as if they are being swallowed into a vacuum where nothing will matter.

Seth is unconscious, but Kate resists the pulling.

Not again. Not again not again not again.

The man towers above her in height and muscle. He's stronger than her but every molecule in her body is telling her to not get into the MV. Her broken nose hums sky-blue. It's not like she's having flashbacks of her childhood kidnapping – nothing as clear as that – it's more like her body is remembering the trauma and refusing to make the same mistake again. Her gun is lost in the wreck of the car. She tries to fight him off, feeling for a moment that she'd rather die brawling right here and now than ever get abducted again. Who are these people who think they can just take others, and take their children? As if their bodies are nothing more than packaged meat, something bloodless to be possessed and traded on a whim. Her anger builds, and with it, her strength. She screams as she lashes out at him. Punches him on his jaw, which remains unmoved, and her knuckles crack. Tries to knee him between the legs but there is some kind of armour there, and it's like she's just slammed her knee against a concrete wall. She's injuring herself more than him. The other man – just a few metres away – is trawling Seth's body towards the van.

Half-thoughts flitter. She'll use her adrenaline-energy to try to get away; she may not be able to fight him but maybe she can escape. Just then there is a flash of light. With a bright crack, the night air is scented with gunpowder and blood. Seth has just shot one of the men, whose head glances backwards, struck by the force of the bullet. The other man hefts his AK47 up for a better grip and starts firing at Seth, who darts to take cover behind the still-smoking cab.

While Kate watches in horror, the man sprays the car with a hundred high-velocity steel bullets. There's the jarring sound of slugs ripping into the car, and an echo as some of the shots ricochet. As he hoists Kate up, ready to throw her over his shoulder, one of the slingshot bullets whizzes towards them, penetrates the man's mask, and bites him on his cheekbone. He exclaims, rips off his mask, and puts a hand up to the fresh flesh. Kate uses the split-second distraction to break his hold on her and run. She sprints and slides in behind the destroyed cab, scraping her legs and knees on the tarmac.

Seth is still alive and a silent sob of pain and relief escapes her open lips. With shaking hands she takes the revolver he offers her, and when her fingers wrap around the grip it's with a grim feeling of satisfaction. When, a split-second later, the man appears beside her, she takes quick aim and shoots him in his bulky tattooed neck. The projectile must have hit an artery because the blood, made black by the night sky, spurts out like an oil fountain. He tries to cover the wound, tries to staunch the bleeding, but out it shoots. He roars in fury and tackles Kate to the ground. Her head slams against the tarred gravel and her vision explodes into stars. The sheer force of his weight knocks the gun out of her hand and the air out of her chest.

Seth turns his gun on the man but is hesitant to take the shot. Kate knows that in the soupy darkness he can't see where the attacker's tank of a body ends and hers begins. She's suffocating under his bulk. Her throat makes a gurgling sound: she can't breathe, can't catch a breath. Her lungs are silent sirens.

"Get him off me," she tries to say, but no words come out. "Get him off." But there is no air to float her words. The blood pours out of the man's neck and soaks her torso. Hot metallic sap – red liquid mercury. The sensation makes her want to scream. Seth wrestles the dying man, forcing his body off her, and suddenly the dead weight is gone and Kate can muster a wet wheeze. Seth looks for the third man but he has disappeared. Slowly the stars disappear from Kate's brain. All that is left is the light blue murmur of her injured shoulder and nose. A Sapphire Ache.

Seth collects the man's handgun from his hip holster, checks the magazine, and shoves it into the waistband of his shiny slaxuit pants. He helps her up off the tar. His face is lunar.

"Ready?" He is asking if she's ready to run.

Kate doesn't trust her voice so she nods instead. He takes her hand, but as they're about to set off, the door of the van rolls open – the sound-memory itself is enough to paralyse them both – and Seth yells "Get down!" and pulls her down to the ground with him. They expect a hailstorm of bullets, but then there is something else. A whisper. A small movement that makes both of them instinctually look up at the vehicle.

"Mommy!" cries the little girl inside the van. She stands, illuminated by the overhead cabin light – a shining aura – with a look of hope on her face that smashes Kate's heart. Silver.

CHAPTER 69

GRIM CLAW

"Silver!" shouts Kate, before Seth slaps his gun-peppery hand over her mouth. The girl hears her voice and starts saying "Mommy? Mommy?" over and over again as her face folds into tears.

Bongi comes into view, puts her hands on Silver's shoulders, strokes her hair.

"Kate," she announces, "you'd better come in."

The image of Bongi touching her daughter makes Kate so furious she's ready to kill.

"We won't hurt you."

The wasted bullet shells that surround the pockmarked cab tell a different story. Kate begins to get up off the ground but Seth pulls her down again.

"They'll kill us," he says.

"I know," says Kate, and stands up anyway. She won't let her little girl die alone. She puts her hands up and walks towards the vehicle. Seth remains down, watching Bongi through the sight of his gun, ready to cover his twin, but then Bongi says, "You too, Seth."

At the mention of Seth's name Silver starts sobbing, then sees Kate emerge from the darkness and falls down under the emotion of it. Bongi yanks her up and she keeps howling. A reluctant Seth surfaces, dusting his hands on his pants. He catches up with Kate, who's almost at the van, when the third man reappears out of the inky background and points his AK47 at them, motioning for them to drop their weapons. Silver tries to shrug off her nanny, tries to run towards Kate, but Bongi's grim claw on her shoulder keeps her inside the vehicle. At last Kate reaches her and the girl breaks free and flies into her arms. Her hiccupping body melts into Kate's, every nook and cranny filled with the sweet sharp smell and sensation of her precious daughter. For a short moment, Kate's world is restored. The child is at once solid and completely weightless. She's wearing the soiled candy-coloured dress Kate had packed for her stay at her grandparents' house; the destination she never reached. The fabric smells of urine.

"My baby," she cries into Silver's neck. "My baby."

Bongi steps aside, gesturing for them to climb into the MV. It's a luxurious cabin surrounded by a hull of smoked glass. The presence of a toddler carseat puzzles Kate.

"Sit down," says Bongi. Silver makes herself as small as possible in her mother's lap – a periwinkle – and Kate hugs her fast. The large door slides closed automatically and the locks click shut. The claustrophobic space sends Kate's brain whirring with fear. She tries to control her breathing; this is not the time for a panic attack.

CHAPTER 70

DEAD MARBLES

"Where are you taking us?" asks Seth.

The tinted glass partition separating the cabin from the front seat slides all the way open. A throne-like chair rotates to face them.

Kate is so shocked by what she sees that she gasps out loud, making Silver jump.

"I thought you'd be able to tell us that," he says in his sonorous – and familiar – voice. "Hello, Kate, Seth. I'm sorry we have to meet under such … difficult circumstances."

Kate's shock is bright orange: It's her version of *deja vu.* She's been experiencing it more and more lately. As if her life is some kind of loop of bad luck. The restaurant conversation, the abduction, and now this. Hadn't they been through all of this before? Same-same but different. It's not Van der Heever who sits before her, although it may as well be. Some duplication, some clone, some glitch in the matrix.

Lumin?

Seth launches out of his seat with his hands stretched in front of him, ready to strangle the man. The Resurrector guard drops his automatic rifle to grab him before he reaches the Maistre then wrestles him back into his seat. Seth puts up a fight, but Bongi pulls her pistol out in a practised, fluid movement and aims it at his skull. Seth clenches his jaw and shows them his dirty lacerated palms in surrender.

The blood on Kate's chest is still drying. Her nose is definitely broken.

"They can't be trusted," says Bongi, gun cocked.

"*We* can't be trusted?" says Kate.

"Tie them up," the woman says, and the guard zips cable ties around their wrists. When he approaches Kate, Silver recoils at his panting shadow. The girl moves away from him as if he's hurt her and she's now afraid of him. Kate glares at the man, then at Bongi: the nanny she trusted with her children's lives. How utterly stupid she has been. There is a hot seething energy just beneath her skin as she clenches her bruised fists.

"We don't know where Mally is," says Seth. "So you're wasting your time."

"Don't do that," says Lumin. "Don't lie. You'll save us all a lot of time if you just tell the truth."

"Fuck you," says Kate. She can't help it. She has so much sudden, blind hatred for the man; she feels like she could snuff him out with her bare hands.

"Perhaps if you let me explain," says the Maistre, steepling his fingers. "It will become clear to you why we very much need to know where he is."

"Go ahead," says Seth. "Explain all you like."

"Nothing," growls Kate, "nothing you can do to us will make us tell you where he is."

Lumin's face twitches with a half-smile. "You see, I don't want to force it out of you. I'd prefer it if we came to an understanding."

Kate's trying to pull her wrists out of the plastic bracelets but all she's managing to do is scrape the skin off her hands and stop her circulation.

"You must let us have the boy."

"He has a name," says Kate. "He has a name, for fuck's sake."

"His name is problematic," says Lumin. "It makes him seem more …"

"Yes?"

"More *human.*"

Kate feels Silver's body tense up.

"He *is* human, you bastard," says Seth. "He is 100% human."

Lumin looks pained. "Well," he says, extending a palm, "the scriptures don't see it that way."

"Scriptures?"

"The Book of Light," says Bongi. "The Prophecy." Kate can see from the luminosity in her eyes that she is absolutely brainbleached.

"The Book of Light says that the last living Genesis Child will lead us to the ledge."

"The ledge?"

"The End of the World. He'll destroy the planet, and everything you know. Mass destruction."

"A little boy, Lumin, really?" says Kate. "You're afraid of a little boy?"

"If that boy survives into his fourth summer," says Lumin, "then he'll live to be sixteen. And that will be the End of Days."

Kate looks at her Helix. 31/10/2024, 21:58. Spring ends in a few hours. Tomorrow it will officially be summer.

"How can you?" says Kate. "How can you purport to be this incredible man of dignity and moral fibre when really you're nothing more than a child-killer?"

"You're just on the wrong side of the fence, dear," he says. "To you, I may appear to be a killer, but to the rest of the world I'll be a saviour. You're trying to save one manufactured boy. I'm trying to save the whole planet."

"So that's it," says Seth. "You want to be a hero."

Lumin shakes his head. "No," he says. "I couldn't care less if I live or die, as long as I fulfil my duty in this matter. In fact –" He laughs. "No one will know either way, will they?"

"I knew about the prophecy before the boy was even printed," says Lumin. "We studied it fervently, not knowing that the boy hadn't even been produced yet. But then the Genesis Project scandal hit the news – the pictures of all those babies in their incubators, courtesy of you and your friends – and we knew. Everything clicked into place."

Click, click, click Betty/Barbara had said, clicking her fingers too close to Kate's face. Like dominoes they fall.

"I knew then that it would be one of those infants that would threaten to lead us all to destruction. But now – "

"It's taken almost four years," says Bongi, "and only Mally is left."

"Why did you wait?" Kate asks Bongi. "You could have done it months ago."

"The scripture says that it's the *last living* Genesis child who will lead us to the ledge. We singled Mally out with Celestia's guidance and got rid of the others. Besides, the boy's life is not for me to take. Maistre Lumin is the one who has been called."

"Everything is on course," says Lumin. "Everything is as it should be. All we need from you, now, is to know where the boy is."

"And, what? You think you'd just appeal to my good nature and I'd hand him over?"

"I wanted to try to make you understand," he says. "I thought there was a chance that if you knew what was at stake, then you would help us with the solution."

"The solution?" says Seth.

"The only thing I know for sure," says Kate, "is that you're delusional. More dangerous than that: you're delusional and charismatic, and that is a very dangerous combination."

"You're wasting your breath, Lumin," says Seth. "Nothing you say is going to make us give up our son."

A searing stab in the soul for Kate, hearing Seth call Mally their son for the first time. It would have been a clean shot of joy if the circumstances were any different. Instead of what it is now, where she can't see any of them surviving the night.

"I don't want to resort to force," says Lumin. "Are you sure we can't come to some kind of agreement? Perhaps, if you change your perspective on the situation, and look at it as saving your daughter, and everyone else you know, instead of sacrificing your son? Because if we don't switch the Genesis Child off tonight, then we will all die. Do you see that? Everyone will die."

"According to you," says Kate.

"According to the Celestia Prophecy."

"You're wasting your time." Seth is restless in his seat.

"May the record reflect," he says to Bongi, sighing, "for all it's worth, that I did try to come to a mutually agreeable arrangement."

Bongi nods at him. She moves her feet a little further apart, as if to ground herself. As if she's preparing for a fight.

"I'll die before handing my son over to you," says Kate.

"Oh, I know that," says Lumin. "That's why I came prepared."

Kate's heart, already hammering away, increases its speed, forcing her lungs to pump with nervous breath. She tries to keep her nerves steady, her hands steady, but the adrenaline is fizzing inside her, confusing her thoughts and making her shake.

"Put her in the chair," says Lumin.

At first Kate doesn't understand what he means. She's already sitting. But then Bongi lunges for Silver and steals her away from Kate's lap. The girl squeals and kicks and tries to fend off the nanny but Bongi is strong, and she manages to force the child into the toddler carseat.

"Give her back to me!" shouts Kate, and struggles to get up, but the guard kicks her in the stomach and she collapses, gasping. The explosion of pain obliterates her thoughts. He hauls her back into her seat and shakes a finger at her in warning. Next time he won't be so gentle.

Bongi is battling with the safety straps because Silver is arching her back, pushing her body out of the bucket shape, and flailing like mad. Her squeal is a needle of ice. Every time Bongi almost gets the mechanism to lock, Silver squirms just enough to unclasp the keys. The nanny's mouth is set in a hard line. Perspiration starts to pop on her forehead.

"Leave her alone!" shouts Seth, and moves to help Silver but is stopped by the sight of the AK47 pointed at him.

"Stop it," Bongi hisses at the child, and pushes the girl's body into the chair with force, causing her to scream even louder. The woman looks at the guard for help but he gestures that he can't take his sight off Kate and Seth. Her jaw muscle ripples as she grinds her teeth and tries to clip Silver in again.

"Silver!" she shouts. "Silver, stop that right now. Keep still! It's time to go into your special chair."

The girl ignores the request and launches into a full-blown tantrum.

That's my girl.

There is a loud crack. The sound reverberates through the vehicle's cabin. Then there is quiet. Bongi has slapped Silver so hard across the face she's silenced by the shock. Her eyes glaze over as a bright red welt appears on her tender cheek-skin.

A smack, a swarm. Kate's rage travels like poison in her veins.

"You fucking bitch," she says to Bongi through clenched teeth. "You fucking bitch. She trusted you!" Tears of fury roll down her face. She fights to get free, tries again to escape the cable ties but all it does is lacerate her wrists.

Bongi finally clicks the carseat lock into place and steps away, wiping the sweat off her face with her forearms. Silver's face begins to swell where she's been struck. She just stares ahead as if she's had her consciousness cut off.

"Silver," says Kate, her throat constricted, "Mommy's here. Mommy's here." She's tied up and she doesn't know what else to say. Silver doesn't register. Her eyes are dead marbles.

CHAPTER 71

THERE ARE NO NEW HEARTS

Themba brings Keke a mug of hot tea. She doesn't take it. She can't bear to lift her hands off Marko's skin. Two of the three cops have left, taking her SnapTile with them; a guard remains at the door. A weird kind of house arrest, but in ICU. He'd taken pity on her, removed her cuffs when the hospital counsellor had come to see her and had not put them back on. Perhaps he can tell that there'll be no running for her: that she won't leave Marko's side.

"I know what you're going to say," says Keke to Themba. They regard each other with grim faces.

"Do you?"

"That it's time to let go."

"I gather the counsellor has come to see you."

"Yes."

"Talked you through it."

"Yes."

"Do *you* think it's time?" asks the nurse.

Keke looks around at all the beeping and humming machinery that's keeping Marko alive.

"We had an agreement," she says, her nose stinging with the beginning of tears. "An understanding."

"What's that?"

"After the Genesis episode."

"The what?"

"Never mind. You don't need to know the details. But I was taken…used as bait. They withheld my insulin – for leverage – and I went into sugar shock. I almost died."

"That's terrible."

"After that, Marko and I agreed that if it had been worse…if I had gone into a hypoglycaemic coma and not recovered, if it looked hopeless, that the life support should be switched off."

"A living will," says Themba.

"Yes. A living agreement, anyway. And Marko said he wanted the same."

"I'm sorry. It's very difficult."

"How do you know when to do it?" asks Keke. "If there's even a one percent chance of him recovering, I want to keep the machines on."

"The doctor was certain," says the nurse. "He said there was no chance – zero chance – of a recovery."

"Unless he gets a new heart," says Keke.

"Yes."

"But there are no new hearts."

"No."

She lets out a long, wobbling sigh. "So then, it's time?"

Themba shrugs. "If you need more time…"

"It'll be going against his wishes, waiting any longer. Already I'm seeing his body atrophy. He's grey, can you see that? He's been grey since the attack." She's holding on to Marko. "This isn't what he looks like. What he used to look like."

"I'm so sorry."

Keke doesn't want sympathy. It wrecks the barrier between acting strong and outright weeping.

"Your family should be here with you. Your friends."

A sharp thought pierces her grief: fear for Kate and Seth, and the kids. Will she ever see them again?

Her eyes rest on Marko. His medical eyepatch, his personalised hospital gown. He's the thinnest he's ever been. This isn't how she wants to remember him.

Keke's eyes are streaming now. "This whole time. It never felt real. I never expected him to *not* wake up."

"Of course," says Themba. "That's normal. It's normal to expect things to get better."

She stifles the sobs that are rising in her throat, and moves towards the life support equipment. She tells herself to be brave. To not be selfish.

"Do I just," she says, tears running down her face, "do I just turn this switch?" The counsellor had shown her how to do it, but surely it wasn't as simple as that?

Is it really that easy to end someone's life? To end Marko's *life?*

She can't believe this is happening. It just seems too prosaic. When you think of death, it's so huge, so final, it's such a mind-boggling concept, but here she stands within arm's reach of her pharmacy-bought deodorant and a mug of tea that's getting cold. Tea. How could she even consider drinking tea, now or ever again?

"I can do it for you," Themba steps forward.

"No. Marko would want me to do it."

It's such an intimate act, after all.

"This switch?" Her voice is gravel.

Themba removes her patient's oxygen supply and nods at her. She has tears in her eyes too. Keke takes a deep, stuttering breath and switches off Marko's life support.

CHAPTER 72

PARAFFIN & GARBAGE

Arronax gets off the private plane and sniffs the night sky; scrunches up her nose. She hates the way Joburg smells. Pollution and smoke. Paraffin and garbage. She much prefers her lab. What's not to love? Brisk white walls, purified sea air, perfect climate control. Her family call her a control freak, but she knows better than that. She just likes to have a handle on things that can be controlled, because God knows that most things in the universe are completely, absolutely, undeniably out of our control. Besides, she's a scientist. She wouldn't be any good at her job if she didn't like playing with variables.

A man in an airport uniform greets her on the strip. He blinks too much. Maybe it's the sight of her mermaid hair. She knows that when she's not in her lab coat she doesn't look like much of a technologist.

He wants to carry something for her. "You didn't bring any luggage?"

"Just this," she says, patting the small transit box she has under one arm. And of course, a sonic toothbrush and a clean pair of panties, which are in her handbag, in case of emergency. She'll fly back home as soon as she's delivered the merchandise, unless Seth asks her to stay the night. The man in uniform leads her off the strip and around the west corner of the private airport, where there is a cab waiting, engine already purring in that soft, dry way hydrocars do. Arronax loves the efficiency of Nautilus, the way that every detail is thoughtfully arranged and on time. In London she would take it for granted, but South Africa is, altogether, a different kettle of fish. She slides into the back seat and waves goodbye to her chaperone before the tinted window glides shut, and the cab skates away.

The car doesn't ask her where she wants to go. Even that detail has been attended to. She relaxes back into the seat then has the image in her head of a hundred other people doing the same thing before her, and sits up straight again. All those bodies. All those heads, all the hair. She sees them like ghosts in the car with her. It's the reason she can't sleep in hotels. The bed linen can be straight off the washing line, smelling of fabric softener and sunshine and a hot iron, but still they bring with them all the people who have lain in them before. Sweating, sleeping, making love. It sets her teeth on edge. A 4DHD microscan of a dust mite is not something you can ever un-see.

"ChinaCity/Sandton," says the cab. "The Gordhan. Estimated arrival time is 23:12."

Arronax looks at her SnapTile, dials the surgeon who's waiting for her to arrive with the product.

"Doctor Gazongo. We'll be there in seventeen minutes."

"Sure," says the surgeon, voice dull with exhaustion. "We'll be ready. The galleria's all set up. The nurses will prep him now and bring him down."

"Excellent. Sorry if I woke you up." She's not really, but it seems like the polite thing to say.

"I'm looking forward to it. It's not every day you get to debut this kind of surgery."

The crispness of her British accent is offset by his softness. "You sound tired."

"I'm drinking a double coffeeberry shot as we speak."

"I hope it's half-caff. I don't want your fingers shaking."

"My fingers don't shake."

The car zooms through the dark. Algaetrees flash on and off as they pass underneath. She tries for the sixth time to call the next of kin of the patient – Kekeletso – but she never answers. Maybe Seth sent through the wrong number. He did seem very distracted in his message to her, but it's possible she wasn't reading it correctly. Difficult, sometimes, to correctly decipher the tone of a bump. She assumes this is the 'Keke' he often thinks about.

They'll need the woman's signature to proceed with the surgery, of course. She'd have to find her at the hospital and get her to double-sig the waiver. Despite her initial hesitation in meeting Seth's first condition in order for him to remotely complete the job, she soon realised that he had done her a significant favour in finding their first human trial subject. Usually it takes months to fight through all the red tape involved in *in vivo* pilots, but he has managed to find the perfect patient. Getting Seth Denicker on board is the very best thing that has happened to this project. She must think of a fitting reward.

CHAPTER 73

A WISP OF HOPE

Marko's flatline trills through the room. Kekeletso turns away from the screen; she doesn't want to see that fatal green line. Themba mutes the cardio monitor. Keke feels as if she's sinking; at the same time wishes she is a ghost so that she can float up and away with Marko's spirit.

There is a commotion outside. The double doors burst open and all of a sudden there are ten nurses and a crash cart in the room.

"Wait, wait!" says Themba with her hands in the air. "It's okay. Leave him. It's a DNR."

"No," says a man in blue scrubs, handing her a Tile. "Not anymore."

A wisp of hope. They re-connect his oxygen and unclamp the brakes on the bed.

Themba frowns at the device and flicks through a few pages while the staff wheel Marko away.

"What's happening?" whispers Keke, suddenly back to earth. "What's going on? Where are you taking him?"

Themba looks at her, utterly bewildered. "Ever heard of Nautilus?"

CHAPTER 74

DARK DREAM

"I knew you'd be fully prepared to give your life for the boy," says Maistre Lumin, "so we had to think of some other way to get you to co-operate."

Kate continues to try to work her hands out of the plastic loop behind her back. It doesn't feel as if she's making any progress and they are throbbing with pooled purple blood (Violent Violet). Seth's face is as white as a dinner plate.

"When you refused to bring him to us in exchange for your daughter we knew we had to ... shall we say ... dig deep."

Bongi adopts her steady pose again. Is this really happening? It's so stupidly surreal that for a second Kate wonders if she's in the middle of one of her nightmares, but the pain in her wrists asserts a deadly reality. This is no dark dream.

"We've done our homework. We know what happened to you, what the Genesis Project did to you. We know everything that's on public record about you, but we also know more. In fact, I'm confident that we know ... Well, perhaps we know even more than you know, about yourself."

Keke was right about her Helix being bugged. Kate shoots a withering look at Bongi, who doesn't even have the grace to look ashamed.

"The VXR sessions you had with Dr. Voges were most revealing."

"Fuck you." Kate says it with such ferocity that some spit lands on her chin. She wipes it away with her good shoulder. Silver is still in a trance.

Maistre Lumin taps his foot. Checks the car's clockologram. Their deadline is rushing to meet them.

"None of it matters, now. We're running out of time. I need to know where Mally is."

"We don't know where he is," says Kate. "He ran off."

Lumin looks at her for a long time. Drills into her, until she has to look away.

"I've brought something with, you see. A tool, to help the truth out of you."

Kate's stomach burns.

"Sebongile," he says, palm outstretched. Bongi takes her eyes off them for a second to pass something to Lumin. It's a zip-up charcoal-coloured clamshell, for which he thanks her and opens, carefully, on his lap. He sits like that for a moment, appearing satisfied with the contents. Kate wants to know what's inside, but at the same time she doesn't. Crimson Cringe: it's a strange sense of rubbernecking when it's your own torture on the table.

Lumin finally lifts the thing out of the box. It's his pair of golden-handled secateurs. Polished to a high shine, the blades catch the interior light as he shows them off. Even though the pruning tool is a metre away, Kate feels the cold, sharp steel on her skin, feels it puncturing her flesh.

"You sick motherfucker," says Seth. "You're not going near Kate with those things."

"Oh," says Lumin, in mock-surprise. "These aren't for Kate." He takes off the safety catch and scissors them in the air between them, making a rasping sound. "These are to use on Silver."

CHAPTER 75
GOLDEN SECATEURS

The terror zings all the way through Kate's body; her nerves fizz with fright.

"No!" she shouts past the bright effervescence. She tries harder to squeeze her hands through the cable-tie bracelet but they're numb, so when she forces it, the cable slices into her heel, spilling the lilac blood. The pain cuts through the numbness.

"No," she growls at Lumin. Her fear and anger is a beast inside her that is ready to take Lumin by the throat, but she can't get at him. He takes a step forward, secateurs in hand, and Kate screams and lashes out at him with her feet, tries to kick him, tries to defend her daughter. He gets closer to the girl and Kate can't stand it and then all of a sudden she's free – the blood from her wound lubricated her escape – and she launches herself at Lumin. She comes at him so hard and so quickly he falls under her weight. Kate doesn't have a weapon. She's not strong enough to strangle him, but she thinks if she can scratch through his throat to his carotid –

But before she can do anything a shadow swarms over her like a cloud of locusts, and as she tries to jam her nail into Lumin's pulsing neck the floor falls away from her as she's lifted off him by the scruff of her jacket and thrown out of the vehicle. She tumbles and rolls away and sees flashes of stars in the night sky. The bruised grass smells green. She ignores the pain – a blue bolt from shoulder to palm – and scrambles to get back inside the vehicle but when she looks up it's straight into the barrel of the Resurrector's automatic weapon.

Bongi is helping Lumin up, dusting him off and adjusting his cloak. He has a smear of Kate's blood on his throat.

"Get her back in here! And tie her up properly this time." His cheeks are blotches of pink. Anger, or embarrassment, or both. He uses a tissue to wipe the blood away.

The guard, despite being twice the size and strength of Lumin, flinches at the scolding. He hauls Kate up into the van and ties her bleeding hands in front of her this time, ties her feet together, and then connects the two loops with another tie so that she can't move. So that she's trussed like a rabid dog on the floor; a lamb to the slaughter. Seth is watching her, but his eyes don't register hers. She can tell by the look on his face that he is in his head, trying to figure out a solution. Whereas her first reaction is to move, his is to think. His eyes skitter to the secateurs that were knocked out of Lumin's hands, and he watches as Bongi picks them up and hands them back to him.

"You've wasted enough of my time," Lumin says, smoothing down his wisp of white hair. She has humiliated him in front of his entourage. His eyes say: *You'll pay for that. I'm telling you, you'll pay for that.*

Kate growls at him. The danger has made her wild.

"Tell me right now where Mally is or your daughter will suffer the consequences."

"You wouldn't," says Kate.

"You're wrong," he says.

His eyes look so deeply into hers it feels as if he is mining them. He speaks slowly, "You see, I know what your nightmares look like."

He holds the secateurs aloft to make his meaning clear.

"No," says Kate. "Please."

"You are giving me no option!"

"Bongi!" says Kate, "Please. It's Silver. Silver! You can't let him hurt her."

Bongi remains fire-eyed for Lumin. "You're the one who's hurting her. Do what he says and she'll be safe."

Lumin sits next to the toddler carseat and casts a detached glance at Silver. Uses the hand that he's holding the secateurs in to move a strand of hair out of her eyes. Her swollen face doesn't flinch. She's gone somewhere far inside herself, as if Bongi's unexpected slap had turned off a switch in her brain.

Kate knows what that's like.

Lumin takes the girl's hand in his. An affectionate uncle. Kate's insides liquefy into neon juice.

"I know what haunts you. What do you think your late lover would say, if he was here?" He wiggles the fingers on his other hand, then hides his thumb so that it looks like it's missing.

"Lumin, please. Please. I beg you."

"Tell me where the boy is."

"I don't know here he is! He ran away from the hospital! He's on the streets, somewhere."

His nostrils flare. "You have an idea. The colours."

He raises the secateurs to Silver's hand, puts her little finger in between the blades. The girl stares ahead, oblivious. Kate yelps and struggles with the ties.

"You spoke in code, on the phone. Tell me what it means."

"Tell him," says Seth.

"They'll kill Mally!"

"Mally isn't here."

What he means is, Mally isn't here with a pair of shiny pruning shears being held to his hand. He could be anywhere. There might be time to save him.

Lumin adjusts the angle of the blades so that Silver's little finger is in the perfect position to be severed at the large knuckle.

"Tell him," says Seth again.

She struggles with the restraints. "How can I?"

Bongi looks at the time, 23:00, and says: "Sixty minutes to midnight."

There is so much tension in the cabin, it's like they are all set in electric jelly.

"This is your last chance," says Lumin, his eyes arresting Kate's. "I'm going to count to three."

This is too much for Kate to handle. She can't stand the vulnerability. She can't stand it. It's like her heart is outside her body, raw and beating.

"One," Lumin says, like a parent losing his patience. "Two."

He looks down and is about to apply pressure when Kate shouts "Okay! Okay. I'll tell you."

He looks up at her, moves the secateurs away from Silver's hand. Waits for her to talk.

"Pink, khaki, dot, purple, brown, purple, dark green, 'S'."

Seth translates. "25.8084° S."

"GPS co-ordinates," says Bongi. She taps the numbers into her Tile.

"Pink, purple, dot, grey, brown, purple, cyan, 'E'."

"28.7081° E" says Seth.

Bongi taps the last digits then frowns. Lumin looks at her, a question mark for a face.

"They're playing with us," she says, showing him the screen. Lumin's cheeks begin to colour again.

"We're not," says Kate. "Those were the exact colours."

"You expect us to believe," he says, grabbing the Tile from Bongi and tilting it in their direction, "that Mally is on his way to the Luminary?"

The realisation stings Kate and Seth at the same time.

Lumin's cross face melts into a pleased one. "Oh, you truly didn't know, but how perfect," he says, smiling at Bongi, who types the co-ordinates into the van's holodash. "We thought we'd have to chase him, but there he is, running towards us."

Kate grunts, wrestles with her binding.

Lumin beams at everyone. "I told you, didn't I? I told you to trust in Celestia."

"Praise the Light," says Bongi.

The vehicle's engine starts, and they move forward.

"Praise the Light," says the Maistre.

CHAPTER 76
DEATH SONG

Keke watches as the cardio surgeon slices open Marko's chest for the second time in a week. The barely healed previous incision is simply cut away and discarded. Keke flinches as it's tossed onto a tray, as if a piece of him is worth nothing. Themba inspects her face, which she can feel is pale and damp.

"Are you okay?" she whispers.

Keke nods and swallows her discomfort. To distract herself from the emotion rising in her chest she watches the director. He's walking around the operating arena, adjusting cameras, changing angles, tapping in lens instructions. He, and all the recording equipment, are dressed in the same white scrubs. The medical team – Dr Gazongo and three assistants, are in Medical Mint. That's what Kate had called the colour, anyway. Her stomach cramps with self-reproach when she thinks about Mally escaping her charge. If she had just been able to stay awake–

Something goes wrong with the surgery. Gazongo's brow darts downwards and he yells some commands at his team. There's a flurry of activity over Marko's body and chittering in the gallery. The machines screech their now-familiar death song. Keke finds that despite everything, she is calm. She's been through this before.

The blue-haired woman who had suddenly appeared in her life bearing the synthetic heart is on the other side of the room, behind the glass. She looks agitated, keeps wringing her hands and checking her Tile. In a way they are polar reflections of one another: one light, the other dark; one water, the other, earth. Keke reminds herself to breathe. The machines stop shrieking and return to their cool, consistent beats, and the clockologram ticks above them all. It's twenty-eight minutes to midnight.

CHAPTER 77

RAT HUNTERS

They arrive at the huge gates of the Luminary, which sparkle with their golden paint even in the dread-dark of almost-midnight. The sentinels have bumped to expect them and the guards are already swinging the ornate metal gates open when the van speeds down the long, straight asphalt path. The vehicle barely slows down as it shoots through the entrance and into the vast property, and after a few twists and turns on the serpentine driveway, the mouth of the wide garage is already open to receive them. The van parks inside, and Kate feels as though they have been swallowed by a monster. The idea she used to have of the Luminary: the picture in her head of this giant white-and-gold monastery, has faded, has inverted to its shadow side: darkness where there was light. Evil where she had presupposed good.

Row upon row of people are shrouded in the dark. An army in arachnasilk and shiny face masks. It makes her feel so cold inside. Lumin was the Good Samaritan. He was the one who took all the urchins off the street. Fed them and trained them in combat: Martial arts, bomb assemblage, sword-fighting. Lumin had recruited the rat hunters as Resurrectors.

The engine turns itself off and the multivan doors roll open. There is the soft warm light of a naked bulb, and the parking garage smells of turpentine and oil. Fertiliser. Pesticides. Earthworm compost. Lumin is helped out of the car by his bodyguard, and Bongi follows, but Kate and Seth are held back by their restraints. Silver is still catatonic. Her eyes are closed, now, but she's not sleeping.

The guard starts to unlock an inter-leading door to the inside of the monastery, but Lumin stops him.

"The boy won't be inside," he says. "He wouldn't have made it past the security system. He'll be in the grounds, somewhere. In the gardens."

The open garage door reveals to Kate a night sky sparkling with danger. Seth squirms in his seat, trying to somehow loosen his binding. Lumin strides into the garden.

"Bring the bait," he says. Bongi unclips Silver's harness and carries her like a sleeping child. It's a poignant image: a sinister *Piéta.* Two meaty Resurrectors grab Kate, sever her ankle restraints, and drag her and Seth out of the vehicle and into the cool moonlit lushness of the sable-leafed garden.

CHAPTER 78

MAZE OF BLACK ROSES

Lumin and the Resurrectors stream into the garden. They're on high alert with only twelve minutes to find their sacrificial lamb. They take turns pushing Kate and Seth to the front, passing hedges fragrant with blooms. Lumin speaks into his wrist and his voice is broadcast all over the property.

"Mally." His voice is warm, welcoming. Kate pictures him as a leathery venus fly trap.

"You can come out now. There's nothing to be afraid of. Your parents are here, and they need your help. They're very anxious to see you."

His voice echoes in the air around them.

"Your mother's here, and your Uncle. Silver's here, too! We're all waiting for you. You can come out. It's safe."

"Don't come out!" shouts Seth, and a masked man slams his fist into his cheekbone, knocking him to the ground. Another Resurrector kicks him in the throat.

Lumin broadcasts his message again, but this time with more urgency.

"I know you're here!" he says, "It's very important that you come out now!"

If Mally can just stay hidden for a little while longer, it will be midnight and the prophecy will crumble.

"Don't listen to these people!" shouts Kate. "Don't come out no matter what –"

Kate's chest explodes with sparks. She's on the ground, she can't talk, the pain takes everything. She doesn't know if it was a fist or a boot. The arachnasilk army drag her along the damp grass. She gasps to get the cold black air into her hollering lungs.

"We don't even know if he's here," she hears Bongi say.

"He's here," says Lumin. "I can feel his presence. I can feel the reckoning in the air."

"Shall we pray?" she asks, in *isiXhosa.* Cosmic cream.

Lumin replies in English, "This is not the time for prayer."

"I just thought – "

"Mally!" shouts Lumin, panic starting to fray his voice. "We need you to come up here now."

The marching bodies wind their way into the maze of black roses.

CHAPTER 79

ALCHYMIST, FOLKSINGER, NEW DAWN.

Alchymist, Folksinger, New Dawn. The rose maze is a masterpiece of landscape design. More than a thousand different rose varieties grow together to form a circular maze: the shape of the sun. Carolinae, Bracteatae, Synstylae. In daylight it's a multi-scented oil painting, at night it's a barbed cage of black roses and thorns. The small, spiteful blades keep catching Kate's coat and scratching her arms. The plants want to hook her, hold her back, but the Resurrectors keep pushing her forward.

The walls aren't impenetrable, like traditional victorian mazes. Instead she can see flashes of movement through the canes and leaves, shadows of shadows. They get deeper into the heart of it. The rhythm of their dread is Lumin's broadcast voice.

At last, the hedges open up to a vast clearing with a raised sundial in the middle. It's the centre of the maze. With Lumin and Bongi so preoccupied with finding Mally, Kates wonders if she'll be able to make a run for it. Seth's face is bleeding and her own body feels broken. Would they even be able to run? And even if they manage to get away from the thugs on either side of them, would they be able to find their way out of this complicated maze? She looks around, tries to identify the best exit, and takes a tentative step away from her captor. He doesn't seem to notice. She'll have to reach Bongi to grab Silver and then –

A petite figure appears, blocking her way and drawing a large silver sword that flashes with starlight.

Jackson's teeth, left naked by her wide smile, glow in the dark. Her scarf trips in the breeze.

"Not so fast," she says, her voice a wounded whisper.

She slowly lowers and rests the blade against Kate's neck. Thirsty for vengeance, no doubt, thinks Kate, remembering in glass-shard detail how she had, just hours before, cut the woman's throat. She wonders what it looks like, now, the wound.

Delicate skin glued together with stem cells. No one would guess she was injured, with that scarf concealing the gash. The only clue is in the way Jackson moves, with a stiff neck, as if she had slept badly the night before.

She fixes Kate with her raisin eyes, and flicks the sword at the guard, warning him off with the glinting metal. Her message is clear: Kate belongs to her. No one but she will have the pleasure of cutting her down. Again the sword is pressed against Kate's throat, harder this time, so that she can feel the run of the blade, the shallow incision. A warm drool of blood down her neck.

Lumin sees the new blood. "Don't kill them yet."

Jackson gives him a disappointed look.

"We need them. To lure the boy."

She purses her rubies, but doesn't move the sword.

Fifty Resurrectors, a hundred.

"Six minutes to go," says a sweating Sebongile.

Lumin gets a pair of men to move the top of the sundial and help him on to the plinth. Although he requires assistance, he is nimble despite his heavy robe, and his age. He stands there, surveying his estate of shadows. "This is your last chance, Mally."

There is a kind of fever in his face. Kate's hatred of him is deep and burning, but she does see in that moment that he truly believes in what he's doing.

As if sensing her thoughts, he looks straight at her, his eyes gleaming with purpose.

"Bring her to me." He has the golden secateurs in his hands.

Kate flinches, tries to move away. "No."

"Don't you touch her, Lumin," growls Seth, "or I swear to God I'll kill you."

"That may prove to be difficult," says Lumin, motioning at his tied hands.

Jackson grabs her arm and forces her forward, towards Lumin. He hops down from the plinth, then turns his attention from Kate and gestures for Bongi to place Silver on the altar and hold her there. The girl doesn't cry or resist: she is a shell.

"Mally!" shouts Lumin. "Mally if you don't come out right now I'm going to hurt your sister!"

"No!" screams Kate.

Seth struggles with his binding. "Lumin! Lumin don't you dare!"

"This is your last chance!" shouts Lumin, lifting the secateurs and shearing the crisp night air. He takes a step closer to Silver.

Bongi frowns, is about to say something, then stops.

Lumin advances. "It's the only way."

"Don't come out!" shouts Seth. "Stay where you are, Mally! Don't come out for anything!"

"Last chance, Mally!" shouts Lumin. "Last chance to save your family. To protect your little sister!"

No one breathes.

Maistre Lumin scissors the secateurs. The evil rasping sound sends a frozen hook into Kate's chest.

"Ready?" Lumin says, and picks up Silver's hand off her lap.

"No!" screams Kate, trying to throw Jackson off, but the woman's grip just gets firmer and the sword cuts deeper.

Lumin holds Silver's hand, and with a hard snick he cuts off her little finger.

Absolute shock silences them all for a moment. Kate's whole body turns into cold water. Seth starts shouting words that she doesn't understand. The pain catapaults Silver out of her stupor. As the blood starts spurting she opens her eyes and jaws and screams. Her wide open mouth is a hurricane. It's a sound Kate has never heard before. The combination of her own horror, her futility, and the piercing sound drilling into her temple, something short-circuits in her brain. and even though she tries to hang on to reality, a noxious grey fog comes and steals away her consciousness.

CHAPTER 80

SMALL WHITE STARFISH

The sound of a child screaming pulls Kate up from murky depths. Her thoughts are muddled. As she gets closer to the surface, she recognises the scream. Silver. The memory of what has just happened assaults her, kicks her in the stomach, and she retches, there, where she's lying. She moves to wipe her mouth but her hands are still bound. Vomit and saliva paints her hair sour. The screaming continues. It's the most awful sound Kate has ever heard in her life. It cuts across her vision like a rusty handsaw and she's in danger of passing out again, but she forces herself to stay there, with her baby who needs her. She blinks hard to try to dislodge the serrated blade that's blinding her. She can hear Seth now, he's also shouting. Struggling. Telling Silver that she's okay, that she's going to be okay. But how can she be, after this? Silver's screaming tells them all she knows it's a lie. The little girl is still pinned down by Bongi, grasping her injured hand with the other. A small white starfish turned in on itself.

"Silver!" she finally manages to say then retches again. "I'm here. Mom's here."

But her words are as futile as her trussed-up arms. The cold ground leaches what is left of her warmth.

Finally the shrieking starts to lose volume, and turns into sobbing. Bongi is still there with them, but there's something different about her now. That mesmerised look has gone out of her eyes as she looks at Silver's leaking hand with horror. Silver's weeping fades; Kate guesses she's entirely in survival mode now .

"Do you hear that, boy?" echoes Lumin's voice all around them. "Your sister needs you!" They keep quiet and listen for him. Twenty guards must be surrounding them, their dark uniforms bleeding into the night. Lumin motions for some of them to hide, and they do.

"You've always been her protector. Her superhero. She told me so. She needs your help now more than ever. Are you going to come and save her?"

All along. All along Bongi had been grooming him for this moment.

The secateurs flash. They make the sound of walking on dead leaves. He approaches Silver again and she starts flailing and screaming.

"I can keep going," Lumin shouts above her. Kate fights the grey fog. There is a whisper of a movement out in the elaborate garden. Automatic guns swivel in the direction of some cream-petalled roses. "Come out and join us."

Seth is about to shout again but he's knocked out cold by the butt of a rifle. More Resurrectors stream into the quad. They're outnumbered twenty to one – and those are only the rat hunters she has managed to see. Her neck sears under the sword.

"Last chance, Mally," Lumin says, eyes trained on the spot in the maze. His guise of sunlight and charm is replaced by seething dry ice. "Or we kill your family."

Everyone holds their breath. After a few beats, there is the sound of a small movement within the dark bushes. Such a soft, gentle sound. Lumin sends his people in the direction with two fingers pointed like a pistol. Go, go, go, his heavy-knuckled gun is saying.

"Run!" screams Kate. "Run!" Her squall rises and breaks in the air around them. The sword is jammed harder against her neck.

The man who gets there first shoots at the small shape – they all jump at the sound of the gunfire in the still night – and heavy blooms explode into fresh confetti. The man curses under his breath, and, lost for words, picks the shuddering body up by its ears for the Maistre to see. Lumin lets out a cry of frustration at the sight of the dying rabbit. The creature kicks his blood onto surrounding petals, painting the roses red (Mad Hare).

Lumin mutters and marches, but Bongi holds him back, motions for him to be quiet. She's got her eye on a different spot, just behind them. She puts Silver down on the grass, who squirms her way to her mother's lap. Sebongile silently inches towards the row of bushes. The night is hushed. Kate holds her ragged breath.

Bongi puts her fingers to her lips and whistles, loud and clear, and there is a high-pitched beeping sound from just behind the roses. She hurls herself through the thorny canes and grabs Mally by the arm with such a firm grip he has no choice but to melt under it.

CHAPTER 81

NIGHT-CHILLED SWORD

Sebongile drags the kicking boy towards the blood-stained altar. It's time to make the sacrifice. There's not a minute to waste. She hauls him up and onto the glittering plinth, and tries to keep him from hitting her and sliding down as he flails. Jackson takes off her scarf and hands it to a nearby Resurrector, who uses it to tie the boy to the sundial stand, tucking the end into his mouth to stop him from screaming. Mally chokes, his body shunts and his eyes roll in panic.

"Three minutes."

The air is charged. Lumin walks up to Mally and puts his hands on either side of his blonde head, as if he is blessing him. He screws up his face and mutters under his breath, anointing him with his thin skin and slithering words. Mally cries and chokes, and doesn't take his eyes off Kate, who has one arm wrapped around Silver's back and the other extended out towards him, held back by the night-chilled sword held hard against her throat.

Lumin's mutters become louder and his face starts to smooth out, his skin seems to catch more moonlight. Mally kicks and kicks and Kate cries out for him with a panic-slack mouth.

"Two minutes," says Bongi.

Lumin then firms his hold on the boy's head, old palms on tender cheeks, and looks into his eyes, and with a quick crack no one sees coming, he snaps Mally's neck.

Kate squeezes Silver and screams. There's an immediate sorrow so keen it threatens to slice her in half. She tries to push forward but Jackson keeps her back with the blade. She's obliterated by the horror; that furious monster that's inside her that means to destroy her on the way out. Mally's eyes close and he lists soundlessly to the side, but the scarf keeps his small body upright. Seth is roaring, Silver is wailing, and Lumin, arms raised to the black sky, is struck silent with ecstasy.

Kate's screaming turns into retching as she vomits onto the wet grass, emptying the poison that's found its way into her body, but it doesn't work. The venom is still right there, in front of her. Lumin turns his shining face to her.

Jackson feels his eyes on them, and turns to him. "Maistre?"

Her neck is covered in a skin-coloured platelet plaster that has beads of dried blood showing through. A red pearl necklace.

"Yes," Lumin says.

"Yes?"

"Kill them all." He begins to walk away.

Jackson's grinning lips bare her fangs. She grasps the handle of her sword and swishes the steel, cutting the midnight air with elegant figure eights. Infinity.

The other Resurrectors move towards them and they're surrounded by muscles and blades and perfumed thorns. Kate grabs Silver again and holds her close. It feels as if they're about to be eaten by a shivering cluster of night-spiders. Oily guns glint with starlight. Jackson swirls her sword. The mask-faced members eat the ground with their feet till there is nothing left between them and Kate realises that this moment, this terrible, dirty, green-bitter moment, will be the last she ever has. Her scratched skin stops stinging, and she can smell the ribbons of rose-scent, like silk streamers floating across her vision. She hugs Silver so hard it's as if she wants their bodies to meld. Seth is back on his feet, ready to fight, to protect them, but his tethered arms are drooping under his realisation – the one that is the mirror-twin of hers – that this time, there is no escape for them.

CHAPTER 82
ELEGANT ARROWS

Cornered by the army of Resurrectors and Jackson's sword, Kate feels her back come up against the petals and thorns of the maze's inner hedge. Torso to torso, Silver's arms are wound around her neck. The lights in Jackson's eyes dance; there is nowhere to go as the killers advance.

Kate closes her eyes against the terror. Heartache threatens to consume her as she waits for the blade to run through her body. Who knew there could be so many different kinds of pain?

She stops fighting. She's not welcoming death – would never welcome death – but at least she won't have to live without Mally. She can't imagine that, and now she won't need to, and she forces herself to focus on that shimmering consolation. She buries herself in her love for Silver, drops her lips to the little girl's neck, and loses herself in the intense embrace. If this is her last moment, let it be one of fierce and exceptional love.

All of a sudden there is the sound of a whistling projectile and Kate's eyelids instinctively click open. A Resurrector in the back row gasps and clutches his chest. Furrowed brows and slippery fingers: blood like ink. He stutters a last breath and falls forward, and everyone jolts at the sight of the long white arrow that's embedded in his back. They're frozen for a moment then there is further whistling, whispering, whizzing as more elegant arrows find their meat targets. A row of ten Resurrectors cries out and falls down, then another ten. Jackson curses, drops something, and vanishes. Seth hurls himself over Kate and Silver to protect them from the missiles. She tries to see what's happening but Seth forces her head down.

Out of the small shape that is left to her through which to witness the battle she sees scores of women appear, dressed in white robes that glow in the lunar light. They're armed with bows, and crossbows, and as Kate picks Solonne out of the crowd of SurroSisters, she watches her extend her arm backwards, pull a diamond-tipped arrow out of her quiver, and with a practised hand place it in the bow and send the shaft straight into the chest of an approaching Resurrector. The white robes dazzle the Resurrectors' night-vision goggles, forcing them to tear off their masks and leave their faces exposed. There are shouts and cries as men and women fall like black dominoes all around them. Lumin climbs up onto his golden plinth and starts shouting to stop the fighting, stop the fighting, while his men writhe and bleed on the ground.

When Seth realises what is happening he lets Kate go, and joins in the battle, scooping up a gun from a nearby dead body. Kate feels drunk with all that has taken place and imagines the SurroTribe as glowing warriors on horseback, or glorious cream centaurs. She watches as their pearlescent bows release bolt after bolt of retribution. Holy avengers. But as Solonne approaches, she sees that there are no horses, that the Surros are on their feet, wearing leggings and sneakers to keep them nimble.

The Resurrectors are camouflaged by the night, so Seth picks up Jackson's dropped Tile and activates a holo flare that rises up like cobalt smoke.

More Resurrectors tumble. Solonne reaches Kate and Silver, slits the cable ties binding her wrists, and pulls them to their feet, then goes to untie Mally. Kate's caught in a wave of anguish as marble-faced Solonne unlashes the boy's limp body, steadies his lolling head, and draws him towards her, listening for breath or a beating heart.

Kate sees a glint of metal through the Delphic maze. Jackson. She passes Silver to a nearby Surro and runs after the steel that is flashing through the thorns and roses.

"Stop!" says the Surro, but Kate keeps running, picking up a relinquished gun as she goes, snapping it into readiness to fire, and placing her finger firmly on the trigger. She dodges the flying arrows and the bodies that litter the ground.

"Stop! We need to stay together!"

Kate hears the words but they burn up in her head. Gun cocked, she runs further into the maze.

CHAPTER 83

THE SOUNDTRACK IS THE SCENT OF ROSES

Kate follows the flashing of the sword. As she enters the first passage, a man jumps out at her, wraps his salty fingers around her mouth, whispers hot breath into her ear. The closeness of his lips – vibrations of Zeebee – makes her body respond automatically and she elbows him in the solar plexus and head-butts him. The knock sends her skull blazing, but she blinks it away just in time to see him lurching for her again, and shoots him squarely in the chest. He falls to his knees, and his gun lands on the ground. The three bullets slow him down but his arachnasilk protects him from serious damage. While he scrambles for the weapon she darts away, and as she turns the corner, she twirls and shoots some more in his direction, not stopping to see if she hit her target.

After a while she slows down, and puts her hands on her knees to catch her breath. Just above the rambling canes she can see Seth, who now has two blazing guns. Solonne is carrying away Mally's body. The battleground is strewn with corpses hemmed to the ground. Pinned with ivory needles. The soundtrack is the scent of roses.

She starts jogging again but something trips her and she sprawls forward, smacking her jaw on the ground. Instinctively she kicks at the object that made her stumble, not knowing if it's a rock or a grasping hand of the enemy, and points her gun at it. It's an arm, which, on closer inspection, turns out to be attached to a body. A Resurrector with a snapped-off arrow in his heart.

Kate's thin coat offers little protection so she strips the dead man of his soft armour and zips it onto herself. The suit is still warm and the front is wet with blood, and it's too big for her so she rolls it up at the bottom and pops the generous collar to shield her neck. She picks up the dead man's gun. It's bigger than hers; an automatic that she doesn't know how to use, but she pockets it anyway. She moves forward again, this time feeling more like a hunter than the hunted. Armed and armoured: the protective suit seems to bring with it a sense of calm. A shape comes around the next corner and Kate shoots it without hesitation. The Resurrector – this time a woman – is taken by surprise, and Kate's blasting gun explodes her skull with ten metres to spare.

Kate jogs on, turning corner after corner. A part of this feels surreal, like a video game; she can even see the VR artwork in her head: a circular rose maze studded with hidden treasures and enemies, but when she stumbles and falls into the brambles, it's a painful reminder that this is very much her reality. She extricates herself from the clawing canes. Without the spider silk her arms would be stripped of skin.

Another woman appears, and despite the darkness, Kate recognises her. Would recognise her anywhere, because she was used to seeing her in her house, in her kitchen, hugging her children when they were both still alive and healthy and undamaged.

Bongi.

Surrounded by blooms, they face each other with loaded guns. Bongi's expression betrays shock and disbelief. She lowers her gun, and holds it, shaking, at her side.

"Ma," she says. "Will you forgive me?"

Kate pictures the dead Safeguard escort, garrotted in the train station's public restroom stall, pictures the discarded pink backpack; the abandoned cuddle-bunny. She thinks of how the nanny slapped Silver, how she handed Lumin the secateurs.

"Ma?" Her beseeching eyes are liquid.

Kate pulls the trigger. An aperture opens up on Bongi's forehead: there is a mist of blood. Kate pushes her sagging body to the side and keeps going.

There is movement ahead of her and she quickens her pace. Suddenly the petalled passages open up to another small clearing where a light-fountain gives the impression of a water feature. The splashing white noise calms her, and it's as if there is a clean light inside her head and she can think clearly.

Now there are ten different lanes to choose from, so she stands on her toes, trying to catch a glimpse of any movement nearby, a clue to where to go. Her pulse is jagged.

"Lumin's long gone," says Jackson's injured voice, making Kate jump. She fires the gun without meaning to, putting a single bullet into the fountain, and scrambles around, looking for Jackson, who steps out from one of the alleys, sword hanging by her side. "You'll never find him."

Kate's hatred bubbles up inside her again, like before, but this time she's got hot bullets in her hand and without thinking she squeezes the trigger as many times as she can until there is a haze of gunpowder all around them and Jackson has disappeared. The blasts ring in her ears, bouncing around like jumping metal spirals and the air is flavoured with flint.

Kate hears the swishing behind her now, and spins around. Jackson comes at her like a panther in the night, growling, and knocking her down with a perfectly-placed kick to the chest. Her head hits something hard and her bruised jaw cracks. She lies spreadeagled on the fragrant ground, trying to visualise Jackson through the camouflage of pain. She tries to stand but her legs aren't listening to her brain. Gun still in hand, she doesn't wait for a clean shot, and just fires into the darkness in front of her. Five bullets make it out of the gun, then she realises she's out of ammo. She tosses the weapon aside and grasps in her pocket for the other one. She fantasises about shooting Jackson through the pocket, surprising her with a face full of bullets, but she can't find the trigger.

She can't find the trigger.

She can't find the trigger.

Her fingers are blind worms. Where the fuck is the trigger? The holo water feature rushes and gurgles.

Jackson appears above her, bright teeth replacing the stars.

"There's no point in struggling," she whispers. "We've won. Don't you see?"

Kate tries to get up but it's as if her legs are sewn to the ground.

"Don't worry," Jackson says. "It's over now. I'll make it quick."

Kate's Helix screams midnight.

Jackson, shiny-faced with sweat and triumph, holds her sword above her.

CHAPTER 84

FATAL CRIMSON

Another whistling sound, one that will feature in Kate's dreams forever. A short shrill whisper in the fresh night.

The whistling and then … it's stopped by a smack of flesh and bone. Jackson's eyes bulge as the arrow shoots straight through her back and emerges from her chest. She blinks and her lips move, but she doesn't say anything. She drops the sword and wraps her hands around the stained shaft of the arrow. She coughs, a wet hack, and blood begins to trickle from her lips. It dyes her teeth fatal crimson. Her eyes begin to close, and she swoons like an actress in a vintage film. One step of an elegant death dance, and then it's over, and she's on the ground. Despite the clear night, a bolt of electricity cracks open the sky, illuminating the entire garden for a split second.

Kate's losing her grip on reality. Is this the end of the world?

The bright white flash reveals the person responsible for Jackson's demise.

Three years old, and shorter than the crossbow she is holding. Lightning highlights in her hair.

Silver.

EPILOGUE

Johannesburg, 2024

"M'lady," rasps Marko. He opens his right eye for the first time since the attack. His hand travels up to the designer eye patch and his fingers run along its edges. He frowns.

Keke pulls his hand away from his face.

"Damn it, Marko," she says, and kisses him hard. "You bastard."

"Why don't you guys get a room," says Kate, and Seth smirks.

"I'd love to," says Keke.

Marko blinks at the blank walls, the antiseptic in the air. A machine next to his head shows a steady green heartbeat.

Themba bustles in, ready to scold. "You need to be gentle with him." Her intern badge has been replaced with a resident brooch. "Nothing too exciting, yet, please."

They stay by his side as he drifts in and out of consciousness. Keke doesn't let go of his hand.

The next time his eye clicks open is when a small body climbs onto the end of his bed.

"Silver."

Silver grins and waves. Her new little finger is made of feather-light aluminium, and printed bone. It's covered in soft, stamped silicone.

As good as the original, the Dark Doc had said, evaluating his work post-surgery. Silver had said *no,* which made Kate want to weep, but then she had looked at the Doc and said, *it's better.*

"Thank you, Marko," says Silver. He frowns. He hasn't yet realised what he's sacrificed to find her. All he can muster is: "Cool finger."

"I also want a cyberfinger," says Mally in a muffled voice.

Kate pulls the curtain along the rings to open up his side of the room. "Good morning!"

"Hello, roomie," he says to Marko. "I've been waiting for you to wake up."

Marko looks so relieved to see Mally, but then he takes in the boy's full-body exocast and it makes his pulse race. He sees the quadriplegic sticker on the headboard.

Kate can see he's trying to talk, trying to figure out what happened. When the words don't come out, emotion takes over and his lips pull to the side. She can see the quiet devastation rolling over him.

"Easy, tiger," says Seth, patting Marko's shin through the cotton sheet. "Everything's okay, now."

Marko, anxious, puts a hand on his chest, feels the stem cell dressing, then traces his eye patch again.

How do you tell someone what we need to tell him?

Arronax clears her throat. "Alright, Mally," she says in her crisp accent, "Marko's awake. You know what that means, right?"

"It's time to put on a show," he says.

"That's right. Are you ready?"

The boy tries to nod, but his cast keeps him from moving his broken neck. Themba fusses around him, adjusts his bespoke hospital gown, removes his catheter. Arronax snaps open the catches on the cast and levers Mally up by the arms, like a baby, while Themba supports his back. They leave his neck-brace on. They lower the bed and help him off, and everyone holds their breath. Kate lets out a small gasp when she sees him standing, and when he starts to walk, one jerking step at a time, something bursts in her chest, and she launches into full-blown sobbing.

"Look, Mom," he says. "I can walk again!"

Silver claps and claps. Keke's also crying now, and Themba joins in.

The picture of Meadon comes loose from the wall and flutters to the tiles below. Arronax had given it to Mally before the surgery, saying that the synth slamander was the perfect mascot for his recovery. Meadon, she had told him, is the reason he'd be able to walk again. The procedure had taken five hours, and they had implanted a 32-electrode stimulator near his C-5 vertebrae in the middle of his neck, just below the site of injury. If the break had been just a millimeter higher –

"Well done, Mally," Arronax says, "well done!"

Mally beams at them. "Can I go home now?"

Kate wipes her face, hugs him gently. "Soon. I promise."

His eyes shine with tears.

Marko whispers: "Who will be my roomie, if you go home?"

They help him back into bed, smooth the starched white cotton over his pallid legs.

"I have a gift for you, Mally," says Arronax, "for being such a strong, brave boy." She picks up a big box from the corner of the room. It's been wrapped in animated gift paper: a cartoon drawing of a boy playing with a dog. They race around and around the box.

Seth shoots her a look of disbelief.

Mally's tears vanish.

"Well?" says Keke. "Open it!"

Mally rips off the paper and opens the white box. His face lights up when he sees what's inside.

"I can't believe it!"

Arronax helps him lift the soft nut-brown puppy out of the box and onto his lap. "It's the brand new version of the K9000." She switches it on and it yaps. "It's a Loyal Labrador. Chocolate Coat. A limited edition."

Mally's face is already soft with love. He brings the small dog up to his chest and buries his lips in her shiny fur. "She's warm," he says, and the dog pants happily. "Thank you, Arro," he says. "I've always wanted a RoboPup."

"I know," she says, winking at Seth.

The word 'RoboPup' and the realistic nature of the bot makes Kate shudder. It makes her feel uncomfortable, but she'll live with it, if it makes Mally less homesick; if it offers him some happiness. God knows he deserves it, after what they've all been through. She looks up at the ceiling, which is crowded with white helium soft-pop balloons: A gift from Solonne.

The puppy barks and chases her tail, and they all laugh. Keke's Patch rings, so she silently excuses herself and leaves the room to answer the call. When she's still not back after ten minutes, Kate goes to check on her.

Keke's not in the hospital corridor, nor at the coldtea vending machine. The unisex restroom icon catches Kate's eye, so she makes her way over and pushes open the door. On her way in, she catches sight of her reflection in one of the mirrors, sees that her eye make-up is smudged from her sobbing, so she takes a moment to rub the mascara tint off her cheeks.

"I'm telling you again," she hears Keke whispering from behind one of the doors. "I'm telling you again to leave me alone."

Kate thinks she must be talking on the phone, so she's shocked when she hears someone else talk. A bright current runs through her veins, making her fingers tremble.

"Keke, please, just hear me out," says a male voice.

"No!" says Keke. "I'm not going to do it. Okay? I'm not."

"I'm not going to hurt her," says the man's voice. "All I need is – "

"Is that what you told the friends of your other victims?"

"Victims? What are you talking about?"

"The cops were here. They told me everything."

The man laughs. "You're going to believe the police? Really?"

"You killed Helena Nash."

"Helena Nash killed herself."

"You helped her. And those others. I'm leaving."

There is a scuffle.

"Let me go."

"Keke. Listen to me, please – "

"I'll pay you back, okay? I'll find a way. Then we'll be square."

"You don't have to pay me back. This isn't about quid pro quo. It's about something far bigger than that. All I need you to do is – "

"No, I won't do it. She's been through enough. Now, I'd appreciate it if you let my arm go."

Kate frowns. Let her arm go? She tiptoes along the room and when she sees two pairs of feet under a shower door she slides it open. Keke and the man turn to look at her at the same time.

"Let go of her arm," says Kate. The man does so.

"Kate," he says. He's good looking, and dressed in a sharp suit. Blue silk tie (Teal Trespasser). "I have something I have to tell you."

"Then tell me." Kate can't remember ever meeting the man but something about him is familiar. As if she had seen him before, on the homescreen, or in a dream.

"Not here," says Zack. "Not like this."

WHAT HAVE WE DONE

BOOK 3

WHAT HAVE WE DONE

WHEN TOMORROW CALLS BOOK THREE

JT LAWRENCE

PROLOGUE

The Gordhan Hospital
Johannesburg, 2024

"I'm telling you again," comes Keke's terse whisper from behind one of the unisex restroom doors. "I'm telling you again to leave me alone."

Kate suspects Keke's talking on her phone, so she's shocked when she hears a reply. Bright nerves flash through her (Cadmium Current). She turns away from the smart mirror and forgets about the spilt mascara on her cheeks.

"Keke, please, just hear me out," says a man.

"No!" says Keke. "I'm not gonna do it. I can't."

"I'm not going to hurt her. I promise. All I need is—"

"Is that what you told the friends of your other victims?"

"Victims? Keke, what are you talking about?"

"The cops were here, Zack. They told me everything."

"You're going to believe the *police?* Really?"

"You killed Helena Nash."

"Helena Nash killed herself."

What the fuck? thinks Kate, adrenaline rising. She sneaks a little closer to the door.

"You helped her. And those others," says Keke. "I'm leaving."

There is a scuffle.

"Let me go. Let me go or I'll scream."

"Keke. Listen to me, please—"

"I'll pay you back, okay? I'll find a way."

Kate frowns. *Pay him back? What the hell is going on here?*

She tiptoes closer, her heart banging in her chest.

"You don't have to pay me back! This isn't about quid pro quo. It's about something far bigger than that. All I need you to do is—"

"No! Kate has been through enough. She can't deal with this. Let me go."

Kate feels a flare of anger. She slides open the door, and Keke and the man turn to look at her. His fingers are wrapped around her forearm.

"Let go of her arm," says Kate.

"Kate." He's good looking, dressed in a sharp dark suit and a silk tie. Teal Trespasser. "I have something I have to tell you."

"Then tell me." Kate can't remember ever meeting the man, but something about him is familiar. As if she's seen him before, on the homescreen, or in a dream.

"Not here," says Zack. "Not like this."

"I don't know who you are, and I'm not gonna play games with you," says Kate. "Tell me what's going on."

"It's complicated."

"Who sent you?"

"Now, that's an interesting question."

Kate glares at him.

He rubs his lips. "You wouldn't believe me if I told you."

There's a purple hammering behind Kate's eyes. It's exhaustion or frustration or, more likely, a debilitating blend of both. She has the inappropriate urge to slink down onto the hard cold floor and close her eyes for a long time. Why does she attract the crazies? She's had enough crackers people in her life. From now on, she only wants conversations with sane people. Nice, non-crackers people who don't drag her into surreal, unpredictable worlds.

"You're wasting our time," says Kate, ready to leave. She wants to get back to Mally and Silver in the hospital ward. The purple hammering gets darker, starts tipping towards indigo.

Zack looks at the micro-camera in the corner of the ceiling, and whispers, "Is there somewhere we can meet?"

Kate scowls at the idea. "You really think I'd agree to that? What's next? Sweets from your trenchcoat pocket? No, there is not *somewhere we can meet*."

Zack shows her his palms in surrender. He has beautiful hands, and Kate's annoyed at herself for noticing. Now is certainly not the time to appreciate them or the depth of his eyes (Stardust Surveillers). She needs to get out of here right now.

"Hurry up!" Keke fidgets, and Zack shoots her a look. What are they not telling her?

"Zack is a suicide agent," says Keke.

"A what-what? I don't know what that means."

The Suicide Contagion is pervasive, but what do the unlucky lemmings have to do with her?

"This will be difficult for you to understand, at first," he says, "but for the sake of your children I need you to have an open mind—"

For the sake of my children? Kate takes a step away from him. He advances on her, gripping her arm. Firm, and thrilling.

"You're not threatening my kids."

"No! No. The opposite. I'm here to save them. To save you all. It's what I've been put here to do. It's the reason I—"

Kate is about to ask—*save us from what?* But there's a crash as a squad of men in black kevlarskin and exoscales break through the main door and flatten Zack against the sonic shower tiles. Kate cries out in alarm as she grabs Keke and they move away from the aggressive men, bumping into the basins behind them. Panic paints her insides a shrill shade of yellow. The men are shouting at Zack, jamming oiled gunmetal into his cheek. Telling him not to move, not to try anything stupid, not to breathe. Kate spots a glint of a police badge. They force his arms up against the wall and frisk him with gloved hands.

Detective Ramphele trails in and nods at a stone-eyed Keke, who nods back.

The men turn Zack around. "Girdler," the detective says, blinking, as if he doesn't quite believe what he's seeing. Zack is calm, his eyes unflecked by fear. Ramphele looks at Zack with something akin to admiration as he caresses the revolver in the harness strapped to his hip. "Zachary Girdler. I never thought I'd see the day."

"Zack. I'm sorry. I didn't have a choice." Keke's face darkens, as if clouds have raced over the sun.

Unspoken words echo in the air: *You always have a choice.*

"They were going to arrest me for conspiring with you in Helena Nash's murder," says Keke. "They had me in cuffs and Marko was dying. The twins were missing. I was desperate. It was the only way they'd agree to—"

Zack clenches his jaw, says, "You did what you needed to do," but his eyes say *Jesus, Keke, what have you done?*

Kate's stomach percolates with dread. Her instinct tells her this shouldn't be happening, that this is not part of the plan.

But what plan? Whose plan?

Violence scents the air. Things are happening too quickly and Kate wants to stop and scroll backwards. The men snap smartcuffs on Zack and shove him forward.

"Don't take your eyes off him," says Detective Ramphele. "Not for a second, d'you hear me?"

"Yes, sir."

"He's a slippery motherfucker."

Zack doesn't take his eyes off Kate. It's as if a live wire connects them.

"Wait!" she shouts, but they don't.

Kate's desperate now to know what he needs to tell her, but the cops are all over him. She has the feeling that something vital is spooling away from her and if she doesn't grab on to it right now she'll regret it forever.

"Please, wait!" she shouts again.

"You have to come and find me," says Zack, "so that I can give you the message. You need to know. Your life depends on it."

The testosterone squad bustle Zack out of the restroom.

"I'll get you the best lawyer!" Keke yells after him. "I'll come see you!"

Ramphele shouts a laugh. "Where Girdler is going, you'll never see him again."

PART 1

CHAPTER 1

FUNERAL CAKE

12 YEARS LATER

Seth's Apartment

Johannesburg, 2036

Kate takes another bite of the funeral cake. "What do you think?"

"Mm," Keke says, still chewing, "If this cake was a person I'd take him home and—"

Seth clears his throat, and she doesn't finish her sentence. At forty-something, Keke still has that violet glint of mischief in her eyes. She winks at Seth, and he winks back.

"It's good." Keke clicks her tongue. "*Imnandi.* I'd go with this one. The other two were good, but ... what's this one called again?"

Kate frowns. When her line of vision connects with the holotag, the name of the cake appears. "Death by Choxolate."

Keke snorts. "Ah, well, at least they have a sense of humour."

"Dark humour," says Kate.

"Perfect for the funeral business."

"They've got a lot to smile about," says Seth. "Have you seen how much they charge? I'm in the wrong business entirely."

"And what business is that, Mr Denicker?" Keke leans her leather-clad hip against the kitchen island's granite counter. "Last time I saw you, you were about to start at The Company That Shall Not Be Named."

"I'm still there."

Keke straightens her back. "Doing?"

"Advanced chemgineering. What else?"

"Home or away?"

"Sorry?"

"Are you working for them, or against them?"

"Ah, you know. The usual. A bit of both."

They snicker, but the truth is that if Bilchen even got a sniff of the fact that Seth was a biopunk hacktivist, he'd probably be thrown into some kind of (trademarked) dungeon.

"I keep expecting them to come to their senses and make me disappear."

Keke taps her chin. "Maybe they have a plan for you."

"Ja," says Kate. "One that involves luring you in and then chopping you up for iguana food."

Seth smiles. "With their reputation, it would hardly come as a surprise."

Keke licks some frosting off her fingertip. "Lucky iguanas."

"And with that sense of humour," says Kate, "you should be in the funeral biz."

Keke eyes what's left of the cake. "Don't tempt me."

"Who knew there'd be so much bank to be made in the urban death industry?"

"I love the way you say 'urban death industry'."

"Ha ha," says Kate, clearing away the confexionary boxes.

"But you guys seem to be coping well with your mom's illness," says Keke. "How are you feeling about everything?"

Seth shrugs. "We're dealing, but it's weird, you know? Planning a funeral for someone who is still … alive."

She won't be for long. Kate blinks away the tears that sting her sinuses.

Funeral parties are trending this spring. Woke wakes are all the rage.

WHY WAIT TILL YOU ARE DEAD? is one of the less-subtle headlines Kate's seen on the forever-hovering city holoboards she wishes she could swat away. It costs more than a million blox to switch off the automatic ads that float into your neuroreality vision. Kate's always called it outright blackmail and refused to pay the ransom, but lately her resolve is sliding. She's tired of the constant laser-targeted marketing trying to scratch her eyes out. She imagines going for an old-fashioned walk along the purple-blossomed jacaranda streets with nothing crowding her vision—just breathing in the fresh air.

I mean, what's next? She'd demanded of Seth. *Are they going to make us pay to* breathe?

Seth had raised his eyebrows as if to say he wouldn't be surprised. As it is, inane people are buying up bags of Alpine Air as if their lives depend on it. Which in a way they will, if the SMOG score climbs much higher. Creeps are digging out their old Superbug masks and adding new bespoke touches: satin patches, copper rivets, intricate stitching, hand-sewn or thread-printed with their latest avatar and/or slogo.

The front door bangs closed. Bonechaser jumps up from her bed and runs to the front of the house. A flurry of happy pink barks peels into the air around Kate.

"Mally? Is that you?"

"We'll be in the cineroom!" shouts Mally, and a different door bangs shut.

What is it about teenagers slamming doors?

"If he breaks that Securodoor again, it's coming out of his allowance," says Seth.

"If a moody sixteen-year-old can break a hundred thousand rand security door, it deserves to be broken," says Keke. "I mean, what are you going to do in event of a Zombiepocalypse? You're going to *not* slam the door?"

"You're like them, you know," says Seth. "You have an answer for everything."

"I'll take that as a compliment!" Keke bats her eyelashes at him.

"No wonder you guys get on so well," says Kate.

There's something about Kekeletso that's always been youthful, quick curiosity and lithe limbs. She's always up for trying something new; just last week she was learning how to fly a Volanter. Her hot energy makes her skin glow.

On the other side of the scale, trauma and the sleep-dep that comes with parenthood has taken its toll on Kate, as she's reminded every morning when her swingbed mirror chime wakes her. She can feel she's growing older but is still surprised when she notices new textures on her skin: hashtags on the sides of her fingers; overnight crêpe on her wrists. Keke, on the other hand, gets work done regularly, after years of saying she'd never. She calls it 'saving face'.

I can't do lunch today. I'm at the spa, saving face.

But even on haggard days, Kate's not tempted to inject neurotoxic proteins and stem cells into her wrinkles. In a way, she's happy to grow older, finds herself less anxious, and more at ease with life, despite the constant challenges the kids throw her way. The vacuumbot glides in, seemingly happy for the opportunity to do some work, and inhales the sweet crumbs off the kitchen floor.

"Would it be wrong to go with the same cake for the twins' party on the weekend?"

"The funeral cake? Probably," says Keke. "But who cares? What have you planned for their birthday, anyway? Barcade? Light Jugglers? Mars Immersia? Drone ballet? None of them quite say *Sweet Sixteen*, do they?"

"Ha," says Seth.

"More like Not-So-Sweet." Kate calls up the twins' party-planning list and ticks off 'CAKE'. All the other boxes remain unchecked.

"*What* are you talking about?" asks Keke. "Your kids are the best. You *know* they're the best."

"Ha," says Seth again.

"Have you *met* other teenagers? They're vile. They're despicable. I cross the street when I see teenagers."

"Okay, so ours aren't that bad," says Kate, "but—"

"What's up? Is it Mally? His new girlfriend?"

Kate shudders.

"I wish you wouldn't do that," says Seth.

She shoots him a look: *sorry-not-sorry*. She can't help it that she gets chills when Vega walks in the door.

"It's just … weird, you know? It takes some getting used to."

First a robotic dog and then—

"And you just let them spend time in there, unchaperoned? That's very *avant-garde* of you."

"Their quality time is the least of our worries," says Seth. "It's Silver who's giving Kate grey hairs."

Kate touches the silver floss in her fringe. The streak of white has multiplied overnight.

"How very Marie Antoinette of you," says Keke, and smiles at the plates, empty of cake.

"I want to get her into some kind of rehab," says Kate.

Keke flinches. "What? Silver? Why?"

"You're overreacting," says Seth. "Silver's behaviour is totally normal."

"Her behaviour is not normal!" says Kate. "She's immersed *all the time*."

"Normal," says Keke.

"Sometimes she doesn't speak to us for days. She forgets to eat, because she eats in the immersion, but then forgets that she has to eat in real life too."

"Normal."

"Have you seen how skinny she is? She fainted the other day, and couldn't figure out why. Then we realised she hadn't eaten in two days."

"So pack her some iso-protein bars and get her jackmate to set a reminder on her interface. And one of those smart sippycups that bump you to hydrate."

"Are you being serious?"

"What? It's a thing."

Kate holds a hand up to her forehead. "That's no way to live."

"It's the new way to live," says Seth.

"She wants to get meshed, and I don't know how to stop her. All her friends are doing it."

"You can't stop her, Kitty," says Keke. The words burn Kate's stomach. "I mean, once the tech gets a bit more sophisticated I'm going to do it too."

"You wouldn't!"

"Me too," says Seth. "It's scary now, but it'll seem completely normal to Silver's and Mally's kids."

Morgan has been nagging Kate to get meshed. He says an analogue brain is only capable of so much; that if they don't lace up soon then they'll be in danger of being on the same level as domestic cats to advanced AI, which is currently lapping them at every turn. Both scenarios fill Kate with a deep sense of foreboding. She doesn't want to be a house cat, and she doesn't want her brain to be upgraded. So where does that leave her?

"And it's normal for us to resist it, just like our parents resisted cell phones and ebooks. Besides, wouldn't it be great to ditch these lenses and mandibles?" Keke touches the translucent transmitter that runs from her ear to lips.

"I don't even feel mine anymore," says Seth.

"Just so that you guys know," Kate massages her temples. "I'm freaking the fuck out right now."

"You look calm to me."

"Years of parental practice."

What does Arronax always say? You can't stop progress. But that doesn't mean she has to like it.

"I just want you creeps to know that if you ever mesh, I'm going to … I don't know. Run away. Join the tribe of Disconnects. Escape to somewhere—"

Bonechaser starts barking.

"What's that sound?" Keke looks behind her, in the direction of the cineroom.

"It's the hound," says Seth.

"No, the *other* sound."

They all cock their heads. It's a siren, and it's getting louder. Bonechaser's barking rises a notch.

Something about the barking sounds off to Kate. It's the wrong note and there's an edge of ferocity to it. She's never heard him sound like that before. Is that siren … coming from this apartment?

A loud snarling sound rushes at them. Mally starts yelling.

"Down, Chaser, down!" comes his muffled shouting. "Down!" and as Kate and Seth rush towards him, Mally begins to scream.

CHAPTER 2

CHASER

Kate, Seth and Keke run towards the rabid growling. The siren, with Mally's screaming, scores yellow lines in Kate's vision. As they tumble into the cineroom, there is a wet, meaty sound of teeth tearing into flesh. Mally shouts in shock and pain; his face is a mask of pure horror.

"Chaser!" shouts Seth. "Down!"

But the snarling dog continues to attack Mally. With another crushing bite to his upper thigh, the boy falls to the floor. When the dog goes for Mally's face, Kate shouts "No!" and there's a blast so loud it blinds her. She can't work out what's happening until she smells the gunpowder and hears Bonechaser whine. Her vision returns in spectral shapes: four people shifting and stirring around her, and a dying dog on the floor. Mally is holding his injured leg, watching his pants bloom with petals of crimson. Kate rushes to him, landing on her knees and throwing her arms around his shoulders.

"You're okay!" she says, as if she's shouting an order.

Mally's pale mouth trembles.

"Are you insane?" Kate yells at Seth, who's gazing down at his gun as if he can't remember what it is. "You could've shot Mally!"

Seth looks up at her. "You'd rather your son be mauled to death by a robotic dog?"

Keke doesn't move. They all look down at Bonechaser, whose whine has faded to a thin whimper, as she pants and follows her tail around and around in a circle, a great big hole blown into her skull.

Kate's shaking inside and out. "The fuck just happened?"

"Bonechaser is sick," says Vega, making Kate start. She'd completely forgotten

Mally's girlfriend. Vega is, as always, perfectly unruffled. "We'll need to take him to the PeTTech vet."

Mally swipes away his tears. Bonechaser and he had been inseparable until Vega arrived on the scene.

Kate peers sadly at the dog. At first Chaser gave her the creeps, but over time they'd become attached. In fact, now more than ever—with the kids being teenagers—it seems that Chaser is the only one who's ever really happy to see her. The dog stumbles, and Kate automatically reaches out to help her, but Seth grabs her arm, shakes his head.

I just want to say goodbye, she thinks, as she watches the K9000 power down. One paw taps the floor in a death tic.

"Mally is in need of medical attention," says Vega.

Seth activates his Scribe. "I'll order an ambudrone."

"That is not necessary," says Vega.

"Of course it's bloody necessary," says Kate, with more venom than she intends. "He has a mangled leg. He's in shock."

"I have performed a thorough body scan," Mally's girlfriend says. "His wounds are superficial."

"Well, I'd still like to take him to a doctor."

"It is not necessary," says Vega. "I have the correct equipment to treat him right here."

She unbuttons her blouse, revealing perfect C-cups in a lacy push-up, and out of the top of her ribcage slides a neat compartment. Vega extricates the first aid kit from inside, and the drawer closes again, with hardly a hint of it on her skin. A headlamp snakes out of her temple, and when it turns on she smiles at them.

"May I use your kitchen table?"

Vega picks up Mally as if he weighs nothing, despite him being almost as tall as Seth, and carries him to the kitchen. She lays him gently on the table and opens her medikit. Kate hovers while Vega scissors his jeans open and sprays the wounds with disinfecting anaesthetic.

"Ah," he says with a sigh. "That's better already."

"Hold still," says Vega, "this will only hurt a bit." She holds the pieces of skin together and runs a surgical autostapler over the wound, leaving a miniature railway track of skin-coloured sutures. Kate finds herself uneasy, but fascinated. It's like Vega's just zipped him up.

"They'll dissolve in a few days," says Vega. "You'll be as good as new." She covers the smaller gashes with platelet plasters and packs the kit back into her ribcage, passing Mally an inhaler. "For the pain."

. . .

Seth puts a call in to Arronax. Her mermaid avatar spins open with a splash. "We've got a problem."

Kate walks out onto the balcony, and Keke follows. She holds onto the rail, then, with shaking hands, presses a button to roll open the invisi-screen, and they look out onto the hot city, grey embroidered with green, and breathe in the toxic air that smells of ozone and ash.

"You know that kind of defeats the object of the screen, right?" says Keke.

When the screen is employed, the air on the balcony is filtered and cooled. It's supposed to make you feel as if you're standing in the fresh air—*sans* pollen and pollution—*Protecting You without Sacrificing the View (TM),* but it just makes Kate feel claustrophobic. Being shut in an invisible box is still being shut in a box.

"Seriously, what the fuck just happened?"

A drone speeds right past them. It's branded with a popular Chinese restaurant chain logo: three chopstix on a plate forming the 'A' symbol for anarchy, because who doesn't love rebellion *and* noodles?

"*Angaz*. No idea. Robopup rabies?"

"Twelve years," says Kate. "Twelve years that robot's been Mally's best friend. The perfect pet. Loyal Labrador, they said. Programmed to be loyal. What's twelve human years in doggie years?"

Keke shrugs. "I don't know. But twelve human years is like twelve centuries in technology. Chaser's ancient. When's the last time you had him upgraded?"

"2029. They don't upgrade his model anymore."

"It makes you think."

"Of?"

"You know—" Keke gestures inside with a subtle flick of her eyebrows. "The Stepford girlfriend."

"Don't go there. I have enough to worry about."

"You must admit—she is kind of handy to have around."

"Yes."

"What else do you think she keeps in those compartments of hers?"

CHAPTER 3

ELECTROSMOG & SUNLIGHT

"Do you ever still think of the … you know, the prophecy?" says Keke.

They're sitting down now, on the balcony floor, barefoot and stripped to their underwear, drinking whisky that looks like liquid gold in the last light of the sunset.

"Of course I do. Every day. Especially when I get frustrated with the kids. Then I feel guilty, because really we're all still here by the grace of … what?"

"Lady Luck," says Keke. "Luck. And love."

An image of Lady Luck appears in Kate's mind, a hallucinogenic mash-up of the Statue of Liberty, Wonder Woman ReDux, and her memory of Solonne with her quiver of diamond-tipped arrows.

They clink their glasses and take a sip.

"You shouldn't feel guilty. You know you've got nothing to feel guilty about."

"It comes with the territory," says Kate. "Being a parent is a sentence to a lifetime of guilt."

They sit in companionable silence for a moment.

"Do you know that Solonne still sends the kids balloons every birthday?"

"Really?"

"White ones. I know she means well, but they spook the shit out of me. They float around for days reminding me of that stupid prophecy."

"I try not to think about it," says Keke, "but—"

"I know," says Kate. "Then another one of their predictions comes true and it's terrifying all over again."

"The Mars one! Shit."

One of the Celestial Prophecies is that the people stealing from the Red Planet would become a burnt offering to the multiverse to appease Celestia. The prophecies are mostly dismissed as charismatic cult claptrap, but people started to pay a bit more attention when the latest returning Mars ship disappeared in space, blipping the lives of fifty-two space miners, twelve tourists, and hundreds of trillions of dollars worth of equipment.

"Seth's always saying that anyone can write a 'prophecy' and then find some kind of data to support it. But it's just ... It's uncanny, right?"

"Downright fucking terrifying," says Keke. The golden threads woven into her cornrows glint in the golden light. The whisky buzzes behind Kate's eyes. Amber Purr.

"Do you still remember the exact words?"

"Of course I do. I couldn't forget them if I tried. It's like they've been carved into my brain with a hot scalpel."

Sometimes she wakes up to Lumin whispering in her ear—

The last living Genesis Child will lead us to the Ledge.

—and she claps the lights on and she's alone, and his words slither away to hide somewhere in her bedroom, only to flicker in on her dreams another night.

"If the boy survives into his fourth summer then he'll live to be sixteen and that will be the end of days."

"And Mally turned sixteen a couple of months ago, right?"

"Right."

"And Silver's birthday is in...thirty-six hours."

"Yebo."

"Do you think the world will end before or after their birthday party?"

"It would save me some planning if it happened before. I still don't have a theme. All I have is some funeral cake."

"Well, that's easy, then," say Keke. "We'll have a rapture party."

Seth opens the balcony door to find the friends chuckling into their glasses. "You two had better come in."

"Nope, nope, nope," says Kate. "This is the most fun I've had since ..."

Kate searches her recent memory and comes up blank.

"She needs some downtime, Seth," says Keke. "It's been a hell of a day."

Seth's eyes rest on Keke's exposed skin for a second too long. There is no time for desire.

"You have no idea," he says, spotting their discarded mandibles. "You're not connected?"

"We disconnected an hour ago. We needed some analogue time. Some electrosmog and sunlight, to feel human again."

"We have a problem," says Seth. "You need to see something."

Kate tips the rest of the whisky into her mouth. Birch and beeswax. "We'll sort out Bonechaser tomorrow."

What do you do with a broken pet, anyway? Is there some kind of memorial party planning service for them too? She wouldn't be surprised. Long gone are the days of choosing between being buried or cremated: humans can now pick from a menu of options including, among hundreds of others, vertical cemeteries, forest pods, essence amulets, and cryogenix. She wouldn't be surprised if the same options weren't available for beloved pets, although she guesses that robotic dogs have a different fate.

"Bonechaser is the least of it," Seth says. His face is pale despite the darkening sky. He throws their clothes at them. "You've got to connect right now."

CHAPTER 4

RUNNING WITH THE RODENTS

Innercity
Johannesburg, 2036

Silver adjusts her vintage gas-mask and picks up her pace. Ironically, it makes it more difficult to breathe, not less, but she puts up with the discomfort because there's no way she's getting The Black Lung. She's seen the 4DHD VR animation at school, where they practically shove you right inside the diseased organ to show you what breathing raw city air can do to healthy tissue. *So* not gonna happen. Besides, the mask is, like, ancient, and totally original thread. Kate tells her that when she was young, like, a hundred years ago, everyone wanted new clothes all the time. They'd spend their weekends in malls spending money on new clothes, even though they had a full wardrobe at home. Even though they knew the shit was mostly FongKong, they wanted the shiny stuff. Bizarro. Imagine working all week for some evil corp and then spending your free time spending what you earned on things you didn't need, and then get into debt so that you can work some more. Suckers. And it's not like they didn't know it, either. They were always saying things like 'rat race' and 'hamster wheel' but what did they do? They kept on fucking running with the rodents, that's what. Running and running until they were all burned out and needed to retire at sixty-five. Sixty-five! That's like giving up on your life when you're only halfway through. Or die from a heart attack. What a joke. What a brainbleach. What a fucked-up way to live.

Her mandible chimes 19:14.

Shifuckfuck, I'm late.

Her appointment has been set for 19:00, and they said the procedure takes ninety minutes, all-in. Silver hopes it doesn't run over—she'll have to hurry if she wants to get home in time for her 21:00 curfew and not make the parental units suspicious.

Although, Silver sighs, Kate would always be suspicious. Can people be born with a paranoid gene? Kate certainly was. Or maybe she wasn't born with it ... maybe it developed over time. Can't blame her, really. Kate gets that haunted look when Silver asks her about stuff, like why Marko disappeared from their lives so suddenly and won't even beam or bullet them, or what happened to James. I mean, she's not dumb, she knows that her dad died before she was born, but why're they never allowed to ask questions about him? Talking, not talking, it hurts either way.

Silver turns a corner, as instructed by her mandible maps, and jogs down an alley wet with greasy puddles that shine in pearlescent colours. 64381, to be exact, if she were to describe it to Kate. She reaches a nondescript door and her dash pings. Silver raps on the painted metal, the same shade of grey as the smoggy dusk sky, and the speakeasy is slid open with a bang. Green eyes like dragon scales.

"Go home, little girl," says the owner of the scales. "This is no place for you."

CHAPTER 5
FROM CHOP TO STAB

Seth's Apartment
Johannesburg, 2036

The women amble reluctantly inside, glowing from the drink and the heat. The air-conditioned apartment wakes them, turns their skin to instabraille. Kate buttons her asymmetrical hoodie right up to her neck. She sees a navy-cream ombré canvas bag on the floor and knows instinctively that Chaser's body is inside, and shivers.

Why is Seth so riled up? What can be worse than what just happened to Mally?

Kate and Keke put their mandibles back on.

"Kate connect," she says, and her dashboard appears, her Scribe blinks.

"Keke connect," says Keke.

They're both hit with a barrage of messages and alerts at the same time. It makes her temples throb and tastes of a scraped metal. She swipes them all away, but as soon as her vision clears, more messages stream in.

Prioritise.

The alerts freeze for a second then swirl around each other till the most important ones are at the top. Kate looks at the first one on the list, an Echo.news headline clip posted less than a minute ago, and opens it by thinking *Play.*

The video is amateurish, shaky, and not properly focused, but it's clearly the outside of The Bent Hotel, in Saxonwold, known for its interstellar prices and political dignitary guests. The giant motorised gate is opening and closing, as if someone is sitting on the remote. Then a commotion comes into view, just for a moment: Kate gasps when she sees a terrified woman slam into the wall of the entrance building, as if she's been thrown at it. Instead of sinking to the floor as Kate expects her to, she scrabbles around, trying to get purchase, trying to get out of the building, but then a hand clamps down on her leg and pulls her back inside. Her mouth is wide open, and Kate feels the woman's silent scream scrape her skin. She shudders again.

"What the fuck!" says Keke.

"Are you watching the same thing as I am?" asks Kate. "Bent?"

"What? No. The Loop."

"Connect to Keke," says Kate, and she watches on Keke's interface as the hyperloop speed train careens straight into a stationary cabin and explodes into a violent cloud of smoke and debris. A graphic at the top right of the screen is counting: a rainbow stopwatch as the numbers tick over. 489. 528. 540. Then Kate realises the units are the confirmed fatalities.

"Watch the Reality DroidChef one," says Seth.

Search. Reality DroidChef.

Hundreds of results come up. Kate chooses the one with the most confirmations. She wants to make sure what she is watching is real news, and not some cyberprankster who thinks it'll be cool to use his home SFX software and splice it into a major newstream's channel. The last time that happened, a fake clip of an actress being beheaded in Belarus made it around the globe more than a thousand times before it was outed as quack. The DroidChef clip has more than six hundred individual confirmation stamps on it.

Play.

Kate's already nervous of what she'll see. The image of the woman being dragged back into the hotel is still jigging in her head. The video opens on the set of RDC; it was a live recording. The camera is trained on a chopping board, where a stamped silicone android's hand is making fast work of a no-tears onion. The knife is made of compressed carbonate. It's easy to see how sharp it is by how little resistance the genetically modified onion offers. Kate has seen the knife's ads: *Extremely sharp: Not recommended for human use.* The camera tilts up to show the chef: a smooth-faced femmebot with a toothy smile, who's not even looking down while the knife dices the onion at supersonic speed. The human host is looking at his watch and laughing as the bot tips the minced onion into a bowl and starts on a new one. He tells her to go faster, and beams some more. Usually Kate would snark at the brainlessness of it all, but for now her heart is pumping hot blood throughout her body. Her breath is shallow, and her fingertips tingle with adrenaline. The bot is smiling widely at the camera, her knifework a blur. The host grins and says something Kate can't hear over her nerves. She knows exactly what's going to happen. Does she have to watch it till the end if she already knows the conclusion? As she considers switching it off, the smiling android starts chopping her hand. The stamped silicone of her skin is lacerated to show titanium bones and latex tendons working underneath.

Keke hisses, an inhalation of cold breath through teeth.

The host's cheery face fades as he realises what's happening, and he blinks and automatically reaches to stop the robot from hurting herself further. Kate wraps her fingers over her eyes and peeps through. The chef tosses the knife a few inches into the air and catches it again at a different angle—so that she can change her grip from chop to stab—and without turning away from the camera or shrinking her smile, in a breathtakingly fluid motion, she drives the knife straight into the host's chest.

CHAPTER 6

YOU SHOULD ALWAYS BE WORRIED

"I don't understand what's happening," says Kate. A moment ago she was on the balcony with her best friend, soaking up whisky and sunshine, and joking about Doomsday. Now they stand huddled in the cool apartment, hugging themselves and grasping for words as clip after clip flashes in on their vision. They were fire, and now they are ash.

Stop thinks Kate, and the news freezes. *Clear.*

She looks around the apartment as if she doesn't know where she is. Where the kids are. The real world punches her in the gut. "Where's Mally?"

"In his room. Resting," says Seth.

"With Vega?"

"Vega went out to replenish her medikit. Said she'd stay at her hostel tonight. Make sure Mally gets a good night's sleep."

"And Silver?"

"She's not answering my bullets."

"Well, that's normal."

"Should we be worried?" asks Kate.

Seth is deadpan. "We're parents. We should always be worried."

Keke chips in, "You're a human. You should always be worried."

Kate tries to stay calm. "At least we know where she is. Where she *always* is. It's the one upside of having a daughter addicted to immersia."

CHAPTER 7

NOT KIDS LIKE YOU

SkinTech Clinic
Johannesburg, 2036

"There's a kid here," transmits the man with dragon scales for eyes. "Says she has a slot booked." He listens to the feedback then looks at Silver's hair. "Ja. Looks funny on a kid."

Despite the variety of artificial dyes and powders and shifting shades out there, creeps find her white hair unsettling.

"If you say so, Boss." Screeching metal on metal as the deadbolt is drawn aside; Silver is allowed access and the man locks the door behind her. They spend a moment eyeing each other. He's younger than he first appeared, head to toe in black, has a jaw-tattoo that incorporates his designer mandible, and kohl smudge on his eyes. He runs a metal detector over her shoulders, her back, her thighs. The machine beeps when it glides over her jacket, which is full of studs and steampunk corsetry. Hollow buttons and copper darts. They do it again without the jacket, and she's given the all clear.

He seems disconcerted by her, won't stop looking. She stands up to his gaze. "I take it you don't get a lot of kids coming around here."

"Oh, we get kids," he says. He means street urchins and child prostitutes, white lobster orphans. A city like this swallows kids whole. "But not kids like you."

Silver moves quickly through the lifi-lit passage, and when she gets to the end she turns into a large waiting room. The creeps sitting in their swingchairs instinctively look up at her. She's used to people staring. She glares back, and they look away. Keke says people stare because of the way Silver dresses. She means it in a good way. Silver's uniform of her bespoke steampunk hooded coat, rubber peelboots, fake-snake leggings—and of course her white hair and heritage gas-mask—is guaranteed to make even the most indifferent stranger take a second look.

Silver counts five patients in front of her. If they all take an hour each she'll never get home in time. It takes so long to get to this side of town, it'll be a shame to turn around and go back again. She's been saving for ages, and it's near damn impossible to get an appointment. Plus, she has her heart set on getting this done before Saturday.

A woman dressed like a Halloween nurse flutters into the room and nods wordlessly at Silver.

The painfully thin man next to her starts chewing his teeth, shaking his head in small, hard tics. A woman wearing a cybercap and cradling a fox in a shawl gazes blankly at the floor. Silver hesitates. Does she really want to go through with this? She follows the nurse.

The doctor stands up from behind his desk and opens his arms.

"Silver," he says warmly. His voice is exactly as she remembers it—a panther, a vibrating sports car engine.

"DarkDoc." She disappears into his arms for a moment. It feels good.

When they separate, the doctor lifts her hand as if to kiss it, but instead he raises it to his eye level and inspects her artificial finger.

"How is it? Giving you any trouble?"

Silver shakes her head. "No. No. Your craftsmanship has stood the test of time."

Morgan smiles and gestures for her to sit. The steel clips in his dreadlox glint in the light.

"Glad to hear it, but then to what do I owe this auspicious occasion?"

"It's my sixteenth birthday on Saturday."

"So it is! Happy birthday."

"I'm here to buy myself a birthday present."

"Well." He clasps his hands together. "You have my full attention."

"I'm stuck on the sixth level in Eden 7.0."

The techdoctor frowns at her. "You're not supposed to be anywhere near that game. It's for adults only."

"I know."

"How did you get in?"

"How do you think?"

"I'm assuming it would have involved hacking, and the best hacker in the country just happens to be your godfather."

"Exactly."

"He shouldn't have done that. There's a reason they don't let kids play that game."

Silver sighs. She's mature enough. The Net knows she's shrewder than most of the adults with whom she comes into contact. The rules aren't for everyone: The DarkDoc should know.

"Anyway," he says, "you can't access the seventh level. You know that. Not without—"

Silver blinks at him. "So then you know why I'm here."

Morgan laughs, and spins the brushed metal levitating sphere on his desk. "You know I can't do that for you."

"Why not?"

"You're underage, for one. You're only allowed neural lace when you turn eighteen."

"Sixteen, if you have your guardian's permission."

Since when does the DarkDoc care about the rule of law?

"And … do you have it? Kate's permission?"

"No," says Silver. "Obviously. But she's a technosaur. The law should make allowances for that."

He chuckles. "You do have a point."

"Please," Silver says. "Please, Doc. I have the Blox."

He doesn't need to know how she got the bank in the first place.

"How can I say no to my favourite kid in the world?"

A spear of excitement runs through her body. "You'll do it?"

"I'll do it."

"Oh, thank you!"

"Not so fast," he says. "I'll make you a deal."

"I'll do anything," Silver says. "Anything."

"Come back when you're sixteen."

"But I am practically sixteen!"

"And bring your mother."

"But we've already said—she'll never agree to it!"

"Then you have some convincing to do."

Disappointment flows through her veins like cold ink.

"Ah, to be so young," he panther-purrs. "So impatient."

Damn it. Damn him. Damn everything. Silver's so disappointed she feels like crying. She stands up, ready to leave, her gas-mask dangling by her side.

"Chin up, Silver. I'll chat to her tonight. I'll help you to get her on board. I'll even book the operating room for tomorrow morning."

It's no use, thinks Silver. *Kate will never sign the consent.*

Morgan pushes a button, and a few seconds later there's a knock at the door. It's the man who let her into the clinic.

"Boss?"

"I'd like you to put this young lady into a cabbie, please, as we discussed earlier."

"I can do that myself," says Silver.

And I'm no lady.

"My treat," the DarkDoc says. "And this way you'll have company."

Silver looks at the time on her holodash. 20:00. She'll make it just in time for her curfew if she leaves now.

"You know where to take her?" asks Doctor Morgan.

"Yes, sir."

The door automatically closes behind Silver, and Morgan leans back against his swivel chair, puts his hands behind his head and thinks for a moment.

Beam Kate Lovell.

It rings three times, and then he hears her voice. Tense. The sound of her saying his name makes his thighs feel warm.

"Kate. Are you okay?"

"Define what you mean by 'okay'."

"We need to talk."

"I don't like the sound of that."

"Silver was just here."

A moment of shocked silence.

"What? Where?"

"Here, at the clinic."

"But … she's supposed to be the at the Atrium. She's always at the Atrium."

"I've put her in a SkinTech cab with one of my most trusted assistants. You'll see her soon."

"Have you been watching the newstream?"

There's a knock at the door. The nurse points at her wrist.

"I've had back-to-back appointments. Speaking of which, I need to go."

"You'd better have a look." She says. "And thank you … for sending Silver home."

"Sure. We still need to talk about her. About why she was here. I'll call you when I punch out."

"Thank you."

"Oh, and Kate—"

"Yes?"

"I don't know why I got this feeling … but … I think she knows about us."

CHAPTER 8

MILK&SILK

Seth's Apartment
Johannesburg, 2036

"Silver's safe." Kate mutes her mandible. "She's on her way to us right now."

"Thank the Net," says Seth.

Keke sighs. "So what do we know about this shitshow that's happening outside right now?"

More and more it seems to Kate that her reality is spinning out of control. The rate of evolution of everything is just too fast. How can anyone keep up? Is she even meant to keep up? Or is that a recipe for insanity? She has a pervading sensation that she doesn't feel safe. An everyday sense of menace hovers, a constant vicious vertigo, and she finds it difficult to believe she's the only one who feels this way.

Seth puts his hands together in a quiet clap, as if he's about to start telling a really good story. "There've been some incidents over the last few days. Random. Seemingly random, anyway."

"Incidents? Like what?"

"Little quirks. Small glitches. At first they didn't seem too sinister."

"Like what happened at MegaMall?" asks Keke.

"Exactly."

On Tuesday a mannequinbot started screaming at a customer in Milk&Silk. The customer said he did nothing to set it off, but the security footage later revealed that he had sexually assaulted her. Except they don't call it sexual assault when it happens to a robot. Interference, they say. He had interfered with the skinbot: had shoved his hand into her designer brassiere in broad daylight. Or artificial mall light, anyway. It's not a criminal offence—not yet—so he'll get away with his story, Kate is sure. After all, what is he expected to do when the goods are flaunted to brazenly? Surely the skin was asking for it, wearing that seductive get-up? And conveniently avoiding the fact that the whole reason for her existence is in fact to model lingerie, and that a 5.0 robot is incapable of 'asking for it'.

"He got off lucky," says Keke, perhaps referring to the DroidChef incident.

"The mannequin didn't," says Kate, picturing her naked body being carted back to the factory if she was lucky, and the recycling yard if she wasn't.

"And then the JungleRumble thing," says Seth.

"Hey?"

"It's under the Blanket. I assume they paid handsomely for that."

"Nah. The CEO is Mashini Wam's daughter."

The president's real name is Mashigo Amahle, but she has the reputation of getting inconvenient people taken care of, hence the nickname. *Umshini Wami* is the one apartheid resistance song that stayed long after the struggle was over. Loosely translated, it means 'my machine': the song is about a fighter calling for his machine gun.

"But seriously, that amusement park was just an accident waiting to happen. I mean, hopped-up kids and robotic wild animals? What could possibly go wrong?"

Kate winces. She's seen the ads showing adults and children alike putting their heads into lion's mouths like old-school circus lion tamers. Riding crocodiles in the river. Winding boa constrictors around their necks. "There're always so many kids there. I don't actually want to know."

"I do!" says Keke.

"Then you need to hack the Blanket."

"Where's a talented hacktivist when you need him?" says Kate, but when she sees Keke roll her eyes, she regrets the joke. She hasn't even asked her how Marko is lately. Or where he is. Or if she thinks he'll ever come back.

Seth smooths over the awkward pause in conversation. "Well, they've closed it till further notice. Pending enquiry and all of that. I'm sure the government will assign a 'task team' to investigate."

"Ha."

"So ... we're hoping that all these glitches are coincidence?" says Keke.

"There's no such thing as coincidence," Kate and Seth say, at the same time.

"When you look at the common denominators—" Seth fetches a glass from the kitchen cupboard and pours them all a whisky. "Then you'll see why this is a real problem."

"What are they? The common denominators?"

"Area, for one."

He projects a map of South Africa from his Scribe and red blisters emerge like a pox. Johannesburg is clearly the eye of the storm.

"Holy fuck," says Keke.

"And, more worryingly—"

"It's spreading," whispers Kate. More and more flags appear at the edges of the tornado. Fear is a yellow zip up her back.

"Yes, but that isn't what I was going to say."

"What's happening out there? What's causing it?"

"That woman who was killed at The Bent," says Seth, "that hand … belonged to the hotel porterbot."

Kate sees it happen again: the woman's crazed eyes and open mouth as the thing clawed at her leg. Porterbots are known for their strength, they're manufactured that way to perform their jobs easily.

Keke's breath is a whisper of terror. "It's AI."

Experts have been warning us for decades.

Enslave AI before it enslaves us.

They'd been lectured about the danger of embracing artificial intelligence without restraint or respect for as long as they can remember. Not by dodgy fringe-dwellers or city disconnects but by the most respected people in the field. The graphic refreshes itself, and a surge of new flags pops up like a Mexican wave.

CHAPTER 9
DRAGON SCALES

Innercity
Johannesburg, 2036

Silver is shown out the clinic. She puts her mask back on, and adjusts her breathing to the claustrophobic filter over her mouth. Her coat feels heavy on her shoulders. She should have known the DarkDoc wouldn't help her without Kate's consent. He's considered to be this renegade biotech specialist on the forefront of science, breaking rules all over the spectrum, but now Silver sees he's just like everyone else: a sheeple bleating the same tune as everybody fucking else. Why can't creeps think for themselves? She's so sick of it. Why can't she be eighteen already?

She's further enraged by the tears that spark her eyes.

Keep cool, Silver.

"Hey," says Dragon Scales.

He's hot in a bad-boy way.

She pulls her mask to the side again. "Hey yourself."

Sexy in a kind of grimy way that makes her feel a tingle of excitement in her pelvis.

He moves to open the cab's door, but stops as if something is just occurring to him.

"You wanna go somewhere?"

Danger strokes her neck.

"I shouldn't," she says.

"Why?" He laughs. "You have a curfew?" He opens the door.

"No," she fibs. "I just have to get back."

"I'll take you," he says, so she climbs in. "I'll take you anywhere you wanna go."

CHAPTER 10

ON ICE

12 YEARS PREVIOUSLY

ICE

Johannesburg, 2024

The security gate judders open and the navy van glides through, its tyres crackling on the tarmac. A guard acknowledges them with his palm as they pass. The sleek vehicle winds around the vast building and enters through a sliding turnstile at the back which elevates the van. They land up on the fifth floor. Once the ignition deactivates, Detective Ramphele turns his head to check on Zack.

"I'm still here," Zack says. "Did you expect me to have vanished?"

Ramphele snorts. "I've seen the footage. I know what you're capable of—I don't understand it, but I've seen it—and I'm not letting you out of my sight."

Of course Ramphele doesn't understand it. He doesn't have the neural capability. He's still 100% bio, as far as Zack can tell. It's like expecting a goldfish to think out of the bowl.

Zack wipes the perspiration from his palms. This arrest is a risky development, and his anxiety is interfering with his regular cool reasoning. Ramphele's got a vice-like grip on him. A wild dog with a bone. Zack's anxiety taps him on the shoulder, insisting that he needs to escape. So much hinges on the successful completion of his mission; a mission he knows is now in jeopardy.

Zack stares forward through the superblack tinted windows, his mind racing. "Where are we?"

"You'll see soon enough."

"You're putting me on ice," Zack says. The Innercity Crim Establishment is the place you stay while you're awaiting trial.

"You'll be lucky," says the detective.

"Lucky to be on ice?"

"Lucky to get a trial."

"So Nash was right, then," says Zack, more to himself than to the cop.

"Helena Nash was a kid-killer."

"She wasn't, though, and you would have known that if you had done your job and hadn't had a complete fucking farce for a trial."

Ramphele grunts.

"It was the trial she deserved," says the detective. "And you—"

The doors unlock after their mandatory two-minute security quarantine. The cop holds up his Tile: Zack's mugshot is front and centre. Next to the picture are 3D icons for various folders. As far as he can see, there is an icon for every one of his deceased clients. Ramphele swipes up to show scores and scores of files. A hundred, two hundred? Dead.

"You'll get the trial you deserve, too."

CHAPTER 11

AMPHIBIAN SUSPICION

Ramphele pushes Zack along by the small of his back; it is an intimate gesture. The entrance to the facility on this floor is modest, with just a hulking black gate that automatically opens after a dull buzzing sound comes from the adjacent security kiosk. Ramphele guides him through the hall and to the scabby timber reception desk that's pitted and tattooed with blue ink—a remnant from another era. No pens here anymore: A silicone stylus is less dangerous than a ball-point.

Never letting Zack out of his peripheral vision, the detective sigs a few holo-leaves and time-stamps them. The bored receptionist yawns them through.

The warden on admission duty is a woman taller than Zack and twice as built. The uniform is powder blue with an angular cut. Her eyes click into his and don't let go.

"So this is him," she says, curling the tip of her tongue over her bottom lip. Her tag reads WARDEN C BERNARD.

"Yebo," says Ramphele. "You ready for him?"

"Oh, yes." She slants her head as if to get a proper look at Zack. There's something cold in her eyes, something hard and shiny, as if her pupils are the point of something sharp: a kitchen knife or, more suitably given their surroundings, an ice-pick.

"Oh yes," Bernard says again, and he imagines her cracking her large knuckles, getting them punch-ready, even though her meaty hands are otherwise occupied. Her calves are solid; Zack guesses she's a walker. Bernard takes a plastic envelope from the detective then turns and pushes the pad of her finger up against the biometric access pad. An arrow lights up above the door.

"I'll call for details about the trial," says the detective.

"You do that," says Bernard. Ramphele looks on as the metal door and then a glass partition, slide open—a double mouth—and watches as the warden and Zack are swallowed up by the elevator.

Warden Bernard has a head of tight, wiry curls that she keeps gelled into submission. Her head is an army barracks of metal pins. She wears a choker with rivets that reminds Zack of a dog collar. Zack stares at the back of her neck as she turns away from him to select the relevant floor. Clammy. Her skin is too white. SPF100 junkie? Or because she spends her life in this prison. He guesses the latter. It lends her a slightly amphibian suspicion.

Zack breathes in deeply through his nose and sighs it out. How long will he be stuck here? Until a trial date is set. When will they decide that? Who knows.

The warden looks at him sharply. "Problem?"

He holds up his cuffed wrists. "More than one."

It's imperative to get on the warden's good side. Zack counts his lucky stars that he's reasonably good looking and that she's a woman. Never a guarantee, mind you, but it's a good start.

They get buzzed through the iron gate.

Christine Bernard collects Zack's ICE-branded prison clothes from a counter, and they walk down a corridor scraped by the thousands of reluctant heels before his. The door to his cell opens automatically, and Zack takes stock of where he'll be sleeping for the foreseeable future: iron bed, stained mattress, dog blankets, bare walls. He wonders off-hand if the absence of art and colour and natural light in prisons is a purposeful or accidental strategy to capture minds as well as bodies. Bernard further darkens the door.

Zack turns to her, and she tosses him his uniform; he catches the orange overalls on his chest, and wonders how many creeps had worn this particular outfit before him.

"Get undressed," she says. He expects her to leave, but she stands there, watching him.

He starts with his tie: unknotting the teal silk and placing it over the back of a chair, then opens his white-collared shirt, button by button. Bernard swats her palm with her baton like a metronome. It has a textured handle for better grip and an expandable, telescopic rod; sixteen inches of solid steel for extra striking power.

Zack unclips his belt, drops his pants, and reaches for the overalls.

"Everything," the warden says. She eats him with her eyes.

Zack hesitates. He doesn't want to wear prison-issue jox, and he certainly doesn't want to be completely naked in front of Bernard. Not because he minds being naked—he's usually rather a fan of nudity—but because it will give her too much power, too quickly.

She sees his hesitation and it hardens her face. Her fingers wrap around the hard steel.

"Everything."

CHAPTER 12

EVEN MY TOASTER IS INTELLIGENT

TWELVE YEARS LATER

Seth's Apartment

Johannesburg, 2036

Seth sets his Scribe to project the running news holo on the large white wall next to where they're standing. Echo.news is showing the hyperloop crash in slow motion.

"Speaker," he says, and the sound of the journalist's voice is amplified throughout the room.

"Mere hours ago we reported that these incidents were not linked. There was nothing to tie the Loop accident to The Bent Hotel murder. However, after consulting a panel of experts—"

"We approached you," says a man in a polka-dot bow-tie. His wiry hair and eccentric outfit make him look like an Andy Warhol-styled Einstein.

"Pardon me," says the journo, "I stand corrected. Dr Kirk called us to set up this piece."

Dr Kirk is sitting behind a desk, his fingers interlaced. His thumbs shoot up and he nods to acknowledge the journalist's apology. Kate gets the idea the doctor doesn't care who called whom, but it's his job to care about facts. His poker cap—a bright green visor with an open top—casts emerald light on his face, which makes Kate think of the Wizard of Oz, and the Tin Man who wanted a heart.

"Since chatting to Dr Kirk, we've changed our position."

The Echo.news ticker tape animates and winds around the room like the 1980s video game Snafu, an ever-extending pink snake flickering the death toll. The numbers keep changing colours.

CONFIRMED FATALITIES

HYPERLOOP: 612

BILCHEN SATELLITE DEPOT (SANDTON): 82

CARBON FACTORY: 39

PRINTADRINK: 14

JUNGLERUMBLE: 3

THE BENT HOTEL: 1

STREAM STUDIOS (DROIDCHEF): 1

MEGAMALL MILK&SILK: 0

When did the world get so utterly broken?

In 2028 more than half of the world's leaders were women. It seemed at the time more of a bitter, hard-won status rather than a triumph. And now it feels like a hollow victory, because really they were handed a poisoned chalice. It's as if the male leaders tossed them the keys to a car that broke down after having its engine fall out onto the highway during rush-hour traffic. The new strains of terrorism, the gummed-up rivers and noxious air. It's like inheriting a bomb that's about to explode and being expected to say thank you.

That's why seeing that old picture of the skinny polar bears is one of the saddest in history. Because at the time the picture was taken, it wasn't yet too late. So they can clone the bears now but where will they live? That's what happens when the polar ice melts and there are more plastic bottles than fish in the sea. That's what happens when humans think they're a superior life form.

And now this.

"Dr Kirk, can you tell us what your take is on these incidents? And what it could mean for the country? Are we facing a robot rebellion?"

Kirk's qualifications run along the bottom of his picture: Dr Kirk (Theoretical Physicist) CH, CBE, FRS, FRSA.

"We knew it would happen eventually, right?" says Keke. "A robot rebellion. The Singularity. I've watched enough sci-fi shorts to know the drill."

"Yes and no," says Seth. "This isn't either of those things, but that doesn't mean—"

"It's not a rebellion," says the scientist.

"Ha," says Kate. "Seth. How did you know?"

"How I know everything: maths."

Kate and Keke shrug at each other.

"Can you put my slide up?" says Kirk to the journalist, and he does so. It looks almost identical to Seth's map, but now has double the number of red flags.

"I've just come from an emergency meeting at NASP, and my associates and my hypothesis is that it's simply an update snag."

The journo pushes his blackrims up the bridge of his nose. "A snag?"

"Robots' codes are being constantly updated. We're exploring new territory all the time. It's hardly surprising that the odd upgrade has some … unexpected consequences."

"Dire consequences, in this case," says the journalist. "Rebellion or not, artificial intelligence is … Well, it's killing human beings."

"Indeed. Just because the spur is at a micro level we shouldn't be fooled into thinking that it's an insignificant problem. If we don't fix this fast, we'll be facing a potential global catastrophe."

'Robot Rebellion' disappears from the ticker tape slugs and is replaced by 'AI Update Malfunction'. It hardly has the same ring to it, but the fatalities keep ticking over, flashing hue after hue.

"How do we fix it?" The journalist's forehead has developed a sheen. "I mean, there must be something we can do?"

"Even my toaster is intelligent," Kirk says with a wry smile. "I mean, I can't even unplug the thing because nothing has cables anymore. Everything just flies through the air."

The journo shifts uncomfortably in his seat.

"I apologise," Kirk says, when he registers the horror on the man's face. "It's just that … well, it's just that we've fully integrated ourselves in this neuroreality where AI is as much part of our lives as our own DNA. And now, well …"

He shrugs. Does he need to point out the obvious?

"What are you saying, Dr Kirk?"

"What am I saying? That's it's already too late. We've walked into the mouth of the monster, and we did it willingly, with our eyes wide open."

"There must be something we can do."

The scientist shrugs. "I guess you can switch off your toasters, but—"

The journalist completes his sentence, "—but they can turn themselves back on again."

CHAPTER 13
REVENGE RE-TARGETING

"Your front door's not working," says a woman with a crisp British accent.

"Arronax." Seth envelopes her in an embrace that immediately makes it clear where she'll be sleeping tonight.

Keke's eye twitches.

"I thought you were in the Cape Republic?" says Kate.

Arronax always makes it clear that she doesn't like Joburg. She shakes her head and her hair changes colour from lavender to navy striped with black.

"I'm up for the *Biomimicry in Robotic Design* convention at the Lipworth Institute."

The Lipworth Institute is Johannesburg's answer to the Cape Republic's Nautilus. Founded and funded by an anonymous donor, it's the continent's premier robotics design outfit.

"I thought you already knew everything there was to know about biomimicry," says Keke.

"Arro's being humble. She's the whole reason for the convention. She was going to be the headline speaker."

"*Was* being the operative word." Arronax sighs. "Of course they'll cancel the whole thing now."

"Sorry you wasted a trip," says Keke.

Arronax casts a hungry look at Seth. "Not at all."

Seth fetches another glass and pours them all a generous shot.

"I need to be here, anyway, with what's going on. Attempt some damage control." Arronax takes a sip and pulls a face. She's not used to hard tack.

Seth motions for her to drink the rest. She's going to need it.

"This is probably the biggest setback I've ever encountered."

Kate laughs without mirth. "You're so English."

"What's that supposed to mean?"

"It's the beginning of the apocalypse, and we'll all probably be dead tomorrow, but you call it a 'setback'."

"Oh." Her cheeks colour. "It's hardly that bad, is it? I was preparing for my talk while I was on the plane. I switched off my news alerts."

"It's bad," says Seth.

"A couple of isolated incidents?" Hope is liquid in her eyes.

"You'd better sit down."

They watch a news update together, which includes new frightening clips that have been sent in from all over the city. Arronax's body seems to wilt with every story, and her face is as grey as tap water. A man was killed at a gym in Lonehill by the orbital stepper he was inside. A pregnant woman was run over by a Turing cab. A patient at the Gordhan died when the nursebot administered a lethal dose of pexidine. The clip shows the surgeon robots being rounded up and locked in the disused hospital chapel, and the human nurses whipping premature newborns from their smart incubators.

"Oh no," says Arronax, pale hands flying up to her face. "Oh no, no, no."

"Those poor babies." Kate can't even think about what will happen to them. It hurts too much.

Arronax begins weeping. They're all taken aback. Kate's never seen Arronax so much as tear up before. Now she's shaking and crying into her hands. Seth tries to comfort her, but she's so full of emotion she can't be touched.

"I'm sorry."

Still reeling from the picture of the newborns, Kate has tears in her eyes, too. "I'm sorry." What else can she say? Arronax's entire career—and her career is her life—wiped out in just a few hours. It's also a death of sorts.

"Can I see him?" she says to Kate, and for a second she thinks Arronax means Mally, but then her gaze skitters to the bag on the floor. Seth picks it up, lays in on the kitchen table, and Arronax tentatively zips it open. She runs her fingers over Bonechaser's damaged head. He smells like an electric storm.

"How is Mally?"

"Shaken up. Sad. He'll be okay."

He's been through worse.

Arronax starts crying again. She shakes her head, and her black highlights take over the rest of her hair (Raven Grief). Kate pours another round.

Arronax has spent the last ten years campaigning for #RoboRights, a charter to ensure that bots of any kind are afforded basic entitlements like the right to say 'no', and to protect themselves from harm. Her dogged determination ensured the Nancies' approval of a law that criminalised violence against robosapiens, and her latest project is pushing a bill that'll allow AI of any kind to refuse a human's instructions if it goes against their inherent moral code, and/or cause harm to any bot or living being.

It was her idea to add a circulatory system to the latest generation of robosapiens. Perhaps if they could bleed like humans, was her thinking, then they'd be treated more humanely. Unfortunately, it backfired.

Arronax came up against massive resistance. Creeps are scared by how very human-like the latest generation of automatons are, and giving them rights just seems to be a step too far. When Nautilus revealed that the new version of androids—7thGen like Vega—would have warm blood, it caused protests all over the country. Where do you draw the line, between humans and robots? Arronax says: Why does there need to be a line at all? The future could be a peaceful and mutually beneficial co-existence, with droids becoming more human, and humans absorbing more tech. Soon there wouldn't need to be a distinction at all. She covered this issue in her latest interview on ANDROID NATION which was widely disseminated on social media and taken out of context in various AI hate-groups. The alt-tech nazis just shared the *"why does there need to be a line at all?"* clip, making some people so riled up that they had beamed her death threats. One man in particular seems obsessed with Arronax and likes to leave poisoned easter eggs for her in all her favourite places. Revenge re-targeting. Not even augmented reality is safe anymore.

Arronax sniffs and pours herself another shot, and downs it. Pulls her seawater cardigan closed as if she is pulling herself together too.

"All right." She wipes aqua-glitter from her eyelids. "Best we come up with a plan."

CHAPTER 14

DEAD CITY SUNBEAMS

Innercity
Johannesburg, 2036

Dragon Scales starts the car. The headlights illuminate the narrow city street, sending the rats scampering. One rat stays perched on top of a dumpster, too hungry or old to care about the ignition of a hydrocar, or the shock of the bright light. He looks straight at them, eyes pinpricks of glow-in-the dark green, whiskers twitching as he nibbles whatever it is he's holding in his hands.

"Tell me about yourself," the man says.

He means, Silver is sure, what's a girl like her doing in a place like this.

They drive past more dumpsters, and more scattering rats, and then past the old sardine-tin security complexes overtaken by squatters and feral woodland creatures. Since the Seasian craze of Forest Critters lit up the local pet scene, the city has a wild animal problem. Foxes, raccoons and squirrels were brought in by unscrupulous animal dealers and sold as sterilised pets, and no one caught on until they were all expecting their first litters. To add to the population explosion (and confusion), sub-crazes streaked in: the sales of bio-identical robotic forest animals shot through the roof, and, more bizarrely, so too did the fad of dye-grooming your cat or dog to look like the original Critters. It's best to not look too closely while driving: Roadkill smears the city streets.

"You tell me first," says Silver.

"What do you want to know?"

"We could start with names. You could tell me your name," she says.

"Names are just a social construct to box people in. I don't believe in names."

Silver guffaws. "You don't believe in names?"

"Not ones that other people have given me."

"Okay …"

"You don't think it's crazy that you live your whole life by the name someone else—who didn't even know you at the time—gave you?"

"It's just a name."

"It's never just a name."

"So what do I call you then?"

"You can call me whatever you like. What were you calling me in your head before we started this conversation?"

Silver hesitates.

"Come on, there must have been something."

"Dragon Scales."

Now it's his turn to laugh.

"Dragon scales. I love it. Do you see? Now we have something more than we had a minute ago. A connection. An agreement. It's so much better than just handing out a random tag that you'd probably forget by tomorrow."

"What will your name be for me?" asks Silver.

He narrows his eyes at her, as if sizing her up. "I haven't decided yet."

"But what were you calling me before?"

"I was calling you 'Kid'," he says. "But that's not right."

"I like it, though," says Silver.

"You like being called a kid?"

"I like it when *you* call me 'Kid'."

"I've got it." He looks at her hair. "Kid Silver."

"That's funny—" she says, about to tell him her real name.

"It was a brilliant band in the late nineties." He scrolls through his Scribe. "I'll play some for you."

"The nineties? Christ, how old *are* you?"

Music fills the car. Twisted rhythm, and subtle layers of drum loops and orchestration. Innocent and sophisticated at the same time.

"Dead City Sunbeams. Electric Sky. It's fucking perfect for you."

Silver can feel the music pulse through her body, a new beat of excitement swelling the inside of her chest.

"Yes," she says, relaxing into the sound. "It's perfect."

A few tracks in, they pass a stuttering solar-sign that says 'DISTRICT 12'. It used to be the meat-packing district, when creeps thought it was still okay to butcher animals for food. Silver shudders, thinking of the pictures she's seen of skinned cow carcasses hanging from hooks. The casual way the men worked on the corpses with heavy cleavers, as if they were cutting timber instead of previously sentient flesh and bone. Bodies traced with nerves, brains spiked with panic. On the heels of the vegan revolution the blood-stained concrete floors gave way to cotton and synthsilk: a bustling fashion district. Bustling, that is, until new clothes became unfashionable, and the industry caved in on itself. New businesses are hesitant to move into the area now, suspicious and/or superstitious, and the city doesn't want to change the sign again. Now it's just called District 12.

Silver's feeling drugged by the strange new music and the novelty of being in a car with a handsome man who keeps looking at her. It's almost like being in one of her RPGs. Why does he keep looking at her? There's something happening. Something he's not telling her. The car takes a right turn, which will drive them further into the CBD. They should have gone left.

"This isn't the way to my home," she says.

Dragon Scales keeps his eyes on her. "I know."

They park in the street, outside a warehouse. He opens the door and as Silver steps out she's assaulted by the stink of the city. She puts on her gas-mask then takes his proffered hand. It's warm. He leads her around the corner, looks both ways, then opens a door camouflaged by a realistic mural of the same smoky brix that make up the rest of the building. Sometimes she thinks of this city as an underground labyrinth: There is the day-time trade and pedestrian city, monochrome, with dots of colour where informal traders sell fruit and junk chips and grey tech, and then there is the underbelly, the mass of narrow alleys and secret doors and underground tunnels. A dark parallel universe. A shadow city.

Silver hesitates outside the door. She has a feeling that if she crosses the threshold there will be some kind of huge consequence, some point of no return. Her nerves light up her stomach and her face, so that she feels as if she's glowing. Not a pretty glow, but a radioactive shine. What is she doing here in this strange place with this strange man? Her clock ticks 21:12. Kate will be starting to worry now. She needs to get home. She needs to get back in the car and get home as soon as possible.

The dragon scales sparkle. His skin feels so good. He has this magnetic pull she's never felt before.

She needs to get home.

She needs to see where he's taking her.

She'll be sixteen soon. Silver's on a cusp, a precipice. If there is a time to turn your life upside down, surely it is now?

CHAPTER 15

PRISONS NEVER SLEEP

12 YEARS PREVIOUSLY

ICE

Johannesburg 2024

Zack starts as he hears a shuffling sound at the door. It's pitch black. As his eyes adjust to the darkness, he can hear the groaning and thudding of the building's innards. Prisons never sleep.

The sound that woke him, real or imagined, pulled him from a dream of another life where he was free. He tries to grab on to the coattails of that dream, tries to make his way back to the light and colour and warmth of the parallel reality, but there's another sound at the door, and Zack knows it's Bernard again. The knowledge sets off a fizz of foreboding inside his stomach.

The door slides open and she floats inside. Stronger than her silhouette is her smell—perhaps a residue of bodywash—cucumber and mint, and something else that he can't name. Dog saliva. Yoghurt. Some kind of curdled dread, or is that his own body, reacting to hers?

She doesn't say anything. Bernard just stands there and watches him sleep.

CHAPTER 16

PIRATE. DESPOILER. BANDIT

Every morning there is a strict routine of exercise at the ICE. It doesn't matter if your muscles are cramping from lying on the nibbled rubber slab they call a mattress, or if you can hardly keep your sleep-deprived eyes open because of the yelling and snoring and swearing that is the 24/7 soundtrack in the hard, cold cells. It doesn't matter if you're healthy or ill, if you drink your three daily nutrishakes or if you're on a hunger strike. You do the exercise.

You strip down to your orange jox and climb into the Orb. The first time you do it, you worry about coming out alive. After that, it gets easier. The holistic fitness machine scans your body and your brain for the exercise that will most benefit you. It identifies Zack's weakest group of muscles—his lower back—and coaches him through various strength training exercises. The Orb knows the drills can get boring, so its additional features can exercise your mind too. Mini holo crossword puzzles and maths games. Slitherlinks. Memory contests. KenKen, Skyscrapers, Futoshiki, Hitori, Nurikabe. Unfortunately, the mental features are shut off for prisoners like him. They want his body to be strong, to complete the work they'll soon employ him to do in the penal labour camps, but they want his brain to be as dull as seaglass.

"Your lawyer's here," says Lovemore, the guard with the lazy eye.

Heady relief melts Zack's muscles. He gives his hands and face a quick shot of cold water, jumps into his overalls, then offers his wrists to the guard to cuff.

Thank fuck, thank fuck, thank fuck, is all he can think as he's led towards the admin wing. At last, someone who will be on his side. Someone who can get him out of this fuck-forsaken nightmare so that he can get on with his job.

The interview room is about as depressing as his cell, but it's a different kind of depressing, which he appreciates. As he sits down, a man arrives, and a new tension chills the room. Zack stares at the interloper's well-tailored suit with something close to envy. Of course, he knows the feeling is not about the suit at all, but a kind of nostalgic pang for the life he used to have—the life he'll never have again. The man approaches the table and offers Zack his palm. Zack doesn't take it. No one shakes hands anymore, especially not with a dangerous serial killer. Isn't that what he's supposed to be? Isn't that why he's in here?

The man retracts his hand and smiles to paper over the sudden awkwardness.

"Mpanghi," he says.

"Excuse me?"

"My name."

Mpanghi sits down, pretends to relax, and interlaces his fingers over the beginning of a potbelly.

"That couldn't have been easy," says Zack.

"What?"

"In school. Your name."

"Ha!" he says, and looks around. He wasn't expecting a laugh. His mirth surprises him. "You're right. It wasn't easy."

uMpanghi: Pirate. Despoiler. Bandit.

"Suits you, though," says Zack.

The man stops smiling.

Zack turns to the guard. "This isn't my lawyer."

Lovemore blinks at him.

"But I am," Mpanghi says. "I am your lawyer. Appointed by the state."

Zack stands up. "There's been a misunderstanding."

"Sit down, Prisoner," says Lovemore.

"I don't need a state-appointed attorney. I have my own lawyer. Detective Ramphele said he would be called."

"Ramphele no longer works for the SAP."

"I don't care about Ramphele, I just want my lawyer. My real lawyer."

Lovemore breathes through his mouth, scratches his cheek with slender fingers. "I don't know anything about that."

"Well," says Zack, taking a step forward, "that's not a problem. Just let me contact him. All it'll take is one call."

"You don't have phone privileges," he says.

Zack swallows his frustration. "Can *you* call him for me?"

When Lovemore looks uncertain, he adds, "I'll pay you more than what you make here in a year."

"That won't be necessary," says Mpanghi.

"You're new here. You don't know what's necessary."

"You don't have banking privileges, either," says Lovemore.

"My lawyer will arrange that. My real lawyer."

Mphangi's eyes crinkle in a false smile. "I'm afraid that's not how it works."

There's something sinister about the man. Zack felt it immediately as he entered the room, thought it was maybe nerves from being cloistered for so long but, no, there's definitely something menacing about him.

"What the fuck does that mean?"

Lovemore says, "It means that just because you're rich, doesn't mean you get to call the shots. Doesn't mean you get special treatment."

"Used to be rich," says Mpanghi.

Zack looks at him. "What did you say?"

"Your accounts have been frozen, pending the outcome of the trial."

"They can't do that."

"They have, already. Don't worry, you'll get it all back ... If you're innocent."

"And if they find me guilty?"

"Your money goes into the pot. You'll be paying for other criminals' trials. But don't worry, once they've enlisted you at one of the crim colonies, you'll be able to start earning bank again. Pray that you get into the space mining programme... I've heard that one pays the best."

It also has the highest fatality rate.

"It's against the constitution." Zack's chest blooms with anxiety. The money was going to be his ticket out of here. This isn't going according to plan.

Mpanghi and Lovemore look at each other and laugh without smiling.

"Haven't you heard? The Nancies keeps changing the constitution."

"Change it every day, like dirty underwear."

"Last week it was the *Amakwerekwere* ban. This week, well, your timing is very bad," says the lawyer. "The Criminal Asset Seizure Act was signed ... last night. It was hardly contested in parly and I can't say I disagree with the tenets. I mean, why should wealthy people be able to get the best lawyers? Hardly seems fair. Now you'll all get equal treatment." He strokes his oiled beard; his eyes rest on Zack. "I mean, a murderer is a murderer, right?"

CHAPTER 17
DOUBLE DECEPTION

12 YEARS LATER

Johannesburg, 2036

Silver is pulled along a dim passageway plastered with old-school bumper stickers, graffiti and chewing gum. Over and over again she sees the letters QE. QE. QE.

"QE?"

"Question Everything," says Dragon Scales.

At the very end she recognises a sticker of an image she grew up with: a neon bunny. Seth would always point them out to her and Mally, when they'd spot them on a park hoverbench or a skateboard ramp.

That's Alba, he used to say, and tell them the story of the DNA-spliced rabbit in the lab. Silver named her cuddle bunny after him, and still secretly sleeps with the threadbare plush tucked into the angle of her elbow, her lips on his balding head.

"That's Alba," she says now, pointing to the sticker, and DS smiles.

They go further and deeper and Silver tries to remember the way but after the first few turns, her mind blanks, and her nerves start zinging again.

What the fuck am I doing?

As if reading her thoughts, he turns to her and says: "Almost there."

They reach another door, and he uses his fingerprint to unlock it. The fluorescent lights detect their motion and flicker on, overhead. It's a double volume room that looks like a disused operating theatre. Cheap white tiles everywhere, scratched and scuffed from years of scrubbing and harsh chemicals. Dusty now, smirched, with sinister black grouting. Pushed up against the walls are old OR spotlights and metallic trays; medical cabinets; IV hooks. Silver is sure she's still green. She starts to sweat.

Dragon Scales pulls a vintage dentist's chair into the centre, then shuttles the overhead spotlight next to it, switches it on, to test it. The bright light hurts Silver's eyes, and she looks away.

"This isn't what I was expecting."

Her voice comes out dull and flat: the room is soundproofed.

A tiny red light glows from the corner of the door, indicating that its locked.

"Don't worry, it's perfect for what we need to do."

Silver's insides have liquefied; at least, that's what it feels like.

"I can see you're nervous," says Dragon Scales. "I don't want you to worry."

Silver slowly steps backwards and knocks over a metal bowl. It clatters and rings on the tiles. "Let me out of here."

"Let me explain."

The hairs on her neck stand up. "I don't want you to explain. I want to get the fuck out of here."

"Why don't you sit down?" He motions at the chair and switches off the spotlight.

"I'll scream," she says, but they both know there is no point.

"There's no need—" he begins, but is interrupted by a shuffling sound at the door.

The small LED switches to green, and Silver breaks for it, but just before she gets there, another man comes in and she almost crashes into him.

"Whoa!" he says, catching her.

"Let me out!" Silver shouts, but the door swings on its hinges and closes softly, and the red light comes back on.

"Whoa!" he says, letting her go. "What the fuck, man?"

"Thank you for coming," says Dragon Scales. "We're almost ready for you. Kid Silver, this is Doctor Smith."

How stupid does he think I am?

Doctor Smith. A double deception, in just two words.

The man seems nervous. "She's just a little girl."

"She'll be sixteen soon."

"I don't know, man." He rubs his ear and then his neck.

"We have a deal," says DS. "Right?"

"I don't know," he says. "I mean, she's so young. Look at her. And I'm not even really a—"

DS interrupts him. "It's a simple procedure, you'll do fine."

'Smith' hunches over in his defeat, and pulls a roll of starched black fabric out of his shoulder bag. He loosens the tie and unrolls it onto a stainless steel tray, revealing surgical implements that glint in the harsh light.

Silver starts to scream. She runs for the door, pounding on it and shouting for help. From behind, Dragon Scales slaps a hot hand over her mouth and shoots a tranqtaser into her neck. The current travels down her limbs, a long, hot shock, and is followed by the warmth of the tranquilliser. It melts her. Silver's body wants to soften all the way to the floor, but Dragon Scales holds her up, carries her to the chair and secures her wrists and feet with the big brown leather straps and copper buckles. He switches the spotlight back on, momentarily blinding her, then angles the light so it's shining on her silver hair. She's woozy with the fear and the drugs; she wants to kick and fight, but her body is a warm, wet sponge.

DS holds something to her head, some buzzing thing, and with the vibration she feels her hair being shaven. A streak of white falls to the floor. She thinks he'll shave her whole head, but he stops at that one line just left of centre, where she used to part her hair. DS fastens a leather strap to her forehead now too. Silver tries to talk, to beg, but even her mouth is paralysed. DS spends a moment caressing her head, her cheek.

"There's nothing to be afraid of," he says, then holds her hopeless hand. "I know it seems scary, but this is the quickest and easiest way. We're not going to hurt you."

Silver's face is frozen; her tongue is numb. All she can manage is a throaty groan.

What has she done what has she done what has she done—

A tear runs down her temple.

Smith's face moves away, then pops up again, holding a mediquill.

"Anaesthetic," he warbles, then jams it into the tender crook of her arm. "Count down from ten."

The scalpel is out now and misted with antiseptic spray. The same spray is cool on her strip of bare scalp. Silver resists counting, but colour-numbers come to her anyway, and float before her. Rainbow sprinkles on soiled bandages. Spinning scalpel cupcakes. 10, 9, 8 … and then they fade to black.

CHAPTER 18

SHORN AND STITCHED

Dragon Scales watches as the med school drop-out applies the dressing to Silver's shorn and stitched scalp. He checks her vitals. Her body is twitching with stress, but she's alive. He touches her cheek, snaps his fingers in her face.

"Silver?" *snap, snap.* "Silver?"

She gasps as if drowning, her back arches and her eyes open and roll back.

"Can you hear me?"

A long, desperate gasp for air, then her body seems to relax. She lists backwards on the chair and her eyes close again.

"Is she okay?" DS asks Smith. "Is that normal?"

Smith shrugs. "What's normal? I told you I've never done this before."

Dragon Scales checks her pulse again, and it seems steady. He touches his mandible to place the call. "It's done."

A woman replies, "Good. Bring her in."

CHAPTER 19
SKIN ZIP

Seth's Apartment
Johannesburg, 2036

Mally switches off his cinescreen and gingerly climbs out of bed. Standing makes his upper thigh throb like a motherfucker. He gives his worst injury a quick inspection—it's already healing, thanks to the stem-cell skin zip—and limps towards the kitchen. He stops short when he hears Kate's terse voice.

"Fuck," says his mother. She doesn't like it when *he* swears, but her mouth is one of the foulest he knows. So much for modelling the behaviour you expect from your kids. There's other stuff too, that she does. He doesn't blame her, though. No one said having a baby made you perfect. And in his case, well, she didn't even give birth to him, so all bets are off.

"What are we going to do?" That's Keke talking.

"Get out before the panic sets in," says Seth.

"Out?"

"Out of the city. Out of AI's reach."

What the hell are they talking about?

"Out of AI's reach? That doesn't even exist."

"The longer we stand here talking about it, the less chance we have of getting out alive."

Mally stares at a poster on his wall. It's a vintage one, a gift from Uncle Marko. It's a

2D cartoon of a Bender from Futurama, and the robot's saying: *Being a robot is great, but we don't have emotions, and sometimes that makes me very sad.*

"But where?" demands Kate. "And how will we live? What will we eat?"

"You know what I mean. Away from any kind of machine that can harm the kids. Besides, what will we eat if we stay here? It's not like the Bilchen Meal drones are going to keep delivering."

"Oh," says Kate, anxiety turning her voice to gravel.

"What's wrong? Kate? It looks like you're about to pass out."

"The kids. Silver. Silver's out there somewhere. Morgan put her in a cab, but that was over an hour ago."

Mally's never heard Seth so worried. "It's past her curfew. Silver never misses her curfew."

"What if she's—"

"She's still not answering her mandible."

"We have to go get her."

"What about Mally? We can't leave him here."

"There's no way he's going out there."

"Shit. What about Vega?"

"He's never seeing her again."

Mally starts tip-toeing backwards, away from the kitchen. He doesn't know what's going on—not yet—but there's no way he's not going to see Vega again. He'd rather die than never see her again. She is his soulmate, his best friend. Some people say that robots don't have souls—some even try to criminalise human/bot relationships—but Mally knows that's not true. Seventh-generation androids have got exactly the same proficiency for love as any bio person. Flesh and blood doesn't make you human, that's for sure. That's what he's seen over and over again in his sixteen years. It's what struck him into existence and what almost bashed him out of it again. Vega has as much vital force as any non-droid he knows. They love each other so much it hurts—well, it hurts him, anyway, deeply and achingly—and there's no way Kate's paranoia is going to come between them.

Seth's Vektor is abandoned on the sideboard. Usually Seth's so careful with storing the gun: Mally's never seen it lying around before. He is obviously more upset with the Bonechaser incident than he lets on. He blinks back tears. He won't think about the dog now, he can't; there'll be time for him to mourn later.

He takes the availability of the Vektor as a sign, clips the weapon onto his utility belt and covers it with his shirt. He's reversed all the way to the front door now, which is still on the blink, allowing him a quick and soundless exit.

CHAPTER 20

A NORMAL KIND OF MIDNIGHT

Mally's about to step into the elevator when he gets a bad feeling.

"Good evening," says the speaker inside the intelligent metal cube.

Best to stay away from anything with smarts, he decides, remembering his mother's tense conversation with the others. As he takes the stairs, he thinks of Silver, and his nerves gnaw at him. He should be trying to find her too, but he needs to keep his eye on the ball. He'll find Vega first, then they'll figure out the rest. Besides, his mother and Seth will probably go out to get Silver, that's what it sounded like. She's probably safe at the Atrium, anyway. Probably forgot to set the timer on her immersion and now she's missed curfew. Unusual for her, he reflects, as he gets a new lining of dread in his stomach. Silver knows that if she misses her curfew she'll be grounded for a week. She's so obsessed with gaming Eden 7.0 that a week without playing will kill her.

The other kids in their virtual class treat Silver differently. Well, they treat them both differently, but for different reasons. Mally because he's the only surviving Genesis kid, and also because of his controversial relationship with Vega. But they kind of revere Silver. It could be because of her eccentric appearance (beautiful, white-haired, bird-boned), her attachment to that grimy gas-mask, or her mad gaming skills. Or it could be because of her bionic finger, and the story that comes with it. The Net knows the kids like to tell that story. He's heard a thousand variations, each one more outlandish than the last, but Mally thinks people feel weird around her mostly due to the feeling you get when she walks into the room, even if it's a virtual room. It's like she has an air of electricity about her. Like there's static in the air. He used to think he was the only one to feel this way, thought maybe it's because they're twins (or kind-of twins) but now he sees it on other people's faces too. A kind of surprise, a curiosity, that she arouses wherever she goes.

She's always had it, her point of difference, whatever it is. He remembers people's reactions to her when she was a child, but with puberty it's been magnified. Intensified. The kids in class who are also into the Atrium Games say that the other players call Silver 'Ghost'.

Mally reaches the bottom of the stairs and his leg feels as if it's on fire. He roots in his pocket for the analgesic inhalant, sucks out a dose, and hobbles out of the front entrance, thankful that the biometric pad is still working, and stands on the hot pavement. It's almost midnight, but it's 36 degrees Celsius.

Coolvest.

His cooling shirt immediately temps him down. He puts on his facemask and swipes the ads out the way to check his newstream. Nothing cosmic seems to be happening in the headlines:

Shini Wam signs off New Nuke deal.

Mars shuttle still missing.

Have you got your flu sticker?

Roguebots vs Bot-Hunters: A Tipping Point.

The Orbital Space Junk Clean-Up Needs Your Help.

Crim Colonies profit up 17%.

Are your smart drugstax killing you?

Killer Porterbot; DroidChef; Hyperloop: What Really Happened?

Universal Basic Income is finally here!

So maybe whatever the parental units were panicking about isn't as serious as they think. Indeed, as people walk and airskate around him, it looks like any normal kind of midnight in Jozi. He stands for a second longer, wondering which tram to climb aboard. The Atrium is twelve blocks east. Vega's hostel is in the opposite direction. Is Silver really in danger? Probably not. Or at least that's what he tells himself, despite his nagging intuition, as he catches a westbound and heads into the smartificial sect of ChinaCity/Sandton.

CHAPTER 21

MISTER GALAXY

12 YEARS PREVIOUSLY

ICE

Johannesburg 2024

Zack uses the mean bar of prison-issue soap to draw on the bag-washed brix of his cell. He uses the whole wall opposite his metal bunkbed as his canvas, and only manages to get the outlines done before running out of soap—a loose-lined sketch of a blooming lotus flower. He likes that it's almost invisible.

It's the best use of the soap he can think of: to add something pretty to look at. Something that embodies beauty and potential and hope because, the Net knows, there's none of that in here. More importantly, it's his daily reminder of The Truth, why he's here, and what he still needs to do. Zack stands there in his small grey cell and looks at the flower. Imagines it blooming and arching and then crumbling away to nothing.

I'm here to wake up the Lotus Eaters.

The arrest has temporarily derailed his plan, but there is always a way forward, and it's imperative that he keeps his nerve.

The small soap lozenge is one of those maddening details he's glad he's now rid of. They give you a pillow-case, but no pillow, a window with no view, and a piece of cheap soap with no water. He can't yet tell if it's lack of attention to detail or, in a more sinister vein: a welcome mat to the house of insanity. Sometimes he feels, psychologically speaking, as if they're giving him just enough rope to hang himself with.

He hears a whistle from outside. Lazy-eyed Lovemore. He knows without a doubt because Lovemore is the only guard who warns you before he enters. He's usually whistling a kind of musty gospel tune. Maybe he thinks prisoners deserve a modicum of privacy, or maybe the whistling is like his protective charm, to shield himself from walking in on cell mates doing things he doesn't want to see.

The door opens, and the guard motions for Zack to follow him.

Lovemore's not his favourite, but at least it's not Bernard.

The light hurts Zack's eyes; he blinks away the burn. "Where're we going?"

"Didn't they tell you?"

They walk down corridors and up stairs and on conveyor belts until Zack loses his sense of direction. It doesn't help that there are no windows and no natural light to gauge the scope of the sun. He wants to think that his lawyer, his real lawyer, has somehow managed to break through the red tape, or that the charges against him have been dropped, but he can't help but have a bad feeling. Everything about this place seems underhanded, opaque. Helena Nash told them so, said they had sped through her trial with one goal only, and that was to put her away forever.

They reach the courtroom, which is already populated by the jury and a sprinkling of press. He inspects the journalists' faces one by one, searching, hoping, for Keke. Surely she would attend? At best, to support him, at worst, to see him grilled and found guilty. But even that, he'd prefer over this: not one familiar face in the crowd.

"It's happening now?" he asks Lovemore. "The trial? Already?"

"You're never happy, you crims," he says, "nag, nag, nag for a speedy trial and then when you get one, you complain. We can't keep you on ICE forever, you know."

Yes, Zack knows. ICE costs the state cash, while the crim colonies pretty much print money. They don't want creeps to stay here for one day longer than absolutely necessary.

"But we don't even have a strategy, yet."

"You had the opportunity to liaise with Mr Mpanghi."

"You're kidding."

He's not kidding.

"That wasn't a meeting. That was an ambush."

Lovemore shrugs. "You weren't very co-operative for a man being offered free legal counsel."

"I haven't even shaved. I'm in prison overalls."

His bright orange suit screams 'dangerous criminal' and he has itchy, three-day stubble. His hair is greasy and his eyes are underlined by dark crescents.

"Don't worry about it, pretty boy, this isn't Mister Galaxy. You're not getting judged on your looks."

Zack knows very well that everyone, everywhere, is always pre-judged on their looks, and he knows for a fact that at the moment he looks exactly how they want him to look: like a degenerate serial killer.

Lovemore leads him to his seat in the front row of the gallery, next to Mpanghi, who nods to acknowledge his presence.

"Do you have a plan?" Zack whispers.

"Of course." He smiles: an ebony Cheshire cat.

Zack searches the gallery again for Keke.

The trio of judges trails in, and everybody stands. Zack doesn't recognise any of them.

His charge sheet is read aloud, and the corner-mounted cameras record the muted exclamations from the crowd behind him. The anchor reels off every victim's name, one by one, so that the jury can feel the mass accusation like a heavy stole on their shoulders. It's their job, is the clear, unspoken message, to secure justice for these people. The jurors take turns to cast suspicious glances at him, their minds perhaps already made up.

The anchor finally gets to the end of his list: 108 counts of premeditated murder. There's a hushed moment, an opportunity to let the gravitas of the charges against him sink in, and then the head judge claps his hands and says "Well! Let us begin."

CHAPTER 22

BREAD & CIRCUSES

TWELVE YEARS PREVIOUSLY

ICE

Johannesburg, 2024

Every day when Zack is brought to the courthouse, he looks for Keke, and every day he's disappointed. Surely, surely one day she'll show? It starts to feel like an unrequited love affair of the criminal variety. Every day he slumps further into despair. He hasn't had a shower or a decent night's sleep in weeks. He's haunted every night by the looming silhouette of Bernard. He lies awake, waiting for her to arrive, and when she does—she always does—then he lies there listening to her breathe while adrenaline combs his nerves and keeps him awake long after she leaves.

Why does Bernard stalk him? Why does she watch him sleep? Does she know who he really is?

Impossible.

He's begged Lovemore for something, anything to read, to stop the slow atrophying of his brain. It's one of the most difficult things about being in here. He can deal with no showers, no company—and lately, no toothbrush—but with no sleep and nothing to read he will surely go insane. Every day in this place is a step closer to delirium.

Mphangi subtly sniffs the air, then moves an inch away from Zack. He doesn't blame him. He'd move away from himself if he could. Far away. Perhaps if he thinks about the metaphysical hangman's noose they're extending to him hard enough it will materialise. Something like Schrödinger's Cat. Schrödinger's Noose?

Stand up! Stand up! Observe!

Zachary Girdler is both alive and dead at the same time.

"When can I take the stand?" he asks Mphangi.

The pirate's eyebrows shoot up. "You're not taking the stand."

"Won't they want my testimony? Won't they need to ask me questions?"

He shakes his head.

"What if I want to say something?"

"What would you say?"

"I could prepare a speech. In my defence."

"This isn't *Law & Order*."

"Mpanghi. I need to get the hell out of here."

"Just let me do my job."

"But you're not doing your job! That's the problem. We just sit here all day watching the prosecutor paint me into a a corner."

"You need to trust in the judicial process."

Zack doesn't even know why he's arguing. It's not like he can tell the truth about what he does, anyway. Maybe he thinks that without any hard evidence—because he knows none exists—they won't be able to convict him. But no one seems to mind this minor detail. In fact, he gets the feeling that most of the time these people aren't even listening. He has his suspicions that one of the junior judges hasn't heard a word of the trial—Zack saw his earbuttons in, and his right foot is always tapping—and the day-dreaming jury don't seem to require any further convincing of his guilt. He can tell from their dagger glares that they were against him from day one.

The prosecutor comes to the end of his examination, and thanks the witness. The woman rises to leave the stand.

"Aren't you going to cross-examine?" Zack whispers.

Mpanghi shrugs, wrinkles his nose. *Nah,* his body language says. *Nah.* As if someone's offered him a tepid cup of tea.

"Next witness!" calls the head judge, and Zack can't help but imagine that he's treading some Kafka-flavoured Möbius strip, a Lewis Carrol trial where everyone's crazy and no one seems to mind. "Next witness!" says judge, but he may as well be shouting "Off with his head!"

What was that quote about bread and circuses? Zack wishes he could remember it, because he thinks it might just sum up exactly what's happening here.

CHAPTER 23

A FUCKING LUCKY PACKET

Lovemore is whistling outside Zack's cell again. Zack stops what he's doing—adding scratch detail to his lotus flower mural by using a small nail he pried from his prison-issue boots—and hides the tack inside a tiny slit inside his mattress.

The door opens, and Lovemore stops mid-tune and greets him in a celebratory manner.

"Prisoner!" Lovemore's never once called him by his name. Do they teach that in guard training, to keep the detainees at a distance? Will he get a number when he's taken to the crim colonies, concentration camp style? It should do a good job of further dehumanising him in the penal scouts' eyes. Maybe Zack is being paranoid. Maybe Lovemore's just not good with names.

Zack expects the guard to admonish him for drawing on the wall, or say something demoralising like, "They're just going to paint over that as soon as you're out of here, you know," or "Get scrubbing, Prisoner!" or maybe worse, but he acts as if he hasn't seen it at all. As if he hasn't seen it grow from a barely invisible soap sketch to a massive toothpaste and boot-polish shaded 3D-looking bloom.

"Jury's out!" says Lovemore, who is clearly having a good day.

"What?"

"Get your stuff, Prisoner. It's moving day!"

"But we didn't even conclude the trial. We haven't heard all the testimony. What kind of trial is over in three days?"

"A successful one," says Lovemore.

Zack almost chokes. "Successful for who?"

The guard shows him his big white teeth. "For everyone."

Mpanghi has a similar attitude. "Very good," he says, when he sees Zack. "A very good trial."

Zack's fuse is lit. "The fuck do you mean? It's been an absolute sham."

"The quicker the trial, the less expensive it is for the people. We all knew the outcome from the beginning, didn't we? There's really no point in dragging these things out."

The judges enter and everyone stands, then sits down again. Zack remains upright.

"Have you reached a verdict?" asks the head judge.

A juror with long white braids stands and says, "We have, your Honour." She clicks a button on the remote she's holding and their jury score is projected onto the evidence cinescreen.

Twelve red men. Twelve out of twelve. A dirty dozen.

"*Eish!*" Mpanghi looks impressed. "Full marks!".

Zack grits his teeth, curls his hand into a fist.

Do not punch your attorney. Do not punch your attorney. Not in front of the whole court, anyway.

The audience is pleased. They clap as if it's been a long but satisfying stage play. The head judge bangs his gavel and the people quieten down.

"Thank you for your service," he says to the jury, who look jolly for the first time. It's as if they've been holding their vote in for three days, and now they can finally relax. Now they're free to get back to their normal lives, spend whatever stipend they'll receive for their work here, root through their ICE-branded goodie bags for their Kool-aid flavoured jelly beans.

"Guilty as charged. We'll now proceed with sentencing."

"Sentencing?" says Zack. "That's not how it works."

The judge puts his gavel down. "Mister Girdler? You have an objection?"

Zack looks down at Mpanghi, who returns his glare with interest. *Is his client really stupid enough,* he seems to be thinking, *to piss off the judge who's about to sentence him?*

"You need time to consider the verdict, and then decide on the sentence."

"I don't need any more time," says the judge. "I've heard and seen enough."

"But—"

"Guilty of 108 charges of pre-meditated murder, Mister Girdler. I didn't need to think very long at all when it came to decide what we should do with you."

The jury has lost its cheer, now. They look on, fascinated. Zack realises then that none of this has been real, from the imposter lawyer to the actors on the jury bench. The head judge narrows his eyes at Zack. It's all been an elaborate ruse, a game, an expert choreography of power vs pawn.

"I'm not falling for this!" Zack shouts. "I can see what's happening here!"

The audience starts tittering. They weren't expecting an encore.

"This isn't a court of law. And you," he says to the judge. "A judge! I bet you don't even have a law degree. I bet you got your certificate out of a fucking lucky packet!"

Now the audience and press have their devices out, recording Zack's outburst. Further proof, he imagines, that he's a madman, deluded and dangerous.

"Girdler," says Mpanghi, "sit down, man. You're making it worse."

"Fuck you!" shouts Zack, and uses all the willpower he possesses not to break the lawyer's nose.

"Where did they get you from?" Zack shouts at the gallery who are hiding behind their recording devices. They are all actors; he can see that now. Flashes from their cameras prick his already scratchy eyes.

The head judge bangs his gavel. "Mister Girdler!"

"Will the accused please sit down," pipes the prosecutor, enjoying the show.

This can't be happening. He can't go to a Penal Labour Colony. He has to get to Kate before it's too late.

"I will not sit down!"

A part of Zack is observing himself as part of the show. He knows the protestations before they leave his mouth. He sees himself wrecked by this insidious system: hungry, dirty, high on sleep-dep, and knows that it will be better for everybody if he just acts obsequious, because raving about the injustice won't solve a damn thing. No one cares about the rights of a person responsible for more than a hundred individually and immaculately orchestrated deaths. They just want to lock him up and throw away the key. This cannot happen. There's something at the very core of him that refuses to be deceived.

"I'm giving you one last chance to sit down!" shouts the head judge. The court security police start to pre-emptively make their way towards him: two navy uniforms in the corners of his vision.

"I can't believe you get away with this shit," says Zack.

Keep calm, now, keep quiet.

The security cops are right here. He prepares to fight them, but his cuffs keep his wrists bound.

"You get away from me!" he shouts at them. They both flinch, as if he's a rabid dog who's tried to bite.

"Come on, Prisoner," says one of the cops, one hand out towards him and the other tickling her thigh holster. "Take it easy."

"I have a name!" shouts Zack. His actions are spinning out of his control now.

"Take it easy and no one gets hurt." She has hazel eyes. Kind eyes. He's lulled into a second of letting his guard down when the other cop tries to grab him. Zack struggles, trying to get away while the creeps watch through their camera lenses. Flash, flash, flash.

He pulls back his arms, ready to right-hook the cop, but as he does so, his handcuffs bite him hard on his wrists. He looks down at them, at once shocked and unsurprised. He immediately feels the warm, comforting rush of TranX as it streamrolls over his adrenaline. It takes away his desire to fight, to run, to reason, and the floor rushes up to meet him.

No, no, no. This isn't part of the plan.

He hears snippets of conversation as his consciousness escapes like vapour out of his skull:

— *unavoidable* —

— *Clearly a danger to himself and others* —

— *Maximum security is the only option* —

— *or psych ward?* —

— *sedation* —

— *paranoid* —

— *delusional* —

— *away for a long, long time* —

It's a relief when the drug washes him away.

CHAPTER 24

HOT TOKYO

TWELVE YEARS LATER

Innercity
Johannesburg, 2036

Mally's mandible buzzes. Vega calling.

Pick up, he thinks, and the call connects.

"Vega. I was just on my way to you."

"Mally," she says. "Mally." But something sounds wrong. Her tone is off.

His heart sprints.

"What's wrong? Where are you?"

"Mally," she warbles, sounding like a robot for the first time Mally can remember.

Find Vega. Find Vega!

His holomap spins out and shows him the destination pin. She's not at her hostel—she's closer than that—three blocks north, at the CBD Night Market. Mally instructs the tram to stop. Other vehicles hoot. He jumps off, and as he lands on the pavement a jolt of pain in his injured leg almost floors him. He can't see any northbound trams, and no cabbies are idling, so he starts to jog towards her location. Every step is a steel rivet in his flesh. He's running and murmuring now, he doesn't care what the people think as they stop to watch him hiss in pain. The teeth of the railway sutures are coming apart, opening his wound.

When he arrives at the market it's buzzing with vendors shouting and shoppers haggling. A mime dressed as a golden statue blows a kiss to a baby in a bubble-pram, and the baby starts to cry. Buskers in bowler hats sing a hundred-year-old song. Mally pushes his way through the crowd that smells of sherry popgrains and roasted nuts, body odour and barbecue sauce. Strawberry XugarSpray. He's fifty metres away from Vega now, and some of the market-goers step out of his way as he hyperventilates into his mask, sweating and bleeding, muttering to himself. It's a good tactic to part the crowds.

There's a booth at the outskirts of the Asian section called Hot Tokyo. It's a brightly lit mini-mart for the regular home staples not supplied by the fresh produce market: alt-dairy milks and cheeses, coconut water, hotwipes, detergents. His dash tells him Vega's in there.

"Vega!" Mally shouts as he stumbles through the wide entrance. The short woman at the till puts her hands up in fright, as if she's expecting to be robbed. Her eyes are magnified by the thick lenses in her old-tech frames.

"Vega!" Mally shouts at her, and the shop owner reverses into the shelves of blunt-vapes, snaffeine, and caramel condoms a decade past their sell-by date. Some of the products clatter to the ground. He shows her Vega's avatar, the ruby Alpha Lyrae star, and her eyes grow wider still. She shows him the panic button on the counter and speaks in Xiang. Mally's mandible insta-translates to English: "The man he took her," she says. "Called the cops. Called the cops."

"Which man?" he shouts, resisting the urge to shake the woman. Vega's location is moving slowly away from him. She babbles and shows him her old-school security screen, rewinds it two minutes by swiping a stubby finger, and Mally watches with horror as a man with a mohawk winds his arm back and punches Vega as hard as he can, smashing her cheek in and almost breaking her neck. There are other men surrounding the two, and Mally thinks they'll step in to help her but instead they laugh and cheer soundlessly.

"No go there. Wait for cops! No go there, he kill you!"

Hot saliva floods Mally's mouth, as if he's about to be sick, but he doesn't have time for that. The man staggers towards Vega and trails his hand over her hip, moves his crotch towards her in clumsy humping jerks while the others laugh. She is frozen; she doesn't have protocol for that. She tries to step away from the man, but slips on some spilled liquid on the floor where her groceries have been smashed. The man lunges at her.

"Where?" Mally shouts, but the woman shakes her head. She won't tell him, doesn't want him endangering his life for a robot. She doesn't understand. He scrubs through to the end of the attack where he sees the other men leave the grocery store, and the mohawk head-butts Vega then drags her by the hair out the back door. Mally tears his eyes away from the screen, looking for the door.

He races towards it, through it, and lands up in a crowded kitchen, then a steaming laundry room, then a black back alley, where the man has Vega's body spreadeagled over a dumpster, her skirt pushed up, her panties torn and hanging off a broken ankle.

"Stop!" Mally says, and the mohawk looks up at him with sour evil in his eyes. Muscles flexed, glaring at him as if he can't believe a kid is going to waste his time.

"Leave her alone," says Mally.

Vega's body is a mannequin.

The man takes his hand off Vega's knee and walks a few steps towards Mally. "Get outta here, boy. Mind your own business."

"I'm not leaving without her," says Mally. "And, anyway, the cops are coming."

The man laughs, then mocks Mally. "Ooh! The cops are coming! The cops are coming!"

"They're on their way," says Mally. "The shop owner called them five minutes ago."

"You think I give a fuck about pigs?" He hawks and spits onto the littered ground. "You think the pigs care about what we do to fucking skins?"

Mally swallows hard.

The police force has had a fair amount of trouble with PR lately, with human cops abusing the new robo recruits.

It's to be expected, the Minister of Security said, *we presumed there would be a certain amount of resistance. Teething problems. Adjustment issues.*

Teething problems. Tell that to the recruit who had his head cut off with a bandsaw by his law enforcement partner.

"It's illegal, what you're doing. She's—" He hates to say the words, but they're true. "She's government property." He gulps the rising acid in his throat. "She's a 7thGen. You're d-damaging government property. And there's video evidence of you doing it."

The mohawk ambles back to Vega, a greasy stride of alpha male, ready to assert his power. He has a swastika scalp tat. He puts his hand back on her knee, starts to move it up her inner thigh, the thigh Mally knows so well. Vega's body shudders. The air is thick, foetid; Mally feels choked with haze and nerves.

The man unhooks the notch on his pants. He winds his arms around Vega's calves and pulls her body towards himself. "You ready for me, robo-whore?" He slaps her caved-in cheek. "I'm going to fuck you till you bleed."

Something inside Mally explodes. Fresh adrenaline flushes through his heart and erupts in every cell of his body. What is it about creeps? What is it about these fucking toxic bastards that compels them to thrust poison into beauty? Why do they have to stain and maim? The fury fills his body, makes his bones vibrate. He unclips the Vektor from his utility belt and holds it up to the man with shaking arms.

"Whoa, cowboy!" he says, putting up his hands. "Where'd you get that?"

Now he's paying attention.

Now who's in charge, thinks Mally, but then there's a short melody of metallic clicks as the man returns Mally's Vektor's aim with his own, bigger weapons which he draws from behind him, one in each hand.

Where are the cops? Where are the fucking cops?

The mohawk advances. His comparative bulk makes Mally feel young, weak, takes him back to the childhood nightmare that still haunts him.

Vega's body jerks again.

He's close now, just a few metres away. Which bullet will reach him first? Panic evaporates what's left of Mally's thoughts. He pulls the trigger, but nothing happens. His brain is as blank as the weapon.

"I almost feel sorry for you," says the man. "You don't even know how to fire a gun."

Mally tries the trigger again. Nothing.

"You don't even know that Vektors can only be fired by their owners," says the man, "which, judging by your position, you are very clearly not."

Mally tries again, tries to force the thing to fire, but it remains stubbornly mute. The realisation slams into him. There's a biometric fingerprint pad on the trigger, of course, and no one but Seth can fire it.

"This is getting more and more interesting," says the mohawk. "A boy, with a stolen gun, rat-running the city streets to protect androids. I'm intrigued. I'm almost tempted to keep you alive—"

Finally, finally, the siren of a police drone wails overhead.

"—but, unfortunately for you, we've run out of time."

He raises his semi-automatic and aims it at Mally's forehead. His lips shrink as he looks through the weapon's sight and a deafening shot explodes the air.

CHAPTER 25

WE'RE NOT SAFE ANYMORE

Mally thinks he's been shot. Thinks he can't feel the pain because of the shock, because of the blinding, eardrum-popping blast that's just happened in front of his eyes. He looks down at his chest, blinking away the bombshell, expecting to find a hole where his heart used to be, but his trembling fingers can't find any damage. If there's no damage, why can't he breathe? The police siren grows louder. Then he sees that the mohawk is sprawled on the ground, and the back half of his skull is missing. Mally can't understand what is happening until he sees Vega, who is now sitting up, her roscoe smoking.

"Vega!" Mally darts over to her. It feels like running on air. His instinct is to ask if she's okay, but her face is conked in and her arm looks dislocated. Her ankle is definitely broken. He pulls her skirt down, unloops the shredded panties carefully from her feet and drops them into the dumpster, and helps her down from the garbage. She packs her radial gun back into the top of her arm.

"Come," Mally says gently. "Come, I'll take you home."

She makes an odd sound—a machine sound he's never heard from her before. A computer shutting down.

"Stay with me," he says, easing her forward. Vega stumbles as she tries to walk on her fractured bones. He'll take her home, to Arronax; Arro will know how to fix her. The two of them limp back through the laundry and the kitchen, then through the convenience store. The shop owner is nowhere to be seen. She's probably trying to flag down the drone. Those police drones are notoriously bad at following their heat seekers. The floor is still a battleground of dropped groceries.

Vega sees the spilt food and says, "I was gathering supplies."

Mally looks at the floor, confused. Dented tins of chickpeas, a box of protein cereal, an up-ended tub of soyghurt, a broken pink jar. Why would she need food?

"For your family," she says. "Something's changed. Something's happening. We're not safe anymore."

CHAPTER 26

SINNER PLEASE

12 YEARS PREVIOUSLY

ICE

Johannesburg, 2024

This time they're letting me use the mental gymnastics, too, thinks Zack, as he wakes up groggy and realises he's lying down inside the Orb. He feels the tightness of the band around his temple; his fingers trace the skin-warmed metal. It seems to be a regular jack-in cable, or, at least, the new, non-invasive, wireless version of the old port and cord. *They've decided I can keep my brain, after all.*

Zack wonders how to select the japuzzle of his choice. He can't see a sidebar. Maybe it's because he's still half asleep. That tranquilizer hit him hard.

He senses movement in the room and then strong fingers lock his hands in place on either side of him. Click, click. The band flashes from opaque to transparent and Zack sees it's Bernard looming over him—who else would it be?—and she's got something in her hands. A black lozenge. Some kind of XDrive.

Bernard leans across him, yoghurt breath, and plugs it into the band squeezing his temple. She's sweating.

"What the …" he begins, but Bernard shoves a rubber ball gag in his mouth.

"Shut up, Prisoner."

Zack's memories are like electric currents. Pictures in his head come alive and zap him with needle pricks and hot shocks, and they build until the whole band starts to burn him.

He groans.

Silver, Mally, Seth, Kate. The quills. The drawing of the lotus on the wall. The picture of Kate is the brightest. Not the haunted woman with mascara spilled down her cheeks he met in the bathroom of the hospital but the real Kate who devours him with her oceanic eyes, her skin like glowsilk.

"Don't fail me," she's saying.

I won't.

"It's the whole reason for your existence."

I know.

"Save her."

Zack tries to hold on to the picture but it burns up like a polaroid on fire. The memories sweep out of his head with a final burst of bright white and then there is peace and darkness. Someone approaches, whistling a gospel tune. Zack knows the song. Has heard it every day since he's been here.

Sinner Please.

Bernard whips the drive out of the band and slips it surreptitiously into her pocket.

"All set?" asks Lovemore as he enters the room.

"Affirmative." Her breathing is heavy.

Lovemore comes into view; he doesn't make eye contact.

"What are you going to do?" asks Zack, but his words leave his mouth as an unintelligible mumble.

Lovemore checks Zack's cuffs, then flicks a switch on the side of the Orb.

The currents fire up again but this time they're not small shocks, they're lightning bolts. There's a searing inside his skull: his brain in a hot pan.

Zack screams and bites down on the gag in his mouth. His whole body seizes.

He feels the blankness coming for him, rolling at him like a storm, ready to wipe out every part of who he is and what he was put here to do, and he knows there is no way he can stop it.

PART 2

CHAPTER 27

BLOOD AND A BRUTAL PAST

TWELVE YEARS LATER

Seth's Apartment
Johannesburg, 2036

"I'm going to find her," says Kate, her anxiety and anger billowing together, neon yellow and green, to create an urgent need to move.

Keke's eyes bulge. "You can't. It's already getting crazy out there. The Blanket's not going to keep this under wraps for much longer. I'm already getting alerts on my tickertape. Creeps are catching on."

"It's way past Silver's curfew now. Something's wrong. I can feel it."

It's not just an expression. Kate can literally feel a sick burning in her stomach. She knows this sensation: One of her kids is in danger. No second-guessing this time. No blaming it on PTSD-flavoured paranoia. Just trusting her instinct, and taking action.

"I need to find her."

"You go out there, you'll get caught in the full-blown panic."

"At least I'll be able to look after her."

"The thing about Silver," says Seth, "is that she can look after herself."

Kate can't believe he's being so blasé about it.

"Her martial arts in the games she plays do not count in the real world, Seth."

"We both know that's not true," he says.

Kate sees, in her mind's eye, the picture of Silver at four years old, bow and diamond-tipped arrow in hand as the lightning highlights her hair.

"That was different. She knew who the enemy was. She was armed."

"All I'm saying is, if someone has a chance of surviving this, it's her."

"You're saying we should just abandon her to the wild city? Expect her to find her own way home? She doesn't know what's happening! A fucking waitbot could kill her! A traffic light! She doesn't know!"

"I'm not saying we should abandon her. I'm saying that if things are escalating out there then it'll take longer than usual to get home."

"That's exactly what I'm saying. She never misses her curfew. She's three hours late!"

"You're just going to go around in circles," says Arronax, looking up from her SnapTile.

"Well, that's helpful," snarks Keke. "We do hope we're not boring you."

Arronax ignores Keke's barbed tone. "All I'm saying is, if anyone's going to go out, they'd better stop standing around and talking about it."

"You think she should go?" says Seth.

"She's going, regardless of what I happen to think. All I'm saying is, the sooner the better."

Kate runs to her room, grabs her ancient revolver. She hasn't opened the secret shoebox for more than ten years, hasn't held the gun, never mind fired it, so she hopes it's still in working order. She takes out the leather thigh holster too, hard with age and neglect, and pulls it over her jeans. Kate jams the old-school revolver into its nook and then snicks closed the click-stud. How many boxes of ammo? She only has two. They'll have to do.

"I'm coming with you," says Seth, zipping up his hoodie.

Of course he's coming with her. They are joined in a way that other twins will never glimpse. They're two halves of the same person, really. Always have been. United by blood and a brutal past.

"I was hoping you'd say that."

Keke runs into the room, almost smashing into them. "Mally," she says. "Mally's gone."

Seth feels for his Vektor, then spins around to look at the table where he left it. "And he's taken my gun."

CHAPTER 28

FOREHEAD TO NAPE

White Mezzanine, 2036

Silver wakes in a startling white room with a headache as bright as the walls. She rubs her wrists where the leather cuffs were, and there's no trace on her pale skin of being previously tied down. She's wearing a starched cotton shift and is naked underneath. Her mouth is dry, dry, dry, and her head is banging with a post-surgery spike hangover. Silver gets off the wheeled stretcher and finds a long mirror on the otherwise blank wall. She pulls off the spearmint gown and inspects her body. All her hair is still there, apart from the band that was shaved off from forehead to nape. The rest of her small body seems unharmed, her face clear and pale without her usual foundation powder and kohl makeup. She runs her hands over her ivory skin: her goose-pimpled stomach, her bony shoulders, her sub-rosa tattoo. Her fingers play on her ribs. When did she get so skinny?

Silver takes a breath then feels, gingerly, for the wound she knows is on the back of her head. When she finds it, her hand recoils at the puckered dressing. She guesses it's a platelet plaster, already mostly dissolved.

There's a simple closet in the room, camouflaged, white against white. Inside are her clothes and her gas-mask, that look filthy against the white walls. She dresses, drawing comfort from their familiar weft and warp. Her mandible is missing. She can't remember ever having been disconnected for this long. How long had she been unconscious? She feels sick when she thinks of how worried Kate must be. Wishes there was a way to tell her mom that she's okay.

Head pounding, she checks herself in the mirror again. *Is* she okay?

CHAPTER 29
POWDER MUSK

Seth's Apartment
Johannesburg, 2036

Kate and Seth embrace on the pavement outside their apartment building. The midnight air is soupy: It makes her eyes water, and her own breath chokes her. Or maybe that's her nerves; maybe the electrosmog has nothing to do with it.

"Take care of yourselves," he says, looking into her eyes, then Keke's, as if he's memorising them.

"Don't say it like that," Keke's voice is deep with emotion. "Like it's the last time."

His shoulders move. A micro-shrug.

They watch as Seth hops on a westbound solartram towards Vega's hostel. They grab a tram heading east, and Kate says a quick prayer to the night sky.

Please let Silver be safe at the Atrium.

Of course she's at the Atrium. She's not home ... where else would she be?

Augmented ads crowd their vision as they travel, hyper-targeted to their individual codes. Kate bought Blunt Kruffins last week from BAKED; now they urge her to try their new Hash Brownies. Athleisure Club wants her to update her jogger leggings with coolpatches; maybe that will encourage her to take up exercise again, as her last run, they note, was 249 days ago. She swipes them away, irritated. Blinks her burning eyes, tries to concentrate. Keke's face is bleak behind her mask too. What products are flashing in on her? Certainly something edgier than joggings. Or maybe she's ignoring the ads entirely. Maybe she's thinking of Marko, missing him. Wondering if she'll ever see him again.

They reach the Atrium. The Victorian structure is lit up spectacularly against the inky sky. Made up almost entirely of old glass framed with lead, the structure features interior lights that make the whole building glow. Long-established plants climb up the sides and curl into the windows, meeting the leaves of the inside plants that seem to want to escape. Some of the panes of glass are cracked or missing, some frosted with age. When the Nancies decreed that all buildings had to be made up of at least 20% living organic matter, most corps added plant pockets to the sides of their structures, and roof-top gardens. Herbsills and airplants. The Atrium let its regular garden grow wild into the building, so from the outside it looks like the plants are trying to consume it.

Kate and Keke walk right in without as much as a bell to announce their entrance. There are no security guards or swivelcams to side-eye them. Kate doesn't know why. Surely they're not immune to the White Lobster junkies looking to score?

She's been here before, of course. She brought Silver here for immersion parties when she was younger. At first it was a session a year, then ten, then all of a sudden Silver couldn't skip a day without feeling antsy. Kate doesn't know when or how it had gotten so out of hand. She wishes she had stopped it before it became such a driving force in her daughter's life. It hadn't been a problem until it was, well, a problem, and by then, it was too late. She walks past a party of jacked-in kids skiing on a mountain. The milieu is projected above the participants for the benefit of the gallery.

It's good exercise, Silver says, *it's completely interactive. I'm adopting skills. Working out. Problem solving. Defending myself. Designing worlds. It's about art and creation; it's not like I'm a crack addict.*

And it's true, but it's also taken her little girl away from her. How many other parents find themselves on this slippery slope, she thinks, as she walks past the guardian area, where parents are drinking coffeeberry shooters, one eye on the screen and the other on their own individual fixes. How many of these other parents had a sweet, strong, loving daughter (or son) and now see only a shell of that child? Kate's photographic memory means there's no lack of the pictures she's taken over the years of that young girl who used to crawl onto her lap with her glow-in-the-dark cuddle bunny. Her heart aches with the loss.

No one here seems particularly concerned about the AI malfunction. There's a hushed tone overall, and the feeling of inclusiveness whether the players are immersed in group experiences or going it alone. They're a tribe. Kate and Keke make their way past a group busy with a scuba diving simulation. Adults, this time. Either doing it to get certified for the real thing, or just happy to do it inside an inner-city building and not having to bother with heavy equipment, sea-sickness, dangerous currents, or the bends. A whale shark swims past them, and they all murmur a drugged-sounding "Who-o-oa."

It's not *real,* Kate would say to Silver, to which Silver would grunt, and spin her eyeballs.

It's as real as *this,* she'd say, gesturing to the apartment with its artificial sunrise and invisi-screen and synthetic ham sandwiches.

She has a point, Seth had chimed in from the couch, Bonechaser snoring on his lap.

What is REAL, anyway? Silver had asked. Mally had looked up from his flexiglass Tile, then, interested.

Kate did not have an answer.

Keke and Kate reach the stairs—the elevator has been out of order since Kate first visited, five years ago—and climb to the second floor. The second level is for recreational gaming: parties, training, team building, while the third is for hard-liners. The basement, well, it's the only place here that has restricted access, so who knows? Strictly 21+, and you have to know someone who knows someone to apply, like some secret underground New York swingers' nightclub. Kate wouldn't know where to start to gain entrance, although she's sure Keke, with all her contacts, would drift in like a breeze.

"What happens in the basement?"

Andy Warhol springs to mind, Studio 54 with a futuristic twist. Alcohash cocktails, cocaine shadowshots, deviant botsex.

Keke shrugs. "Never been."

"If you were to guess? From what you've heard?"

"Hardcore bot nooky. V-XXX-R. Kinky shit. I mean, it must be bizarro sex, right? Or why bother coming here?"

"Excuse the pun," jokes Kate.

Keke cackles her wild laugh, and people turn to look at her.

"Everywhere you look there's a novel neuroreality porn hub popping up."

"Adult Planet," says Kate. "Every time I see that flashing pink sign it makes me think of some kind of old-school cartoon. A pink animated planet. It tastes like those old lucky packet sweets. Powder Musk. Totally inappropriate."

"Now why … " says Keke, giving Kate an eyeful, "is Adult Planet targeting *you* with their ads?"

Kate's cheeks warm. "I don't know," she mutters. "Their algorithms must be off."

Keke looks at her. "Right."

She clears her throat.

"Kate Lovell, you are not having *sex* are you? I thought you'd sworn it off forever."

Kate blushes some more. Why, she doesn't know. She's almost forty years old, for Net's sake.

"Don't take it the wrong way," says Keke.

"Is that supposed to be another pun?"

"Ha! You *are*! You wily slut. Who? How? Tell me everything."

But even if Kate wants to answer the question—which she doesn't—they've run out of time. They've reached Silver's regular jack-in console, and her pod is bare.

CHAPTER 30

GRAVEYARD TREES

TWELVE YEARS PREVIOUSLY

Johannesburg, 2024

When Zack opens his bleary eyes, he sees a human shape sitting across from him. They're in a vehicle. He squints at the shape, tries to make out who it is. As he is rocked by the motion of the van he feels strangely at peace. The nagging feeling he's had for as long as he can remember is gone. There was something important he had to do, but it's faded now, and only cool relief remains.

In fact, he can't remember much of anything, anymore. He has vague recollections of life before his arrest, but it all seems so faraway.

He knows his name is Prisoner, and that the shape across from him is his warden, Bernard. She doesn't acknowledge his waking, but doesn't look away either. He knows he does not like Bernard.

Which crim colony are they taking him to? Lovermore told him that the space mining programme is the most dangerous, but also pays the most, and that the sky-scraping vertical farms are one of the easiest options: those aeroponic crops basically take care of themselves. Maybe they'll put him in a kitchen or a laundry. Maybe he'll have to clean toilets for the other crims. Or a hard labour option—they've probably put him down for that—laying trax for the first phase of the new smart Hyperloop.

The van slows and turns a corner. The windows are tinted the colour of tar. Zack tries to move, to get more comfortable, but when he looks down, he sees he's strapped into some kind of wheelchair.

"Where're we going?" he asks the warden. "How much longer?"

She doesn't reply. You would think she didn't know he existed if it weren't for her glare of cold steel.

They move at an unhurried pace, the speed of an extra-cautious cabbie, or a human driver with nothing better to do for the rest of the day, then they pull up and park. For a second there's a glint of paranoia: Will they even take him to a penal colony? Or will they just stop at an abandoned strip of veld and put a bullet in his brain? They'll tell the task team hired to investigate that he tried to get away, and what choice did they have? After all, they couldn't allow a serial murderer to escape.

The back of the van is opened, and the ramp folds itself down to the ground. Bernard kicks the brake off Zack's wheelchair and pushes him out. She brings a small black kitbag with her. The fresh blue of the sky is almost blinding. He tilts back his head and relishes the feeling of the sun on his face.

"Feels good?" Bernard casts her shadow over him.

Zack cracks open one eye to look at her. Could she not just allow him this one moment of bliss?

"Well, lap it up, Prisoner—"

I would if you let me.

"Because this is the last bit of sunshine you're ever gonna see."

Bernard drives Zack's chair roughly, swinging him away from the view of graveyard trees—tall, fragrant pines—to face the main building.

Zack is expecting some kind of ugly state structure—utilitarian concrete and chipstone and very little imagination—but the architecture he sees takes his breath away. It must be at least twelve storeys high, and is made from some kind of glossy white material. Its outline is irregular—like a shard planted in the earth—but it's made up of hundreds of hexagons. It looks like a giant piece of shiny white honeycomb. The grounds are carpeted in lush green grass, freshly mown, and perennials blooming and bursting with petal and seed, and there's a dense forest behind the shard.

Zack's confused. There's no branding outside, no state banner. Now that he thinks of it, there's not even a security wall around the place. What kind of crim colony is this? Bernard pushes him up the ramp to the entrance. Her breathing is ragged with anger and effort. The glass doors slide open to admit them, and a friendly security guard greets them as if they are day visitors, instead of a convict strapped into a prison-issue wheelchair and a huffing ham-cheeked warden.

"We've been expecting you," says the pretty receptionist, smiling warmly. "Welcome to SkyRest."

CHAPTER 31
PUREST HUMAN

TWELVE YEARS LATER

Seth's Apartment
Johannesburg, 2036

Mally and Vega finally reach Seth's apartment building. A feeling has crept into the black city air that wasn't there an hour ago: slow, insidious, as if there is an undetected gas leak and all it'll take is an accidental spark to blow up the whole place. Maybe it's just them, the glances they're attracting. Vega is in pretty bad shape.

As they cross the road to get to the apartment, a cabbie speeds up, as if to mow them down. Mally launches them out of the way, onto the hard pavement, and the taxi just misses them. Pain burns a hole in his thigh. His wound is open again, his trousers are double-dyed by blood, old and new.

He gets up, helps Vega stand again, loops her arm over his shoulder. He knows he's supposed to report the malfunctioning cabbie, but now he's shaking again, and he just wants to get home and tend to his love. They eventually get inside and he breathes a sigh of relief as he feels the cool, conditioned air on his skin. The stairs are waiting.

"Almost there," Mally says, more to himself than to Vega.

Only Arronax is home.

"Mally!" she says "Where the hell were you?" but then she sees Vega, and she understands.

"You went to fetch her?" She starts weeping again.

Mally puts Seth's Vektor on the kitchen counter. "Don't worry, Arro, we're safe now." He's not sure why Arronax is crying.

"Safe?" she says, incredulous. "I need to let your parents know you're home." She wipes her tears on her shell-studded sleeves, sniffs, attempts to pull herself together. She tries to beam Seth and Kate three times each, but is met with a busy signal.

"The commstation must be down. We'll try again later. In the mean time," she says to Vega, "let's see if we can fix you up."

"I'd really appreciate that," says Vega.

Arronax winces at the android's crushed face. She takes her gently by the hand and sits her down on a wingback. Then she grabs her utility bag and pulls up a stool next to her to survey the damage.

Does it hurt? Mally feels like asking, but realises it's a stupid question. She's been viciously attacked, humiliated, assaulted. Of course it fucking hurts.

Arronax sets to work. She fixes the ankle first, so that Vega can walk again. She is a nimble surgeon with her needle-nosed pliers and blowtorch. The room smells like burnt rubber and bitumen. Metal on metal. A car crash. Arronax moves on to Vega's fractured arm, her sprained hand.

"This part might be difficult to watch," she says to Mally. "Why don't you go get yourself a drink, or something?"

"No," says Mally. "I want to be here for her."

Just hours ago Vega was the one tending to his wounds. He holds her uninjured hand.

Arronax breathes deeply, and nods.

She peels off half of Vega's face. The stamped silicone gives way to a titanium skull—shiny, apart from the damaged cheek bone, which is like crumpled tinfoil. Arronax sculpts the structure back to its original shape and folds the silicone back over it, sealing it with some bright flashes of purple light.

"There," Arronax says, arranging some of Vega's lustrous long hair over the seam. "As good as new." She swallows hard.

Vega smiles. "Thank you."

Of course, it's not nearly as good as new, and Mally gets a twinge of sorrow every time he looks at Vega's face. It certainly looks a lot better than it did before.

"Thank you," Mally says to Arronax, eyes glistening with gratitude, and regret.

"What were you doing out there, anyway?"

"I went to gather supplies," says Vega.

"What supplies? You're almost 100% stocked, according to your meter. What did you need?"

"She went to buy groceries," says Mally. "For us."

He sees the floor of the convenience store again, littered with broken glass and spilled food. The owner of the shop, hugging herself and chattering in Xiang.

Arronax pauses, looks concerned. "That's not in your protocol."

"I am very fond of Mally," she says, "and he needs food to live. Things are happening out there. I knew it wouldn't be safe for Mally's family to go out for food. Mally's family are important to him. It will be best if they stay alive."

Arronax shakes her head, a shudder, and her hair turns a dark shade of purple. She packs up the rest of her tools. "Okay, kids. I'm going to try to reach Seth again. Promise me you'll stay here? Stay out of trouble?"

Once Arronax has moved back to her makeshift desk, Mally takes Vega's hand again. He wants to say something loving and profound, but the words don't come to him.

All he can manage is: "I love you."

"I know," says Vega.

"If you love me too, you can say it back."

"Okay," says Vega.

"I love you," he says again.

"I know," says Vega.

Mally laughs, strokes her abraded skin.

"You saved my life," she says.

"That's not true."

"You saved my life. I wouldn't be here now if it weren't for you. I'd be in the dumpster. You know that's true."

"But—"

"I owe you my life."

"No, you don't."

"I owe you my life, and you know what? I'm glad I do."

"Why?"

"Because you're the purest human."

"That's a weird thing to say."

"You have the cleanest heart in the city," says Vega.

"Again, a weird thing to say. But thank you."

"It's true. I can see it."

They look into each others' eyes.

“What else can you see?” asks Mally.

“I wish I could tell you.”

“Tell me.”

“I can’t. It will fuck your mind.”

Mally laughs. He’s been trying to teach Vega to swear, but her code resists it, and muddles the words up.

“Do you mean, it will be a mind-fuck?” He laughs.

“Mind-fuck,” she says. “Mind-fuck.” As if she’s a toddler learning a new word.

“It will blow your brain out,” she says. This time he doesn’t correct her; he just sighs and looks away.

“Your happiness score is low,” Vega says. “Shall I make you some pancakes?”

He thinks of that mohawk man and how he punched Vega with all his strength. Thinks of her body spreadeagled on the trash. Would he ever forget those visuals? Would *she?*

“Vega. I need you to help me understand something.”

“Of course. What is it?”

He struggles with the words, looks down and clasps and unclasps his hands, still grimy from the altercation.

“When you were … when we were … when you were being attacked. By that man.”

Vega looks at him, clear-eyed.

“You had your roscoe—your radial gun—the whole time. Why didn’t you defend yourself?”

“Defending myself is not in my protocol,” she says.

“You’re not allowed to defend yourself?”

“Not against humans. Human life is more valuable than robosapien life.”

Mally winces. “But then, later, you did shoot him.”

“That’s because he turned on you.”

CHAPTER 32
CURSED WHITE

White Mezzanine, 2036

"Let me out!" Silver screams, holding her humming head. "Let me out of here!"

She bangs on the walls, kicks the furniture. Tries to smash the glass of the tiny square window in her room, but it's reinforced flexiglass and she knows it's unbreakable. She thrashes around, shatters the plate of food that magically appears every time she wakes, upends the metal trolley, punches her stretcher.

The architecture of her prison is infuriating. The door to her room remains unlocked, but outside there is only a passage with walls as white as her ward. If she walks down the passage, she's forced to turn right four times and is then, of course, back at her door. The white membrane keeping her in is thin and elastic, like biolatex, but impossible to tear from the inside. It's like being trapped in a white soft-pop balloon.

Silver can't figure out if it's meant to be a unique kind of torture or a puzzle. Surely a puzzle would have some kind of clue? But this place is just a bleached rubber groundhog day.

Is someone keeping her captive? Or did she die in that grimy ex-abattoir and this is some kind of wretched middle earth? Some limbo? How long has she been here? It could be hours or days. Every time she wakes, she's back in her starched cotton shift, bathed and sweet-smelling.

Silver stops her tantrum and sits down on the floor, against one of the cursed white walls, and draws her legs up, hugs them, tries to comfort herself. Her bandwidth isn't coping with anything but the sincere desire to stop her headsplosion, which is a solid eight out of ten on her own personal Richter scale. The blue pain pills are there again, on their peach-coloured porcelain saucer. She crawls over to the tablets, holds them in her hand. The volume control of brainpain is on the rise, and she doesn't think she'll survive it if it gets any worse. It already feels as if it's scrambling her signals. Reluctantly, she puts the pills back on their plate.

The food lies spilled on the floor: transparent cubes of nutrijelly. She misses her mother with a keen sorrow she hasn't felt in a long time. Seth. Mally. If only there were a way to reach them, to let them know where she is. But how can she do that? She has no idea herself. Maybe Kate would re-trace Silver's steps, figure something out.

Her gaze alights on her boots, which she hasn't bothered putting on this time, and travels up to her jacket, which is hanging on its lone ivory hanger. The back of the jacket is shaped with metal corsetry. Steel bones and five elegant darts of copper. Silver gets up and pulls the jacket off its hanger, starts chewing at the stitching.

With no tools at hand apart from her teeth and short nails, it takes two hours to release the first swatch of metal. She has stars in her vision as her headache reaches nine out of ten. She begins to unpick the next one.

CHAPTER 33

MAYBE THIS IS THE FUTURE

TWELVE YEARS PREVIOUSLY

SkyRest
Johannesburg, 2024

The SkyRest receptionist picks up her Tile and comes around the sleek concierge counter, and is immediately replaced by an almost identical woman behind the desk. Same crisp snow uniform, sage-green silk scarf, claret lipstick, immaculate hair. Same automatic smile.

"I'll take Mister Girdler from here," the woman says.

Girdler? thinks Zack. He thought his name was 'Prisoner'.

The room is cavernous, light, and everything looks new and expensive. Tight-fisted Bernard doesn't relinquish the wheelchair.

"Didn't you get the transfer documents?" she asks.

The receptionist looks confused. "Yes, we did. We're all set up to receive Mister Girdler. Everything is in order."

"I'm not talking about his intake papers. I'm talking about my transfer papers." Bernard holds up her black bag.

"No," says Zack. *No, please no.*

"Shut up, Prisoner," she says to him through clenched, tea-coloured teeth.

The receptionist's perfect forehead creases into the beginnings of a frown. V-tox, Zack guesses, assuming that face-sculpting is part of the uniform. She looks back towards the new receptionist behind the counter, who swipes away a leaf and nods.

"I do apologise," she says, her face clear again. "I wasn't up to speed." Her name badge reads 'Gaelyn'.

Bernard wipes her hand-sweat onto her hips.

"There'll be someone along shortly to escort you to your new staff quarters," she says to Bernard.

"I won't be going to my quarters right now."

"But—"

"I'm staying with the prisoner."

"It's not necessary—"

"I'll let you know what is necessary and unnecessary," the warden growls. "You don't know this one, okay? You don't know what he's capable of."

The receptionist looks at Zack, adjusts her scarf. He gives her a friendly shrug.

"Can he walk?"

"Of course I can walk."

"We strapped him into the chair for the commute."

"Can you … un-strap him?"

Bernard doesn't answer her. Instead, she glares in Gaelyn's direction while she unbuckles Zack's straps with more force than necessary. Now he can stand, and walk, but he still has his smartcuffs on.

Yet another woman in the same mould (snow, sage, claret) appears out of nowhere and whisks the ugly wheelchair out of the building.

"Please, follow me," says Gaelyn, and clicks away in her silver-spiked stilettos.

They step onto a fast-track line, which is no small feat for someone in heels as high as hers. He feels a little in love with Gaelyn. Of course, he doesn't know her from a bar of soap, but she's just so different—the polar opposite, really—of Bernard. Neat, slim frame, beautifully styled hair and make-up. He can't remember the last time someone was nice to him; he craves more of her clear-eyed attention.

They hop off the line and walk towards an elevator. When they're inside and the doors close, Zack says, "You're very good with people."

Bernard sighs.

"Thank you!" says Gaelyn.

"You make people feel very welcome here."

"That's our warmth score," Gaelyn says, and chooses a floor on her Tile.

"Excuse me?" snarks the warden.

The elevator starts to rise.

"Our warmth score. All potential employees are measured according to certain traits. The points allocated then reveal which job will suit us best. There are one hundred categories. I scored highest in the warmth section. That's a combination of joy and empathy. Emotional intelligence."

"I can tell," says Zack, and in the background, Bernard rolls her eyes.

It's so nice to speak to someone relatively normal after all this time on ice. For now he'll overlook her Stepford aspect and appreciate her for what she's good at. You do, after all, have to have some serious talent to make a crim feel welcome at a penal colony.

The elevator climbs higher and higher, and when they reach the top, Zack is relieved to see they're still in Johannesburg. Far in the distance, he can see the Ponte tower, best known for the number of residents who have hurtled to their deaths from its multicoloured windows.

When they reach the top floor, the metal doors open with a *ping*. The interior, as expected, reflects the exterior design: brutally minimalist, and empty. It's like some kind of exclusive VIP lounge. Zack moves to exit the lift but Gaelyn holds him back.

"We don't leave the elevator for this part of the tour."

The doors close, they drop a few floors, and they open again.

Now it's an open-plan office with young people working from their pods. Holo design pads are floating around with sketches and scribbled ideas on them. Some kind of brainstorming unit.

"We like to show the new intakes the whole building, so that you have a holistic idea of what happens here. So that you know how you can grow in the company if you're dedicated and you work hard."

Bernard snorts, but Gaelyn has the good grace to ignore her.

A few floors below that is a vast room buzzing with people speaking into small mics that are plastered near their mouths.

"Call centre."

There's also a smart canteen, where you can swipe a meal straight off a menu, a gym floor, a play centre, and a napping pad. Zack's hopes start climbing. He's never heard of a crim colony like this before, but maybe this is the future? Maybe the government has realised they can get the best out of their prisoners if they treat them well. This may be a prototype for future PLCs. Look at all these happy, productive workers! It's a far cry from the automatons in grey uniforms he has a vague recollection of seeing in what feels like a previous life. Are these people, these young, vital people … are they all criminals? It doesn't seem likely. Zack inspects Gaelyn. Is *she* a convict? Surely not. So how does this work?

She catches him staring at her and smiles. The elevator slides further down, till they reach the ground floor. Zack thinks they'll get out now but Gaelyn holds him back again. He likes the feel of her hand on his chest.

"You don't start here," she says.

Bernard smirks.

The elevator goes down past ground level, down, down, down, till Zack feels as if they are in the bowels of the earth, till the air is heavy and the only light is from the LEDs in the ceiling of the lift, giving both women disturbing white masks for faces.

Ping! goes the elevator, and the doors open for them one last time.

Gaelyn steps into darkness and smiles. "This is where you start."

They walk along a dark passage deep underground. Motion-sensitive LEDs flicker on to light their way. The walls are raw rock face and there's a hint of an odd smell—what is it? Damp? Mould? Old laundry detergent. Zack feels the weight of the earth all around him.

I should have known. I should have known I wouldn't be working up there in the light.

Gaelyn's heels provide a staccato soundtrack to his feelings of doom.

They reach a massive steel door. Gaelyn inserts her wafer key and looks, unblinking, into the retina scanner, and it beeps and unlocks. It becomes clear to Zack why the security outside the SkyRest building is light. They keep all the crims right here in this hulking subterranean lock-up, and there is no way to escape. A shroud of claustrophobia wraps around his head.

Once they're through the steel door, Gaelyn takes off her shoes and motions for them to do the same. Bernard's boots are bigger than his. They make their way into the Residence: decent looking recreation rooms, neat accommodation. Spick and span cafeteria that only stinks a little. There's even a ping pong table and a vintage jukebox in the corner. An air sanitiser spills a constant plume of humidified air into the space. It's not pleasant by any stretch of the imagination, but better than Zack expected after seeing that dungeon passage. Was that also done on purpose?

"Where is everyone?"

"They're working. We encourage a very strict work ethic here."

I'm sure you do.

She trains her cloudless eyes on him. "Keeps everyone out of trouble."

Gaelyn slides open the door to his room. It couldn't be any more different to the dirty, overcrowded South African prisons pre-crimcol days where you'd be in danger of being shivved for a cracked plastic dinner plate. Here there are no jail cell bars in sight, and the tiny room is Asian in style: a sleeping mat on the tatami floor, minimal, and spotless. A perfect cube of folded clothes sits on the corner of the mat.

Gaelyn asks Bernard to remove Zack's cuffs, and she does so. She then takes Zack's hands in hers, and before he knows what's happening she's clicked a single polished black band on his left wrist. It beeps.

"More comfortable?"

He runs his finger over its smooth surface, nods.

"Lewis?" Gaelyn calls down the passage. There's a muted sound of someone moving in the next room, then they hear that door slide open. Determined footsteps arrive, attached to what can only be described as an old Hipster Hell's Angel: seventy-something in the shade with a perfectly groomed grey beard, and hair to match; a cappuccino-skinned body that's seen a hundred pull-ups a day for decades; and a huge, elaborate tattoo that snakes its way out of his frayed vest—down his vein-mapped arms and up his neck. Hard scales and dangerous eyes. A dragon. He lifts his chin to acknowledge Zack.

"Mister Girdler, Lewis is one of our most experienced residents. If you have any questions, ask him. He'll show you around."

Lewis nods.

"You're going to be just fine, Zack," Gaelyn says.

Zack?

Is that my name? Yes, it feels right. Zack.

"All right!" Gaelyn says, hugging her Tile to her chest. "My job here is done."

Zack wants to say: *Don't leave me here.* For a moment, psychologically, he is reduced to a child hanging on to his mother's skirt, head buried in hard shins. *Don't leave me here.* He doesn't move, just watches as she turns and walks away from him. The only kind face he's seen in months. *Don't leave me here.* What have these people done to him? He forces his thoughts away from the retreating shape of the receptionist and looks Lewis directly in the eyes.

"Where do we start?"

CHAPTER 34

A MAP TO NOWHERE

TWELVE YEARS LATER

White Mezzanine, 2036

Once Silver's unpicked two pieces of copper, she uses the edge of one piece to sharpen the other. It already has a good shape—a long triangle—so all it needs is some friction to turn it into a more efficient weapon. She finishes it and is satisfied with her work, happy with what she's made despite the knowledge of what it will be used for.

Her head is still pounding off the scale. Even swallowing what little saliva she has sends lightning bolts of pain through her skull. Soon it will be over. She blows the metallic dust off the blade—copper glitter—and polishes it with her cotton shift.

Silver doesn't know why it's taken her so long to realise this is what is required of her. It should have been obvious from the start.

The bathtub is bright porcelain and so clean it's as if no one has ever looked at it, never mind bathed in it. Silver clicks the five-finger option and warm water rushes out of the tap. The water is as clear as drinking water. Silver's fascinated: She's never bathed in transparent water before. She adds another five fingers so that the tub is half-full. Over the top, vulgar luxury, she knows, but in her situation it's forgivable. She pulls her starched shift off over her head and slowly climbs in. It's like sliding into warm liquid glass. She lies back against the white slope, then slips under the water, feeling the warmth wash over her whole scalp and face and shoulders, and it feels so good—such a relief. She sighs out bubbles and stays under until her lungs protest.

When she surfaces, she's thinking of her family. Tears come. The warmth of the water tinges her usually ivory skin with pink, and the blue veins on her wrists are showing off. Beautifully sketched lines of navy. A map to nowhere.

Silver leans over the edge of the tub and picks up her hand-fashioned copper razor.

She cuts lengthways along the veins on both arms. Silver moans in pain as the skin parts. Doubt flickers in on her. Is she really doing this? Is this really the only way? But there's no going back now.

Of course she's expecting the blood. The more, the better. The quicker. But the starkness of the vermilion against the bath, the pulsing flow, startles her. She watches as the red spills down and creates underwater clouds, like upside-down atom bombs. Soon the porcelain is painted; the water is dyed.

Crimson Cascade, Kate would say.

Silver leans back again, resting her arms on the lip of the bath. She watches the last of her consciousness leak out of her wrists, and her eyelids swoon.

CHAPTER 35

GHOST

The Atrium

Johannesburg, 2036

"Hey," Keke says to a passerby.

"Hey yourself," says the man, looking Keke up and down approvingly.

Jesus, does she never get sick of the attention? Kate's sure it would drive her mad—that constant gnawing of her body by every stranger she meets. Doesn't she ever feel that one day there'll be nothing left?

Instead, it has the opposite effect on Keke. Her back straightens, showing off the perfect shape of her breasts, the flat board that is her stomach.

"We're looking for Silver. You seen her?"

"Silver?"

"She usually jacks in here." Kate motions at the empty pod. At least, she thinks she does. The initials 'GK' are scratched into the smooth shell, making Kate second-guess herself. She hasn't been here with Silver for a long time. It's one of the ways she's let her drift away. Again: the ache.

"Teenage girl, long white hair."

On the wall there's a slogan splashed in violet: *As we design, so, perhaps, we were designed.*

"Small," says Kate. "She's quite small for her age."

The man's eyes widen. "You mean, 'Ghost'?"

"What?" snaps Kate. For some reason, the name unsettles her. Her hair stands on end.

"Ghost?" says Keke. "That could be her."

The man looks impressed. "She's a legend around here, you know. She's, like, the best player in the whole place."

Kate remembers when Silver was a toddler and used to put a white serviette over her head at dinnertime.

I'm a gho-o-ost, she used to say. *I'm a gho-o-ost.*

What do they know? What's going on? Paranoia, as familiar and shocking as cold water, splashes her in the face. "Why do you call her that?"

The man looks puzzled at her reaction. "It's her avatar," he says, frowning. What he means is: *You don't know your own daughter's avatar?*

"And …"

"And what?"

"And it fits her perfectly."

"What's that supposed to mean?"

His eyes meet Kate's. "She's impossible to kill."

"When's the last time you saw her?" Keke slips easily into her investigative journo cloak.

"She was here earlier." The man's wearing a perfumed shirt and the fragrance comes off him in feathers of invisible smoke. Amber, pepperwood, juniper berry. Kate tried out a perfumed bra when the trend hit, but her kids kept on sniffing the air around her and saying *Can you smell that? Can you smell that?* as if someone had stepped in dog shit instead of what it was supposed to be: Citrus Burn.

"When?" asks Keke. "And where did she go?"

"I don't know. Time gets a bit foggy in here." The lights are always set to daylight-bright and there are no clocks on the walls. "I'd guess at late afternoon? I don't know where she went, but she did say something."

This gets Kate's attention. "Yes?"

"Well, Nova was teasing her, saying she'd beat Silver to the win."

"Win the game?"

"Ja. All in good fun, because everyone knows that when Silver turns sixteen she's going to dominate Eden 7.0. I mean, we don't stand a chance. The only reason we're ahead of her at the moment is because we're meshed and she's not."

"You need to be meshed to win?"

"You need to be meshed to access 7.0."

"And she said she was going to get meshed when she turned sixteen?"

"It goes without saying. She's a fucking prodigy. Have you *seen* the worlds she's designed? She's like a freaking space architect. And her colonies are brilliant. Even her bio systems—"

"So," Kate interrupts, "Nova was goading her—"

"Not goading," he says, "not really. We're always just stinging each other. We're all close friends and we look out for one another. Nova loves Silver like a little sister."

Along with the warm fragrance coming off him there are other scents: tea, and timber. It's difficult to see his face when there are so many shapes in the air between them.

"And then?"

"And then Silver said she was leaving early, which she never does, so we asked her why, and she said that she was going to get her sixteenth birthday present."

The bright bulbs start hurting Kate's head, as if somehow the light is seeping into her brain and dehydrating her thoughts.

"Which is?"

The man smiles, showing the distinctive grey, ground-down teeth of a hard-line gamer.

"Well, she didn't say, but … isn't it obvious?"

"She wouldn't," says Kate as they jog out of the Atrium.

Keke glances at her, purses her lips.

"Silver wouldn't do that. Go out on her own and get it done against my wishes. Would she?"

"Get meshed?" says Keke. "Of course she would. She's been talking about it for two years. You just haven't been listening."

"I thought it was a phase. Everything's a phase, with kids, you know?"

"Not this."

"And I *was* listening. Just because I didn't want her to get it, doesn't mean I wasn't listening."

"What I mean is … and don't take this the wrong way … that you weren't *listening*-listening."

"What the fuck is that supposed to mean?"

"You heard Silver asking if she could get the neural lace. She wasn't really asking. What she was saying was that she was going to get it with or without you."

"Well, then, in that case, there's nothing I could have done to stop her, right?"

"No, but you could have gone with her. You could have made sure she got it done safely."

Kate's face burns: anger swirls with regret. A whirlpool on fire.

"Wow, Keke, look at you. All the answers. Why don't *you* try to parent fifteen-year-old twins and see how you do with that?"

Keke grabs Kate's arm, makes her stop walking, arrests her with her ice-blue biolenses.

"KittyKat. I'd never be able to do what you do. It's terrifying."

"You're not helping."

"I wouldn't even like to *try* to be a mother. Not for a day. I'd rather shoot myself."

"Again, not helping."

"Sorry. I don't know what to say."

"They always tell you everything," says Kate.

"Well, they wouldn't if I was their parent!"

They hurry out of the Atrium and stop on the pavement outside, not sure where to go next.

Kate's mandible begins to ring.

"Kate," purrs the DarkDoc. "I've been trying to reach you."

The combination of the static and his gruff voice blows silver streamers into her vision.

"The commlines are a mess," she says. "It'll get worse."

She doesn't hear the next few words.

"...I need you to come here as soon as you can."

"I can't," says Kate.

"I need to see you before—"

"Before the world ends?"

There's a pause. More shimmering static.

"Something like that."

Usually when he says those words—*I need to see you*—Kate feels an immediate rush of warmth to her pelvis, but today the yellow adrenaline is splattering over all her other emotions.

"I can't."

"Things are getting dangerous out there. Please come to me."

"I can take care of myself."

"I know. It doesn't change how I feel."

"I want to be with you too," says Kate, and Keke makes googly eyes at her. She turns away. "But I can't. Silver is missing."

"No, she's not," says Morgan. "That's what I'm calling to tell you."

"She is," says Kate. "She's not at home. We're at the Atrium. She's not here, either."

"I know. That's because she's here, with us."

CHAPTER 36

IS THIS THE REAL WORLD?

"You're fucking the DarkDoc?" asks Keke.

"Language," scolds Kate, not because she minds the word—god knows it's one of her favourites—but because it's become a habit to try to keep things clean with the twins around.

Keke is genuinely shocked. "I did not see that coming!"

"Stop with the sex puns already."

"How? Where? When?"

They pass a mean posse of men with automatic rifles, clubs, and hunting knives. It says *Fuck Robots* on one of the men's wide chests. Another man wears a face mask emblazoned with a pixellated swastika and an anthrobot's severed arm around his neck like a mantle. Badly drawn prison tattoos scribble their skin.

Bot Hunters. Science deniers. Alt-tech nazis.

The hate group gathered momentum last year when a few of the older generation of anthrobots started spontaneously activating their self-destruct buttons in crowded places. There were six bomb blasts and more than twenty fatalities before they were all seized and taken off the market.

TERRORBOTS! the newstream tickertape had screamed, whipping people into a frenzy of panic and suspicion of all things AI, but then when the terror attacks had been properly investigated, it turned out that an unidentified human had hacked the switches, so it hadn't really been a robot rebellion at all. Of course, the alt-tech nazis didn't let the truth get in the way of their mission to 'enslave the enemy' and drive other violent propaganda. And, while the new anthrobots still have baked-in self-destruct switches, the only way to deploy them now is for both the bot and a human to activate it at the same time. Unlike humans, 7thGen robosapiens are untouched by the Suicide Contagion, which in theory ensures that the detonator will only be deployed in true emergencies.

One of the men glares at Kate. She feels for her gun and is relieved when it's still there in its holster, thigh-warmed.

"I want to know everything," says Keke. "Spill!"

"It's not important. We've got bigger things to worry about."

"Oh no, you're not going to get away with that. I want details."

Kate motions for a northbound tram to stop and they hop on, relieved to put space between themselves and the creeps.

Keke's still looking at her. "This is a mindfuck on so many levels."

"So the world has gone completely mad and we're practically in the midst of a civil war but you think that my sex life is a mindfuck."

"It is!"

"Why?" asks Kate. "Am I that out of the game?"

"You're as hot-damn sexy as ever, and you know that," says Keke. "But—"

"Yes? Get it all out of your system. We're on our way to see him, and I don't want you acting crackers around him."

"The DarkDoc!"

"He has a name, you know. Morgan. I don't call him the DarkDoc in bed."

"You should," says Keke. "That's hot."

"No," Kate shakes her head, laughing. "No. It's not."

"That voice," says Keke, pretending to be enraptured.

"I know," says Kate. "It's the voice that did it."

"I thought you hated doctors."

"I do. I did. It's complicated."

They ride past 4D street art. Animations of characters and slogans. Japanimé. Logos and tags and avatar stamps. Two-dimensional bumper stickers read 'QE'; 'Wake Up' and 'Is this the Real World?'

"You're gonna tell me where we're going?" asks Keke.

"You haven't given me a chance!"

There's a screeching on the other side of the street. A cabbie drives off the road and straight into a Mexican food truck. A big bang and smoke and yelling, but no one seems too badly hurt. Pedestrians hurry past the tacos and salsa on tar. The wall in the background says 'The Internet is God', and it animates so that the words 'The Internet' and 'God' swap places every few seconds.

The Internet is God. God is the Internet. The Internet is God.

"Holy shit," says Keke. "What the fuck. This is so surreal."

"Morgan's with Silver. That's why we're going there."

"She's safe?"

"He didn't say that."

"What did he say?"

"That we need to get there as soon as possible."

"That doesn't sound good."

"He wouldn't say more than that. Said he didn't want me to worry. He'll tell us everything when we get there."

"Get where?"

"The Lipworth Institute."

CHAPTER 37

SMUDGED WITH ASH AND HEARTACHE

The Android Pod

Johannesburg, 2036

Any hope of finding Mally at Vega's hostel evaporates as soon as Seth arrives. The front door has been blown wide open, and now the entrance to the building is a gaping, smoking maw. Looters stream out with chips and roscoe bullets they'll never be able to use. Seth hears shouting and mad laughter. Broken glass crunches underfoot as he makes his way inside. Whoops of victory ring out as people kick cabinet locks in and smash the expensive tech with baseball bats. *Fuck Robots* is emblazoned on more than one of the fire-smoked walls.

Some robosapien bodies lie in pieces on the floor, completely human-looking at a glance. Human from the outside, anyway: stamped silicone, padded by flesh-coloured sponge—it's just the colour of their blood that gives them away. That, and, if you look closely enough, the white titanium bones.

A man in a camouflaged exo-suit walks with purpose through the trashed hall, finger on the trigger of a large automatic weapon: a metal-melter. Instead of bullets, it's specifically designed to fry a robot's circuitry. Seth recognises the type. These people are usually underground, but it seems that the AI uprising has coaxed them out of their secret bunkers.

This is not good news, he thinks as he stops and looks around at the chaos.

The Bot Hunter sidles past Seth, bumping him just hard enough to send a message. Seth automatically feels for his Vektor, but remembers it's not there just before his hand comes away empty. He turns to look at the man, and they exchange hard looks before letting go.

There's another small explosion a few rooms away. The looters jump, but recover quickly, then seem energised by the destruction. They remind Seth of grinning hyenas, come to steal the scraps from the Grim Reaper's table.

Seth grabs one of the young men running past.

"Where are they?" Seth asks. "The robots?"

The man shakes himself loose from Seth, shrugs, then takes off.

A woman's shaking voice sounds from behind him. "They took them."

Seth turns around to see a woman smudged with ash and heartache. Was she there all along? She's so grey he didn't even noticed her when he walked in.

"They took them," she says. Her shoulder is bleeding: some kind of black shrapnel is poking out, pointing towards Seth.

"Are you all right?" he says. "Can I help you? Take you somewhere? Hospital?"

"What's the point." It's not a question.

Seth leaves the exploding building with the feeling that it will devour itself before dawn. He sees a NASP policeman—code for Roguebot Cop—handcuffing an anthrobot.

"I don't understand," the bot is saying. She looks like a fourth-generation model, quite obviously not human, so an easy target for brutes like this. "There is no reason for my arrest. I didn't break protocol."

The cop swipes perspiration from his eyebrow. "It's for your own safety."

"I don't understand," she says.

A distraught woman in a faded yellow dress is arguing with the cop. She has a wailing toddler on her hip. A small patch of blood and dirt is visible where the kid's knee is bleeding onto her.

"She was helping us!" the mother keeps saying. "Don't you understand? She was helping!"

"It doesn't matter," says the cop.

The toddler cries and cries.

"My child fell in the street. This robot helped her. Why are you handcuffing her?"

The cop's lips shrink; he doesn't have time for this. He's got a whole city to clean up.

"I don't understand," the bot says.

"You don't need to understand, buttercup." He finally clicks the cuffs in place. A van with the NASP insignia rolls up and he walks her over, helps her up into the pen, which Seth sees is crowded with all kinds of anthrobots.

"Where are you taking them?" asks Seth.

The cop ignores him.

"Hey!" shouts Seth. "Where are you taking them?"

They slam shut the back door and the vehicle speeds away.

CHAPTER 38

YOU USED TO BE ABLE TO SEE THE STARS

The Lipworth Institute

Johannesburg, 2036

When Kate and Keke arrive at the Lipworth Institute they are scanned and frisked and interviewed and snapped. Their DNA code is verified by the bottle of water they are offered on arrival.

“Someone’s paranoid,” mumbles Keke.

“Not paranoid,” says Kate. “Safe.”

“Now they’ve got our numbers,” says Keke. “They could print a copy of you right now. They could clone your ass and keep you in a cage in the basement and no one would be any the wiser.”

“Jesus. Now who’s being paranoid?”

“I’m just saying. Stranger things have happened.”

“I’d like to think that my family would know the difference between me and a facsimile.”

“Ha,” says Keke.

“What’s that supposed to mean?”

Keke shrugs. “This place just gives me the creeps. It’s so …clean. White.”

“Really.”

“It doesn’t bother you?”

"It doesn't bother me. In fact, I like it. It gives me a break from my synaesthesia. It's like a palate cleanser for my brain."

"What did you say about me being crackers earlier? For the record, I am not the one who is crackers."

A smooth white robot cycles up to them. "Good morning."

Is it morning already?

"Good morning," says Kate. "Doctor Morgan said I should meet him here."

"Of course, Miss Denicker, please follow me."

After a few steps the droid stops and addresses Keke, "I'm sorry, but your access has been denied."

"Excuse me?"

"Your code has not been pre-approved."

"What the fuck does that mean?"

"Your record," says Kate.

"My record?"

"Your criminal record," says the bot, helpfully.

"My record is clean!"

"Not according to the SACRKS. I'm sorry."

"If you're talking about what happened in 2024, they dropped the charges."

"Hmm," says the droid.

Keke stands her ground.

"And the 2021 charge was also dropped."

Sensing Keke's persistence, the droid shifts into peace-making mode. "Please feel free to wait for Miss Denicker in our Metro Revolvorant."

Keke's mandible beeps.

"Please accept this credit to treat yourself to a complimentary beverage of your choice."

Keke acquiesces with a sigh. "Fine. Whatever. I'll wait for you at their crap-o-rant. Keep me posted!"

Keke zooms up in their external elevator that only has one stop: The Metro Revolvorant. It's empty apart from a bored waitbot vacuuming the glass floor with its skirt. The vertiginous view reminds her of that old club they used to go to in the 20s. *What was it called?* She met many a contact there.

The restaurant is superglass from floor to ceiling, and, as the name suggests, it slowly revolves to offer the patrons a view of the whole city, which would be magnificent if it wasn't for the electrosmog that covers Johannesburg like a static dirty dog blanket.

You used to be able to see the stars.

When did the air become unbreathable? Slowly, slowly, then all at once.

How things can change so much in a decade. Now the outside sky is grey-black, with only the slightest hint of dawn. Keke grabs a seat and punches in her order for an iced coffeeberry. Despite her melancholia, it's not the worst place to watch a sunrise.

"Welcome to the Metro Revolvo!" says an electronic voice, and Keke almost jumps out of her leathers. The waitbot's LED eyes regard her with a neutral expression. It puts her drink on the table, and Keke thanks it, despite always making fun of Kate for doing the same thing.

It's a fucking droid, Kate, she would say.

Manners are manners, Kate would fire back, especially if the kids were with them.

The bot goes back to vacuuming the already spotless floor. Keke thinks it might be the loneliest thing she's ever seen. Without warning, she feels a heaviness on her chest, as if the whole sad empty restaurant is itself a vacuum, and it's crushing her.

This is not the time for an existential crisis. Pull yourself together.

She knows what she needs to do.

CHAPTER 39

BALLS IN A BEAR TRAP

TWELVE YEARS PREVIOUSLY

SkyRest

Johannesburg, 2024

Lewis takes Zack around the residence. He's a man of few words, and of those words at least half are swearwords, but Zack gets the general gist of how the system operates. The three separate wings are all identical to this one. They work eight-hour shifts then replace one another, like a relay team. Work, leisure, sleep. Work, leisure, sleep. Work, leisure, sleep. Cogs in a machine.

Zack expects the rooms to be cold, but a warmth emanates from the walls. Their residence will still be vacant for another half hour.

"Let's grab a sandwich before the mob gets back," says Lewis as they pass by the cafeteria. He skims two subs off a tray and hands one to Zack, who doesn't have an appetite—hasn't had an appetite in days—but accepts it anyway. They sit at a plastic table.

"It's your day off?" asks Zack.

Lewis laughs, wipes invisible crumbs from his beard. "No. No such thing in here." He takes another bite. "They always get me to do the babysitting."

Zack's never been the ingénue before; he's used to being the mentor. He's used to being the one with the silk tie and all the answers.

"No offence," Lewis adds.

"None taken," says Zack. "I'm just ... adjusting."

"You'll get used to it soon enough," says the old hippie. "Things are simple in here, which is more than I can say for the outside world. You work hard, you get Rewards. You keep working hard, you level up."

Level up? thinks Zack. Something about the phrase ignites a flame of anxiety in his chest. An important thought is hovering, just out of his reach.

"You level up all the way," continues Lewis, "and you get out of the dungeon. Up to where all the pretty white space is with entertainment rooms and cinescreens and virtual gyms and office pods. And decent food," he says, crumpling up his serviette and shooting it into the corner bin. "Not this cardboard panini shit. Or so I've heard."

Zack notices for the first time the lapel on Lewis's vest.

"These are my stages," he says, tapping the five colours on his chest. They're like military stripes. "Two more to go before I get elevated."

"Elevated?"

"Promoted. To up there," he points to the ceiling.

"How long have you been here?"

"Jesus. I don't know. How'm I supposed to know? You see a fucking calendar in here?"

"Longer than the rest?"

"Most of them."

"Are we talking years? Or decades? How long does it take to get up there?"

Lewis shrugs. "It depends how hard you work." He looks at Zack's sandwich, untouched. "Good decision," he says.

In the remaining time before the work shift is over, Zack learns how to slam the side of the jukebox in exactly the right position to get it to play 'A Little Less Conversation' (which kicks him in the gut with nostalgia for a nameless woman with burnt caramel skin), how to hack the sonic shower so that it gives you an extra thirty seconds of spray (*believe me, on some days you'll need it*), and what you have to do to get Rewards.

"Rewards? Like treats? Like, for a dog," says Zack.

"Sure, you can think of it that way."

"What's the best way to think of it?"

"Ways to make your life here more comfortable."

Lewis shows Zack his own room. It's pimped out with body-building equipment, a long mirror, a comfortable looking bed, and a beard-grooming kit.

"Some inmates use Rewards for snax. Chocolate and nutnut cookies and shit. Not me. I want to look my best when I get up to civilisation."

Zack eyes out the SkyRest-branded shaving foam canister and cut-throat razor. It looks well used. "They're not worried that you use that as a weapon?"

"Ah, no," says Lewis. "No bad behaviour in here. It's not worth it. They'll strip you of all your stages. It's a fate worse than death."

Lewis points at the corner of the ceiling. Zack assumes a microcam is there.

"Every room. They watch everything we do. Real time. No one gets away with anything. It's a clean way to live, you know. Transparent. Puts you on your best behaviour. In the real world if someone pissed me off, I'd probably fuck them up. That's one of the reasons I'm in here. Now I let shit slide. All actions have consequences. I meditate the anger away. It's a lot fucking healthier."

"What happens to you in here if you break the rules?"

"No one breaks the rules."

"That can't be true."

"Listen," says Lewis, looking up at the camera again, then back to Zack. "I'm only going to say this once."

Zack looks at him.

"Do not break the rules in here. Do not break the fucking rules. Got it?"

He nods.

"Do not start trouble. Show up for work. Don't wander off. Don't cause fights. Okay?"

"Okay," says Zack.

"You do not want to be thrown in solcon. Not in this place."

Lewis looks away now, and there's something in his eyes that wasn't there before. What has he seen?

Zack tries to lighten the atmosphere. "So there're never any punch-ups?"

"Well, I wouldn't say that. Put a bunch of men in a dungeon and there are going to be skirmishes. But they're rare. There's just too much at stake. Plus—"

"Plus?"

He taps his black bracelet. "They can stop a brawl before it escalates. They've got eyes on you, right? Plus they monitor your heart rate, your blood sugar, your adrenaline, and this thing packs a hell of a current. Someone up there gets antsy, and they can floor every single one of us with a push of a button."

"They can taser us all? All at once?"

"Taser, monitor, drug..." he polishes the cuff with his sleeve. "Basically, they've got our fucking balls in a bear trap. So my best advice is to act accordingly."

CHAPTER 40
MIDNIGHT ELVES

"You ready for your first shift, Girdler?"

Lewis stands at Zack's sliding door. The bell rings.

"I think so." Zack doesn't mind the idea of hard work today. It might help with his nerves. Lewis gestures for him to follow, and they join the rest of the crims as they stream out of the residence and into the adjacent factory. Zack calls it a factory, but to be honest he still doesn't know what products SkyRest makes. He receives a few mildly interested looks from the others, but most of them ignore him. Soldier ants, worker bees: all in the same grey soft-cotton kit.

"What is the actual work?" asks Zack.

"That's not an easy one to answer."

Zack laughs without humour. "What do you mean?"

"It's not like we're working on an assembly line, right? We're not manufacturing shit. This isn't fucking Bilchen."

"Then ... what?"

"They identify what needs doing and they funnel us accordingly."

"But what? What work?"

Why is Lewis being so evasive?

"Anything. Anything that requires labour as long as—"

"Yes?"

"As long as we're not seen."

"By who?"

"By the clients. By the pretty people in the honeycomb. We're like ... the midnight elves. You know, the little crims who steal inside and do all the work. Like an invisible workforce, you know? The ghost in the machine. No one wants to see the elves. It breaks the spell."

They keep walking.

"So, give me some examples, so that I know what to expect."

Lewis sighs. Zack can see him thinking: *I'm too old for this shit.*

"Okay, so ... the day before yesterday we were chopping wood for the incinerator. The day before that, we were creating seed eggs. Before that: chopping fucking onions. Before that: re-potting saplings. Birch, I think they were. Silver birch."

"What are seed eggs?"

Lewis holds up a hand to stop him from asking more questions.

"You're not ready to know that shit yet. You're going to be in here a long time. You're gonna need to learn some fucking patience."

"Sorry," says Zack.

"I'm not mad. I'm just telling you like it is."

They trot into an artificial greenhouse. There are no windows, because it's deep underground, but the ceiling is covered in thousands of lo-glo bulbs, and the plants —thousands upon thousands of plants—reach up to their fake suns like disciples who don't yet know they've been swindled.

They line up along the rows of aeroponic vegetation. How many are there of them? Zack does a quick headcount. Two hundred? Each row seems to contain a different plant. Theirs has a purple flower.

"Slow and steady," says Lewis, tapping his stages. "Slow and steady wins the race."

Zack looks at Lewis's lapel. "Hey. You got another stripe."

Lewis's eyes twinkle. "Close now," he says, "real close. I think you had something to do with it."

"I doubt it," says Zack.

"You filled in the satisfaction report, right?"

"Well, there was a form. It asked how I would rate my initiation experience."

"Right," says Lewis. "I think that's what tipped the scales. I mean, I knew I was close."

"What's the first thing you're going to do?" asks Zack. "You know, when you're up there?"

"I'm gonna go for a swim. Did you see that swimming pool?"

"No," says Zack. "I thought pools were illegal."

"Not in state institutions. Not when they service a community like this."

"You saw it?"

"Oh yeah. Oh man, that pool. As blue as the fucking Atlantic. I haven't been for a swim since 2009."

"That does sound pretty good."

"And then, then…I'm going to have a meal. A proper meal. And a CinnaCola, with ice. Real ice. Not fake ice."

"I don't think they make that anymore. CinnaCola, I mean."

"Ah." Lewis looks disappointed.

"Listen up, residents," says a familiar voice from the front of the greenhouse.

A medium close-up of Bernard's toad-skinned face is beamed into a hexagonal-framed hologram above them.

"We're going to be spraying the plants today. It's important that you spray them hard enough to dislodge any insects—"

Insects? Down here? And: *So they've given her a job to do.*

"—but not so hard that you damage the leaves or uproot the organism."

Bernard nods at the creep holding the holocam and they track down to her hands, where she demonstrates the correct procedure. Zack can't help cringing when there's a close-up of her hands and her broad, flat fingernails. She was in his room again last night. He heard the door slide open and something inside him shriveled up like it would never be the same again. And now she's here to stay.

"What are these plants, anyway?" he whispers to Lewis.

"It's fucking alfalfa," says Lewis. "Can't you tell?"

CHAPTER 41
HOLLOW BUTTONS

TWELVE YEARS LATER

White Mezzanine, 2036

Silver wakes in the same white room, in the same spearmint shift. At first she's confused, and then disappointed. She pulls the linen off her body and inspects her wrists. No wounds, no scars, as if her suicide didn't happen at all.

"Fuck," she says.

Her disappointment grows bigger inside her, out of control—a veld fire—and changes quickly to a hot white fury. She takes it out on the furniture again: the side table, the chair, the plate of breakfast nutrijelly. Silver tries to smash the small square of reinforced flexiglass that should be her portal to the outside world but all she manages to do is hurt her hand. She stops shouting when the tears come, not because she's no longer angry but because she can't yell and cry and breathe at the same time without hyperventilating. Silver cries until her eyes are swollen and her head pounds with its terrible ache, and she has to lie with her cheek and temple on the cool floor for relief.

She stares at the two cobalt-coloured tablets lying on the tiles. Slowly, slowly, she crawls towards them and picks them up. She knows that if she swallows them they'll take away her pain. Her unremitting headache, her glowing hand, her heartbreak. They'd make this hell-flavoured purgatory easier to handle. She wants to take them so badly, but instead she stands up and walks to the cupboard and finds her jacket, and pushes the pills into the hollow buttons of her coat. She checks on the other buttons, feeling them with the tips of her fingers, as if her eyes are not to be trusted. Twenty-four have now been filled. Twelve to go. That should be enough to escape.

CHAPTER 42
UNDER THE SURFACE

TWELVE YEARS PREVIOUSLY

SkyRest
Johannesburg, 2024

Once the plants are sprayed and inspected for any kind of malformations or disease, the workers move on to other things. Some go to help in the kitchen, some, the laundry. Zack and Lewis are enlisted to saw and chip wood, along with another ten men. What surprises Zack most is how much space there is down here. The outside building—that white honeycomb shard planted into the earth—is the tip of an iceberg. An anthill that is rooted deeply and widely under the surface.

"Be careful," warns Lewis, looking at the humming machine. "These are industrial chippers. They'll chew your fucking arm off if you daydream."

They start feeding the appliance with the hunks of wood supplied. It makes short work of even the hardest wedges of timber. They both grunt and sweat with the effort of hauling the heavy pieces.

"No offence, but … aren't you too old for this kind of work?" Zack is only half joking.

"Fuck off," says Lewis. They both know he is the stronger of the two.

It's gratifying labour, and the air is filled with a dusty forest fragrance that penetrates their paper masks. They bag all the wood chips, and pack them into trolley cages which are wheeled away by another team. They sweep the floor till it's spotless; so that no one would be able to say there were twelve men in here making whole trees disappear.

After an exhausting eight hours, the bell rings, and they amble back to their residence, stretching sore muscles and rubbing dirt off their skin. Bernard follows them from behind. Zack ruffles his hair and sawdust falls onto his shoulders. His cuff beeps green.

"Hey," says Lewis. "The gods approve!"

Zack looks at him, and Lewis slaps him on the back.

"You got your first Reward. What are you going to choose?"

"I don't know."

"You don't know?" Lewis wipes his arms and hands with a damp rag.

"I guess I'll look through the catalogue."

"You need to set up your wishlist, man. Most of us have lists a mile long. You don't even have an idea?"

Zack still doesn't have an appetite, and there's nothing he's seen in Lewis's room that he wants to replicate, but then he gets it.

"A book," says Zack. It's exactly what his atrophying brain requires. "I'll request a book."

Lewis shakes his head. "Sorry, man. Down here? No books allowed."

CHAPTER 43

GOOD ANGEL, BAD ANGEL

TWELVE YEARS LATER

The Lipworth Institute

Johannesburg, 2036

"Morgan!" Kate runs up to the DarkDoc and hugs him. He's standing outside a private ward in the medical wing of the Lipworth Institute. Why Africa's premier robotics lab needs a medical wing is not clear to Kate, but more pressing questions are crowding her head.

"Kate." His arms and his voice envelop her, and she allows herself to be held for a minute before she breaks away. Morgan's solid frame is always a comfort. She feels grounded when they're together: When he's touching her there's no danger of flying off into space. He holds her by her upper arms now, as if to inspect her. His warm skin is cedar leaves and cardamom: a fresh winter fire. She doesn't see her shapes when he talks, despite his voice's dark resonance. Instead it goes deep inside her.

Kate swallows hard. "Silver?"

"Before you see her …" the DarkDoc says, "let's talk."

"Let me see her first. Is she in there?" She moves towards the closed door.

"Kate. Please. I don't want you to—"

But it's too late. Kate leans against the door and rushes in, and when she sees Silver, she's so shocked that the blood drains away from her head.

"Whoa," says Morgan as her knees give way, and he grabs her.

"What happened to her?" Kate tries to blink away the dizziness. "What the fuck happened to her?"

Silver is bone-white. She's in a spherical oxygen tent, unconscious. IV bags hang on steel arms above her shoulders. One white, one red. Good Angel, Bad Angel. Her head is bandaged, her wrists shackled to the bed with velcro strips. Silver looks so small and defenceless on the hospital bed it makes her want to cry.

Kate approaches the transparent plastic dome and unzips it just enough to hold her daughter's cold, sleeping hand. She looks so young. Too thin and too fragile. A bird with a smashed wing. The skin on her inner arms has bright red welts, a few platelet plasters dress where the skin is broken.

"It's her sixteenth birthday tomorrow." Kate doesn't know why she says it.

"I know," says Morgan.

"How did you find her? How did you know she was here?"

"I got a med-alert from the institute. They must have scanned her dynap code. I'm still listed as her primary physician."

"Why didn't they call me?"

"The commlines have been unstable. I couldn't get hold of you either, but I kept trying until I did."

Kate re-sets her mandible.

You have three hundred and eight missed calls, it says.

"You called me three hundred times?" she asks Morgan.

A half-smile. "That sounds about right."

Kate blinks at him. "Thank you."

"It's nothing. Besides, it's the good samaritan who brought her in here you should thank. And the Institute. She couldn't be in better hands."

"Why are her arms strapped down?"

"She was harming herself. Scratching. She almost hit a vein before we realised what she was doing."

"What happened to her?"

The DarkDoc pulls her to the visitors' couch where they sit down. He hands her a paper cup of some kind of lukewarm flower tea. Chamomile? No. The shape of chamomile is oval and rough-edged. This is soft. Palest yellow on white (Pee Snow). She puts it down on the ledge beside her.

"I want to know everything. Don't leave anything out."

"I don't know much, yet, but as far as I can see, Silver's had a bad reaction."

"A bad reaction? To what?"

"I've examined the wound on her head. She got laced. I don't know where or how—"

"Oh no," says Kate. "Oh no. It's my fault."

Liquid guilt spreads inside her, blackening and embittering her organs. Cold Tar.

"It's not your fault."

"I should have done it with her. Gone with her. Given her permission. Then *you* could have done it. Instead of … instead of *this*."

They both look over at Silver's still body. Morgan squeezes her hands.

"You were trying to protect her. Besides, I should have known when she came to see me that she wasn't going to take no for an answer. Silver's stubborn … like someone else I know."

He's trying to lighten the mood, but it doesn't work.

"I'm sorry," Morgan says. "I should have accompanied her home."

"I should have gone with her in the first place!"

"You did what you thought was best."

"Did I?"

"Kitty. Of course you did."

"Did I do what I thought was best, or what suited me best?"

Kate's so angry with herself, she feels like bashing her head on the wall. "I've just been … trying to stop her from drifting away, you know?"

"I know."

"It's like immersion just takes her further and further away from me. And now look at her!"

"She's catatonic."

"Is she in a coma?"

"No. Her vitals are there. Shallow, but all there. She's just not … conscious."

"I don't understand."

Morgan steeples his fingers. "It's like she's … somewhere else. Like she's slipped away from us and left her body behind."

Kate buries her face in her hands for a moment then looks at him. "Can you fix her?"

His immediate expression tells her all she needs to know.

"There are so many ways to mesh," he says, "so many different laces on the market. And on the grey market. It's impossible to regulate any of it, never mind creating proper peer-reviewed studies of how it affects different people in different ways. The tech evolves every single day … it's just spinning away from us."

Kate's hopes drag. The DarkDoc is the southern hemisphere's pre-eminent biotech doctor. If he can't fix her, who can?

"You'll try, though? You'll do what you can?"

Kate can see he's already rehearsed his answer.

"It's too risky."

"You have to try!"

"I'd be going in blind. The chance of causing irreversible damage is just too high. I wouldn't take the risk with a patient I didn't know, never mind with Silver."

Kate blinks at him, waiting for the information to sink in.

"So. There's nothing we can do?"

The DarkDoc smooths his black beard. "I didn't say that."

CHAPTER 44

TRUMPET OF DEATH

TWELVE YEARS PREVIOUSLY

SkyRest

Johannesburg, 2024

This time when they are led into the hall to work they are given special protective gear. Thin plastic overalls that crunch when you walk, wide face masks, and biolatex gloves. The air is less stale than usual.

The guard with grey hair and a voice like dusk stands in front of them. The younger guard—a blond, fresh-faced assistant—films him so that his face is broadcast in the hexagonal holoframe above the residents.

“Good morning,” he says, and the men mutter their replies. Zack picks up that the guard’s name is Xoli. He seems to enjoy the attention. “You’ll be wondering why you’ve been given extra kit. It’s because we’re dealing with a new substance today. It’s part of our experimentation in a new, cutting-edge technology, and we need your help. It’s not without risk, though, so please be careful and keep your prophylactix on at all times.”

There’s a murmur of interest. Virgin tasks are few and far between, from what Zack’s seen, so getting to do new work seems like something to look forward to. The men are instructed to move towards the trestle tables, and the day leaders peel away the covers to reveal large tubs of dark brown organic matter.

“Now for those of you with foraging experience,” says Xoli, and there are a few laughs, “You’ll know that this—” He holds up a large lily-shaped, charcoal-coloured mushroom. "—is called a Black Trumpet. Cornucopioides. Also known as black chanterelle, and … Trumpet of Death."

Zack studies the tub in front of him. He can see the fungi between the humus and brittle leaves.

"Now, mycologists would usually tell you that there's nothing to fear from a black chanterelle, and they'd be right. In fact, these mushrooms, in the wild, are really quite delicious and will do you no harm."

Xoli holds up his specimen, and the camera zooms in.

"However, this batch of fungi has been adapted by our bioburial scientists, who spliced its helix with Dermestid."

The room is quiet.

"Anyone?"

A few frowns and head-shakes.

"Derme-stid. Skin Beetle. A Dermestid is a flesh-eating beetle."

Zack's skin crawls with imaginary insect legs.

"So, I introduce to you … *Carnacraterellus cornucopioides*."

"A man-eating mushroom," says someone at the front.

Xoli looks pleased. "Correct."

The men murmur. Xoli talks them through the process: find the mushrooms, identify the mycelia, harvest the spores, store them safely in the envelopes or soil trays provided.

"Please work carefully," he says. "And, whatever you do, don't breathe the spores in. As you can imagine, you don't want these suckers seeding your lungs."

Later, in his room, Zack lies on his mat and swipes through the Reward catalogue. What he really wants now is sleeping pills. He hasn't had a good night's sleep since he was arrested. Although, even if he has the pills, he probably won't take them. Only one thing is worse than Bernard watching him sleep, and that's not even knowing she's watching him sleep.

He might request a bed or a decent mattress at least, but those cost a lot more than one Reward. He'd have to save up if he wants a big purchase like that. A small mirror, perhaps, for above the sink? He doesn't know what he looks like anymore. Maybe it's best to keep it that way. Prison pyjamas and artificial light, atrophying brain. Thinking about looking at himself every day in these conditions make him decide against it. He imagines himself as hollow-eyed and hollow-boned. That's what it feels like, anyway.

He scrolls and scrolls until he eventually finds something to buy. The app congratulates him on his redemption (if only it was that easy) and informs him to expect delivery in the next open chute.

. . .

The dinner bell rings, and Zack silently congratulates himself for getting through most of the day.

Zack joins Lewis's table in the cafeteria. Lewis points at him and says "Girdler" for the benefit of the other diners. The men shoot him cursory glances. One or two mumble *hello*.

"You're not eating?" asks Lewis.

Zack shakes his head. "Not hungry."

"You gotta eat."

"What is it?" asks Zack.

"Who fucking knows," says Lewis, and some of the other men laugh.

Zack grabs a tray and chooses the least unattractive option at the counter. Some kind of tofurkey with grey sauce and matching mash. Some pretty leaves on the side that makes the food look slightly less dire.

Back at the table, he takes a bite of mashed potato. Or, at least, he thinks it's mashed potato. It's difficult to swallow.

"You'll get used to it," says Lewis.

I doubt it.

"Soon you'll be eating decent food," says a shiny-scalped man to Lewis. He lifts his eyebrows at Lewis's lapel and points his fork up to the ceiling.

"Ah," says Lewis, relishing the thought.

"I heard they've got an artisanal ice cream shop up there," says a man who looks like a professional wrestler. "There are, like, a hundred different flavours. And if they don't have the flavour you want, you can make a request and they'll make it for you."

"Ah," says Lewis again.

"I'd ask for salted butterscotch," says the wrestler. "In a cinnamon cone."

"Black Choxolate," says the bald man, but there's not much hope in his voice. He only has two stages on his lapel.

"Eighties Bubblegum," says Lewis. "Remember that? Summers at the South Coast. Blue ice-cream dripping down your chin."

For a moment they all look lost in their memories of childhood treats and open skies.

"And you'll forget all about us," says baldy.

"I fucking won't," says Lewis.

"Yes, you will," says the wrestler. "And you should."

"I'm ready," says Zack to Lewis as they finish their game of table tennis.

"Hmm?"

Lewis is buoyed by the dinner conversation about his inevitable elevation, and Zack wants to take advantage of his good mood. "You said you'd tell me what SkyRest does when I was ready."

Lewis scoffs. "You're not ready."

"Lewis. Please."

He puts his bat down and takes a long, hard look at Zack. The ball vibrates on the table, then comes to a stop. Eventually Lewis capitulates with a shrug. "All right," he says, and Zack follows him to the cineroom.

CHAPTER 45

MENACING HALO

TWELVE YEARS LATER

Metro Revolvorant
Johannesburg, 2036

Keke projects her contact list and hesitates before tapping on Marko's avatar, a saffron silhouette of a man meditating with a giant ball of fire behind him. She knows she's not supposed to call him, but this is an emergency. Besides, the chance of the call actually going through, all the way to an out-of-the-way ashram in India, when there's chaos on the ground here, is infinitesimal.

She's surprised when, on the third attempt, the phone buzzes. It's ringing on his side. Her pulse quickens. There's a click. All of a sudden Marko's face is right there in the restaurant, projected over Keke's empty glass. His eyepatch remains an accusation—will always be an accusation, whether he ends up forgiving her or not.

"Keke." He smiles.

He looks like a different person.

"You've lost weight," she says, past the tears.

"Have I? I suppose I have. That's what a fruitarian diet does. And fasting. We do a lot of fasting here."

"I know we agreed I wouldn't contact you," says Keke. "I'm sorry."

"Don't be. It's absolutely lovely to see your face."

Don't get emotional. Don't say anything tender.

"I miss you." The tears spill down her cheeks. "Sorry. Sorry. I promised myself I wouldn't cry."

"It's okay," says Marko. "It's okay."

She sniffs and angrily swipes away the tears. Clears her throat. This isn't why she called him.

"How's your mom?"

"I don't know, actually," Marko says. "She's still travelling. The last time we chatted she was feeding orphans in Udaipur."

The line is bad. Marko's face keeps snowing over.

"I'm surprised you answered. You're still unplugged?"

"Yes. This is the first time this old Tile has rung in … months."

"When will you … Do you know yet, when you'll come home?"

"This is my home now, Keke."

Keke swallows more tears, tries to un-crumple her face.

"It's not."

"You're right. There's no such thing as 'home'. Not really. It's just an emotional attachment to a place, which serves no one."

Keke feels her heart harden against him. If she's honest with herself, really honest, she can't stand this version of Marko. This bean-eating, meditating, philosophising, asexual silhouette. Yes, he's probably a 'better' man, but not for her. The essence of him is gone. What makes it more difficult, of course, is that she's the one who caused this emergence, this evolution, and she still hates herself for it, even though she felt at the time, and still feels, that she had no other choice. Her decision to sacrifice Marko's eye saved Silver's life. How could he resent her for that? Of course he's never admitted it: He didn't want to cause any further pain. But it became too difficult for them to live together. When he first came home after being discharged from The Gordhan, he found it hard to talk to her, to look her in the eye. As he grew stronger, Keke tried to initiate sex—nothing too strenuous—but he wouldn't (couldn't?) get it up. Then, before she could get a handle on the situation, he was off to visit his mother in Goa, and suddenly an ashram had swallowed him whole. He hadn't been connected since.

"You're not going to like this," she says, "but I need your help."

What he used to say: *Anything for you, M'lady.*

What he says now: "Keke … you know I can't."

"You don't understand."

As if the emotional static isn't bad enough, the phone connection is crackling too.

"We're all in danger, Marko. There's something going on here."

"What?" Marko snaps to attention. His dreamy look is replaced by worry. "What's going on?"

"There's some kind of ... artificial intelligence malfunction, they're calling it. A robot rebellion. An uprising. There've been over a hundred fatalities—and those are only the ones that we know of—and it's spreading."

Marko stares at her. "Wait. What?"

"Did you hear me? People are being killed by AI."

"AI doesn't rebel. Their code prohibits it."

"I told you, they're malfunctioning."

"Impossible."

The line is dropped. Keke calls him back, fifth time lucky.

"That's why we need your help."

"That is totally out of my area of expertise."

"Bullshit."

"It's not! I don't know the first thing about defective droids, and even if I did, how would I do anything from here?"

"You've got that Tile."

"This Tile is ancient. The tech is, like, eight years old. That's, like, ninety-six in tech years. And the signal here is terrible."

"I feel like you haven't yet grasped what is going on here."

"I—"

"Forget about our problems. Forget about being disconnected. We're in danger, Marko. Kate, Seth, the kids." She thinks of Mally and Vega. Wonders about Silver. "Especially the kids."

Marko bunches his hair up in his fists.

"I'll get on a plane. I'll get on the first plane."

"Jesus, Marko. Aren't you listening? AI wants to kill us."

Keke side-eyes the waitbot who is still vacuuming the restaurant floor. No wonder they've gone postal. Imagine that is your entire existence.

"What are you saying? That they've closed the airports?"

"Of course they've fucking closed the airports!"

Everyone knows how much damage can be done when a plane is used as a weapon. Finally something clicks in Marko's brain. Keke can see a sudden clarity in his expression.

"You say it's spreading?"

"The Nancies are trying to keep it under the blanket. The danger of mass hysteria, blah. But yes, it's spreading. Twenty-four hours ago there were a couple of seemingly isolated incidents reported. Since then it's just exploded."

"It doesn't make any sense. AI is specifically programmed to never harm humans or animals."

"Something's changed."

Marko scratches his head again. "Those initial incidents. Were they spread out? Or did they come from a common point of origin?"

"As far as we could tell, a common point, but none of the reports were official. Just first-hand accounts posted on SMstreams by civilians."

She brings up a sub-screen showing red pins on the map. There's a definite concentration over Sandton. Within a few seconds it updates, adding hundreds of new pins in a menacing halo.

"Holy Hedy Lemarr," says Marko.

For a second Keke glimpses the old Marko, and it twists her heart. *Not that it matters anymore.*

"This isn't a malfunction, Keke."

His face flickers in the static. She loses him for a while then he comes back.

"Keke?" he says. "I've lost you. Keke?"

"I'm here," she says, "Marko. I'm here."

"Listen to me. If you can hear me. This isn't a malfunction."

And just as Keke's about to ask what it is, and what they can do, they get cut off, and she doesn't get through to him again.

CHAPTER 46
CRAVING KEKE

Ashram Ramanana
Panchagiri Hills, India, 2036

Marko smacks his Tile in frustration. The signal here is worse than the itch on a neckbeard. No wonder these mountain yogis preach unplugging. It's like being back in the dark ages for Net's sake.

"Sorry," he whispers to the device. "It's not your fault that quantum tech hasn't reached us yet."

He needs to be nice to the Tile. He polishes it with his sleeve. It might be the only way to keep Keke safe.

There's a faint knock on the door. A swami sweeps in, and stops in his tracks when he sees Marko with an electronic device in his hands. There's confusion in his frown, and disappointment, even though he tries to not show it.

"Marko, it's time for the retreat to begin."

They've planned a three-day silence retreat, which they'll finish off with a *yajna.* Suddenly Marko thinks if he has to scrub one more stone floor he'll turf himself out of a window.

"I can't," says Marko. "Sorry. I have an emergency."

"An emergency is a manmade concept." The sage's voice is a calm, clear pond. "Look around you. There are no emergencies here."

Marko's hand shoots up to his eye-patch. He traces the edges with clammy fingertips.

"It's my friend. In South Africa. She's in trouble."

"It's not up to you to fix her situation. Do not take that power from her."

"It's important. I just need some time. Half an hour. I'll join you as soon as I can." The fib flushes his cheeks.

"As you wish," says the swami, and starts to leave. He puts his hand on the door. "I hope that you will not undo all we have accomplished in dealing with your technology addiction."

If Marko could push the man out of the room he would.

"Yes," says Marko. Yes. Whatever it takes to get rid of the guy.

Knowing that Keke and the others are in danger has burst the incense-fragrant bubble in which Marko's been living. He's been trying his best to sort out his head, to fix himself before he can try to repair his relationship with Keke, but knowing that she's in trouble now and he can't go to her feels like someone is punching his lungs. Will he ever see her again? He thinks of all the time he's wasted, being here, when he could have been with her.

To be frank, his stay here has been pretty lame. He realises now that he was after some kind of eighties Hollywood spiritual training, some kind of Karate Kid/Sensei shit. Wax on, wax off. But really he's been playing along. Hoping that if he drinks the Ashram Kool-Aid for long enough he really will find peace and forgiveness. Pretending that he can be happy in this analogue world of mindful physical chores and meditation when really he's been jonesing for his online life: being completely in the flow when he's doing what he's best at. Most of all, of course, he's been missing Keke, although 'missing' is too weak a word. Images of her hold his sleep hostage: the warm fingers of his memories keep him wide awake. The feel of her, the scent. 'Craving' is more accurate a word. It could pretty much sum up the past few months. Years? Whether he admits it to himself or not, he's been craving Keke.

He restarts the Tile, hoping a new connection will be cleaner, but the call to Keke won't go through. He wants to tell her he might be able to help, after all. It's true he has no experience in defective droids, but he suspects something else is going on: something more sinister. Yes, he's a conspiracy theorist, and yes, he's naturally paranoid, but something about this 'rebellion' feels dirty, and he has an idea what it is.

He tries to call her again, without luck, so instead he concentrates on finding out what he can about the attacks. He thinks it'll take a while to get back into the saddle, hacking-wise—especially on this troglodyte of a Tile—that maybe he'll be a bit rusty and need time to adjust, but he's wrong. As soon as he's in, it's as if he's a bullet in a greased chamber, and within twelve minutes he's scraped enough darkdata to prove his theory correct. It feels good. He doesn't want it to, but damn, it feels fucking fantastic. His synth-heart is pounding. The footage of the Bent Hotel murder plays over and over in his head.

The bad news is that he was right about the so-called rebellion not being a code malfunction. As soon as he saw those red pins multiplying he knew. He recognised the pattern immediately. It's not a coincidence, or an uprising, or a defect. It has all the hallmarks of an infective agent that multiplies within the host.

It's a virus, and it's the scariest thing he's ever seen.

CHAPTER 47

CORPORATE VIDEO OF DEATH

TWELVE YEARS PREVIOUSLY

SkyRest
Johannesburg, 2024

Lewis and Zack enter the dim cineroom, and Lewis dials up the lights, interrupting the crims watching an old nature documentary.

"Hey!" some of them say, before realising who it is.

"Sorry to interrupt, gents," Lewis says, pausing the film. "We need the room."

The men complain under their breath, but no one dares confront Lewis. They stand up and amble out.

"Scram!" he says to a laggard then closes the door behind him. "It's not like they haven't seen that grizzly documentary a hundred times before."

Zack flips through the available titles on DVD. The titles are milquetoast. No new releases, no sex or violence. Just old wildlife shows, clean sitcoms, and vintage feel-good films. He picks one out, cracks open the cover and inspects it. 'Eternal Sunshine of the Spotless Mind'.

Lewis laughs at the old tech. "When's the last time you saw one of those?"

Even the dusty DVD player looks a hundred years old.

Lewis changes the amp source then types in a code to unlock a SkyRest-branded video. When prompted to confirm, he looks at Zack. "You sure you want to know this shit?"

Zack nods.

"It's like bad porn," he says.

"What?"

"I mean, it's not something you can un-see."

Zack nods again, and Lewis shrugs and clicks play.

They grab a seat in the front row, and the film begins. The introductory shot is drone-footage of the architecture: some flattering angles of the white honeycomb shard among the deep green of the surrounding forest, and a woman's honey-tongued voice-over begins.

"Welcome," she says, "to SkyRest."

Is that Gaelyn's voice? Or do they all just sound the same?

An ultra realistic animation of a tree falling in a forest occurs. The tree soon greys and shrinks as it breaks down, and new growth—bright green saplings—shoots up from the nurse log.

"It's easy to become disconnected from nature when you're living a high-speed urban life. Part of this disconnect is thinking of death as an inherently negative experience."

Something about the death industry feels familiar to him, but he's not sure why.

Is this why I was sent to this particular crim colony?

"But what makes SkyRest different from other urban vertical cemeteries?"

Unseen things click into place one after another in Zack's mind, like someone shuffling a deck of cards.

"SkyRest offers clients a variety of burial options—"

Hexagonal frames appear on the screen to illustrate the available alternatives, and the first frame is enlarged: Inside is a tombstone.

"Our traditional burial contains all the hallmarks of a conventional burial, except that it takes place on one of our sky storeys. You are welcome to visit the resting place of your loved one any time of day or night."

The next frame is an urn on a mantelpiece. "If you end up selecting customary cremation, we have a variety of options to deal with the ashes. These include, amongst others: having them mixed with oil paint, and commissioning an artist to create a unique work for you. Having them distilled and turned into jewellery, or having them buried under the rootball of a sapling that you can take home and plant in your garden."

Seems sensible. Zack doesn't see what the big deal is so far.

"If you don't want to keep the remains, we also offer water cremation."

Okay, that's a new one, but still, hardly controversial.

"These are all popular burial solutions," says the speaker, "but none of them is environmentally friendly, and at SkyRest we strive for a carbon-double-negative footprint. If it's also important to you to leave the world with causing minimal damage, you may consider our earth-friendly options."

Zack's ears prick up; the SkyRest logo animates on screen.

"SkyRest introduces ... Recomposition™. Your Doorway to Immortality."

Immediately Zack thinks of zombies. Does this place bring dead bodies back to life? A shameful amount of bank has been spent on immortality tech, but as he thinks it, he knows this isn't that kind of place. Everything he's seen has been deep green and eco-devoted—and he's petty sure zombies don't fit into that equation.

"For most people, the suddenness and permanence of death is difficult to accept, especially when it's a loved one. With SkyRest's trademarked Recomposition™ technology, your spirit can live on by nurturing the earth that sustained you during your lifetime."

Zack hardly blinks.

"Traditional burials are anything but natural. Bodies are preserved with the known carcinogen, formaldehyde, and then sealed in caskets that further embalm them, taking up valuable land and leaching poison into the ground. Even cremations are not without environmental damage: a single cremation pumps a toxic cocktail of chemicals into the air. In fact, our legal team here at SkyRest predicts that both of these options will be banned by 2040. Recomposition™ offers a positive solution to those looking for an earth-friendly burial."

The animation of the nurse log returns.

"Recomposition™ interlaces the cycles of life into the meaning-hungry, time-starved urban fabric and reminds us that, as humans, we're deeply connected to the natural ebb and flow of Mother Earth."

A young woman is lying on a forest floor, asleep. Dead? Naked, apart from some strategically placed autumn leaves. Her long blonde hair is styled against the dark ground. More and more dead leaves cover her pale skin until she is no longer visible. The earth has swallowed her up.

"There you go." Lewis pauses the video. "Happy now?"

"Yes," says Zack. "No. I don't understand what the big deal is. Why the secrecy?"

"What can I say? It's death. People get cagey."

"How does it work?"

"You want me to draw you a fucking picture?"

"Can we watch to the end?" Zack already knows the answer and is frustrated. He's not sleeping, not eating, and he just wants answers. Is it too much to ask?

Lewis turns off the screen. "You're not ready for the end."

The video has jogged Zack's degraded memory. Pictures of dead people flash in on him: Face after face of obliteration.

Ramphele's file.

Then in a dreamlike scenario he sees himself injecting a young girl, and she collapses and dies in his arms. The disjointed memory fills Zack with bewilderment and fury.

"Do you know why I'm in here, Lewis? Do you know what I was convicted of?"

"Don't know. Don't wanna know."

"I was found guilty of killing over a hundred people."

Lewis's hand freezes on his beard.

"So don't tell me that I can't handle the end of a fucking video. Don't tell me I can't handle a sanitised corporate video of death. I am Death's friend, okay? I'm the Grim Fucking Reaper."

CHAPTER 48
COSMIC CHESS GAME

TWELVE YEARS LATER

The Lipworth Institute
Johannesburg, 2036

Kate finds Keke at a booth in the dawn-lit Revolvo. Bathed in an orange glow, she's staring out the window with tears streaming down her cheeks. Her face is still: There's no sniffing or fussing, the tears just flow. It's as if she's one of those cinegraphs that used to be in fashion where only one element of the picture moves. Kate approaches Keke slowly, not wanting to wreck her reverie.

"What's happened?" she asks. "Keke?"

"It's beautiful, isn't it?"

Kate looks at the view. The daybreak colours are insane. It's as if someone has painted the regular sunrise with liquid LSD.

Keke has a faraway look in her eyes. "I mean, I hate that air pollution 99.9 percent of the time. But, hot damn! This is not one of those times."

They spend a moment absorbing the magnificence.

"The last sunrise will be the prettiest," says Keke.

"Who said that? Confucius? The Dalai Lama?"

"Nope," says Keke, draining her third drink. "Yours truly."

"Don't. It's not our last sunrise."

"I've got a bad feeling, Kitty. A very bad feeling."

"Silver's really sick," says Kate.

This shakes Keke out of her daydream. "Shit! I've been so deep into the Doomsday and Marko shit that I completely forgot why we were here."

"You were right. She got meshed. Some backstreet job that Morgan doesn't know how to treat."

"Brain damage?"

"We're not sure yet."

"Fuck! I'm so sorry. I don't know what to say."

"There's nothing to say, really."

Keke climbs out of the booth, knocking over her empty glass as she does so, and hugs Kate. They kiss each other's cheeks, then sit down again. Kate tastes Keke's salt on her lips.

"Wait," says Kate. "Did you say you spoke to Marko? Seriously? He took your call?"

"Reluctantly."

"It's been, what? How many years?"

"I don't know," fibs Keke. "I've lost count."

"Motherfucker. How is he?"

"Skinny."

"And he just answered? Like, 'Hi Keke'?"

"Pretty much."

"Did you tell him you've been waiting for him?"

"No. It wasn't that kind of conversation. I asked him for help. To hack the roguebots."

"And?"

"And … not his speciality."

"I guess not."

"Ja, well. He could have fucking tried."

"Morgan said much the same when I asked him to treat Silver. Hands off. Said it's too dangerous."

"He probably knows best."

"Yes."

"Well," says Keke, rubbing the tear-marks off her face. "Looks like we'll have to do it our-own-fucking-selves."

"Looks like it," says Kate, and they smile at each other.

There is some kind of reckoning in the air, as if they've reached the end of something. Kate senses a new kind of nostalgia—a wistful pre-remembering. Would this really be their last day together?

Keke takes a deep breath, as if she's ready to rush off and save the world. "Doomsday or not, we'll make it count."

The servbot cycles over and picks Keke's glass up off the floor.

"Welcome to the Metro Revolvorant!" it says to Kate. They wait for it to leave before speaking again.

"I do have a favour to ask," says Kate.

"Anything."

"Well, if I'm honest it's a shitload more than a 'favour'."

"You know I'll do anything for you," says Keke.

"This is different."

"Spit it out, woman!"

"Morgan told me something about Silver. He didn't think it was important, but—"

"But?"

"I think it might be. Something is telling me it is, or I swear I wouldn't ask you."

"For Net's sake. Do I need to wrestle it out of you?"

"Okay. So Silver's in this, like, dream state? And she's been mumbling things. Urgent things. So I was trying to listen to her and she wasn't making sense, but then she said very clearly…she said 'Zack'."

Keke's eyes flare. "Zack?"

"Yes. As clear as day. Zack, Zack, and then she said 'Get Zack'."

"I don't understand the connection."

"Nor do I! But remember that day at The Gordhan when he said he needed to tell me something important? But then he was arrested before he had the chance to say anything else and then—I'm sure I told you—it kept bothering me, not knowing. So I tried to track him down. I wanted to visit him in prison and talk to him. But when I started asking questions…the police closed ranks."

"I know," says Keke.

"You know? You know what?"

"They wouldn't tell me where he was, either. They said it was a special case because he was so dangerous. Didn't want the press sniffing around. Didn't want anything to be reported above the Blanket. I tried to get details about his trial but no one I spoke to could tell me anything."

"Exactly. It was like the system just swallowed him whole."

"It happens," says Keke. "Remember that politician who challenged Shini Wam in parly? She also disappeared with no trace. And that journo—Mpumi—remember him? You always said that he looked like a *Drum* magazine cover model."

Mpumi had a balling retrosexual Sophiatown afro-vintage chic look going on when they met. Now Kate imagines him as a little older: just as immaculate as before, but perhaps with a little grey salting his hair.

"Oh shit! He helped me on the Betty/Barbara story."

"Gone. One day he was promoted to chief editor at Echo.news. The next day his boyfriend reported him missing. Like they've just been plucked from reality. Like some kind of cosmic chess game."

"That's terrible. Why would they snatch *him*? Was he reporting on corruption?"

"Nah. Nothing as innocent as that. According to the rumours on the ground, he was some kind of double agent. He was pretty ruthless. He'd do anything for a story. He made a lot of deals with a lot of dangerous people."

Kate sighs, taps the table. "Oh, well then. Never mind about the favour."

"You wanted me to find Zack?"

"Yes. I realise this is a serious leap of logic, but … something is telling me that he might be our only chance to break Silver out of her state."

"Well, I have reasonably good news for you then."

"Hey? But you've just said—"

"I said the police wouldn't tell me where he was. I didn't say I stopped looking."

CHAPTER 49
BLOOMS OF YOUR BELOVED

TWELVE YEARS PREVIOUSLY

SkyRest
Johannesburg, 2024

"I'm sorry about last night," says Zack to Lewis over breakfast. Lewis raises his white eyebrows at him and motions for him to sit.

"No worries. I expected it. It's always difficult for initiates to process the work they do here. But," he says, pushing his plate away, "after what you told me, I think you'll have no problem fitting in."

Zack sits and looks at the abandoned food. No-egg omelette? Dutch baby pancake? He can't stand the idea of eating food he can't identify.

"What I said … isn't really the truth," says Zack. "Not the whole truth, anyway."

"I don't need to know, man. I'm not your priest. I'm not your lawyer."

"But I want you to know that it's not what it sounded like. It's not what I made it sound like."

"All right."

"I'm not a serial killer," says Zack.

Lewis looks at him over his coffee mug. "Really."

"It's complicated."

"Okay," says Lewis.

"Okay?"

"No one's perfect, right? We've all done wrong. Inside of here and out."

Has Lewis accepted his apology?

"But there is one thing." Lewis traces a scar on the table. "And I don't mean to offend."

Zack looks at him.

"Have you looked in the mirror, lately?"

"What?"

"You look like shit, man."

Zack finger-combs his hair, rubs his eyes. "I haven't been sleeping."

"I can see that. Your eyes have more baggage than a supermodel."

"I actually think I feel worse than I look."

"Not fucking possible," says Lewis, and throws his head back, laughing. A few residents stop eating their omelette/pancake to look at him, and Zack laughs too.

"Any advice?" he asks.

"Advice? Sure. Get a fucking mirror."

Zack laughs.

"No, seriously," says Lewis. "You'd better start sleeping. And start eating! The way you're looking ... well ..." He gestures at the building above them. "If you're not careful, they'll be using you in their next video."

The now-familiar siren sounds, letting them know that their work shift is beginning. The men sigh, bin what's left on their plates, and lope out of the cafeteria. This time they're led to a hall Zack has not yet seen. A warden shows them how to re-pot plants that have grown out of their containers. Roses, hydrangeas, maples, trailing Boston ivy, Virginia creeper. Considering yesterday's video, he reckons taking a thriving Boston ivy plant home instead of ashes is a good thing. You could have this urn of ashes in your house that you don't know what do do with, or you could have this plant that can cover a whole wall—a whole building—and flicker from season to season between green and red. An everyday reminder that the person you've lost is not really lost at all. Or a rose bush: you can forever have the blooms of your beloved.

They tap the plants' containers to release the roots, then ease them into the soft new soil. It's therapeutic work, and Zack starts relaxing for the first time since being here. They play classical music over the sound system. His shoulders unknot; his brain untangles. After the re-potting, they have to shift some soil in wheelbarrows, then they're instructed to sweep up and bag the sawdust and kindling in the wood-chipping room. The exercise feels good. The work is easy and monotonous and becomes like meditation. He keeps checking his cuff for his next Reward, and wonders how long it will be till he gets the first stage on his lapel.

This place isn't so bad. Then he corrects himself: *It could be worse.*

When their shift is over and they've showered, and they're waiting for dinner, they hang out in Lewis's room. Lewis is still in good spirits, doing arm-lifts and eating protein pretzels. His bare chest ripples with muscles a man half his age would be proud to have, and his tattoo seems darker than usual, the colours richer. The illustration seems to pulse on his skin, as if the dragon is alive.

"Getting ready for that swim?" Zack asks.

"I can taste that water, you know. I can feel it streaming through my hair in that first dive. Cooling my scalp."

"Going to be a good feeling," says Zack. "After all this time."

"Oh, yes." He drops from the bar then downs half a bottle of water. "Oh, yes."

Lewis offers him the SkyRest-branded packet of pretzels. Zack hesitates.

"Go on," says Lewis. "They're not going to bite you."

Zack reaches his hand inside the bag, grabs a few then sprinkles them on his other palm. Tentatively puts one in his mouth. It's not too bad.

"Will you tell me the rest of it?" asks Zack.

"The rest of what?"

"The rest of the video. Tell me how they do it?"

"All right," he says, sitting down. "Sure. Why the fuck not?"

Zack eats another pretzel. They're quite good, actually.

"What do you want to know?"

"Everything."

CHAPTER 50

NITROGEN-RICH MATERIAL

"Ever heard of Ouroboros?" asks Lewis.

"Your tattoo," says Zack. "The serpent that devours its own tail."

Zack knows the ancient Egyptian circular symbol of eternal return that has been re-used and recycled by philosophical trains from Greek magic to alchemy to Kundalini health goths.

"Right. So they have this system going here. It's completely self-sustaining. Everything you eat, wear, or touch in this place comes from this place. *It is its own* immortality."

"Recomposition."

"Recomp's the main technology, yes. There are others on the menu, and even more that they're experimenting with."

"How does the recomp work?"

"Recomp is when they take the ... nitrogen-rich material—"

"The what?"

"The nitrogen-rich material. That's what they call it."

"Do you mean, the bodies? The dead bodies?"

"Yes, that's what it means."

"So they take the nitrogen-rich—the bodies—and place it inside a mound of carbon-rich material ... so that's the sawdust, and the wood chips. They add a bit of moisture, some extra nitro on top to get it going. Maybe some alfalfa."

Zack remembers the pretty purple alfalfa blooms they had worked on during a previous shift. What had Lewis said about them? That they're a feminine herb, element of the earth, and especially good on sandwiches.

"Then the microbes do their thing. The microbial activity gets the pile cooking. Their heat kills the bad shit. The pathogens. That's what you can feel."

"What do you mean?"

"We call it our underfloor heating. The warmth, from the middle of the building? That's the core. That's where it all happens. Bodies in the top. Compost out the bottom."

Human compost.

Saliva rushes into Zack's mouth. He tries to swallow his revulsion.

"Then they cure the compost. Sometimes the clients want to take the compost home. They plant a fucking tree or whatever. Or they let someone here do it for them. They plant one of those saplings in the forest at the back. Put a tag on the tree, or a bench with a silver plaque underneath it. But most of the compost goes unclaimed. That's the stuff we use for the aeroponics. It's what we use to grow everything in here."

Zack spits out the pretzel he had in his mouth.

Lewis laughs. "Ja, that's pretty much the standard reaction."

Zack looks around the room. His uniform, the linen, Lewis's snax, the soap, the toothpaste, all emblazoned with the SkyRest logo.

"Yes," says Lewis. "Even the toiletries. Hemp oil and Miswak and Homosapien. So best get used to it."

Zack reaches for his water and rinses his mouth out, spits the water into Lewis's basin.

"Once you've had time to process it, you'll see that it makes complete sense. It's the full circle, you know? None of that embalming shit. No poisoning the well. None of that hanging onto dead bodies. If you think about it, being attached to a dead body is way weirder than letting it go back to the earth, you know? No waste, no harm, just energy doing its thing. Going round and round like it should. The process is actually a fucking beautiful thing."

"Does everyone in here ... Do the rest of the residents know?"

"Most of them. Some have been red-flagged. Admin decided it's best to not tell them. The truth doesn't serve everybody."

Zack feels ill.

The bell rings for dinner time.

CHAPTER 51

NO ONE LIKES TO KEEP A SECRET

TWELVE YEARS LATER

The Lipworth Institute

Johannesburg, 2036

"You know where Zack is?" Kate asks Keke.

"Of course I know where he is."

"You found him?"

"It wasn't easy, but when I couldn't find any kind of record for him, or anything about his trial or sentencing, I tracked down that cop."

"The cop that—"

"Yes. Ramphele. The guy who cuffed me while I was with Marko in hospital. Aiding and abetting a serial killer, he said. Bullshit."

"I can't believe you've known all this time. Why didn't you tell me?"

"You had enough to deal with. Lumin. The Resurrectors. Mally's surgery and recuperation. I'd already unwillingly unleashed his crazy on you that day at The Gordhan. I thought you'd sooner forget."

"I still dream about him," says Kate. "It's crackers, because, really, I don't know him. I mean I met him for a few seconds but when I dream about him, his face is as clear as day. It was like we had this weird, intense connection."

"I know. I think about him every day," says Keke, "but for a different reason."

"Why?"

"Isn't it obvious? Because I'm the reason he's in there."

"You're not."

"I am. I'm the one who made the deal with Ramphele. Zack trusted me, and I set him up."

"You're not the one who killed people. He's in there because he killed people."

Keke shakes her head. "Zack's not a killer."

"Twelve years," Kate says, shaking her head in disbelief. "Feels like yesterday we were in that hospital. Can you imagine being in prison for that long? Especially when you're innocent. Can you imagine what that does to you?"

"I tried to tell the detective that, but he wasn't interested. He'd been chasing Zack for years."

"You must have made him so happy by agreeing to help him."

"It was weird because he was so desperate to arrest Zack, right? It was like his life depended on it. But then when I saw him afterwards he was ... upset."

"Upset?"

"Like ... properly depressed. We met at a hole in Randburg. The place was disgusting. Faux-flagstones that smelt like week-old beer. Broken glass on the floor. The autoloos were broken. They were literally serving cockroaches at the bar." Keke shudders. "I could tell he was a regular there. The beer was cheap; I know because I kept buying him round after round. It's like he had an uncontrollable thirst, like no amount of booze would ever slake it."

"You've always been so good at your grind."

"Yes, well. It's easy, actually. No one likes to keep a secret. That's what I've learnt. A secret has too much power. It builds up ... it makes people feel uncomfortable. Most people are just waiting for an excuse to spill."

"It's a relief," says Kate, "it diffuses the power."

"Exactly."

"So what did the depressed detective have to confess?"

"Ramphele wouldn't confess. He wouldn't tell me anything about the case—but there was definitely something dodgy going on—I could feel it ... I could see that it was eating him up on the inside. And then after our meeting? Guess what?"

"What?"

"He went missing. The station I called said he'd retired, but there were no documents to prove it. His file just blipped out of existence. Someone else I spoke to said that he just stopped coming to work one day."

"What the fuck?"

"So I figure, either he did something that he couldn't live with—like putting an innocent man away—and pretty much erased himself … or someone didn't like what he told me. Considered him too much of a liability."

"The cosmic chess game."

"The fucking cosmic chess game. But I did manage to find out where they were keeping Zack."

"Where is he?"

"SkyRest."

Kate's quiet for a moment. She feels her cheeks warm. "SkyRest. Seriously? That's in Fourways. That's, like, twenty minutes away in a tuk-tuk. Zack's been living less than half an hour away from us for twelve years and you've never fucking said anything?"

"What would be the point?"

"To ask him what he was going to tell me!"

"Just because it's close, it doesn't mean that you can just pop in for tea and scones. SkyRest has the highest security out of all the PLCs. It where they send only the dangerous crims. There is a strict no-visitor, no-contact policy. And there are, like, three layers of biometric security. Besides, knowing he's so close … it would've just made you more frustrated."

"How do we know he's still alive?"

"Because if he was dead they'd have to report it. That's true for any crim colony. Remember the vertical mine shaft colony in Phokeng? The crims lived in the shaft?"

"They were shut down. Not profitable enough."

"Yes, they were shut down, but not because of the business. That was the Nancies spinning their usual bullshit our way. The business was going well—well enough, anyway—they were shut down because their crim death rate was above the acceptable threshold."

"But can't they just *jook* the numbers?"

"They would if they could. No doubt. But the UN Human Rights Council audit them, so they have to add up or they're in for a world of pain. If there's even a hint of creative accounting with bodycount the HRC will shut them down before you can say penal labour camp."

"And that would bite our economy."

"In a big way. Last numbers I saw said that the colonies made up thirty-eight percent of our GDP."

"Holy shit."

"Imagine closing them down and going back to the prison system that costs the country money instead of making it money. Now you see the motivation to keep their operations clean. Or at least clean enough to stay out of trouble."

They spend a moment just looking at each other.

"So Zack is alive. At SkyRest," says Kate.

"All facts point to that conclusion, yes."

"We need to break him out," says Kate, cool as TranX.

Keke chokes. "Have you not heard what I've been saying? It's impossible."

"It's the only way to save Silver."

"You don't know that."

"It's my best guess. Why else would she be asking for him? She's never even met him. Never heard his name."

"I can't explain that. I mean—"

"She hasn't said one other word. Not one. Not 'help me' or 'Mom' or 'Mally' or anything. 'Zack', she said. 'Get Zack'."

"How?" says Keke. "On a normal day it would be impossible. Now we're dealing with the roguebots and the Bot Hunters too. Have you seen the reports? They're killing each other in the streets. Civilians too. It's only going to get worse."

They both look at the servbot, who has stopped vacuuming. Its eyes are closed, as if it's powered down for a nano-nap. The overhead lights flicker, then stabilise again.

CHAPTER 52

HER MOUTH IS LEMON PITH

Keke stands and gathers her things.

"Where are you going?"

"Where do you think?" says Keke. "To SkyRest. To get Zack."

"No," says Kate. "It's too dangerous."

"Ah, well," says Keke. "It'll be exciting, if nothing else."

"Don't fuck around, Keke."

"I'm not."

"When I asked you the favour … to find out where Zack is … I didn't mean I wanted you to go out and find him. I'd never ask you to risk your life for me."

"I'm not doing it for you. I'm doing it for Silver."

A lilac rush of sad gratitude spirals in Kate's peripheral vision. "You can't. You're right, it's impossible. You won't even be able to get in."

"What kind of fairy godmother would I be if I wasn't willing to duel with a few roguebots and break into a maximum security crim colony to find a character in Silver's dream?"

Kate smiles. "No ways. *I'll* go after Zack. You stay here and be with Silver."

"I'm not welcome here," says Keke.

"This place is safe."

"No place is safe. If artificial intelligence is really trying to kill us, then … no place is safe. I may as well go out with all guns blazing."

Then what's the point of anything? What's the point of finding Zack and saving Silver if they're all going to die, anyway? But Kate knows she has to do something. She thinks of Silver's body lying in that white room, so close to living and so close to dying. She has to try, despite the odds, because that is what having children does to your heart. It cleaves it in two—or in her case, three—and it feels as if you have your heart beating outside your body, just out of your reach, pulsing along and weathering the elements.

"I'm doing it no matter what you say," says Keke, "so you can wipe that look of desolation off your face."

"Don't," says Kate, but she only half means it, and hates herself for it. She's already asked so much of Keke.

Keke is halfway out of the restaurant when she turns and says: "I'm sticking you with the bill!"

"Ha ha," says Kate. "The drink was complimentary!"

"Ha ha!" shouts Keke. "I had ten!" and then she's gone, and there is a blue watercolour wash all over, and Kate has the very real feeling that she'll never see her best friend again.

All of a sudden her mandible beeps with an outgoing call response. When she couldn't get hold of Seth earlier she had set her device to perpetual silent dialling. It's taken more than two hours to place the call.

"Seth!" she yells.

"No need to shout."

"I've been trying to … Never mind. Have you found Mally?"

"Not yet. I've been to Vega's hostel. It's not good."

"What?"

"It's like civil war here. It's like the fucking apocalypse. Looting. Explosions. Bot Hunters in full force, taking out anything without a pulse."

"Oh no."

"Now that the light's coming up I can see the full extent of it. It's … terrible, Kate. It's terrible."

Kate's body tenses with anxiety; her mouth is lemon pith.

Seth clears his throat. "They're rounding up anthrobots. The AI Security Branch."

"And doing what with them?"

Usually this news wouldn't dye her insides yellow but she knows Mally is out there and would do anything to protect Vega.

"I don't know," says Seth. "They're saying it's for their own protection, but I doubt it."

Kate remembers the revolver strapped to her thigh.

"Oh, shit." There's a bright green spike in her anxiety. She runs after Keke, calling her name, but she's already gone. She breathes hard into the mandible. "Shit!"

"What's wrong?" says Seth, still on the line.

"Keke. I forgot to give her my gun. If it's as bad as you say it is out there, then—"

"She's going out into the city? Unarmed? That's insane. Stop her!"

"It's too late. She's gone."

"Where?"

"She's going to SkyRest. For me. For Silver."

"What?"

"I'll explain later. I need to go after her."

"I'll meet you there."

CHAPTER 53

BONE BARK

TWELVE YEARS PREVIOUSLY

SkyRest

Johannesburg, 2024

Zack is in the forest. Dark as dread. He's running from something. Someone? The leaves hit his face, the thin black branches whipping his cheeks and arms as he races away from the danger. Where is he? This must be the forest that surrounds the crim colony. Has he escaped? He runs despite the dark, despite not being able to see more than a metre in front of him, despite the soft mounds of earth that threaten to swallow his feet and twist his ankles. He runs and runs despite not having any energy left in his limbs. Panic pushes him forward; makes his legs feel weightless.

He's wearing his suit and tie. He doesn't know how. He doesn't know in which direction he's running. He'll just keep going until he reaches the edge then strategise when he gets there. He needs to leave the threat behind.

But there's a problem with his plan or, rather, a problem with the forest. Because he keeps running but he's not getting anywhere. He can sense that despite his frantic pace, he hasn't moved an inch—an enchanted forest, a cursed forest. All of a sudden, he's flying through the air and lands in a shallow ditch full of leaves. The air is knocked out of him. He touches the soil on the banks that surround him and realises it's not a ditch at all. It's way too deep. It's a rectangular hole, six feet down. A grave. The realisation doesn't help to get the oxygen he needs into his lungs. The air is thick with the aroma of humus and clay. Leaf mould. Too thick to breathe. He scrabbles to climb out of the hole; he can't find a foothold.

He makes it halfway up the bank of soil when a rock gives way and he falls back down. He collapses hard, onto his back, and the shock of it keeps him lying like that until his head stops buzzing. But in the place of the buzzing is another sound: a whispering, rustling, an animal ticking, hundreds of insect legs. There's a pin prick on his ankle, then on his hand. He jumps up and shakes off the things. One is trying to get inside his ear and he swipes at it with a yell. Another sharp pain, on his leg, and then there are stings all over as the beetles swarm over him. Zack screams as he tries to sweep them off. As if sensing his panic they bite down. They want to get their feed before their dinner disappears. He starts to feel the wetness of the trails of blood mixing together. His fingers frantically scrape at the walls of black soil, and one of his nails tears off. Eventually he finds a root to grab onto and uses all the strength the adrenaline gives him to haul himself up and out of the death cube.

Zack pulls off what's left of the flesh-eating beetles and crunches them underfoot. He's dripping blood. Once he's sure he's free of the bugs, he puts his hands on his knees and waits for his lungs to catch up with him. The danger is still present, some unseen evil in the forest, but there's also the danger of him passing out and then there'll be no way he gets out of here alive. How did he get here? All he can remember is—

There's a sound behind him, a dead branch snapping. He spins around, his heart already trying to judder out of his body. Zack tries to make out what—who?—made the noise. He starts reversing and backs into a wide tree trunk. He puts his hands out to steady himself against the bark, but as his palms touch it, he recoils. It doesn't feel right. He turns towards it and yells in fright. Bits of bone are embedded in the bark. Bone bark. The branches further up are cartilage and sinew. There is some hair, some cheekbone. Teeth. Fragments of the pale woman from the video are part of this tree. An eyeball swivels to look at him, and he yells again, wants to run but his horror keeps him rooted to the spot. A shaft of moonlight casts the softest light on the tree, and Zack realises it's not the woman from the video. It's him.

Zack is yelling into the dark. A large hand is covering his mouth. Spongey, cold skin over his fevered jaw. His eyes click open. It's Bernard trying to suffocate him. He tries to fight her but she has the advantage of being above him, and uses all her heft to pin him down, knee on shoulder. He struggles and struggles, but is made weak by the starvation, the sleep-dep, the forest nightmare. Zack tries to call for Lewis, but her hand cancels out any trace of his voice. Gradually he stops struggling, thinking she will kill him now, she'll kill him and would that be that bad? But as he stops fighting her, she eases off too, until there is just one soft hand on his mouth the other goes to her own, an index finger crosses her lips telling him to be quiet.

"Shhh," Bernard says.

CHAPTER 54

ELEVATION

The day's chute delivery arrives with a neatly wrapped Rewards parcel for Zack. The bald resident—Spud, they call him—hands it over.

"Congratulations!" Spud says, slapping Zack on the shoulder. Zack thinks he means for the Reward but then he looks down at what Spud is eyeing: he has a colour stripe on his lapel. His first Stage.

Zack swings by Lewis's room and is shocked when it's empty—not only of Lewis but also all his things. It's completely stripped down to the basics, with just a sleeping mat on the floor.

"Isn't it great?" says a voice in his ear.

Zack spins around, holding his Reward parcel against his chest. It was meant to be a gift for Lewis. Spud is grinning.

Zack's mind is furry with last night's events. "What?"

"Isn't it great?" Spud says again. "He's gone! Promoted!"

Zack shakes his head. Of course. Lewis has been Elevated. That's good news. That's really good news, but why does it make his stomach simmer with dread? He looks down at the gift. His nails are lined with dirt, and one of his fingernails is torn.

CHAPTER 55

STAINED FOR SLAUGHTER

TWELVE YEARS LATER

Fourways
Johannesburg, 2036

Keke hops off the northbound solartram and stands still for a second, adjusting to her new reality. On her way to Fourways she's seen things she'd never believe if someone else had told her about them. It's as if the city has begun to eat itself.

Right now, right in front of her, a school smokes in the early morning light. A teenager in a blackened, frayed school uniform stumbles towards her, and Keke catches her. Ash floats like grey snow in the air.

"Hey," says Keke. "Are you all right?"

The injured girl's having problems talking. Too traumatised? But then Keke sees she's having trouble with her mouth. It looks as if her bottom jaw is stuck.

Jesus.

"Are you okay? What happened?" but the girl still can't talk. She's just leaning into Keke and drilling into her with wide eyes. Suddenly Keke realises none of the girl's wounds are bleeding, and she jumps backwards, causing the schoolgirl to fall onto the pocked pavement and skin her knee. No blood.

Keke shows the girl her palm. "Sorry. I got a fright."

The anthrobot keeps trying to talk through her closed jaw. She's becoming more frantic now. She stumbles towards Keke, who reverses, not wanting to be touched again.

"I didn't mean for you to fall. I just didn't realise—"

The non-bleeding girl keeps coming; Keke almost trips over a blown-out tyre.

"Stay where you are," says Keke. "We'll get you some help."

Her promise rings hollow in the hazy air. All around her she sees broken tarmac, maroon soil, sharp rocks.

The schoolbot starts crying. She's terrified.

Of what?

Then the answer becomes clear as a dozen other schoolgirls come out from behind the redberry pines adjacent to the slowly burning building.

Like a cackle of hyenas the girls prowl round them. They're armed with various make-shift weapons: a fragment of glass, a hammer, a rock. A palm of stones. The anthrobot is crying: a long, shrill wail that is almost human. Keke pulls the bot towards her. Her burnt uniform dusts Keke's hands with black.

"It's okay," Keke tells her. "You'll be okay." It's only then she sees the blue circle spray-painted on the back of the bot's uniform. Marked as non-human: stained for slaughter.

They're surrounded. The girls kick up red dust and inch forward, tightening the circle.

"What's going on here?" demands Keke with an authority she doesn't feel.

"*What's going on here,*" mocks the bobbed girl with the hammer. She wears her school dress's collar pointing up and has a illustration of a lobotomised chimp on her face mask.

Keke has read about the bullying of teenbots in schools. Her first reaction was that they should not put anthrobots in school—what is the point?—but apparently there are many advantages to doing so. It's important that the human kids get used to having AI around, and the machine-teens help the kids with extra lessons. They're also well stocked, so you could always ask them for an extra stylus, a needle and thread, a platelet plaster or a protein bar. The bots' presence makes the kids more competitive, which is great for the schools' academic and sports performance, but it's a double-edged sword: The most competitive take exception to the over-performing bots and abuse them.

"Hand her over," says the blonde girl holding the shard of glass. She has blue paint on her fingers.

"Why?" says Keke. "Why are you trying to hurt her?"

"*Her?* It's not a *her.* It's an *it.* It's a *robot.*"

Keke flicks her eyes over to the bot's uniform. XARINA, the holotag says.

"Her name's Xarina," says Keke.

"We don't call her that."

Keke takes a step backwards. “Robots are here to help us.”

The girls snort and snarl.

“Looks like we’ve got a robo-sympathiser,” says the blue-fingered girl, angling her head. “They’re even worse than the robots.”

The kids step closer and there is more dust, like red smoke in the air. Their practised movements send ice water down Keke’s spine. Choreographed cruelty.

“What did she do to you?” demands Keke.

“She’s not *real*, don’t you get it?”

A swarm of Special Task drones buzz in the sky above them. They’re in a hurry.

“But why hurt her?”

“Where have you been?” demands the freckled one. “The machines have gone mad. They’re killing people. We need to protect ourselves.”

Xarina whimpers and shakes. Strangers walk past their sinister huddle, turning their eyes away, seeing, but not seeing.

Fuckers. Who are the robots, now?

“This android isn’t violent. Look at her. Look at her!”

“We can’t take that chance,” says the blonde. “Terry’s aunt was killed by a supermall escalator.”

The plain girl Keke assumes is Terry nods.

“And Mrs Nduli was attacked by her Elfbot.”

When Keke looks confused, the girl adds, “Her home security bot. The one that’s supposed to *protect* you.”

Glass shard says, “They’ll kill us all, if we don’t stop them.”

“I’ll take her with me,” says Keke. “I’ll make sure that she doesn’t hurt anyone.”

“*You!*” The brunette laughs. “What are *you* going to do?”

“I can take care of myself.”

“Whatever,” says Freckles.

“Let’s see, then,” says the schoolgirl with the hammer. “Let’s see how well you can protect yourself.”

CHAPTER 56

COLD-BUTTER BODIES

TWELVE YEARS PREVIOUSLY

SkyRest
Johannesburg, 2024

There is a jovial atmosphere in the cafeteria at breakfast time. Word has spread that Lewis has finally been elevated and the other residents are exuberant. Part of it is for Lewis, and part is the stoking of their hopes that they, too, will one day be promoted. Two men at an adjacent table each have only one more Stage to go. They laugh over their salty French toast at the inmates who joke around them about the clear blue pool and the craft ice cream and the all-you-can-watch film suites.

Zack's stomach is still roiling when it's time to start the work shift. He's left Lewis's gift in his room—still wrapped—even though he's sure he'll never see him again. They walk over to a hall where trestle tables are set out with old-school sewing machines, and the men are divided into those who can sew and those who can't. Zack is in the latter group, so he is tasked with unrolling and cutting fabric according to overhead projector templates. They set to work as the machines hum in the background. Usually the white noise would be calming, but today it's as if the buzzing is inside his head. His new shift-partner is a slimy man with nervous eyes, and adds to Zack's feeling of unease.

After two hours of work, a bell rings and the men sigh and stretch their arms and backs before they're shepherded to the next task. Zack trails behind the group, trying to avoid his new partner. There will be a five-minute toilet break before the next grind begins. Without really thinking, without even meaning to, Zack peels off from the crowd and slips into a dark room. He knows they're constantly monitored—knows they're watching his every move—so he doesn't understand why he's doing it. If he gets caught, he'll get docked any Rewards due to him. He may even get stripped of his first Stage. But there is an instinct stronger than fear, stronger than the desire to climb the ladder that leads him away from the others.

Zack slips in quietly, and waits for his eyes to adjust to the low light. The space has an earthy smell—is it one of the potting rooms?—but he doesn't see any plants or soil. He blinks, trying to make out what it is in front of him. He inches forward, towards a large dark shape. When he's closer, he sees it's a dozen make-shift platforms built from old building palettes, and they each hold up a large burlap bag with hand-sewn, re-purposed zips.

Wood chips? Sawdust?

But the shape of the bag is wrong. It's too long. It's horizontal. That, and the zip, makes it look like a—

He moves towards the bag closest to him. As he touches it, the bell rings for the next shift to start, and he jolts. Time to go, but he stays there, his body and brain frozen.

They'll miss him soon. He'll be in trouble. His hand travels back to the zip. The smell is stronger now, the dark humus scent reminding him of his nightmare last night. Damp soil and something else. What is it? He pulls down the handle of the zip.

Inside the bag is more brown burlap, wrapped around a sphere, like a dressing. Zack keeps unzipping the rest of it and flinches when he sees that the round bandaged thing is attached to a neck, and a torso. There's a noise in his ears, a humming. It's the adrenaline telling him to run.

So it's a dead body. So what? It's to be expected, isn't it, in a place like this?

The body is ivory, veined with blue. Zack zips it up again. He really needs to go. They've probably noticed he's missing. If he goes now he can still use the excuse of an extended toilet break or—less convincingly—that he got lost. If he doesn't get back now there'll be someone in here to drag him away. He moves to the next bag and opens it. An ash marble torso, waiting to be recycled. One more, he tells himself, he doesn't know why. The Net knows he doesn't want to see another one of these cold-butter bodies. But the next body isn't pale. The skin of the strong neck is loam-coloured and wrinkled, and as the zip moves, tooth by tooth, opening the bag, something in Zack knows what's inside before his brain clicks. He sees the top of the tattoo that he knows so well: Ouroboros.

It's Lewis. It's Lewis.

Lewis, who is supposed to be ten storeys above him, swimming laps in a crystal pool.

Zack stares at the rest of the tattoo: the dragon's head, its circular body, eating its own tail. He draws away, realises he's close to hyperventilating. Then he opens the bag further, and there's a strong ribbon of that soil smell—and now Zack identifies it—mushrooms. Forest mushrooms. And he sees openings in Lewis's skin—his stomach and thighs—like a sea-sponge, dark holes stretched by and embroidered with thriving funghi where they have rolled spikes over his skin and sprinkled in the shroomspores of the fungi that is eating his flesh. Dark meat with mushroom gills.

Zack turns his head away from the body bag and sprays vomit onto the black concrete floor. Water and bile splashes out of him. He wants to run, but his body heaves and heaves. When he straightens up, there is a silhouette at the door.

CHAPTER 57
THE COOLER

Two guards come running, almost falling over Bernard in their hurry to get to Zack. They stumble, and shine their powerful flashlights into his eyes.

"Don't do anything stupid," she says.

It's a bit late for that.

The guards—Xoli and Samuel—move forward and Zack puts his arms up in surrender, wonders distractedly why they didn't just drop him with a current from the cuff. In his blinded state he has a flashback of Lewis's myco-ravaged flesh and almost vomits again. He covers his mouth with the back of his hand. He feels arms around him as the men guide him away from Lewis and the other body bags in the room.

"Where to?" asks Samuel.

"Solitary, for now," says Xoli. "Till they tell us otherwise."

What had Lewis said about solitary confinement? To avoid it at all costs. You go in the Cooler, you'll never be the same. That's if you're lucky enough to come out. Lewis said that 'luck' and 'solitary' do not often go hand in hand. Zack's head is spinning. He just can't get around the fact that Lewis is dead.

The young guard blinks. He seems surprised at the harshness of the punishment, but sets his jaw and moves Zack along.

"Stop," says Bernard, as they get to the door. "I'll deal with him." She looks smug. A cat that finally has the canary in her claws.

"But—"

"Girdler has been a menace from the start. There's only one way to deal with him and I know how." She runs her fingers up and down her baton, moistens her lips.

The guards look uncertain, but hand him over anyway. She pushes Zack in front of her.

"Start walking, Prisoner," she says. "The Cooler's got nothing on me."

Zack expects to be taken somewhere dark and beaten to within an inch his life, so when he figures out where they're going he slows down and waits for his brain to catch up. Bernard pushes him forward.

"Stop dawdling, Prisoner."

His mind is a spiderweb of questions and pictures that won't fade. Bernard grabs two chairs from the common room and marches him to his room, makes him sit in one; she takes the other for herself. The residence is empty: Everyone else is still working. He should be used to her observance by now, but can still feel her ugly dishwater eyes washing all over him. Should he be grateful that she saved him from solcon? Or does she have something worse planned?

Heeled footsteps approach. Gaelyn. She arrives and beams at Zack.

"Mister Girdler!" she says, as if they're meeting by coincidence somewhere light and sunny—on a cruise ship, maybe, Cinnacola cocktails in hand—instead of in an underground penal colony cell.

"I do hope you're settling in nicely?"

Zack just blinks at her.

"I heard we had an incident," Gaelyn says, but Zack doesn't answer. "Now, I don't want you to worry too much about that. It's natural that you are curious as to how SkyRest functions. I only wish that you had come to me instead of exploring on your own."

"I was just—"

"I know, I know. There's no need to explain yourself." She squeezes his arm. The contact, the human touch, is a surge of warmth. "Now, I see that we need to start taking better care of you."

Bernard snorts.

"You're half the size you were when you arrived a week ago. Is anything the matter?"

What a strange question to ask.

"Tell me what I can do to help you," says Gaelyn. "It's my job to take care of you."

He finds himself gradually defrosting. "I've been battling to eat."

"I can see that!" Gaelyn says. "Your cuff is reporting very low blood sugar. Don't worry, I know just the thing." She makes a note on her Tile. "We'll have you sorted out in no time. I don't want you to worry about anything. Are we all okay?"

She searches his face for agreement. Zack wants to agree. He wants to stay on her good side.

"What happened to Lewis?" he asks.

Gaelyn's eyes flicker for a moment, then return to their friendly shine. Her smile is wide. "Oh, we're so thrilled to have him upstairs with us!"

Zack frowns at her.

"If anyone deserved a promotion, it was Lewis! Always such a pleasure to have around. And the way he embraced our philosophy, well, we couldn't be happier to have him with us. We hope that, after this hiccup, you'll work hard to join us too."

"But he's not up there," says Zack, and Bernard's eyes flare.

Shut up, she's saying. *Shut the hell up, Prisoner.*

"What do you mean?"

"Lewis isn't upstairs. He's in a body bag."

"What?"

"Lewis wasn't elevated. He's dead. You can deny it as much as you want, but I saw his dead body in that room."

Gaelyn looks concerned. "No wonder you're not yourself! If you think you saw Lewis's body you must have had quite a shock."

"I know what I saw."

She frowns again, and feigned worry pouts her lips. "Hmm. This is unfortunate. Maybe the others were right."

"What do you mean? Who are the others?"

"The Residents' Care Team. Your history … during the trial. They predicted you'd need some pharmaceutical assistance."

"I don't."

Gaelyn makes another note on her Tile.

"Just for a while. Till you adjust. Moving here can be a traumatic experience! We need you to be able to cope with your new environment. We can't have people making waves, upsetting the others."

"Maybe the others need upsetting," whispers Zack.

"Excuse me?" says Gaelyn.

Bernard stomps on his foot. *Shut up!* she's saying.

"I said maybe the other residents need upsetting."

"If I were you," says Gaelyn, "I'd be very careful of what you say next."

Zack wants to shout at her, yell in their faces. He holds himself back. Getting thrown in solitary isn't going to help his cause.

"I'm going to let you off with a friendly warning. You can even keep your first Stage. I think you'll find that life is a lot easier down here if you co-operate."

Gaelyn tucks her Tile into her utility harness, and turns to leave.

"What's the first thing he did?" says Zack to her retreating back.

She turns around. "Excuse me?"

"What's the first thing Lewis did when he got up there?"

Gaelyn turns on her most winning smile. "He stripped off the new clothes we gave him and jumped in the pool!"

CHAPTER 58

TINTED MIRROR

TWELVE YEARS LATER

Fourways
Johannesburg, 2036

"Stay away from me!" Keke shouts as the schoolgirls close in on her. "You just stay the fuck away."

The injured anthrobot keeps up her high whine.

"Judas," someone hisses.

Judas? What have these kids been reading? Anyway, they have the story the wrong way around.

"You're a traitor," says the blue-fingered girl. "Taking a robot's side."

"I'm not taking anyone's side, but I'm not going to let you hunt someone down."

She's about to add, *What would your parents say?* But then thinks better of it. Where did they learn to hate so easily in the first place? Who taught them to be so vicious? She guesses it started at home.

The girl with the hammer strikes a blow on Xarina's shoulder. The pitch of the whining goes up a notch.

"You stop that right now," says Keke. *You little bitch!*

Freckles throws a stone at the anthrobot, and it glances off her chest.

"Harder!" says the girl with mirror braids.

The next stone hits Keke on her cheekbone and temporarily replaces her vision with sparkling stars and pops.

Keke touches her cheek where the stone has drawn blood.

Motherfucker! It hurts.

She needs to run. She wasn't convinced the kids were going to go through with the attack. She should have bolted as soon as she saw them sauntering up like pack animals. Why did she hesitate? Now it's too late.

The hammer strikes the bot again. The blonde girl with the blue fingers and sharp piece of glass eyes Keke nervously. Is this really how it's going to end? At the clammy hands of these schoolyard jackals?

The combination of Xarina's high-pitched whine and Keke's glowing cheekbone makes her feel out of control. Suddenly the rock slams into the bot's chest, and something in Keke snaps. She takes the blood from the cut under her eye and with two fingers, paints lines on her face with it: across her forehead, down her cheeks, over her nose and chin. Then she starts screaming as loudly as she can. She launches herself at the hammer-wielder, wrestles it from her, then starts swinging it and shouting at the others like a madwoman, hoping to scare them off. She smacks the stones out of Freckles' palm, breaking a knuckle in the process. Freckles cries out and cradles her hand.

The girl grasps to retrieve her hammer, but Keke shouts "Away! Away!" and when she doesn't move, Keke hits her on her shoulder with it, exactly as she had done to Xarina. The girl squeals and shrinks away.

From behind Keke comes the unmistakable buzz of a taser, and Keke feels it bite into her hip: an electric cobra. She shouts in surprise and pain, but really it's no more than a short shock: nothing like the usual debilitating current—and she sees that's because Xarina had moved to shield her, and the jolt she'd felt was just the residual current from where she's in contact with the bot's body. Keke smashes the taser out of the girl's hand so that it lands on the littered ground, right in front of Xarina, who picks it up.

"You don't scare us," says the girl with venomous eyes. She goes for the taser, but Xarina gets to the trigger first, and the bot sends a perfectly aimed clean shot of cobalt electricity right into the girl's chest. The current is so strong it flings the schoolgirl's vibrating body onto the pavement, knocking her out. She's still shivering on the ground when Freckles makes exactly the same mistake and gets the same treatment. The other girls yelp and shout, but they don't help their friends. Xarina shows the taser around, as if asking them who wants to be next. Three members of the gang step down from the fray and slowly reverse out of the circle. Keke feints at the timid one—Terry?—with her upraised hammer, and she backs away too. A girl with a neon pink face-mask high-kicks Xarina in the chest. It does no damage—except perhaps to the girl's ankle—but it sets off the others to attack too, and soon there are four of them kicking the anthrobot. The bot drops the taser as they begin tearing into her with their fists and nails and teeth. They strip her singed clothes and stamped silicone skin. Her hair comes out in clumps. They kick her in her most vulnerable joints and she falls to her knees, then just as she looks like she's about to succumb, the bot looks up at Keke with bright eyes, as if something has clicked in her processing and she realises that she is much stronger than them.

Xarina's shrill screaming now transforms into a deeper bray as she roars and flings the attackers off her body as if they're nothing more than dolls. She forces her fingers into her own mouth and pulls off her lower jaw, then uses the disembodied titanium to slam one of the girls on the side of the head, and she spins away from them. Xarina's still shouting when she picks up a saucer-eyed girl and throws her twenty metres away, into a dirty bricked wall. Bones break. Xarina turns on the next girl; there are still three left, including the blonde with the glass, a girl with mirror braids, and a mean-looking blunt-cut brunette. Keke looks around at the injured girls' bodies with horror, keeps hearing the sound of those young bones breaking, and feels as if she's caught in a dream.

The brunette drops her rock. Mirror braids holds up her hands in surrender.

"Stop," Keke says to the anthrobot. "Don't hurt them." She can't bear to see any more violence.

Xarina turns to look at Keke. Half of the anthrobot's face is peeled off, most of her hair is gone.

"We're out of danger," says Keke, "you don't need to fight anymore."

The skinned bot blinks. She lowers her arms and stops shouting; she's still for a moment, processing the information. Her body seems to relax and, seemingly exhausted, she drops her metal jaw to the ground.

Without hesitating, the brunette slams Xarina from behind, causing the schoolbot to fall face forward into the red sand. The girl with mirror braids picks up the taser and jams her finger down on the trigger, sending fifty thousand volts into Xarina's body, paralysing her. She keeps going, sending pulse after pulse into the synthetic schoolgirl's body, until they can smell burning rubber and metal, and still she doesn't stop. Braids has this spooky look on her face, a cold indifference. The wrecked face of the robot, turned sideways out of the dirt, watches Keke as it jerks: desperate, beseeching: an image Keke knows she'll never forget. Some pedestrians have slowed to watch, now that the opportunity to help has passed. Multi-coloured face-masks seem to flow past in a weird stop-animation in Keke's peripheral vision.

"Enough," Keke says, putting her hand out, even though she knows it's too late, but the girl ignores her and keeps melting Xarina.

"Enough now," Keke says, moving to take the taser away, and then she feels a hot, sharp stinging in her lower back, and the stinging turns to a searing pain, as if someone has stabbed her with a hot knife, and she turns around and sees the blonde girl looking up at her with a shocked expression, as if she had never really expected the glass to penetrate Keke's skin. As if it was too easy to slide the transparent dagger into sinew and organ. For that moment, connected by weapon and flesh, it's as if Keke can hear the blue-fingered girl's thoughts, and it's like she's wondering how something so simple and quick can have such dire consequences.

They stare at each other with matching shocked expressions, a tinted mirror of panic.

Is this what most violence is like? thinks Keke as the stars come back to reclaim her vision. *Ordinary people shocked by their own and others' swift actions?*

It feels as if the blood in her head drains out all at once through the new wound, her life flowing out of her. Keke's mind is as light as the sky above; her consciousness is floating upwards to join the grey clouds. She never expected death to be so welcoming, or so brisk.

Then there's no more time for philosophizing as she swoons to the ground.

Keke collapses next to Xarina, two cut-down bodies on the rough rusted soil. Creeps begin to gather around them, snapping footage for their Flitter feeds. Keke's vibrant blood puddles around them. The anthrobot tries to say something but without the modulator in her jaw-part the words just stream out as a sad sigh. Keke matches the sound with her own. Xarina moves her palm towards Keke, and they hold hands and look into each other's eyes as they both power down.

CHAPTER 59
RETCH

TWELVE YEARS PREVIOUSLY

SkyRest
Johannesburg, 2024

Xoli and Samuel arrive at Zack's door. Xoli is carrying a SkyRest-branded suitcase.

"Mister Girdler," Xoli says, gravel for a voice.

Zack looks from them to Bernard and back again.

"Where do you want him?" asks Samuel.

Xoli glances up from opening the silver catches on the case. "That chair he's in will do."

Zack frowns. "What are you going to do to me?"

The older man coughs and says, "Nothing to worry about, brother. We're just going to fix you up."

"I don't need fixing up."

The guard shrugs, points to the ceiling. "Orders from above."

Samuel ties Zack to his chair with some kind of wide elastic strap that he fastens at the back. He pulls another one over his arms. Zack struggles against the restraints but knows it's no use. The older guard pulls a transparent silicone bag from the suitcase—it's filled with a creamy liquid—then a thin plastic pipe. He tears the packaging open with his teeth and connects the two.

"Ready?"

"Ready," says Sam, holding Zack's head still. Xoli pushes the pipe up Zack's nose and threads it through down into his throat, causing him to retch. He struggles and some of the white stuff splatters on the floor.

"Take it easy," Xoli says, re-threading the pipe. "Just take it easy." He casts hard eyes at Bernard. "Can we have some help here?"

Bernard approaches and wraps her meaty forearms around Zack's head, holding it still.

Zack shouts and retches some more, and then he can feel the cool liquid running down his throat.

His vision becomes blurred before Gaelyn comes in. It takes twelve minutes for the bag to drain, and by the thirteenth minute he is lying, untethered and asleep, on his mat.

When Zack wakes, he's alone. There is a cool mist of relief. His tongue is swollen, his throat dry and scratched from when they force-fed him. Force-fed him what? Some kind of triple-strength nutrishake. Spiked, no doubt. He knows a sedation headache when he feels one.

What else did they give him? Some kind of psychotropic: an antipsychotic would be his guess.

"Something to control your hallucinations," Gaelyn had said. "Something to help you get some rest." What happened after that is a blur.

Zack tries to stand, but he falls back down again. His brain is slushed ice.

They wouldn't have to resort to feeding him if he just ate his meals, they said. The drugs they can administer via his cuff, but, unfortunately, nutrition still requires a manual approach. Zack crawls to his basin, splashes his face. Swigs half a bottle of water. The cool liquid balms his bruised throat; his thoughts are scudding clouds.

What did he do to get into trouble? He can't remember. There's a constant niggle of foreboding you get when you know you've done something wrong. Vague memories come to him: a circular dragon tattoo. A clear blue pool: empty. A beautiful biker with burnt caramel for skin. He can't think of her name, or how they met. Then a more urgent thought about a woman with long red hair. Kirsten? Katherine? He needs to see her. Has to tell her something really important but he can't put his finger on what. It's there in his head, right there, and just as he thinks he can grab onto it, it disappears behind the pharma fog.

CHAPTER 60

HONEYED HALLUCINATION

TWELVE YEARS LATER

Fourways
Johannesburg, 2036

"Move out of my way!" shouts Kate as she elbows the voyeurs. "Keke!"

Keke opens her eyes. She looks drunk, as if she's seeing some kind of vision, some incandescent daybreak honeyed hallucination. Kate almost stumbles over in her hurry to reach her friend.

"Keke!" she shouts, without meaning to, because the crimson spill scares her. She kneels down in it, anyway, and examines Kekeletso for injuries. A large fragment of glass in embedded in her lower back. Where did it come from? Some kind of explosion? Or an accident? Kate can't tell. She shields her eyes and looks up at the flashing mandibles surrounding them.

"Has someone called an ambudrone?" she asks, and someone answers "They're offline."

They're offline?

"Is anyone here a doctor?"

Heads shake.

"A nurse?"

A small man steps forward, hand half-raised. He sheepishly turns his camera function off. "I did a first aid course once."

Kate holds Keke's face; she's still conscious. Good. A rush of bright green relief.

James had told her once when they were watching a film about a man who had an axle perforate his chest that you shouldn't remove the foreign object, because you could make it worse. The object could be holding the body together, in a way, and/or staunching the bleeding. Depending on the shape, removing it could cause more harm than the initial penetration. Think of a ninja star, James said. But this isn't a barbed object, and that advice is fifteen years old, before skin zips and platelet sprays. Does the same advice apply? *Leave it up to the trauma team at the hospital,* she can hear him say, but right now the hospital ERs are overflowing, and even the closest one is a too-risky cab drive away.

Kate doesn't know what to do. She shakes her hands out as she thinks, then feels for Keke's pulse. It's weak. Or is that just the pulsing of blood in her own nervous fingers making Keke's seem faint?

"Don't worry, Kex," she says, trying to smooth her worried face into something more comforting. "It's not as bad as it looks." The last sentence is for her own benefit.

Kate reaches over to Xarina's metal corpse and levers open her chest cavity with the back of a hammer she finds. She retrieves the medikit and rifles through it. It's well stocked. Maybe she will be able to help, after all. She hauls it over to Keke, shakes her hands again, and gets to work. First is the hand sanitiser for herself, and the disinfecting anaesthetic spray for Keke's wound, which she uses liberally. The camera flashes from the crowd are little tinfoil shimmers in her head, and make her teeth hurt.

"I'm going to take care of you," says Kate. "You'll be fine."

"Ha," says Keke, attempting a smile. "You forget that I know you don't have any kind of medical training whatsoever."

"True," says Kate, "But what I lack in expertise I will make up for in charm and extra anaesthetic."

"That's a deal I can live with."

Keke's bravery makes Kate falter.

What if—

She'd never be able to live with herself. The shard glitters in the rising sun.

"Now," says Kate. "Do you think I should take the glass out?"

Keke's eyes open a little wider. "What do you mean, do I think you should take the glass out? Of course you need to take the fucking glass out. What kind of fake doctor are you?"

"It might make you bleed more."

"I have a glass dagger in my back for fuck's sake. What other option is there? Jesus Christ, can you at least pretend to know what you're doing?"

All right, thinks Kate. *All right.* A spray of relief. If there's a consensus it takes the pressure off her. She'll take it out. She prepares by laying out her instruments on the medikit white apron on the ground: PainStop Pen; pliers; saline wash; gauze, stemcell gel, skin zip. As an afterthought, she pulls on the biolatex gloves that smell like young tree sap and talcum. Seeing the surgical setup, Kate's boldness returns. She can do this. A Special Task volanter arrives in the sky, chops the air above them, kicking up the dry red sand, then moves on.

Nothing to see here. Just your regular Doomsday hustle.

Kate uses the painkiller injection pen to blast six shots of lidocaine into Keke's lower back. She also squirts the painkiller inhalant up her nose.

"Ahhhh." Keke sighs. "Thank you."

"I haven't done anything yet."

"Oh, yes you have," Keke says. "You're a fucking goddess."

Kate laughs out loud.

"Seriously. Has no one ever told you that?" says Keke.

"Go home, Keke, you're drunk."

"Ha! Wishful thinking."

Kate picks up the pliers and steels herself. "Ready?"

"Ready," says Keke, and Kate secures the teeth of the tool around the glass shard, prepares to use some muscle, and pulls it smoothly out. They both gasp: Keke in pain, and Kate in sympathy. At first the wound hardly bleeds, and for a second Kate is so relieved she feels as if she can fly, but then it starts pouring out, like a pump has been turned on, and Kate grabs clumsily for the saline wash. She works as quickly as she can, gritting her teeth as she washes the gaping wound that makes her want to faint, drying it with the gauze, filling it with the gel and tearing the paper off the back of the skin zip with her shaking fingers. Finally she places the zip, closes up the gash and covers it with a large platelet plaster which is probably unnecessary, but makes her feel better.

"Done." Kate snaps off her gloves. The sound smells like freshly starched sheets.

Keke open her eyes. "Seriously?"

The voyeur creeps begin to leave.

"I know. I surprise even myself with my superior surgical skills."

"When I stand up am I going to find my ass sewed to my elbow?"

"No." Kate laughs. The feeling of relief is back. "But you've lost a lot of blood, and I don't know how much internal damage there is, so …"

"Don't worry. I'm not going to sue you for malpractice."

"Seriously. Your kidney may be sliced in half, for all I know."

"Ah, well, luckily I have another one."

"You're still drunk."

"I like it this way. What's in that inhalant, anyway?"

Kate checks the bottle. "Pexidine."

"It's a thing of wonder and beauty."

Kate hands it over. "It's all yours."

Keke struggles to get up.

"Whoah!" says Kate. "Whoah. I don't think you should be standing."

"Nonsense," says Keke, "I'm as good as new." She lets out a sharp exhalation, screws up her face, and lies back down again.

Kate looks around at the dead robot and discarded weapons. Flashes of white violence spark in her brain. "What the fuck happened?"

"I'll tell you later. What are you doing here, anyway?" asks Keke. "You're supposed to be with Silver."

"I couldn't let you do it on your own, and I forgot to give you this." Kate points at her gun.

"That would have come in handy," says Keke.

"Besides, I thought I could help Silver more by getting Zack instead of sitting in a hospital ward holding her hand."

"I guess that in my condition, breaking into a crim colony is now out of the question?"

"You guess correctly. Ten minutes ago I wasn't even sure if you were going to live."

"Yay?"

"The only place you're going is the Lipworth Foundation."

"They won't let me in," says Keke.

"Not as a visitor," says Kate, "but as a patient they're obliged to."

One last question hangs in the air. Who will accompany Keke? She's not well enough to make it there on her own on a solartram, and the mutinous cabbies are too dangerous. But if Kate takes her, she'll be too late to get Zack and save Silver. They huddle there at an unspoken impasse with everything at stake—Keke not asking, Kate not wanting to refuse.

CHAPTER 61

SHELL

TWELVE YEARS PREVIOUSLY

SkyRest

Johannesburg, 2024

Zack completes his grind—making hemp oil soap—and shuffles back to the residence with the rest of the men. How many shifts has he done now? They all seem to blur into one. They automatically move from one thing to another: work, shower, rest, eat. Butternut wedges for dinner, spongey reconstituted peaches with soywhip for dessert. Zack's learnt to eat the food now. No matter how unappetising, it's the better option. He's regaining some muscle mass. He never wants to be as weak as he was when Bernard held him down to force feed him. He needs to be able to work.

Zack has two stripes on his lapel now, and he's working hard to win his third. He needs to fast-track up that ladder. He doesn't know why his need is urgent, but it is. Every time he finds himself exhausted, he thinks of the Stages he needs to earn to get up, to get out, and it keeps him going.

Despite the sedative effects of the psychotropics, he still wakes every night to Bernard in the room. He needs to be strong. He needs to be able to defend himself.

The wrestler resident has also been elevated. It came about suddenly. He still had two Stages to go before promotion but on Tuesday last week he was gone and his room was stripped bare. It caused some excitement. What did the man do to level up so quickly? What was his secret? Could anyone remember what he was saying or doing differently? Everyone had worked doubly hard that day, thinking of the ex-resident relishing his longed-for salted butterscotch ice cream.

Elevation through Hard Work.

The residents are happy for the wrestler, but Zack feels uneasy. Is it envy, or something more? For some reason he just can't imagine the wrestler up there, among the savvy-looking worker bees. Something about it just doesn't feel right to him.

Zack climbs on top of his new bed and holds the unopened gift on his chest. He can't remember what it is or who he'd bought it for, but every time he's tempted to open it, a deep sense of foreboding stops him. He's been able to save up enough Rewards for a new mattress and a few other home comforts. He's requested books a few times but his requests disappear into thin air. "What do you need books for?" Zack can imagine Gaelyn saying. "You've got everything you need right here."

Because I need waking up, he would tell her.

Because I've lost myself.

Because I feel like I'm stuck in a shell.

CHAPTER 62

12 YEARS LATER

12 YEARS LATER

SkyRest
Johanneburg, 2036

Zack hears Gaelyn call his name. He finishes up-combing his salt-and-pepper hair and runs a bit of styling clay through it. Uses a SkyRest soluble steri-wipe to clean his hands before heading down the residency passage. When he reaches the open door of the blank room, Gaelyn greets him with a wide smile, and motions towards the new resident.

"Zack," she says, "this is David."

Zack nods at the man.

"David, Zachary is one of our most experienced residents."

"If you have any questions, ask him. He'll show you around."

The men size each other up.

"Right!" says Gaelyn, who hasn't seemed to have aged at all since the day Zack first arrived. "My job here is done. Call me if you need anything."

Zack lifts his chin to the newbie. "Let's grab a sandwich before the rest of the mob gets back."

David watches Zack eat his shamwich with an expression that can only be described as revolted.

"Go on," says Zack. "Eat something. You'll need your strength. There's a lot of work to do."

"What kind of work?" asks the man.

"All kinds," says Zack, wiping his mouth with a rice-paper serviette. "To keep it interesting. You do your Quota, you get your Rewards."

"And then you get promoted?" he says.

"Elevated. Yes."

"You get to go up there?"

"Yip," says Zack. "You work hard, you climb the ladder."

"How long does it take? How long have you been here?"

He looks at Zack's lapel which is fully striped apart from one last Stage.

Zack shrugs. These whippersnappers are always so damn nervy.

"Twelve years," says Spud.

"What?" David looks around. The other residents are sauntering in: dirty, sweat-soaked. They shuffle towards the showers. Spud wipes perspiration off his forehead with his arm.

"Zack's been here twelve years."

"Really?" says Zack. It feels so strange to put a number on the time he's been down here.

"I've been here sixteen. I started a calendar when I first arrived. Not that the years matter. The only things that matter are these babies," he taps his lapel.

David looks at Spud's shirt and blinks away the start of tears. After sixteen years, Spud only has eight Stages out of twelve.

"Cheer up, Snapper," says Zack, scrunching up his serviette and launching it into the corner bin. "You'll be okay."

CHAPTER 63

THE INVERSE OF PANDORA'S BOX

SkyRest
Johanneburg, 2036

Zack's dreaming again. It's a similar variation every night, as if his subconscious is trying to pull him into some kind of realisation—characters from a previous life trying to get through to him. A man with a dragon tattoo is telling him something but his voice is so distorted Zack can't make out any of the words. Sometimes the dream takes a sinister turn and he lands up in a forest under dead leaves. Sometimes worse: sometimes he's buried alive. The real nightmares are when he's covered in beetles that bite his back and his legs and leave small trails of dark blood.

There's no evil in the dream tonight. Tonight it's the biker woman who, in slow-motion, kisses his cheek and whispers something into his ear. Her vitality radiates off her. He wants to hold her, wants to climb inside her, would do anything to feel her vibrance against his lonely skin.

Then a miracle happens. She breaks out of the dream and is right there in his room with him. He can feel her hand on his face. How is this happening? He's wanted this moment for . . .has it really been twelve years?

But something feels wrong. He ignores it at first, so desperate for the dream to be true, but the skin feels wrong. And the smell. It's not nutmeg, like it should be, but yoghurt.

Zack flinches, his eyes click open, and he knows who it is before his eyes adjust. Of course it's Bernard. It's always Bernard. But she's never woken him like this before, her toady palm on his cheek. Her too-white face is a sinister moon. He hears a gasp, realises it must have come from him. Zack scrambles backwards into his pillow, away from her.

"What do you want?" he asks. "What the ever-loving fuck do you want?"

He hates her. Hates every part of her, even the way she breathes. He wishes she would stop breathing. She doesn't answer him.

He can't do this anymore, can't stand it one night longer. One way or another, this will stop tonight.

"Why do you do it?" Zack asks.

He's surprised when she finally speaks. "What?"

"Why do you watch me sleep?"

"Isn't it obvious?" Bernard asks.

Twelve years. Twelve years! Something about that makes Zack want to blow this place up, with Bernard in it. Without any warning, he's reached his tipping point. Something is twisting inside him, coiling, ready to strike.

One Stage to go. Just one more Stage and you'll be elevated. DON'T DO ANYTHING STUPID.

"It's not obvious," says Zack.

"Then I've done my job."

"Is it over?" asks Zack. "Your job? Are you going somewhere?"

"You're the one who's going somewhere. It's time."

A warm breeze of hope.

"Do you mean … I'm being elevated?"

His heart lifts in his chest.

"Is that why you woke me? Are we going now?"

"You're due to get your last Stage tomorrow night."

Zack's besieged by conflicting emotions. He covers his face with his hands.

Twelve years.

He should be feeling a clean hit of joy, shouldn't he? Instead, his stomach is a cement mixer of longing and dread and something else he can't identify.

"That's good news. That's really good news." His voice is flat.

Bernard screws up her face. Her contempt is almost palpable; it's like the room is crowded with her scorn.

"Good news?" she snarls. "Don't you understand anything?"

"You're upset that I'll be gone," says Zack. "You'll have no one to harass."

She snorts in disbelief. "Harass?"

"What would you call it? You've worn me down so much that I don't even know who I am anymore."

"Well, I'll remind you who you are. You are Zachary Girdler. And you had better start acting like it, before it's too late."

Zack is taken aback. She's never called him by his name before.

"What's that ... What's that supposed to mean?"

"It means you need to wake the fuck up."

He's never heard her swear before, either. Never seen her so riled up.

"Wake *up*!" she says, and he senses she wants to shake him, but holds herself back. "Remember *why you exist*."

"I—"

"Do you really believe that Lewis was promoted? After what you saw?"

Lewis?

He has a vague recollection of the man.

Lewis? What is she talking about? What did he see?

"Lewis was elevated," Zack says, as if hypnotised. The words don't seem to come from him.

"What about Mulalo? Steven? Azwi? You think they're all up there?" She skewers the air with her finger. "Playing fucking foosball?"

Suddenly it seems unlikely, but where else would they be? Out on parole?

"I thought you were smarter than that!" Bernard punches the bed.

"What do you mean?"

"You of all people should know the truth about this place."

Bernard's words echo in Zack's head. Something is resonating through the smog that is his brain.

He knows. He knows. He knows. But why isn't he seeing it? Because he's been worn down by this place. Worn down, beaten down, dumbed down. They've drugged the memory out of him. Zack doesn't know anything anymore. He gave up a long time ago. He lost the plan.

"On the first day here I saw the upstairs levels," Zack says. "I saw the different floors. The VR room, the restaurant, the open-plan offices."

"You saw what you wanted to see," says Bernard. "Lewis saw a pool. Steven saw an ice cream shop. That initiation tour is a fucking hologram. Why do you think we didn't get out of the elevator?"

As he hears it, he knows it's true.

"But then where do the promoted men go?"

"You know the answer to that. You saw the body bags."

"What?"

"Karōshi," says Bernard.

"No," Zack shakes his head. Thinks of the friends he's lost.

"Karōshi," she says again. "They monitor your declining health as you work yourself to death. And then, one day, the circle is complete."

Zack sees the dragon tattoo clearly now. Ourobos. Lewis. The circle is complete.

Bernard is agitated. Her fingers keep flying up to her hard-gelled curls. "You want to know why I'm in here every night? Why I watch you sleep?"

Of course he does. He does and he doesn't.

"I'm protecting you."

"What?"

"Don't you understand anything? I've been protecting you all along."

Zack's head is spinning. Bernard grabs his leg, forces him back into the moment.

"You need to focus," she says. "We don't have much time."

"Focus on what?"

"On your end game."

"I don't know what that is anymore."

"Think, Zack. *Think.* I don't know the details. It's up to you to remember them."

Bernard places a band over his temple, and plugs the black lozenge XDrive into it. There's a flicker of light in his head and hot sparks in his skull as his backed-up memories are restored. He remembers the cardboard cut-out trial, the Orb, the first of the zombie drugs. Other concepts come to him, too, but he doesn't understand them yet.

"I've been able to access your cuff. Over the past forty-eight hours I've been weaning you off your SkyRest medication. You should be seeing things more clearly now."

That's why he had the dream. The reaching for the truth. Pictures, moments, names are coming to him, slowly at first. It's as if his mind is opening up and is in danger of absorbing every starless concept around: the inverse of Pandora's Box. The zombie spike is wearing off and exposing what he's always known, deep down. It gains layers and scope and force and speed and he feels like it's going to bowl him over and leave him for dead.

A lotus flower blooms in Zack's head. "I need to get out of here."

Bernard's eyes glint. "I can help you."

PART 3

CHAPTER 64

REDPEPPER PROXIES

Ashram Ramanana

Panchagiri Hills, India, 2036

Marko's done what he can to warn the Nancies about the V1R1S, and sent them his recommended shutdown procedure. He made it clear that it's imperative to cut the power to the entire country, and the neighbouring countries, to stop it from spreading. If the contagion beats the shutdown they'll have to use the Kill Switch, and no one wants to resort to that; if it comes to that they may as well nuke the whole country. He doesn't know yet if they've taken his advice.

Now Marko fistpumps as he finally finds the IPX of the person responsible for creating the V1R1S. He's been working for fifteen hours solid. He's been knee-deep in darkweb dungeons and redpepper proxies. He's sweated through his scratchy roughcotton robe. There's a plate of congealed dhal on his side-table. The swami urged him to eat, but he doesn't have time. He hasn't been able to get hold of Keke, and he has a terrible twisting feeling in his gut that is telling him she's in real danger.

Marko's longed-for epiphany finally arrives, and it's nothing to do with sun salutations or silent retreats. It's all about Keke.

He's been such a fool. Once this disaster is over he's going to kick himself like no man in history has ever kicked himself before. And then he's going to rush back to South Africa and give every remaining second to Keke. Keke! Love of his life; fuel for his fire. What a damned fool stupid bastard he has been. What had he been thinking? He loves her like fire loves wood. If he is the bird then she is the join between his breast and wing. He was nothing before he met her and he's nothing now. Keke is his creator. She makes him into the best version of himself. He'll worship her the way she loves to be worshipped. The way she deserves to be worshipped. Gradually, with his tongue, in slow circles. Until she shouts out and squeezes him between her godly and glorious thighs. Marko feels himself get hard. He adjusts himself, and a notification pops up on screen.

The image of Keke fades slightly as he discovers the IPX.

"Come to Papa," he whispers, squirming in his seat. When he licks his dry lips, his tongue comes away salty. He needs electrolytes. He needs hydration. He doesn't care; he's so close to the answer he can feel nipping at his fingertips.

"Yes, yes, yes." It's the right place. An unmistakable server signature. Now it's as simple as finding out who it belongs to and shutting the motherfucker down. He sends a dummy NASP email to the address he finds. If the owner of the address opens it, it'll escalate Marko's privileges and he'll be able to identify and destroy the Root. He automates a SMPR flash where the fucker's identity and physical address will be broadcast to every South African with a mandible. He smacks the 'send' key and then stares at the screen, waiting. He's going to catch the ratbastard who put Keke in danger if it's the last thing he ever does.

Marko plays an invisible piano on the table top. He hums a made-up tune. He searches for his secret stash of nutnut cookies, and he waits.

He starts when there's a knock on the door. Damn it, is he going to have to wrestle the swami to get out of *yajna*? But when he looks up there's a young local boy holding out a white courier satchel to him. More kids hop on their bare feet and giggle from the doorway. They're excited about something. Marko takes the bag and looks at the waybill, dated last week. He gives the kids all a cookie and tells them to scram.

It's a drone delivery from Johannesburg, but the sender's address is blank.

CHAPTER 65

HAPPY HOUR

Fourways

Johannesburg, 2036

When Kate hears the annoying buzz of the Volanter again she feels like swatting it out of the toxic sky. She can't stand the hovering, hovering, hovering. Can't they just land or fly away? Anything but this supremely irritating humming giant mosquito that feels as if it's inside her head. Then, as if by magic, it does start to descend, whipping up the red smoke and litter as it does so, and they both have to cover their eyes to prevent them being sandblasted.

It's not a Special Task sunchopper. It's a handsome metallic navy affair with a pinstriped belly and bling on the blades. It lands, and as the dust begins to settle, Seth steps out.

"How?" is all Kate can manage to say. Relief, certainly, and also perhaps the after-effects of the trauma of finding Keke bleeding—what she at first thought was dying—on the ground. She blinks away the tears.

"How?" The answer is not important. What is important is that Seth is here in a Volanter—a Volanter!—and she knows the Lipworth Foundation has a dronepad.

"She's hurt!" Kate yells at Seth, who nods and tenderly picks up Keke and carries her to the aircraft, helps her up into the bucketseat, straps her in. Keke winces, then puts on the headset and clicks the ignition button. She switches off the smartpilot; she knows she has to fly it manually. The blades start whirring above them.

"You okay?" shouts Seth, and Keke nods. Gives them a thumbs-up. He leans into her, kisses her cheek, stays there a moment longer than expected.

"See you on the other side!" she shouts, and pulls the stick backwards. The Volanter begins to rise, and within seconds it's humming high in the sky, then it's gone.

Seth watches the sky.

They start walking towards SkyRest, two blocks away. Questions crowd Kate's head.

"Mally?"

Seth's lips turn down. "I didn't find him."

Her heart contracts. She can't think about that now. Unknowingly, she's stopped in her tracks.

"Come on." Seth pulls her gently along. "One thing at a time."

"Did you steal that Volanter?"

"I don't like to use the word *steal*. It has negative connotations."

"Who does it belong to?"

"I don't know. Some billionaire? I found it at the golf course."

"The golf course."

Kate thought that golf had gone the way of cigarettes and swimming pools. She hasn't even heard the word for over a decade.

"That AstroGolf place."

"You stole a sunchopper from a billionaire at a fake golf course."

"It was happy hour."

Kate looks at her digital clock display.

"It's 9AM."

Seth shrugs. "Billionaires don't care."

Kate laughs. It feels good. How life can be so dire and so stupid all at once makes her feel slightly human again. She still has Keke's blood on her knees.

"I pulled a giant piece of glass out of Keke's back."

Seth glances at her, perhaps to see if she's joking.

"Forgive me if I find that difficult to believe."

"I swear."

"You can't even look at a needle without passing out."

"That's not true. Not anymore."

Having kids has toughened Kate. She's dealt with smashed faces, broken bones, even … an image of Meadon flashes in on her vision. A dark night, the long ribbon scent of roses, Lumin's swift hands, and a crunching sound she'll never forget as long as she lives. No, she's not going to think about that. Not now. She has to focus on getting Zack.

"What's your plan?" asks Seth as they get to the SkyRest building.

"I don't have one," says Kate. "Don't look at me like that."

"You think we'll just be able to walk right in and collect him? A serial killer. From the PLC with the highest security in South Africa."

"When the situation is so impossible I tend to not overthink things."

"Or not think at all."

"Shut it. I'm in survival mode. I'm moving on instinct alone. It's the best I can do."

It's always been like that between them. Seth for thinking, Kate for feeling. Maths and colour.

She's tempted to add *Just trust me,* but Seth has a rule that you should never trust people who say that.

The receptionist at the entrance greets them with a wide smile. Kate's auto-targeting adstream had delivered a few of SkyRest's marketing messages to her while she was researching the funeral party.

Was it really just yesterday that they were eating those funeral cake samples?

SkyRest is the leading innovator in the urban death industry. The last ad she saw informed her that she could have the ashes printed into anything she likes: a flashdisk brimmed with downloaded memories; a decorative ceramic fruit bowl; a knock-off of a designer garden chair.

The guard cheerfully relieves them of their weapons.

"Welcome to SkyRest!" The receptionist points to her holotag. "I'm Gaelyn." Despite the situation outside, her make-up is perfect, her forehead uncreased.

In fact, the whole place looks remarkably orderly, given the chaos on the streets. Maybe they're even happy about the apocalypse. It is, after all, what they specialise in. More bodies to turn into soap and FongKong trinkets. Gaelyn doesn't bat an eyelid at Kate's dirty and blood-stained clothes.

"I'd like a tour of your products and services, please," says Kate.

"Forgive me being so bold," says Gaelyn. "But when you walked in, the system scanned your dynap codes."

Kate flushes. "Is there a problem?"

"Not at all. I just wanted to offer you both my sincere condolences about your mother."

"Thank you," says Kate.

"Has she been ill long?"

"Not too long."

Anne has stage four uterine cancer. It spread to her lymph nodes before she agreed to see a doctor, so although there are many different and effective cures for cancer, it's too late for her. The disease has already ravaged her insides. Her senior smartwatch SOS suffer-score is a solid eight out of ten. Rather than languish in hospital, she's chosen elective death. The living funeral is scheduled for next week, and the plan is for her to be surrounded by her loved ones, say goodbye, and take the pentobarbital.

"We hope that here at SkyRest you'll come to understand a more positive experience when it comes to death. In ancient times it was regarded as a passage and celebrated accordingly. It's only the modern western way that has shrouded it in fear. Soon your mother will no longer be suffering, and we'll take care of the rest. I hope you take comfort in that."

Gaelyn sticks a small green dot on each of them, then takes them past the front desk, past a watercooler, the door to the emergency fire stairwell, and through to the exhibition hall. The second she steps away from the reception desk, a carbon copy replaces her.

Suddenly a deafening siren rings through the air. It fills the space with red zigzags. Kate and Seth both flinch at the sudden noise, but Gaelyn remains completely unperturbed. There is chatter at the front entrance. Men in kevlarskin onesies appear, holding long, smooth weapons with two handles that look like they're straight out of a space opera film. Where did they come from? It's like they jumped out of the walls.

"Stay where you are," says the SkyRest announcer. "Stay where you are."

Two of the guards jog towards Kate and Seth. Apart from the bulletproof suits, they wear graphene face armour with moving parts that agitate when they talk.

"Come with us," they say.

CHAPTER 66

KILL SWITCH

"No," says Kate.

The SkyRest guard looks at her. "It's for your own safety."

"I've heard that before," says Seth.

"What is the situation?" Gaelyn's smile is as wide as ever.

"We have a TX599. All visitors are to come with us."

Seth looks around. As expected, there are no other visitors.

Gaelyn takes a step forward. "I'm afraid we'll have to continue this tour another time. We have an unusual situation."

"What's happening?"

"We've never had a situation like this before, but don't worry. If we all just follow the protocol, everything will be fine."

Kate doesn't know what to do. There's no way she's going with the thugs. No way she's being trawled into another dark van, not without kicking and screaming.

Gaelyn shakes her head in what looks like a nervous tic. "Will be fine," she says. "Will be fine."

"Reset," says one of the guards.

"Reset," says Gaelyn. "Affirmative." She cocks her head and looks at Kate. "If we all just follow the protocol everything will be fine." The receptionist tries to take a step forward, but her body arrests in that awkward position, and she can't seem to get out of it. "Will be fine."

The guard picks her up and throws her over his shoulder. The other motions with a nod to take her away.

"Come with me," says the remaining guard.

The twins stand their ground.

"I'm not offering you a choice," he says. "You have to come with me right now. We're about to have a serious security breach, and it's not safe to be in here."

"What do you mean," says Seth, "that you're *about* to have a security breach. What does that mean?"

"You don't need to know the details. You need to—"

"We do if you want us to move," says Kate.

The guard looks at the green sticker with annoyance. He would have carried them away just like Gaelyn if he was allowed to. Something about the sticker is putting him off.

"Due to a situation that is out of our control, we need to shut down the building."

"What situation?" asks Kate. "Do you mean the rebellion?"

"Shut it down? What?" says Seth, "The whole building? You can't."

That would be a disaster. Or would it?

The guard bites down and his jaw muscles ripple. He's clearly annoyed to be wasting time with stubborn civilians, but he can't touch them, and he can't leave them here. The siren is ringing and the red zigzags are still scraping Kate's eyeballs. Seth checks his newstream.

International Texpert in India Confirms 'Malfunction' is a Virus

V1R1S Spreading with Deadly Consequences

Switch Off, Unplug, You Can Stop the V1R1S

V1R1S Reaches Cape Republic, Thousands Dead

Prepare for National Shutdown

Call for the KILL SWITCH Now

Roguebots Not Rebels: Meet the V1R1S that's spreading at the speed of light

"They've confirmed it's a virus," says Seth. "They're going to be shutting down the city one band at a time."

"Shutting down?"

"Cutting the power."

"The government? They can't do that. This place is solar."

"It's not the government. It's everyone, everywhere. Doesn't matter if they're on the grid or not. Doesn't matter where the power comes from. Everyone's responsible for shutting their own power off over the next few hours by staggered deadlines, north to south, or face the consequences of the V1R1S spreading."

"Why *staggered?*"

"I don't know. To give them time to loot the national treasury before it goes offline forever?"

"But don't the roguebots have back-up battery packs?"

"They won't last forever. And, combined with the Kill Switch, it'll stop most of the AI from icing any more people."

"They're going to trigger the Kill Switch?"

"It looks like it."

It's a three-signature government decision. Not only will the Kill Switch terminate all robot consciousness, including surgeons and nurses and teachers, it'll kill every iteration of artificial intelligence in the country, from smart fridges to traffic lights to artificial hearts. Activating the Switch will cause planes to drop out of the sky. It'll break the country in half, wipe out trillions on the Cryptox Exchange, and take out thousands of civilians. Would Mashini Wam really have the ovaries to do that? Do they want her to? Kate pictures the premature babies in their smart incubators and wants to cry. Then she thinks of her own baby, Silver, and can feel the blood drain out of her face.

"Silver," she says. "She won't be able to get back."

Seth's mouth is a hard line. In a low voice he says "We need to get Zack and get back to her before the Lipworth shuts down."

Kate looks around for evidence of the blackout, and, as if by magical thinking, things start fading. First it's the display LEDs lighting up the products at the back of the exhibition hall, then the darkness bangs towards them and mechanisms all around are frozen in time. Seth and Kate stand in the dark, momentarily lost in space.

"How long do we have?" she asks.

"Not long enough."

CHAPTER 67

GHOST CUTLASSES

If the mission to find Zack seemed difficult before, it seems impossible now. Yes, Kate had wished for SkyRest's power to be cut to disable the security system, but she hadn't thought further than that. She hadn't thought of standing here in the dark, in a building that goes up eleven storeys and down—who knows how many?—She hadn't thought of being marooned here surrounded by thick black unfiltered air with no clue how to find Zack. She also hadn't thought of how the disabled security system wouldn't just let Zack out, but the rest of the dangerous crims too. Without wanting to, she imagines being stuck down in the bowels of this building, being stuck with murderers and rapists and never getting out again. Silver fading away in her hospital bed, Mally being killed in his sleep by his Stepford girlfriend. Sudden bright yellow panic squeezes her lungs, imaginary voices shout at her, and Seth hears her breathing become ragged and holds her arm.

"Don't panic," he says, as if it's that easy to avoid a panic attack.

Kate tries to keep her heart from climbing into her throat. She thinks of other situations more dangerous than this that she's survived, and not only survived, but dominated, and slowly this thought, the memories, take the fright out of her adrenaline, and replace it with energy. Her chest is still galloping, but her mind is clear.

One by one, individual torches come on, like white sabres in the dark (Ghost Cutlasses). They're coming from the guards' heads; their face armour has some kind of built-in headlamp.

"We don't have much time," says the guard. "Come with me."

"Give us your head lamp," says Kate.

He hesitates.

"Give us your headlamp, and we'll go with you."

The guard shakes his head then unbuttons something on his utility belt. He swivels the head to turn it on, and hands it to Kate. She's never been so happy to see a penlight in her life. It's the new tech one, the glow-worm, that you can break in half. She does so, and hands the other half to Seth. As agreed, they follow the guard out of the product display room, and as they get near the front entrance, Kate grabs Seth's arm, and they peel away into the emergency stairwell.

They run down the stairs as fast as they can without falling. Kate has that familiar burnt-orange feeling again, *deja vu*, and remembers being in The Office stairway with Seth on the day they found each other again, discussing The Genesis Project and Non-Lizards. They climb down, down, down, and the air gets cooler. Space opens up around them: the stairs are designed in a wentletrap. Winding green, bruise-blue, iced magenta, dry khaki, lemon zest, until they hit fresh pomegranate and can hear voices. They leave the spiral stairwell and run along a stone hewn passage, pushing open a disabled securodoor. This darkness is different: it's redolent of yeasty dough and hand sanitiser and sore throats. Despite the lack of light, Kate's vision is shot through with soft, wobbling blox of colour: Jailhouse Nutrijelly.

"Who's there?" says a man, making Kate almost drop her torch in fright. She shines it in the direction of the voice. A monochrome face appears. He shields his eyes and squints, trying to see who's holding the light.

"What's going on?" asks someone else. "Why are the lights off?"

"Has something happened?"

"Are we being punished?"

Kate surveys the room. There must be fifty of them. Why are they gathered here? Why haven't they bolted for the open door, to escape?

"When will it come back on?"

"The water dispenser isn't working."

"It's getting difficult to breathe."

The men, faces shining, begin squirming in agitation. Sweat slick.

Seth tests the waters. "Gaelyn sent us."

"Ah," some of them say. There is audible relief. Gaelyn knows about their situation. It will be fixed soon.

"You're not being punished," says Kate.

The mood changes; everything is going to be okay.

"It's a scheduled break in supply for maintenance reasons. Gaelyn apologises for not warning you in advance."

"Ah," they say. Gaelyn's the best. Everyone loves Gaelyn.

The door is standing wide open. Kate knows the lights are off, but ... surely with no guards in the immediate vicinity at least a few of them would have tried to escape?

Irrationally, the fact that the men are so meek in the face of what is probably their one and only chance of ever escaping, makes Kate more uncomfortable than the fact that she's surrounded by dangerous crims. Something about this setup feels very wrong.

Seth grabs her arm and it jolts her out of her anxious thoughtloop. "Listen," he says.

Far above them there is the sound of metallic thunder, and it's getting louder.

"Where is Zack?" Kate says.

"Zack?" they say. *Zack zack zack? What has this to do with Zack?*

"He's gone," says a man towards the front of the group. The light hits his shiny scalp.

"What do you mean, 'gone'?"

"He's been elevated," says the man. The others murmur.

"Elevated?" asks Kate. Seth is pulling Kate away.

"Promoted!" he shouts. "He was promoted last night."

Seth pulls Kate away from the clammy residence, out into the stone passage where the emergency staircase is, and a breath of cooler air. They race down the steps, but only get down one flight when they hear the thunder coming towards them again, hard boots on metal stairs, and see the urgent beams of torches above them, and have to jump off the iron spiral and crouch in the dark corner behind it.

Seconds later the kevlar-skinned guards smash past them and stream into the passage and whatever room is on the other side of it. Kate waits a moment, then they go for the stairs again. Seth is first up, and just as Kate puts her foot on the first step, a large body grabs her from behind and smacks a meaty hand over her mouth. Kate shouts, but Seth doesn't hear her, and keeps going. Kate struggles and tries to throw the person off, but all she manages to do is drop her torch, and it goes skittering off the edge of the step and falls down into the black vortex, smashing on the stone floor far below.

CHAPTER 68

ROCKY RABBIT HOLE

Kate elbows the attacker in the kevlar-padded ribs and yells for Seth, but the hand over her mouth is firm and hardly a sound escapes.

"Sh-sh-sh-sh-sh," is the hissing, too close to her ear, and the sensation makes her shout louder. She imagines a giant hissing cockroach scuttling next to her head, and she wants to faint with the creepiness, the crackliness of it. She half expects the insect's scratchy leg to brush her face but the thing that caresses her ear is not carapace but soft cheek skin, female, and smells of *tsatsiki.*

The woman slams Kate sideways, and in the dark Kate expects her head to be smashed against the rocky wall. She's surprised when the wall is missing and she falls hard into a room, cracking her elbow on the stone floor. She gasps in pain, but keeps quiet when she hears the guards running again.

"Don't make a sound," whispers the woman. Is it a Gaelyn? No, she's far too substantial for that. Too strong. Her white sabre cuts through the air, illuminating another door on the opposite side of the narrow room—or is it a passage?—they're in. She offers Kate a hand up.

"Who are you?"

The woman doesn't answer. Kate gets up on her own.

Kate holds her elbow while the electric blue current buzzes inside the bone. "What do you want from me?"

"Come," she says.

"No," says Kate, and starts walking back towards the staircase, towards Seth.

"We've been waiting for you for twelve years," the woman says, and Kate's legs stop working.

"What?"

"We don't have much time."

The torch is again throwing light on the doorway where the woman wants her to go.

I'd be mad to trust this woman, Kate thinks, but then she remembers Betty/Barbara in the basement with the warning and the key, and the message that had led her back to Seth and saved her life. She'd also thought B/B was crackers, with her barbecue sauce BO and dog-hair jersey, spouting about assassins and Doomsday, but she'd been right, and Kate wouldn't be here without her.

With a deep breath to steady her nerves, Kate follows the woman through the doorway, and they hurry down a hall then another passage that snakes its way around one way and then another so that Kate loses her sense of direction. Just as she starts second-guessing her decision to follow the woman, they reach a door with an antique padlock which the woman unlocks with a small silver key attached to a lanyard around her neck. Seeing the key makes Kate's thoughts tumble down around her—*is she dreaming? When the lights come back on will this woman have Betty/Barbara's face and start babbling about hit lists and seed banks?* But it's just Kate's panic murmuring. She knows that B/B is dead, has been dead for almost two decades, and that this woman is another brand of insanity altogether, and she is just as crazy for having followed her so deep into this godforsaken rocky rabbit hole.

The woman opens the door and pushes Kate inside. The sound of the lock clicking closed behind her sends ice into her veins. No more passages, no more doors, just a small blank room crowded with claustrophobia. The cell is just concrete and dripping water, and a thin, dirty mattress, grey and blue stripes, and Kate's sudden panic makes her want to fling her whole body at the door, break through it, fractured elbow be damned, and run away as fast as she can. She'll die down here if she doesn't fight her way back up to the light and the air. Kate feels the weight of all the people who have beaten her to it, leaden on her chest. Who knew souls could be so heavy?

Kate turns to the woman and braces herself, ready to fight with everything she's got, when a familiar voice comes from the corner behind her. Kate spins around.

There is a grey mask at the end of the beam of light.

"You've come," says Zack, and there is a look of wonder on his face.

CHAPTER 69
DEAD MEN DON'T CARE

Seth ascends the stairs, boots hitting the metal steps, but something immediately feels wrong. He stops and turns around, and Kate is gone.

"Kate?" he whispers urgently. "Kate?"

Now the panic claws at him. He doesn't want to go back down. He doesn't want to die down here. It shouldn't make a difference, really. Dead men don't care, but he can't help feeling that he'd rather die somewhere in the open, where he can see the sky or the faces of the people he loves, instead of having this great hulking weight over him.

"Kate?"

Dread and terror roil in his stomach. His body is warning him to get out while he can. Each step down ramps his anxiety higher. When he reaches the platform it feels as if the coolness of the rock face is seeping into the marrow of his bones. Where could she have gone?

Seth moves as quietly as he can, back towards the warm core of the building. How would he possibly be able to find Kate in this lightless labyrinth? Already he's made his way through passages and openings that all look identical. Empty black barns and doorways to nowhere. His foreboding sits high in his chest.

Eventually there's a room that's not empty. There's no one in it, as far as he can see, but there are pallets in the centre, with some kind of high-tech cooler boxes stacked on top. What could be on those pallets? He shouldn't look. He really shouldn't look. He has to find Kate and get out of this sour netherworld as soon as he can.

But, really, what could it be? It will drive him crazy not knowing. He'd be thinking of this room for the rest of his days, wondering what is inside the bloody coolers. Anyway, it'll only take a couple of seconds to check it out.

There is a row of brown boxes and a row of red. He walks up to the first row and flicks his flashlight beam over the lids.

Extremely hazardous, it says. *Biohazard.* It has a 3D tag of a man in a hazmat suit. *Danger. Ingozi. Don't touch.*

That old trick.

Seth's seen that gimmick a hundred times in the black clinics and evil corps he's exposed. They slap a couple of 'biohazard' stickers on anything they don't want nosy staffers knowing about. Put a half-convincing 'radioactive' label on a safe door and you'll never have to worry about anyone ever breaking in.

Fucking amateurs, he thinks, as he snaps open the catches of the first lid.

Inside the box are neatly filed flexiglass envelopes, all labelled with a numeric code. He lifts a random one out and shines his penlight at its centre. It looks like some kind of print. A round stamp the size of his palm made up of pinpricks of black material with a blank circle inside. Geometric, but certainly organic, like the iris of an eye. He think he recognises the pattern, but he can't think what it is. There's something about the network architecture of the thing: the Fibonacci fractals are clear, but why a stamp, and why here, in this box, in this subterranean cavern? He lifts another, then another. They're almost identical.

Seth peels one of the envelopes apart to get a closer look. The radiating lines and dots are indeed some kind of organic matter. Mycelium? He brings it even closer to his face, and when he does, he knows for sure. He sniffs a bit closer. There's no mistaking that earthy scent, like rainforest soil, truffle shavings. The circular designs makes sense now: the gills. These are mushroom spore stamps.

Seth doesn't bother to close the box, just moves on to the next one. Again, similar designs, but slight—evolving—differences in size and density, as if they are working on crisping the subspecies. He figures all the brown boxes contain mushroom spores, so he moves to the other side of the pallets where the red cooler boxes are. They have the same biohazard warnings, and the lids are secured with matching yellow-and-black chevron tape. The lid itself is slightly different too. It has a pattern of tiny holes. Whatever's inside needs air, and he hesitates to open it. He really shouldn't do it. He shouldn't even be in here. He needs to find Kate, but it will only take another ten seconds and then he'll be out.

He puts his ear to the breathing holes. There's a faint crackling from inside, a susurration. There's definitely something alive in there. Seth begins peeling the tape off the sides as quickly as he can without making too much noise. He snicks open the catches and lifts the top tentatively, his heart thumping, half expecting something to jump out at him. The rustling is louder now and it smells like old leaves and decay and something else that makes his stomach lurch. The light from his torch illuminates the contents, and Seth flinches and almost drops the lid. Hundreds of beetles scuttle and swarm over each other, their nutty carapaces vibrating, frantic with hunger. Seth is about to close the box when he sees something else in there: a large round shape at the bottom that they're all flitting over. He wants to look closer but can't stand putting his face any nearer to the insects. What is it? What has got them so excited?

He puts his hands on either side of the container and gives it a good shake, dislodging the beetles from the object, and then immediately wishes he hadn't. The cooler box is suspended half on, half off the pallet. A severed head stares back at him. Half of the skin has been eaten away, revealing large patches of clean white skullbone. Both eye sockets gape with black vacuums for eyes—tea-coloured teeth grimace.

Seth's fright makes him fumble with the container and he half-falls, and the box falls with him, spilling the colony on to the concrete screed floor. Sensing a long-awaited freedom, the beetles scatter, and the decomposing skull rolls and knocks into the wall.

Fuck. Shit. And then, totally inappropriately: *Own goal.*

A beetle bites his hand and Seth shakes it off, stands, and crunches it underfoot. He brushes his body with his fingers, pulling the hungry beetles off his clothes; finds one in his hair and throws it across the room.

Seth has seen enough, and he moves to leave the room. He tries to close the door behind him to keep the bugs contained, but the smartlock isn't working. When he hears footsteps coming in his direction, he pushes himself up against a wall, out of sight. It's a trio of prison guards; they must have heard the box hitting the floor. He holds his breath as they rush past him, torches blazing, into the *biohazard* room. Their boots crush the early insect escapees.

"The fuck?" says one.

"We're not supposed to be in here," says the other.

"Holy shit. This is not good."

Seth folds around the corner they've just rushed past. He breathes as quietly as he can.

The first guard talks into his mandible: "We need a clean-up in the bio section."

There is static.

"Hello?"

"Jesus, Samuel. You really think they care about some bugs right now?"

"I can't get through to Gaelyn."

"There's no one at the desk, you idiot. We have two hundred convicted murderers and paedos and no way to keep them down here. Do you think they're gonna send a fucking janitor? Wake the fuck up!"

"I just ..." Samuel says, "The signs, you know. The hazard warnings. I just think we have to contain this somehow or there'll be trouble."

"You're as thick as pig shit, Sam. You know that?"

"Sam's got a point," says the third man. "Remember when we lived in the barracks for training?"

"Not you too. What the fuck are you two on about? We've got a catastrophic security breach here. We're probably going to be lynched by the mob before cereal time and you two are worried about some fucking bugs."

"I just mean, remember the roaches there? One day there was one and the next day there were a hundred. These things know how to breed."

He's got a point. Seth's pretty sure the flesh-eating insects are laying eggs in invisible crevices as they speak. He shudders. *Samuel's right. This does not bode well.*

"You two are un-fucking-believable. Hurry up, we need to get to the convicts."

"Yes, sir."

The man shakes his head and he walks towards the residence, away from Seth, muttering under his breath. "Trust my luck to get stuck with these morons on fucking D-Day. Tweedle-dee and Tweedle-fucking-dumb."

"I just really think, Sir—" says Samuel.

"Oh for Christ's sake!" the man explodes. "Fine! Fine, Pig Shit! You stay here and clean up this mess, and when you're done you can join the grown-ups in the residence, okay?"

"Yes, Sir."

The two guards march off, and the man in charge smacks the wall for good measure, in case his yelling did not adequately convey his frustration.

Samuel takes his automatic rifle off his back and plants it down against the wall. Maybe Seth has overestimated his intelligence after all. The man steps back inside the *biohazard* room and by the sounds of things, begins to swat the bugs with an unseen tool.

As soon as the two guards are far enough gone, Seth sneaks towards the gun and nabs it, then steals away. Kate is close; he can feel her through the warm walls. Seth clasps the weapon to his torso.

Thank you, Pig Shit.

CHAPTER 70

GREY SKULL

Zack's appearance is so shocking that Kate has to look twice to make sure it's him. His body is strong, firm with the kind of muscle you get from hard labour, not like the bicep-kissers in coolvests you see all over your adstream. But his face … is a grey skull. Bone ash. What have they done to him? The years in here have stripped him of his spark.

"Zack?" She's still uncertain.

"You've come," he says, as if in a trance.

"I told you she'd come," says Bernard. "Even though she took her sweet time."

"What now?" says Zack.

"Don't look at me." Bernard motions at Kate. "She's the one who's supposed to be setting you free."

"I don't know how to get out of here," says Kate.

"Yes, but you have that," says Bernard, gesturing at the green pixel on her chest. "And that's our ticket. Guards can't touch customers, and that means if you protect Zack, they can't stop us from leaving."

Kate looks down at the green dot. "That's all it'll take? A pixel?"

Well, a pixel and an apocalypse.

"There's no way to escape without it. Zack would be shot on his first step out of here. They would have put a bullet in me, too. The order was to wait for you, and we did."

Bernard gestures that they should follow her.

. . .

Kate sees through the guard's brusqueness. She can see by the way the woman looks at Zack—what is left of Zack—that she very much cares if he stays alive. They follow her out the door and turn right into the passage.

"This isn't the way we came in," says Kate.

"We're going out the back," says Bernard.

They hurry along what seems like a Möbius strip, and Kate feels as lost as ever, but then she hears people, faint at first, then louder. Excited gabble, like bubbles in the air.

Kate grabs Bernard's arm. "We can't go that way. There're people there."

"It's the only way." Bernard pulls her baton off her utility belt.

They get closer to the clamour. Kate's adrenaline is now flashing neon yellow at her, and her instinct is to run in the opposite direction. The image of the small damp cell drives her forward.

"Watch out," says Bernard. "The other pods aren't as well behaved as the one you've seen."

"Not as heavily medicated, you mean," says Kate.

Bernard looks at her. "Yes."

They all slow down as they approach the residence.

"Be as quiet as you can." Bernard switches off her torch and Kate follows suit. They slip into the dark common room where a crowd of excited men are chattering like monkeys. They have two flashlights between them—*where did they get them?*—and they're hopping and kicking something in the middle of the room. Cursing. It's a guard. No, two guards, curled up on the floor in an attempt to protect themselves from the blows.

Kate tries to ignore the terror that slams into her chest. The darkness takes on a sinister quality and the air curdles around her. She tries not to breathe too hard but her anxiety is crushing her lungs.

They flatten themselves against the wall as much as they are able, and slowly move around the room to get to the door on the other side. Smoothly and quickly they go, averting their faces, hoping the men will be too distracted by the guards to notice them sliding along the walls in the dark. Kate can't help but glance at the men, shadow rubbernecking, horrified by the naked violence in stuttering monochrome. An action scene in an old movie—an avant-garde stage play.

Kate, Zack and Bernard are just a few footsteps from the door when there is a loud "Hey!" and a man with a bulging face is looking right at Kate, caught in the scattered light.

"Run!" shouts Bernard.

They launch forward, but stumble in the dark. Kate falls hard on the concrete floor. A hand reaches out and grabs her leg.

Kate screams and kicks at him. Her adrenaline is like a current zipping up inside her body.

"Help us!" yells one of the prisoners. "Get us out of here! We'll die if you leave us here!"

She kicks the man in the face but he just shouts, firms his grip, and pulls her along the floor towards the centre of the room. She lashes out, but he's much stronger than her. Bernard appears and strikes him on the head with her baton and he lets go and rolls away, but then another prisoner takes his place and grabs Kate around the hips. She yells and punches him in the face, struggling against him while Bernard lands as many blows as she can on the other approaching men and their greedy hands. Kate's fear is smothering her; she chokes on bile as she kicks and screams and is dragged further into the mob. Zack is fumbling with something in his uniform pocket while men shove and punch him. He's not even fighting back. It's as if he's gone inside himself, some protective measure to block what is happening.

Fight! Kate wants to yell at him. *Fight!* But all he does is look down and fumble.

Kate screams and scrabbles, trying to get away. Her elbow fizzes with bright blue pain as she flails against them. Her voice is fading, her muscles trembling from fear and fatigue.

This is not how I die.

She lands a well-placed kick to a man's jaw, and he lets her go. Another grabs her, an insane leer on his pale face. She tries to kick him, too, but he catches her foot and twists it, and she yells as the pain jolts up her leg.

Bernard is using her strong arms to hand off attackers and strike down anyone in her way. She whacks the man whose hands are wrapped around Kate's pelvis, whacks him so hard on the temple Kate hears a crack, and he falls away without further resistance, leaving a comet of red on her chest.

"Help us!" they keep saying. "Get us out of here!" they shout as they attack.

Kate's able to get to her knees but is pulled back by her hair, and she roars as she turns to elbow the man in the groin, and he sinks to the floor. Another man climbs on top of Kate, then another, and she's flattened against the hard ground, smacking the side of her head on the way down. She can't find the oxygen she needs to stay conscious. Static blows into her brain and threatens to close her eyes. Her whole body throbs navy. Despite the close moaning and babbling, Kate hears Bernard yelling and whipping the prisoners with her baton. Kate's eyes are closed now but she imagines the woman as twice her normal size, roaring and smashing the men in her way like Godzilla. Kate's consciousness is streaming out of her but if she passes out now she's dead. Not only dead, but worse: because she can feel the men's hands all over her, grabbing for her breasts, her stomach, between her legs, pulling her hair and fingers and lips as if they mean to dismember her. They are wild dogs ready to carry off parts of her, and when one prisoner digs his nails in behind her ear and tries to peel it off, it gives Kate the furious energy to buck and shove the heel of her hand hard up into his nose. The cartilage gives way with a crunch and he hoses her with his hot, sick blood.

Her terror feeds her energy.

"This is not how I die!" she shouts, and jumps up and kicks the next man high in the chest, sending him lurching backwards, then knees the next attacker in the groin. Another man, about to jump on her, is side-swiped by Bernard's baton, as is the next, and then there is finally some space to make an escape out of the room.

"Zack!" shouts Kate.

Still Zack fumbles.

For fuck's sake!

Bernard moves to grab his arm, to yank him out of the room, when a convict shocks her with a punch to her jawbone, then wrestles the baton out of her hand and cracks Bernard on the back of the head with it. Her body hits the floor with a hefty smack.

The man is about to kick Bernard's bleeding head when Kate punches him as hard as she can in his stomach, cracking her knuckles. He exhales hard, but doesn't move. He sets his sights on Kate. Shaking out her stinging hand, she steadies her stance, ready to defend herself, but her confidence drains out of her as more men come, and more men, and Kate gets the idea that no matter how hard she fights, they'll just keep coming at her. Multiplying like Agent Smiths over and over again until there are hundreds of them and nothing left of her.

CHAPTER 71

DARKMEAT VENUS FLYTRAP

Kate's heart is wild. She manages to floor one of the men with a well-timed kick to the groin, and smashes another convict's nose, temporarily blinding him. She has to keep on fighting, but there's just one of her and seemingly dozens of them. The prisoners move together now as one, wanting to swallow her up: a darkmeat venus fly trap. Kate's muscles are burnt out, she has no more energy to fight them off. She loses a sleeve to the mob, then feels them tugging at the naked arm as if to pop it from its socket. They descend on her. Kate's voice is hoarse but she screams anyway, a ragged moan that is lost in the chaos of bodies. Bernard bleeds black on black.

Kate trains her eyes on flashes of Zack, who finally stops fidgeting with his uniform pocket and pulls out a piece of sharp glinting metal. He starts swiping at the men and they cry out in surprise and pain as he slashes their throats and arms and anything else he can reach. They spin away from him, spraying blood, and he cuts and cuts as if he is mowing down a field of weeds. The floor is slippery with the warm artery oil. The men over Kate disappear one by one. Finally, the stragglers, not fancying their odds of survival, back away and leak into adjacent rooms. Kate is coughing up vomit. Her face is wet with tears, although she doesn't remember crying.

Zack puts the cut-throat razor back in his pocket, and levers Kate off the ground. He's shiny with sweat and other fluids. Bernard has surfaced, shaking her head, dizzy, unsure on her feet. She finds her steel baton and hugs it to her stomach. They run out of the residents' room and along a passage, turn left and then right. As they run, Bernard trails her hand along the wall, inspecting it as she goes. Suddenly she stops and her hand wraps around the edge of a camouflaged door.

"Here." Bernard unhooks the catch and slides it open, revealing a doorway to a dark tunnel. The air flowing out is cool and scented with soil. They climb through, and Bernard slides the door closed after them. Despite the steep slope they quicken their pace and leave the heat of the silo core behind. The secret subway has rails on the ground, like a makeshift mining shaft.

"What is this?" asks Kate.

"The best way to shuttle bodies out of here without being seen," says Bernard.

"Bodies?" says Kate.

"Corpses."

Kate shivers. She's seen enough dead bodies for the day. Her wrecked state of mind spills over into her imagination, and she daydreams of the tunnel interior being studded with eyeballs and teeth, and whips her hand away from the sandy wall.

"We're almost there," Bernard says, mostly for Zack's benefit, who seems to be flagging. As Kate gets her hopes up that they'll be in the fresh air soon, Bernard curses and Kate almost walks into her back. The flashlight illuminates a huge heap of soil where the shaft has collapsed, blocking the tunnel. Bernard issues a string of expletives so coarse even Kate is surprised. Sounds are coming from behind them now.

Guards? Criminals?

"They'll find us in here," says Zack. "They'll follow our trail."

Kate and Bernard look at the ground where fresh crimson drops shine. Betrayed by their own blood.

Bernard uses her baton to tap the ceiling. Clods of sand rain down on them. It's loose: loose enough to move. Bernard dislodges more of the soil. It's their only option.

"Dig," she says.

They dig and dig the hard soil above them. It coats them in dust and mud and the grains on the ground becomes their step up so that they can dig some more. The baton is especially helpful, and they take turns with it. Zack dislodges a small, sharp rock and uses it as a hammer to speed up the work. When Bernard has the baton Kate uses her hands, scraping the skin off her fingers and palms and tearing her nails off while she frantically claws to get to the fresh air and light. Whenever they hear a sound from silo-side they stop to listen.

"Hurry, hurry," says Kate, more to herself than the others. They all know what the stakes are. Zack gives Kate his cut-throat razor. Perhaps he'll use his digging rock as a weapon if the stragglers decide to take another chance with them. It's hard work digging upwards because you lose circulation in your arms if you hold them up for too long, never mind trying to move stubborn soil. And there is just so much of the stuff. It's everywhere, including Kate's mouth and eyes. Eventually they hit something, some kind of weak strata, and there is a rumbling sound above them.

"Watch out!" shouts Bernard, just before the landslide buries all of them and they have to fight to breathe, and crawl and kick so they don't drown in it, have to swim upwards through the silt, but they all do it and when their heads are above the mound that's just almost swallowed them they whoop and smile with their soil-covered faces—just white eyes and grins—because the outside air has rushed to meet them: dappled light and cool forest air and the smell of decomposing leaves. They've made it. It was like digging her way out of her grave, as if she'd been buried alive, but here she is, here they are, alive, with the worst behind them.

They struggle to wrench their limbs free from the heavy soil, and once they're all above ground level they look at each other again with stupid grins. Kate laughs, ridiculously, frantically, because of course there's nothing to laugh about. Yet here she is, with two virtual strangers, and they've just escaped a certain death not once but twice. Now they're standing in a godforsaken forest and she has what—or, rather, who—she came for.

For a moment it seems like time stops, and her urgent issues seem far away: Silver unspooling in a hospital bed, Mally staring into Vega's dangerous eyes. Keke butchered by a schoolgirl. For now she just breathes in the chlorophyll-rich air and rubs the sand off her cheeks, reminded as she does so that her elbow is probably broken—at the very least fractured—and of course it's the same arm she broke in 2021, and damaged again in 2024, and she thinks: perfect. Because she's alive.

And then the clock starts ticking again, and she remembers that she needs to get to Silver before the Lipworth powers down. And this makes her think of Seth, and her heart turns grey.

CHAPTER 72
CORPSE COMPOST

The three of them hurry along in the brindled light of the forest. It's the first time Zack has been outside in twelve years. It's utterly peaceful, a block away from the SkyRest building and its subterranean cells, and further still from the jagged Jozi skyline and all the mayhem contained therein.

Kate trips over what feels like a root of a tree but as her body pitches forward, and she softens the fall with her good arm, her face comes close enough to the ground to see the slipping-off skin of a marbled arm escaping the ground. She yells in alarm and backs away, reverse crawling, but then her elbow sinks into the soft soil and there's another limb—a short leg—and a half-decomposed face with teeth bared in a death snarl. She shoots up, stumbles again, and suddenly Zack is right there, catching her hand.

"Don't panic," he says, and she looks at him as if he is crazy. "They can't hurt us."

They're ankle-deep in decaying flesh and bone, soil and leaf mould (Corpse Compost). The idea is sickening to Kate, but the truth Zack speaks evaporates her fright. These skeletons are harmless. The men trying to tear her apart underground were the real danger. Roguebots and Bot Hunters and the V1R1S are a real danger. Anyway, there's no time for fear.

With her mind on her kids, Kate's able to half-ignore the bones she feels cracking under her boots, and the squelching of putrefied flesh she hears.

"This is one of their experimentation fields," says Bernard, slightly breathless with the effort of walking through the soft matter.

"I've dreamed of this forest," says Zack. "Dreamed of it enough times to know that it can't hurt us."

Kate steps on a particularly slimy part and slides a little, then gags.

"Keep your focus on the trees," he says.

Kate looks up, and Zack's right, the trees are shimmering with health and energy and fresh new leaves. The new life that is nourished by the death below. She realises they're all breathing easily without their face-masks on, as if they're in a bubble of oxygen.

Kate wants to call Seth, but realises that her mandible is gone; ripped off by the crims. She says a quick nonsense-prayer to the multiverse, hoping he's making his way back to the Lipworth Foundation. She has a bad feeling.

Kate shudders. "I need to find Seth. What if he went back down to find me?"

"He wouldn't want you going back," says Zack. "He'd want you to save Silver."

CHAPTER 73

ANTHROBOT ACADEMY

Seth's Apartment
Johannesburg, 2036

Mally and Vega sit on Mally's bed, facing each other and holding hands. He leans forward and kisses her on the mouth, tentatively, tenderly. Her body warms and arches. She runs her fingers through his hair, and his scalp comes alive under her touch. Other parts of his body, too. She knows exactly what sets him on fire.

Vega starts pulling at his cargo pants. He stops her with gentle hands.

"Don't," he says. "Not today. Not after what you've been through."

"I want to," says Vega. "I am very fond of you."

"I love you," Mally says, "but we don't have to have sex to prove it."

"I want to," says Vega. "Things are happening in this world. What if this is our last chance?"

Vega opens her shirt to Mally. He traces the perfect outline of her breasts over her smooth brassiere, feels her pulse through her warm silicone skin. Spends a moment with his hand covering her heart pocket which contains her living hard drive, her Soul Shard. Vega slips her fingers under the waistband of his pants and pulls them down. His desire is clear. She kisses him, and he melts under her, sinking into his pillow. She moves her lips and tongue down his body.

"This isn't why—" Mally starts saying, but then his yearning overcomes him and the sentence turns into a groan.

Vega knows, anyway.

She knows this isn't the reason he dates her. Other men do it, of course, commissioning girlfriends from the anthrobot academy to use as house-cleaning sex slaves, but not him. He thinks he fell in love with Vega the first time he saw her in virtual class. His feelings were so strong that first meeting he lost his usual shyness and asked her if he could meet her IRL. Since then they've been practically inseparable, but he's turned down every sexual advance of hers—apart from kissing and some light fondling—because he doesn't want to treat her like an object. He loves her superintelligence, her skewed humour, her spirit. He loves the spark in her eyes, the way they learn from each other all the time, and the way they just get each other in every way.

Net, he loves her, Mally thinks, as she starts to pull down his cooljox.

And she's right. Who knows what's happening out there, or what's going to happen tomorrow? *Will there even be a tomorrow?*

He doesn't know, but what he does know, now, and the knowledge surges inside of him, feeding his desire, is that it *is* time. They've waited long enough; it's the perfect time to consummate their relationship. He sits up and starts to tug off Vega's shirt, and she one-handedly snaps her bra off behind her back. The sight of her naked breasts makes his heart swoop, and he's light-headed for a second as he moves his mouth down to kiss them.

The doorbell rings, and they both jump. His parents, perhaps, or an errant Silver. Would Kate ring the doorbell instead of using the biopad? Possibly. The front door has been giving problems. Either way they sigh, smiling, and pull their clothes back on.

"Purest human," Vega whispers, buttoning up her shirt as Mally leaves to answer the door.

Arronax has beaten him to it.

"... here as a representative from the National Android Safety..." a stranger is saying.

Arronax senses Mally behind her and turns to include him in the conversation.

The man looks at Mally, as if sizing him up. Beady eyes. Twitching fingers. He's wearing a cheap blue suit so new it makes Mally immediately suspicious. How does he not get egged in the street wearing that? He could at least fray the edges a little.

"Good morning." His holotag flashes with the NASP logo. Govender is his name. "I was just saying ... that I'm here to interview Miss Alpha Lyrae about the incident last night."

"Why?" asks Mally.

"It's regulation," says Arronax. "All anthrobot assaults need to be reported."

"Well, it doesn't matter anymore," says Mally.

The man nervously adjusts his mandible. "Why do you say that?"

"Let's just say ... the creep responsible for the attack won't be doing it again."

"We know," says Govender. "A man is dead and Miss Lyrae's roscoe bullets were found at the scene. I'm sure you can appreciate how this needs to be investigated."

Arronax frowns. "What are you saying?"

"Vega's in trouble?" Mally can feel his cheeks colour. "For defending herself? For saving my life?"

"Not in trouble," says the man. "Not unless she did something off-protocol."

"Well, she didn't," says Mally, and tries to close the door, but Govender jams his foot in the way.

"I'm going to have to interview her," he says.

"She's been through enough," says Mally.

"It won't take long."

"Then you'll leave?"

"Then I'll leave."

They set up in the open plan kitchen. The 'interview' comprises Govender downloading Vega's memory of the assault. Arronax is busy on her SnapTile while they complete the transaction. The rep watches Vega's version of the attack and flinches with every shot fired. Once he has a copy of the video, he inserts his diagnostic key into the back of her neck and it flashes red.

"This is bad," Govender says. "This is worse that I thought."

"What's that supposed to mean?"

"It means we're going to have to take her in."

Vega stands up, dusts the creases in her outfit, ready to go.

"Hell no," says Mally. "You're not taking Vega anywhere."

"I'm afraid it's not up to you, Mister Lovell," says the man. "Alpha Lyrae has undergone significant damage, both on a hard- and software level. She needs to be tended to."

"Tended to?"

"She's not safe as she is, but don't worry, we'll be able to help her."

"No," says Mally. "No way."

He's seen the news. Seen how the Special Task Police are rounding up bots of all kinds and keeping them in electric wire-festooned concentration camps.

"We'll fix her up. Reboot her. She'll be as good as new."

"I'm not going to let you do that," says Mally.

"With all due respect," says Govender, "it's not up to you. Under section 17C of the NASP act we're to claim all damaged bots and—"

"Don't speak about her like that. Like she's someone's property."

"But ... she is," he says. "I realise you're young and—"

"It's got nothing to do with age," Mally says. "It's about being decent."

"Alpha Lyrae is government property." Govender starts to approach Vega, puts a hand out to take her arm. "And as such, she's—"

"You leave her alone!"

"It's okay, Mally," says Vega. "It's protocol."

"I don't give a fuck about protocol," Mally says. "I'm sick of hearing about fucking protocol. He's not taking you anywhere."

"I'm going to have to arrest you for obstructing reclamation," says Govender.

"No," says Vega, giving the NASP representative her best smile. "There's no need for arrests. I'll come with you."

Mally blocks the man's way. "There's no way I'm going to let that happen."

Arronax looks up from her device, and Mally watches as her face drains of colour. She flashes her eyes at him and grabs Seth's Vektor gun from behind the instakettle. It won't fire without his bioprint, but Govender won't know that.

"Get out," Arronax flicks the weapon in the direction of the door.

Govender shoots up with his hands in the air. "What are you doing?"

"Get out," Arronax growls. Her hair changes from silver-lilac to deep purple edged with black.

Vega looks confused. "What is happening?"

"Now is your last chance to walk out of here," says Arronax.

The man keeps his hands in the air and stumbles backwards, towards the front door.

As he crosses the threshold he says "She'll kill you too, you know. There's no such thing as a good robot."

"Bullshit," says Mally. "You don't know who you're talking to. You should show some respect."

This catches Govender off guard. He looks from Mally, to Arronax, to Mally again.

"Keep quiet, Mally," says Arronax.

Mally ignores her. "This is Doctor Arronax."

"Shut up, Mally!" says Arronax, but Mally can't help himself.

"She's lead engineer on 7thGen robosapiens and the founder of the RoboRights movement."

Govender's eyes widen, and he stumbles as he backs into a cabinet. "Well, then," he says, when he's regained some composure, "Doctor Arronax. Maybe you deserve to die at the hands of one of the monsters you've created."

Mally moves to punch him in the face, but Vega holds him back. Govender doesn't need any more encouragement to get out. As he leaves, he narrows his eyes and says, "My advice is to kill the robot. Kill her before she kills you."

"So much for NASP being around to protect anthrobots," says Mally.

"That man wasn't from NASP." Arronax shows Mally her screen. She's deep in the NASP intersite, and there's no such staff member.

Now it's Mally's turn to be confused. "Then who was he?"

"I don't know, but his agenda's clear. And by now he would have broadcast this address and our identities to all his Bot Hunter mates."

"Oh, shit," says Mally. "I wasn't thinking. I'm so sorry."

"Don't worry. You didn't know. The important thing is to get out of here as soon as possible."

Arronax is packing her cardigan and Tile as she talks. She opens a few kitchen cupboards and grabs crackling packets of food: mango biltong, butter popgrains, and protein pretzel stix, and shoves them into her backpack. The Vektor goes into her lab coat pocket.

"Where will we go?"

"I have a safe room. In the city. We can stay there till—"

Till what? Till the danger's passed? Probably not going to happen. Till we run out of food? Till we die?

He can't see a positive outcome. He doesn't even know if he'll ever see his family again. There's a hand on his back and he turns to look at Vega. Her eyes are electric. "Let's go," she says.

CHAPTER 74

YOU ARE EXCUSED FROM YOUR DAILY GRIND

ChinaCity/Sandton
Johannesburg, 2036

Kate, Zack and Bernard rush through the city, tram-hopping and skirting the worst of the flash civil war zones. Kate's head is still bleeding from the hit she took at SkyRest. As they hurry they grab a pack of hotwipes from a vandalized vending machine so they can at least clean their faces of the blood and dirt that covers them. Kate's arm is glowing with pain. She can't help but stare at Zack's grey face.

What did they do to you? she wants to ask, but it's not the time.

On the southbound solartram they zip past pedestrians: shell-shocked, angry, bewildered. Some people look as if they're on their way to work, but they're not quite convinced they need to go in. It's not like there's a Doomsday memo, thinks Kate. An apocalyptic announcement.

DEAR CIVILIANS. TODAY IS THE END OF THE WORLD. YOU ARE EXCUSED FROM YOUR REGULAR DAILY GRIND. ENJOY THE DAY.

"Keke will be so damn happy to see you."

Zack's face animates. "Keke?"

"She tried to go to your trial."

"There was no trial."

"That's what she was worried about."

"They hired some actors and a cardboard court. And just like that …"

"Are you angry with her?" asks Kate.

"Angry with Keke? No. Never."

"But—"

"She's not the reason I went to the crim colony. My job is the reason I was arrested in the first place. Because creeps don't understand the big picture."

"What is that? What is your job?" asks Kate.

"Do you know the allegory of Plato's Cave?"

Kate shakes her head. She's heard of if before, but has no idea what it means, and she's certainly not in the mood for riddles.

"What about the Lotus Eaters?" asks Zack.

"No," says Kate. "So can you please just tell me what the hell is going on?"

They pass a giant bonfire spewing acrid smoke. People are tossing pavement detritus into the flames. Broken furniture, boxes, anthrobot limbs. Some of the people are bare-chested and they've stained themselves with some kind of war paint: blood? Ash and spit? They've got wild eyes and shout randomly as they feed the fire.

"Yes," says Zack, taking her hand. They arrive at their destination and jump off the tram. "It's almost time."

There's no way the Lipworth Foundation's security system will let an escaped convict in. Bernard senses Kate's hesitation and says, "Leave it to me."

She has a word with the guardbot and there's a call to someone else, and with a ping of green their entry is authorised. Bernard is clearly more influential than Kate imagined. The receptionist advises them that the power will be cut by 14:00. They hurry through the shiny, brightly lit white corridors, avoiding the elevator. "It's 12:39," says Kate, looking at her bare wrist: a habit she's never been able to kick.

They arrive at Silver's private ward. Kate pushes open the door and sees her daughter in the oxygen tent, in the same position and state, and it's as if she'd just left a moment ago.

The DarkDoc stands up, relief splashing his face. "Kate."

He takes her by the shoulders and holds her an arm's length away, inspecting her.

"Jesus Christ. What happened? Are you okay?"

Kate squeezes her elbow and winces. "I could do with some painkillers."

"I'm afraid we're all out," Morgan says.

"You're kidding," says Kate. "You're kidding, right?"

"They've put all the narcotics on double lockdown. It's to stop the looters from coming in here."

"How's Keke?" Kate asks.

Doctor Morgan replies in his vintage-engine purr: "She's fine. I checked in on her half an hour ago. She's a tough cookie. She wanted to be discharged … wanted to go looking for you. I told her to hang tight, that you'd be back."

"Surgery?"

"No. The surgery bots have been powered down."

"What about human? Human surgeons?"

"Not here. This isn't a hospital. My bet is they're all working their third or fourth shifts in a row in ERs all over the city."

More people who didn't get the memo. Or maybe they want to spend their last day helping strangers. That kind of generosity of spirit doesn't come naturally to Kate. Her first instinct has always been selfish: to protect her own before anyone else.

"I'm so glad you're back," says Morgan. "I was worried."

Zack walks up to the oxygen tent, unzips it, sticks his head in and scans the back of Silver's head. He looks worried.

"So you're Zack," says Morgan. "Silver's been saying your name over and over. She seems to think that you're the one who knows how to save her."

Kate thinks of the mob at SkyRest. "She'd better be right."

"It's not going to be easy." Zack's face remains the shade of overcooked oatmeal.

"What do we do? How do we wake her up?"

Zack blinks, deep in thought. "It's not so much about waking her up. She's actually awake, even though she doesn't look it."

"Then?"

"You're really not going to want to hear this."

"Tell me," says Kate.

"It's going to be an extremely … difficult thing for you to do."

Jesus, this man with his non-answers. If he hadn't just saved her life she'd want to throttle him. He is just not capable of a straight answer. Her face heats up: anger, desperation (Fraught French Rose). "I'll do anything."

This seems to snap him out of his trance. "Silver's mesh …"

"I know," Kate says. "It's like some backstreet … I can't believe—"

"No," Zack says. "Not backstreet. The opposite is actually true. It's a highly sophisticated piece of—"

DarkDoc jumps in, “I’ve never seen neural lace like that before. It looks to me like some biopunk put it together with what he could get drone-delivered to his basement. And the way it was implanted, well, it’s a quack-job at best.”

“I agree that the surgery itself was badly done,” says Zack, “but—”

“Doctor Morgan is the leading techdoctor on the continent,” says Kate. “If anyone knows about mesh, it’s him.”

“Look,” says Zack. “The reason you don’t recognise the lace is because …”

Zack has the doctor’s full attention.

“It’s because this technology hasn’t been invented yet.”

CHAPTER 75

SLATE SORROW

"Um..." says the DarkDoc, scratching his scalp, perhaps thinking Zack is delusional. "Hasn't been invented yet?"

"I know," says Zack, "it's not easy to understand."

"Help me."

Kate's brain is also whirring. *Not been invented yet?*

"Aliens?" she ventures, and it does a good job of breaking the tension. They all cough out a single laugh, apart from Bernard, who seems to be the victim of a permanent humour failure. Kate pictures Bernard suddenly as a chubby baby in a vintage highchair, with a cooing young mother pulling faces and playing peekaboo in an attempt to make her ever-serious baby laugh. In Kate's imagination, baby Bernard ignores her mother and just stares ahead.

"Not quite." Zack finally has some colour in his face. He's looking more vital, more like the Zack Kate met that day at the Gordhan when her twins were toddlers. It's as if his sense of purpose, being here, helping her, is making him age backwards.

"Then?" asks Doctor Morgan.

Kate says, "Why you? Why would she ask for *you* of all people?"

Words drift unsaid in the sanitised air like white balloons.

"I promise you I'll answer all your questions," says Zack.

As his eyes find Kate's, she realises they still have a connection—a strange, electric, impossible connection—after all this time.

"I'll answer every single one of them, but right now we need to get you meshed as soon as possible if you want to save Silver before they cut the power to this part of the grid."

Kate blanches. "What?"

"According to my calculations," says Zack, "This power will be on for another…" He checks the clock on the wall. "Seventy-three minutes. That's barely enough time to implant the lace, get you immersed, and for you to bring Silver out."

"It's too risky," says Doctor Morgan. "It's way too risky. And even if it weren't, we'd need more time than that."

"I need to get meshed?" asks Kate, still shocked at the turn of the conversation.

"Honestly: the risk is substantial," says Zack.

"It's more than substantial," says Morgan. "We don't know what we're dealing with here."

Zack stands his ground. "It's the only way."

"You can't do it," the DarkDoc turns to Kate. "You'll end up … you'll end up like Silver."

They all look at the bone-white body inside the oxygen tent.

Kate drags her gaze back to Morgan. *Don't you see?* Her eyes say, *I can't not do it.*

"It's a simple procedure," Zack says to the DarkDoc.

"Don't look at me!" says Morgan. "There's no way I'm going to perform that surgery."

"You've performed tech surgeries that are way more grey market than this," says Kate. It was, funnily enough, how they had met. Morgan had agreed to perform a surgery that was dangerous and illegal—one that had at the same time cost Marko's eye and saved Silver's life—and here they are again. "You've never let red tape stand in the way."

"It's not about red tape."

It's about you, his eyes say, but she turns away so she doesn't have to see his plea.

"Those were patients," Morgan says. "Virtual strangers."

Kate paces as they talk. They're running out of time. Her nervous energy is making her feel as though she's walking on air. "It doesn't matter."

"Of course it matters!"

"This thing, right now, saving Silver," says Kate. "That's all that matters."

"I can't be responsible for sending you into catatonia. Because that's exactly what I'd be doing."

"You'll be doing what I'm asking you to do. It's my decision."

"Look at the clock," says Zack. "We don't have time to argue."

It's twelve forty-nine. The ChinaCity/Sandton band will be shut down at fourteen hundred.

"Please," says Kate. They've been in this position before. It was Keke who had finally convinced him to go through with it. Keke is uniquely persuasive when it comes to people of the opposite sex. Or any sex, really. "Please, Morgan. Please. It's our only chance."

He turns inwards, steps closer to her, and says in his low voice, "I don't want to lose you." When she can't think of a reply, he continues, "But something tells me I already have."

They start moving to the operating room. Bernard pushes Silver's bed along so they can all stay together. They get Kate settled in what looks like an operating chair. Zack pulls a hospital gown over her head and adds another layer of linen while Morgan washes his hands and collects the implements he needs. The tools clatter in the silver tray, and the cold metallic sound sends slush down Kate's spine. Zack and Bernard throw on cotton gowns and scrub their hands, too.

Why are they helping her?

The DarkDoc has a cold, hard edge of desolation around him (Slate Sorrow). He's holding his freshly sanitised hands up like surgeons do in old films. He automatically looks around for his team, expecting them to know what to do, but it's only the escaped criminal and his warden.

The DarkDoc shakes his head, closes his eyes and is quiet for a moment. He fills a syringe with an orange liquid, fits a needle, then takes Kate's arm in his tender, gloved hands.

"What's that?" asks Zack.

"Anaesthetic," says Morgan, and brings the needle to the crook of Kate's arm.

"Stop," says Zack. The doctor frowns at him.

"You can't use general anaesthetic for this. Kate has to be fully conscious in the immersion. We can't afford any downtime."

"The local anaesthetic is on lockdown," says the DarkDoc. "I can't do this without anaesthetic."

"Yes, you can," says Kate. Her knuckles are white.

CHAPTER 76

GALAXY OF BRIGHT ROLLING PAIN

"Jesus, Kate. Do you even know what you're saying?"

"Get on with it," says Zack. "We don't have a second to lose. I'll brief her. I'll talk her through the difficult parts."

"The 'difficult parts'?" says the DarkDoc. "We're about to perform brain surgery without any kind of anaesthetic. We don't even have painkillers, for Net's sake."

They all look at Morgan, waiting. The flash of anger passes, and his face clears. "Fine," he says. "We need a laser blade. The surgical ones are locked away."

Zack thinks of Lewis and pulls out the old cutthroat razor, bought with his first SkyRest Reward twelve years ago. A gift that was never given. "Will this do?"

It's patterned with dried blood. A landscape of dark brown blooms and grasses on a flashing silver background.

"Is it sharp?" asks the DarkDoc.

"Yes."

"Then it'll do."

Zack quickly washes it at the sterile station while Bernard parts Kate's hair and uses scissors to cut away the long strands. Zack brings the soap spray with him on the way back, spritzes the area of her scalp that needs shaving, then picks up the razor and puts a hand on Kate's shoulder.

"Hold still."

As Zack shaves the back of her head, Kate's practically blinded by the burnt orange of *deja vu.* Of course, she knows why. She's done this before, except last time she was cutting a chip out of her own scalp to save her life. The orange throbs in her temples; she's never felt it as intensely as this before.

"We'll need to secure her," the DarkDoc says. "If she moves during a sensitive time in the surgery it will be catastrophic."

Bernard finds large surgical bands and they tie Kate down. Every part of her body is fixed to the operating chair. In a strange way the restriction is comforting, but when she hears Morgan picking up a scalpel, the terror comes running at her. A ferocious dog of fear.

"I need to score through your lambdoid suture to insert the mesh properly."

Kate tries to nod, but she can't move. Zack comes into view.

"Okay, talk to me," says Kate, her teeth buzzing with nerves.

Zack takes a seat in front of her and levers it right down so that they can look each other in the eyes.

"This whole procedure will only take ten minutes," says Zack.

"Eight," says Morgan.

"Eight minutes, Kate. Okay? It's gonna be hell, but then it'll be over."

"Okay."

"I'm going to talk you through the whole thing. Focus on what I'm saying, not what you can feel happening."

"Okay."

"Eight minutes."

"Okay."

Zack nods at the DarkDoc, and he makes the first incision.

Kate draws in a sharp breath through her teeth. The pain is acute, but it's manageable.

"First I'm going to brief you on what you need to do to bring Silver back. Then, when the pain gets unbearable, you must find a place in your mind, in your memory, where you can go, and leave this room behind. Think of a place you want to go. Get it ready in your mind. You'll need to disassociate. Got it?"

"Got it." Kate knows which memory she'll use. She can feel the scalpel make two more incisions, and the small flap of skin is folded back. She clenches her jaws. It's a low blue flame of pain.

"All right," says Zack. "Once you're meshed, you'll be able to become totally immersed."

"How?"

"You'll just see it. It'll be all around you. Like a projection, but deeper. More real."

"Like my synaesthesia?"

"Like your synaesthesia on MDMA."

"Where will I find Silver?"

"Let your subconscious do the work. You two are connected in a way that's difficult to explain. You know where she is, you just need to find her, and you need to do it quickly, and get out."

"I'm worried I won't be good at this. That I won't be able to find her."

There's a sharp stinging at the back of Kate's head and she cries out.

"Just remember that the immersion isn't a foreign thing. It's not someone else's design. It's all yours. It uses your thoughts to create itself. The lace is just the connector. You are the operating system."

"Yes." Kate remembers that from the VXR therapy she had for her PTSD. The experiences were so vivid because they came directly from her brain. It was like living and breathing in the actual downloaded memory.

"So you go, follow your instinct, and find Silver as fast as you can. She'll be close."

There's another sharp pain, as if someone has stabbed her in her brain stem, and stars explode in her head. Zack keeps talking but she can't hear him over the pain. All she manages is a low groan. Blue fireworks, silver stars, hissing agony—it's as if there's no space for her brain anymore, it's all being crowded out by the galaxy of bright, rolling pain.

"Can you hear me, Kate?" says Zack, but she can't talk and she can't move her head. She's desperate to know what else Zack is saying, needs to know what he's telling her, but all she can hear is the groan she can't keep inside.

Bernard hands Morgan the bonesaw beam.

"It's almost over," says Zack. "This is going to be the worst part, now. And then it's over."

Kate feels water on her face. Is she crying? Sweating? Clear liquid drips onto the expensive tiles below her. She can't imagine how the pain can get any worse.

"Get ready to leave the room," coaches Zack. "Visit your memory now."

Morgan begins to score through her lambdoid suture. The laser makes a crackling sound as it cuts through the fissure in Kate's skull. It's so intense her body begins to shake. Saliva splashes out of her mouth.

"Two minutes," says the DarkDoc.

Kate wants them to stop, would do anything to make them stop. She struggles and tries to tell them she can't survive this pain.

"Leave the room," says Zack, but she can't. The pain is so overbearing it holds her right there in its terrible vice: It's like being frozen but burning hot at the same time. She wants to scream but her voice is no longer working.

The buzzing continues, and it feels as if her brain is exploding in slow motion. Kate vomits. The bile splatters the floor with bitter green. Zack wipes her mouth for her, her nose, and cleans the floor. “Leave the room,” he says in a hard whisper, and Kate closes her eyes and swims away from the operating room. Swims through the ceiling and out of the building till she’s way above it and it’s not smoggy anymore: It’s 2022 and the sky is a brilliant clear cold blue.

CHAPTER 77

A DIFFERENT KIND OF FAMILY

Kate's flying through the sky, away from the city and towards the South Coast, back in time, back to a memory that's so dear it feels as if she's climbing back into a warm bed. She's ripping through the air, over towns and cities, and slows almost to a stop when she reaches Westville, KZN, where she was born.

From above, Kate recognises her hired electric car, idling by the river embroidered by weeping willows and rushes and reeds. She sees her mother, her real biological mother, walking towards the river, and all of a sudden she's pulled out of the sky as if caught in a giant vacuum, sucked down with a force, and she finds herself shunted into her younger body that's sitting in the car. The rearview mirror tells her she's in her late twenties again, and when Kate looks down at her belly it's stretched and round. She runs her hand over it. Silver.

Kate breathes and lets go; she allows herself to relax fully into the memory.

Westville, KZN, 2022

Kate sits in her hired car, parked a little way away from the river, under the glittering dappled shade of willow trees. She takes off her safety belt, adjusts her tender back in the chair. Her left arm is slightly paler and thinner than her right, still recovering from being in the exoskeletal cast she had to wear for months.

She breathes in the muddy green smell of the river (Wilted Waterlily): a smooth, undulating smell. Balmy Verdant. Rolling Hills.

God, Kate has missed driving, the freedom of the open road to the thrumming soundtrack of your choice. Stopping for a hydrogen refuel—not as pungent a memory as petrol—and greasy toasted cheese in a wax paper envelope. Flimsy paper serviette. Vanilla whipped Soy-Ice in a hard chocolate coating that you get to crack open with your teeth. Noticing, inside the store, that all the Fontus fridges are gone. Kate imagines them yawning in recycle tips, stripped of any valuable metal, or re-purposed as beds or dining-room tables in townships.

Kate winds down her window further, allowing more of the clear air into the car. After tossing out the air-freshener at the car rental agency (Retching Pink) she drove the first hour with all the windows open to try to flush out the fragrance. Artificial roses: the too-sweet scent painted thick vertical lines in her vision. Her sense of smell seems to be in overdrive lately, and the shapes more vivid than ever.

It's a superb day: warm, the humidity mitigated by a cool breeze, and the sky brighter than she's ever remembered seeing it. The branches of the weeping willows stroke the ground, whispering, as if to soothe it. She can smell a hundred different shades of green in the motion of leaves.

A woman pops up in the distance, walking towards the river. She has handsome silver hair, a thick mass of it, twisted up and fixed in place with a clip and a fresh flower. A stained wicker picnic basket in her hand. She is tall and moves in elegant strides: not rushing, nor dawdling, her sense of purpose clear. She doesn't look around for a good spot; she knows exactly where the good spot is.

The woman sets down her basket, lays out a picnic blanket, smoothes it down in a practised movement. Once she's removed her shoes, she sits with her legs out in front of her, crossed at the ankles, leaning back on her hands with her eyes closed and her face to the sky.

The woman takes out her clip and lets her hair tumble down like mercury. Kate unthinkingly touches her own short hair, rakes her fingers though the awkward length of re-growth. The woman relaxes like that for a while, then sits up and opens her basket, bringing out a plastic plate and knife, a packet of crackers, cheese triangles. A small yellow juicebox.

Kate snaps a photo of her with her LocketCam, then retrieves the cooler-box from the back seat that she packed that morning. She takes out a dripping bottle of iced tea, a packet of Blacksalt crisps, and a CaraCrunch chocolate bar. Watching the woman by the river, she opens the foil packet and starts to eat; then she remembers the bright green apple in her bag—Granny Smith—and eats that too.

So this is what her real mother looks like. Not just her non-abductor mother, more than just her biological mother, but her real mother. She can feel it. She sees Seth/Sam in her body language, her straight nose. But the hair and the eyes are hers.

She looks again at her reflection in the rear-view mirror, touches the new streak of grey at her temple (Silver Floss). Kate feels a welling up in her chest, an inflating of her ribcage, and breathes deeply to stay calm. Warm tears rush down her face; she is used to the feeling now, even welcomes the release. During the past few months she has made up for a lifetime of not crying.

The woman looks so peaceful, so at ease with the world, a trait Kate hasn't been lucky enough to inherit, but she hasn't always been like this; she has also had her dark days. They never moved house—they still live at 22 Hibiscus Road—as if they thought if they moved, they would lose all hope of the twins finding their way home.

Anne Chapman visits the river almost every day, the spot where she used to sit in the shade while the twins splashed around, and then later, their subsequent children: another son and daughter, born five years after Kate and Sam, spaced three years apart. The children, now grown, visit often, and the family looks like any normal, happy, loving family. It would be difficult, seeing them laughing and joking at family dinners, to guess at their sad, fragmented past.

Kate's yearning crowds the car. How she would love to meet her mother, grasp her hand, taste her cooking, ask her about the years before the kidnapping, and after. But looking at her, seeing how content she is, how restful her spirit seems, she knows she can't do it. It would be like smashing a shattered mirror that has taken decades to put together. Its hold is tenuous, gossamer, and she won't be the one to re-splinter it.

No fresh heartbreak.

She has a new life, *thinks Kate,* like I do now. *She thinks of Seth at home in Illovo with Baby Marmalade: how good he is with him, how gentle. Seth who wants to keep his Genesis name, instead of 'Sam,' says it doesn't suit him, and he's right.*

He has a new life too, despite not changing his name. She pictures what she guesses they are doing now, sitting on the couch in front of the homescreen, Baby Marmalade asleep in his arms, Betty/Barbara the Beagle snoring in her usual spot, her snout on Seth's lap. The wooden floor littered with nappies and wipes and teething rings and toys.

A different kind of family, *James said.*

An unusual family, but a family nonetheless: waiting for her to return home, and anticipating its new addition.

She thinks of her Black Hole, which is still there but has been sewn up to the size of her skin-warm silver locket. It's the smallest she can ever remember it being, but it yawns when she thinks of James.

Kate watches her mother pack up, shake the blanket, fold it and put it away, then start walking back in the direction from which she came. Kate reaches for the door handle, then stops herself.

No. No. *But when that feels too harsh, she allows herself a concession, thinks,* at least: not today. Maybe tomorrow, but not today.

After a few steps, her mother turns and looks directly at the car in the distance. Kate can't see her expression. A moment goes by, and Anne turns back and continues her walk home.

Kate takes a few breaths with her head back and her eyes closed, then snicks her safety belt in and starts the car, swinging it into reverse. Her back is aching again, her ankles puffy. She adjusts her position, rubs her swollen belly.

"Time to get you back home, little one."

Born seven months apart, her babies will be almost like twins. A different kind of twin.

Kate begins to drive away and gets as far as the stop sign at the top of the road when she changes her mind. She turns the car around and races back to the parking lot at the river. Her mother is gone.

CHAPTER 78
GLASS MERCURY

Westville, KZN, 2022

Kate clambers out of the car, fighting with her safety belt with dumb fingers, almost tripping in her rush to catch her mother. She leaves the door open, not caring, and runs as fast as she can, hands on her pregnant stomach, down the peppermint slope and shouting, "Anne! Anne!"

A small, faraway thought occurs to her: that she must look completely crackers with her strange, short haircut, her mismatched arms hugging her round belly, running and shouting after a woman who she thinks might be her real mother—the mother she was taken from so long ago. She doesn't care. She's near the river now, can hear it gurgling, and looks frantically for the woman who was just here. Shields her eyes from the sunshine and squints up in the direction she was walking. There's just an empty path.

Her desperation flashes monochrome. It cat-claws at her: needles in her skin.

"Anne!" she shouts as loudly as she can. "Anne Chapman!" but there's not a soul in sight. Just the river and the green-flavoured breeze and the birds.

Kate stops running, and rests her hands on her knees. Her lungs are hard elastic. When she straightens up again, the woman has stepped out from behind the willows, a look of unabashed wonder on her face, still grasping her picnic things.

"Anne Chapman?" asks Kate, whispering now, also stung by the quiet hope in the moment. They're only a few metres away from each other.

The woman blinks, drops the basket with a grassy thud. Her hands go up to her face and she touches her nose, her mouth, as if to test if the moment is real, or a dream.

"Sorry," says Kate. "I know it's a lot to take in. I wasn't going to—" She stumbles over her words. "I was going to wait and—"

"It can't be," the woman says, hope now like flames in her cheeks. "Can it?"

Kate's heart is sprinting; she puts her palm over her chest as if to tell it to slow down.

Calm. Calm. Stress is not good for the baby.

They stand marvelling at each other. Silver floss for hair, and eyes the colour of the sound of the sea. It's like looking into a time-travelling mirror (Glass Mercury). Then Anne reaches out through the mirror and touches Kate's chin, and it's so tender that Kate just wants to melt under her touch and the poignancy of the moment. The sense of her immense loss—thirty years of tender, unconditional love she missed out on—almost bowls her over. A life stolen. The overwhelming feeling of her own personal tragedy splashes her world purple.

The abducted two-year-old in Kate wants to yell Mom! *and fling her arms around her mother, but the moment is strange and disjointed and not the Hallmark scene she imagined it could be. Yes, they're bound by warm flesh and blood—always would be—but their relationship is eternally eroded by deprivation. The heart-bending truth is that they are virtual strangers, and this realisation, coupled with the rolling feeling of squandered time she feels, punches Kate in the stomach, and it hurts so much she winces, and holds on to her belly.*

"Oh!" says Anne, stepping towards her, taking her by a shoulder, "Are you okay?"

There's another jab, and Kate exclaims with a sharp intake of breath. Anne lays the blanket out and, holding her good arm, helps Kate to sit down.

"I think," says Kate, recovering, "I think the baby just kicked."

Immediately the pane of cold glass that's between them shatters and falls away, and they both start weeping. They hug and hold hands and cry and cry. Their salty cheeks touch, their tears run together. Sniffing, they both search for tissues but come up empty-handed. Kate uses her sleeve to wipe her face.

"Kate. My darling Kate. After all this time. Is it really you?" but Kate doesn't need to answer.

CHAPTER 79

BRAIN ON FIRE

The Lipworth Foundation
Johannesburg, 2036

As the memory comes to its end, Kate is pulled back into the operating room. The back of her head is still sizzling with pain, but it's not the overbearing, black-hammer kind that knocks you into oblivion.

The DarkDoc smoothes a thin platelet plaster over the wound. "Done."

"Kate?" says Zack. "Are you with us?"

Kate lets out a low groan. "Fu-u-u-uck. That was—" But she doesn't have a word to describe it.

"It'll take you a while to adjust to the mesh," says the doctor.

"I don't have time."

They unwrap her limbs so she can move freely again. Morgan shines a pen-light into her eyes. "How do you feel?"

Woozy, she's going to say. *Brain on fire.* But there's something else. She looks around the room, looks at the people's faces. It's like there's an extra dimension.

"Intense," is all she manages to say. The pain is fading.

There's the ordinary world, real life, which is how regular creeps experience reality —Kate calls it 'monochrome'—without the extra shapes and sounds and colours that she sees, then on top of that is her synaesthesia. But now, now there's an additional layer, and it's rich and beautiful. Enhanced. Like you've only ever seen black-and-white films but then you turn on a switch and all of a sudden it's 4DHD hypercolour with textures that come right out at you, as if you can feel them with your eyes.

"Kate?" says Zack, moving into her field of vision.

My god *he's beautiful.* He is the most beautiful thing she's ever seen. She wants to touch him.

"It feels like," says Kate, "it feels like my eyeballs are drunk."

"It's not your eyeballs," says the DarkDoc, coming into view.

He's a magnificent man too. So strong, so gruff and handsome. Is he really her lover? It suddenly seems unlikely.

"It's your brain." The doctor emanates deep red energy. It's as if his chakras are glowing in short bursts. Kate thinks she can see his heart beating, as if she has some kind of new real-time X-ray heat-sensing ability. She wants to touch him, too. She was wrong to say it felt as if her eyeballs are drunk. It's more accurate to say that every neuron and nerve ending in her whole body is tripping on some kind of futuristic neat-tech rainbow crack version of LSD.

"I understand now," Kate says. "I understand why Silver wanted to get this."

"This is just the beginning," says Zack.

"How much time do we have left?"

Kate has forgotten about the warden. She looks at her, takes in her stocky frame, her firm muscles. *How strong she is, like an Amazon warrior! But more royal than that, with her silver baton. A military queen.*

"Forty-eight minutes," says Zack, bringing Kate to attention. "That's if they shut off the power at fourteen hundred exactly."

"It's not enough time," says Morgan.

"It's all we have."

Kate stares over at Silver inside the dome of the transparent tent. It looks like a bubble to her now, as if they are all underwater and the sleeping Silver is protected by her own special pocket of air. It's like a fairytale.

"Tell me what I need to do."

CHAPTER 80
BRIGHTCANDY CANAL

"All right," says Zack. "Doctor Morgan's and my theory is that Silver got stuck in between reality and her RPG immersion."

Kate splutters. "Theory? That's all you have?"

"That's all we have."

Jesus Christ on a cracker.

Kate's mind is racing, and her thoughts feel as if they leave heat trails in their path. Words tumble out of her mouth. "RPG? How do you get stuck? I've never heard of that before. Is it because it was a backstreet mesh? It wasn't done properly ... it didn't work well enough?"

"We think it's because it worked *too* well," says Morgan. "That particular lace is so advanced ... and Silver so adept at immersion that we think she went too deep, too quickly, and ...yes, she got stuck."

"Usually when you have trouble immersing, you just come out and restart. But for some reason Silver's not doing that. We know she's not in Eden 7.0, and we know she's not here with us, so our theory is that she's somewhere in between."

"Eden 7.0?"

"It's the updated version of the role-playing game she's always in. It's so advanced now that you can only play if you're meshed."

"How do you know she's not in the game?"

"Doctor Morgan has patients at the Atrium. They haven't seen Silver since she left the building yesterday. Not in the game or in real life."

Kate remembers her earlier trip to the Atrium, but now in her memory it has a glow to it, a promise, irresistible potential.

"They were on high alert there, when I called," says Morgan. "Rushing to fetch everyone out before the grid goes down. Do you understand the implications, Kate, if you're immersed when the power is cut?"

"Yes," says Kate. "No power, no Net. No Net, no way out."

Morgan nods at her, slow and sad.

"Forty-six minutes," says Bernard.

"All right," says Zack, "You've gotta go."

Kate's blood rushes through her veins; there's a lightness in her head. "But I don't know what I'm doing!"

"I'm going to dial you in." Morgan clicks something on his mandible and talks softly to it. "Going through."

Kate grabs Zack's hand.

"You've got the greatest chance of finding her. She came from you."

"But I don't even know how to—"

And just like that, Kate's body goes limp. Her consciousness is sucked out of her flesh and bone and transported through a rushing-light fibre-optic tunnel (BrightCandy Canal) and the ether goes cold and dark around her.

CHAPTER 81
MEZZANINE PUZZLE

Kate's consciousness is rushing and rushing as if she is being teleported through space and time and her heart is going mad in her chest—even though, looking down, she doesn't have a chest (or a heart, for that matter)—until she reaches some kind of plateau where it feels as if she's standing on top of a skyscraper, and then she tumbles—her soul tumbles—back down and into her body. It's a soft landing, and it smells of rosemary blooms and bright moss.

A version of her body, anyway, where neither of her arms is broken and her scalp is untouched. She stands up, dusts herself off. She can feel it's not her real body: can feel that she's not really standing. It's like being in a super-realistic dream. How long has it taken her to get here? There's no way to tell. All she can do is find Silver and get her out as soon as she can.

Kate's standing in an overgrown garden, rampant with new buds and tangled vines. Warm, humid air streams into her shocked lungs. No roses in sight, thank the Net. She's never felt comfortable with them since what happened at the Luminary. The thorns always remind her of Bongi's betrayal, of Mally's almost-fatal injury at the hands of Lumin, and it paints her heart cold black. The plants here have the opposite effect: the promise and innocence of bursting blooms; the scent of citrus leaf and Penny Royal and apple blossoms form a soft invisible lattice, lifting Kate's spirit. As she is lifted, she sees where she is.

The Atrium looms large, glowing in the fading light. Kate makes her way through the creeping jungle, almost expecting the tendrils to snake up and around an ankle, keeping her back, not to consume her, but to protect her from the danger ahead.

Kate's relieved. She had pictured being delivered into some low-oxygen cosmos where she'd have no idea how to find Silver, but this is easy; she knows exactly where to go.

Kate runs towards the Atrium. She rushes through the entrance, expecting to see the regulars jacked in at their pods, but the place is deserted. The whole floor looks disused, as if everyone left in a hurry and a dust-storm has swirled through. Kate climbs the stairs to Silver's level, but before she gets there she knows it will be barren too. And indeed, Silver's spot is as empty as the others'.

'Ghost' it says on the outside of her booth, 'GK', and Kate shudders.

"Hello?" Kate's voice bounces off the glass walls.

Silver must be close. Why else would Kate be here? She trawls through the abandoned building, thinking, looking for a clue. She remembers being here earlier and talking about the basement. Wonders how Keke is. Kate's loath to go down there —still spooked by what happened at SkyRest—but she doesn't have a choice. Once she's decided, it's easier, and she makes her way past the stained mugs, half-eaten fauxburgers and forgotten lockets of snaffeine. She pockets a red lanyard she finds with an Atrium chipcard attached to it. The 4D mugshot is of the man she met here previously. She doesn't remember his name, just the scent of his perfumed shirt: amber, pepperwood, juniper berry.

As Kate descends to the basement the levels get darker. The dust is so thick here it's like sand. Where does it all come from? She looks at the cracked windows and the vines that wind themselves around them and anything else in their path. Left to their own devices Kate is sure the jungle would consume the Atrium altogether. She follows the darkness down.

"Hello?" Kate calls. No answer, and no echo this time, either.

She reaches the basement door with the 'off limits' sign, holds up the chipcard and it clicks from red to green, just like she knew it would. This isn't real life. Not a game, not quite, but somewhere in between: a mezzanine puzzle. She'll take advantage of her virgin clover while it lasts. The heavy door swings open.

CHAPTER 82

HOT IN HER POCKET

In the Atrium underground, the only light is the warm buzzing coming from the occasional levitating lightbulb Kate passes. There are doors everywhere. How will she know which one is right? She walks along, minding her step, trying not to stumble on the mounds of sand that cover the ground. The sand is her reminder that this is not real, that her real body is passed out in the OR under the watchful eye of Morgan and Zack. Where is Seth? Being underground again makes her nerves fizz with the recent trauma of the SkyRest crim colony. Deep breaths of the musty, cool air keep her calm, or calm enough. It'll take her hours, days, to check out all these private immersion rooms; hopefully she'll strike it lucky.

The first door Kate opens leads to a dark, sound-proofed room, with a VXR shell in the centre. One of many identical spaces, she guesses. She steps inside the capsule and reaches for her mandible but remembers now that she's meshed, she doesn't need one anymore. Kate brings up the interface just by thinking about it, and blinks 'go'.

She's immediately transported to a dim, overcrowded, high-ceilinged hall of shouting creeps, mostly brawny men with popping veins, but some women too. Their skin is slick with sweat and oil, and the sour smell of body odour and liquor hovers like a low cloud. The woman next to Kate is shouting and pumping her fist in the air. Her dark lipstick is smudged; perspiration glints from her eyebrows. The navy scent of danger perfumes the air. Kate moves forward a little, trying to glimpse what they're all shouting about, and then she sees the boxing ring in the centre. Batcam drones flap and squeal above the elevated stage, recording the action.

Two men are up on the platform, but they're not boxers. The man with a peroxided box-cut and emerald silk shorts slams his opponent—a man in red with a metal mouth—against the corner pillar then smashes his fist into his jaw with such force that it riles the crowd up even more. Metal teeth scatter like spent bullets onto the platform and into the crowd, and they cheer.

"Finish him!"

Kate tries to turn around so she can leave, but heaving bodies are pressed against her now, and they're not letting her through.

It's a simulation, Kate tells herself, *it's a simulation. Keep calm.*

These are all real people. They may not physically be in the room with her but they're all real somewhere, just like she is. The thought makes her feel sick.

The box-cut drives his fist into the man's stomach now, causing him to double over, and when he does so, the attacker knees him hard in the face, forcing him back again. He pins his opponent against the pillar and lays into him so viciously his eyes close and he slides to the floor.

This isn't an ordinary fight club. It's some kind of death match. The audience screams and spits and gesticulates. "Kill him!"

The man in the green shorts starts yelling and kicking his opponent's unconscious body. He kicks him as hard as he can, shouting for the coward to get up and fight. The crowd boos the half-dead man for not rising to the occasion. Kate tries to leave, but the crowd's noise and the flashing of the batcams interfere with her vision, and she can't call up her interface to escape. Finally the fighter's eyes open and he gets up on one elbow, and the box-cut jumps on him, smashing his head onto the stage's white tarp.

"Finish him!"

Someone throws a knife into the ring. Without hesitating, the man in green grabs the knife and drives it with both hands into the neck of his opponent, and the crowd goes mental. There's a jet of blood, a slow-motion arc of red mist that spray-paints the tarp. The killer stabs him again and again to the cheering, and just when Kate thinks the fight is over, the man who seems to be lying dead on the floor reaches up and grabs the box-cut and throws him a metre into the air. He roars and pulls the knife out and uses it to hack at the box-cut, who is now screaming and slipping in the crimson spill. The graphic violence shocks Kate, but it's the colour of the box-cut's blood that spins her head. The fluid that dribbles out of his fresh gashes is apple green. It forms its own splashes and smears on the tarp, which is beginning to look like a Jackson Pollock canvas. Kate tries to look away but the shrieking batdrone footage is projected everywhere. It's impossible to not look.

Red shorts hacks at the box-cut until his arm comes away from his torso and he throws the limb into the hungry crowd, then he starts sawing the man's neck. The green-blooded man gasps and gurgles as the tendons in his neck spring apart.

Knowing that they are robots doesn't make it any easier to watch. Kate's been pushed to the front now, and she doesn't know how to get back to the Atrium. The box-cut is dismembered, bit by bit, and fed to the baying crowd. Once there is nothing left of him, the remaining fighter throws up his arms and yells in manic victory, and the noise in the hall becomes deafening. In his excited state, the man drops the knife and it goes scudding across the platform with just enough momentum to drop off the stage, right in front of Kate. Without hesitating—without thinking, really—she quickly picks it up and slips it into her coat pocket. Her hand comes away sticky with green blood (Robo Sap).

The winner is carried away while some feral-looking young kids—rat hunters—loosen the tarp at its corners, taking care to not step on the still-wet artwork, and clip one side of it to a rod, which is then lifted on a pulley system, displaying the painting for everyone to see. The creeps cheer and cheer, and then the auction begins. The street urchins disappear into the crowd: they move along by crawling along the floor, where there is more space to manoeuvre, and no doubt pick a few pockets on their way. Kate won't judge them, her own plunder glowing hot in her pocket. Copying them, she goes down on her hands and knees and pushes her way out. Glass shards lacerate her palms, and some careless boots and heels find her head and back, but she just puts her head down and moves as fast as she can. Eventually Kate reaches the edge of the room and cooler air, and she covers her ears and calls up her dashboard. This time it works, and she blinks 'escape'. When her eyes open again she's sitting, with tight lungs, in the VXR shell. She leans back for a moment to appreciate the solitary cool, dim room, and when she opens her white fists they are clean and injury free.

CHAPTER 83

DOOMSDAY DEBRIS

Fourways
Johannesburg, 2036

Seth is on his way to the Lipworth Foundation. Despite the clusterfuck that is the current satellite situation he somehow manages to receive the occasional bullet from Arronax. Mally is safe, they're together, and they're heading to the Lipworth. More than that: He knows exactly where in the building they'll be, and he has the code to get in. There's a specific room he and Arronax use there for their meetings. She hates hotels and feels uncomfortable in his apartment, so the safe room at the Lipworth is perfect for what Arronax has taken to calling her 'layovers'.

There's the tastefully decorated office she gets to use when she's in Jozi to consult, and the safe room is *en suite.* That's where they usually end up, on the floor or up against the wall. Sex with Arronax never disappoints.

Seth walks along the city street, dodging broken bottles, burning cars and litter bunting. There's a feeling of wildness, of savagery. Seth reaches back and his fingers play on the automatic rifle he snatched from SkyRest. Jozi isn't the prettiest or the safest place to be right now, but it's better than being in that surreal, subterranean prison with the building weighing down on your every pore. He is still creeped out by it, as if he needs a sonic shower and memory detox to get those damn scuttling, biting beetles out of his head. Seth had searched and searched for Kate, but had just become more lost. Eventually he'd found the staircase again, and couldn't resist climbing up and out, into the open air. He had to trust Kate found her way out too. His intuition was telling him she was no longer underground, and he had to trust it. They've always had an eerie sense of connection: those first milk years in Durban, followed by the gaping absence of each other, growing up. And now that they've been living together for sixteen years it's as if they're joined at the hip, telepathically speaking. This doesn't mean they always agree. They drive each other insane sometimes. Seth knows his twin sister better than he knows himself, knows how strong she is. She would have found her way out. All he can do is hope he's not wrong.

Even the solartrams have stopped working now, despite their promise of 24/7/365. It's always a problem, thinks Seth absent-mindedly, when companies use numbers as slogans. Numbers are steady, stable, incontrovertible. There are no terms and conditions attached; they are not punctuated by spinning asterisks. Not that it matters now. Not that anything matters anymore.

A naked woman streaked with dirt ambles along the pavement towards him. Blood on her cheek, non-seeing eyes. Seth can't tell if she's human or droid. He skips out of her path. He's five minutes away from the Lipworth, and he needs to keep going.

Seth coughs into his face-mask. He blames the toxic-smelling smoke in the air. He's had this irritating niggle in his chest since leaving SkyRest, like an itch in his lungs he can't scratch.

There's a wolf-whistle from across the road. A flaming car passes in slow motion. The wolf-whistle again, this time louder. Despite his instinct telling him to keep walking, he looks around. He can't help it. Monochrome cityscape and interactive street art. The rolling, burning car. Then he sees the man, a barbarian with a tank for a body, and he's not alone. It's a group of them—five? Six apoca-pirates—and they're leering and passing around a bottle. The whistler holds a dirty timber baseball bat over his massive shoulders. It's studded with nails and shards of glass. Doomsday Debris.

The gang begins to cross the road, clearly headed in the direction of the naked woman. They whistle and catcall and call her a 'pretty bitch'.

Keep walking, Seth tells himself. *Keep fucking walking.*

"What you doin'?" asks the biggest man, adjusting his pace to walk alongside her. He has rocky shoulders and a black vest that says 'Fuck Robots'. The woman doesn't answer him. Seth doesn't even think she hears him, considering the state she's in. Seth forces himself to ignore the situation and keep walking. He's almost there.

"Hey!" shouts the barbarian right into the woman's face. "Answer me when I speak to you, bitch!"

Seth slows down, his shoulders sag. He was so close to getting to safety.

"Larry asked you a fucking question," says one of the men, slapping her on her back. "Have some fucking respect."

Another man throws a crushed can at her, and it glances off her temple, opening up a dribble of new blood. Seth's fury heats his stomach; his veins pulse. He is so goddamned sick of these entitled sadobastards.

"You know what I think, Larry?" says a woman—there's a woman in the gang too. "I think she wants to suck your cock."

The men laugh and make animal sounds: grunting; licking; laughing. Dirty tongues wagging. Seth's hands turn into fists.

"Slow down now, missus. Where are you going in such a hurry?"

The barbarian with the baseball bat takes her hand. If Seth didn't know better it would look like a loving gesture, but when she resists, tries to keep walking, he yanks her arm so hard it swipes her whole body sideways.

"I said slow down!" Larry shouts, and now that Seth is closer, he sees the man's saliva fleck her face, and she betrays her consciousness by flinching.

Seth still can't tell if she's human. Does it even matter? He used to think it did.

"Leave her alone," says Seth, but the gang is so busy heckling and taunting the woman they don't even notice him. He pulls the automatic rifle up and out of the makeshift holster on his back.

"Leave her alone!" he shouts.

The rifle is a powerhouse. Branded—appropriately—with the SkyRest logo, loaded with frangible bullets designed for maximum surface damage. That's code for maximum pain. Designed to injure instantly, intensely, without the lethality of hollow points. Perfect for keeping prisoners on their best behaviour—perfect for trigger-happy guards who aren't allowed to kill their charges but who like the feel of a large automatic weapon in their hands.

"Who the fuck are you?" says Larry, twirling his bespoke bat.

"Get lost," says one of his henchmen. "Does she belong to you?"

"She doesn't belong to anyone. She doesn't have to. Step away from her right now," says Seth, the weapon thrumming with potential in his hands.

"The fuck is that thing?"

The naked woman tries to slip away, but Larry catches her wrist.

"You don't want to find out," says Seth. "Leave now and you won't have to."

The barbarian smiles. "Is that right?" He hands the woman to the pack and addresses Seth squarely, runs his hand over the nail- and glass-studded bat and squeezes, puncturing his own palm, and the blood begins to run. If he feels pain, it doesn't register on his face. He's even bigger than he looked before.

Seth feels strangely calm. This might be the end, but, looking around at the air, thick with pollution, the immutable damage, the quick-breeding fires, the sorry excuses for humankind right in front of him, he feels at peace with the idea of dying. This world is broken. It's been broken for a long time. Sure, he was used to some kind of privileged existence, binge-watching series streams in his air-filtered, temperature-regulated, drone-delivered-processed-food-on-demand apartment, but that is no way to live. It's not really living, at all.

His survival instinct is still strong, but his fear of death swirls up and away into the electrosmog that surrounds him.

"I'm going to ask you one more time to keep walking," says Seth, lifting the gun so he can look through the sight. He softens his shoulder where he's expecting the impact from the butt. There's that annoying tickle in his lungs, so he coughs hard to try clear it before taking aim. It's changing from a tickle to a sharp prickling sensation: more pain that itch.

One of the men starts touching the woman. His filthy, callused hands trail over the distressed woman's stomach, then over her hip to squeeze her butt. His nails are outlined in grime. Another man begins to approach Seth, and he trains the rifle on him. The man gets closer. Deciding against a second warning, Seth pulls the trigger.

Three frangibles rocket out of the weapon, and all of them connect with the greasy man: face, chest, thigh. Designed to come apart as soon as they leave the barrel, the bullets separate into a spiralling core and three sharp petals. The lead alloy blooms in the air, as if breathing, then embeds itself in the flesh of the target.

The man roars, confused as to why there is so much pain, like a rolling flame over his body, and tries to pull out the strange bullet that has bitten into his cheek. This causes more damage and he shouts again. His other wounds bleed oily black through his dark clothes. Angry, he wants to swipe at Seth, but his limbs are contracting with the pain, and he lands on the tar. While watching him writhe, Larry advances, lifting his bat, preparing to swing. The woman with the denim-dyed hair flanks him, her spiked knuckleduster glinting in the afternoon light. Seth fires at the barbarian and gets him in the chest and stomach. Larry doesn't acknowledge the bullets at all; he just keeps coming. Seth realises the man doesn't feel pain, and he has to rely on his agility alone as the bat comes rushing for his head. He sidesteps Larry and manages to shoot two of the others as they advance. They roll away in pain. The bat comes for Seth again, and he gets out of its way just in time. There's a sudden sharp pain in his lower back, and a wet sensation. Seth turns around to see that the woman has slashed him with her spikes. Before he can respond, she punches him in the stomach with them. It's like being stabbed four times at once, and he shouts in surprise, looking into her dilated irises as the consequences sink in. Satisfied, she pulls them out, and it feels as if she's taking his organs with her. Then there's a loud thump and all the air is knocked out of Seth's lungs. The tarmac scrapes his face. He can feel the bleeding where he's been struck across the back with the bat, and where he's been stabbed in front. A pair of boots walks up, and before he can raise his arms to protect himself, they kick him in the face. It's the loudest thing he's ever heard.

The naked woman stares at him, as if she's thinking.

The bat comes for him again, and takes out his left knee. Seth rocks and shouts in pain, coughs up some blood. There are five of them now, surrounding him—a circle of tormentors. They're all in the sky, and he's eating dirt. They discuss among themselves what they should do with him, if there's any more fun to be had before he flatlines.

"You know what?" says the barbarian. "I feel like watching a show."

CHAPTER 84

BRAIN BLEACH

Kate stumbles out into the corridor with its gentle, stuttering light and examines the doors. She's already seen too much violence in her life, too much pain. She's going to have to summon up all the courage she has to open another door, never mind the number of doors needed to find Silver. And, when all of this is over, she promises herself, she'll go in to a nice padded room somewhere in the mountains. One of those places that remove unwanted memories and lets you download happy ones in their place. Brain Bleach, the dubsters call it.

There must be more than twenty identical doors here. Kate walks down the passage, trying to get a feel for which one could be the right one. She calls up her interface again, and now that it's on, when she looks at a door, a green holotag comes up.

DNA CASINO WITH TOPLESS BARSTAFF, says the one she's standing near. She keeps moving down the passage.

PLASTIC SURGERY PRACTICE IN VIVO XXX-HOT MODELS

ROMAN FEAST (WITH LIVE ORTOLAN) AND SODO-ORGY

BDSMXV SEX DUNGEON X-GRAPHIC DUBCON & OFF-LABEL BE WARNED 21+

Kate steps back, to see which one she's already visited.

. . .

ROBO DEATH MATCH ART CIRCUIT AUCTION

She keeps walking, reading the green tags on the doors as she goes. When she finds a red holotag, she stops. Does that mean the room is not vacant? It doesn't say what the immersion's theme is. She puts her hand on the doorknob. Metallic, cold. Canary-coloured adrenaline kicks her in the head. Kate takes a deep breath and opens the door.

CHAPTER 85
HANSEL & GRETEL

White Mezzanine, 2036

It's not a door but some kind of portal to another place altogether, because now she's standing in a white passage and it's clean and beautiful and there's light everywhere.

Yes! I've reached the next level. But then she's immediately worried. Has she really reached the next level? Is she closer to finding Silver now? Or has she done something wrong and she's back at the Lipworth Foundation?

It's all the white that's bothering her. This is what the Lipworth looks like, but then she interrogates the setting further: She kicks a wall and it doesn't hurt. She runs down the corridor and she's so full of energy and stamina she feels as if she can run all day. Indeed, she'd have to, because it looks like an infinity corridor with no beginning and no end. There are strips of mirrors, too, silver reflecting white. She stops in front of one, inspects herself.

Kate has her mane of red hair, slick-styled and shiny, and her scalp is uncut. There's no more pain. Her wrinkles are gone, her eyes have a cosmic sparkle. She lifts her damaged arm to see she has full mobility, and it no longer hurts at all. Not only that, but she's wearing some kind of body-hugging superhero catsuit in ombre orange. The colour pops against the white and it's as if it's feeding her body energy, like when you lace up your runners tightly and it makes you want to sprint. She can't stand still; she needs to move. Needs to hurry. She moves away from the mirror, sees entrances to more passages, all identical.

"Silver?" Kate knows she has to find some way to step up. What is she missing? "Silver?"

The dark orange. Her brain is trying to tell her something, but she's removed from her clear, real-life thinking. It's like there's a filter on her thoughts down here—up here?—wherever she is, and she can't grab on to the nagging idea that's trying to present itself.

Think!

The burnt orange is *deja vu,* right? So what is familiar about this moment? It's the white corridor.

Lipworth. We've been through this already.

But, no, it's not that. The memory isn't of the Lipworth Foundation. It's a lot deeper than that. Further away, but more entrenched.

Of course, when she's got it. Of course. It's so obvious. It's the white interior of the Genesis Project headquarters—also subterranean, also bright white. But what does it mean? Then she thinks of fairytales: of Silver stuck in her sleeping body like Snow White. Of the thorny rose maze of the Luminary. Of the one she knows best, the one she lived through, herself, and still has the book James gave her: Hansel and Gretel. Kate and Sam. Toaster waffle roof tiles. She thinks of the breadcrumb trail of scuffmarks that had led her out of Genesis and saved her life, and looks down at the floor. Kate doesn't notice anything but white, but then she squats and sees them. Tiny multicoloured dots. It's weird because they're not part of the floor, not really. It's like her neural lace is projecting her synaesthesia onto the floor, as if she feels lost but something in her brain knows the way.

Kate follows the pixels for a while and, just as she begins to second-guess her fairytale theory, the breadcrumbs veer left, and after a while they lead her sharp right, and then something tells her she's close and she calls: "Silver?"

Kate hears someone's voice and stops in her tracks. Someone is there.

Silver?

"Mom?"

"Silver! I'm coming!" Kate runs towards the voice but there's just white mist everywhere, and she can't see where she's going. She trips on air, somersaults and falls, but it doesn't hurt. She doesn't feel anything but relief as she scrambles up again to follow the sound of her daughter's voice.

"Mom!" shouts Silver, and there she is, on the other side of some kind of thin white membrane, a biolatex film. Kate can see the outline of her hands and elbows as she pushes through the screen. She starts pushing too, tries to tear the elastic with her nails, her teeth. It tastes like the rubber of soft-pop balloons. Kate thinks of the Gordhan, of Mally in a body cast, of Solonne.

"Can you cut it?" asks Silver.

"Cut it? With what?"

"Don't you have anything?"

"What do you mean? No."

"Look at your weapons."

"Silver," Kate says, touching her forehead against the screen. She wants to say: *my silly girl. I didn't bring any weapons.*

"Look down, Mom. Look at your utility belt."

And she's going to say *I don't have a utility belt,* but then she looks down and she does have one. It's the knife she picked up at the death match, which she pulls out of its sheath and stares at. A thought nags at her: *this is all too easy.* Finding the Atrium, finding the chipcard, then the knife, the portal, the breadcrumbs, and now, finding her daughter. But she doesn't have time to waste so she ignores the idea and goes with her good fortune. Maybe it's her virgin clover. Maybe it's something else.

"Stand back," Kate says as she slices through the white.

CHAPTER 86
CAR CARCASS

Innercity
Johannesburg 2036

The gang hauls Seth up and strips his clothes off with a hunting knife.

"You're going to do it," says the barbarian with the bat.

"Do what?" asks Seth, but he already knows the answer.

Two of the gang members push the naked woman face forward over the bonnet of a burnt-out car carcass and spread her legs with coarse hands. The front of her body is stamped with the dark residue of the vehicle: white and black; negative, positive. She doesn't resist, and they step back, dust their hands, and put away their weapons. The nunchux are clipped away, the hunting knife goes back into its sheath. One of the men makes lewd gestures over his own junk while another pushes Seth's broken body towards the woman.

"I can't," Seth says, coughing and gesturing at his dripping wounds.

The woman licks Seth's blood off her spiked knuckleduster. "I can help you with that."

The men snigger. One of them has picked up the automatic rifle Seth dropped. He aims it at Seth and motions with its nose for him to obey the instruction. Larry looks on, amused, bat hanging at his side. Seth limps as slowly as possible towards the splayed woman, trying to buy time to think. Every step on his shattered knee sends an arrow of pain up his body, and he's coughing up what looks like bits of raw kidney. When he gets to the woman, he gingerly levers himself over her. She recoils beneath him.

"I won't hurt you," Seth whispers.

His blood trickles on her. One of the men throws a broken bottle at him. "That isn't how you do it!" and the rest of the gang laughs.

"Hurry up, you cunt," says the denim-haired knuckleduster. "We're waiting for our show."

Seth's earlier thought, before he was stabbed, was to run; he was sure he could outrun them. Now every step is agony, and they're bristling with weapons, including his.

I was so close. He thinks of his family, and of Keke. Always of Keke. He knows he should have told her years ago how he felt about her, but it was never the right time. She's in love with Marko, despite his insane decision to leave her.

He pictures Kate, his better half, his puzzle piece. The kids. God! To see them one more time.

The woman beneath him shifts slightly, bringing him back. She's saying something under her breath. He can't hear her.

"What?" he whispers into her neck, hiding his lips from the enemy.

"That's more like it," says the barbarian. "Let's see some action."

Another piece of debris comes flying at them. It bounces off Seth's shoulder.

"What did you say?"

The man with the SkyRest gun aims it at Seth.

The woman whispers, "I said get ready to get down."

"What?"

"On the count of three."

Seth couldn't be more confused.

"One," she says. "Two. Three."

Seth hits the deck, and the woman spins around and releases her roscoe. The smart steel barrel of the gun pops out of her forearm and she fires round after round into the yelling gang members, flattening them with its firepower. They're all cut down apart from the barbarian, who seems indestructible. He must have ten bullets in him now, but he keeps advancing. The naked woman keeps firing. Seth can taste the gunpowder. He leopard crawls to where the freshly dead bodies lie and wrenches the hunting knife from the man's holster. Larry reaches the woman and starts to throttle her. She's out of bullets. Seth crawls quickly towards the savage and slices through both of his heel's tendons. He may not be able to feel pain, but he won't be able to walk without his achilles. Seth expects to see yellow cartilage and bone, but instead is shocked by a flash of silver titanium before the blood washes over it.

The robot barbarian falls down, slamming the woman down with him, and Seth lurches in his direction, knife raised, ready to slit his throat.

The woman tries to stop him. "He can't hurt us now," she says.

"I don't care," says Seth, as he severs the head from the barrel-chested body.

They pick a few garments off the still-warm dead bodies. The clothes have an evil stink. The femmebot pulls on a pair of dark jeans. Her carbon-dusted breasts are still bare. Seth retrieves his gun, and gives the bat to her.

"Bye," he says, and starts limping away. He can only shuffle along, anything quicker and the pain stops him in his tracks. He's still bleeding from the spike-holes in his stomach.

"Let me help you," she says. Her ribcage drawer slides open.

"I don't have time. I need to go." He coughs up more clots and spits them out on to the hot tarmac.

"You won't get anywhere in that state."

"I will, or I'll die trying."

"Wait," she says, touching his arm. "Take this. I don't have anything else left in my medikit." She hands him an inhaler. Pexidine. Seth unscrews it and gives himself a large dose of the painkiller in each nostril, then pockets the bottle.

"Thanks."

"I can't do anything about your knee," she says. "My scanner surmises that your tibia is shattered and the patellar tendon is shredded, presumably by the splintered bone. You'll need surgery."

"That sounds about right," he says, grimacing from the jolting pain he feels every time he puts his weight on it.

"But that's not your biggest concern," she says.

Seth looks at her.

"You have severe internal bleeding in your lungs. As things stand, I can't tell if you'll die from the blood loss or the oxygen deprivation. Both seem just as likely."

"Wow," says Seth, lungs gurgling. "Don't sugarcoat it."

"I'm sorry," she says. "Is there a way to sugarcoat death?"

"Ha," he says. "Good point."

The bot closes her drawer, and the skin there is almost seamless. She props him up with a steel shoulder and helps him walk.

"I'll help you to where you're going," she says. "But I can't stay. I have something I need to do."

"Thank you," Seth says. "Do you want to put a shirt on?"

"Do you want me to put a shirt on?"

Seth shrugs, and they stagger together towards the Lipworth Foundation.

CHAPTER 87

FORCE QUIT

White Mezzanine, 2036

Kate and Silver fall into each other with yelps of relief. Silver's body is bird-boned and brittle, and it makes Kate want to keep holding her. It feels so real Kate can even smell Silver's signature scent: white apple flesh, rum and sage. She wonders how long it's been since they hugged like this. Not since Silver was small, she's sure. As a toddler, Silver would steal into her room at night and slip into her bed. Mally would do it too, of course. Sometimes they'd even climb into each other's beds and she'd find them snoring sweetly together in their twin pyjamasuits. She had read something about how you shouldn't let your small kids come to your bed at night, how becoming dependent on a parent to fall back to sleep would give them insomnia issues for life.

They need to learn to self-soothe, Kate used to tell herself as she carried the small bodies back to their KidKocoons. A stab of guilt when they'd cry in their sleep that they wanted their mama, and there she was, alone and lonely in her own bed; and a stab of guilt when she'd let them stay cuddled up to her, their imagined future insomnia fuelling hers.

Of course, after Lumin she couldn't give a toss who wrote what in which parenting stream. If the twins padded through to her bed during the night, she'd pull their little bodies as close to hers as they'd let her and they'd sleep with tangled limbs, breathing each other in all night.

Silver's the first to let go, and this breaks Kate's reverie. What is this place? It looks like an executive hospital room, but the periphery is wavy, as if the VXR designer didn't finish the full render. Kate picks up the plate of nutrijelly cubes for a closer look when Silver smacks the dish out of her hand. It clatters and vibrates on the tiles, the jelly-like blocks of soft lego on the floor, reminding Kate again of a simpler time. She moves to clean it up.

"Don't!" Silver's eyes are wide.

"I was just going to ask you what it was."

"Don't even touch it, and don't eat or drink anything while you're here."

"What is this place?" asks Kate.

"I don't know."

"We need to get out right now," says Kate. "They're shutting down the grid."

"I'm ready," says Silver. Pale, brave.

"How do we do it?"

Silver bites her lip. "You really don't know?"

"No."

"Zack didn't tell you?"

"For Net's sake, Silver—"

"He didn't tell you what we need to do?"

"All he said was, it would be good practice."

"What?"

"It would be good practice. I don't know what that means. We were rushing—*are rushing*—to get you out in time."

"I don't think you would have agreed to come if you knew—"

"Of course I would have!" Kate takes her shoulders. "I'd do anything for you. Don't you know that?" Her sinuses sting with new tears.

"But—"

"Just tell me."

Silver blinks away her own tears. "This isn't going to work."

"We'll make it work!"

Kate feels the time ticking away, and her mind is awash with blue watercolour: aquamarine exasperation. "You kept asking for Zack. How do you know him?"

"He comes to me in my dreams."

"You have dreams in here?"

"Only of him."

"He came to you in your dreams and told you how to get out of here?"

"I've always known how to get out. It's the same as my games."

Kate frowns. "Then why are you still here?"

"Because it's not working. It's like this place is some weird limbo that you can't—"

Silver's lost for words. Anxiety climbing, Kate motions for her to continue.

"—but then Zack told me that you'd be able to do it. That it would work if *you* did it. That he'd send you. And he did."

Kate feels like shaking some of the urgency she feels into Silver. It's time to go.

"In order to leave a game or an immersion when you're still alive, you usually just say 'escape', right? Or blink the 'quit' button," says Silver.

Kate nods. She thinks she may have known that.

"But sometimes it doesn't work. Not often, but sometimes. Like, if the software hangs or there's some kind of update blitz or whatever."

"Right."

"Then you have to force quit."

"Right."

"But this place ... blocks your interface, blocks the voice commands. So you can't force quit the regular way. You need to ... action it."

"Okay," says Kate. "How do you action it?"

Silver looks at her. Electric eyes. Then Kate understands.

"Oh."

"It gets a little more complicated," says Silver.

"Tell me."

"Ever since I started playing RPG with Seth when I was little ..."

"You've always been so good at the games. He was always saying so."

"But it's more than that. It's more than my skill set. It's that ... I realised that I couldn't die."

The understanding begins to snow down on Kate in large indigo flakes.

"No matter what. No matter which war I fight in, which bridge I jump off, I stay alive."

"That's why they call you 'Ghost'," says Kate. "Because you never die."

"It's always been a gift," says Silver. "My secret weapon."

"Until now."

"I tried to force quit here. I cut my wrists in the bath."

Silver shows her pale arms to Kate. The skin is flawless.

"When I woke up I was washed clean and back in bed."

Kate's heart swells in empathy. "I'm sorry you had to go through that. Especially on your own."

"I'm starving myself—" She plucks at her loose gown. "—but it's not working."

Silver seems manic now. She opens a cupboard door and grabs her jacket, throws it on the bed, starts pulling at the copper buttons.

"What are you doing?"

Silver extricates a pill from inside the hollow button at the collar, then moves down to the next one, and the next, till she has a pile of capsules.

"I've been saving up pain pills. Hiding them. I have over fifty, now."

"You were planning to take them all at once?"

"But it won't work. I realised after the bath. It won't work."

"What I don't understand is how I can help. If you can't die, then what can I do?"

Silver picks up the dagger Kate dropped when they first embraced, and hands it to her, handle first. She closes Kate's confused fingers over it. Kate looks down at it. The knife is brassy and intricate; a dragon with pearlescent eyes has been engraved into the metal. Its tail whips out the end of the handle and back to its mouth, forming a scaled loop.

"You know what Uncle Marko always used to say."

"What?"

"That there's always a hack for everything."

"That's probably true."

"Mom," says Silver. "You're my hack."

CHAPTER 88

SMOKE & SHIMMER

Lipworth Foundation
Johannesburg, 2036

"Come on, Kate," says Zack, searching her face for clues. "Come on. You're running out of time."

Mally bursts through the operating room swing-doors and sees both his sister and his mother lying unconscious on the clinic beds. He freezes.

"What the fuck are you doing to them?"

"Take it easy, Mally," says the DarkDoc, his palm pleading patience. "We're helping them."

Arronax and Vega enter the room too, then Keke limps in.

"Zack!" Keke says, eyes sparkling despite her obvious pain.

Zack looks up and smiles at her. "Keke."

Arronax looks at the bodies. "We've got to move them."

"We can't," says Morgan. "Not till they emerge. Too risky."

"We have to."

"What if there's some kind of break in connection? It's better to wait."

"Listen to me," says Arronax. "The world outside is mayhem, and it's ramping up."

"There are people after us," says Mally, thinking of Govender and those whom he has no doubt told about Arronax. "It's just a matter of time before they find us."

"Which people?" asks Zack.

"Bot Hunters."

"Because of me," says Vega.

"Not because of you," says Mally. "Because they're mouth-breathing meatbags who have less intelligence in their whole body than you have in your little finger."

"I killed a human," says Vega.

Keke stares. "What?"

"It was self-defence," says Mally. "Vega saved my life, but now they want her RTS-ed."

Zack blinks and shakes his head. Despite his inherent knowledge of where he originally comes from, a lot of this strange 2036 world is new to him.

"Return To Sender," says Morgan. "The Special Task force has been briefed to round up all the roguebots. The problem is, you can't tell if an android is corrupt just by looking at them, so now they're just arresting indiscriminately."

"If they focussed on the Bot Hunters instead, things would be better."

"Mally," says Morgan, gently, "I don't think you realise the gravity of the situation. The special police—"

"I do realise! I'm not a child! But if—"

"The V1R1S is spreading quicker than any pandemic in history. They're saying it's got an infection rate of one thousand. One thousand! Do you know what that means? For every one robot with the disorder they will infect another thousand." The DarkDoc's face is ashen, as if he, too, didn't understand the implications of the V1R1S until he spoke it out loud. It's all happened so quickly.

Arronnax moves towards the exterior glass wall, looks down at the city they have just traversed. Fires smoke and shimmer. Apoca-pirates throw rocks at storefronts and grab jewellery they'll never need. Roguebots and alt-tech nazis clash in the streets with vektors and tasers and roscoes and hand-to-hand combat. She watches as a few city cowboys look up at the building and decide to enter.

"We all need to move to the safe room right now."

"You didn't tell us there was a safe room," says Morgan.

Sounds start emanating from the lower floors: it won't be long till the security has been compromised.

"It's not safe to move them," says Morgan, "but it's not as dangerous as staying in here."

Zack unclamps the break on Silver's gurney, and the DarkDoc takes Kate's. Arronax leads the way.

"I expected Seth to be here by now," says Zack in a low voice. "He needs to be here for it to work."

Bernard grunts in agreement.

"For what to work?" asks Keke.

"Nothing."

Keke whips around to face Zack. "It doesn't sound like nothing."

"I'll re-phrase it. It's nothing for you to worry about."

Keke side-eyes him. "I'm watching you, Zachary Girdler."

"Noted," says Zack.

"I'm not fucking around. I've got my eagle eye on you."

"Damn, I missed you," says Zack.

Their eyes connect for a moment; they keep moving forward.

The steel gurneys rattle down the wide white passage.

CHAPTER 89

SKELETON TURNS TO ICE

Arronax receives an emergency email from an anonymous source at NASP. Thinking it's about the security breach at the hands of Govender, she opens it, and immediately regrets her decision. She tries to close it, delete it, but it's too late. Shaking, she switches off her interface. Whoever is hacking her is already boring his way in, and there's no getting him out. He'll find out who she is and what she's done and broadcast it, and it'll be the end of everything for her. Her whole skeleton turns to ice.

CHAPTER 90
DRAGON DAGGER

White Mezzanine, 2036

Kate feels the weight of the knife in her hand. "I'm not going to kill you."

"It's the only way," says Silver.

"There must be another way."

"There's not!"

"It's impossible."

"You won't be killing me. You'll be saving me. If you don't do it, I'll be stuck here forever, and you know what? I'd rather die! I'd rather die a hundred times over than be in this place."

At last there's some colour in her cheeks; her eyes are feral.

"Please!" she says. "Please, Mom. I can't do it myself. You have to do it for me."

"You know I can't!" Kate throws the dagger on the bed. "How could I?"

"How could you? Think of me! Think of me in the real world, stuck in my useless body forever."

Kate holds her head as if her cool palms will stop her thoughts from exploding her brain.

This is crazy. This is so crazy. It's all a dream. It must be.

Kate's countdown timer clicks over to nine minutes.

"Nine minutes," says Kate.

Silver scrambles for the dragon dagger, puts it back into Kate's hand.

"We have to do it now. Right now."

"How can I?"

"Straight into my heart. It'll be the quickest."

"I can't!" shouts Kate.

"Stop being so selfish!"

Kate splutters. "What?"

"The reason you can't do it is because you're thinking about yourself! How it will make *you* feel. Not what it will do for me."

Kate stutters.

"Please, Mom. Please. I'm asking you to set me free."

Eight minutes.

Seven and a half minutes.

Kate swallows hard. "Lie on the bed."

Silver sobs in relief and climbs onto the stretcher, eyes stunned wide. Pills scatter to the floor. Silver clasps her hands together over her stomach. Her hair splays: silver thread on the white pillowcase.

"Thank you!" She sobs. "Thank you, Mom."

"Sh-sh-sh," says Kate. "Don't say anything else."

Before I change my mind.

Don't say anything else.

This isn't real life.

I'm not killing her. I'm setting her free.

Still the dagger feels too heavy in her hands.

Seven minutes.

"I'm ready," says Silver. "I love you."

Kate's eyes burn. She swallows again and lifts the dagger using both her hands.

It's not real.

It's a fairytale.

She is the huntsman after Snow White's heart.

"I love you," Kate says, and drives the knife into Silver's chest.

. . .

Kate feels the blade penetrating the rib-bone, then with an extra push it gives way. Silver shrills in pain, and Kate lets go of the dagger as if it's shocked her.

Fuck!

She instantly regrets what she's done; she must be insane. Certifiable. To do something as depraved as this. Silver keeps screaming, thrashing on the bed. Blood begins to wick into the white cotton of her gown.

"I'm sorry!" Kate's tears drip down onto the bed. She hadn't even realised she was crying.

What have I done? What the fuck have I done?

Silver's screaming transforms into a low moan, and her writhing slows. She's half-sobbing again, relieved, her eyes alight as if she can see the other side. Her small damaged starfish of a hand searches blindly for Kate's, and they hold onto each other while Silver's chest bleeds and her heart drifts away.

Is she dead?

Silver's image starts deconstructing. Blocks like giant pixels shift and dissolve. Right there on the bed in front of her, as she's holding Silver's hand, she fades away as if she's a computer-generated dandelion blown in the wind. And just like that, the room is empty and Silver is free.

CHAPTER 91

CRIMSON CHEMICAL COPPER

Kate's shattered. She needs time to recover, but there is none.

Six minutes.

She calls up her interface but it doesn't work. She tries again.

"Escape," she says. "Escape." She's still there in the white room.

I'm going to be lost inside here forever.

She tries blinking 'force quit' but the button isn't there. Barbed tendrils of adrenaline reach up and unfurl inside her.

Don't panic, she tells herself. *You know what to do. You know how to force quit.*

Kate reaches for the knife so she can open her own veins, but it's gone—disappeared with Silver.

Fu-u-uck!

Desperate, she looks around the room. What did Silver use on her first attempt? Kate spots the mirror and tries to smash it, but it's self-healing mercury glass and just knits itself back together. She casts around, trying to swallow her panic, trying to stay calm so that she can think clearly.

Five minutes.

Then she sees the pills on the porcelain tiles, knocked off the bed in Silver's rush to climb on. Kate falls to her knees and begins to pick them up, starts shoving them in her mouth and looking for water before realising they will never work in time. And Silver said to not eat or drink anything here, anything that could tie her body to this place. She imagines Silver smashing the glass of water out of her hand. Kate spits the bitter blue pills out into her palm. She needs a quicker way, but they are all she has.

Kate thinks of Seth's snaffeine, of Keke's pexidine, knows how quickly and efficiently drugs can work if they're inhaled. She put the mound of pills on the white tiled floor and smashes them under her boot heel, grinds them as quickly as she can into a rocky powder, then snorts the blue talc off the thumb joint of her hand. The first hard sniff is like a sapphire bullet in her brain. The sparks shoot up her nose and detonate. Kate cries out, covers her nose with both hands—a reflex—and gasps in pain. Her eyes stream, her brain chokes.

Holy fuck, what is in *these things?*

Kate can hardly see what she's doing for the second round as the sparks obliterate her vision. She does the best she can to line up the next dose and sniffs again. Another bullet, another explosion. The jerk of pain sends her body reeling backwards.

"A-a-a-h," is all she can say as the drug burns into her brain. It's like eating a fresh birdseye chilli and having brain freeze at the same time, squared, cubed, times a hundred, and in flashing neon blue. But it's working. Kate can feel the synapses begin to shut off, the electrical impulses lose their juice. She has to get all of this in before she passes out. Her heart is slowing already.

Three minutes.

She lines up another shot, then another, then another, till all that's left of the powder is a fine dust on the floor tiles. The last dose is the trickiest, but the least painful, because her whole face is now completely numb. Kate struggles to keep her eyes open as the drugs pull her eyelids down, start dragging her whole body onto the floor, as if gravity is leaking into the room and pushing on every part of her, even her cheek-skin into her skull, even her eyeballs into their sockets.

It's working, she thinks, but then there's a strange fluid sensation at the back of her damaged sinuses and Kate thinks it's her body's way of fighting back, that it's all going to come back out again, and she can feel the pressure build and the next thing there is liquid gushing out of her nose and mouth. She expects it to be snot and saliva but when she forces open her eyes for the last time sees it's blood. It flows out of her and puddles on the tiles. Liquid crimson chemical copper. Then an invisible tidal wave flattens her and she lies spreadeagled on the floor, waiting for oblivion. She doesn't see the clock tick down to 00:00.

CHAPTER 92

BLOOD HANDKERCHIEF

The Lipworth Foundation
Johannesburg, 2036

The door to Arronax's office stands ajar. Arronax hesitates outside. Has the power already been cut? Is it too late for Silver and Kate? She tentatively pushes open the door.

Seth is sitting inside the room. He looks up at her, relief washing down his face. The door to the adjoining safe room is closed and a small red light flashes.

Arronax is about to run to hug him but stops when she sees his state. Seth's body is perforated, his knee is swollen to twice its normal size, and he's holding a piece of cloth in his hand, stained red. A blood handkerchief.

"What… Are you okay?"

"Define 'okay'," he says, coughing.

"Why is the safe room closed?" she asks.

"I don't know, I tried my code but it's not working."

Arronax tries to unlock the safe room door with her retina but it doesn't work. She punches in a code manually but it stays locked and the red light keeps flashing.

"Is Kate here?"

Arronax doesn't have to answer, because from behind her hurry in Zack, Bernard, the DarkDoc, Keke, Mally and Vega, and they're pushing two gurneys between them. He shoots up, grimacing when he sees it's Kate and Silver on the beds.

Arronax notices how Seth looks at Keke. Relief that she's alive, but that's not all.

Mally hugs Seth.

"What the hell happened?"

"The power's still on?" asks Zack. No one answers; they don't need to. The lights are on. The power has not yet been cut. They still have some time: minutes, maybe seconds. The clock reads 13:58.

"Come on, Kate," says Keke, holding on to the bed rails. "Come back to us."

Kate's face is pale and without expression.

Silver starts gasping, and they all crowd around her.

"What is it?" asks Seth, his eyes mad. "What's happening to her?"

Morgan takes Seth by the shoulder and leads him to a chair. "You need to sit down. You look like you're about to pass out."

Seth shakes him off. "Just tell me what the fuck is going on. What did you do to them?"

Silver gasps for air as if she is drowning.

"What's happening?" Keke is desperate. "Can't you help her?"

"It's good. It means she's surfacing."

"She's choking to death!"

"She's not," says Arronax. "She's coming back to us."

Silver writhes and gulps. Her eyes roll back so far it looks like she has giant pearls for eyes.

Seth elbows his way to the side of Silver's bed, unties her wrists. He levers her limp torso against his chest, cradles her small body. He holds the back of her bandaged head, pushes his cheek up against hers, tries to infuse her with his warmth and what's left of his vitality. He kisses her cheek hard.

Silver starts blinking, and her eyes spin back to normal. One last gasp that seems to take all the oxygen out of the atmosphere and then she's there, back in the room with them, body and mind.

"Silver!" says Mally, and grabs her other hand.

Silver sits there, taking in the surroundings. She looks down at her chest, then back up at her family. She swallows hard and is about to say something when Kate starts gasping in exactly the same way, and they crowd around her, too. Kate's surfacing is more violent. She thrashes around as if she's fighting someone in a dream. She retches and shouts.

"Kate," says Morgan. "Everything's okay. Can you hear me? Silver's okay."

Kate retches again, and then her body starts vibrating with some kind of seizure. Bright blood trickles out of her nose.

"Shit!" shouts Keke. "What's happening to her?"

"I don't know," says the DarkDoc. "Kate? Kate? Can you hear me?" He tries to feel her pulse with his fingers but she is flailing too much.

"Mom!" shouts Mally.

"If she doesn't come out of it right now then it's too late," says Arronax.

The thin blood runs and gets onto everything. Her whole body shakes, every part of her. Seth takes her hand like he did with Silver and the seizure stops. And then it's worse because her limbs and mouth go slack and she looks dead. The only colour in her face is that bright red smear of blood. It's as if her body cools and shrinks right in front of them.

"Kate?" Unadulterated fear tears Seth's voice like a piece of paper. "Kate!"

Enormous seconds tick by.

"Mom," says Silver, in a little-girl voice.

There's a hint of movement on Kate's face, an almost invisible twitch of an eyebrow.

"It's over," says Arronax. "We're out of time."

The clock ticks over to 14:00.

Zack swears loudly and kicks a nearby chair. Bernard covers her face with her hands. Keke's eyes stream.

In the distance: wild whooping and crashing. Clattering.

"They're going to be able to get in here, now," says Arronax, eyes flashing with fear. It's only a safe room when the power is on. They know I'm here. They'll kill us all."

"Mom," Silver says again, with more power, and she reaches over and takes her mother's limp hand. As Silver touches Kate, it's as if she's given her an electric shock, because Kate jolts up and her eyes click open. Kate turns her head to see Silver and they look into each other's eyes. Their chests rise and fall with hard breaths, and then the lights go out.

CHAPTER 93

TWEAK

"Silver?" says Kate, "are you okay?"

Silver nods. The two of them are helped out of their beds, and the others push the gurneys to the side of the room. Keke cleans the blood off Kate's face, and Mally brings them water to drink.

"Barricade the doors," says Arronax, and Morgan and Bernard do so, fumbling in the dark.

"It's not going to hold," says Morgan. "We need something heavier."

"We need to get into the safe room."

Arronax tries to unlock the safe room door again, and is again denied access.

Instead they lock the latch of the office door manually with the deadbolt, then they push a couch and a filing cabinet against the door. "They'll just batter it open, anyway," says Morgan. "They'll find their way in."

"I don't understand," says Mally. "Why would they want to come in here? Isn't there enough to plunder in the rest of the building?"

"It's because I'm in here," says Arronax.

Mally turns to her in the dark. "But why?"

"They blame me for the roguebot attack."

"Because Nautilus engineered them? Because you champion their rights?" asks Mally.

Arronax taps a spherical battery-powered touch lamp and brings it to the middle of the room, and it's like the moon is there with them. Their long shadows paint the walls.

Arronax's face is a mask. "Because I designed the V1R1S."

CHAPTER 94

BLOODTHIRSTY BOT HUNTERS

Mally's affronted. "You did *not.*"

Arronax looks at him with cold pools for eyes. "I'm afraid I did."

Kate can't think of anything to say. *Is this really happening? Is this the real world?*

"Arro," says Seth, deadly serious. "What the fuck are you talking about?"

Arronax takes a deep breath. Her skin is ceramic in the lunar light. "It's my fault. All of this. Everything. I designed the V1R1S."

"No, you didn't." Kate's voice is hoarse. "You wouldn't."

"That doesn't make any sense," says Seth, coughing into his handkerchief. "Why would you want your machines to malfunction?"

Kate notices Seth's blood and her stomach turns to stone.

"I didn't. I don't. I just made a mistake with … I didn't think the design through properly. Rather … the actual design is perfect, I know it is. It's the delivery system that—"

"I can't believe what you're saying."

"It was supposed to be an improvement! It was the smallest tweak in code. All it was supposed to do was to allow the robosapiens to say 'no'."

"You programmed artificial intelligence to refuse humans' instructions."

"They deserve the right to say 'no'!"

"Jesus, Arronax."

"It was meant to improve their existence."

Keke crosses her arms in front of her. "Have you seen the clips? That hotel butler who crushed that woman? That school bus that drove off the bridge with fifty kids in it?"

Arronax's hands fly up to her face. "I know."

"Do you?"

"I know!" Arronax shouts. "I know, okay? Do you think this is easy for me? None of it was meant to happen. The tweak was supposed to be an insignificant upgrade. But, somehow—"

Seth paces, limping, in the near-dark. "I can't fucking believe this."

Kate's again caught by the idea that this isn't really happening.

"Part of the problem was I couldn't access all the machines, I couldn't do a recall. Not without drawing attention to what I was trying to do. So … I had this idea. I was looking at my flu vax sticker and then it came to me. I made the code … contagious. It was the only way to spread it. I tested it and tested it till I was certain it was safe. But I think that it must have somehow, I don't know … mutated. Like a real virus does when faced with resistance. I can't explain it."

Seth sits down with a grimace, and rubs his eyes.

"Regardless of who is responsible for the uprising," says Zack, "we have more important things to discuss."

"More important?" Mally looks at him. "Are you serious? There is a horde of vicious Bot Hunters moments away from breaking down that door and killing us all, and you have something else you'd like to discuss."

Zack regards everyone in the room. "What if I told you there's a way to escape?"

Mally looks at the barricaded door. "Not very likely."

There is a huge bang from outside, then another one.

"Fuck," says Kate. Not particularly eloquent, but at the moment it's all she can manage.

Bernard and Morgan shore up the barricade with whatever pieces of furniture they can grab in the dark. The hammering continues. They'll break right through soon. The Bot Hunters outside are yelling and the sound makes Kate's heart pulse neon green.

"She should be here by now," says Bernard.

"Who?" asks Kate. She's so relieved to have made it back but this, here and now, feels just as much of a dream as her immersion did. A dark room, Arro confessing, bloodthirsty Bot Hunters baying at the door. She grabs Silver and holds her close. Bernard doesn't answer her.

"She'll be here," says Zack.

CHAPTER 95

SHOULDER CROW

The horde finally manages to break a hole in the door. An arm comes through, crusted and grimy, and searches for the handle. It can't reach. Instead they continue to chip away at the aperture, through which flows a stream of angry cursing, and the smoky scent of civil war. Kate clutches Silver to her; imagines what the savages would do to her delicate daughter.

A hologram avatar appears in the middle of the room: an ivory crossbow with a diamond-tipped arrow on a white disc.

Zack and Bernard both look relieved. The light on the safe room door changes from red to green, and then it swings open. Solonne walks out, glowing in her trademark white robe.

"Solonne," Kate says. Could this scene be any more surreal? The robe is like a beacon of light in the dim room.

"What are you doing here?"

Arronax touches the top of her head, as if something has occurred to her for the first time. Her mouth hangs open.

"It's you. *You're* the anonymous founder of the Lipworth."

Kate considers all the white everywhere, from the tiles to the ceiling—she should have guessed Solonne had something to do with it. The limbo where Silver was trapped was white too.

How long had Solonne been in the safe room? How did she manage to get here unscathed? Then Kate remembers the SurroTribe, and how handy they are at guarding important people. She pictures hundreds of SurroSisters all over the city with their white uniforms and bows and arrows, like glowing sentinels, or angels. The green light on the safe room door fades and dies. There will be no more locking it now.

There's a howl from behind the main door, and the hole is quickly widening.

"We don't have much time," says Solonne to Zack. "Have you explained the situation?"

"Not yet. Kate's just come out of the Mezzanine. I haven't told her anything."

Not for lack of trying. Kate remembers the day she met Zack in the unisex bathroom at The Gordhan so long ago. *I have to tell you something,* he had said urgently to her, before he was whisked away by the cops. It's haunted her for twelve years; a grey-feathered shoulder crow. Kate is ready to listen.

The opening in the door is now large enough for a man to claw his way through. As he crams his arms and shoulders in, Bernard whips him on the back of the head with her steel baton, knocking him out and temporarily plugging the hole.

"You get out here, you robofucker!" shouts one of the mob from outside.

"Your machines killed my brother!" yells someone else.

"Come out here or we'll kill you all!"

Kate trembles as the dread billows and swirls around her like dirty wind. They'll break in here. Who will they murder first?

"Ow, Mom," says Silver, and Kate loosens her grip.

Arronax's face is a tight mask; her hair is pulsing purple.

"Don't even think about it," says Seth, coughing. Kate imagines his lungs bubbling with blood.

"I have to."

"Are you crazy? Do you know what they'll do to you?"

Arronax's body language is firm with resolve. "I'm going."

"That's insane," says Kate. "You'll be dead within a minute."

"If they have me they'll leave you alone."

"No, they won't," says Seth.

Keke and the kids watch with wide eyes.

"Even if they don't, it'll buy you some extra time."

"You're not going out there, Arro," says Seth. "No way."

Solonne clears her throat. "It's the right thing to do."

"It's crazy!" says Seth. "I won't let you!"

Arronax moves closer to Seth and lowers her voice. "You've never told me what to do. Don't start now."

"Please don't do it. They'll rip you to shreds."

"I'll get what I deserve."

The thudding on the door is louder now, as if the men outside have found something heavy to barge it with.

"No one deserves that. You made a mistake."

"A mistake that killed a hundred thousand people."

"You meant well."

"You know what they say about the road to hell, right?"

"All we need is five minutes," says Solonne. "Then we'll be safe."

Arronax nods. "It's the least I can do."

CHAPTER 96
SOUL SHARD

"I'll go with you," says Vega. "Protect you."

"So you'll *both* die? No way!" says Mally.

"We won't die. My roscoe is fully loaded and my jujitsu is on fleek."

"It's too risky."

"Mally," says Solonne. "Do you trust me?"

Mally turns towards her. "Of course." Everyone in the room knows he wouldn't be alive if it weren't for Solonne.

"Then, please, listen to reason. Let Arro and Vega distract them while we escape."

"Escape?" says Keke, motioning at the battered door. "There's nowhere to escape to!"

"What if they're killed?"

"At least *we'll* be alive," Solonne says. "If they don't go out there … it's over for all of us."

Morgan says in a low voice, "They're going to die either way."

The words hang in the air.

"I don't want to live without Vega." Mally blinks away hot tears. "She's everything."

"Think of your mother, and Seth, and Silver. Everyone in this room will die if you don't let them go."

Mally starts sobbing.

"Don't worry, Purest Human," says Vega. She unbuttons her top again, just like she did hours ago, for a completely different reason. Sex and death, magnetically entwined, forever pushing and pulling at one another.

Vega reveals her chest, and opens the pocket that lies over her heart. She clicks out a ruby DNA chip with her star-shaped Alpha Lyrae logo on it: her Soul Shard.

"Everything I am is in this chip."

"It's not *you,* though," cries Mally.

"It is," Vega says, touching her breastbone: warmed titanium under stamped silicone. "This body, this is the thing that's not me. I can get another one of these, but that chip is nothing but me. Do you understand?"

"No!" Mally shouts through his tears. "If you're going out there, I am too!"

There's a massive thud on the door that dislodges the shored-up furniture. Bernard and Zack rush to pack it back.

Zack gives Arronax a soft look. "If you're going, now is the time."

"You're not going!" Mally sobs.

"Mally. Mally. I need to tell you something," whispers Vega.

"It won't change anything," cries Mally. "Nothing you say will change how I feel about you."

"I have the V1R1S."

"What? No, you don't."

"I do. That man from NASP—"

Mally remembers Govender interfering with Vega's hardware. Remembers the flash disk he plugged into Vega's neck, the LED lighting up, and then the quick stashing of it in the inside pocket of his flashy new suit.

"No." Mally shakes his head. "Oh, no."

"This body is broken." Vega takes Mally's chin in her hand. "Look at it."

Mally blinks and studies Vega. Her head is still conked in from last night's attack, and the silicone skin is coming away from where Arronax sutured it back onto her silver skull. She has a frozen neck joint, and a pronounced limp from her broken ankle. He imagines the insidious virus teeming all over her insides, painting over her code with evil. Once it takes over completely, she'll kill him as if he means nothing to her.

Oh, his heart is breaking. Right there, right then, it's as if someone is squeezing it right inside his chest cavity. The pain blooms inside his chest like the smoke of an atom bomb. It takes every ounce of will he has to stay standing, instead of melting down to his knees.

It hurts so much.

"This body is broken, but my Shard is pure." Vega puts it in Mally's hand and closes his fingers over it.

Mally tries to rise above the ache. "I love you," he says, almost knocking her over with a bear hug. "I love you, Alpha Lyrae."

Vega steps away. "I know."

Mally looks as if he's about to say something, and Vega smiles. "I love you too, Purest Human."

"It's settled, then," says Arronax, smoothing her hair. It turns a serious shade of aubergine and makes her look even paler than before. Another huge bang on the door and the furniture is again dislodged.

Zack moves to kiss Arronax on the cheek, and as he does so, he slips a quill into her pocket. They exchange a look of understanding.

Seth hugs Arronax, grasps her hand. She offers Seth his Vektor back, but he refuses. He disables the bio-info in his name and adds her dynap code in its place. He shows her the trigger, and how to hold the Vektor so it doesn't kick back too hard. They look into each other's eyes as if there is more to say.

Arronax breaks away and hammers on the door with the heel of her hand. "I'm coming out!" she shouts. "Stand down! Stand down and I'll come out!"

Seth coughs up more blood. The horde outside quietens a little.

Mally puts the Shard in his pocket, and he kisses Vega goodbye. The tears are still running down his face. Kate catches Vega's eye and nods, and Vega nods back. They move the furniture away from the door to allow Arronax and Vega passage. Seth puts his arm around the still-sobbing Mally. They open the door just enough, and the two women slip out.

"Get into the safe room," says Solonne. "Quickly."

CHAPTER 97

SHIELD

Arronax and Vega hold on to each other as they move out of the room and into the clutches of the mob. Arronax holds the Vektor in a way she hopes makes her look like she's used the weapon before.

"Why did you lie to Mally?" she whispers to Vega, "about being infected?"

The deceit had shocked Arronax. Not because she knows Vega doesn't have the V1R1S, but because she built, refined, and polished the design for 7thGen robosapiens, and she knows for a fact it's impossible for them to be dishonest.

"It was the only way he'd let me go."

The dirty pack grabs at the women and pulls them away from the door, to the middle of the crowd. There must be two dozen people there, all shouting at them. A man hawks and spits in Arronax's face. When she wipes the saliva away, her trembling hands betray her fear. The barbarians are armed with solar lamps and makeshift weapons and guns. Arronax and Vega turn around slowly within the circle, not wanting to turn their backs on any one of them for too long. When Arronax sees Govender, the NASP imposter, she trains the gun on him. He's out of place in his smart blue suit in the tide of ripped and grimy ragbag uniforms of the Bot Hunters.

Arronax stiffens with anxiety; her mouth is cotton.

"Ah, look," says one of them. "She's brought her robowhore with her."

A man with a Vektor takes aim, and Vega moves instinctively in front of Arronax to act as a shield.

"Wait," Govender says. "I've been dreaming of this moment for months. I want to enjoy this."

Arronax realizes Govender is the one who's been beaming her death threats.

"Fuck that," says one of the men. "They're mine." He takes aim again and the suit knocks the weapon out of his hand. "What the—" He rolls his hands into fists, ready to fight, and Govender pulls out a subrocket from the breast pocket of his shiny jacket and shoots the Bot Hunter in the head. Maroon brain matter sprays out of the back of his skull and he falls to the floor. This shocks a few people in the crowd, arouses others. Ready for blood, they rumble forward.

It's only been a minute. Not long enough for the others to escape.

Govender points his rocket at Arronax now, and searches her face. She returns his scowl with the glare of the Vektor. Her trigger finger twitches, but if she shoots him it might set off the rest of them.

Arronax needn't have worried; the men advance steadily without any encouragement from her. Her hair turns white.

It's a strange thing, when you know you're about to die. It's not like your life flashes before your eyes, not really. It's more like a total surrender of everything, from your fondest childhood memories to the designs you'll never complete, to the feeling of your lover's skin on yours. Regrets and joy swirl together into a strange bittersweet moment of absolute clarity, a crystal instant when you realise you'll never see the ocean again, never again sink your feet into the soft warm sand or hear the waves crash and roar, and you're strangely accepting of it because the knowledge pulses in your chest that in this lifetime you've loved more than you've lost.

"All right," Govender says to the hopped-up horde, "take them apart."

The Bot Hunters are an arm's length from them, now less, and Arronax starts shooting. She takes out four or five of the men before they wrench the gun out of her hands and she screams as they struggle. Their hungry paws grab at her body. A blue-eyed man with a rusted blade is ready to drive it into Arro's stomach.

Arronax roots around in her lab coat pocket for the quill, uncaps the injection pen, and, beneath her lab coat, jams it into her thigh. There is a hot current to her heart.

She hugs Vega close.

"Ready?" Arronax whispers, feeling the drug taking hold. Vega nods.

"Now."

Vega pops open her shoulder cap and Arronax presses the red self-destruct button. There's a flash of impossible white as Vega detonates, and the concentrated explosion takes out everybody in the room so quickly no one lives to hear the sound of the bomb.

CHAPTER 98

GENESIS CHILD

They rush into the darkness of the safe room. Solonne closes the door behind them and stands with her back against it. Bernard lends her weight to it, too. She can't lock it without power, but the heavy steel door will offer some measure of protection.

"Get down," she says, and they do. Kate pushes Silver to the floor and covers her with her own body.

There's a loud flash and a boom.

The building shakes.

"The fuck was that?" says Seth, not wanting to know the answer.

Debris rains down around them. Kate lets Silver go. The safe door swings open, allowing them a dim view of the main door that has been knocked off its hinges. Shrapnel from the exploded furniture crackles on the floor. The barbarians are dead, but Kate knows there'll be more on their way.

Seth and Mally look desolate.

"Let's run for it," says Keke.

"No," says Solonne. "There're a hundred more of them on their way in. There's no way we'll get out in time."

Kate breathes in the heavy black air. Smoke burns her eyes.

There's a scratching sound, and then a spark and the smell of phosphorous and chlorate as Solonne lights a match, and then a candle.

. . .

"You need to listen very carefully for the next minute," says Zack. He has everyone's attention. "There's only one way to get out of here, and we need to move fast."

Kate looks at the broken door and the dead bodies outside, coated in blood and ash.

"Kate, Silver, you're the ones who know how to do it."

"No I don't," says Kate. "I have no idea."

"You do, because you've just done it. You two escaped the Mezzanine, which is a lot more difficult than this will be. It was essential practice, and you succeeded."

"Experience Points," says Silver.

"Exactly," says Zack. "And now you're ready."

Keke touches her bandaged back and grimaces. "Ready for what?"

"For the next level," says Solonne.

Kate's brain whirrs. "I don't understand. This is real life, not an immersion. There is no next level. Unless you mean—"

Zack looks into her eyes and Kate finds she can't look away. Violet Velcro.

"Unless you mean *dying*," says Kate.

Zack doesn't break eye contact. "Think of it as levelling up."

Kate feels as if her head is imploding in a hundred shades of neon.

"Did you just say what I thought you said?"

"We don't have much time," says Solonne, flames in her cheeks. "We need to do it now. The others are close."

"That day at The Gordhan when I said I needed to tell you something. It wasn't the right time or place then because you weren't ready to hear it."

"Zack's entire existence is for you, about you," says Solonne. "You think it was a coincidence that he worked with Keke on that trial?" She gestures around the room. "Do you think any of this is a coincidence?"

"The prophecy," says Keke.

Solonne nods. "Yes."

"That prophecy was about *Mally,*" says Kate. "The Genesis Child will lead us to the ledge. Mally's the Genesis child."

"Are you sure about that?" asks the Matriarx.

"Of course I am. You told me so, yourself."

"You heard what you wanted to hear. You think of Mally as the stronger child, but Silver is the one. You've seen her super-abilities. Silver's always been the one."

Kate thinks of Silver's Atrium jack-in pod. 'GK' the engraving had said. Kate knows there's always been something different about Silver, knows deep down that what

Solonne is saying is true. *Impossible to kill,* the guy at the Atrium had said. *Ghost. Genesis Kid.*

"But what does it mean?"

"What does it mean?" says Solonne. "It means that when Silver turns sixteen it'll be the end of everything."

"I'll be sixteen in a few hours," says Silver.

"Which is why I created the Mezzanine," says Solonne.

Kate splutters.

"I needed you to break Zack out of SkyRest, and I needed you to both get meshed in order to understand what we're about to tell you. There was no way you'd agree to free Zack or get the neural lace without me forcing your hand by trapping Silver in the Mezzanine."

"Forcing my hand?" Kate says, fury burning a hole in her stomach. "I almost died at SkyRest. I was almost torn apart. I had brain surgery without anaesthetic. *I had to kill my daughter.* Do you have any idea—?"

"I'm sorry. I wish it had been easier for both of you."

"You're *sorry?*" says Kate.

"The V1R1S mutation," says Keke, looking at Solonne, her understanding beginning to dawn, "That was also you."

"I had help," Solonne says, looking at the DarkDoc, who has a shadow on his face Kate's never seen before. Bernard stands guard at the door.

"You fuckers," says Keke. "Solonne. Zack. Morgan. You were all in on it."

Kate's rage builds, her hands are fists.

Seth coughs and spits blood on the floor. "And you let Arro believe she had caused the rebellion when all she was trying to do was to make the world a better place. And you let her walk out of here to claim a redemption she didn't even need."

"Don't worry about Arronax," says Solonne. "We took care of her."

"You certainly did." The candelight flickers in Seth's eyes.

Kate looks at Morgan and thinks of being in bed with him, how uninhibited she was. How sick she feels with the intimate betrayal. How could she have allowed this to happen to her again, to trust and be betrayed like this *again?* She thinks of Marmalade James and wants to scream and pull out her hair. She wants to punch them all. She wants get out of this room where tentacles of claustrophobia are reaching for her breath.

"You said you sent Silver *home.*"

"I know it's difficult to hear, Kate," says Morgan, "but we did it for you."

CHAPTER 99

WORLD'S WORST JEHOVAH'S WITNESS

Too many far-out concepts hover in the air around Kate; she can't get a handle on what is happening, what is really happening. Not what people want her to believe, not what is easy to believe, but the real truth of this moment. How does this all fit together? The betrayal is a stab of bitter on her tongue, a hint of cyanide, like chewing an apple seed. How fitting.

"So how do we get out of here?" asks Keke.

"They want us to kill ourselves," says Kate. "That's how we surfaced from the Mezzanine."

"Seems a little counterintuitive," says Seth, coughing. "We're trying to stay alive here, in case you've forgotten." Kate can tell he's finding it harder and harder to breathe.

"After all we've been through!" Kate paces. "Van der Heever, Mouton, Jackson, Lumin. Fighting to stay alive, fighting to keep the kids alive. After all of that, you want us to kill ourselves."

"Don't think of it as killing yourself," says Zack.

"Ha," says Seth. "I know where this is going. Here's a gun! But don't think of it as a gun. Here's a knife! But don't think of it as a knife. The power of positive thinking, right?"

Zack shakes his head. "All those people I helped—"

"Killed," says Keke. "All those people you killed."

"I saved them."

"Saved them? Is that what they're calling it nowadays?"

"What Ramphele didn't tell you is that all those people wanted to die."

"So … you're an angel of mercy now."

"They were all suffering. All I did was introduce them to the truth."

"And what's that?"

"That they could escape this reality for a better one. That they can enter the larger domain of reality above this world."

"Oh my God," says Keke. "Seriously? Escape this reality for a better one? You're a fucking evangelist? Are you going to tell us you're the world's worst Jehovah's Witness now?"

"Best Jehovah's Witness," says Kate.

"What?"

"Well, he'd be the world's best Jehovah's Witness, wouldn't he? By getting this far?"

"I know it's a difficult concept to get your head around," says Zack.

"Understatement," says Keke.

Kate puts a warm hand on her forehead, as if it will help her to understand. "You're saying … Heaven exists?"

"No," says Zack. "Not unless your version of Heaven means stepping up into the real world."

"Fuck." Seth knuckle-scrubs his hair.

"I'm not asking you to kill yourself," says Zack.

"Really?" says Keke. "That's what it sounds like."

"What I mean is, it's not coming from me. The message."

"Who, then?" asks Kate. "Who sent you?"

Zack's eyes are alight. "You did."

CHAPTER 100

THIS IS WHAT KOOL-AID TASTES LIKE

"Bullshit," says Kate. "I think I would have remembered that."

"It's not something you can remember here."

"Remember *here*?"

"We're not on the same plane of consciousness here. Think of it … think of the place you're going to … as the future."

"Holy fuck. We're time travelling now."

"Not quite."

"Well, that's a relief," snarks Keke.

"Put it this way," says Zack. "The future has already happened."

Kate sits down and gives her thigh a hard pinch. It hurts. "So …" she says, looking up at Zack, speaking slowly and clearly. "You're saying I sent you from the future."

"No, but that's probably the easiest way for you to understand it right now."

There's hollering in the distance. The new barbarians have entered the building. More apoca-pirates are bashing to get in.

"I'm trying to explain it to you in the simplest and quickest way possible, because if this is going to work, we need to do it right now. But I know you won't do it if you don't understand the stakes."

"Tell me, then. Tell me in the simplest way possible."

Zack and Kate's eyes connect. "I need you to have an open mind."

Seth's breathing is worse than ever. He smacks himself on the chest, trying to clear his airways, but it just makes him cough more. His handkerchief is now dripping red.

"Christ on a cracker. Just get on with it," says Keke.

Zack draws a breath. It's clear he has to build himself up to what he's about to say.

"Did you ever wonder how I was able to wipe myself off the security footage at the Carbon Factory?"

"Of course we did," says Keke. "Not just from the footage, but from people's minds too. I questioned every one of those jury members we did duty with and not one of them remembered you from the Lundy trial."

"Impossible," says Kate.

"Not impossible," says Zack. "We've been doing it forever."

"Doing what?"

"Re-programming thoughts. Tweaking memories. Smoothing over glitches."

"What the fuck are you talking about?"

"Are you sure you don't know?" asks Zack. "Because I think that, deep down, you do."

"I don't know anything," Kate says. "Tell me what's going on."

Zack clears his throat, steeples his fingers. "This is a simulation."

Kate blinks. She doesn't understand. "What's a simulation? This room? This day?"

"He means everything," says Keke. "Everything's a simulation. He means our lives have been a simulation."

"*Are* a simulation," says Zack.

"Shut up," says Kate.

"I know it's difficult to hear—really difficult to hear—but I promise you it's true."

Kate stares at him. She was beginning to believe some of the things he said, but now he's gone too far. He's delusional and dangerous and belongs back in the crim colony. Why the fuck had she risked her life to break him out?

"That's why there's a suicide contagion," Zack says. "That's why more and more people are ending their lives here. Not because people are suicidal but because they've learnt the truth—that you need to die in this sim to get back to the real world."

"Whoah," says Keke. "Go home, Girdler, you're drunk."

"It's expected, of course. That you'd be skeptical," he says.

Keke laughs. "The Net knows I like a good mind-fuck, Zachary Girdler, but you have gone too far."

Kate doesn't find it funny at all. "Okay, I can't," she says. "I give up. I can't do this anymore."

Seth coughs. "It's not impossible."

"What?" Kate spins to look at him.

"What he's saying. It's a well-endorsed theory. Scientifically speaking, the odds of this world being a simulation are much higher than it *not* being a simulation."

"Not you too," says Kate. "Mister Never-Drink-the-Kool-Aid. I've got news for you. *This* is the Kool-Aid. This is exactly what the fucking Culty Kool-Aid tastes like."

"No," says Seth. "Kate. I know you don't want to hear this, but mathematically, it makes complete sense. There's very little probability of us *not* living in a simulation."

"Shut up," says Keke, blinking her wide eyes.

"But I can feel that I'm real," says Kate. "I know deep down that I'm real. Nothing you can say will change that."

Zack is gentle with her. "You feel real because that is how you've been programmed to feel. Like a robosapien is programmed to feel human, and they do, because they don't know any better. That's why it's so hard for you to grasp this. You were never meant to hear the truth. You were designed to function within the rules of the game, not to subvert them. By its very nature, it's a box you cannot think outside of."

Being shut in an invisible box is still being shut in a box.

"But the neural lace expands your consciousness," says Solonne. "You've never been able to see the whole truth before, but now you can, if you choose to."

"Quarks," mutters Seth.

"What now?" says Keke.

"Quarks. The rules that govern subatomic particles' behaviour are almost identical to computer codes that correct for errors in manipulating data in computers." When Kate stares at him, he says, "Basically, it looks like everyday particles are being run on computer codes. The universe *is* mathematics. That can only point to one thing: that it's been *designed.* You know the Fibonacci ratio, Kate. We spoke about it the day we found each other again."

"I remember," she says.

"It occurs in so many aspects of the cosmos, and that's just the beginning. The constants of nature—like the strength of fundamental forces—have values that look fine tuned. Even the smallest alterations would mean that atoms would become unstable. That planets would be catapaulted out of their orbits. There's only one possible explanation. The universe—this universe, anyway—has been constructed."

Kate wants to reject what her brother is saying. It's just too far out, too conspiracy-theorist. The conspiracy to end all conspiracies.

"Look at the hyper-reality achieved in the games Silver plays at the Atrium. Our tech is still lagging, but the time will come when it'll be possible for us to create something similar to our universe—allowing us to play God—then it'll stand to reason that a civilisation one level above us with advanced computing power has done the same thing, and that their work is the reason you and I are living and breathing."

"You of all people," Kate says to Seth. Brilliant, cynical Seth. "How can you believe this?"

"It's not about belief, Kate. It's mathematics. I'm not the only one. Bostrom. Minsky. Musk. They all said the same thing. You can't deny science. It's not just plausible, but … inescapable. If you look closely—some might say, too closely—on a molecular level, you'll see that you can only zoom in so much before it gets blurry. Fuzzy."

"Like it's pixellated?" asks Keke.

"Exactly," says Seth. "Look closely enough, and everything is fucking pixellated."

CHAPTER 101

CYBERCOSMIC DUST

"You know all those times you've wondered if this is all there is?" asks Zack. "You know that feeling? Like, surely there must be more to life? Well, now you know why. Because intuitively, you've always known that there's more out there. Kate, you've always known."

Kate understands this is true—the black hole that has been with her forever. Gaping all through her life despite finding her lost twin, despite being reunited with her biological parents, despite giving birth to a child of her own and getting the gift of Mally. The dark vacuum has haunted her for as long as she can remember.

Seth rubs his face. "I feel it too."

"There are other clues," says Zack. "Clues you couldn't understand before now. Before you laced up."

"Like what?" asks Kate.

"Your synaesthesia. Your numbers and colours, the shapes and smells. It's residue from the real world."

Kate thinks of Silver's jack-in pod again, and remembers the slogan splashed in violet on the wall.

As we design, so, perhaps, we were designed.

Kate looks at Silver. "The game you play. You design simulations."

Silver nods.

"Simulations like this."

Silver nods again. "It's called co-creation. It's about beauty and purpose, like art. The players co-construct the worlds they play in."

"So this all makes sense to you."

"Yes," says Silver.

"Silver will lead you," says Solonne. "It's what she was born to do."

The chaos is closer now. Soon they'll be here and then it will all be over, anyway. Even if nothing Zack says is true, a quick, painless suicide in here will be better than being killed by the bloodthirsty barbarians. Who knows what they'll do to her, do to Silver?

The players co-construct the worlds they play in.

The new knowledge shines like a light in Kate's head. She's starting to understand. The beginning thoughts of new concepts stream into her head. Things start to become obvious, when before they were obscured by the everyday drama of her life. The idea of artifice nags at Kate. Hasn't she thought it a hundred times, herself? That her life seems to be on some kind of cruel fictive loop? The burnt orange *deja vu.*

The same story told in spiralling, parallel ways with slight variations: Evil doctor van Heerden; Evil cult leader Lumin. Kate and Seth being abducted as toddlers; Mally and Silver being abducted as small children. Kate breaking her arm—the same arm—over and over. Cutting a chip out of her head in 2021; cutting her head open to insert the mesh in 2034. Rescuing Silver from the Resurrectors; Rescuing Silver from the Mezzanine. Mally falling in love with his robotic puppy; Mally falling in love with Vega. Kate being betrayed by James; Kate being betrayed by Morgan. Kate cutting off James's thumb; Lumin cutting off Silver's little finger. Now, looking at Zack, the familiar stranger, she can't help thinking that she's lived this story before.

You've always known.

A breeze of hot sparks blows inside Kate's head. The fairytale retellings now also make sense. That's what her subconscious was trying to tell her when she was newly meshed and immersed in the Mezzanine. Whoever designed this sim was playing with the story arcs of classic fairytales. Hansel and Gretel was, of course, Kate and Seth being kidnapped as children. After that came The Pied Piper: The outwardly benevolent-looking Maistre Lumin and his rathunters leading the children away. Today's story is Snow White, or Sleeping Beauty: porcelain-skinned Silver under the spell of Solonne, catatonic, waiting to be brought back to life. Kate in the rose maze, Kate in the labyrinth. Abduction, hypnosis, poison, roses, thorns, rescuing, redemption, re-awakening. She knew this. Inherently, she knew this.

As we design, so, perhaps, we were designed.

"This simworld is ending," says Zack. "Soon it'll be nothing more than cybercosmic dust. It's always had this expiry date."

Solonne takes a step closer. "That's what Lumin didn't understand. He thought if he killed the Genesis Child he'd save the world, but this world is broken beyond repair. The fact that the expiry date is the same as Silver's sixteenth birthday is symbolic more than anything else. Nothing anyone does in this sim would change that. Of course, Lumin has a God Complex, and he doesn't listen to sense. He believed his own interpretation of the prophecy, and that he could influence the algorithms by killing Mally. He thought he was saving the world."

"You're in touch with Lumin?" asks Kate.

"I wouldn't say that."

"But he's around?"

"Loosely speaking, yes." Solonne's eyes say: *We haven't seen the last of him.* "He's caused me such headaches, that man."

"He almost derailed the mission when he got me arrested," says Zack. "Twelve brain-bleached years in SkyRest was *not* part of the plan."

"Lumin got you arrested?"

"In an indirect way, yes. Keke only made that deal with Ramphele to avoid arrest so that she could help find the twins and be with Marko when he way dying. Both of those situations were caused by the Resurrectors, led by Lumin."

"But why couldn't you just ... write yourself out of SkyRest?" asks Kate.

"We can smooth over glitches," says Zack. "Breaking out of a high security underground penal labour colony is not a glitch. I never expected to be convicted, but when I was, I thought I'd have time to work something out. Then they drugged me and wiped my memory before I could come up with a strategy to escape. I lost who I was when I was in there. Lost the plan. Lost everything."

"It all worked out, though," says Solonne. "Just like I knew it would. Sometimes we have to trust the process. It actually wrapped up quite neatly. Breaking you out of SkyRest was the perfect qualification challenge for Kate."

"Easy for you to say," says Zack. "You weren't the one getting your brains vacuumed out of your head."

"You needed some Suffering Points, anyway," says Solonne. "Yours were way down."

"Suffering Points are like karma," says Silver to Kate. "You need a certain number before you can level up."

I'm pretty sure we all qualify, now, thinks Kate, looking around at the people she loves. Seth coughing up blood, Keke with her back sliced open, Mally with his heartache, Silver still recovering from the Mezzanine.

"So, the expiry date of this simulation can't be changed," says Zack. "But the sim creator wants you levelled up before that happens."

CHAPTER 102

POISON & LACE

Solonne retrieves a neat metallic case from her white pine-leather shoulder bag.

"This part is easy," says Zack. "Luckily. You've been through the worst."

A light blue breeze of relief.

Solonne opens the case to reveal a neat row of ten narrow gulleys in black foam. Three are empty, and the rest cushion seven injection pens. They're made of the most delicate glass and steel.

"Why the fancy tech?" says Seth. "If what you're saying is true then surely a quick bullet would do the job?"

"No." Zack takes the case from Solonne and snaps out the first of the pens. "Dying is not enough to level up. People think they can just kill themselves to escape this simulation—like they do in Eden 7.0—but this sim is a far more sophisticated system. It's not a game. Its technology is hundreds of years ahead of this reality. You can't just die. You need the tech, too. You need the neural lace."

"An injectable mesh?" says the DarkDoc, inspecting the quill Zack hands him.

"Not just mesh. It's the perfect combination of poison and lace. Think of escaping this sim as a portal that is only open for a couple of seconds. You only get to see that portal as you die, and you only get to go through it if you're meshed. It's a delicate thing."

Zack hands everyone a pen, apart from Solonne.

"You're not coming?" asks Bernard.

"No," says Solonne. "I've done the job I was meant to do."

Kate knows it's not quite as simple as that. There are eight of them in the room, and only seven quills.

"Who has the other three?"

"Arronax had one," says Zack. "Then we sent one to Marko, and one to your mother, but we have no way of knowing if they reached them, and if they'll use them in time."

Her mother! Kate pictures Anne in another dimension, healthy, unravaged, and out of her wheelchair.

The voices are close now.

"Hurry," Solonne urges.

Kate stands on an imaginary ledge. There's nothing underneath her but air the colour of Skiss Sky, wisps, cool trails of cirrus. Open sky everywhere, the crispest air to breathe. She takes giant lungfuls of it. Will she jump? Will she make her kids jump? After all she's been through to keep them alive, is she going to now leap into oblivion with them?

"Fuck," she says.

Keke looks at her with wide eyes. "You can say that again."

"What do we do?"

"We level up or die trying," says Seth.

"Kill ourselves?" says Kate. "Kill the twins?"

Her body feels like it's filled with acid.

"You can't," says Keke. "No way."

Zack steps forward with the case of quills. "It's the only way."

Kate moves to take one but hesitates. "I can't believe we're going to do this."

"Are we?" asks Mally. His eyes are still swollen.

"Holy fuck," says Keke. "Are you really going to do it? You believe this is real?"

"I don't know what I believe," says Kate. "All I know is that if we don't jump right now, someone will be in here to push us. And I'd rather jump."

"Me too," says Silver. "I'm not letting those men touch me."

"I'm dying, anyway," says Seth. "I can feel it. I won't make it through the night."

"You don't know that," says Keke.

"I do. My lungs are liquefying. I won't be able to breathe soon, and I don't want to be here for that. Sim or not, I'm claiming one of those quills."

"Me too," says Mally. "I've got nothing left to live for, anyway."

"Jesus," says Keke.

Kate turns to her. "Come with us."

Keke shakes her head. "I don't like this. I'd rather stay and fight."

"We're completely outnumbered," says Kate. "They're going to stream in here any second. I was almost ... I was almost pulled apart by the creeps at SkyRest ... I'm not letting it happen again. And I'm not going to let it happen to you, either."

Keke still seems undecided. She doesn't have the neural lace that Kate has, so she can't see outside the box, can't see the beginnings of the truth that Kate is glimpsing. How can Kate convince her? Keke's never been one to feel much fear, so Kate changes her angle.

"It'll be an adventure," she says. It's mostly a lie, because she doesn't even know if she believes Zack yet. "It could be one of the best fucking things that ever happens to us."

Or it could be plain suicide.

Keke taps her foot, crosses her arms as she thinks. There is clattering next door.

"It's a gamble, I know," says Kate. "It's fucking metaphysical Russian Roulette. But if there is a way out of here," she gestures at the twins, "I need to take that chance. And I don't want to go without you."

As Kate pictures the spinning barrel of a star-dusted revolver hovering in the air between them, a real gunshot rings out, then another, and her vision is scored by the hard, sharp zigzags of someone's serrated scream of horror. Shark teeth. A clatter and a crystalline crash as more windows are broken. It seems the savages have claimed another victim.

"Keke, please!"

The wound on Keke's back is bleeding again.

"Okay," Keke says. "Okay. I'll do it."

And Kate wonders, with a neon jab in her stomach, if she's doing the right thing, convincing her best friend to poison herself.

CHAPTER 103

RAPTURE PARTY

It's easy enough to inject your own quill, but in an unspoken agreement the family decide to inject each other. They hug, and Seth approaches Mally first, who sets his jaw and offers his right shoulder, and Seth, pale as ivory, administers the mesh. Mally's eyes roll back and Seth lowers him slowly to the floor. A sob catches in Kate's throat. Seth's eyes are also wet.

Kate looks into Silver's eyes.

"Are you sure you want to do this?"

"Yes," she says. "Yes, Mom."

Kate hugs her as tightly as she can, takes her face into her hands and kisses her cheek.

"Brave girl," she says. "You've always been such a brave girl." Kate's crying as she pushes the quill into Silver's arm and catches her as she wilts into her arms. She lays her delicate body next to Mally's.

Morgan gives Kate a flat wave and administers his own shot, as does Bernard. Zack checks each one of their wrists with his fingers to make sure their hearts have stalled.

Keke hugs Kate goodbye. "So, you got what you wanted."

"What?"

"A rapture party! It's perfect. Apart from the distinct lack of funeral cake."

Kate almost laughs. "How can you joke at a time like this?"

"What do you mean?" asks Keke. "Apocalypses are always the best times to joke."

Post-diabetic Keke doesn't flinch at having to inject herself, but Seth takes the pen from her and holds her tightly. She returns the embrace. They're all weeping.

Seth hesitates before shooting her up. "Keke."

"Seth. You don't have to say anything."

"I want to."

Footsteps outside. The smell of the horde reaches them first: The scent of malevolence seethes into the room, sweat and blood and gunpowder.

"We don't have time," says Keke.

"I want you to know how I feel about you."

Keke's eyes soften. She covers his hand with her own shaking fingers and takes her quill back.

"We don't have time," she says, and drives it into her arm.

Keke's body sinks into him, and Kate watches as he holds her, breathing her in for a moment longer, then lays her gently down.

Kate is still crying when she and Seth sit on the floor and squeeze each other's hands.

"Will it work?" Kate asks, looking at her dead children, anxiety like a bright bomb in her skull.

"I don't know," Seth's breath comes in gasps.

She takes a deep, shuddering breath. Her whole body is shaking from the inside out. "I guess there's only one way to find out."

Kate and Seth squeeze each others hands, whispering "I love you," and then tenderly inject one other.

Kate's shocked by the sharp sting of the quill. She can feel the poison painting the inside of her veins. It's exactly as she imagines a jellyfish sting to feel. A swarm, a smack. A bright blue current of venom shooting towards her heart. A rushing feeling in her head.

The barbarians hurtle in. Three, five, then ten of them, slick with fresh blood and stained by death and depravity. Kate sees them leer at Solonne in her white robe and feels sick for her. The rushing sound is taking over Kate's vision now, but she can still make out Zack injecting himself. Zack looks over at Solonne, who nods back, her face betraying her naked fear for just an instant.

Kate's eyeballs spin back and she expects to see darkness, realising then that she doesn't expect to wake up again, but instead there is white thunder, like she's standing in front of a giant waterfall. Kate and Seth fall backwards onto the floor together, still holding hands, and it feels as if they're falling through the floor. They take their last breath, and their souls swoop out of their bodies.

EPILOGUE

NIRVANA 1.0

It's not like waking up.

Not quite. It's more like when you've been daydreaming and then something happens to snap you out of it. You weren't sleeping, but now you're certainly awake. There's a green rush of clear consciousness (Mint Crackle).

Kate's standing in a field of seeding wildflowers. Symbolic, she's sure, of life and death and regeneration. She remembers the garden in her small apartment with James, the black-petalled rose maze at the Luminary, and the creeping wild weeds at the glass-paned Atrium. The word 'atrium' is another word for heart, and it makes sense—a glass heart—as other seemingly unconnected things also all start to make sense to her now: like her colours and shapes. As if she has a more developed perspective now that she's here, as if she's above, or beyond, her previous existence.

Kate's wearing her body-fitting orange catsuit again. It energises her, makes her feel as if she can do anything, like fly through the air. She touches her stomach, her hips, to make sure she's all there. The dragon dagger is back in its sheath on her utility belt.

"Mom," says Silver, and it is, at the same time, as if she has just appeared there and has been there all along. She looks so healthy in this dimension; Kate doesn't think Silver's ever looked this vital before. She has colour in her skin: sun-ripened peaches; vanilla ice cream flecked with cinnamon. She's dressed in white, and has a SurroSis-style crossbow and a quiver of diamond-tipped arrows on her back. Her shoulders and arms are strong and ribboned with muscles.

The others are there too, and it feels right. Keke and Morgan stand behind Kate, dressed like steampunk assassins. Mally's a sophisticated robot, sleek and strong in his titanium and silicone armour. He wears Vega's Soul Shard on his chest, over his heart.

Bernard has taken the form of a large woolly dog, and is huffing warm, wet air into the grasses. Saint Bernard, of course, named after the monk who helped distressed travellers along their treacherous journey across the highest part of the Alpine path and founded a hospice there. The marching partners of travel and death.

Has everything always been so obvious? It's like Kate can see clearly—really clearly—for the first time.

Zack appears next to Bernard, and he has also taken an avatar. He looks like himself but taller, with a glowing bronze skin, and giant fire-feather wings.

Saint Zachariah.

Ouroboros appears as a fluttering gold leaf tattoo on his chest: a serpent eating its own tail. Eternal death; eternal return.

"Where is Seth?"

"We'll find him."

"My mom? Marko? Arronax?"

"We're not sure if they all made it, but we'll try to find them too."

Kate looks around. Outside of this lush natural field there is a white desert to the left, and a sparkling cityscape to the right.

"This is it?" asks Kate. "This is the real world?"

"Not quite," says Zack. "Not yet."

"What?"

"It's the first step."

"But you said the lace … would lead us out of the simulation?"

"And it did. Now you have to level up. You can't just get straight in. You have to prove your worth."

"It's a game," says Silver.

"I'm not good at games."

"You have help." Zack gestures at the others, and then at Silver. "Including the best player we've ever seen."

"You didn't tell me this," says Kate.

"I knew you wouldn't have come. You'd be cyberdust, and I would have failed."

"What do I do now?"

"There's only one thing you can do. Win."

"Win? And if I can't? There's nothing to go back to."

"That's right," says Zack, feathers flaming. "So I recommend you win."

He begins walking ahead, in the direction of the shimmering city, leaving sparks and singed grasses rustling in his path. Bernard the dog pants and joins his side, parting the plants with her ample, wiry-haired flanks.

Kate's nerves and energy rise in a wave, up her body. "But how?" she asks. "How do I play?"

Zack turns. Burning feathers float to the ground. "You'll figure it out. After all, you invented it."

<<<<>>>>

ALSO BY JT LAWRENCE

~

FICTION

SCI-FI THRILLER

WHEN TOMORROW CALLS

• *SERIES* •

The Stepford Florist: A Novelette

The Sigma Surrogate (prequel)

1. Why You Were Taken
2. How We Found You
3. What Have We Done

When Tomorrow Calls Box Set: Books 1 - 3

~

URBAN FANTASY

BLOOD MAGIC SERIES

1. The HighFire Crown
2. The Dream Drinker
3. The Witch Hunter
4. The Ember Isles
5. The Chaos Jar
6. The New Dawn Throne

~

STANDALONE NOVELS

The Memory of Water

Grey Magic

EverDark

~

SHORT STORY COLLECTIONS

Sticky Fingers

Sticky Fingers 2

Sticky Fingers 3

Sticky Fingers 4

Sticky Fingers: 36 Deliciously Twisted Short Stories: The Complete Box Set Collection (Books 1 - 3)

~

NON-FICTION

The Underachieving Ovary

ABOUT JT LAWRENCE

JT Lawrence is a bestselling author and
playwright. She lives in Parkview, Johannesburg, in a house with a red front door.

~

Be notified of giveaways, special deals & new releases
by signing up to JT's mailing list.

www.jt-lawrence.com

facebook.com/JanitaTLawrence

twitter.com/pulpbooks

amazon.com/author/jtlawrence

bookbub.com/profile/jt-lawrence

When Tomorrow Calls is a work of fiction.

Names, characters, places and incidents are the product of the author's imagination or are used fictitiously. Any resemblance to actual persons, living or dead, events, or locales is entirely coincidental.

1st Edition

Published in South Africa by Fire Finch Press, an imprint of Pulp Books.

www.jt-lawrence.com

Cover images by Shutterstock and Covervault.com

❀ Created with Vellum

Printed in Great Britain
by Amazon